DESPERATE REMEDIES

DESPERATE REMEDIES

Thomas Hardy

'Though an unconnected course of adventure is what most frequently occurs in nature, yet the province of the romance-writer being artificial, there is more required from him than a mere compliance with the simplicity of reality.'

Sir W. Scott

CHIVERS

British Library Cataloguing in Publication Data available

First published in 1871
This Large Print edition published by BBC Audiobooks Ltd, Bath, 2010.

U.K. Hardcover ISBN 978 1 408 49190 4

Printed and bound in Great Britain by CPI Antony Rowe, Chippenham
and Eastbourne

PREFATORY NOTE

The following novel, the first published by the author, was written nineteen years ago, at a time when he was feeling his way to a method. The principles observed in its composition are, no doubt, too exclusively those in which mystery, entanglement, surprise, and moral obliquity are depended on for exciting interest; but some of the scenes, and at least one of the characters, have been deemed not unworthy of a little longer preservation; and as they could hardly be reproduced in a fragmentary form the novel is reissued complete—the more readily that it has for some considerable time been reprinted and widely circulated in America.

January 1889.

To the foregoing note I have only to add that, in the present edition of 'Desperate Remedies,' some Wessex towns and other places that are common to the scenes of several of these stories have been called for the first time by the names under which they appear elsewhere, for the satisfaction of any reader who may care for consistency in such matters.

This is the only material change; for, as it happened that certain characteristics which provoked most discussion in my latest story were present in this my first—published in 1871, when there was no French name for them it has seemed best to let them stand unaltered.

February 1896.

The reader may discover, when turning over this sensational and strictly conventional narrative, that certain scattered reflections and sentiments therein are the same in substance with some in the *Wessex Poems* and others, published many years later. The explanation of such tautology is that the poems were written before the novel, but as the author could not get them printed, he incontinently used here whatever of their content came into his head as being apt for the purpose—after dissolving it into prose, never anticipating at that time that the poems would see the light.

T.H.

August 1912.

CONTENTS

I.
THE EVENTS OF THIRTY YEARS   1

II.
THE EVENTS OF A FORTNIGHT   24

III.
THE EVENTS OF EIGHT DAYS   46

IV.
THE EVENTS OF ONE DAY   77

V.
THE EVENTS OF ONE DAY   86

VI.
THE EVENTS OF TWELVE HOURS   117

VII.
THE EVENTS OF EIGHTEEN DAYS   150

VIII.
THE EVENTS OF EIGHTEEN DAYS   175

IX.
THE EVENTS OF TEN WEEKS   219

X.
THE EVENTS OF A DAY AND NIGHT 256

XI.
THE EVENTS OF FIVE DAYS 291

XII.
THE EVENTS OF TEN MONTHS 328

XIII.
THE EVENTS OF ONE DAY 367

XIV.
THE EVENTS OF FIVE WEEKS 430

XV.
THE EVENTS OF THREE WEEKS 447

XVI.
THE EVENTS OF ONE WEEK 466

XVII.
THE EVENTS OF ONE DAY 490

XVIII.
THE EVENTS OF THREE DAYS 508

XIX.
THE EVENTS OF A DAY AND NIGHT 533

XX.
THE EVENTS OF THREE HOURS 583

XXI.
THE EVENTS OF EIGHTEEN HOURS   594

SEQUEL   621

I.

THE EVENTS OF THIRTY YEARS

1. DECEMBER AND JANUARY, 1835–36

In the long and intricately inwrought chain of circumstance which renders worthy of record some experiences of Cytherea Graye, Edward Springrove, and others, the first event directly influencing the issue was a Christmas visit.

In the above-mentioned year, 1835, Ambrose Graye, a young architect who had just begun the practice of his profession in the midland town of Hocbridge, to the north of Christminster, went to London to spend the Christmas holidays with a friend who lived in Bloomsbury. They had gone up to Cambridge in the same year, and, after graduating together, Huntway, the friend, had taken orders.

Graye was handsome, frank, and gentle. He had a quality of thought which, exercised on homeliness, was humour; on nature, picturesqueness; on abstractions, poetry. Being, as a rule, broadcast, it was all three.

Of the wickedness of the world he was too forgetful. To discover evil in a new friend is to most people only an additional experience: to him it was ever a surprise.

1

While in London he became acquainted with a retired officer in the Navy named Bradleigh, who, with his wife and their daughter, lived in Dunkery Street, not far from Russell Square. Though they were in no more than comfortable circumstances, the captain's wife came of an ancient family whose genealogical tree was interlaced with some of the most illustrious and well-known in the kingdom.

The young lady, their daughter, seemed to Graye by far the most beautiful and queenly being he had ever beheld. She was about nineteen or twenty, and her name was Cytherea. In truth she was not so very unlike country girls of that type of beauty, except in one respect. She was perfect in her manner and bearing, and they were not. A mere distinguishing peculiarity, by catching the eye, is often read as the pervading characteristic, and she appeared to him no less than perfection throughout—transcending her rural rivals in very nature. Graye did a thing the blissfulness of which was only eclipsed by its hazardousness. He loved her at first sight.

His introductions had led him into contact with Cytherea and her parents two or three times on the first week of his arrival in London, and accident and a lover's contrivance brought them together as frequently the week following. The parents liked young Graye, and having few friends (for their equals in blood were their superiors in position), he was received on very generous terms. His passion for Cytherea grew not only strong, but ineffably exalted: she, without positively encouraging him, tacitly assented to his schemes for being near her. Her father and mother seemed to have lost all confidence in nobility of birth, without money to give effect to its presence, and looked upon the budding consequence of the young people's reciprocal glances with placidity, if not actual favour.

Graye's whole impassioned dream terminated in a sad and unaccountable episode. After passing through three weeks of sweet experience, he had arrived at the last stage—a kind of moral Gaza—before plunging into an emotional desert. The second week in January had come round, and it was necessary for the young architect to leave town.

Throughout his acquaintanceship with the lady of his heart there had been this marked peculiarity in her love: she had delighted in his presence as a sweetheart should do, yet from first to last she had repressed all recognition of the true nature of the thread which drew them together, blinding herself to its meaning and only natural tendency, and appearing to dread his announcement of them. The present seemed enough for her without cumulative hope: usually, even if love is in itself an end, it must be regarded as a beginning to be enjoyed.

In spite of evasions as an obstacle, and in

3

consequence of them as a spur, he would put the matter off no longer. It was evening. He took her into a little conservatory on the landing, and there among the evergreens, by the light of a few tiny lamps, infinitely enhancing the freshness and beauty of the leaves, he made the declaration of a love as fresh and beautiful as they.

'My love—my darling, be my wife!'

She seemed like one just awakened. 'Ah—we must part now!' she faltered, in a voice of anguish. 'I will write to you.' She loosened her hand and rushed away.

In a wild fever Graye went home and watched for the next morning. Who shall express his misery and wonder when a note containing these words was put into his hand?

'Good-bye; good-bye for ever. As recognized lovers something divides us eternally. Forgive me—I should have told you before; but your love was sweet! Never mention me.'

That very day, and as it seemed, to put an end to a painful condition of things, daughter and parents left London to pay off a promised visit to a relative in a western county. No message or letter of entreaty could wring from her any explanation. She begged him not to follow her, and the most bewildering point was that her father and mother appeared, from the tone of a letter Graye received from them, as vexed and sad as he at this sudden renunciation. One thing was plain: without admitting her reason as valid, they knew what that reason was, and did not intend to reveal it.

A week from that day Ambrose Graye left his friend Huntway's house and saw no more of the Love he mourned. From time to time his friend answered any inquiry Graye made by letter respecting her. But very poor food to a lover is intelligence of a mistress filtered through a friend. Huntway could tell nothing definitely. He said he believed there had been some prior flirtation between Cytherea and her cousin, an officer of the line, two or three years before Graye met her, which had suddenly been terminated by the cousin's departure for India, and the young lady's travelling on the Continent with her parents the whole of the ensuing summer, on account of delicate health. Eventually Huntway said that circumstances had rendered Graye's attachment more hopeless still. Cytherea's mother had unexpectedly inherited a large fortune and estates in the west of England by the rapid fall of some intervening lives. This had caused their removal from the small house in Bloomsbury, and, as it appeared, a renunciation of their old friends in that quarter.

Young Graye concluded that his Cytherea had forgotten him and his love. But he could not forget her.

2. FROM 1843 TO 1861

Eight years later, feeling lonely and depressed—a man without relatives, with many acquaintances but no friends—Ambrose Graye met a young lady of a different kind, fairly endowed with money and good gifts. As to caring very deeply for another woman after the loss of Cytherea, it was an absolute impossibility with him. With all, the beautiful things of the earth become more dear as they elude pursuit; but with some natures utter elusion is the one special event which will make a passing love permanent for ever.

This second young lady and Graye were married. That he did not, first or last, love his wife as he should have done, was known to all; but few knew that his unmanageable heart could never be weaned from useless repining at the loss of its first idol.

His character to some extent deteriorated, as emotional constitutions will under the long sense of disappointment at having missed their imagined destiny. And thus, though naturally of a gentle and pleasant disposition, he grew to be not so tenderly regarded by his acquaintances as it is the lot of some of those persons to be. The winning and sanguine receptivity of his early life developed by degrees a moody nervousness, and when not picturing prospects drawn from baseless hope he was the victim of indescribable depression. The practical issue of such a condition was improvidence, originally almost an unconscious improvidence, for every debt incurred had been mentally paid off with a religious exactness from the treasures of expectation before mentioned. But as years revolved, the same course was continued from the lack of spirit sufficient for shifting out of an old groove when it has been found to lead to disaster.

In the year 1861 his wife died, leaving him a widower with two children. The elder, a son named Owen, now just turned seventeen, was taken from school, and initiated as pupil to the profession of architect in his father's office. The remaining child was a daughter, and Owen's junior by a year.

Her christian name was Cytherea, and it is easy to guess why.

3. OCTOBER THE TWELFTH, 1863

We pass over two years in order to reach the next cardinal event of these persons' lives. The scene is still the Grayes' native town of Hocbridge, but as it appeared on a Monday afternoon in the month of October.

The weather was sunny and dry, but the ancient borough was to be seen wearing one of its least attractive aspects. First on account of the time. It was that stagnant hour of the twenty-four when the practical garishness of Day, having escaped from the fresh long shadows and enlivening newness of the morning, has not yet made any perceptible advance towards acquiring those mellow and soothing tones which grace its decline. Next, it was that stage in the progress of the week when business—which, carried on under the gables of an old country place, is not devoid of a romantic sparkle—was well-nigh extinguished. Lastly, the town was intentionally bent upon being attractive by exhibiting to an influx of visitors the local talent for dramatic recitation, and provincial towns trying to be lively are the dullest of dull things.

Little towns are like little children in this respect, that they interest most when they are enacting native peculiarities unconscious of beholders. Discovering themselves to be watched they attempt to be entertaining by putting on an antic, and produce disagreeable caricatures which spoil them.

The weather-stained clock-face in the low church tower standing at the intersection of the three chief streets was expressing half-past two to the Town Hall opposite, where the much talked-of reading from Shakespeare was about to begin. The doors were open, and those persons who had already assembled within the building were noticing the entrance of the new-comers—silently criticizing their dress—questioning the genuineness of their teeth and hair—estimating their private means.

Among these later ones came an exceptional young maiden who glowed amid the dulness like a single bright-red poppy in a field of brown stubble. She wore an elegant dark jacket, lavender dress, hat with grey strings and trimmings, and gloves of a colour to harmonize. She lightly walked up the side passage of the room, cast a slight glance around, and entered the seat pointed out to her.

The young girl was Cytherea Graye; her age was now about eighteen. During her entry, and at various times whilst sitting in her seat and listening to the reader on the platform, her personal appearance formed an interesting subject of study for several neighbouring eyes.

Her face was exceedingly attractive, though artistically less perfect than her figure, which approached unusually near to the standard of faultlessness. But even this feature of hers yielded the palm to the gracefulness of her movement, which was fascinating and delightful to an extreme degree.

Indeed, motion was her speciality, whether shown on its most extended scale of bodily progression, or minutely, as in the uplifting of her eyelids, the bending of her fingers, the pouting of her lip. The carriage of her head—

motion within motion—a glide upon a glide—was as delicate as that of a magnetic needle. And this flexibility and elasticity had never been taught her by rule, nor even been acquired by observation, but, *nullo cultu*, had naturally developed itself with her years. In childhood, a stone or stalk in the way, which had been the inevitable occasion of a fall to her playmates, had usually left her safe and upright on her feet after the narrowest escape by oscillations and whirls for the preservation of her balance. At mixed Christmas parties, when she numbered but twelve or thirteen years, and was heartily despised on that account by lads who deemed themselves men, her apt lightness in the dance covered this incompleteness in her womanhood, and compelled the self-same youths in spite of resolutions to seize upon her childish figure as a partner whom they could not afford to contemn. And in later years, when the instincts of her sex had shown her this point as the best and rarest feature in her external self, she was not found wanting in attention to the cultivation of finish in its details.

Her hair rested gaily upon her shoulders in curls and was of a shining corn yellow in the high lights, deepening to a definite nut-brown as each curl wound round into the shade. She had eyes of a sapphire hue, though rather darker than the gem ordinarily appears; they possessed the affectionate and liquid sparkle of loyalty and good faith as distinguishable from that harder brightness which seems to express faithfulness only to the object confronting them.

But to attempt to gain a view of her—or indeed of any fascinating woman—from a measured category, is as difficult as to appreciate the effect of a landscape by exploring it at night with a lantern—or of a full chord of music by piping the notes in succession. Nevertheless it may readily be believed from the description here ventured, that among the many winning phases of her aspect, these were particularly striking:—

During pleasant doubt, when her eyes brightened stealthily and smiled (as eyes will smile) as distinctly as her lips, and in the space of a single instant expressed clearly the whole round of degrees of expectancy which lie over the wide expanse between Yea and Nay.

During the telling of a secret, which was involuntarily accompanied by a sudden minute start, and ecstatic pressure of the listener's arm, side, or neck, as the position and degree of intimacy dictated.

When anxiously regarding one who possessed her affections.

She suddenly assumed the last-mentioned bearing in the progress of the present entertainment. Her glance was directed out of the window.

Why the particulars of a young lady's

presence at a very mediocre performance were prevented from dropping into the oblivion which their intrinsic insignificance would naturally have involved—why they were remembered and individualized by herself and others through after years—was simply that she unknowingly stood, as it were, upon the extreme posterior edge of a tract in her life, in which the real meaning of Taking Thought had never been known. It was the last hour of experience she ever enjoyed with a mind entirely free from a knowledge of that labyrinth into which she stepped immediately afterwards—to continue a perplexed course along its mazes for the greater portion of twenty-nine subsequent months.

The Town Hall, in which Cytherea sat, was a building of brown stone, and through one of the windows could be seen from the interior of the room the housetops and chimneys of the adjacent street, and also the upper part of a neighbouring church spire, now in course of completion under the superintendence of Miss Graye's father, the architect to the work.

That the top of this spire should be visible from her position in the room was a fact which Cytherea's idling eyes had discovered with some interest, and she was now engaged in watching the scene that was being enacted about its airy summit. Round the conical stonework rose a cage of scaffolding against the blue sky, and upon this stood five men—

four in clothes as white as the new erection close beneath their hands, the fifth in the ordinary dark suit of a gentleman.

The four working-men in white were three masons and a mason's labourer. The fifth man was the architect, Mr. Graye. He had been giving directions as it seemed, and retiring as far as the narrow footway allowed, stood perfectly still.

The picture thus presented to a spectator in the Town Hall was curious and striking. It was an illuminated miniature, framed in by the dark margin of the window, the keen-edged shadiness of which emphasized by contrast the softness of the objects enclosed.

The height of the spire was about one hundred and twenty feet, and the five men engaged thereon seemed entirely removed from the sphere and experiences of ordinary human beings. They appeared little larger than pigeons, and made their tiny movements with a soft, spirit-like silentness. One idea above all others was conveyed to the mind of a person on the ground by their aspect, namely, concentration of purpose: that they were indifferent to—even unconscious of—the distracted world beneath them, and all that moved upon it. They never looked off the scaffolding.

Then one of them turned; it was Mr. Graye. Again he stood motionless, with attention to the operations of the others. He appeared to be lost in reflection, and had directed his face towards a new stone they were lifting.

'Why does he stand like that?' the young lady thought at length—up to that moment as listless and careless as one of the ancient Tarentines, who, on such an afternoon as this, watched from the Theatre the entry into their Harbour of a power that overturned the State.

She moved herself uneasily. 'I wish he would come down,' she whispered, still gazing at the skybacked picture. 'It is so dangerous to be absent-minded up there.'

When she had done murmuring the words her father indecisively laid hold of one of the scaffold-poles, as if to test its strength, then let it go and stepped back. In stepping, his foot slipped. An instant of doubling forward and sideways, and he reeled off into the air, immediately disappearing downwards.

His agonized daughter rose to her feet by a convulsive movement. Her lips parted, and she gasped for breath. She could utter no sound. One by one the people about her, unconscious of what had happened, turned their heads, and inquiry and alarm became visible upon their faces at the sight of the poor child. A moment longer, and she fell to the floor.

The next impression of which Cytherea had any consciousness was of being carried from a strange vehicle across the pavement to the steps of her own house by her brother and an older man. Recollection of what had passed

14

evolved itself an instant later, and just as they entered the door—through which another and sadder burden had been carried but a few instants before—her eyes caught sight of the south-western sky, and, without heeding, saw white sunlight shining in shaft-like lines from a rift in a slaty cloud. Emotions will attach themselves to scenes that are simultaneous—however foreign in essence these scenes may be—as chemical waters will crystallize on twigs and wires. Ever after that time any mental agony brought less vividly to Cytherea's mind the scene from the Town Hall windows than sunlight streaming in shaft-like lines.

4. OCTOBER THE NINETEENTH

When death enters a house, an element of sadness and an element of horror accompany it. Sadness, from the death itself: horror, from the clouds of blackness we designedly labour to introduce.

The funeral had taken place. Depressed, yet resolved in his demeanour, Owen Graye sat before his father's private escritoire, engaged in turning out and unfolding a heterogeneous collection of papers—forbidding and inharmonious to the eye at all times—most of all to one under the influence of a great grief. Laminae of white paper tied with twine were indiscriminately intermixed with other white

15

papers bounded by black edges—these with blue foolscap wrapped round with crude red tape.

The bulk of these letters, bills, and other documents were submitted to a careful examination, by which the appended particulars were ascertained:—

First, that their father's income from professional sources had been very small, amounting to not more than half their expenditure; and that his own and his wife's property, upon which he had relied for the balance, had been sunk and lost in unwise loans to unscrupulous men, who had traded upon their father's too open-hearted trustfulness.

Second, that finding his mistake, he had endeavoured to regain his standing by the illusory path of speculation. The most notable instance of this was the following. He had been induced, when at Plymouth in the autumn of the previous year, to venture all his spare capital on the bottomry security of an Italian brig which had put into the harbour in distress. The profit was to be considerable, so was the risk. There turned out to be no security whatever. The circumstances of the case tendered it the most unfortunate speculation that a man like himself—ignorant of all such matters—could possibly engage in. The vessel went down, and all Mr. Graye's money with it.

Third, that these failures had left him

burdened with debts he knew not how to meet; so that at the time of his death even the few pounds lying to his account at the bank were his only in name.

Fourth, that the loss of his wife two years earlier had awakened him to a keen sense of his blindness, and of his duty by his children. He had then resolved to reinstate by unflagging zeal in the pursuit of his profession, and by no speculation, at least a portion of the little fortune he had let go.

Cytherea was frequently at her brother's elbow during these examinations. She often remarked sadly—

'Poor papa failed to fulfil his good intention for want of time, didn't he, Owen? And there was an excuse for his past, though he never would claim it. I never forget that original disheartening blow, and how that from it sprang all the ills of his life—everything connected with his gloom, and the lassitude in business we used so often to see about him.'

'I remember what he said once,' returned the brother, 'when I sat up late with him. He said, "Owen, don't love too blindly: blindly you will love if you love at all, but a little care is still possible to a well-disciplined heart. May that heart be yours as it was not mine," father said. "Cultivate the art of renunciation." And I am going to, Cytherea.'

'And once mamma said that an excellent woman was papa's ruin, because he did not

17

know the way to give her up when he had lost her. I wonder where she is now, Owen? We were told not to try to find out anything about her. Papa never told us her name, did he?'

'That was by her own request, I believe. But never mind her; she was not our mother.'

The love affair which had been Ambrose Graye's disheartening blow was precisely of that nature which lads take little account of, but girls ponder in their hearts.

5. FROM OCTOBER THE NINETEENTH TO JULY THE NINTH

Thus Ambrose Graye's good intentions with regard to the reintegration of his property had scarcely taken tangible form when his sudden death put them for ever out of his power.

Heavy bills, showing the extent of his obligations, tumbled in immediately upon the heels of the funeral from quarters previously unheard and unthought of. Thus pressed, a bill was filed in Chancery to have the assets, such as they were, administered by the Court.

'What will become of us now?' thought Owen continually.

There is in us an unquenchable expectation, which at the gloomiest time persists in inferring that because we are *ourselves*, there must be a special future in store for us, though our nature and antecedents to the remotest

18

particular have been common to thousands. Thus to Cytherea and Owen Graye the question how their lives would end seemed the deepest of possible enigmas. To others who knew their position equally well with themselves the question was the easiest that could be asked—'Like those of other people similarly circumstanced.'

Then Owen held a consultation with his sister to come to some decision on their future course, and a month was passed in waiting for answers to letters, and in the examination of schemes more or less futile. Sudden hopes that were rainbows to the sight proved but mists to the touch. In the meantime, unpleasant remarks, disguise them as some well-meaning people might, were floating around them every day. The undoubted truth, that they were the children of a dreamer who let slip away every farthing of his money and ran into debt with his neighbours—that the daughter had been brought up to no profession—that the son who had, had made no progress in it, and might come to the dogs—could not from the nature of things be wrapped up in silence in order that it might not hurt their feelings; and as a matter of fact, it greeted their ears in some form or other wherever they went. Their few acquaintances passed them hurriedly. Ancient pot-wallopers, and thriving shopkeepers, in their intervals of leisure, stood at their shop-doors—their toes hanging over the edge of the step, and their obese waists hanging over their toes—and in discourses with friends on the pavement, formulated the course of the improvident, and reduced the children's prospects to a shadow-like attenuation. The sons of these men (who wore breastpins of a sarcastic kind, and smoked humorous pipes) stared at Cytherea with a stare unmitigated by any of the respect that had formerly softened it.

Now it is a noticeable fact that we do not much mind what men think of us, or what humiliating secret they discover of our means, parentage, or object, provided that each thinks and acts thereupon in isolation. It is the exchange of ideas about us that we dread most; and the possession by a hundred acquaintances, severally insulated, of the knowledge of our skeleton-closet's whereabouts, is not so distressing to the nerves as a chat over it by a party of half-a-dozen—exclusive depositaries though these may be.

Perhaps, though Hocbridge watched and whispered, its animus would have been little more than a trifle to persons in thriving circumstances. But unfortunately, poverty, whilst it is new, and before the skin has had time to thicken, makes people susceptible inversely to their opportunities for shielding themselves. In Owen was found, in place of his father's impressibility, a larger share of his father's pride, and a squareness of idea which, if coupled with a little more blindness, would have amounted to positive prejudice. To him humanity, so far as he had thought of it at all, was rather divided into distinct classes than blended from extreme to extreme. Hence by a sequence of ideas which might be traced if it were worth while, he either detested or respected opinion, and instinctively sought to escape a cold shade that mere sensitiveness would have endured. He could have submitted to separation, sickness, exile, drudgery, hunger and thirst, with stoical indifference, but superciliousness was too incisive.

After living on for nine months in attempts to make an income as his father's successor in the profession—attempts which were utterly fruitless by reason of his inexperience—Graye came to a simple and sweeping resolution. They would privately leave that part of England, drop from the sight of acquaintances, gossips, harsh critics, and bitter creditors of whose misfortune he was not the cause, and escape the position which galled him by the only road their great poverty left open to them—that of his obtaining some employment in a distant place by following his profession as a humble under-draughtsman.

He thought over his capabilities with the sensations of a soldier grinding his sword at the opening of a campaign. What with lack of employment, owing to the decrease of his late father's practice, and the absence of direct and

21

uncompromising pressure towards monetary results from a pupil's labour (which seems to be always the case when a professional man's pupil is also his son), Owen's progress in the art and science of architecture had been very insignificant indeed. Though anything but an idle young man, he had hardly reached the age at which industrious men who lack an external whip to send them on in the world, are induced by their own common sense to whip on themselves. Hence his knowledge of plans, elevations, sections, and specifications, was not greater at the end of two years of probation than might easily have been acquired in six months by a youth of average ability—himself, for instance—amid a bustling London practice.

But at any rate he could make himself handy to one of the profession—some man in a remote town—and there fulfil his indentures. A tangible inducement lay in this direction of survey. He had a slight conception of such a man—a Mr. Gradfield—who was in practice in Budmouth Regis, a seaport town and watering-place in the south of England.

After some doubts, Graye ventured to write to this gentleman, asking the necessary question, shortly alluding to his father's death, and stating that his term of apprenticeship had only half expired. He would be glad to complete his articles at a very low salary for the whole remaining two years, provided payment could begin at once.

The answer from Mr. Gradfield stated that he was not in want of a pupil who would serve the remainder of his time on the terms Mr. Graye mentioned. But he would just add one remark. He chanced to be in want of some young man in his office—for a short time only, probably about two months—to trace drawings, and attend to other subsidiary work of the kind. If Mr. Graye did not object to occupy such an inferior position as these duties would entail, and to accept weekly wages which to one with his expectations would be considered merely nominal, the post would give him an opportunity for learning a few more details of the profession.

'It is a beginning, and, above all, an abiding-place, away from the shadow of the cloud which hangs over us here—I will go,' said Owen.

Cytherea's plan for her future, an intensely simple one, owing to the even greater narrowness of her resources, was already marked out. One advantage had accrued to her through her mother's possession of a fair share of personal property, and perhaps only one. She had been carefully educated. Upon this consideration her plan was based. She was to take up her abode in her brother's lodging at Budmouth, when she would immediately advertise for a situation as governess, having obtained the consent of a lawyer at Aldbrickham who was winding up her father's affairs, and who knew the history of her position, to allow himself to be referred to in the matter of her past life and respectability.

Early one morning they departed from their native town, leaving behind them scarcely a trace of their footsteps.

Then the town pitied their want of wisdom in taking such a step. 'Rashness; they would have made a better income in Hocbridge, where they are known! There is no doubt that they would.'

But what is Wisdom really? A steady handling of any means to bring about any end necessary to happiness.

Yet whether one's end be the usual end—a wealthy position in life—or no, the name of wisdom is seldom applied but to the means to that usual end.

II.

THE EVENTS OF A FORTNIGHT

1. THE NINTH OF JULY

The day of their departure was one of the most glowing that the climax of a long series of summer heats could evolve. The wide expanse of landscape quivered up and down like the flame of a taper, as they steamed along through the midst of it. Placid flocks of sheep reclining under trees a little way off appeared of a pale blue colour. Clover fields were livid with the brightness of the sun upon their deep red flowers. All waggons and carts were moved to the shade by their careful owners, rain-water butts fell to pieces; well-buckets were lowered inside the covers of the well-hole, to preserve them from the fate of the butts, and generally, water seemed scarcer in the country than the beer and cider of the peasantry who toiled or idled there.

To see persons looking with children's eyes at any ordinary scenery, is a proof that they possess the charming faculty of drawing new sensations from an old experience—a healthy sign, rare in these feverish days—the mark of an imperishable brightness of nature.

Both brother and sister could do this; Cytherea more noticeably. They watched the undulating corn-lands, monotonous to all their companions; the stony and clayey prospect succeeding those, with its angular and abrupt hills. Boggy moors came next, now withered and dry—the spots upon which pools usually spread their waters showing themselves as circles of smooth bare soil, over-run by a net-work of innumerable little fissures. Then arose plantations of firs, abruptly terminating beside meadows cleanly mown, in which high-hipped, rich-coloured cows, with backs horizontal and straight as the ridge of a house, stood motionless or lazily fed. Glimpses of the sea now interested them, which became more and more frequent till the train finally drew up beside the platform at Budmouth Regis.

'The whole town is looking out for us,' had been Graye's impression throughout the day. He called upon Mr. Gradfield—the only man who had been directly informed of his coming—and found that Mr. Gradfield had forgotten it.

However, arrangements were made with this gentleman—a stout, active, grey-bearded burgher of sixty—by which Owen was to commence work in his office the following week.

The same day Cytherea drew up and sent off the advertisement appended:—

A YOUNG LADY is desirous of meeting with an engagement as GOVERNESS or COMPANION. She is competent to teach English, French, and Music. Satisfactory references—Address, C. G., Post-Office, Budmouth.

It seemed a more material existence than her own that she saw thus delineated on the paper. 'That can't be myself; how odd I look!' she said, and smiled.

2. JULY THE ELEVENTH

On the Monday subsequent to their arrival in Budmouth, Owen Graye attended at Mr. Gradfield's office to enter upon his duties, and his sister was left in their lodgings alone for the first time.

Despite the sad occurrences of the preceding autumn, an unwonted cheerfulness pervaded her spirit throughout the day. Change of scene—and that to untravelled eyes—conjoined with the sensation of freedom from supervision, revived the sparkle of a warm young nature ready enough to take advantage of any adventitious restoratives. Point-blank grief tends rather to seal up happiness for a time than to produce that attrition which results from griefs of anticipation that move onward with the days: these may be said to furrow away the capacity for pleasure.

Her expectations from the advertisement began to be extravagant. A thriving family, who had always sadly needed her, was already definitely pictured in her fancy, which, in its exuberance, led her on to picturing its individual members, their possible peculiarities, virtues, and vices, and obliterated for a time the recollection that she would be separated from her brother.

Thus musing, as she waited for his return in the evening, her eyes fell on her left hand. The

27

contemplation of her own left fourth finger by symbol-loving girlhood of this age is, it seems, very frequently, if not always, followed by a peculiar train of romantic ideas. Cytherea's thoughts, still playing about her future, became directed into this romantic groove. She leant back in her chair, and taking hold of the fourth finger, which had attracted her attention, she lifted it with the tips of the others, and looked at the smooth and tapering member for a long time.

She whispered idly, 'I wonder who and what he will be?

'If he's a gentleman of fashion, he will take my finger so, just with the tips of his own, and with some fluttering of the heart, and the least trembling of his lip, slip the ring so lightly on that I shall hardly know it is there—looking delightfully into my eyes all the time.

'If he's a bold, dashing soldier, I expect he will proudly turn round, take the ring as if it equalled her Majesty's crown in value, and desperately set it on my finger thus. He will fix his eyes unflinchingly upon what he is doing— just as if he stood in battle before the enemy (though, in reality, very fond of me, of course), and blush as much as I shall.

'If he's a sailor, he will take my finger and the ring in this way, and deck it out with a housewifely touch and a tenderness of expression about his mouth, as sailors do: kiss it, perhaps, with a simple air, as if we were children playing an idle game, and not at the very height of observation and envy by a great crowd saying, "Ah! they are happy now!"

'If he should be rather a poor man—noble-minded and affectionate, but still poor—'

Owen's footsteps rapidly ascending the stairs, interrupted this fancy-free meditation. Reproaching herself, even angry with herself for allowing her mind to stray upon such subjects in the face of their present desperate condition, she rose to meet him, and make tea.

Cytherea's interest to know how her brother had been received at Mr. Gradfield's broke forth into words at once. Almost before they had sat down to table, she began cross-examining him in the regular sisterly way.

'Well, Owen, how has it been with you to-day? What is the place like—do you think you will like Mr. Gradfield?'

'O yes. But he has not been there to-day; I have only had the head draughtsman with me.'

Young women have a habit, not noticeable in men, of putting on at a moment's notice the drama of whosoever's life they choose. Cytherea's interest was transferred from Mr. Gradfield to his representative.

'What sort of a man is he?'

'He seems a very nice fellow indeed; though of course I can hardly tell to a certainty as yet. But I think he's a very worthy fellow; there's no nonsense in him, and though he is not a public school man he has read widely, and has a sharp appreciation of what's good in books and art. In fact, his knowledge isn't nearly so exclusive as most professional men's.'

'That's a great deal to say of an architect, for of all professional men they are, as a rule, the most professional.'

'Yes; perhaps they are. This man is rather of a melancholy turn of mind, I think.'

'Has the managing clerk any family?' she mildly asked, after a while, pouring out some more tea.

'Family; no!'

'Well, dear Owen, how should I know?'

'Why, of course he isn't married. But there happened to be a conversation about women going on in the office, and I heard him say what he should wish his wife to be like.'

'What would he wish his wife to be like?' she said, with great apparent lack of interest.

'O, he says she must be girlish and artless: yet he would be loth to do without a dash of womanly subtlety, 'tis so piquant. Yes, he said, that must be in her; she must have womanly cleverness. "And yet I should like her to blush if only a cock-sparrow were to look at her hard," he said, "which brings me back to the girl again: and so I flit backwards and forwards. I must have what comes, I suppose," he said, "and whatever she may be, thank God she's no worse. However, if he might give a final hint to Providence," he said, "a child among pleasures, and a woman among pains

30

was the rough outline of his requirement." '

'Did he say that? What a musing creature he must be.'

'He did, indeed.'

3. FROM THE TWELFTH TO THE FIFTEENTH OF JULY

As is well known, ideas are so elastic in a human brain, that they have no constant measure which may be called their actual bulk. Any important idea may be compressed to a molecule by an unwonted crowding of others; and any small idea will expand to whatever length and breadth of vacuum the mind may be able to make over to it. Cytherea's world was tolerably vacant at this time, and the young architectural designer's image became very pervasive. The next evening this subject was again renewed.

'His name is Springrove,' said Owen, in reply to her. 'He is a thorough artist, but a man of rather humble origin, it seems, who has made himself so far. I think he is the son of a farmer, or something of the kind.'

'Well, he's none the worse for that, I suppose.'

'None the worse. As we come down the hill, we shall be continually meeting people going up.' But Owen had felt that Springrove was a little the worse nevertheless.

'Of course he's rather old by this time.'

'O no. He's about six-and-twenty—not more.'

'Ah, I see . . . What is he like, Owen?'

'I can't exactly tell you his appearance: 'tis always such a difficult thing to do.'

'A man you would describe as short? Most men are those we should describe as short, I fancy.'

'I should call him, I think, of the middle height; but as I only see him sitting in the office, of course I am not certain about his form and figure.'

'I wish you were, then.'

'Perhaps you do. But I am not, you see.'

'Of course not, you are always so provoking. Owen, I saw a man in the street to-day whom I fancied was he—and yet, I don't see how it could be, either. He had light brown hair, a snub nose, very round face, and a peculiar habit of reducing his eyes to straight lines when he looked narrowly at anything.'

'O no. That was not he, Cytherea.'

'Not a bit like him in all probability.'

'Not a bit. He has dark hair—almost a Grecian nose, regular teeth, and an intellectual face, as nearly as I can recall to mind.'

'Ah, there now, Owen, you have described him! But I suppose he's not generally called pleasing, or—'

'Handsome?'

'I scarcely meant that. But since you have

32

said it, is he handsome?'

'Rather.'

'His *tout ensemble* is striking?'

'Yes—O no, no—I forgot: it is not. He is rather untidy in his waistcoat, and neck-ties, and hair.'

'How vexing! . . . it must be to himself, poor thing.'

'He's a thorough bookworm—despises the pap-and-daisy school of verse—knows Shakespeare to the very dregs of the foot-notes. Indeed, he's a poet himself in a small way.'

'How delicious!' she said. 'I have never known a poet.'

'And you don't know him,' said Owen dryly.

She reddened. 'Of course I don't. I know that.'

'Have you received any answer to your advertisement?' he inquired.

'Ah—no!' she said, and the forgotten disappointment which had showed itself in her face at different times during the day, became visible again.

Another day passed away. On Thursday, without inquiry, she learnt more of the head draughtsman. He and Graye had become very friendly, and he had been tempted to show her brother a copy of some poems of his—some serious and sad—some humorous—which had appeared in the poets' corner of a magazine from time to time. Owen showed them now to

Cytherea, who instantly began to read them carefully and to think them very beautiful.

'Yes—Springrove's no fool,' said Owen sententiously.

'No fool!—I should think he isn't, indeed,' said Cytherea, looking up from the paper in quite an excitement: 'to write such verses as these!'

'What logic are you chopping, Cytherea? Well, I don't mean on account of the verses, because I haven't read them; but for what he said when the fellows were talking about falling in love.'

'Which you will tell me?'

'He says that your true lover breathlessly finds himself engaged to a sweetheart, like a man who has caught something in the dark. He doesn't know whether it is a bat or a bird, and takes it to the light when he is cool to learn what it is. He looks to see if she is the right age, but right age or wrong age, he must consider her a prize. Sometime later he ponders whether she is the right kind of prize for him. Right kind or wrong kind—he has called her his, and must abide by it. After a time he asks himself, "Has she the temper, hair, and eyes I meant to have, and was firmly resolved not to do without?" He finds it is all wrong, and then comes the tussle—'

'Do they marry and live happily?'

'Who? O, the supposed pair. I think he said—well, I really forget what he said.'

34

'That *is* stupid of you!' said the young lady with dismay.

'Yes.'

'But he's a satirist—I don't think I care about him now.'

'There you are just wrong. He is not. He is, as I believe, an impulsive fellow who has been made to pay the penalty of his rashness in some love affair.'

Thus ended the dialogue of Thursday, but Cytherea read the verses again in private. On Friday her brother remarked that Springrove had informed him he was going to leave Mr. Gradfield's in a fortnight to push his fortunes in London.

An indescribable feeling of sadness shot through Cytherea's heart. Why should she be sad at such an announcement as that, she thought, concerning a man she had never seen, when her spirits were elastic enough to rebound after hard blows from deep and real troubles as if she had scarcely known them? Though she could not answer this question, she knew one thing, she was saddened by Owen's news.

4. JULY THE TWENTY-FIRST

A very popular local excursion by steamboat to Lulwin Cove was announced through the streets of Budmouth one Thursday morning by the weak-voiced town-crier, to start at six o'clock the same day. The weather was lovely, and the opportunity being the first of the kind offered to them, Owen and Cytherea went with the rest.

They had reached the Cove, and had walked landward for nearly an hour over the hill which rose beside the strand, when Graye recollected that two or three miles yet further inland from this spot was an interesting mediaeval ruin. He was already familiar with its characteristics through the medium of an archaeological work, and now finding himself so close to the reality, felt inclined to verify some theory he had formed respecting it. Concluding that there would be just sufficient time for him to go there and return before the boat had left the shore, he parted from Cytherea on the hill, struck downwards, and then up a heathery valley.

She remained on the summit where he had left her till the time of his expected return, scanning the details of the prospect around. Placidly spread out before her on the south was the open Channel, reflecting a blue intenser by many shades than that of the sky overhead, and dotted in the foreground by half-a-dozen small craft of contrasting rig, their sails graduating in hue from extreme whiteness to reddish brown, the varying actual colours varied again in a double degree by the rays of the declining sun.

Presently the distant bell from the boat was heard, warning the passengers to embark. This was followed by a lively air from the harps and violins on board, their tones, as they arose, becoming intermingled with, though not marred by, the brush of the waves when their crests rolled over—at the point where the check of the shallows was first felt—and then thinned away up the slope of pebbles and sand.

She turned her face landward and strained her eyes to discern, if possible, some sign of Owen's return. Nothing was visible save the strikingly brilliant, still landscape. The wide concave which lay at the back of the hill in this direction was blazing with the western light, adding an orange tint to the vivid purple of the heather, now at the very climax of bloom, and free from the slightest touch of the invidious brown that so soon creeps into its shades. The light so intensified the colours that they seemed to stand above the surface of the earth and float in mid-air like an exhalation of red. In the minor valleys, between the hillocks and ridges which diversified the contour of the basin, but did not disturb its general sweep, she marked brakes of tall, heavy-stemmed ferns, five or six feet high, in a brilliant light-green dress—a broad riband of them with the path in their midst winding like a stream along the little ravine that reached to the foot of the hill, and delivered up the path to its grassy area. Among the ferns grew holly bushes deeper in

37

tint than any shadow about them, whilst the whole surface of the scene was dimpled with small conical pits, and here and there were round ponds, now dry, and half overgrown with rushes.

The last bell of the steamer rang. Cytherea had forgotten herself, and what she was looking for. In a fever of distress lest Owen should be left behind, she gathered up in her hand the corners of her handkerchief, containing specimens of the shells, plants, and fossils which the locality produced, started off to the sands, and mingled with the knots of visitors there congregated from other interesting points around; from the inn, the cottages, and hired conveyances that had returned from short drives inland. They all went aboard by the primitive plan of a narrow plank on two wheels—the women being assisted by a rope. Cytherea lingered till the very last, reluctant to follow, and looking alternately at the boat and the valley behind. Her delay provoked a remark from Captain Jacobs, a thickset man of hybrid stains, resulting from the mixed effects of fire and water, peculiar to sailors where engines are the propelling power.

'Now then, missy, if you please. I am sorry to tell 'ee our time's up. Who are you looking for, miss?'

'My brother—he has walked a short distance inland; he must be here directly.

Could you wait for him—just a minute?'

'Really, I am afraid not, m'm.' Cytherea looked at the stout, round-faced man, and at the vessel, with a light in her eyes so expressive of her own opinion being the same, on reflection, as his, and with such resignation, too, that, from an instinctive feeling of pride at being able to prove himself more humane than he was thought to be—works of supererogation are the only sacrifices that entice in this way—and that at a very small cost, he delayed the boat till some among the passengers began to murmur.

'There, never mind,' said Cytherea decisively. 'Go on without me—I shall wait for him.'

'Well, 'tis a very awkward thing to leave you here all alone,' said the captain. 'I certainly advise you not to wait.'

'He's gone across to the railway station, for certain,' said another passenger.

'No—here he is!' Cytherea said, regarding, as she spoke, the half hidden figure of a man who was seen advancing at a headlong pace down the ravine which lay between the heath and the shore.

'He can't get here in less than five minutes,' a passenger said. 'People should know what they are about, and keep time. Really, if—'

'You see, sir,' said the captain, in an apologetic undertone, 'since 'tis her brother, and she's all alone, 'tis only nater to wait a minute, now he's in sight. Suppose, now, you were a young woman, as might be, and had a brother, like this one, and you stood of an evening upon this here wild lonely shore, like her, why you'd want us to wait, too, wouldn't you, sir? I think you would.'

The person so hastily approaching had been lost to view during this remark by reason of a hollow in the ground, and the projecting cliff immediately at hand covered the path in its rise. His footsteps were now heard striking sharply upon the flinty road at a distance of about twenty or thirty yards, but still behind the escarpment. To save time, Cytherea prepared to ascend the plank.

'Let me give you my hand, miss,' said Captain Jacobs.

'No—please don't touch me,' said she, ascending cautiously by sliding one foot forward two or three inches, bringing up the other behind it, and so on alternately—her lips compressed by concentration on the feat, her eyes glued to the plank, her hand to the rope, and her immediate thought to the fact of the distressing narrowness of her footing. Steps now shook the lower end of the board, and in an instant were up to her heels with a bound.

'O, Owen, I am so glad you are come!' she said without turning. 'Don't, don't shake the plank or touch me, whatever you do . . . There, I am up. Where have you been so long?' she continued, in a lower tone, turning round to him as she reached the top.

Raising her eyes from her feet, which, standing on the firm deck, demanded her attention no longer, she acquired perceptions of the new-comer in the following order: unknown trousers; unknown waistcoat; unknown face. The man was not her brother, but a total stranger.

Off went the plank; the paddles started, stopped, backed, pattered in confusion, then revolved decisively, and the boat passed out into deep water.

One or two persons had said, 'How d'ye do, Mr. Springrove?' and looked at Cytherea, to see how she bore her disappointment. Her ears had but just caught the name of the head draughtsman, when she saw him advancing directly to address her.

'Miss Graye, I believe?' he said, lifting his hat.

'Yes,' said Cytherea, colouring, and trying not to look guilty of a surreptitious knowledge of him.

'I am Mr. Springrove. I passed Corvsgate Castle about an hour ago, and soon afterwards met your brother going that way. He had been deceived in the distance, and was about to turn without seeing the ruin, on account of a lameness that had come on in his leg or foot. I proposed that he should go on, since he had got so near; and afterwards, instead of walking back to the boat, get across to Anglebury

Station—a shorter walk for him—where he could catch the late train, and go directly home. I could let you know what he had done, and allay any uneasiness.'

'Is the lameness serious, do you know?'

'O no; simply from over-walking himself. Still, it was just as well to ride home.'

Relieved from her apprehensions on Owen's score, she was able slightly to examine the appearance of her informant—Edward Springrove—who now removed his hat for a while, to cool himself. He was rather above her brother's height. Although the upper part of his face and head was handsomely formed, and bounded by lines of sufficiently masculine regularity, his brows were somewhat too softly arched, and finely pencilled for one of his sex; without prejudice, however, to the belief which the sum total of his features inspired—that though they did not prove that the man who thought inside them would do much in the world, men who had done most of all had had no better ones. Across his forehead, otherwise perfectly smooth, ran one thin line, the healthy freshness of his remaining features expressing that it had come there prematurely.

Though some years short of the age at which the clear spirit bids good-bye to the last infirmity of noble mind, and takes to house-hunting and investments, he had reached the period in a young man's life when episodic periods, with a hopeful birth and a disappointing death, have begun to accumulate, and to bear a fruit of generalities; his glance sometimes seeming to state, 'I have already thought out the issue of such conditions as these we are experiencing.' At other times he wore an abstracted look: 'I seem to have lived through this moment before.'

He was carelessly dressed in dark grey, wearing a rolled-up black kerchief as a neck-cloth; the knot of which was disarranged, and stood obliquely—a deposit of white dust having lodged in the creases.

'I am sorry for your disappointment,' he continued, glancing into her face. Their eyes having met, became, as it were, mutually locked together, and the single instant only which good breeding allows as the length of such a look, became trebled: a clear penetrating ray of intelligence had shot from each into each, giving birth to one of those unaccountable sensations which carry home to the heart before the hand has been touched or the merest compliment passed, by something stronger than mathematical proof, the conviction, 'A tie has begun to unite us.'

Both faces also unconsciously stated that their owners had been much in each other's thoughts of late. Owen had talked to the young architect of his sister as freely as to Cytherea of the young architect.

A conversation began, which was none the

less interesting to the parties engaged because it consisted only of the most trivial and commonplace remarks. Then the band of harps and violins struck up a lively melody, and the deck was cleared for dancing; the sun dipping beneath the horizon during the proceeding, and the moon showing herself at their stern. The sea was so calm, that the soft hiss produced by the bursting of the innumerable bubbles of foam behind the paddles could be distinctly heard. The passengers who did not dance, including Cytherea and Springrove, lapsed into silence, leaning against the paddle-boxes, or standing aloof—noticing the trembling of the deck to the steps of the dance—watching the waves from the paddles as they slid thinly and easily under each other's edges.

Night had quite closed in by the time they reached Budmouth harbour, sparkling with its white, red, and green lights in opposition to the shimmering path of the moon's reflection on the other side, which reached away to the horizon till the flecked ripples reduced themselves to sparkles as fine as gold dust.

'I will walk to the station and find out the exact time the train arrives,' said Springrove, rather eagerly, when they had landed.

She thanked him much.

'Perhaps we might walk together,' he suggested hesitatingly. She looked as if she did not quite know, and he settled the question by showing the way.

They found, on arriving there, that on the first day of that month the particular train selected for Graye's return had ceased to stop at Anglebury station.

'I am very sorry I misled him,' said Springrove.

'O, I am not alarmed at all,' replied Cytherea.

'Well, it's sure to be all right—he will sleep there, and come by the first in the morning. But what will you do, alone?'

'I am quite easy on that point; the landlady is very friendly. I must go indoors now. Good-night, Mr. Springrove.'

'Let me go round to your door with you?' he pleaded.

'No, thank you; we live close by.'

He looked at her as a waiter looks at the change he brings back. But she was inexorable.

'Don't—forget me,' he murmured. She did not answer.

'Let me see you sometimes,' he said.

'Perhaps you never will again—I am going away,' she replied in lingering tones; and turning into Cross Street, ran indoors and upstairs.

The sudden withdrawal of what was superfluous at first, is often felt as an essential loss. It was felt now with regard to the maiden. More, too, after a meeting so pleasant and so enkindling, she had seemed to imply that they

45

would never come together again. The young man softly followed her, stood opposite the house and watched her come into the upper room with the light. Presently his gaze was cut short by her approaching the window and pulling down the blind—Edward dwelling upon her vanishing figure with a hopeless sense of loss akin to that which Adam is said by logicians to have felt when he first saw the sun set, and thought, in his inexperience, that it would return no more.

He waited till her shadow had twice crossed the window, when, finding the charming outline was not to be expected again, he left the street, crossed the harbour-bridge, and entered his own solitary chamber on the other side, vaguely thinking as he went (for undefined reasons),

> One hope is too like despair
> For prudence to smother.

III.

THE EVENTS OF EIGHT DAYS

1. FROM THE TWENTY-SECOND TO THE TWENTY-SEVENTH OF JULY

But things are not what they seem. A responsive love for Edward Springrove had made its appearance in Cytherea's bosom with all the fascinating attributes of a first experience, not succeeding to or displacing other emotions, as in older hearts, but taking up entirely new ground; as when gazing just after sunset at the pale blue sky we see a star come into existence where nothing was before.

His parting words, 'Don't forget me,' she repeated to herself a hundred times, and though she thought their import was probably commonplace, she could not help toying with them,—looking at them from all points, and investing them with meanings of love and faithfulness,—ostensibly entertaining such meanings only as fables wherewith to pass the time, yet in her heart admitting, for detached instants, a possibility of their deeper truth. And thus, for hours after he had left her, her reason flirted with her fancy as a kitten will sport with a dove, pleasantly and smoothly through easy attitudes, but disclosing its cruel and unyielding nature at crises.

To turn now to the more material media through which this story moves, it so happened that the very next morning brought round a circumstance which, slight in itself, took up a relevant and important position between the past and the future of the persons herein concerned.

At breakfast time, just as Cytherea had again seen the postman pass without bringing her an answer to the advertisement, as she had fully expected he would do, Owen entered the room.

'Well,' he said, kissing her, 'you have not been alarmed, of course. Springrove told you what I had done, and you found there was no train?'

'Yes, it was all clear. But what is the lameness owing to?'

'I don't know—nothing. It has quite gone off now . . . Cytherea, I hope you like Springrove. Springrove's a nice fellow, you know.'

'Yes. I think he is, except that—'

'It happened just to the purpose that I should meet him there, didn't it? And when I reached the station and learnt that I could not get on by train my foot seemed better. I started off to walk home, and went about five miles along a path beside the railway. It then struck me that I might not be fit for anything to-day if I walked and aggravated the bothering foot, so I looked for a place to sleep at. There was no available village or inn, and I eventually got the keeper of a gate-house, where a lane crossed the line, to take me in.'

They proceeded with their breakfast. Owen yawned.

'You didn't get much sleep at the gate-house last night, I'm afraid, Owen,' said his sister.

'To tell the truth, I didn't. I was in such very close and narrow quarters. Those gate-houses are such small places, and the man had only his own bed to offer me. Ah, by-the-bye, Cythie, I have such an extraordinary thing to tell you in connection with this man!—by Jove, I had nearly forgotten it! But I'll go straight on. As I was saying, he had only his own bed to offer me, but I could not afford to be fastidious, and as he had a hearty manner, though a very queer one, I agreed to accept it, and he made a rough pallet for himself on the floor close beside me. Well, I could not sleep for my life, and I wished I had not stayed there, though I was so tired. For one thing, there were the luggage trains rattling by at my elbow the early part of the night. But worse than this, he talked continually in his sleep, and occasionally struck out with his limbs at something or another, knocking against the post of the bedstead and making it tremble. My condition was altogether so unsatisfactory that at last I awoke him, and asked him what he had been dreaming about for the previous hour, for I could get no sleep at all. He begged my pardon for disturbing me, but a name I had casually let fall that evening had led him to think of another stranger he had once had visit him, who had also accidentally mentioned the same name, and some very strange incidents connected with that meeting. The affair had occurred years and years ago; but what I had said had made him think and dream about it as if it were but yesterday. What was the word? I said. "Cytherea," he said. What was the story?

49

I asked then. He then told me that when he was a young man in London he borrowed a few pounds to add to a few he had saved up, and opened a little inn at Hammersmith. One evening, after the inn had been open about a couple of months, every idler in the neighbourhood ran off to Westminster. The Houses of Parliament were on fire.

'Not a soul remained in his parlour besides himself, and he began picking up the pipes and glasses his customers had hastily relinquished. At length a young lady about seventeen or eighteen came in. She asked if a woman was there waiting for herself—Miss Jane Taylor. He said no; asked the young lady if she would wait, and showed her into the small inner room. There was a glass-pane in the partition dividing this room from the bar to enable the landlord to see if his visitors, who sat there, wanted anything. A curious awkwardness and melancholy about the behaviour of the girl who called, caused my informant to look frequently at her through the partition. She seemed weary of her life, and sat with her face buried in her hands, evidently quite out of her element in such a house. Then a woman much older came in and greeted Miss Taylor by name. The man distinctly heard the following words pass between them:—

' "Why have you not brought him?"

' "He is ill; he is not likely to live through the night."

'At this announcement from the elderly woman, the young lady fell to the floor in a swoon, apparently overcome by the news. The landlord ran in and lifted her up. Well, do what they would they could not for a long time bring her back to consciousness, and began to be much alarmed. "Who is she?" the innkeeper said to the other woman. "I know her," the other said, with deep meaning in her tone. The elderly and young woman seemed allied, and yet strangers.

'She now showed signs of life, and it struck him (he was plainly of an inquisitive turn), that in her half-bewildered state he might get some information from her. He stooped over her, put his mouth to her ear, and said sharply, "What's your name?" "To catch a woman napping is difficult, even when she's half dead; but I did it," says the gatekeeper. When he asked her her name, she said immediately—

'"Cytherea"—and stopped suddenly.'

'My own name!' said Cytherea.

'Yes—your name. Well, the gateman thought at the time it might be equally with Jane a name she had invented for the occasion, that they might not trace her; but I think it was truth unconsciously uttered, for she added directly afterwards: "O, what have I said!" and was quite overcome again—this time with fright. Her vexation that the woman now doubted the genuineness of her other name was very much greater than that the innkeeper did, and it is evident that to blind the woman was her main object. He also learnt from words the elderly woman casually dropped, that meetings of the same kind had been held before, and that the falseness of the *soi-disant* Miss Jane Taylor's name had never been suspected by this dependent or confederate till then.

'She recovered, rested there for an hour, and first sending off her companion peremptorily (which was another odd thing), she left the house, offering the landlord all the money she had to say nothing about the circumstance. He has never seen her since, according to his own account. I said to him again and again, "Did you find any more particulars afterwards?" "Not a syllable," he said. O, he should never hear any more of that! too many years had passed since it happened. "At any rate, you found out her surname?" I said. "Well, well, that's my secret," he went on. "Perhaps I should never have been in this part of the world if it hadn't been for that. I failed as a publican, you know." I imagine the situation of gateman was given him and his debts paid off as a bribe to silence; but I can't say. "Ah, yes!" he said, with a long breath. "I have never heard that name mentioned since that time till to-night, and then there instantly rose to my eyes the vision of that young lady lying in a fainting fit." He then stopped talking and fell asleep. Telling the story must have relieved him as it did the Ancient Mariner, for he did not move a muscle or make another sound for the remainder of the night. Now isn't that an odd story?'

'It is indeed,' Cytherea murmured. 'Very, very strange.'

'Why should she have said your most uncommon name?' continued Owen. 'The man was evidently truthful, for there was not motive sufficient for his invention of such a tale, and he could not have done it either.'

Cytherea looked long at her brother. 'Don't you recognize anything else in connection with the story?' she said.

'What?' he asked.

'Do you remember what poor papa once let drop—that Cytherea was the name of his first sweetheart in Bloomsbury, who so mysteriously renounced him? A sort of intuition tells me that this was the same woman.'

'O no—not likely,' said her brother sceptically.

'How not likely, Owen? There's not another woman of the name in England. In what year used papa to say the event took place?'

'Eighteen hundred and thirty-five.'

'And when were the Houses of Parliament burnt?—stop, I can tell you.' She searched their little stock of books for a list of dates, and found one in an old school history.

'The Houses of Parliament were burnt down

in the evening of the sixteenth of October, eighteen hundred and thirty-four.'

'Nearly a year and a quarter before she met father,' remarked Owen.

They were silent. 'If papa had been alive, what a wonderful absorbing interest this story would have had for him,' said Cytherea by-and-by. 'And how strangely knowledge comes to us. We might have searched for a clue to her secret half the world over, and never found one. If we had really had any motive for trying to discover more of the sad history than papa told us, we should have gone to Bloomsbury; but not caring to do so, we go two hundred miles in the opposite direction, and there find information waiting to be told us. What could have been the secret, Owen?'

'Heaven knows. But our having heard a little more of her in this way (if she is the same woman) is a mere coincidence after all—a family story to tell our friends if we ever have any. But we shall never know any more of the episode now—trust our fates for that.'

Cytherea sat silently thinking.

'There was no answer this morning to your advertisement, Cytherea?' he continued.

'None.'

'I could see that by your looks when I came in.'

'Fancy not getting a single one,' she said sadly. 'Surely there must be people somewhere who want governesses?'

'Yes; but those who want them, and can afford to have them, get them mostly by friends' recommendations; whilst those who want them, and can't afford to have them, make use of their poor relations.'

'What shall I do?'

'Never mind it. Go on living with me. Don't let the difficulty trouble your mind so; you think about it all day. I can keep you, Cythie, in a plain way of living. Twenty-five shillings a week do not amount to much truly; but then many mechanics have no more, and we live quite as sparingly as journeymen mechanics . . . It is a meagre narrow life we are drifting into,' he added gloomily, 'but it is a degree more tolerable than the worrying sensation of all the world being ashamed of you, which we experienced at Hocbridge.'

'I couldn't go back there again,' she said.

'Nor I. O, I don't regret our course for a moment. We did quite right in dropping out of the world.' The sneering tones of the remark were almost too laboured to be real. 'Besides,' he continued, 'something better for me is sure to turn up soon. I wish my engagement here was a permanent one instead of for only two months. It may, certainly, be for a longer time, but all is uncertain.'

'I wish I could get something to do; and I must too,' she said firmly. 'Suppose, as is very probable, you are not wanted after the beginning of October—the time Mr. Gradfield mentioned—what should we do if I were dependent on you only throughout the winter?'

They pondered on numerous schemes by which a young lady might be supposed to earn a decent livelihood—more or less convenient and feasible in imagination, but relinquished them all until advertising had been once more tried, this time taking lower ground. Cytherea was vexed at her temerity in having represented to the world that so inexperienced a being as herself was a qualified governess; and had a fancy that this presumption of hers might be one reason why no ladies applied. The new and humbler attempt appeared in the following form:—

NURSERY GOVERNESS OR USEFUL COMPANION. A young person wishes to hear of a situation in either of the above capacities. Salary very moderate. She is a good needle-woman—Address G., 3 Cross Street, Budmouth Regis.

In the evening they went to post the letter, and then walked up and down the Parade for a while. Soon they met Springrove, said a few words to him, and passed on. Owen noticed that his sister's face had become crimson. Rather oddly they met Springrove again in a few minutes.

This time the three walked a little way

together, Edward ostensibly talking to Owen, though with a single thought to the reception of his words by the maiden at the farther side, upon whom his gaze was mostly resting, and who was attentively listening—looking fixedly upon the pavement the while. It has been said that men love with their eyes; women with their ears.

As Owen and himself were little more than acquaintances as yet, and as Springrove was wanting in the assurance of many men of his age, it now became necessary to wish his friends good-evening, or to find a reason for continuing near Cytherea by saying some nice new thing. He thought of a new thing; he proposed a pull across the bay. This was assented to. They went to the pier; stepped into one of the gaily painted boats moored alongside and sheered off. Cytherea sat in the stern steering.

They rowed that evening; the next came, and with it the necessity of rowing again. Then the next, and the next, Cytherea always sitting in the stern with the tiller ropes in her hand. The curves of her figure welded with those of the fragile boat in perfect continuation, as she girlishly yielded herself to its heaving and sinking, seeming to form with it an organic whole.

Then Owen was inclined to test his skill in paddling a canoe. Edward did not like canoes, and the issue was, that, having seen Owen on board, Springrove proposed to pull off after him with a pair of sculls; but not considering himself sufficiently accomplished to do finished rowing before a parade full of promenaders when there was a little swell on, and with the rudder unshipped in addition, he begged that Cytherea might come with him and steer as before. She stepped in, and they floated along in the wake of her brother. Thus passed the fifth evening on the water.

But the sympathetic pair were thrown into still closer companionship, and much more exclusive connection.

2. JULY THE TWENTY-NINTH

It was a sad time for Cytherea—the last day of Springrove's management at Gradfield's, and the last evening before his return from Budmouth to his father's house, previous to his departure for London.

Graye had been requested by the architect to survey a plot of land nearly twenty miles off, which, with the journey to and fro, would occupy him the whole day, and prevent his returning till late in the evening. Cytherea made a companion of her landlady to the extent of sharing meals and sitting with her during the morning of her brother's absence. Midday found her restless and miserable under this arrangement. All the afternoon she sat alone, looking out of the window for she scarcely knew whom, and hoping she scarcely knew what. Half-past five o'clock came—the end of Springrove's official day. Two minutes later Springrove walked by.

She endured her solitude for another half-hour, and then could endure no longer. She had hoped—while affecting to fear—that Edward would have found some reason or other for calling, but it seemed that he had not. Hastily dressing herself she went out, when the farce of an accidental meeting was repeated. Edward came upon her in the street at the first turning, and, like the Great Duke Ferdinand in 'The Statue and the Bust'—

He looked at her as a lover can;
She looked at him as one who awakes—
The past was a sleep, and her life began.

'Shall we have a boat?' he said impulsively.

How blissful it all is at first. Perhaps, indeed, the only bliss in the course of love which can truly be called Eden-like is that which prevails immediately after doubt has ended and before reflection has set in—at the dawn of the emotion, when it is not recognized by name, and before the consideration of what this love is, has given birth to the consideration of what difficulties it tends to create; when on the man's part, the mistress appears to the mind's eye in picturesque, hazy, and fresh morning

59

lights, and soft morning shadows; when, as yet, she is known only as the wearer of one dress, which shares her own personality; as the stander in one special position, the giver of one bright particular glance, and the speaker of one tender sentence; when, on her part, she is timidly careful over what she says and does, lest she should be misconstrued or under-rated to the breadth of a shadow of a hair.

'Shall we have a boat?' he said again, more softly, seeing that to his first question she had not answered, but looked uncertainly at the ground, then almost, but not quite, in his face, blushed a series of minute blushes, left off in the midst of them, and showed the usual signs of perplexity in a matter of the emotions.

Owen had always been with her before, but there was now a force of habit in the proceeding, and with Arcadian innocence she assumed that a row on the water was, under any circumstances, a natural thing. Without another word being spoken on either side, they went down the steps. He carefully handed her in, took his seat, slid noiselessly off the sand, and away from the shore.

They thus sat facing each other in the graceful yellow cockle-shell, and his eyes frequently found a resting-place in the depths of hers. The boat was so small that at each return of the sculls, when his hands came forward to begin the pull, they approached so near to her that her vivid imagination began to thrill her with a fancy that he was going to clasp his arms round her. The sensation grew so strong that she could not run the risk of again meeting his eyes at those critical moments, and turned aside to inspect the distant horizon; then she grew weary of looking sideways, and was driven to return to her natural position again. At this instant he again leant forward to begin, and met her glance by an ardent fixed gaze. An involuntary impulse of girlish embarrassment caused her to give a vehement pull at the tiller-rope, which brought the boat's head round till they stood directly for shore.

His eyes, which had dwelt upon her form during the whole time of her look askance, now left her; he perceived the direction in which they were going.

'Why, you have completely turned the boat, Miss Graye?' he said, looking over his shoulder. 'Look at our track on the water—a great semicircle, preceded by a series of zigzags as far as we can see.'

She looked attentively. 'Is it my fault or yours?' she inquired. 'Mine, I suppose?'

'I can't help saying that it is yours.'

She dropped the ropes decisively, feeling the slightest twinge of vexation at the answer.

'Why do you let go?'

'I do it so badly.'

'O no; you turned about for shore in a masterly way. Do you wish to return?'

'Yes, if you please.'

'Of course, then, I will at once.'

'I fear what the people will think of us—going in such absurd directions, and all through my wretched steering.'

'Never mind what the people think.' A pause. 'You surely are not so weak as to mind what the people think on such a matter as that?'

Those words might almost be called too firm and hard to be given by him to her; but never mind. For almost the first time in her life she felt the charming sensation, although on such an insignificant subject, of being compelled into an opinion by a man she loved. Owen, though less yielding physically, and more practical, would not have had the intellectual independence to answer a woman thus. She replied quietly and honestly—as honestly as when she had stated the contrary fact a minute earlier—

'I don't mind.'

'I'll unship the tiller that you may have nothing to do going back but to hold your parasol,' he continued, and arose to perform the operation, necessarily leaning closely against her, to guard against the risk of capsizing the boat as he reached his hands astern. His warm breath touched and crept round her face like a caress; but he was apparently only concerned with his task. She looked guilty of something when he seated himself. He read in her face what that something was—she had experienced a pleasure from his touch. But he flung a practical glance over his shoulder, seized the oars, and they sped in a straight line towards the shore.

Cytherea saw that he noted in her face what had passed in her heart, and that noting it, he continued as decided as before. She was inwardly distressed. She had not meant him to translate her words about returning home so literally at the first; she had not intended him to learn her secret; but more than all she was not able to endure the perception of his learning it and continuing unmoved.

There was nothing but misery to come now. They would step ashore; he would say good-night, go to London to-morrow, and the miserable She would lose him for ever. She did not quite suppose what was the fact, that a parallel thought was simultaneously passing through his mind.

They were now within ten yards, now within five; he was only now waiting for a 'smooth' to bring the boat in. Sweet, sweet Love must not be slain thus, was the fair maid's reasoning. She was equal to the occasion—ladies are—and delivered the god—

'Do you want very much to land, Mr. Springrove?' she said, letting her young violet eyes pine at him a very, very little.

'I? Not at all,' said he, looking an

astonishment at her inquiry which a slight twinkle of his eye half belied. 'But you do?'

'I think that now we have come out, and it is such a pleasant evening,' she said gently and sweetly, 'I should like a little longer row if you don't mind? I'll try to steer better than before if it makes it easier for you. I'll try very hard.'

It was the turn of his face to tell a tale now. He looked, 'We understand each other—ah, we do, darling!' turned the boat, and pulled back into the Bay once more.

'Now steer wherever you will,' he said, in a low voice. 'Never mind the directness of the course—wherever you will.'

'Shall it be Creston Shore?' she said, pointing to a stretch of beach northward from Budmouth Esplanade.

'Creston Shore certainly,' he responded, grasping the sculls. She took the strings daintily, and they wound away to the left.

For a long time nothing was audible in the boat but the regular dip of the oars, and their movement in the rowlocks. Springrove at length spoke.

'I must go away to-morrow,' he said tentatively.

'Yes,' she replied faintly.

'To endeavour to advance a little in my profession in London.'

'Yes,' she said again, with the same preoccupied softness.

'But I shan't advance.'

'Why not? Architecture is a bewitching profession. They say that an architect's work is another man's play.'

'Yes. But worldly advantage from an art doesn't depend upon mastering it. I used to think it did; but it doesn't. Those who get rich need have no skill at all as artists.'

'What need they have?'

'A certain kind of energy which men with any fondness for art possess very seldom indeed—an earnestness in making acquaintances, and a love for using them. They give their whole attention to the art of dining out, after mastering a few rudimentary facts to serve up in conversation. Now after saying that, do I seem a man likely to make a name?'

'You seem a man likely to make a mistake.'

'What's that?'

'To give too much room to the latent feeling which is rather common in these days among the unappreciated, that because some remarkably successful men are fools, all remarkably unsuccessful men are geniuses.'

'Pretty subtle for a young lady,' he said slowly. 'From that remark I should fancy you had bought experience.'

She passed over the idea. 'Do try to succeed,' she said, with wistful thoughtfulness, leaving her eyes on him.

Springrove flushed a little at the earnestness of her words, and mused. 'Then, like Cato the Censor, I shall do what I despise, to be in the fashion,' he said at last . . . 'Well, when I found all this out that I was speaking of, what ever do you think I did? From having already loved verse passionately, I went on to read it continually; then I went rhyming myself. If anything on earth ruins a man for useful occupation, and for content with reasonable success in a profession or trade, it is the habit of writing verses on emotional subjects, which had much better be left to die from want of nourishment.'

'Do you write poems now?' she said.

'None. Poetical days are getting past with me, according to the usual rule. Writing rhymes is a stage people of my sort pass through, as they pass through the stage of shaving for a beard, or thinking they are ill-used, or saying there's nothing in the world worth living for.'

'Then the difference between a common man and a recognized poet is, that one has been deluded, and cured of his delusion, and the other continues deluded all his days.'

'Well, there's just enough truth in what you say, to make the remark unbearable. However, it doesn't matter to me now that I "meditate the thankless Muse" no longer, but . . .' He paused, as if endeavouring to think what better thing he did.

Cytherea's mind ran on to the succeeding lines of the poem, and their startling harmony with the present situation suggested the fancy that he was *sporting* with her, and brought an awkward contemplativeness to her face.

Springrove guessed her thoughts, and in answer to them simply said 'Yes.' Then they were silent again.

'If I had known an Amaryllis was coming here, I should not have made arrangements for leaving,' he resumed.

Such levity, superimposed on the notion of *sport*, was intolerable to Cytherea; for a woman seems never to see any but the serious side of her attachment, though the most devoted lover has all the time a vague and dim perception that he is losing his old dignity and frittering away his time.

'But will you not try again to get on in your profession? Try once more; do try once more,' she murmured. 'I am going to try again. I have advertised for something to do.'

'Of course I will,' he said, with an eager gesture and smile. 'But we must remember that the fame of Christopher Wren himself depended upon the accident of a fire in Pudding Lane. My successes seem to come very slowly. I often think, that before I am ready to live, it will be time for me to die. However, I am trying—not for fame now, but for an easy life of reasonable comfort.'

It is a melancholy truth for the middle classes, that in proportion as they develop, by the study of poetry and art, their capacity for conjugal love of the highest and purest kind, they limit the possibility of their being able to exercise it—the very act putting out of their power the attainment of means sufficient for marriage. The man who works up a good income has had no time to learn love to its solemn extreme; the man who has learnt that has had no time to get rich.

'And if you should fail—utterly fail to get that reasonable wealth,' she said earnestly, 'don't be perturbed. The truly great stand upon no middle ledge; they are either famous or unknown.'

'Unknown,' he said, 'if their ideas have been allowed to flow with a sympathetic breadth. Famous only if they have been convergent and exclusive.'

'Yes; and I am afraid from that, that my remark was but discouragement, wearing the dress of comfort. Perhaps I was not quite right in—'

'It depends entirely upon what is meant by being truly great. But the long and the short of the matter is, that men must stick to a thing if they want to succeed in it—not giving way to over-much admiration for the flowers they see growing in other people's borders; which I am afraid has been my case.' He looked into the far distance and paused.

Adherence to a course with persistence sufficient to ensure success is possible to widely appreciative minds only when there is also found in them a power—commonplace in its nature, but rare in such combination—the power of assuming to conviction that in the outlying paths which appear so much more brilliant than their own, there are bitternesses equally great—unperceived simply on account of their remoteness.

*   *   *

They were opposite Ringsworth Shore. The cliffs here were formed of strata completely contrasting with those of the further side of the Bay, whilst in and beneath the water hard boulders had taken the place of sand and shingle, between which, however, the sea glided noiselessly, without breaking the crest of a single wave, so strikingly calm was the air. The breeze had entirely died away, leaving the water of that rare glassy smoothness which is unmarked even by the small dimples of the least aerial movement. Purples and blues of divers shades were reflected from this mirror accordingly as each undulation sloped east or west. They could see the rocky bottom some twenty feet beneath them, luxuriant with weeds of various growths, and dotted with pulpy creatures reflecting a silvery and spangled radiance upwards to their eyes.

At length she looked at him to learn the effect of her words of encouragement. He had let the oars drift alongside, and the boat had come to a standstill. Everything on earth seemed taking a contemplative rest, as if waiting to hear the avowal of something from his lips. At that instant he appeared to break a resolution hitherto zealously kept. Leaving his seat amidships he came and gently edged himself down beside her upon the narrow seat at the stern.

She breathed more quickly and warmly: he took her right hand in his own right: it was not withdrawn. He put his left hand behind her neck till it came round upon her left cheek: it was not thrust away. Lightly pressing her, he brought her face and mouth towards his own; when, at this the very brink, some unaccountable thought or spell within him suddenly made him halt—even now, and as it seemed as much to himself as to her, he timidly whispered 'May I?'

Her endeavour was to say No, so denuded of its flesh and sinews that its nature would hardly be recognized, or in other words a No from so near the affirmative frontier as to be affected with the Yes accent. It was thus a whispered No, drawn out to nearly a quarter of a minute's length, the O making itself audible as a sound like the spring coo of a pigeon on unusually friendly terms with its mate. Though conscious of her success in producing the kind of word she had wished to produce, she at the same time trembled in suspense as to how it would be taken. But the time available for doubt was so short as to admit of scarcely more than half a pulsation: pressing closer he kissed her. Then he kissed her again with a longer kiss.

It was the supremely happy moment of their experience. The 'bloom' and the 'purple light' were strong on the lineaments of both. Their hearts could hardly believe the evidence of their lips.

'I love you, and you love me, Cytherea!' he whispered.

She did not deny it; and all seemed well. The gentle sounds around them from the hills, the plains, the distant town, the adjacent shore, the water heaving at their side, the kiss, and the long kiss, were all 'many a voice of one delight,' and in unison with each other.

But his mind flew back to the same unpleasant thought which had been connected with the resolution he had broken a minute or two earlier. 'I could be a slave at my profession to win you, Cytherea; I would work at the meanest, honest trade to be near you—much less claim you as mine; I would—anything. But I have not told you all; it is not this; you don't know what there is yet to tell. Could you forgive as you can love?' She was alarmed to see that he had become pale with the question.

'No—do not speak,' he said. 'I have kept something from you, which has now become the cause of a great uneasiness. I had no right—to love you; but I did it. Something forbade—'

'What?' she exclaimed.

'Something forbade me—till the kiss—yes, till the kiss came; and now nothing shall forbid it! We'll hope in spite of all . . . I must, however, speak of this love of ours to your brother. Dearest, you had better go indoors whilst I meet him at the station, and explain everything.'

Cytherea's short-lived bliss was dead and gone. O, if she had known of this sequel would she have allowed him to break down the barrier of mere acquaintanceship—never, never!

'Will you not explain to me?' she faintly urged. Doubt—indefinite, carking doubt had taken possession of her.

'Not now. You alarm yourself unnecessarily,' he said tenderly. 'My only reason for keeping silence is that with my present knowledge I may tell an untrue story. It may be that there is nothing to tell. I am to blame for haste in alluding to any such thing. Forgive me, sweet— forgive me.' Her heart was ready to burst, and she could not answer him. He returned to his place and took to the oars.

They again made for the distant Esplanade, now, with its line of houses, lying like a dark grey band against the light western sky. The sun had set, and a star or two began to peep out. They drew nearer their destination, Edward as he pulled tracing listlessly with his eyes the red stripes upon her scarf, which grew to appear as black ones in the increasing dusk of evening. She surveyed the long line of lamps on the sea-wall of the town, now looking small and yellow, and seeming to send long tap-roots of fire quivering down deep into the sea. By-and-by they reached the landing-steps. He took her hand as before, and found it as cold as the water about them. It was not relinquished till he reached her door. His assurance had not removed the constraint of her manner: he saw that she blamed him mutely and with her eyes, like a captured sparrow. Left alone, he went and seated himself in a chair on the Esplanade.

Neither could she go indoors to her solitary room, feeling as she did in such a state of desperate heaviness. When Springrove was out of sight she turned back, and arrived at the corner just in time to see him sit down. Then she glided pensively along the pavement behind him, forgetting herself to marble like Melancholy herself as she mused in his neighbourhood unseen. She heard, without heeding, the notes of pianos and singing voices from the fashionable houses at her back, from the open windows of which the lamp-light streamed to join that of the orange-hued full moon, newly risen over the Bay in front. Then Edward began to pace up and down, and Cytherea, fearing that he would notice her, hastened homeward, flinging him a last look as she passed out of sight. No promise from him to write: no request that she herself would do so—nothing but an indefinite expression of hope in the face of some fear unknown to her. Alas, alas!

When Owen returned he found she was not in the small sitting-room, and creeping upstairs into her bedroom with a light, he discovered her there lying asleep upon the coverlet of the bed, still with her hat and jacket on. She had flung herself down on entering, and succumbed to the unwonted oppressiveness that ever attends full-blown love. The wet traces of tears were yet visible upon her long drooping lashes.

Love is a sowre delight, and sugred griefe,
   A living death, and ever-dying life.

'Cytherea,' he whispered, kissing her. She awoke with a start, and vented an exclamation before recovering her judgment. 'He's gone!' she said.

'He has told me all,' said Graye soothingly. 'He is going off early to-morrow morning. 'Twas a shame of him to win you away from me, and cruel of you to keep the growth of this attachment a secret.'

'We couldn't help it,' she said, and then jumping up—'Owen, has he told you *all*?'

'All of your love from beginning to end,' he said simply.

Edward then had not told more—as he

ought to have done: yet she could not convict him. But she would struggle against his fetters. She tingled to the very soles of her feet at the very possibility that he might be deluding her.

'Owen,' she continued, with dignity, 'what is he to me? Nothing. I must dismiss such weakness as this—believe me, I will. Something far more pressing must drive it away. I have been looking my position steadily in the face, and I must get a living somehow. I mean to advertise once more.'

'Advertising is no use.'

'This one will be.' He looked surprised at the sanguine tone of her answer, till she took a piece of paper from the table and showed it him.

'See what I am going to do,' she said sadly, almost bitterly. This was her third effort:—

LADY'S-MAID.   Inexperienced.   Age eighteen.—G., 3 Cross Street, Budmouth.

Owen—Owen the respectable—looked blank astonishment. He repeated in a nameless, varying tone, the two words—

'Lady's-maid!'

'Yes; lady's-maid. 'Tis an honest profession,' said Cytherea bravely.

'But *you*, Cytherea?'

'Yes, I—who am I?'

'You will never be a lady's-maid—never, I am quite sure.'

'I shall try to be, at any rate.'

'Such a disgrace—'

'Nonsense! I maintain that it is no disgrace!' she said, rather warmly. 'You know very well—'

'Well, since you will, you must,' he interrupted. 'Why do you put "inexperienced"?'

'Because I am.'

'Never mind that—scratch out "inexperienced." We are poor, Cytherea, aren't we?' he murmured, after a silence, 'and it seems that the two months will close my engagement here.'

'We can put up with being poor,' she said, 'if they only give us work to do . . . Yes, we desire as a blessing what was given us as a curse, and even that is denied. However, be cheerful, Owen, and never mind!'

In justice to desponding men, it is as well to remember that the brighter endurance of women at these epochs—invaluable, sweet, angelic, as it is—owes more of its origin to a narrower vision that shuts out many of the leaden-eyed despairs in the van, than to a hopefulness intense enough to quell them.

IV.

THE EVENTS OF ONE DAY

1. AUGUST THE FOURTH. TILL FOUR O'CLOCK

The early part of the next week brought an answer to Cytherea's last note of hope in the way of advertisement—not from a distance of hundreds of miles, London, Scotland, Ireland, the Continent—as Cytherea seemed to think it must, to be in keeping with the means adopted for obtaining it, but from a place in the neighbourhood of that in which she was living—a country mansion not twenty miles off. The reply ran thus:—

> KNAPWATER HOUSE,
> *August* 3, 1864.
> Miss Aldclyffe is in want of a young person as lady's-maid. The duties of the place are light. Miss Aldclyffe will be in Budmouth on Thursday, when, should G. still not have heard of a place, she would like to see her at the Belvedere Hotel, Esplanade, at four o'clock. No answer need be returned to this note.

A little earlier than the time named,

77

Cytherea, clothed in a modest bonnet, and a black silk jacket, turned down to the hotel. Expectation, the fresh air from the water, the bright, far-extending outlook, raised the most delicate of pink colours to her cheeks, and restored to her tread a portion of that elasticity which her past troubles, and thoughts of Edward, had well-nigh taken away.

She entered the vestibule, and went to the window of the bar.

'Is Miss Aldclyffe here?' she said to a nicely-dressed barmaid in the foreground, who was talking to a landlady covered with chains, knobs, and clamps of gold, in the background.

'No, she isn't,' said the barmaid, not very civilly. Cytherea looked a shade too pretty for a plain dresser.

'Miss Aldclyffe is expected here,' the landlady said to a third person, out of sight, in the tone of one who had known for several days the fact newly discovered from Cytherea. 'Get ready her room—be quick.' From the alacrity with which the order was given and taken, it seemed to Cytherea that Miss Aldclyffe must be a woman of considerable importance.

'You are to have an interview with Miss Aldclyffe here?' the landlady inquired.

'Yes.'

'The young person had better wait,' continued the landlady. With a money-taker's intuition she had rightly divined that Cytherea

78

would bring no profit to the house.

Cytherea was shown into a nondescript chamber, on the shady side of the building, which appeared to be either bedroom or dayroom, as occasion necessitated, and was one of a suite at the end of the first-floor corridor. The prevailing colour of the walls, curtains, carpet, and coverings of furniture, was more or less blue, to which the cold light coming from the north easterly sky, and falling on a wide roof of new slates—the only object the small window commanded—imparted a more striking paleness. But underneath the door, communicating with the next room of the suite, gleamed an infinitesimally small, yet very powerful, fraction of contrast—a very thin line of ruddy light, showing that the sun beamed strongly into this room adjoining. The line of radiance was the only cheering thing visible in the place.

People give way to very infantine thoughts and actions when they wait; the battle-field of life is temporarily fenced off by a hard and fast line—the interview. Cytherea fixed her eyes idly upon the streak, and began picturing a wonderful paradise on the other side as the source of such a beam—reminding her of the well-known good deed in a naughty world.

Whilst she watched the particles of dust floating before the brilliant chink she heard a carriage and horses stop opposite the front of the house. Afterwards came the rustle of a lady's skirts down the corridor, and into the room communicating with the one Cytherea occupied.

The golden line vanished in parts like the phosphorescent streak caused by the striking of a match; there was the fall of a light footstep on the floor just behind it: then a pause. Then the foot tapped impatiently, and 'There's no one here!' was spoken imperiously by a lady's tongue.

'No, madam; in the next room. I am going to fetch her,' said the attendant.

'That will do—or you needn't go in; I will call her.'

Cytherea had risen, and she advanced to the middle door with the chink under it as the servant retired. She had just laid her hand on the knob, when it slipped round within her fingers, and the door was pulled open from the other side.

2. FOUR O'CLOCK

The direct blaze of the afternoon sun, partly refracted through the crimson curtains of the window, and heightened by reflections from the crimson-flock paper which covered the walls, and a carpet on the floor of the same tint, shone with a burning glow round the form of a lady standing close to Cytherea's front with the door in her hand. The stranger appeared to the maiden's eyes—fresh from the blue gloom, and assisted by an imagination fresh from nature—like a tall black figure standing in the midst of fire. It was the figure of a finely-built woman, of spare though not angular proportions.

Cytherea involuntarily shaded her eyes with her hand, retreated a step or two, and then she could for the first time see Miss Aldclyffe's face in addition to her outline, lit up by the secondary and softer light that was reflected from the varnished panels of the door. She was not a very young woman, but could boast of much beauty of the majestic autumnal phase.

'O,' said the lady, 'come this way.' Cytherea followed her to the embrasure of the window.

Both the women showed off themselves to advantage as they walked forward in the orange light; and each showed too in her face that she had been struck with her companion's appearance. The warm tint added to Cytherea's face a voluptuousness which youth and a simple life had not yet allowed to express itself there ordinarily; whilst in the elder lady's face it reduced the customary expression, which might have been called sternness, if not harshness, to grandeur, and warmed her decaying complexion with much of the youthful richness it plainly had once possessed.

She appeared now no more than five-and-thirty, though she might easily have been ten or a dozen years older. She had clear steady eyes, a Roman nose in its purest form, and also the round prominent chin with which the Caesars are represented in ancient marbles; a mouth expressing a capability for and tendency to strong emotion, habitually controlled by pride. There was a severity about the lower outlines of the face which gave a masculine cast to this portion of her countenance. Womanly weakness was nowhere visible save in one part—the curve of her forehead and brows—there it was clear and emphatic. She wore a lace shawl over a brown silk dress, and a net bonnet set with a few blue cornflowers.

'You inserted the advertisement for a situation as lady's-maid giving the address, G., Cross Street?'

'Yes, madam. Graye.'

'Yes. I have heard your name—Mrs. Morris, my housekeeper, mentioned you, and pointed out your advertisement.'

This was puzzling intelligence, but there was not time enough to consider it.

'Where did you live last?' continued Miss Aldclyffe.

'I have never been a servant before. I lived at home.'

'Never been out? I thought too at sight of you that you were too girlish-looking to have done much. But why did you advertise with such assurance? It misleads people.'

'I am very sorry: I put "inexperienced" at first, but my brother said it is absurd to trumpet your own weakness to the world, and would not let it remain.'

'But your mother knew what was right, I suppose?'

'I have no mother, madam.'

'Your father, then?'

'I have no father.'

'Well,' she said, more softly, 'your sisters, aunts, or cousins.'

'They didn't think anything about it.'

'You didn't ask them, I suppose.'

'No.'

'You should have done so, then. Why didn't you?'

'Because I haven't any of them, either.'

Miss Aldclyffe showed her surprise. 'You deserve forgiveness then at any rate, child,' she said, in a sort of drily-kind tone. 'However, I am afraid you do not suit me, as I am looking for an elderly person. You see, I want an experienced maid who knows all the usual duties of the office.' She was going to add, 'Though I like your appearance,' but the words seemed offensive to apply to the ladylike girl before her, and she modified them to, 'though I like you much.'

'I am sorry I misled you, madam,' said Cytherea.

Miss Aldclyffe stood in a reverie, without replying.

'Good afternoon,' continued Cytherea.

'Good-bye, Miss Graye—I hope you will

succeed.'

Cytherea turned away towards the door. The movement chanced to be one of her masterpieces. It was precise: it had as much beauty as was compatible with precision, and as little coquettishness as was compatible with beauty.

And she had in turning looked over her shoulder at the other lady with a faint accent of reproach in her face. Those who remember Greuze's 'Head of a Girl,' have an idea of Cytherea's look askance at the turning. It is not for a man to tell fishers of men how to set out their fascinations so as to bring about the highest possible average of takes within the year: but the action that tugs the hardest of all at an emotional beholder is this sweet method of turning which steals the bosom away and leaves the eyes behind.

Now Miss Aldclyffe herself was no tyro at wheeling. When Cytherea had closed the door upon her, she remained for some time in her motionless attitude, listening to the gradually dying sound of the maiden's retreating footsteps. She murmured to herself, 'It is almost worth while to be bored with instructing her in order to have a creature who could glide round my luxurious indolent body in that manner, and look at me in that way—I warrant how light her fingers are upon one's head and neck . . . What a silly modest young thing she is, to go away so suddenly as that!' She rang the bell.

'Ask the young lady who has just left me to step back again,' she said to the attendant. 'Quick! or she will be gone.'

Cytherea was now in the vestibule, thinking that if she had told her history, Miss Aldclyffe might perhaps have taken her into the household; yet her history she particularly wished to conceal from a stranger. When she was recalled she turned back without feeling much surprise. Something, she knew not what, told her she had not seen the last of Miss Aldclyffe.

'You have somebody to refer me to, of course,' the lady said, when Cytherea had re-entered the room.

'Yes: Mr. Thorn, a solicitor at Aldbrickham.'

'And are you a clever needlewoman?'

'I am considered to be.'

'Then I think that at any rate I will write to Mr. Thorn,' said Miss Aldclyffe, with a little smile. 'It is true, the whole proceeding is very irregular; but my present maid leaves next Monday, and neither of the five I have already seen seem to do for me . . . Well, I will write to Mr. Thorn, and if his reply is satisfactory, you shall hear from me. It will be as well to set yourself in readiness to come on Monday.'

When Cytherea had again been watched out of the room, Miss Aldclyffe asked for writing materials, that she might at once communicate with Mr. Thorn. She indecisively played with the pen. 'Suppose Mr. Thorn's reply to be in any way disheartening—and even if so from his own imperfect acquaintance with the young creature more than from circumstantial knowledge—I shall feel obliged to give her up. Then I shall regret that I did not give her one trial in spite of other people's prejudices. All her account of herself is reliable enough—yes, I can see that by her face. I like that face of hers.'

Miss Aldclyffe put down the pen and left the hotel without writing to Mr. Thorn.

V.

THE EVENTS OF ONE DAY

1. AUGUST THE EIGHTH. MORNING AND AFTERNOON

At post-time on that following Monday morning, Cytherea watched so anxiously for the postman, that as the time which must bring him narrowed less and less her vivid expectation had only a degree less tangibility than his presence itself. In another second his form came into view. He brought two letters for Cytherea.

One from Miss Aldclyffe, simply stating that she wished Cytherea to come on trial: that she would require her to be at Knapwater House by Monday evening.

The other was from Edward Springrove. He told her that she was the bright spot of his life: that her existence was far dearer to him than his own: that he had never known what it was to love till he had met her. True, he had felt passing attachments to other faces from time to time; but they all had been weak inclinations towards those faces as they then appeared. He loved her past and future, as well as her present. He pictured her as a child: he loved her. He pictured her of sage years: he loved her. He pictured her in trouble; he loved her. Homely friendship entered into his love for her, without which all love was evanescent.

He would make one depressing statement. Uncontrollable circumstances (a long history, with which it was impossible to acquaint her at present) operated to a certain extent as a drag upon his wishes. He had felt this more strongly at the time of their parting than he did now— and it was the cause of his abrupt behaviour, for which he begged her to forgive him. He saw now an honourable way of freeing himself, and the perception had prompted him to write. In the meantime might he indulge in the hope of possessing her on some bright future day, when by hard labour generated from her own encouraging words, he had placed himself in a position she would think worthy to be shared with him?

Dear little letter; she huddled it up. So much more important a love-letter seems to a girl than to a man. Springrove was unconsciously clever in his letters, and a man with a talent of that kind may write himself up to a hero in the mind of a young woman who loves him without knowing much about him. Springrove already stood a cubit higher in her imagination than he did in his shoes.

During the day she flitted about the room in an ecstasy of pleasure, packing the things and thinking of an answer which should be worthy of the tender tone of the question, her love bubbling from her involuntarily, like prophesyings from a prophet.

In the afternoon Owen went with her to the railway-station, and put her in the train for Carriford Road, the station nearest to Knapwater House.

Half-an-hour later she stepped out upon the platform, and found nobody there to receive her—though a pony-carriage was waiting outside. In two minutes she saw a melancholy man in cheerful livery running towards her from a public-house close adjoining, who proved to be the servant sent to fetch her. There are two ways of getting rid of sorrows: one by living them down, the other by drowning them. The coachman drowned his.

He informed her that her luggage would be fetched by a spring-waggon in about half-an-hour; then helped her into the chaise and drove off.

Her lover's letter, lying close against her neck, fortified her against the restless timidity she had previously felt concerning this new undertaking, and completely furnished her with the confident ease of mind which is required for the critical observation of surrounding objects. It was just that stage in the slow decline of the summer days, when the deep, dark, and vacuous hot-weather shadows are beginning to be replaced by blue ones that have a surface and substance to the eye. They trotted along the turnpike road for a distance of about a mile, which brought them just outside the village of Carriford, and then turned through large lodge-gates, on the heavy stone piers of which stood a pair of bitterns cast in bronze. They then entered the park and wound along a drive shaded by old and drooping lime-trees, not arranged in the form of an avenue, but standing irregularly, sometimes leaving the track completely exposed to the sky, at other times casting a shade over it, which almost approached gloom—the under surface of the lowest boughs hanging at a uniform level of six feet above the grass—the extreme height to which the nibbling mouths of the cattle could reach.

'Is that the house?' said Cytherea expectantly, catching sight of a grey gable between the trees, and losing it again.

'No; that's the old manor-house—or rather

all that's left of it. The Aldycliffes used to let it sometimes, but it was oftener empty. 'Tis now divided into three cottages. Respectable people didn't care to live there.'

'Why didn't they?'

'Well, 'tis so awkward and unhandy. You see so much of it has been pulled down, and the rooms that are left won't do very well for a small residence. 'Tis so dismal, too, and like most old houses stands too low down in the hollow to be healthy.'

'Do they tell any horrid stories about it?'

'No, not a single one.'

'Ah, that's a pity.'

'Yes, that's what I say. 'Tis jest the house for a nice ghastly hair-on-end story, that would make the parish religious. Perhaps it will have one some day to make it complete; but there's not a word of the kind now. There, I wouldn't live there for all that. In fact, I couldn't. O no, I couldn't.'

'Why couldn't you?'

'The sounds.'

'What are they?'

'One is the waterfall, which stands so close by that you can hear that there waterfall in every room of the house, night or day, ill or well. 'Tis enough to drive anybody mad: now hark.'

He stopped the horse. Above the slight common sounds in the air came the unvarying steady rush of falling water from some spot unseen on account of the thick foliage of the grove.

'There's something awful in the timing o' that sound, ain't there, miss?'

'When you say there is, there really seems to be. You said there were two—what is the other horrid sound?'

'The pumping-engine. That's close by the Old House, and sends water up the hill and all over the Great House. We shall hear that directly . . . There, now hark again.'

From the same direction down the dell they could now hear the whistling creak of cranks, repeated at intervals of half-a-minute, with a sousing noise between each: a creak, a souse, then another creak, and so on continually.

'Now if anybody could make shift to live through the other sounds, these would finish him off, don't you think so, miss? That machine goes on night and day, summer and winter, and is hardly ever greased or visited. Ah, it tries the nerves at night, especially if you are not very well; though we don't often hear it at the Great House.'

'That sound is certainly very dismal. They might have the wheel greased. Does Miss Aldclyffe take any interest in these things?'

'Well, scarcely; you see her father doesn't attend to that sort of thing as he used to. The engine was once quite his hobby. But now he's getten old and very seldom goes there.'

'How many are there in family?'

91

'Only her father and herself. He's a' old man of seventy.'

'I had thought that Miss Aldclyffe was sole mistress of the property, and lived here alone.'

'No, m—' The coachman was continually checking himself thus, being about to style her miss involuntarily, and then recollecting that he was only speaking to the new lady's-maid.

'She will soon be mistress, however, I am afraid,' he continued, as if speaking by a spirit of prophecy denied to ordinary humanity. 'The poor old gentleman has decayed very fast lately.' The man then drew a long breath.

'Why did you breathe sadly like that?' said Cytherea.

'Ah! . . . When he's dead peace will be all over with us old servants. I expect to see the old house turned inside out.'

'She will marry, do you mean?'

'Marry—not she! I wish she would. No, in her soul she's as solitary as Robinson Crusoe, though she has acquaintances in plenty, if not relations. There's the rector, Mr. Raunham—he's a relation by marriage—yet she's quite distant towards him. And people say that if she keeps single there will be hardly a life between Mr. Raunham and the heirship of the estate. Dang it, she don't care. She's an extraordinary picture of womankind—very extraordinary.'

'In what way besides?'

'You'll know soon enough, miss. She has had seven lady's-maids this last twelvemonth. I

92

assure you 'tis one body's work to fetch 'em from the station and take 'em back again. The Lord must be a neglectful party at heart, or he'd never permit such overbearen goings on!'

'Does she dismiss them directly they come!'

'Not at all—she never dismisses them—they go theirselves. Ye see 'tis like this. She's got a very quick temper; she flees in a passion with them for nothing at all; next mornen they come up and say they are going; she's sorry for it and wishes they'd stay, but she's as proud as a lucifer, and her pride won't let her say, "Stay," and away they go. 'Tis like this in fact. If you say to her about anybody, "Ah, poor thing!" she says, "Pooh! indeed!" If you say, "Pooh, indeed!" "Ah, poor thing!" she says directly. She hangs the chief baker, as mid be, and restores the chief butler, as mid be, though the devil but Pharaoh herself can see the difference between 'em.'

Cytherea was silent. She feared she might be again a burden to her brother.

'However, you stand a very good chance,' the man went on, 'for I think she likes you more than common. I have never known her send the pony-carriage to meet one before; 'tis always the trap, but this time she said, in a very particular ladylike tone, "Roobert, gaow with the pony-kerriage." . . . There, 'tis true, pony and carriage too are getten rather shabby now,' he added, looking round upon the vehicle as if to keep Cytherea's pride within reasonable limits.

' 'Tis to be hoped you'll please in dressen her to-night.'

'Why to-night?'

'There's a dinner-party of seventeen; 'tis her father's birthday, and she's very particular about her looks at such times. Now see; this is the house. Livelier up here, isn't it, miss?'

They were now on rising ground, and had just emerged from a clump of trees. Still a little higher than where they stood was situated the mansion, called Knapwater House, the offices gradually losing themselves among the trees behind.

2. EVENING

The house was regularly and substantially built of clean grey freestone throughout, in that plainer fashion of classicism which prevailed at the latter end of the eighteenth century, when the copyists called designers had grown weary of fantastic variations in the Roman orders. The main block approximated to a square on the ground plan, having a projection in the centre of each side, surmounted by a pediment. From each angle of the inferior side ran a line of buildings lower than the rest, turning inwards again at their further end, and forming within them a spacious open court, within which resounded an echo of astonishing clearness. These erections were in their turn backed by ivy-covered ice-houses, laundries, and stables, the whole mass of subsidiary buildings being half buried beneath close-set shrubs and trees.

There was opening sufficient through the foliage on the right hand to enable her on nearer approach to form an idea of the arrangement of the remoter or lawn front also. The natural features and contour of this quarter of the site had evidently dictated the position of the house primarily, and were of the ordinary, and upon the whole, most satisfactory kind, namely, a broad, graceful slope running from the terrace beneath the walls to the margin of a placid lake lying below, upon the surface of which a dozen swans and a green punt floated at leisure. An irregular wooded island stood in the midst of the lake; beyond this and the further margin of the water were plantations and greensward of varied outlines, the trees heightening, by half veiling, the softness of the exquisite landscape stretching behind.

The glimpses she had obtained of this portion were now checked by the angle of the building. In a minute or two they reached the side door, at which Cytherea alighted. She was welcomed by an elderly woman of lengthy smiles and general pleasantness, who announced herself to be Mrs. Morris, the housekeeper.

'Mrs. Graye, I believe?' she said.

'I am not—O yes, yes, we are all mistresses,' said Cytherea, smiling, but forcedly. The title accorded her seemed disagreeably like the first slight scar of a brand, and she thought of Owen's prophecy.

Mrs. Morris led her into a comfortable parlour called The Room. Here tea was made ready, and Cytherea sat down, looking, whenever occasion allowed, at Mrs. Morris with great interest and curiosity, to discover, if possible, something in her which should give a clue to the secret of her knowledge of herself, and the recommendation based upon it. But nothing was to be learnt, at any rate just then. Mrs. Morris was perpetually getting up, feeling in her pockets, going to cupboards, leaving the room two or three minutes, and trotting back again.

'You'll excuse me, Mrs. Graye,' she said, 'but 'tis the old gentleman's birthday, and they always have a lot of people to dinner on that day, though he's getting up in years now. However, none of them are sleepers—she generally keeps the house pretty clear of lodgers (being a lady with no intimate friends, though many acquaintances), which, though it gives us less to do, makes it all the duller for the younger maids in the house.' Mrs. Morris then proceeded to give in fragmentary speeches an outline of the constitution and government of the estate.

'Now, are you sure you have quite done tea? Not a bit or drop more? Why, you've eaten nothing, I'm sure . . . Well, now, it is rather inconvenient that the other maid is not here to show you the ways of the house a little, but she left last Saturday, and Miss Aldclyffe has been making shift with poor old clumsy me for a maid all yesterday and this morning. She is not come in yet. I expect she will ask for you, Mrs. Graye, the first thing . . . I was going to say that if you have really done tea, I will take you upstairs, and show you through the wardrobes—Miss Aldclyffe's things are not laid out for to-night yet.'

She preceded Cytherea upstairs, pointed out her own room, and then took her into Miss Aldclyffe's dressing-room, on the first-floor; where, after explaining the whereabouts of various articles of apparel, the housekeeper left her, telling her that she had an hour yet upon her hands before dressing-time. Cytherea laid out upon the bed in the next room all that she had been told would be required that evening, and then went again to the little room which had been appropriated to herself.

Here she sat down by the open window, leant out upon the sill like another Blessed Damozel, and listlessly looked down upon the brilliant pattern of colours formed by the flower-beds on the lawn—now richly crowded with late summer blossom. But the vivacity of spirit which had hitherto enlivened her, was fast ebbing under the pressure of prosaic realities, and the warm scarlet of the geraniums, glowing most conspicuously, and mingling with the vivid cold red and green of the verbenas, the rich depth of the dahlia, and the ripe mellowness of the calceolaria, backed by the pale hue of a flock of meek sheep feeding in the open park, close to the other side of the fence, were, to a great extent, lost upon her eyes. She was thinking that nothing seemed worth while; that it was possible she might die in a workhouse; and what did it matter? The petty, vulgar details of servitude that she had just passed through, her dependence upon the whims of a strange woman, the necessity of quenching all individuality of character in herself, and relinquishing her own peculiar tastes to help on the wheel of this alien establishment, made her sick and sad, and she almost longed to pursue some free, out-of-doors employment, sleep under trees or a hut, and know no enemy but winter and cold weather, like shepherds and cowkeepers, and birds and animals—ay, like the sheep she saw there under her window.

She looked sympathizingly at them for several minutes, imagining their enjoyment of the rich grass.

'Yes—like those sheep,' she said aloud; and her face reddened with surprise at a discovery she made that very instant.

The flock consisted of some ninety or a

hundred young stock ewes: the surface of their fleece was as rounded and even as a cushion, and white as milk. Now she had just observed that on the left buttock of every one of them were marked in distinct red letters the initials 'E. S.'

'E. S.' could bring to Cytherea's mind only one thought; but that immediately and for ever—the name of her lover, Edward Springrove.

'O, if it should be—!' She interrupted her words by a resolve. Miss Aldclyffe's carriage at the same moment made its appearance in the drive; but Miss Aldclyffe was not her object now. It was to ascertain to whom the sheep belonged, and to set her surmise at rest one way or the other. She flew downstairs to Mrs. Morris.

'Whose sheep are those in the park, Mrs. Morris?'

'Farmer Springrove's.'

'What Farmer Springrove is that?' she said quickly.

'Why, surely you know? Your friend, Farmer Springrove, the cider-maker, and who keeps the Three Tranters Inn; who recommended you to me when he came in to see me the other day?'

Cytherea's mother-wit suddenly warned her in the midst of her excitement that it was necessary not to betray the secret of her love. 'O yes,' she said, 'of course.' Her thoughts had

99

run as follows in that short interval:—

'Farmer Springrove is Edward's father, and his name is Edward too.

'Edward knew I was going to advertise for a situation of some kind.

'He watched the *Times*, and saw it, my address being attached.

'He thought it would be excellent for me to be here that we might meet whenever he came home.

'He told his father that I might be recommended as a lady's-maid; and he knew my brother and myself.

'His father told Mrs. Morris; Mrs. Morris told Miss Aldclyffe.'

The whole chain of incidents that drew her there was plain, and there was no such thing as chance in the matter. It was all Edward's doing.

The sound of a bell was heard. Cytherea did not heed it, and still continued in her reverie.

'That's Miss Aldclyffe's bell,' said Mrs. Morris.

'I suppose it is,' said the young woman placidly.

'Well, it means that you must go up to her,' the matron continued, in a tone of surprise.

Cytherea felt a burning heat come over her, mingled with a sudden irritation at Mrs. Morris's hint. But the good sense which had recognized stern necessity prevailed over rebellious independence; the flush passed, and she said hastily—

'Yes, yes; of course, I must go to her when she pulls the bell—whether I want to or no.'

However, in spite of this painful reminder of her new position in life, Cytherea left the apartment in a mood far different from the gloomy sadness of ten minutes previous. The place felt like home to her now; she did not mind the pettiness of her occupation, because Edward evidently did not mind it; and this was Edward's own spot. She found time on her way to Miss Aldclyffe's dressing-room to hurriedly glide out by a side door, and look for a moment at the unconscious sheep bearing the friendly initials. She went up to them to try to touch one of the flock, and felt vexed that they all stared sceptically at her kind advances, and then ran pell-mell down the hill. Then, fearing any one should discover her childish movements, she slipped indoors again, and ascended the staircase, catching glimpses, as she passed, of silver-buttoned footmen, who flashed about the passages like lightning.

Miss Aldclyffe's dressing-room was an apartment which, on a casual survey, conveyed an impression that it was available for almost any purpose save the adornment of the feminine person. In its hours of perfect order nothing pertaining to the toilet was visible; even the inevitable mirrors with their accessories were arranged in a roomy recess not noticeable from the door, lighted by a window of its own, called the dressing-window.

The washing-stand figured as a vast oak chest, carved with grotesque Renaissance ornament. The dressing-table was in appearance something between a high altar and a cabinet piano, the surface being richly worked in the same style of semi-classic decoration, but the extraordinary outline having been arrived at by an ingenious joiner and decorator from the neighbouring town, after months of painful toil in cutting and fitting, under Miss Aldclyffe's immediate eye; the materials being the remains of two or three old cabinets the lady had found in the lumber-room. About two-thirds of the floor was carpeted, the remaining portion being laid with parquetry of light and dark woods.

Miss Aldclyffe was standing at the larger window, away from the dressing-niche. She bowed, and said pleasantly, 'I am glad you have come. We shall get on capitally, I dare say.'

Her bonnet was off. Cytherea did not think her so handsome as on the earlier day; the queenliness of her beauty was harder and less warm. But a worse discovery than this was that Miss Aldclyffe, with the usual obliviousness of rich people to their dependents' specialities, seemed to have quite forgotten Cytherea's inexperience, and mechanically delivered up her body to her handmaid without a thought of details, and with a mild yawn.

Everything went well at first. The dress was removed, stockings and black boots were taken off, and silk stockings and white shoes were put on. Miss Aldclyffe then retired to bathe her hands and face, and Cytherea drew breath. If she could get through this first evening, all would be right. She felt that it was unfortunate that such a crucial test for her powers as a birthday dinner should have been applied on the threshold of her arrival; but set to again.

Miss Aldclyffe was now arrayed in a white dressing-gown, and dropped languidly into an easy-chair, pushed up before the glass. The instincts of her sex and her own practice told Cytherea the next movement. She let Miss Aldclyffe's hair fall about her shoulders, and began to arrange it. It proved to be all real; a satisfaction.

Miss Aldclyffe was musingly looking on the floor, and the operation went on for some minutes in silence. At length her thoughts seemed to turn to the present, and she lifted her eyes to the glass.

'Why, what on earth are you doing with my head?' she exclaimed, with widely opened eyes. At the words she felt the back of Cytherea's little hand tremble against her neck.

'Perhaps you prefer it done the other fashion, madam?' said the maiden.

'No, no; that's the fashion right enough, but you must make more show of my hair than that, or I shall have to buy some, which God

103

forbid!'

'It is how I do my own,' said Cytherea naively, and with a sweetness of tone that would have pleased the most acrimonious under favourable circumstances; but tyranny was in the ascendant with Miss Aldclyffe at this moment, and she was assured of palatable food for her vice by having felt the trembling of Cytherea's hand.

'Yours, indeed! *Your* hair! Come, go on.' Considering that Cytherea possessed at least five times as much of that valuable auxiliary to woman's beauty as the lady before her, there was at the same time some excuse for Miss Aldclyffe's outburst. She remembered herself, however, and said more quietly, 'Now then, Graye—By-the-bye, what do they call you downstairs?'

'Mrs. Graye,' said the handmaid.

'Then tell them not to do any such absurd thing—not but that it is quite according to usage; but you are too young yet.'

This dialogue tided Cytherea safely onward through the hairdressing till the flowers and diamonds were to be placed upon the lady's brow.

Cytherea began arranging them tastefully, and to the very best of her judgment.

'That won't do,' said Miss Aldclyffe harshly.

'Why?'

'I look too young—an old dressed doll.'

'Will that, madam?'

'No, I look a fright—a perfect fright!'

'This way, perhaps?'

'Heavens! Don't worry me so.' She shut her lips like a trap.

Having once worked herself up to the belief that her head-dress was to be a failure that evening, no cleverness of Cytherea's in arranging it could please her. She continued in a smouldering passion during the remainder of the performance, keeping her lips firmly closed, and the muscles of her body rigid. Finally, snatching up her gloves, and taking her handkerchief and fan in her hand, she silently sailed out of the room, without betraying the least consciousness of another woman's presence behind her.

Cytherea's fears that at the undressing this suppressed anger would find a vent, kept her on thorns throughout the evening. She tried to read; she could not. She tried to sew; she could not. She tried to muse; she could not do that connectedly. 'If this is the beginning, what will the end be!' she said in a whisper, and felt many misgivings as to the policy of being overhasty in establishing an independence at the expense of congruity with a cherished past.

3. MIDNIGHT

The clock struck twelve. The Aldclyffe state dinner was over. The company had all gone, and Miss Aldclyffe's bell rang loudly and jerkingly.

Cytherea started to her feet at the sound, which broke in upon a fitful sleep that had overtaken her. She had been sitting drearily in her chair waiting minute after minute for the signal, her brain in that state of intentness which takes cognizance of the passage of Time as a real motion—motion without matter—the instants throbbing past in the company of a feverish pulse. She hastened to the room, to find the lady sitting before the dressing shrine, illuminated on both sides, and looking so queenly in her attitude of absolute repose, that the younger woman felt the awfullest sense of responsibility at her Vandalism in having undertaken to demolish so imposing a pile.

The lady's jewelled ornaments were taken off in silence—some by her own listless hands, some by Cytherea's. Then followed the outer stratum of clothing. The dress being removed, Cytherea took it in her hand and went with it into the bedroom adjoining, intending to hang it in the wardrobe. But on second thoughts, in order that she might not keep Miss Aldclyffe waiting a moment longer than necessary, she flung it down on the first resting-place that came to hand, which happened to be the bed, and re-entered the dressing-room with the noiseless footfall of a kitten. She paused in the middle of the room.

She was unnoticed, and her sudden return

had plainly not been expected. During the short time of Cytherea's absence, Miss Aldclyffe had pulled off a kind of chemisette of Brussels net, drawn high above the throat, which she had worn with her evening dress as a semi-opaque covering to her shoulders, and in its place had put her night-gown round her. Her right hand was lifted to her neck, as if engaged in fastening her night-gown.

But on a second glance Miss Aldclyffe's proceeding was clearer to Cytherea. She was not fastening her night-gown; it had been carelessly thrown round her, and Miss Aldclyffe was really occupied in holding up to her eyes some small object that she was keenly scrutinizing. And now on suddenly discovering the presence of Cytherea at the back of the apartment, instead of naturally continuing or concluding her inspection, she desisted hurriedly; the tiny snap of a spring was heard, her hand was removed, and she began adjusting her robes.

Modesty might have directed her hasty action of enwrapping her shoulders, but it was scarcely likely, considering Miss Aldclyffe's temperament, that she had all her life been used to a maid, Cytherea's youth, and the elder lady's marked treatment of her as if she were a mere child or plaything. The matter was too slight to reason about, and yet upon the whole it seemed that Miss Aldclyffe must have a practical reason for concealing her neck.

With a timid sense of being an intruder Cytherea was about to step back and out of the room; but at the same moment Miss Aldclyffe turned, saw the impulse, and told her companion to stay, looking into her eyes as if she had half an intention to explain something. Cytherea felt certain it was the little mystery of her late movements. The other withdrew her eyes; Cytherea went to fetch the dressing-gown, and wheeled round again to bring it up to Miss Aldclyffe, who had now partly removed her night-dress to put it on the proper way, and still sat with her back towards Cytherea.

Her neck was again quite open and uncovered, and though hidden from the direct line of Cytherea's vision, she saw it reflected in the glass—the fair white surface, and the inimitable combination of curves between throat and bosom which artists adore, being brightly lit up by the light burning on either side.

And the lady's prior proceedings were now explained in the simplest manner. In the midst of her breast, like an island in a sea of pearl, reclined an exquisite little gold locket, embellished with arabesque work of blue, red, and white enamel. That was undoubtedly what Miss Aldclyffe had been contemplating; and, moreover, not having been put off with her other ornaments, it was to be retained during the night—a slight departure from the custom of ladies which Miss Aldclyffe had at first not cared to exhibit to her new assistant, though now, on further thought, she seemed to have become indifferent on the matter.

'My dressing-gown,' she said, quietly fastening her night-dress as she spoke.

Cytherea came forward with it. Miss Aldclyffe did not turn her head, but looked inquiringly at her maid in the glass.

'You saw what I wear on my neck, I suppose?' she said to Cytherea's reflected face.

'Yes, madam, I did,' said Cytherea to Miss Aldclyffe's reflected face.

Miss Aldclyffe again looked at Cytherea's reflection as if she were on the point of explaining. Again she checked her resolve, and said lightly—

'Few of my maids discover that I wear it always. I generally keep it a secret—not that it matters much. But I was careless with you, and seemed to want to tell you. You win me to make confidences that . . .'

She ceased, took Cytherea's hand in her own, lifted the locket with the other, touched the spring and disclosed a miniature.

'It is a handsome face, is it not?' she whispered mournfully, and even timidly.

'It is.'

But the sight had gone through Cytherea like an electric shock, and there was an instantaneous awakening of perception in her, so thrilling in its presence as to be well-nigh insupportable. The face in the miniature was the face of her own father—younger and fresher than she had ever known him—but her father!

Was this the woman of his wild and unquenchable early love? And was this the woman who had figured in the gate-man's story as answering the name of Cytherea before her judgment was awake? Surely it was. And if so, here was the tangible outcrop of a romantic and hidden stratum of the past hitherto seen only in her imagination; but as far as her scope allowed, clearly defined therein by reason of its strangeness.

Miss Aldclyffe's eyes and thoughts were so intent upon the miniature that she had not been conscious of Cytherea's start of surprise. She went on speaking in a low and abstracted tone.

'Yes, I lost him.' She interrupted her words by a short meditation, and went on again. 'I lost him by excess of honesty as regarded my past. But it was best that it should be so . . . I was led to think rather more than usual of the circumstances to-night because of your name. It is pronounced the same way, though differently spelt.'

The only means by which Cytherea's surname could have been spelt to Miss Aldclyffe must have been by Mrs. Morris or Farmer Springrove. She fancied Farmer Springrove would have spelt it properly if Edward was his informant, which made Miss

Aldclyffe's remark obscure.

Women make confidences and then regret them. The impulsive rush of feeling which had led Miss Aldclyffe to indulge in this revelation, trifling as it was, died out immediately her words were beyond recall; and the turmoil, occasioned in her by dwelling upon that chapter of her life, found vent in another kind of emotion—the result of a trivial accident.

Cytherea, after letting down Miss Aldclyffe's hair, adopted some plan with it to which the lady had not been accustomed. A rapid revulsion to irritation ensued. The maiden's mere touch seemed to discharge the pent-up regret of the lady as if she had been a jar of electricity.

'How strangely you treat my hair!' she exclaimed.

A silence.

'I have told you what I never tell my maids as a rule; of course *nothing* that I say in this room is to be mentioned outside it.' She spoke crossly no less than emphatically.

'It shall not be, madam,' said Cytherea, agitated and vexed that the woman of her romantic wonderings should be so disagreeable to her.

'Why on earth did I tell you of my past?' she went on.

Cytherea made no answer.

The lady's vexation with herself, and the accident which had led to the disclosure swelled little by little till it knew no bounds. But what was done could not be undone, and though Cytherea had shown a most winning responsiveness, quarrel Miss Aldclyffe must. She recurred to the subject of Cytherea's want of expertness, like a bitter reviewer, who finding the sentiments of a poet unimpeachable, quarrels with his rhymes.

'Never, never before did I serve myself such a trick as this in engaging a maid!' She waited for an expostulation: none came. Miss Aldclyffe tried again.

'The idea of my taking a girl without asking her more than three questions, or having a single reference, all because of her good l—, the shape of her face and body! It was a fool's trick. There, I am served right, quite right—by being deceived in such a way.'

'I didn't deceive you,' said Cytherea. The speech was an unfortunate one, and was the very 'fuel to maintain its fires' that the other's petulance desired.

'You did,' she said hotly.

'I told you I couldn't promise to be acquainted with every detail of routine just at first.'

'Will you contradict me in this way! You are telling untruths, I say.'

Cytherea's lip quivered. 'I would answer the remark if—if—'

'If what?'

'If it were a lady's!'

'You girl of impudence—what do you say? Leave the room this instant, I tell you.'

'And I tell you that a person who speaks to a lady as you do to me, is no lady herself!'

'To a lady? A lady's-maid speaks in this way. The idea!'

'Don't "lady's-maid" me: nobody is my mistress, I won't have it!'

'Good Heavens!'

'I wouldn't have come—no—I wouldn't! if I had known!'

'What?'

'That you were such an ill-tempered, unjust woman!'

'Possest beyond the Muse's painting,' Miss Aldclyffe exclaimed—

'A Woman, am I! I'll teach you if I am a Woman!' and lifted her hand as if she would have liked to strike her companion. This stung the maiden into absolute defiance.

'I dare you to touch me!' she cried. 'Strike me if you dare, madam! I am not afraid of you—what do you mean by such an action as that?'

Miss Aldclyffe was disconcerted at this unexpected show of spirit, and ashamed of her unladylike impulse now it was put into words. She sank back in the chair. 'I was not going to strike you—go to your room—I beg you to go to your room!' she repeated in a husky whisper.

Cytherea, red and panting, took up her

113

candlestick and advanced to the table to get a light. As she stood close to them the rays from the candles struck sharply on her face. She usually bore a much stronger likeness to her mother than to her father, but now, looking with a grave, reckless, and angered expression of countenance at the kindling wick as she held it slanting into the other flame, her father's features were distinct in her. It was the first time Miss Aldclyffe had seen her in a passionate mood, and wearing that expression which was invariably its concomitant. It was Miss Aldclyffe's turn to start now; and the remark she made was an instance of that sudden change of tone from high-flown invective to the pettiness of curiosity which so often makes women's quarrels ridiculous. Even Miss Aldclyffe's dignity had not sufficient power to postpone the absorbing desire she now felt to settle the strange suspicion that had entered her head.

'You spell your name the common way, G, R, E, Y, don't you?' she said, with assumed indifference.

'No,' said Cytherea, poised on the side of her foot, and still looking into the flame.

'Yes, surely? The name was spelt that way on your boxes: I looked and saw it myself.'

The enigma of Miss Aldclyffe's mistake was solved. 'O, was it?' said Cytherea. 'Ah, I remember Mrs. Jackson, the lodging-house keeper at Budmouth, labelled them. We spell our name G, R, A, Y, E.'

'What was your father's trade?'

Cytherea thought it would be useless to attempt to conceal facts any longer. 'His was not a trade,' she said. 'He was an architect.'

'The idea of your being an architect's daughter!'

'There's nothing to offend you in that, I hope?'

'O no.'

'Why did you say "the idea"?'

'Leave that alone. Did he ever visit in Dunkery Street, Bloomsbury, one Christmas, many years ago?—but you would not know that.'

'I have heard him say that Mr. Huntway, a curate somewhere in that part of London, and who died there, was an old college friend of his.'

'What is your Christian name?'

'Cytherea.'

'No! And is it really? And you knew that face I showed you? Yes, I see you did.' Miss Aldclyffe stopped, and closed her lips impassibly. She was a little agitated.

'Do you want me any longer?' said Cytherea, standing candle in hand and looking quietly in Miss Aldclyffe's face.

'Well—no: no longer,' said the other lingeringly.

'With your permission, I will leave the house tomorrow morning, madam.'

'Ah.' Miss Aldclyffe had no notion of what she was saying.

'And I know you will be so good as not to intrude upon me during the short remainder of my stay?'

Saying this Cytherea left the room before her companion had answered. Miss Aldclyffe, then, had recognized her at last, and had been curious about her name from the beginning.

The other members of the household had retired to rest. As Cytherea went along the passage leading to her room her skirts rustled against the partition. A door on her left opened, and Mrs. Morris looked out.

'I waited out of bed till you came up,' she said, 'it being your first night, in case you should be at a loss for anything. How have you got on with Miss Aldclyffe?'

'Pretty well—though not so well as I could have wished.'

'Has she been scolding?'

'A little.'

'She's a very odd lady—'tis all one way or the other with her. She's not bad at heart, but unbearable in close quarters. Those of us who don't have much to do with her personally, stay on for years and years.'

'Has Miss Aldclyffe's family always been rich?' said Cytherea.

'O no. The property, with the name, came from her mother's uncle. Her family is a branch of the old Aldclyffe family on the maternal side. Her mother married a Bradleigh—a mere nobody at that time—and was on that account cut by her relations. But very singularly the other branch of the family died out one by one—three of them, and Miss Aldclyffe's great-uncle then left all his property, including this estate, to Captain Bradleigh and his wife—Miss Aldclyffe's father and mother—on condition that they took the old family name as well. There's all about it in the *Landed Gentry*. 'Tis a thing very often done.'

'O, I see. Thank you. Well, now I am going. Good-night.'

VI.

THE EVENTS OF TWELVE HOURS

1. AUGUST THE NINTH. ONE TO TWO O'CLOCK A.M.

Cytherea entered her bedroom, and flung herself on the bed, bewildered by a whirl of thought. Only one subject was clear in her mind, and it was that, in spite of family discoveries, that day was to be the first and last of her experience as a lady's-maid. Starvation itself should not compel her to hold such a humiliating post for another instant. 'Ah,' she thought, with a sigh, at the martyrdom of her last little fragment of self-conceit, 'Owen knows everything better than I.'

She jumped up and began making ready for her departure in the morning, the tears streaming down when she grieved and wondered what practical matter on earth she could turn her hand to next. All these preparations completed, she began to undress, her mind unconsciously drifting away to the contemplation of her late surprises. To look in the glass for an instant at the reflection of her own magnificent resources in face and bosom, and to mark their attractiveness unadorned, was perhaps but the natural action of a young woman who had so lately been chidden whilst passing through the harassing experience of decorating an older beauty of Miss Aldclyffe's temper.

But she directly checked her weakness by sympathizing reflections on the hidden troubles which must have thronged the past years of the solitary lady, to keep her, though so rich and courted, in a mood so repellent and gloomy as that in which Cytherea found her; and then the young girl marvelled again and again, as she had marvelled before, at the strange confluence of circumstances which had brought herself into contact with the one woman in the world whose history was so romantically intertwined with her own. She almost began to wish she were not obliged to go away and leave the lonely being to loneliness still.

In bed and in the dark, Miss Aldclyffe haunted her mind more persistently than ever. Instead of sleeping, she called up staring visions of the possible past of this queenly lady, her mother's rival. Up the long vista of bygone years she saw, behind all, the young girl's flirtation, little or much, with the cousin, that seemed to have been nipped in the bud, or to have terminated hastily in some way. Then the secret meetings between Miss Aldclyffe and the other woman at the little inn at Hammersmith and other places: the commonplace name she adopted: her swoon at some painful news, and the very slight knowledge the elder female had of her partner in mystery. Then, more than a year afterwards, the acquaintanceship of her own father with this his first love; the awakening of the passion, his acts of devotion, the unreasoning heat of his rapture, her tacit acceptance of it, and yet her uneasiness under the delight. Then his declaration amid the evergreens: the utter change produced in her manner thereby, seemingly the result of a rigid determination: and the total concealment of her reason by herself and her parents, whatever it was. Then the lady's course dropped into darkness, and nothing more was visible till she was discovered here at Knapwater, nearly fifty years old, still unmarried and still beautiful,

119

but lonely, embittered, and haughty. Cytherea imagined that her father's image was still warmly cherished in Miss Aldclyffe's heart, and was thankful that she herself had not been betrayed into announcing that she knew many particulars of this page of her father's history, and the chief one, the lady's unaccountable renunciation of him. It would have made her bearing towards the mistress of the mansion more awkward, and would have been no benefit to either.

Thus conjuring up the past, and theorizing on the present, she lay restless, changing her posture from one side to the other and back again. Finally, when courting sleep with all her art, she heard a clock strike two. A minute later, and she fancied she could distinguish a soft rustle in the passage outside her room.

To bury her head in the sheets was her first impulse; then to uncover it, raise herself on her elbow, and stretch her eyes wide open in the darkness; her lips being parted with the intentness of her listening. Whatever the noise was, it had ceased for the time.

It began again and came close to her door, lightly touching the panels. Then there was another stillness; Cytherea made a movement which caused a faint rustling of the bed-clothes.

Before she had time to think another thought a light tap was given. Cytherea breathed: the person outside was evidently bent upon finding her awake, and the rustle she had made had encouraged the hope. The maiden's physical condition shifted from one pole to its opposite. The cold sweat of terror forsook her, and modesty took the alarm. She became hot and red; her door was not locked.

A distinct woman's whisper came to her through the keyhole: 'Cytherea!'

Only one being in the house knew her Christian name, and that was Miss Aldclyffe. Cytherea stepped out of bed, went to the door, and whispered back, 'Yes?'

'Let me come in, darling.'

The young woman paused in a conflict between judgment and emotion. It was now mistress and maid no longer; woman and woman only. Yes; she must let her come in, poor thing.

She got a light in an instant, opened the door, and raising her eyes and the candle, saw Miss Aldclyffe standing outside in her dressing-gown.

'Now you see that it is really myself; put out the light,' said the visitor. 'I want to stay here with you, Cythie. I came to ask you to come down into my bed, but it is snugger here. But remember that you are mistress in this room, and that I have no business here, and that you may send me away if you choose. Shall I go?'

'O no; you shan't indeed if you don't want to,' said Cythie generously.

The instant they were in bed Miss Aldclyffe

freed herself from the last remnant of restraint. She flung her arms round the young girl, and pressed her gently to her heart.

'Now kiss me,' she said. 'You seem as if you were my own, own child!'

Cytherea, upon the whole, was rather discomposed at this change of treatment; and, discomposed or no, her passions were not so impetuous as Miss Aldclyffe's. She could not bring her soul to her lips for a moment, try how she would.

'Come, kiss me,' repeated Miss Aldclyffe.

Cytherea gave her a very small one, as soft in touch and in sound as the bursting of a bubble.

'More earnestly than that—come.'

She gave another, a little but not much more expressively.

'I don't deserve a more feeling one, I suppose,' said Miss Aldclyffe, with an emphasis of sad bitterness in her tone. 'I am an ill-tempered woman, you think; half out of my mind. Well, perhaps I am; but I have had grief more than you can think or dream of. But I am a lonely woman, and I want the sympathy of a pure girl like you and so I can't help loving you—your name is the same as mine—isn't it strange?'

Cytherea was inclined to say no, but remained silent.

'Now, don't you think I must love you?' continued the other.

'Yes,' said Cytherea absently. She was still thinking whether duty to Owen and her father, which asked for silence on her knowledge of her father's unfortunate love, or duty to the woman embracing her, which seemed to ask for confidence, ought to predominate. Here was a solution. She would wait till Miss Aldclyffe referred to her acquaintanceship and attachment to Cytherea's father in past times: then she would tell her all she knew: that would be honour.

'Why can't you kiss me as I can kiss you? Why can't you!' She impressed upon Cytherea's lips a warm motherly salute, given as if in the outburst of strong feeling, long checked, and yearning for something to love and be loved by in return.

'Do you think badly of me for my behaviour this evening, child? I don't know why I am so foolish as to speak to you in this way. I am a very fool, I believe. Yes. How old are you?'

'Eighteen.'

'Eighteen! . . . Well, why don't you ask me how old I am?'

'Because I don't want to know.'

'Never mind if you don't. I am forty-six; and it gives me greater pleasure to tell you this than it does to you to listen. I have not told my age truly for the last twenty years till now.'

'Why haven't you?'

'I have met deceit by deceit, till I am weary of it—weary, weary—and I long to be what I

123

shall never be again—artless and innocent, like you. But I suppose that you, too, will, prove to be not worth a thought, as every new friend does on more intimate knowledge. Come, why don't you talk to me, child? Have you said your prayers?'

'Yes—no! I forgot them to-night.'

'I suppose you say them every night as a rule?'

'Yes.'

'Why do you do that?'

'Because I have always done so, and it would seem strange if I were not to. Do you?'

'I? A wicked old sinner like me! No, I never do. I have thought all such matters humbug for years—thought so so long that I should be glad to think otherwise from very weariness; and yet, such is the code of the polite world, that I subscribe regularly to Missionary Societies and others of the sort . . . Well, say your prayers, dear—you won't omit them now you recollect it. I should like to hear you very much. Will you?'

'It seems hardly—'

'It would seem so like old times to me—when I was young, and nearer—far nearer Heaven than I am now. Do, sweet one.'

Cytherea was embarrassed, and her embarrassment arose from the following conjuncture of affairs. Since she had loved Edward Springrove, she had linked his name with her brother Owen's in her nightly supplications to the Almighty. She wished to keep her love for him a secret, and, above all, a secret from a woman like Miss Aldclyffe; yet her conscience and the honesty of her love would not for an instant allow her to think of omitting his dear name, and so endanger the efficacy of all her previous prayers for his success by an unworthy shame now: it would be wicked of her, she thought, and a grievous wrong to him. Under any worldly circumstances she might have thought the position justified a little finesse, and have skipped him for once; but prayer was too solemn a thing for such trifling.

'I would rather not say them,' she murmured first. It struck her then that this declining altogether was the same cowardice in another dress, and was delivering her poor Edward over to Satan just as unceremoniously as before. 'Yes; I will say my prayers, and you shall hear me,' she added firmly.

She turned her face to the pillow and repeated in low soft tones the simple words she had used from childhood on such occasions. Owen's name was mentioned without faltering, but in the other case, maidenly shyness was too strong even for religion, and that when supported by excellent intentions. At the name of Edward she stammered, and her voice sank to the faintest whisper in spite of her.

'Thank you, dearest,' said Miss Aldclyffe. 'I have prayed too, I verily believe. You are a good girl, I think.' Then the expected question came.

' "Bless Owen," and whom, did you say?'

There was no help for it now, and out it came. 'Owen and Edward,' said Cytherea.

'Who are Owen and Edward?'

'Owen is my brother, madam,' faltered the maid.

'Ah, I remember. Who is Edward?'

A silence.

'Your brother, too?' continued Miss Aldclyffe.

'No.'

Miss Aldclyffe reflected a moment. 'Don't you want to tell me who Edward is?' she said at last, in a tone of meaning.

'I don't mind telling; only . . .'

'You would rather not, I suppose?'

'Yes.'

Miss Aldclyffe shifted her ground. 'Were you ever in love?' she inquired suddenly.

Cytherea was surprised to hear how quickly the voice had altered from tenderness to harshness, vexation, and disappointment.

'Yes—I think I was—once,' she murmured.

'Aha! And were you ever kissed by a man?'

A pause.

'Well, were you?' said Miss Aldclyffe, rather sharply.

'Don't press me to tell—I can't—indeed, I won't, madam!'

Miss Aldclyffe removed her arms from

126

Cytherea's neck. ' 'Tis now with you as it is always with all girls,' she said, in jealous and gloomy accents. 'You are not, after all, the innocent I took you for. No, no.' She then changed her tone with fitful rapidity. 'Cytherea, try to love me more than you love him—do. I love you more sincerely than any man can. Do, Cythie: don't let any man stand between us. O, I can't bear that!' She clasped Cytherea's neck again.

'I must love him now I have begun,' replied the other.

'Must—yes—must,' said the elder lady reproachfully. 'Yes, women are all alike. I thought I had at last found an artless woman who had not been sullied by a man's lips, and who had not practised or been practised upon by the arts which ruin all the truth and sweetness and goodness in us. Find a girl, if you can, whose mouth and ears have not been made a regular highway of by some man or another! Leave the admittedly notorious spots—the drawing-rooms of society—and look in the villages—leave the villages and search in the schools—and you can hardly find a girl whose heart has not been had—is not an old thing half worn out by some He or another! If men only knew the staleness of the freshest of us! that nine times out of ten the "first love" they think they are winning from a woman is but the hulk of an old wrecked affection, fitted with new sails and re-used.

127

O Cytherea, can it be that you, too, are like the rest?'

'No, no, no,' urged Cytherea, awed by the storm she had raised in the impetuous woman's mind. 'He only kissed me once—twice I mean.'

'He might have done it a thousand times if he had cared to, there's no doubt about that, whoever his lordship is. You are as bad as I—we are all alike; and I—an old fool—have been sipping at your mouth as if it were honey, because I fancied no wasting lover knew the spot. But a minute ago, and you seemed to me like a fresh spring meadow—now you seem a dusty highway.'

'O no, no!' Cytherea was not weak enough to shed tears except on extraordinary occasions, but she was fain to begin sobbing now. She wished Miss Aldclyffe would go to her own room, and leave her and her treasured dreams alone. This vehement imperious affection was in one sense soothing, but yet it was not of the kind that Cytherea's instincts desired. Though it was generous, it seemed somewhat too rank and capricious for endurance.

'Well,' said the lady in continuation, 'who is he?'

Her companion was desperately determined not to tell his name: she too much feared a taunt when Miss Aldclyffe's fiery mood again ruled her tongue.

'Won't you tell me? not tell me after all the affection I have shown?'

'I will, perhaps, another day.'

'Did you wear a hat and white feather in Budmouth for the week or two previous to your coming here?'

'Yes.'

'Then I have seen you and your lover at a distance! He rowed you round the bay with your brother.'

'Yes.'

'And without your brother—fie! There, there, don't let that little heart beat itself to death: throb, throb: it shakes the bed, you silly thing. I didn't mean that there was any harm in going alone with him. I only saw you from the Esplanade, in common with the rest of the people. I often run down to Budmouth. He was a very good figure: now who was he?'

'I—I won't tell, madam—I cannot indeed!'

'Won't tell—very well, don't. You are very foolish to treasure up his name and image as you do. Why, he has had loves before you, trust him for that, whoever he is, and you are but a temporary link in a long chain of others like you: who only have your little day as they have had theirs.'

' 'Tisn't true! 'tisn't true! 'tisn't true!' cried Cytherea in an agony of torture. 'He has never loved anybody else, I know—I am sure he hasn't.'

Miss Aldclyffe was as jealous as any man

129

could have been. She continued—

'He sees a beautiful face and thinks he will never forget it, but in a few weeks the feeling passes off, and he wonders how he could have cared for anybody so absurdly much.'

'No, no, he doesn't—What does he do when he has thought that—Come, tell me—tell me!'

'You are as hot as fire, and the throbbing of your heart makes me nervous. I can't tell you if you get in that flustered state.'

'Do, do tell—O, it makes me so miserable! but tell—come tell me!'

'Ah—the tables are turned now, dear!' she continued, in a tone which mingled pity with derision—

'Love's passions shall rock thee
As the storm rocks the ravens on high,
Bright reason will mock thee
Like the sun from a wintry sky.

'What does he do next?—Why, this is what he does next: ruminate on what he has heard of women's romantic impulses, and how easily men torture them when they have given way to those feelings, and have resigned everything for their hero. It may be that though he loves you heartily now—that is, as heartily as a man can—and you love him in return, your loves may be impracticable and hopeless, and you may be separated for ever. You, as the weary, weary years pass by will fade and fade—bright

130

eyes *will* fade—and you will perhaps then die early—true to him to your latest breath, and believing him to be true to the latest breath also; whilst he, in some gay and busy spot far away from your last quiet nook, will have married some dashing lady, and not purely oblivious of you, will long have ceased to regret you—will chat about you, as you were in long past years—will say, "Ah, little Cytherea used to tie her hair like that—poor innocent trusting thing; it was a pleasant useless idle dream—that dream of mine for the maid with the bright eyes and simple, silly heart; but I was a foolish lad at that time." Then he will tell the tale of all your little Wills and Wont's and particular ways, and as he speaks, turn to his wife with a placid smile.'

'It is not true! He can't, he c-can't be s-so cruel—and you are cruel to me—you are, you are!' She was at last driven to desperation: her natural common sense and shrewdness had seen all through the piece how imaginary her emotions were—she felt herself to be weak and foolish in permitting them to rise; but even then she could not control them: be agonized she must. She was only eighteen, and the long day's labour, her weariness, her excitement, had completely unnerved her, and worn her out: she was bent hither and thither by this tyrannical working upon her imagination, as a young rush in the wind. She wept bitterly.

'And now think how much *I* like you,'

resumed Miss Aldclyffe, when Cytherea grew calmer. 'I shall never forget you for anybody else, as men do—never. I will be exactly as a mother to you. Now will you promise to live with me always, and always be taken care of, and never deserted?'

'I cannot. I will not be anybody's maid for another day on any consideration.'

'No, no, no. You shan't be a lady's-maid. You shall be my companion. I will get another maid.'

Companion—that was a new idea. Cytherea could not resist the evidently heartfelt desire of the strange-tempered woman for her presence. But she could not trust to the moment's impulse.

'I will stay, I think. But do not ask for a final answer to-night.'

'Never mind now, then. Put your hair round your mamma's neck, and give me one good long kiss, and I won't talk any more in that way about your lover. After all, some young men are not so fickle as others; but even if he's the ficklest, there is consolation. The love of an inconstant man is ten times more ardent than that of a faithful man—that is, while it lasts.'

Cytherea did as she was told, to escape the punishment of further talk; flung the twining tresses of her long, rich hair over Miss Aldclyffe's shoulders as directed, and the two ceased conversing, making themselves up for sleep. Miss Aldclyffe seemed to give herself over to a luxurious sense of content and quiet, as if the maiden at her side afforded her a protection against dangers which had menaced her for years; she was soon sleeping calmly.

2. TWO TO FIVE A.M.

With Cytherea it was otherwise. Unused to the place and circumstances she continued wakeful, ill at ease, and mentally distressed. She withdrew herself from her companion's embrace, turned to the other side, and endeavoured to relieve her busy brain by looking at the window-blind, and noticing the light of the rising moon—now in her last quarter—creep round upon it: it was the light of an old waning moon which had but a few days longer to live.

The sight led her to think again of what had happened under the rays of the same month's moon, a little before its full, the ecstatic evening scene with Edward: the kiss, and the shortness of those happy moments—maiden imagination bringing about the apotheosis of a *status quo* which had had several unpleasantnesses in its earthly reality.

But sounds were in the ascendant that night. Her ears became aware of a strange and gloomy murmur.

She recognized it: it was the gushing of the waterfall, faint and low, brought from its source to the unwonted distance of the House by a faint breeze which made it distinct and recognizable by reason of the utter absence of all disturbing sounds. The groom's melancholy representation lent to the sound a more dismal effect than it would have had of its own nature. She began to fancy what the waterfall must be like at that hour, under the trees in the ghostly moonlight. Black at the head, and over the surface of the deep cold hole into which it fell; white and frothy at the fall; black and white, like a pall and its border; sad everywhere.

She was in the mood for sounds of every kind now, and strained her ears to catch the faintest, in wayward enmity to her quiet of mind. Another soon came.

The second was quite different from the first—a kind of intermittent whistle it seemed primarily: no, a creak, a metallic creak, ever and anon, like a plough, or a rusty wheelbarrow, or at least a wheel of some kind. Yes, it was, a wheel—the water-wheel in the shrubbery by the old manor-house, which the coachman had said would drive him mad.

She determined not to think any more of these gloomy things; but now that she had once noticed the sound there was no sealing her ears to it. She could not help timing its creaks, and putting on a dread expectancy just before the end of each half-minute that brought them. To imagine the inside of the engine-house, whence these noises proceeded, was now a necessity. No window, but crevices in the door, through which, probably, the moonbeams streamed in the most attenuated and skeleton-like rays, striking sharply upon portions of wet rusty cranks and chains; a glistening wheel, turning incessantly, labouring in the dark like a captive starving in a dungeon; and instead of a floor below, gurgling water, which on account of the darkness could only be heard; water which laboured up dark pipes almost to where she lay.

She shivered. Now she was determined to go to sleep; there could be nothing else left to be heard or to imagine—it was horrid that her imagination should be so restless. Yet just for an instant before going to sleep she would think this—suppose another sound *should* come—just suppose it should! Before the thought had well passed through her brain, a third sound came.

The third was a very soft gurgle or rattle—of a strange and abnormal kind—yet a sound she had heard before at some past period of her life—when, she could not recollect. To make it the more disturbing, it seemed to be almost close to her—either close outside the window, close under the floor, or close above the ceiling. The accidental fact of its coming so immediately upon the heels of her supposition, told so powerfully upon her excited nerves that she jumped up in the bed. The same instant, a little dog in some room near, having probably heard the same noise, set up a low whine. The watch-dog in the yard, hearing the moan of his associate, began to howl loudly and distinctly. His melancholy notes were taken up directly afterwards by the dogs in the kennel a long way off, in every variety of wail.

One logical thought alone was able to enter her flurried brain. The little dog that began the whining must have heard the other two sounds even better than herself. He had taken no notice of them, but he had taken notice of the third. The third, then, was an unusual sound.

It was not like water, it was not like wind; it was not the night-jar, it was not a clock, nor a rat, nor a person snoring.

She crept under the clothes, and flung her arms tightly round Miss Aldclyffe, as if for protection. Cytherea perceived that the lady's late peaceful warmth had given place to a sweat. At the maiden's touch, Miss Aldclyffe awoke with a low scream.

She remembered her position instantly. 'O such a terrible dream!' she cried, in a hurried whisper, holding to Cytherea in her turn; 'and your touch was the end of it. It was dreadful. Time, with his wings, hour-glass, and scythe, coming nearer and nearer to me—grinning and mocking: then he seized me, took a piece of me only . . . But I can't tell you. I can't bear to think of it. How those dogs howl! People say it means death.'

The return of Miss Aldclyffe to consciousness was sufficient to dispel the wild fancies which the loneliness of the night had woven in Cytherea's mind. She dismissed the third noise as something which in all likelihood could easily be explained, if trouble were taken to inquire into it: large houses had all kinds of strange sounds floating about them. She was ashamed to tell Miss Aldclyffe her terrors.

A silence of five minutes.

'Are you asleep?' said Miss Aldclyffe.

'No,' said Cytherea, in a long-drawn whisper.

'How those dogs howl, don't they?'

'Yes. A little dog in the house began it.'

'Ah, yes: that was Totsy. He sleeps on the mat outside my father's bedroom door. A nervous creature.'

There was a silent interval of nearly half-an-hour. A clock on the landing struck three.

'Are you asleep, Miss Aldclyffe?' whispered Cytherea.

'No,' said Miss Aldclyffe. 'How wretched it is not to be able to sleep, isn't it?'

'Yes,' replied Cytherea, like a docile child.

Another hour passed, and the clock struck four. Miss Aldclyffe was still awake.

'Cytherea,' she said, very softly.

Cytherea made no answer. She was sleeping soundly.

The first glimmer of dawn was now visible. Miss Aldclyffe arose, put on her dressing-gown, and went softly downstairs to her own room.

'I have not told her who I am after all, or found out the particulars of Ambrose's history,' she murmured. 'But her being in love alters everything.'

3. HALF-PAST SEVEN TO TEN O'CLOCK A.M.

Cytherea awoke, quiet in mind and refreshed. A conclusion to remain at Knapwater was already in possession of her.

Finding Miss Aldclyffe gone, she dressed herself and sat down at the window to write an answer to Edward's letter, and an account of her arrival at Knapwater to Owen. The dismal and heart-breaking pictures that Miss Aldclyffe had placed before her the preceding evening, the later terrors of the night, were now but as shadows of shadows, and she smiled in derision at her own excitability.

But writing Edward's letter was the great consoler, the effect of each word upon him being enacted in her own face as she wrote it. She felt how much she would like to share his trouble—how well she could endure poverty with him—and wondered what his trouble was. But all would be explained at last, she knew.

At the appointed time she went to Miss Aldclyffe's room, intending, with the contradictoriness common in people, to perform with pleasure, as a work of supererogation, what as a duty was simply intolerable.

Miss Aldclyffe was already out of bed. The bright penetrating light of morning made a vast difference in the elder lady's behaviour to her dependent; the day, which had restored Cytherea's judgment, had effected the same for Miss Aldclyffe. Though practical reasons forbade her regretting that she had secured such a companionable creature to read, talk, or play to her whenever her whim required, she was inwardly vexed at the extent to which she had indulged in the womanly luxury of making confidences and giving way to emotions. Few would have supposed that the calm lady sitting aristocratically at the toilet table, seeming scarcely conscious of Cytherea's presence in the room, even when greeting her, was the passionate creature who had asked for kisses a few hours before.

It is both painful and satisfactory to think how often these antitheses are to be observed in the individual most open to our observation—ourselves. We pass the evening with faces lit up by some flaring illumination or other: we get up the next morning—the fiery jets have all gone out, and nothing confronts us but a few crinkled pipes and sooty wirework, hardly even recalling the outline of the blazing picture that arrested our eyes before bedtime.

Emotions would be half starved if there

were no candle-light. Probably nine-tenths of the gushing letters of indiscreet confession are written after nine or ten o'clock in the evening, and sent off before day returns to leer invidiously upon them. Few that remain open to catch our glance as we rise in the morning, survive the frigid criticism of dressing-time.

The subjects uppermost in the minds of the two women who had thus cooled from their fires, were not the visionary ones of the later hours, but the hard facts of their earlier conversation. After a remark that Cytherea need not assist her in dressing unless she wished to, Miss Aldclyffe said abruptly—

'I can tell that young man's name.' She looked keenly at Cytherea. 'It is Edward Springrove, my tenant's son.'

The inundation of colour upon the younger lady at hearing a name which to her was a world, handled as if it were only an atom, told Miss Aldclyffe that she had divined the truth at last.

'Ah—it is he, is it?' she continued. 'Well, I wanted to know for practical reasons. His example shows that I was not so far wrong in my estimate of men after all, though I only generalized, and had no thought of him.' This was perfectly true.

'What do you mean?' said Cytherea, visibly alarmed.

'Mean? Why that all the world knows him to be engaged to be married, and that the wedding is soon to take place.' She made the remark bluntly and superciliously, as if to obtain absolution at the hands of her family pride for the weak confidences of the night.

But even the frigidity of Miss Aldclyffe's morning mood was overcome by the look of sick and blank despair which the carelessly uttered words had produced upon Cytherea's face. She sank back into a chair, and buried her face in her hands.

'Don't be so foolish,' said Miss Aldclyffe. 'Come, make the best of it. I cannot upset the fact I have told you of, unfortunately. But I believe the match can be broken off.'

'O no, no.'

'Nonsense. I liked him much as a youth, and I like him now. I'll help you to captivate and chain him down. I have got over my absurd feeling of last night in not wanting you ever to go away from me—of course, I could not expect such a thing as that. There, now I have said I'll help you, and that's enough. He's tired of his first choice now that he's been away from home for a while. The love that no outer attack can frighten away quails before its idol's own homely ways; it is always so . . . Come, finish what you are doing if you are going to, and don't be a little goose about such a trumpery affair as that.'

'Who—is he engaged to?' Cytherea inquired by a movement of her lips but no sound of her voice. But Miss Aldclyffe did not answer. It mattered not, Cytherea thought. Another woman—that was enough for her: curiosity was stunned.

She applied herself to the work of dressing, scarcely knowing how. Miss Aldclyffe went on:—

'You were too easily won. I'd have made him or anybody else speak out before he should have kissed my face for his pleasure. But you are one of those precipitantly fond things who are yearning to throw away their hearts upon the first worthless fellow who says good-morning. In the first place, you shouldn't have loved him so quickly: in the next, if you must have loved him off-hand, you should have concealed it. It tickled his vanity: "By Jove, that girl's in love with me already!" he thought.'

To hasten away at the end of the toilet, to tell Mrs. Morris—who stood waiting in a little room prepared for her, with tea poured out, bread-and-butter cut into diaphanous slices, and eggs arranged—that she wanted no breakfast: then to shut herself alone in her bedroom, was her only thought. She was followed thither by the well-intentioned matron with a cup of tea and one piece of bread-and-butter on a tray, cheerfully insisting that she should eat it.

To those who grieve, innocent cheerfulness seems heartless levity. 'No, thank you, Mrs. Morris,' she said, keeping the door closed.

Despite the incivility of the action, Cytherea could not bear to let a pleasant person see her face then.

Immediate revocation—even if revocation would be more effective by postponement—is the impulse of young wounded natures. Cytherea went to her blotting-book, took out the long letter so carefully written, so full of gushing remarks and tender hints, and sealed up so neatly with a little seal bearing 'Good Faith' as its motto, tore the missive into fifty pieces, and threw them into the grate. It was then the bitterest of anguishes to look upon some of the words she had so lovingly written, and see them existing only in mutilated forms without meaning—to feel that his eye would never read them, nobody ever know how ardently she had penned them.

Pity for one's self for being wasted is mostly present in these moods of abnegation.

The meaning of all his allusions, his abruptness in telling her of his love, his constraint at first, then his desperate manner of speaking, was clear. They must have been the last flickerings of a conscience not quite dead to all sense of perfidiousness and fickleness. Now he had gone to London: she would be dismissed from his memory, in the same way as Miss Aldclyffe had said. And here she was in Edward's own parish, reminded continually of him by what she saw and heard. The landscape, yesterday so much and so bright to her, was now but as the banquet-hall deserted—all gone but herself.

Miss Aldclyffe had wormed her secret out of her, and would now be continually mocking her for her trusting simplicity in believing him. It was altogether unbearable: she would not stay there.

She went downstairs and found Miss Aldclyffe had gone into the breakfast-room, but that Captain Aldclyffe, who rose later with increasing infirmities, had not yet made his appearance. Cytherea entered. Miss Aldclyffe was looking out of the window, watching a trail of white smoke along the distant landscape— signifying a passing train. At Cytherea's entry she turned and looked inquiry.

'I must tell you now,' began Cytherea, in a tremulous voice.

'Well, what?' Miss Aldclyffe said.

'I am not going to stay with you. I must go away—a very long way. I am very sorry, but indeed I can't remain!'

'Pooh—what shall we hear next?' Miss Aldclyffe surveyed Cytherea's face with leisurely criticism. 'You are breaking your heart again about that worthless young Springrove. I knew how it would be. It is as Hallam says of Juliet—what little reason you may have possessed originally has all been whirled away by this love. I shan't take this notice, mind.'

'Do let me go!'

Miss Aldclyffe took her new pet's hand, and said with severity, 'As to hindering you, if you are determined to go, of course that's absurd. But you are not now in a state of mind fit for deciding upon any such proceeding, and I shall not listen to what you have to say. Now, Cythie, come with me; we'll let this volcano burst and spend itself, and after that we'll see what had better be done.' She took Cytherea into her workroom, opened a drawer, and drew forth a roll of linen.

'This is some embroidery I began one day, and now I should like it finished.'

She then preceded the maiden upstairs to Cytherea's own room. 'There,' she said, 'now sit down here, go on with this work, and remember one thing—that you are not to leave the room on any pretext whatever for two hours unless I send for you—I insist kindly, dear. Whilst you stitch—you are to stitch, recollect, and not go mooning out of the window—think over the whole matter, and get cooled; don't let the foolish love-affair prevent your thinking as a woman of the world. If at the end of that time you still say you must leave me, you may. I will have no more to say in the matter. Come, sit down, and promise to sit here the time I name.'

To hearts in a despairing mood, compulsion seems a relief; and docility was at all times natural to Cytherea. She promised, and sat down. Miss Aldclyffe shut the door upon her and retreated.

She sewed, stopped to think, shed a tear or two, recollected the articles of the treaty, and sewed again; and at length fell into a reverie which took no account whatever of the lapse of time.

4. TEN TO TWELVE O'CLOCK A.M.

A quarter of an hour might have passed when her thoughts became attracted from the past to the present by unwonted movements downstairs. She opened the door and listened.

There were hurryings along passages, opening and shutting of doors, trampling in the stable-yard. She went across into another bedroom, from which a view of the stable-yard could be obtained, and arrived there just in time to see the figure of the man who had driven her from the station vanishing down the coach-road on a black horse—galloping at the top of the animal's speed.

Another man went off in the direction of the village.

Whatever had occurred, it did not seem to be her duty to inquire or meddle with it, stranger and dependent as she was, unless she were requested to, especially after Miss Aldclyffe's strict charge to her. She sat down again, determined to let no idle curiosity influence her movements.

Her window commanded the front of the house; and the next thing she saw was a clergyman walk up and enter the door.

All was silent again till, a long time after the first man had left, he returned again on the same horse, now matted with sweat and trotting behind a carriage in which sat an elderly gentleman driven by a lad in livery. These came to the house, entered, and all was again the same as before.

The whole household—master, mistress, and servants—appeared to have forgotten the very existence of such a being as Cytherea. She almost wished she had not vowed to have no idle curiosity.

Half-an-hour later, the carriage drove off with the elderly gentleman, and two or three messengers left the house, speeding in various directions. Rustics in smock-frocks began to hang about the road opposite the house, or lean against trees, looking idly at the windows and chimneys.

A tap came to Cytherea's door. She opened it to a young maid-servant.

'Miss Aldclyffe wishes to see you, ma'am.' Cytherea hastened down.

Miss Aldclyffe was standing on the hearthrug, her elbow on the mantel, her hand to her temples, her eyes on the ground; perfectly calm, but very pale.

'Cytherea,' she said in a whisper, 'come here.'

Cytherea went close.

'Something very serious has taken place,' she said again, and then paused, with a tremulous movement of her mouth.

'Yes,' said Cytherea.

'My father. He was found dead in his bed this morning.'

'Dead!' echoed the younger woman. It seemed impossible that the announcement could be true; that knowledge of so great a fact could be contained in a statement so small.

'Yes, dead,' murmured Miss Aldclyffe solemnly. 'He died alone, though within a few feet of me. The room we slept in is exactly over his own.'

Cytherea said hurriedly, 'Do they know at what hour?'

'The doctor says it must have been between two and three o'clock this morning.'

'Then I heard him!'

'Heard him?'

'Heard him die!'

'You heard him die? What did you hear?'

'A sound I heard once before in my life—at the deathbed of my mother. I could not identify it—though I recognized it. Then the dog howled: you remarked it. I did not think it worth while to tell you what I had heard a little earlier.' She looked agonized.

'It would have been useless,' said Miss Aldclyffe. 'All was over by that time.' She addressed herself as much as Cytherea when she continued, 'Is it a Providence who sent you here at this juncture that I might not be left entirely alone?'

Till this instant Miss Aldclyffe had forgotten the reason of Cytherea's seclusion in her own room. So had Cytherea herself. The fact now recurred to both in one moment.

'Do you still wish to go?' said Miss Aldclyffe anxiously.

'I don't want to go now,' Cytherea had remarked simultaneously with the other's question. She was pondering on the strange likeness which Miss Aldclyffe's bereavement bore to her own; it had the appearance of being still another call to her not to forsake this woman so linked to her life, for the sake of any trivial vexation.

Miss Aldclyffe held her almost as a lover would have held her, and said musingly—

'We get more and more into one groove. I now am left fatherless and motherless as you were.' Other ties lay behind in her thoughts, but she did not mention them.

'You loved your father, Cytherea, and wept for him?'

'Yes, I did. Poor papa!'

'I was always at variance with mine, and can't weep for him now! But you must stay here always, and make a better woman of me.'

The compact was thus sealed, and Cytherea, in spite of the failure of her advertisements, was installed as a veritable Companion. And, once more in the history of human endeavour, a position which it was impossible to reach by any direct attempt, was come to by the seeker's swerving from the path, and regarding the original object as one of secondary importance.

VII.

THE EVENTS OF EIGHTEEN DAYS

1. AUGUST THE SEVENTEENTH

The time of day was four o'clock in the afternoon. The place was the lady's study or boudoir, Knapwater House. The person was Miss Aldclyffe sitting there alone, clothed in deep mourning.

The funeral of the old Captain had taken place, and his will had been read. It was very concise, and had been executed about five years previous to his death. It was attested by his solicitors, Messrs. Nyttleton and Tayling, of Lincoln's Inn Fields. The whole of his estate, real and personal, was bequeathed to his daughter Cytherea, for her sole and absolute use, subject only to the payment of a legacy to the rector, their relative, and a few small amounts to the servants.

Miss Aldclyffe had not chosen the easiest

chair of her boudoir to sit in, or even a chair of ordinary comfort; but an uncomfortable, high, narrow-backed, oak framed and seated chair, which was allowed to remain in the room only on the ground of being a companion in artistic quaintness to an old coffer beside it, and was never used except to stand in to reach for a book from the highest row of shelves. But she had sat erect in this chair for more than an hour, for the reason that she was utterly unconscious of what her actions and bodily feelings were. The chair had stood nearest her path on entering the room, and she had gone to it in a dream.

She sat in the attitude which denotes unflagging, intense, concentrated thought—as if she were cast in bronze. Her feet were together, her body bent a little forward, and quite unsupported by the back of the chair; her hands on her knees, her eyes fixed intently on the corner of a footstool.

At last she moved and tapped her fingers upon the table at her side. Her pent-up ideas had finally found some channel to advance in. Motions became more and more frequent as she laboured to carry further and further the problem which occupied her brain. She sat back and drew a long breath: she sat sideways and leant her forehead upon her hand. Later still she arose, walked up and down the room—at first abstractedly, with her features as firmly set as ever; but by degrees her brow relaxed, her footsteps became lighter and more leisurely; her head rode gracefully and was no longer bowed. She plumed herself like a swan after exertion.

'Yes,' she said aloud. 'To get him here without letting him know that I have any other object than that of getting a useful man—that's the difficulty—and that I think I can master.'

She rang for the new maid, a placid woman of forty with a few grey hairs.

'Ask Miss Graye if she can come to me.'

Cytherea was not far off, and came in.

'Do you know anything about architects and surveyors?' said Miss Aldclyffe abruptly.

'Know anything?' replied Cytherea, poising herself on her toe to consider the compass of the question.

'Yes—know anything,' said Miss Aldclyffe.

'Owen is an architect and surveyor's draughtsman,' the maiden said, and thought of somebody else who was likewise.

'Yes! that's why I asked you. What are the different kinds of work comprised in an architect's practice? They lay out estates, and superintend the various works done upon them, I should think, among other things?'

'Those are, more properly, a land or building steward's duties—at least I have always imagined so. Country architects include those things in their practice; city architects don't.'

'I know that, child. But a steward's is an

152

indefinite fast and loose profession, it seems to me. Shouldn't you think that a man who had been brought up as an architect would do for a steward?'

Cytherea had doubts whether an architect pure would do.

The chief pleasure connected with asking an opinion lies in not adopting it. Miss Aldclyffe replied decisively—

'Nonsense; of course he would. Your brother Owen makes plans for country buildings—such as cottages, stables, homesteads, and so on?'

'Yes; he does.'

'And superintends the building of them?'

'Yes; he will soon.'

'And he surveys land?'

'O yes.'

'And he knows about hedges and ditches— how wide they ought to be, boundaries, levelling, planting trees to keep away the winds, measuring timber, houses for ninety-nine years, and such things?'

'I have never heard him say that; but I think Mr. Gradfield does those things. Owen, I am afraid, is inexperienced as yet.'

'Yes; your brother is not old enough for such a post yet, of course. And then there are rent-days, the audit and winding up of tradesmen's accounts. I am afraid, Cytherea, you don't know much more about the matter than I do myself . . . I am going out just now,' she continued. 'I shall not want you to walk with me to-day. Run away till dinner-time.'

Miss Aldclyffe went out of doors, and down the steps to the lawn: then turning to the left, through a shrubbery, she opened a wicket and passed into a neglected and leafy carriage-drive, leading down the hill. This she followed till she reached the point of its greatest depression, which was also the lowest ground in the whole grove.

The trees here were so interlaced, and hung their branches so near the ground, that a whole summer's day was scarcely long enough to change the air pervading the spot from its normal state of coolness to even a temporary warmth. The unvarying freshness was helped by the nearness of the ground to the level of the springs, and by the presence of a deep, sluggish stream close by, equally well shaded by bushes and a high wall. Following the road, which now ran along at the margin of the stream, she came to an opening in the wall, on the other side of the water, revealing a large rectangular nook from which the stream proceeded, covered with froth, and accompanied by a dull roar. Two more steps, and she was opposite the nook, in full view of the cascade forming its further boundary. Over the top could be seen the bright outer sky in the form of a crescent, caused by the curve of a bridge across the rapids, and the trees above. Beautiful as was the scene she did not look in that direction. The same standing-ground afforded another prospect, straight in the front, less sombre than the water on the right or the trees all around. The avenue and grove which flanked it abruptly terminated a few yards ahead, where the ground began to rise, and on the remote edge of the greensward thus laid open, stood all that remained of the original manor-house, to which the dark margin-line of the trees in the avenue formed an adequate and well-fitting frame. It was the picture thus presented that was now interesting Miss Aldclyffe—not artistically or historically, but practically—as regarded its fitness for adaptation to modern requirements.

In front, detached from everything else, rose the most ancient portion of the structure—an old arched gateway, flanked by the bases of two small towers, and nearly covered with creepers, which had clambered over the eaves of the sinking roof, and up the gable to the crest of the Aldclyffe family perched on the apex. Behind this, at a distance of ten or twenty yards, came the only portion of the main building that still existed—an Elizabethan fragment, consisting of as much as could be contained under three gables and a cross roof behind. Against the wall could be seen ragged lines indicating the form of other destroyed gables which had once joined it there. The mullioned and transomed windows, containing five or six lights, were mostly bricked up to the extent of two or three, and the remaining portion fitted with cottage window-frames carelessly inserted, to suit the purpose to which the old place was now applied, it being partitioned out into small rooms downstairs to form cottages for two labourers and their families; the upper portion was arranged as a storehouse for divers kinds of roots and fruit.

The owner of the picturesque spot, after her survey from this point, went up to the walls and walked into the old court, where the paving-stones were pushed sideways and upwards by the thrust of the grasses between them. Two or three little children, with their fingers in their mouths, came out to look at her, and then ran in to tell their mothers in loud tones of secrecy that Miss Aldclyffe was coming. Miss Aldclyffe, however, did not come in. She concluded her survey of the exterior by making a complete circuit of the building; then turned into a nook a short distance off where round and square timber, a saw-pit, planks, grindstones, heaps of building stone and brick, explained that the spot was the centre of operations for the building work done on the estate.

She paused, and looked around. A man who had seen her from the window of the workshops behind, came out and respectfully lifted his hat to her. It was the first time she had been seen walking outside the house since her father's death.

'Strooden, could the Old House be made a decent residence of, without much trouble?' she inquired.

The mechanic considered, and spoke as each consideration completed itself.

'You don't forget, ma'am, that two-thirds of the place is already pulled down, or gone to ruin?'

'Yes; I know.'

'And that what's left may almost as well be, ma'am.'

'Why may it?'

' 'Twas so cut up inside when they made it into cottages, that the whole carcase is full of cracks.'

'Still by pulling down the inserted partitions, and adding a little outside, it could be made to answer the purpose of an ordinary six or eight-roomed house?'

'Yes, ma'am.'

'About what would it cost?' was the question which had invariably come next in every communication of this kind to which the superintending workman had been a party during his whole experience. To his surprise, Miss Aldclyffe did not put it. The man thought her object in altering an old house must have been an unusually absorbing one not to prompt what was so instinctive in owners as hardly to require any prompting at all.

'Thank you: that's sufficient, Strooden,' she

157

said. 'You will understand that it is not unlikely some alteration may be made here in a short time, with reference to the management of the affairs.'

Strooden said 'Yes,' in a complex voice, and looked uneasy.

'During the life of Captain Aldclyffe, with you as the foreman of works, and he himself as his own steward, everything worked well. But now it may be necessary to have a steward, whose management will encroach further upon things which have hitherto been left in your hands than did your late master's. What I mean is, that he will directly and in detail superintend all.'

'Then—I shall not be wanted, ma'am?' he faltered.

'O yes; if you like to stay on as foreman in the yard and workshops only. I should be sorry to lose you. However, you had better consider. I will send for you in a few days.'

Leaving him to suspense, and all the ills that came in its train—distracted application to his duties, and an undefined number of sleepless nights and untasted dinners, Miss Aldclyffe looked at her watch and returned to the House. She was about to keep an appointment with her solicitor, Mr. Nyttleton, who had been to Budmouth, and was coming to Knapwater on his way back to London.

2. AUGUST THE TWENTIETH

On the Saturday subsequent to Mr. Nyttleton's visit to Knapwater House, the subjoined advertisement appeared in the *Field* and the *Builder* newspapers:—

LAND STEWARD.

A gentleman of integrity and professional skill is required immediately for the MANAGEMENT of an ESTATE, containing about 1000 acres, upon which agricultural improvements and the erection of buildings are contemplated. He must be a man of superior education, unmarried, and not more than thirty years of age. Considerable preference will be shown for one who possesses an artistic as well as a practical knowledge of planning and laying out. The remuneration will consist of a salary of 220 £, with the old manor-house as a residence—Address Messrs. Nyttleton and Tayling, solicitors, Lincoln's Inn Fields.

A copy of each paper was sent to Miss Aldclyffe on the day of publication. The same evening she told Cytherea that she was advertising for a steward, who would live at the old manor-house, showing her the papers containing the announcement.

What was the drift of that remark? thought the maiden; or was it merely made to her in confidential intercourse, as other arrangements were told her daily. Yet it seemed to have more meaning than common. She remembered the conversation about architects and surveyors, and her brother Owen. Miss Aldclyffe knew that his situation was precarious, that he was well educated and practical, and was applying himself heart and soul to the details of the profession and all connected with it. Miss Aldclyffe might be ready to take him if he could compete successfully with others who would reply. She hazarded a question:

'Would it be desirable for Owen to answer it?'

'Not at all,' said Miss Aldclyffe peremptorily.

A flat answer of this kind had ceased to alarm Cytherea. Miss Aldclyffe's blunt mood was not her worst. Cytherea thought of another man, whose name, in spite of resolves, tears, renunciations and injured pride, lingered in her ears like an old familiar strain. That man was qualified for a stewardship under a king.

'Would it be of any use if Edward Springrove were to answer it?' she said, resolutely enunciating the name.

'None whatever,' replied Miss Aldclyffe,

again in the same decided tone.

'You are very unkind to speak in that way.'

'Now don't pout like a goosie, as you are. I don't want men like either of them, for, of course, I must look to the good of the estate rather than to that of any individual. The man I want must have been more specially educated. I have told you that we are going to London next week; it is mostly on this account.'

Cytherea found that she had mistaken the drift of Miss Aldclyffe's peculiar explicitness on the subject of advertising, and wrote to tell her brother that if he saw the notice it would be useless to reply.

3. AUGUST THE TWENTY-FIFTH

Five days after the above-mentioned dialogue took place they went to London, and, with scarcely a minute's pause, to the solicitors' offices in Lincoln's Inn Fields.

They alighted opposite one of the characteristic entrances about the place—a gate which was never, and could never be, closed, flanked by lamp-standards carrying no lamp. Rust was the only active agent to be seen there at this time of the day and year. The palings along the front were rusted away at their base to the thinness of wires, and the successive coats of paint, with which they were overlaid in bygone days, had been completely undermined by the same insidious canker, which lifted off the paint in flakes, leaving the raw surface of the iron on palings, standards, and gate hinges, of a staring blood-red.

But once inside the railings the picture changed. The court and offices were a complete contrast to the grand ruin of the outwork which enclosed them. Well-painted respectability extended over, within, and around the doorstep; and in the carefully swept yard not a particle of dust was visible.

Mr. Nyttleton, who had just come up from Margate, where he was staying with his family, was standing at the top of his own staircase as the pair ascended. He politely took them inside.

'Is there a comfortable room in which this young lady can sit during our interview?' said Miss Aldclyffe.

It was rather a favourite habit of hers to make much of Cytherea when they were out, and snub her for it afterwards when they got home.

'Certainly—Mr. Tayling's.' Cytherea was shown into an inner room.

Social definitions are all made relatively: an absolute datum is only imagined. The small gentry about Knapwater seemed unpractised to Miss Aldclyffe, Miss Aldclyffe herself seemed unpractised to Mr. Nyttleton's experienced old eyes.

'Now then,' the lady said, when she was alone with the lawyer; 'what is the result of our advertisement?'

It was late summer; the estate-agency, building, engineering, and surveying worlds were dull. There were forty-five replies to the advertisement.

Mr. Nyttleton spread them one by one before Miss Aldclyffe. 'You will probably like to read some of them yourself, madam?' he said.

'Yes, certainly,' said she.

'I will not trouble you with those which are from persons manifestly unfit at first sight,' he continued; and began selecting from the heap twos and threes which he had marked, collecting others into his hand. 'The man we want lies among these, if my judgment doesn't deceive me, and from them it would be advisable to select a certain number to be communicated with.'

'I should like to see every one—only just to glance them over—exactly as they came,' she said suasively.

He looked as if he thought this a waste of his time, but dismissing his sentiment unfolded each singly and laid it before her. As he laid them out, it struck him that she studied them quite as rapidly as he could spread them. He slyly glanced up from the outer corner of his eye to hers, and noticed that all she did was look at the name at the bottom of the letter, and then put the enclosure aside without further ceremony. He thought this an odd way of inquiring into the merits of forty-five men who at considerable trouble gave in detail reasons why they believed themselves well qualified for a certain post. She came to the final one, and put it down with the rest.

Then the lady said that in her opinion it would be best to get as many replies as they possibly could before selecting—'to give us a wider choice. What do you think, Mr. Nyttleton?'

It seemed to him, he said, that a greater number than those they already had would scarcely be necessary, and if they waited for more, there would be this disadvantage attending it, that some of those they now could command would possibly not be available.

'Never mind, we will run that risk,' said Miss Aldclyffe. 'Let the advertisement be inserted once more, and then we will certainly settle the matter.'

Mr. Nyttleton bowed, and seemed to think Miss Aldclyffe, for a single woman, and one who till so very recently had never concerned herself with business of any kind, a very meddlesome client. But she was rich, and handsome still. 'She's a new broom in estate-management as yet,' he thought. 'She will soon get tired of this,' and he parted from her without a sentiment which could mar his habitual blandness.

The two ladies then proceeded westward. Dismissing the cab in Waterloo Place, they went along Pall Mall on foot, where in place of the usual well-dressed clubbists—rubicund with alcohol—were to be seen, in linen pinafores, flocks of house-painters pallid from white lead. When they had reached the Green Park, Cytherea proposed that they should sit down awhile under the young elms at the brow of the hill. This they did—the growl of Piccadilly on their left hand—the monastic seclusion of the Palace on their right: before them, the clock tower of the Houses of Parliament, standing forth with a metallic lustre against a livid Lambeth sky.

Miss Aldclyffe still carried in her hand a copy of the newspaper, and while Cytherea had been interesting herself in the picture around, glanced again at the advertisement.

She heaved a slight sigh, and began to fold it up again. In the action her eye caught sight of two consecutive advertisements on the cover, one relating to some lecture on Art, and addressed to members of the Institute of Architects. The other emanated from the same source, but was addressed to the public, and stated that the exhibition of drawings at the Institute's rooms would close at the end of that week.

Her eye lighted up. She sent Cytherea back to the hotel in a cab, then turned round by Piccadilly into Bond Street, and proceeded to the rooms of the Institute. The secretary was sitting in the lobby. After making her payment, and looking at a few of the drawings on the walls, in the company of three gentlemen, the only other visitors to the exhibition, she turned back and asked if she might be allowed to see a list of the members. She was a little connected with the architectural world, she said, with a smile, and was interested in some of the names.

'Here it is, madam,' he replied, politely handing her a pamphlet containing the names.

Miss Aldclyffe turned the leaves till she came to the letter M. The name she hoped to find there was there, with the address appended, as was the case with all the rest.

The address was at some chambers in a street not far from Charing Cross. 'Chambers,' as a residence, had always been assumed by the lady to imply the condition of a bachelor. She murmured two words, 'There still.'

Another request had yet to be made, but it was of a more noticeable kind than the first, and might compromise the secrecy with which she wished to act throughout this episode. Her object was to get one of the envelopes lying on the secretary's table, stamped with the die of the Institute; and in order to get it she was about to ask if she might write a note.

But the secretary's back chanced to be turned, and he now went towards one of the men at the other end of the room, who had called him to ask some question relating to an etching on the wall. Quick as thought, Miss Aldclyffe stood before the table, slipped her hand behind her, took one of the envelopes and put it in her pocket.

She sauntered round the rooms for two or three minutes longer, then withdrew and returned to her hotel.

Here she cut the Knapwater advertisement from the paper, put it into the envelope she had stolen, embossed with the society's stamp, and directed it in a round clerkly hand to the address she had seen in the list of members' names submitted to her:—

ÆNEAS MANSTON, ESQ.,
WYKEHAM CHAMBERS,
SPRING GARDENS.

This ended her first day's work in London.

4. FROM AUGUST THE TWENTY-SIXTH TO SEPTEMBER THE FIRST

The two Cythereas continued at the Westminster Hotel, Miss Aldclyffe informing her companion that business would detain them in London another week. The days passed as slowly and quietly as days can pass in a city at that time of the year, the shuttered windows about the squares and terraces confronting their eyes like the white and sightless orbs of blind men. On Thursday Mr. Nyttleton called, bringing the whole number of replies to the advertisement. Cytherea was present at the interview, by Miss Aldclyffe's request—either from whim or design.

Ten additional letters were the result of the second week's insertion, making fifty-five in all. Miss Aldclyffe looked them over as before. One was signed—

ÆNEAS MANSTON,
133, TURNGATE STREET,
LIVERPOOL.

'Now, then, Mr. Nyttleton, will you make a selection, and I will add one or two,' Miss Aldclyffe said.

Mr. Nyttleton scanned the whole heap of letters, testimonials, and references, sorting them into two heaps. Manston's missive, after a mere glance, was thrown amongst the summarily rejected ones.

Miss Aldclyffe read, or pretended to read after the lawyer. When he had finished, five lay in the group he had selected. 'Would you like to add to the number?' he said, turning to the lady.

'No,' she said carelessly. 'Well, two or three additional ones rather took my fancy,' she added, searching for some in the larger collection.

She drew out three. One was Manston's.

'These eight, then, shall be communicated with,' said the lawyer, taking up the eight letters and placing them by themselves.

They stood up. 'If I myself, Miss Aldclyffe, were only concerned personally,' he said, in an off-hand way, and holding up a letter singly, 'I should choose this man unhesitatingly. He writes honestly, is not afraid to name what he does not consider himself well acquainted with—a rare thing to find in answers to advertisements; he is well recommended, and possesses some qualities rarely found in combination. Oddly enough, he is not really a steward. He was bred a farmer, studied building affairs, served on an estate for some time, then went with an architect, and is now well qualified as architect, estate agent, and surveyor. That man is sure to have a fine head for a manor like yours.'

He tapped the letter as he spoke. 'Yes, I should choose him without hesitation—speaking personally.'

'And I think,' she said artificially, 'I should choose this one as a matter of mere personal whim, which, of course, can't be given way to when practical questions have to be considered.'

Cytherea, after looking out of the window, and then at the newspapers, had become interested in the proceedings between the clever Miss Aldclyffe and the keen old lawyer, which reminded her of a game at cards. She looked inquiringly at the two letters—one in Miss Aldclyffe's hand, the other in Mr. Nyttleton's.

'What is the name of your man?' said Miss Aldclyffe.

'His name—' said the lawyer, looking down the page; 'what is his name?—it is Edward Springrove.'

Miss Aldclyffe glanced towards Cytherea, who was getting red and pale by turns. She looked imploringly at Miss Aldclyffe.

'The name of my man,' said Miss Aldclyffe, looking at her letter in turn; 'is, I think—yes—Æneas Manston.'

5. SEPTEMBER THE THIRD

The next morning but one was appointed for the interviews, which were to be at the lawyer's offices. Mr. Nyttleton and Mr. Tayling were both in town for the day, and the candidates were admitted one by one into a private room. In the window recess was seated Miss Aldclyffe, wearing her veil down.

The lawyer had, in his letters to the selected number, timed each candidate at an interval of ten or fifteen minutes from those preceding and following. They were shown in as they arrived, and had short conversations with Mr. Nyttleton—terse, and to the point. Miss

Aldclyffe neither moved nor spoke during this proceeding; it might have been supposed that she was quite unmindful of it, had it not been for what was revealed by a keen penetration of the veil covering her countenance—the rays from two bright black eyes, directed towards the lawyer and his interlocutor.

Springrove came fifth; Manston seventh. When the examination of all was ended, and the last man had retired, Nyttleton, again as at the former time, blandly asked his client which of the eight she personally preferred. 'I still think the fifth we spoke to, Springrove, the man whose letter I pounced upon at first, to be by far the best qualified, in short, most suitable generally.'

'I am sorry to say that I differ from you; I lean to my first notion still—that Mr.—Mr. Manston is most desirable in tone and bearing, and even specifically; I think he would suit me best in the long-run.'

Mr. Nyttleton looked out of the window at the whitened wall of the court.

'Of course, madam, your opinion may be perfectly sound and reliable; a sort of instinct, I know, often leads ladies by a short cut to conclusions truer than those come to by men after laborious round-about calculations, based on long experience. I must say I shouldn't recommend him.'

'Why, pray?'

'Well, let us look first at his letter of answer

to the advertisement. He didn't reply till the last insertion; that's one thing. His letter is bold and frank in tone, so bold and frank that the second thought after reading it is that not honesty, but unscrupulousness of conscience dictated it. It is written in an indifferent mood, as if he felt that he was humbugging us in his statement that he was the right man for such an office, that he tried hard to get it only as a matter of form which required that he should neglect no opportunity that came in his way.'

'You may be right, Mr. Nyttleton, but I don't quite see the grounds of your reasoning.'

'He has been, as you perceive, almost entirely used to the office duties of a city architect, the experience we don't want. You want a man whose acquaintance with rural landed properties is more practical and closer—somebody who, if he has not filled exactly such an office before, has lived a country life, knows the ins and outs of country tenancies, building, farming, and so on.'

'He's by far the most intellectual looking of them all.'

'Yes; he may be—your opinion, Miss Aldclyffe, is worth more than mine in that matter. And more than you say, he is a man of parts—his brain power would soon enable him to master details and fit him for the post, I don't much doubt that. But to speak clearly' (here his words started off at a jog-trot) 'I wouldn't run the risk of placing the

172

management of an estate of mine in his hands on any account whatever. There, that's flat and plain, madam.'

'But, definitely,' she said, with a show of impatience, 'what is your reason?'

'He is a voluptuary with activity; which is a very bad form of man—as bad as it is rare.'

'Oh. Thank you for your explicit statement, Mr. Nyttleton,' said Miss Aldclyffe, starting a little and flushing with displeasure.

Mr. Nyttleton nodded slightly, as a sort of neutral motion, simply signifying a receipt of the information, good or bad.

'And I really think it is hardly worth while to trouble you further in this,' continued the lady. 'He's quite good enough for a little insignificant place like mine at Knapwater; and I know that I could not get on with one of the others for a single month. We'll try him.'

'Certainly, Miss Aldclyffe,' said the lawyer. And Mr. Manston was written to, to the effect that he was the successful competitor.

'Did you see how unmistakably her temper was getting the better of her, that minute you were in the room?' said Nyttleton to Tayling, when their client had left the house. Nyttleton was a man who surveyed everybody's character in a sunless and shadowless northern light. A culpable slyness, which marked him as a boy, had been moulded by Time, the Improver, into honourable circumspection.

We frequently find that the quality which,

conjoined with the simplicity of the child, is vice, is virtue when it pervades the knowledge of the man.

'She was as near as damn-it to boiling over when I added up her man,' continued Nyttleton. 'His handsome face is his qualification in her eyes. They have met before; I saw that.'

'He didn't seem conscious of it,' said the junior.

'He didn't. That was rather puzzling to me. But still, if ever a woman's face spoke out plainly that she was in love with a man, hers did that she was with him. Poor old maid, she's almost old enough to be his mother. If that Manston's a schemer he'll marry her, as sure as I am Nyttleton. Let's hope he's honest, however.'

'I don't think she's in love with him,' said Tayling. He had seen but little of the pair, and yet he could not reconcile what he had noticed in Miss Aldclyffe's behaviour with the idea that it was the bearing of a woman towards her lover.

'Well, your experience of the fiery phenomenon is more recent than mine,' rejoined Nyttleton carelessly. 'And you may remember the nature of it best.'

VIII.

THE EVENTS OF EIGHTEEN DAYS

1. FROM THE THIRD TO THE NINETEENTH OF SEPTEMBER

Miss Aldclyffe's tenderness towards Cytherea, between the hours of her irascibility, increased till it became no less than doting fondness. Like Nature in the tropics, with her hurricanes and the subsequent luxuriant vegetation effacing their ravages, Miss Aldclyffe compensated for her outbursts by excess of generosity afterwards. She seemed to be completely won out of herself by close contact with a young woman whose modesty was absolutely unimpaired, and whose artlessness was as perfect as was compatible with the complexity necessary to produce the due charm of womanhood. Cytherea, on her part, perceived with honest satisfaction that her influence for good over Miss Aldclyffe was considerable. Ideas and habits peculiar to the younger, which the elder lady had originally imitated as a mere whim, she grew in course of time to take a positive delight in. Among others were evening and morning prayers, dreaming over out-door scenes, learning a verse from some poem whilst dressing.

Yet try to force her sympathies as much as she would, Cytherea could feel no more than thankful for this, even if she always felt as much as thankful. The mysterious cloud hanging over the past life of her companion, of which the uncertain light already thrown upon it only seemed to render still darker the unpenetrated remainder, nourished in her a feeling which was scarcely too slight to be called dread. She would have infinitely preferred to be treated distantly, as the mere dependent, by such a changeable nature—like a fountain, always herself, yet always another. That a crime of any deep dye had ever been perpetrated or participated in by her namesake, she would not believe; but the reckless adventuring of the lady's youth seemed connected with deeds of darkness rather than of light.

Sometimes Miss Aldclyffe appeared to be on the point of making some absorbing confidence, but reflection invariably restrained her. Cytherea hoped that such a confidence would come with time, and that she might thus be a means of soothing a mind which had obviously known extreme suffering.

But Miss Aldclyffe's reticence concerning her past was not imitated by Cytherea. Though she never disclosed the one fact of her knowledge that the love-suit between Miss Aldclyffe and her father terminated abnormally, the maiden's natural ingenuousness on subjects not set down for special guard had enabled Miss Aldclyffe to worm from her, fragment by fragment, every detail of her father's history. Cytherea saw how deeply Miss Aldclyffe sympathized—and it compensated her, to some extent, for the hasty resentments of other times.

Thus uncertainly she lived on. It was perceived by the servants of the House that some secret bond of connection existed between Miss Aldclyffe and her companion. But they were woman and woman, not woman and man, the facts were ethereal and refined, and so they could not be worked up into a taking story. Whether, as old critics disputed, a supernatural machinery be necessary to an epic or no, an ungodly machinery is decidedly necessary to a scandal.

Another letter had come to her from Edward—very short, but full of entreaty, asking why she would not write just one line— just one line of cold friendship at least? She then allowed herself to think, little by little, whether she had not perhaps been too harsh with him; and at last wondered if he were really much to blame for being engaged to another woman. 'Ah, Brain, there is one in me stronger than you!' she said. The young maid now continually pulled out his letter, read it and re-read it, almost crying with pity the while, to think what wretched suspense he must be enduring at her silence, till her heart

177

chid her for her cruelty. She felt that she must send him a line—one little line—just a wee line to keep him alive, poor thing; sighing like Donna Clara—

> Ah, were he now before me,
> In spite of injured pride,
> I fear my eyes would pardon
> Before my tongue could chide.

2. SEPTEMBER THE TWENTIETH.
THREE TO FOUR P.M.

It was the third week in September, about five weeks after Cytherea's arrival, when Miss Aldclyffe requested her one day to go through the village of Carriford and assist herself in collecting the subscriptions made by some of the inhabitants of the parish to a religious society she patronized. Miss Aldclyffe formed one of what was called a Ladies' Association, each member of which collected tributary streams of shillings from her inferiors, to add to her own pound at the end.

Miss Aldclyffe took particular interest in Cytherea's appearance that afternoon, and the object of her attention was, indeed, gratifying to look at. The sight of the lithe girl, set off by an airy dress, coquettish jacket, flexible hat, a ray of starlight in each eye and a war of lilies and roses in each cheek, was a palpable

178

pleasure to the mistress of the mansion, yet a pleasure which appeared to partake less of the nature of affectionate satisfaction than of mental gratification.

Eight names were printed in the report as belonging to Miss Aldclyffe's list, with the amount of subscription-money attached to each.

'I will collect the first four, whilst you do the same with the last four,' said Miss Aldclyffe.

The names of two tradespeople stood first in Cytherea's share: then came a Miss Hinton: last of all in the printed list was Mr. Springrove the elder. Underneath his name was pencilled, in Miss Aldclyffe's handwriting, 'Mr. Manston.'

Manston had arrived on the estate, in the capacity of steward, three or four days previously, and occupied the old manor-house, which had been altered and repaired for his reception.

'Call on Mr. Manston,' said the lady impressively, looking at the name written under Cytherea's portion of the list.

'But he does not subscribe yet?'

'I know it; but call and leave him a report. Don't forget it.'

'Say you would be pleased if he would subscribe?'

'Yes—say I should be pleased if he would,' repeated Miss Aldclyffe, smiling. 'Good-bye. Don't hurry in your walk. If you can't get easily through your task to-day put off some of it till to-morrow.'

Each then started on her rounds: Cytherea going in the first place to the old manor-house. Mr. Manston was not indoors, which was a relief to her. She called then on the two gentleman-farmers' wives, who soon transacted their business with her, frigidly indifferent to her personality. A person who socially is nothing is thought less of by people who are not much than by those who are a great deal.

She then turned towards Peakhill Cottage, the residence of Miss Hinton, who lived there happily enough, with an elderly servant and a house-dog as companions. Her father, and last remaining parent, had retired thither four years before this time, after having filled the post of editor to the *Casterbridge Chronicle* for eighteen or twenty years. There he died soon after, and though comparatively a poor man, he left his daughter sufficiently well provided for as a modest fundholder and claimant of sundry small sums in dividends to maintain herself as mistress at Peakhill.

At Cytherea's knock an inner door was heard to open and close, and footsteps crossed the passage hesitatingly. The next minute Cytherea stood face to face with the lady herself.

Adelaide Hinton was about nine-and-twenty years of age. Her hair was plentiful, like Cytherea's own; her teeth equalled Cytherea's in regularity and whiteness. But she was much paler, and had features too transparent to be in place among household surroundings. Her mouth expressed love less forcibly than Cytherea's, and, as a natural result of her greater maturity, her tread was less elastic, and she was more self-possessed.

She had been a girl of that kind which mothers praise as not forward, by way of contrast, when disparaging those warmer ones with whom loving is an end and not a means. Men of forty, too, said of her, 'a good sensible wife for any man, if she cares to marry,' the caring to marry being thrown in as the vaguest hypothesis, because she was so practical. Yet it would be singular if, in such cases, the important subject of marriage should be excluded from manipulation by hands that are ready for practical performance in every domestic concern besides.

Cytherea was an acquisition, and the greeting was hearty.

'Good afternoon! O yes—Miss Graye, from Miss Aldclyffe's. I have seen you at church, and I am so glad you have called! Come in. I wonder if I have change enough to pay my subscription.' She spoke girlishly.

Adelaide, when in the company of a younger woman, always levelled herself down to that younger woman's age from a sense of justice to herself—as if, though not her own age at common law, it was in equity.

'It doesn't matter. I'll come again.'

'Yes, do at any time; not only on this errand. But you must step in for a minute. Do.'

'I have been wanting to come for several weeks.'

'That's right. Now you must see my house—lonely, isn't it, for a single person? People said it was odd for a young woman like me to keep on a house; but what did I care? If you knew the pleasure of locking up your own door, with the sensation that you reigned supreme inside it, you would say it was worth the risk of being called odd. Mr. Springrove attends to my gardening, the dog attends to robbers, and whenever there is a snake or toad to kill, Jane does it.'

'How nice! It is better than living in a town.'

'Far better. A town makes a cynic of me.'

The remark recalled, somewhat startlingly, to Cytherea's mind, that Edward had used those very words to herself one evening at Budmouth.

Miss Hinton opened an interior door and led her visitor into a small drawing-room commanding a view of the country for miles.

The missionary business was soon settled; but the chat continued.

'How lonely it must be here at night!' said Cytherea. 'Aren't you afraid?'

'At first I was, slightly. But I got used to the solitude. And you know a sort of commonsense will creep even into timidity. I

182

say to myself sometimes at night, "If I were anybody but a harmless woman, not worth the trouble of a worm's ghost to appear to me, I should think that every sound I hear was a spirit." But you must see all over my house.'

Cytherea was highly interested in seeing.

'I say you *must* do this, and you *must* do that, as if you were a child,' remarked Adelaide. 'A privileged friend of mine tells me this use of the imperative comes of being so constantly in nobody's society but my own.'

'Ah, yes. I suppose she is right.'

Cytherea called the friend 'she' by a rule of ladylike practice; for a woman's 'friend' is delicately assumed by another friend to be of their own sex in the absence of knowledge to the contrary; just as cats are called she's until they prove themselves he's.

Miss Hinton laughed mysteriously.

'I get a humorous reproof for it now and then, I assure you,' she continued.

'"Humorous reproof:" that's not from a woman: who can reprove humorously but a man?' was the groove of Cytherea's thought at the remark. 'Your brother reproves you, I expect,' said that innocent young lady.

'No,' said Miss Hinton, with a candid air. ' 'Tis only a professional man I am acquainted with.' She looked out of the window.

Women are persistently imitative. No sooner did a thought flash through Cytherea's mind that the man was a lover than she became a Miss Aldclyffe in a mild form.

'I imagine he's a lover,' she said.

Miss Hinton smiled a smile of experience in that line.

Few women, if taxed with having an admirer, are so free from vanity as to deny the impeachment, even if it is utterly untrue. When it does happen to be true, they look pityingly away from the person who is so benighted as to have got no further than suspecting it.

'There now—Miss Hinton; you are engaged to be married!' said Cytherea accusingly.

Adelaide nodded her head practically. 'Well, yes, I am,' she said.

The word 'engaged' had no sooner passed Cytherea's lips than the sound of it—the mere sound of her own lips—carried her mind to the time and circumstances under which Miss Aldclyffe had used it towards herself. A sickening thought followed—based but on a mere surmise; yet its presence took every other idea away from Cytherea's mind. Miss Hinton had used Edward's words about towns; she mentioned Mr. Springrove as attending to her garden. It could not be that Edward was the man! that Miss Aldclyffe had planned to reveal her rival thus!

'Are you going to be married soon?' she inquired, with a steadiness the result of a sort of fascination, but apparently of indifference.

'Not very soon—still, soon.'

'Ah-ha! In less than three months?' said Cytherea.

'Two.'

Now that the subject was well in hand, Adelaide wanted no more prompting. 'You won't tell anybody if I show you something?' she said, with eager mystery.

'O no, nobody. But does he live in this parish?'

'No.'

Nothing proved yet.

'What's his name?' said Cytherea flatly. Her breath and heart had begun their old tricks, and came and went hotly. Miss Hinton could not see her face.

'What do you think?' said Miss Hinton.

'George?' said Cytherea, with deceitful agony.

'No,' said Adelaide. 'But now, you shall see him first; come here;' and she led the way upstairs into her bedroom. There, standing on the dressing table in a little frame, was the unconscious portrait of Edward Springrove.

'There he is,' Miss Hinton said, and a silence ensued.

'Are you very fond of him?' continued the miserable Cytherea at length.

'Yes, of course I am,' her companion replied, but in the tone of one who 'lived in Abraham's bosom all the year,' and was therefore untouched by solemn thought at the fact. 'He's my cousin—a native of this village. We were engaged before my father's death left me so lonely. I was only twenty, and a much greater belle than I am now. We know each other thoroughly, as you may imagine. I give him a little sermonizing now and then.'

'Why?'

'O, it's only in fun. He's very naughty sometimes—not really, you know—but he will look at any pretty face when he sees it.'

Storing up this statement of his susceptibility as another item to be miserable upon when she had time, 'How do you know that?' Cytherea asked, with a swelling heart.

'Well, you know how things do come to women's ears. He used to live at Budmouth as an assistant-architect, and I found out that a young giddy thing of a girl who lives there somewhere took his fancy for a day or two. But I don't feel jealous at all—our engagement is so matter-of-fact that neither of us can be jealous. And it was a mere flirtation—she was too silly for him. He's fond of rowing, and kindly gave her an airing for an evening or two. I'll warrant they talked the most unmitigated rubbish under the sun—all shallowness and pastime, just as everything is at watering places—neither of them caring a bit for the other—she giggling like a goose all the time—'

Concentrated essence of woman pervaded the room rather than air. 'She *didn't*! and it *wasn't* shallowness!' Cytherea burst out, with brimming eyes. ' 'Twas deep deceit on one side, and entire confidence on the other—yes, it was!' The pent-up emotion had swollen and swollen inside the young thing till the dam could no longer embay it. The instant the words were out she would have given worlds to have been able to recall them.

'Do you know her—or him?' said Miss Hinton, starting with suspicion at the warmth shown.

The two rivals had now lost their personality quite. There was the same keen brightness of eye, the same movement of the mouth, the same mind in both, as they looked doubtingly and excitedly at each other. As is invariably the case with women when a man they care for is the subject of an excitement among them, the situation abstracted the differences which distinguished them as individuals, and left only the properties common to them as atoms of a sex.

Cytherea caught at the chance afforded her of not betraying herself. 'Yes, I know her,' she said.

'Well,' said Miss Hinton, 'I am really vexed if my speaking so lightly of any friend of yours has hurt your feelings, but—'

'O, never mind,' Cytherea returned; 'it doesn't matter, Miss Hinton. I think I must leave you now. I have to call at other places. Yes—I must go.'

Miss Hinton, in a perplexed state of mind,

showed her visitor politely downstairs to the door. Here Cytherea bade her a hurried adieu, and flitted down the garden into the lane.

She persevered in her duties with a wayward pleasure in giving herself misery, as was her wont. Mr. Springrove's name was next on the list, and she turned towards his dwelling, the Three Tranters Inn.

3. FOUR TO FIVE P.M.

The cottages along Carriford village street were not so close but that on one side or other of the road was always a hedge of hawthorn or privet, over or through which could be seen gardens or orchards rich with produce. It was about the middle of the early apple-harvest, and the laden trees were shaken at intervals by the gatherers; the soft pattering of the falling crop upon the grassy ground being diversified by the loud rattle of vagrant ones upon a rail, hencoop, basket, or lean-to roof, or upon the rounded and stooping backs of the collectors—mostly children, who would have cried bitterly at receiving such a smart blow from any other quarter, but smilingly assumed it to be but fun in apples.

The Three Tranters Inn, a many-gabled, mediaeval building, constructed almost entirely of timber, plaster, and thatch, stood close to the line of the roadside, almost opposite the churchyard, and was connected with a row of cottages on the left by thatched outbuildings. It was an uncommonly characteristic and handsome specimen of the genuine roadside inn of bygone times; and standing on one of the great highways in this part of England, had in its time been the scene of as much of what is now looked upon as the romantic and genial experience of stage-coach travelling as any halting-place in the country. The railway had absorbed the whole stream of traffic which formerly flowed through the village and along by the ancient door of the inn, reducing the empty-handed landlord, who used only to farm a few fields at the back of the house, to the necessity of eking out his attenuated income by increasing the extent of his agricultural business if he would still maintain his social standing. Next to the general stillness pervading the spot, the long line of outbuildings adjoining the house was the most striking and saddening witness to the passed-away fortunes of the Three Tranters Inn. It was the bulk of the original stabling, and where once the hoofs of two-score horses had daily rattled over the stony yard, to and from the coaches without, thick grass now grew, whilst the line of roofs—once so straight—over the decayed stalls, had sunk into vast hollows till they seemed like the cheeks of toothless age.

On a green plot at the other end of the

building grew two or three large, wide-spreading elm-trees, from which the sign was suspended—representing the three men called tranters (irregular carriers), standing side by side, and exactly alike to a hair's-breadth, the grain of the wood and joints of the boards being visible through the thin paint depicting their forms, which were still further disfigured by red stains running downwards from the rusty nails above.

Under the trees now stood a cider-mill and press, and upon the spot sheltered by the boughs were gathered Mr. Springrove himself, his men, the parish clerk, two or three other men, grinders and supernumeraries, a woman with an infant in her arms, a flock of pigeons, and some little boys with straws in their mouths, endeavouring, whenever the men's backs were turned, to get a sip of the sweet juice issuing from the vat.

Edward Springrove the elder, the landlord, now more particularly a farmer, and for two months in the year a cider-maker, was an employer of labour of the old school, who worked himself among his men. He was now engaged in packing the pomace into horsehair bags with a rammer, and Gad Weedy, his man, was occupied in shovelling up more from a tub at his side. The shovel shone like silver from the action of the juice, and ever and anon, in its motion to and fro, caught the rays of the declining sun and reflected them in bristling stars of light.

Mr. Springrove had been too young a man when the pristine days of the Three Tranters had departed for ever to have much of the host left in him now. He was a poet with a rough skin: one whose sturdiness was more the result of external circumstances than of intrinsic nature. Too kindly constituted to be very provident, he was yet not imprudent. He had a quiet humorousness of disposition, not out of keeping with a frequent melancholy, the general expression of his countenance being one of abstraction. Like Walt Whitman he felt as his years increased—

I foresee too much; it means more than
I thought.

On the present occasion he wore gaiters and a leathern apron, and worked with his shirt-sleeves rolled up beyond his elbows, disclosing solid and fleshy rather than muscular arms. They were stained by the cider, and two or three brown apple-pips from the pomace he was handling were to be seen sticking on them here and there.

The other prominent figure was that of Richard Crickett, the parish clerk, a kind of Bowdlerized rake, who ate only as much as a woman, and had the rheumatism in his left hand. The remainder of the group, brown-faced peasants, wore smock-frocks

191

embroidered on the shoulders with hearts and diamonds, and were girt round their middle with a strap, another being worn round the right wrist.

'And have you seen the steward, Mr. Springrove?' said the clerk.

'Just a glimpse of him; but 'twas just enough to show me that he's not here for long.'

'Why mid that be?'

'He'll never stand the vagaries of the female figure holden the reins—not he.'

'She pays en well,' said a grinder; 'and money's money.'

'Ah—'tis: very much so,' the clerk replied.

'Yes, yes, neighbour Crickett,' said Springrove, 'but she'll vlee in a passion—all the fat will be in the fire—and there's an end o't . . . Yes, she is a one,' continued the farmer, resting, raising his eyes, and reading the features of a distant apple.

'She is,' said Gad, resting too (it is wonderful how prompt a journeyman is in following his master's initiative to rest) and reflectively regarding the ground in front of him.

'True: a one is she,' the clerk chimed in, shaking his head ominously.

'She has such a temper,' said the farmer, 'and is so wilful too. You may as well try to stop a footpath as stop her when she has taken anything into her head. I'd as soon grind little green crabs all day as live wi' her.'

' 'Tis a temper she have,' the clerk replied, 'though I be a servant of the Church that say it. But she isn't goen to flee in a passion this time.'

The audience waited for the continuation of the speech, as if they knew from experience the exact distance off it lay in the future.

The clerk swallowed nothing as if it were a great deal, and then went on, 'There's some'at between 'em: mark my words, neighbours—there's some'at between 'em.'

'D'ye mean it?'

'I know it. He came last Saturday, didn't he?'

' 'A did, truly,' said Gad Weedy, at the same time taking an apple from the hopper of the mill, eating a piece, and flinging back the remainder to be ground up for cider.

'He went to church a-Sunday,' said the clerk again.

'He did.'

'And she kept her eye upon en all the service, her face flickeren between red and white, but never stoppen at either.'

Mr. Springrove nodded, and went to the press.

'Well,' said the clerk, 'you don't call her the kind o' woman to make mistakes in just trotten through the weekly service o' God? Why, as a rule she's as right as I be myself.'

Mr. Springrove nodded again, and gave a twist to the screw of the press, followed in the

193

movement by Gad at the other side; the two grinders expressing by looks that, if Miss Aldclyffe were as right at church as the clerk, she must be right indeed.

'Yes, as right in the service o' God as I be myself,' repeated the clerk. 'But last Sunday, when we were in the tenth commandment, says she, "Incline our hearts to keep this law," when 'twas "Laws in our hearts, we beseech Thee," all the church through. Her eye was upon *him*—she was quite lost—"Hearts to keep this law," says she; she was no more than a mere shadder at that tenth time—a mere shadder. You might have mouthed across to her "Laws in our hearts we beseech Thee," fifty times over—she'd never ha' noticed 'e. She's in love wi' the man, that's what she is.'

'Then she's a bigger stunpoll than I took her for,' said Mr. Springrove. 'Why, she's old enough to be his mother.'

'The row'll be between her and that young Curly-wig, you'll see. She won't run the risk of that pretty face being near.'

'Clerk Crickett, I fancy you knowing everything about everybody,' said Gad.

'Well so's,' said the clerk modestly. 'I do know a little. It comes to me.'

'And I know where from.'

'Ah.'

'That wife o' thine. She's an entertainen woman, not to speak disrespectful.'

'She is: and a winnen one. Look at the

husbands she've had—God bless her!'

'I wonder you could stand third in that list, Clerk Crickett,' said Mr. Springrove.

'Well, 't has been a power o' marvel to myself oftentimes. Yes, matrimony do begin wi' "Dearly beloved," and ends wi' "Amazement," as the prayer-book says. But what could I do, neighbour Springrove? 'Twas ordained to be. Well do I call to mind what your poor lady said to me when I had just married. "Ah, Mr. Crickett," says she, "your wife will soon settle you as she did her other two: here's a glass o' rum, for I shan't see your poor face this time next year." I swallered the rum, called again next year, and said, "Mrs. Springrove, you gave me a glass o' rum last year because I was going to die—here I be alive still, you see." "Well thought of, clerk! Here's two glasses for you now, then," says she. "Thank you, mem," I said, and swallered the rum. Well, dang my old sides, next year I thought I'd call again and get three. And call I did. But she wouldn't give me a drop o' the commonest. "No, clerk," says she, "you are too tough for a woman's pity." . . . Ah, poor soul, 'twas true enough! Here be I, that was expected to die, alive and hard as a nail, you see, and there's she moulderen in her grave.'

'I used to think 'twas your wife's fate not to have a liven husband when I zid 'em die off so,' said Gad.

'Fate? Bless thy simplicity, so 'twas her fate;

but she struggled to have one, and would, and did. Fate's nothing beside a woman's schemen!'

'I suppose, then, that Fate is a He, like us, and the Lord, and the rest o' 'em up above there,' said Gad, lifting his eyes to the sky.

'Hullo! Here's the young woman comen that we were a-talken about by-now,' said a grinder, suddenly interrupting. 'She's comen up here, as I be alive!'

The two grinders stood and regarded Cytherea as if she had been a ship tacking into a harbour, nearly stopping the mill in their new interest.

'Stylish accoutrements about the head and shoulders, to my thinken,' said the clerk. 'Sheenen curls, and plenty o' 'em.'

'If there's one kind of pride more excusable than another in a young woman, 'tis being proud of her hair,' said Mr. Springrove.

'Dear man!—the pride there is only a small piece o' the whole. I warrant now, though she can show such a figure, she ha'n't a stick o' furniture to call her own.'

'Come, Clerk Crickett, let the maid be a maid while she is a maid,' said Farmer Springrove chivalrously.

'O,' replied the servant of the Church; 'I've nothing to say against it—O no:

"The chimney-sweeper's daughter Sue
As I have heard declare, O,

Although she's neither sock nor shoe
Will curl and deck her hair, O.""

Cytherea was rather disconcerted at finding that the gradual cessation of the chopping of the mill was on her account, and still more when she saw all the cider-makers' eyes fixed upon her except Mr. Springrove's, whose natural delicacy restrained him. She neared the plot of grass, but instead of advancing further, hesitated on its border.

Mr. Springrove perceived her embarrassment, which was relieved when she saw his old-established figure coming across to her, wiping his hands in his apron.

'I know your errand, missie,' he said, 'and am glad to see you, and attend to it. I'll step indoors.'

'If you are busy I am in no hurry for a minute or two,' said Cytherea.

'Then if so be you really wouldn't mind, we'll wring down this last filling to let it drain all night?'

'Not at all. I like to see you.'

'We are only just grinding down the early rathe-ripes and griffins,' continued the farmer, in a half-apologetic tone for detaining by his cider-making any well-dressed woman. 'They rot as black as a chimney-crook if we keep 'em till the regulars turn in.' As he spoke he went back to the press, Cytherea keeping at his elbow. 'I'm later than I should have been by rights,' he continued, taking up a lever for propelling the screw, and beckoning to the men to come forward. 'The truth is, my son Edward had promised to come to-day, and I made preparations; but instead of him comes a letter: "London, September the eighteenth, Dear Father," says he, and went on to tell me he couldn't. It threw me out a bit.'

'Of course,' said Cytherea.

'He's got a place 'a b'lieve?' said the clerk, drawing near.

'No, poor mortal fellow, no. He tried for this one here, you know, but couldn't manage to get it. I don't know the rights o' the matter, but willy-nilly they wouldn't have him for steward. Now mates, form in line.'

Springrove, the clerk, the grinders, and Gad, all ranged themselves behind the lever of the screw, and walked round like soldiers wheeling.

'The man that the old quean have got is a man you can hardly get upon your tongue to gainsay, by the look o' en,' rejoined Clerk Crickett.

'One o' them people that can contrive to be thought no worse of for stealen a horse than another man for looken over hedge at en,' said a grinder.

'Well, he's all there as steward, and is quite the gentleman—no doubt about that.'

'So would my Ted ha' been, for the matter o' that,' the farmer said.

'That's true: 'a would, sir.'

'I said, I'll give Ted a good education if it do cost me my eyes, and I would have done it.'

'Ay, that you would so,' said the chorus of assistants solemnly.

'But he took to books and drawing naturally, and cost very little; and as a wind-up the womenfolk hatched up a match between him and his cousin.'

'When's the wedden to be, Mr. Springrove?'

'Uncertain—but soon, I suppose. Edward, you see, can do anything pretty nearly, and yet can't get a straightforward living. I wish sometimes I had kept him here, and let professions go. But he was such a one for the pencil.'

He dropped the lever in the hedge, and turned to his visitor.

'Now then, missie, if you'll come indoors, please.'

Gad Weedy looked with a placid criticism at Cytherea as she withdrew with the farmer.

'I could tell by the tongue o' her that she didn't take her degrees in our county,' he said in an undertone.

*   *   *

'The railways have left you lonely here,' she observed, when they were indoors.

Save the withered old flies, which were quite tame from the solitude, not a being was in the

199

house. Nobody seemed to have entered it since the last passenger had been called out to mount the last stage-coach that had run by.

'Yes, the Inn and I seem almost a pair of fossils,' the farmer replied, looking at the room and then at himself.

'O, Mr. Springrove,' said Cytherea, suddenly recollecting herself; 'I am much obliged to you for recommending me to Miss Aldclyffe.' She began to warm towards the old man; there was in him a gentleness of disposition which reminded her of her own father.

'Recommending? Not at all, miss. Ted—that's my son—Ted said a fellow-draughtsman of his had a sister who wanted to be doing something in the world, and I mentioned it to the housekeeper, that's all. Ay, I miss my son very much.'

She kept her back to the window that he might not see her rising colour.

'Yes,' he continued, 'sometimes I can't help feeling uneasy about him. You know, he seems not made for a town life exactly: he gets very queer over it sometimes, I think. Perhaps he'll be better when he's married to Adelaide.'

A half-impatient feeling arose in her, like that which possesses a sick person when he hears a recently-struck hour struck again by a slow clock. She had lived further on.

'Everything depends upon whether he loves her,' she said tremulously.

'He used to—he doesn't show it so much

now; but that's because he's older. You see, it was several years ago they first walked together as young man and young woman. She's altered too from what she was when he first courted her.'

'How, sir?'

'O, she's more sensible by half. When he used to write to her she'd creep up the lane and look back over her shoulder, and slide out the letter, and read a word and stand in thought looking at the hills and seeing none. Then the cuckoo would cry—away the letter would slip, and she'd start wi' fright at the mere bird, and have a red skin before the quickest man among ye could say, "Blood rush up."'

He came forward with the money and dropped it into her hand. His thoughts were still with Edward, and he absently took her little fingers in his as he said, earnestly and ingenuously—

''Tis so seldom I get a gentlewoman to speak to that I can't help speaking to you, Miss Graye, on my fears for Edward; I sometimes am afraid that he'll never get on—that he'll die poor and despised under the worst o' mind conditions, a keen sense of having been passed in the race by men whose brains are nothing to his own, all through his seeing too far into things—being discontented with make-shifts—thinking o' perfection in things, and then sickened that there's no such thing as

201

perfection. I shan't be sorry to see him marry, since it may settle him down and do him good ... Ay, we'll hope for the best.'

He let go her hand and accompanied her to the door saying, 'If you should care to walk this way and talk to an old man once now and then, it will be a great delight to him, Miss Graye. Good evening to ye . . . Ah look! a thunderstorm is brewing—be quick home. Or shall I step up with you?'

'No, thank you, Mr. Springrove. Good evening,' she said in a low voice, and hurried away. One thought still possessed her; Edward had trifled with her love.

4. FIVE TO SIX P.M.

She followed the road into a bower of trees, overhanging it so densely that the pass appeared like a rabbit's burrow, and presently reached a side entrance to the park. The clouds rose more rapidly than the farmer had anticipated: the sheep moved in a trail, and complained incoherently. Livid grey shades, like those of the modern French painters, made a mystery of the remote and dark parts of the vista, and seemed to insist upon a suspension of breath. Before she was half-way across the park the thunder rumbled distinctly.

The direction in which she had to go would take her close by the old manor-house. The air was perfectly still, and between each low rumble of the thunder behind she could hear the roar of the waterfall before her, and the creak of the engine among the bushes hard by it. Hurrying on, with a growing dread of the gloom and of the approaching storm, she drew near the Old House, now rising before her against the dark foliage and sky in tones of strange whiteness.

On the flight of steps, which descended from a terrace in front to the level of the park, stood a man. He appeared, partly from the relief the position gave to his figure, and partly from fact, to be of towering height. He was dark in outline, and was looking at the sky, with his hands behind him.

It was necessary for Cytherea to pass directly across the line of his front. She felt so reluctant to do this, that she was about to turn under the trees out of the path and enter it again at a point beyond the Old House; but he had seen her, and she came on mechanically, unconsciously averting her face a little, and dropping her glance to the ground.

Her eyes unswervingly lingered along the path until they fell upon another path branching in a right line from the path she was pursuing. It came from the steps of the Old House. 'I am exactly opposite him now,' she thought, 'and his eyes are going through me.'

A clear masculine voice said, at the same instant—

'Are you afraid?'

She, interpreting his question by her feelings at the moment, assumed himself to be the object of fear, if any. 'I don't think I am,' she stammered.

He seemed to know that she thought in that sense.

'Of the thunder, I mean,' he said; 'not of myself.'

She must turn to him now. 'I think it is going to rain,' she remarked for the sake of saying something.

He could not conceal his surprise and admiration of her face and bearing. He said courteously, 'It may possibly not rain before you reach the House, if you are going there?'

'Yes, I am.'

'May I walk up with you? It is lonely under the trees.'

'No.' Fearing his courtesy arose from a belief that he was addressing a woman of higher station than was hers, she added, 'I am Miss Aldclyffe's companion. I don't mind the loneliness.'

'O, Miss Aldclyffe's companion. Then will you be kind enough to take a subscription to her? She sent to me this afternoon to ask me to become a subscriber to her Society, and I was out. Of course I'll subscribe if she wishes it. I take a great interest in the Society.'

'Miss Aldclyffe will be glad to hear that, I know.'

204

'Yes; let me see—what Society did she say it was? I am afraid I haven't enough money in my pocket, and yet it would be a satisfaction to her to have practical proof of my willingness. I'll get it, and be out in one minute.'

He entered the house and was at her side again within the time he had named. 'This is it,' he said pleasantly.

She held up her hand. The soft tips of his fingers brushed the palm of her glove as he placed the money within it. She wondered why his fingers should have touched her.

'I think after all,' he continued, 'that the rain is upon us, and will drench you before you reach the House. Yes: see there.'

He pointed to a round wet spot as large as a nasturtium leaf, which had suddenly appeared upon the white surface of the step.

'You had better come into the porch. It is not nearly night yet. The clouds make it seem later than it really is.'

Heavy drops of rain, followed immediately by a forked flash of lightning and sharp rattling thunder compelled her, willingly or no, to accept his invitation. She ascended the steps, stood beside him just within the porch, and for the first time obtained a series of short views of his person, as they waited there in silence.

He was an extremely handsome man, well-formed, and well-dressed, of an age which seemed to be two or three years less than thirty. The most striking point in his appearance was the wonderful, almost preternatural, clearness of his complexion. There was not a blemish or speck of any kind to mar the smoothness of its surface or the beauty of its hue. Next, his forehead was square and broad, his brows straight and firm, his eyes penetrating and clear. By collecting the round of expressions they gave forth, a person who theorized on such matters would have imbibed the notion that their owner was of a nature to kick against the pricks; the last man in the world to put up with a position because it seemed to be his destiny to do so; one who took upon himself to resist fate with the vindictive determination of a Theomachist.

Eyes and forehead both would have expressed keenness of intellect too severely to be pleasing, had their force not been counteracted by the lines and tone of the lips. These were full and luscious to a surprising degree, possessing a woman-like softness of curve, and a ruby redness so intense, as to testify strongly to much susceptibility of heart where feminine beauty was concerned—a susceptibility that might require all the ballast of brain with which he had previously been credited to confine within reasonable channels.

His manner was rather elegant than good: his speech well-finished and unconstrained.

The pause in their discourse, which had been caused by the peal of thunder was unbroken by either for a minute or two, during which the ears of both seemed to be absently following the low roar of the waterfall as it became gradually rivalled by the increasing rush of rain upon the trees and herbage of the grove. After her short looks at him, Cytherea had turned her head towards the avenue for a while, and now, glancing back again for an instant, she discovered that his eyes were engaged in a steady, though delicate, regard of her face and form.

At this moment, by reason of the narrowness of the porch, their dresses touched, and remained in contact.

His clothes are something exterior to every man; but to a woman her dress is part of her body. Its motions are all present to her intelligence if not to her eyes; no man knows how his coat-tails swing. By the slightest hyperbole it may be said that her dress has sensation. Crease but the very Ultima Thule of fringe or flounce, and it hurts her as much as pinching her. Delicate antennae, or feelers, bristle on every outlying frill. Go to the uppermost: she is there; tread on the lowest: the fair creature is there almost before you.

Thus the touch of clothes, which was nothing to Manston, sent a thrill through Cytherea, seeing, moreover, that he was of the nature of a mysterious stranger. She looked out again at the storm, but still felt him. At last to escape the sensation she moved away, though by so doing it was necessary to advance a little into the rain.

'Look, the rain is coming into the porch upon you,' he said. 'Step inside the door.'

Cytherea hesitated.

'Perfectly safe, I assure you,' he added, laughing, and holding the door open. 'You shall see what a state of disorganization I am in—boxes on boxes, furniture, straw, crockery, in every form of transposition. An old woman is in the back quarters somewhere, beginning to put things to rights . . . You know the inside of the house, I dare say?'

'I have never been in.'

'O well, come along. Here, you see, they have made a door through, here, they have put a partition dividing the old hall into two, one part is now my parlour; there they have put a plaster ceiling, hiding the old chestnut-carved roof because it was too high and would have been chilly for me; you see, being the original hall, it was open right up to the top, and here the lord of the manor and his retainers used to meet and be merry by the light from the monstrous fire which shone out from that monstrous fire-place, now narrowed to a mere nothing for my grate, though you can see the old outline still. I almost wish I could have had it in its original state.'

'With more romance and less comfort.'

'Yes, exactly. Well, perhaps the wish is not deep-seated. You will see how the things are tumbled in anyhow, packing-cases and all.

The only piece of ornamental furniture yet unpacked is this one.'

'An organ?'

'Yes, an organ. I made it myself, except the pipes. I opened the case this afternoon to commence soothing myself at once. It is not a very large one, but quite big enough for a private house. You play, I dare say?'

'The piano. I am not at all used to an organ.'

'You would soon acquire the touch for an organ, though it would spoil your touch for the piano. Not that that matters a great deal. A piano isn't much as an instrument.'

'It is the fashion to say so now. I think it is quite good enough.'

'That isn't altogether a right sentiment about things being good enough.'

'No—no. What I mean is, that the men who despise pianos do it as a rule from their teeth, merely for fashion's sake, because cleverer men have said it before them—not from the experience of their ears.'

Now Cytherea all at once broke into a blush at the consciousness of a great snub she had been guilty of in her eagerness to explain herself. He charitably expressed by a look that he did not in the least mind her blunder, if it were one; and this attitude forced him into a position of mental superiority which vexed her.

'I play for my private amusement only,' he said. 'I have never learned scientifically. All I know is what I taught myself.'

The thunder, lightning, and rain had now increased to a terrific force. The clouds, from which darts, forks, zigzags, and balls of fire continually sprang, did not appear to be more than a hundred yards above their heads, and every now and then a flash and a peal made gaps in the steward's descriptions. He went towards the organ, in the midst of a volley which seemed to shake the aged house from foundations to chimney.

'You are not going to play now, are you?' said Cytherea uneasily.

'O yes. Why not now?' he said. 'You can't go home, and therefore we may as well be amused, if you don't mind sitting on this box. The few chairs I have unpacked are in the other room.'

Without waiting to see whether she sat down or not, he turned to the organ and began extemporizing a harmony which meandered through every variety of expression of which the instrument was capable. Presently he ceased and began searching for some music-book.

'What a splendid flash!' he said, as the lightning again shone in through the mullioned window, which, of a proportion to suit the whole extent of the original hall, was much too large for the present room. The thunder pealed again. Cytherea, in spite of herself, was frightened, not only at the weather, but at the general unearthly weirdness which seemed to

210

surround her there.

'I wish I—the lightning wasn't so bright. Do you think it will last long?' she said timidly.

'It can't last much longer,' he murmured, without turning, running his fingers again over the keys. 'But this is nothing,' he continued, suddenly stopping and regarding her. 'It seems brighter because of the deep shadow under those trees yonder. Don't mind it; now look at me—look in my face—now.'

He had faced the window, looking fixedly at the sky with his dark strong eyes. She seemed compelled to do as she was bidden, and looked in the too-delicately beautiful face.

The flash came; but he did not turn or blink, keeping his eyes fixed as firmly as before. 'There,' he said, turning to her, 'that's the way to look at lightning.'

'O, it might have blinded you!' she exclaimed.

'Nonsense—not lightning of this sort—I shouldn't have stared at it if there had been danger. It is only sheet-lightning now. Now, will you have another piece? Something from an oratorio this time?'

'No, thank you—I don't want to hear it whilst it thunders so.' But he had begun without heeding her answer, and she stood motionless again, marvelling at the wonderful indifference to all external circumstance which was now evinced by his complete absorption in the music before him.

'Why do you play such saddening chords?' she said, when he next paused.

'H'm—because I like them, I suppose,' said he lightly. 'Don't you like sad impressions sometimes?'

'Yes, sometimes, perhaps.'

'When you are full of trouble.'

'Yes.'

'Well, why shouldn't I when I am full of trouble?'

'Are you troubled?'

'I am troubled.' He said this thoughtfully and abruptly—so abruptly that she did not push the dialogue further.

He now played more powerfully. Cytherea had never heard music in the completeness of full orchestral power, and the tones of the organ, which reverberated with considerable effect in the comparatively small space of the room, heightened by the elemental strife of light and sound outside, moved her to a degree out of proportion to the actual power of the mere notes, practised as was the hand that produced them. The varying strains—now loud, now soft; simple, complicated, weird, touching, grand, boisterous, subdued; each phase distinct, yet modulating into the next with a graceful and easy flow—shook and bent her to themselves, as a gushing brook shakes and bends a shadow cast across its surface. The power of the music did not show itself so much by attracting her attention to the subject of the piece, as by taking up and developing as its libretto the poem of her own life and soul, shifting her deeds and intentions from the hands of her judgment and holding them in its own.

She was swayed into emotional opinions concerning the strange man before her; new impulses of thought came with new harmonies, and entered into her with a gnawing thrill. A dreadful flash of lightning then, and the thunder close upon it. She found herself involuntarily shrinking up beside him, and looking with parted lips at his face.

He turned his eyes and saw her emotion, which greatly increased the ideal element in her expressive face. She was in the state in which woman's instinct to conceal has lost its power over her impulse to tell; and he saw it. Bending his handsome face over her till his lips almost touched her ear, he murmured, without breaking the harmonies—

'Do you very much like this piece?'

'Very much indeed,' she said.

'I could see you were affected by it. I will copy it for you.'

'Thank you much.'

'I will bring it to the House to you to-morrow. Who shall I ask for?'

'O, not for me. Don't bring it,' she said hastily. 'I shouldn't like you to.'

'Let me see—to-morrow evening at seven or a few minutes past I shall be passing the waterfall on my way home. I could conveniently give it you there, and I should like you to have it.'

He modulated into the Pastoral Symphony, still looking in her eyes.

'Very well,' she said, to get rid of the look.

The storm had by this time considerably decreased in violence, and in seven or ten minutes the sky partially cleared, the clouds around the western horizon becoming lighted up with the rays of the sinking sun.

Cytherea drew a long breath of relief, and prepared to go away. She was full of a distressing sense that her detention in the old manor-house, and the acquaintanceship it had set on foot, was not a thing she wished. It was such a foolish thing to have been excited and dragged into frankness by the wiles of a stranger.

'Allow me to come with you,' he said, accompanying her to the door, and again showing by his behaviour how much he was impressed with her. His influence over her had vanished with the musical chords, and she turned her back upon him. 'May I come?' he repeated.

'No, no. The distance is not a quarter of a mile—it is really not necessary, thank you,' she said quietly. And wishing him good-evening, without meeting his eyes, she went down the steps, leaving him standing at the door.

'O, how is it that man has so fascinated me?'

was all she could think. Her own self, as she had sat spell-bound before him, was all she could see. Her gait was constrained, from the knowledge that his eyes were upon her until she had passed the hollow by the waterfall, and by ascending the rise had become hidden from his view by the boughs of the overhanging trees.

5. SIX TO SEVEN P.M.

The wet shining road threw the western glare into her eyes with an invidious lustre which rendered the restlessness of her mood more wearying. Her thoughts flew from idea to idea without asking for the slightest link of connection between one and another. One moment she was full of the wild music and stirring scene with Manston—the next, Edward's image rose before her like a shadowy ghost. Then Manston's black eyes seemed piercing her again, and the reckless voluptuous mouth appeared bending to the curves of his special words. What could be those troubles to which he had alluded? Perhaps Miss Aldclyffe was at the bottom of them. Sad at heart she paced on: her life was bewildering her.

On coming into Miss Aldclyffe's presence Cytherea told her of the incident, not without a fear that she would burst into one of her ungovernable fits of temper at learning

Cytherea's slight departure from the programme. But, strangely to Cytherea, Miss Aldclyffe looked delighted. The usual cross-examination followed.

'And so you were with him all that time?' said the lady, with assumed severity.

'Yes, I was.'

'I did not tell you to call at the Old House twice.'

'I didn't call, as I have said. He made me come into the porch.'

'What remarks did he make, do you say?'

'That the lightning was not so bad as I thought.'

'A very important remark, that. Did he—' she turned her glance full upon the girl, and eyeing her searchingly, said—

'Did he say anything about me?'

'Nothing,' said Cytherea, returning her gaze calmly, 'except that I was to give you the subscription.'

'You are quite sure?'

'Quite.'

'I believe you. Did he say anything striking or strange about himself?'

'Only one thing—that he was troubled.'

'Troubled!'

After saying the word, Miss Aldclyffe relapsed into silence. Such behaviour as this had ended, on most previous occasions, by her making a confession, and Cytherea expected one now. But for once she was mistaken, nothing more was said.

When she had returned to her room she sat down and penned a farewell letter to Edward Springrove, as little able as any other excitable and brimming young woman of nineteen to feel that the wisest and only dignified course at that juncture was to do nothing at all. She told him that, to her painful surprise, she had learnt that his engagement to another woman was a matter of notoriety. She insisted that all honour bade him marry his early love—a woman far better than her unworthy self, who only deserved to be forgotten, and begged him to remember that he was not to see her face again. She upbraided him for levity and cruelty in meeting her so frequently at Budmouth, and above all in stealing the kiss from her lips on the last evening of the water excursions. 'I never, never can forget it!' she said, and then felt a sensation of having done her duty, ostensibly persuading herself that her reproaches and commands were of such a force that no man to whom they were uttered could ever approach her more.

Yet it was all unconsciously said in words which betrayed a lingering tenderness of love at every unguarded turn. Like Beatrice accusing Dante from the chariot, try as she might to play the superior being who contemned such mere eye-sensuousness, she betrayed at every point a pretty woman's jealousy of a rival, and covertly gave her old lover hints for excusing himself at each fresh indictment.

This done, Cytherea, still in a practical mood, upbraided herself with weakness in allowing a stranger like Mr. Manston to influence her as he had done that evening. What right on earth had he to suggest so suddenly that she might meet him at the waterfall to receive his music? She would have given much to be able to annihilate the ascendency he had obtained over her during that extraordinary interval of melodious sound. Not being able to endure the notion of his living a minute longer in the belief he was then holding, she took her pen and wrote to him also:—

> KNAPWATER HOUSE
> *September 20th.*
> I find I cannot meet you at seven o'clock by the waterfall as I promised. The emotion I felt made me forgetful of realities.
>
> C. GRAYE.

A great statesman thinks several times, and acts; a young lady acts, and thinks several times. When, a few minutes later, she saw the postman carry off the bag containing one of the letters, and a messenger with the other, she, for the first time, asked herself the question whether she had acted very wisely in writing to either of the two men who had so influenced her.

IX.

THE EVENTS OF TEN WEEKS

1. FROM SEPTEMBER THE TWENTY-FIRST TO THE MIDDLE OF NOVEMBER

The foremost figure within Cytherea's horizon, exclusive of the inmates of Knapwater House, was now the steward, Mr. Manston. It was impossible that they should live within a quarter of a mile of each other, be engaged in the same service, and attend the same church, without meeting at some spot or another, twice or thrice a week. On Sundays, in her pew, when by chance she turned her head, Cytherea found his eyes waiting desirously for a glimpse of hers, and, at first more strangely, the eyes of Miss Aldclyffe furtively resting on him. On coming out of church he frequently walked beside Cytherea till she reached the gate at which residents in the House turned into the shrubbery. By degrees a conjecture grew to a certainty. She knew that he loved her.

But a strange fact was connected with the development of his love. He was palpably making the strongest efforts to subdue, or at

219

least to hide, the weakness, and as it sometimes seemed, rather from his own conscience than from surrounding eyes. Hence she found that not one of his encounters with her was anything more than the result of pure accident. He made no advances whatever: without avoiding her, he never sought her: the words he had whispered at their first interview now proved themselves to be quite as much the result of unguarded impulse as was her answer. Something held him back, bound his impulse down, but she saw that it was neither pride of his person, nor fear that she would refuse him—a course she unhesitatingly resolved to take should he think fit to declare himself. She was interested in him and his marvellous beauty, as she might have been in some fascinating panther or leopard—for some undefinable reason she shrank from him, even whilst she admired. The keynote of her nature, a warm 'precipitance of soul,' as Coleridge happily writes it, which Manston had so directly pounced upon at their very first interview, gave her now a tremulous sense of being in some way in his power.

The state of mind was, on the whole, a dangerous one for a young and inexperienced woman; and perhaps the circumstance which, more than any other, led her to cherish Edward's image now, was that he had taken no notice of the receipt of her letter, stating that she discarded him. It was plain then, she said, that he did not care deeply for her, and she thereupon could not quite leave off caring deeply for him:—

Ingenium mulierum,
Nolunt ubi velis, ubi nolis cupiunt ultro.

The month of October passed, and November began its course. The inhabitants of the village of Carriford grew weary of supposing that Miss Aldclyffe was going to marry her steward. New whispers arose and became very distinct (though they did not reach Miss Aldclyffe's ears) to the effect that the steward was deeply in love with Cytherea Graye. Indeed, the fact became so obvious that there was nothing left to say about it except that their marriage would be an excellent one for both;—for her in point of comfort—and for him in point of love.

As circles in a pond grow wider and wider, the next fact, which at first had been patent only to Cytherea herself, in due time spread to her neighbours, and they, too, wondered that he made no overt advances. By the middle of November, a theory made up of a combination of the other two was received with general favour: its substance being that a guilty intrigue had been commenced between Manston and Miss Aldclyffe, some years before, when he was a very young man, and she still in the enjoyment of some womanly beauty,

221

but now that her seniority began to grow emphatic she was becoming distasteful to him. His fear of the effect of the lady's jealousy would, they said, thus lead him to conceal from her his new attachment to Cytherea. Almost the only woman who did not believe this was Cytherea herself, on unmistakable grounds, which were hidden from all besides. It was not only in public, but even more markedly in secluded places, on occasions when gallantry would have been safe from all discovery, that this guarded course of action was pursued, all the strength of a consuming passion burning in his eyes the while.

2. NOVEMBER THE EIGHTEENTH

It was on a Friday in this month of November that Owen Graye paid a visit to his sister.

His zealous integrity still retained for him the situation at Budmouth, and in order that there should be as little interruption as possible to his duties there, he had decided not to come to Knapwater till late in the afternoon, and to return to Budmouth by the first train the next morning, Miss Aldclyffe having made a point of frequently offering him lodging for an unlimited period, to the great pleasure of Cytherea.

He reached the house about four o'clock, and ringing the bell, asked of the page who answered it for Miss Graye.

When Graye spoke the name of his sister, Manston, who was just coming out from an interview with Miss Aldclyffe, passed him in the vestibule and heard the question. The steward's face grew hot, and he secretly clenched his hands. He half crossed the court, then turned his head and saw that the lad still stood at the door, though Owen had been shown into the house. Manston went back to him.

'Who was that man?' he said.

'I don't know, sir.'

'Has he ever been here before?'

'Yes, sir.'

'How many times?'

'Three.'

'You are sure you don't know him?'

'I think he is Miss Graye's brother, sir.'

'Then, why the devil didn't you say so before!' Manston exclaimed, and again went on his way.

'Of course, that was not the man of my dreams—of course, it couldn't be!' he said to himself. 'That I should be such a fool—such an utter fool. Good God! to allow a girl to influence me like this, day after day, till I am jealous of her very brother. A lady's dependent, a waif, a helpless thing entirely at the mercy of the world; yes, curse it; that is just why it is; that fact of her being so helpless against the blows of circumstances which

223

renders her so deliciously sweet!'

He paused opposite his house. Should he get his horse saddled? No.

He went down the drive and out of the park, having started to proceed to an outlying spot on the estate concerning some draining, and to call at the potter's yard to make an arrangement for the supply of pipes. But a remark which Miss Aldclyffe had dropped in relation to Cytherea was what still occupied his mind, and had been the immediate cause of his excitement at the sight of her brother. Miss Aldclyffe had meaningly remarked during their intercourse, that Cytherea was wildly in love with Edward Springrove, in spite of his engagement to his cousin Adelaide.

'How I am harassed!' he said aloud, after deep thought for half-an-hour, while still continuing his walk with the greatest vehemence. 'How I am harassed by these emotions of mine!' He calmed himself by an effort. 'Well, duty after all it shall be, as nearly as I can effect it. "Honesty is the best policy;"' with which vigorously uttered resolve he once more attempted to turn his attention to the prosy object of his journey.

The evening had closed in to a dark and dreary night when the steward came from the potter's door to proceed homewards again. The gloom did not tend to raise his spirits, and in the total lack of objects to attract his eye, he soon fell to introspection as before. It was along the margin of turnip fields that his path lay, and the large leaves of the crop struck flatly against his feet at every step, pouring upon them the rolling drops of moisture gathered upon their broad surfaces; but the annoyance was unheeded. Next reaching a fir plantation, he mounted the stile and followed the path into the midst of the darkness produced by the overhanging trees.

After walking under the dense shade of the inky boughs for a few minutes, he fancied he had mistaken the path, which as yet was scarcely familiar to him. This was proved directly afterwards by his coming at right angles upon some obstruction, which careful feeling with outstretched hands soon told him to be a rail fence. However, as the wood was not large, he experienced no alarm about finding the path again, and with some sense of pleasure halted awhile against the rails, to listen to the intensely melancholy yet musical wail of the fir-tops, and as the wind passed on, the prompt moan of an adjacent plantation in reply. He could just dimly discern the airy summits of the two or three trees nearest him waving restlessly backwards and forwards, and stretching out their boughs like hairy arms into the dull sky. The scene, from its striking and emphatic loneliness, began to grow congenial to his mood; all of human kind seemed at the antipodes.

A sudden rattle on his right hand caused

him to start from his reverie, and turn in that direction. There, before him, he saw rise up from among the trees a fountain of sparks and smoke, then a red glare of light coming forward towards him; then a flashing panorama of illuminated oblong pictures; then the old darkness, more impressive than ever.

The surprise, which had owed its origin to his imperfect acquaintance with the topographical features of that end of the estate, had been but momentary; the disturbance, a well-known one to dwellers by a railway, being caused by the 6.50 down-train passing along a shallow cutting in the midst of the wood immediately below where he stood, the driver having the fire-door of the engine open at the minute of going by. The train had, when passing him, already considerably slackened speed, and now a whistle was heard, announcing that Carriford Road Station was not far in its van.

But contrary to the natural order of things, the discovery that it was only a commonplace train had not caused Manston to stir from his position of facing the railway.

If the 6.50 down-train had been a flash of forked lightning transfixing him to the earth, he could scarcely have remained in a more trance-like state. He still leant against the railings, his right hand still continued pressing on his walking-stick, his weight on one foot, his other heel raised, his eyes wide open towards the blackness of the cutting. The only movement in him was a slight dropping of the lower jaw, separating his previously closed lips a little way, as when a strange conviction rushes home suddenly upon a man. A new surprise, not nearly so trivial as the first, had taken possession of him.

It was on this account. At one of the illuminated windows of a second-class carriage in the series gone by, he had seen a pale face, reclining upon one hand, the light from the lamp falling full upon it.

The face was a woman's.

At last Manston moved; gave a whispering kind of whistle, adjusted his hat, and walked on again, cross-questioning himself in every direction as to how a piece of knowledge he had carefully concealed had found its way to another person's intelligence. 'How can my address have become known?' he said at length, audibly. 'Well, it is a blessing I have been circumspect and honourable, in relation to that—yes, I will say it, for once, even if the words choke me, that darling of mine, Cytherea, never to be my own, never. I suppose all will come out now. All!' The great sadness of his utterance proved that no mean force had been exercised upon himself to sustain the circumspection he had just claimed.

He wheeled to the left, pursued the ditch beside the railway fence, and presently emerged from the wood, stepping into a road which crossed the railway by a bridge.

As he neared home, the anxiety lately written in his face, merged by degrees into a grimly humorous smile, which hung long upon his lips, and he quoted aloud a line from the book of Jeremiah—

A woman shall compass a man.

3. NOVEMBER THE NINETEENTH. DAYBREAK

Before it was light the next morning, two little naked feet pattered along the passage in Knapwater House, from which Owen Graye's bedroom opened, and a tap was given upon his door.

'Owen, Owen, are you awake?' said Cytherea in a whisper through the keyhole. 'You must get up directly, or you'll miss the train.'

When he descended to his sister's little room, he found her there already waiting with a cup of cocoa and a grilled rasher on the table for him. A hasty meal was despatched in the intervals of putting on his overcoat and finding his hat, and they then went softly through the long deserted passages, the kitchen-maid who had prepared their breakfast walking before them with a lamp held high above her head, which cast long wheeling shadows down corridors intersecting the one they followed, their remoter ends being lost in darkness. The door was unbolted and they stepped out.

Owen had preferred walking to the station to accepting the pony-carriage which Miss Aldclyffe had placed at his disposal, having a morbid horror of giving trouble to people richer than himself, and especially to their men-servants, who looked down upon him as a hybrid monster in social position. Cytherea proposed to walk a little way with him.

'I want to talk to you as long as I can,' she said tenderly.

Brother and sister then emerged by the heavy door into the drive. The feeling and aspect of the hour were precisely similar to those under which the steward had left the house the evening previous, excepting that apparently unearthly reversal of natural sequence, which is caused by the world getting lighter instead of darker. 'The tearful glimmer of the languid dawn' was just sufficient to reveal to them the melancholy red leaves, lying thickly in the channels by the roadside, ever and anon loudly tapped on by heavy drops of water, which the boughs above had collected from the foggy air.

They passed the Old House, engaged in a deep conversation, and had proceeded about twenty yards by a cross route, in the direction of the turnpike road, when the form of a woman emerged from the porch of the

229

building.

She was wrapped in a grey waterproof cloak, the hood of which was drawn over her head and closely round her face—so closely that her eyes were the sole features uncovered.

With this one exception of her appearance there, the most perfect stillness and silence pervaded the steward's residence from basement to chimney. Not a shutter was open; not a twine of smoke came forth.

Underneath the ivy-covered gateway she stood still and listened for two, or possibly three minutes, till she became conscious of others in the park. Seeing the pair she stepped back, with the apparent intention of letting them pass out of sight, and evidently wishing to avoid observation. But looking at her watch, and returning it rapidly to her pocket, as if surprised at the lateness of the hour, she hurried out again, and across the park by a still more oblique line than that traced by Owen and his sister.

These in the meantime had got into the road, and were walking along it as the woman came up on the other side of the boundary hedge, looking for a gate or stile, by which she, too, might get off the grass upon the hard ground.

Their conversation, of which every word was clear and distinct, in the still air of the dawn, to the distance of a quarter of a mile, reached her ears, and withdrew her attention from all other matters and sights whatsoever. Thus arrested she stood for an instant as precisely in the attitude of Imogen by the cave of Belarius, as if she had studied the position from the play. When they had advanced a few steps, she followed them in some doubt, still screened by the hedge.

'Do you believe in such odd coincidences?' said Cytherea.

'How do you mean, believe in them? They occur sometimes.'

'Yes, one will occur often enough—that is, two disconnected events will fall strangely together by chance, and people scarcely notice the fact beyond saying, "Oddly enough it happened that so and so were the same," and so on. But when three such events coincide without any apparent reason for the coincidence, it seems as if there must be invisible means at work. You see, three things falling together in that manner are ten times as singular as two cases of coincidence which are distinct.'

'Well, of course: what a mathematical head you have, Cytherea! But I don't see so much to marvel at in our case. That the man who kept the public-house in which Miss Aldclyffe fainted, and who found out her name and position, lives in this neighbourhood, is accounted for by the fact that she got him the berth to stop his tongue. That you came here was simply owing to Springrove.'

'Ah, but look at this. Miss Aldclyffe is the woman our father first loved, and I have come to Miss Aldclyffe's; you can't get over that.'

From these premises, she proceeded to argue like an elderly divine on the designs of Providence which were apparent in such conjunctures, and went into a variety of details connected with Miss Aldclyffe's history.

'Had I better tell Miss Aldclyffe that I know all this?' she inquired at last.

'What's the use?' he said. 'Your possessing the knowledge does no harm; you are at any rate comfortable here, and a confession to Miss Aldclyffe might only irritate her. No, hold your tongue, Cytherea.'

'I fancy I should have been tempted to tell her too,' Cytherea went on, 'had I not found out that there exists a very odd, almost imperceptible, and yet real connection of some kind between her and Mr. Manston, which is more than that of a mutual interest in the estate.'

'She is in love with him!' exclaimed Owen; 'fancy that!'

'Ah—that's what everybody says who has been keen enough to notice anything. I said so at first. And yet now I cannot persuade myself that she is in love with him at all.'

'Why can't you?'

'She doesn't act as if she were. She isn't— you will know I don't say it from any vanity, Owen—she isn't the least jealous of me.'

232

'Perhaps she is in some way in his power.'

'No—she is not. He was openly advertised for, and chosen from forty or fifty who answered the advertisement, without knowing whose it was. And since he has been here, she has certainly done nothing to compromise herself in any way. Besides, why should she have brought an enemy here at all?'

'Then she must have fallen in love with him. You know as well as I do, Cyth, that with women there's nothing between the two poles of emotion towards an interesting male acquaintance. 'Tis either love or aversion.'

They walked for a few minutes in silence, when Cytherea's eyes accidentally fell upon her brother's feet.

'Owen,' she said, 'do you know that there is something unusual in your manner of walking?'

'What is it like?' he asked.

'I can't quite say, except that you don't walk so regularly as you used to.'

The woman behind the hedge, who had still continued to dog their footsteps, made an impatient movement at this change in their conversation, and looked at her watch again. Yet she seemed reluctant to give over listening to them.

'Yes,' Owen returned with assumed carelessness, 'I do know it. I think the cause of it is that mysterious pain which comes just above my ankle sometimes. You remember the first time I had it? That day we went by steam-packet to Lulstead Cove, when it hindered me from coming back to you, and compelled me to sleep with the gateman we have been talking about.'

'But is it anything serious, dear Owen?' Cytherea exclaimed, with some alarm.

'O, nothing at all. It is sure to go off again. I never find a sign of it when I sit in the office.'

Again their unperceived companion made a gesture of vexation, and looked at her watch as if time were precious. But the dialogue still flowed on upon this new subject, and showed no sign of returning to its old channel.

Gathering up her skirt decisively she renounced all further hope, and hurried along the ditch till she had dropped into a valley, and came to a gate which was beyond the view of those coming behind. This she softly opened, and came out upon the road, following it in the direction of the railway station.

Presently she heard Owen Graye's footsteps in her rear, his quickened pace implying that he had parted from his sister. The woman thereupon increased her rapid walk to a run, and in a few minutes safely distanced her fellow-traveller.

The railway at Carriford Road consisted only of a single line of rails; and the short local down-train by which Owen was going to Budmouth was shunted on to a siding whilst the first up-train passed. Graye entered the waiting-room, and the door being open he listlessly observed the movements of a woman wearing a long grey cloak, and closely hooded, who had asked for a ticket for London.

He followed her with his eyes on to the platform, saw her waiting there and afterwards stepping into the train: his recollection of her ceasing with the perception.

4. EIGHT TO TEN O'CLOCK A.M.

Mrs. Crickett, twice a widow, and now the parish clerk's wife, a fine-framed, scandal-loving woman, with a peculiar corner to her eye by which, without turning her head, she could see what people were doing almost behind her, lived in a cottage standing nearer to the old manor-house than any other in the village of Carriford, and she had on that account been temporarily engaged by the steward, as a respectable kind of charwoman and general servant, until a settled arrangement could be made with some person as permanent domestic.

Every morning, therefore, Mrs. Crickett, immediately she had lighted the fire in her own cottage, and prepared the breakfast for herself and husband, paced her way to the Old House to do the same for Mr. Manston. Then she went home to breakfast; and when the steward had eaten his, and had gone out on his rounds, she returned again to clear away, make his bed, and put the house in order for the day.

On the morning of Owen Graye's departure, she went through the operations of her first visit as usual—proceeded home to breakfast, and went back again, to perform those of the second.

Entering Manston's empty bedroom, with her hands on her hips, she indifferently cast her eyes upon the bed, previously to dismantling it.

Whilst she looked, she thought in an inattentive manner, 'What a remarkably quiet sleeper Mr. Manston must be!' The upper bed-clothes were flung back, certainly, but the bed was scarcely disarranged. 'Anybody would almost fancy,' she thought, 'that he had made it himself after rising.'

But these evanescent thoughts vanished as they had come, and Mrs. Crickett set to work; she dragged off the counterpane, blankets and sheets, and stooped to lift the pillows. Thus stooping, something arrested her attention; she looked closely—more closely—very closely. 'Well, to be sure!' was all she could say. The clerk's wife stood as if the air had suddenly set to amber, and held her fixed like a fly in it.

The object of her wonder was a trailing brown hair, very little less than a yard long, which proved it clearly to be a hair from some woman's head. She drew it off the pillow, and took it to the window; there holding it out she looked fixedly at it, and became utterly lost in meditation: her gaze, which had at first actively settled on the hair, involuntarily dropped past its object by degrees and was lost on the floor, as the inner vision obscured the outer one.

She at length moistened her lips, returned her eyes to the hair, wound it round her fingers, put it in some paper, and secreted the whole in her pocket. Mrs. Crickett's thoughts were with her work no more that morning.

She searched the house from roof-tree to cellar, for some other trace of feminine existence or appurtenance; but none was to be found.

She went out into the yard, coal-hole, stable, hay-loft, green-house, fowl-house, and piggery, and still there was no sign. Coming in again, she saw a bonnet, eagerly pounced upon it; and found it to be her own.

Hastily completing her arrangements in the other rooms, she entered the village again, and called at once on the postmistress, Elizabeth Leat, an intimate friend of hers, and a female who sported several unique diseases and afflictions.

Mrs. Crickett unfolded the paper, took out the hair, and waved it on high before the perplexed eyes of Elizabeth, which immediately mooned and wandered after it like a cat's.

'What is it?' said Mrs. Leat, contracting her

eyelids, and stretching out towards the invisible object a narrow bony hand that would have been an unmitigated delight to the pencil of Carlo Crivelli.

'You shall hear,' said Mrs. Crickett, complacently gathering up the treasure into her own fat hand; and the secret was then solemnly imparted, together with the accident of its discovery.

A shaving-glass was taken down from a nail, laid on its back in the middle of a table by the window, and the hair spread carefully out upon it. The pair then bent over the table from opposite sides, their elbows on the edge, their hands supporting their heads, their foreheads nearly touching, and their eyes upon the hair.

'He's been mad after my lady Cytherea,' said Mrs. Crickett, 'and 'tis my very belief the hair is—'

'No 'tidn'. Hers idn' so dark as that,' said Elizabeth.

'Elizabeth, you know that as the faithful wife of a servant of the Church, I should be glad to think as you do about the girl. Mind I don't wish to say anything against Miss Graye, but this I do say, that I believe her to be a nameless thing, and she's no right to stick a moral clock in her face, and deceive the country in such a way. If she wasn't of a bad stock at the outset she was bad in the planten, and if she wasn't bad in the planten, she was bad in the growen, and if not in the growen, she's made bad by what she's gone through since.'

'But I have another reason for knowing it idn' hers,' said Mrs. Leat.

'Ah! I know whose it is then—Miss Aldclyffe's, upon my song!'

' 'Tis the colour of hers, but I don't believe it to be hers either.'

'Don't you believe what they d' say about her and him?'

'I say nothen about that; but you don't know what I know about his letters.'

'What about 'em?'

'He posts all his letters here except those for one person, and they he takes to Budmouth. My son is in Budmouth Post Office, as you know, and as he sits at desk he can see over the blind of the window all the people who post letters. Mr. Manston unvariably goes there wi' letters for that person; my boy knows 'em by sight well enough now.'

'Is it a she?'

' 'Tis a she.'

'What's her name?'

'The little stunpoll of a fellow couldn't call to mind more than that 'tis Miss Somebody, of London. However, that's the woman who ha' been here, depend upon't—a wicked one— some poor street-wench escaped from Sodom, I warrant ye.'

'Only to find herself in Gomorrah, seemingly.'

'That may be.'

'No, no, Mrs. Leat, this is clear to me. 'Tis no miss who came here to see our steward last night—whenever she came or wherever she vanished. Do you think he would ha' let a miss get here how she could, go away how she would, without breakfast or help of any kind?'

Elizabeth shook her head—Mrs. Crickett looked at her solemnly.

'I say I know she had no help of any kind; I know it was so, for the grate was quite cold when I touched it this morning with these fingers, and he was still in bed. No, he wouldn't take the trouble to write letters to a girl and then treat her so off-hand as that. There's a tie between 'em stronger than feelen. She's his wife.'

'He married! The Lord so 's, what shall we hear next? Do he look married now? His are not the abashed eyes and lips of a married man.'

'Perhaps she's a tame one—but she's his wife still.'

'No, no: he's not a married man.'

'Yes, yes, he is. I've had three, and I ought to know.'

'Well, well,' said Mrs. Leat, giving way. 'Whatever may be the truth on't I trust the Lord will settle it all for the best, as He always do.'

'Ay, ay, Elizabeth,' rejoined Mrs. Crickett with a satirical sigh, as she turned on her foot

240

to go home, 'good people like you may say so, but I have always found the Lord a different sort of feller.'

5. NOVEMBER THE TWENTIETH

It was Miss Aldclyffe's custom, a custom originated by her father, and nourished by her own exclusiveness, to unlock the post-bag herself every morning, instead of allowing the duty to devolve on the butler, as was the case in most of the neighbouring county families. The bag was brought upstairs each morning to her dressing-room, where she took out the contents, mostly in the presence of her maid and Cytherea, who had the entrée of the chamber at all hours, and attended there in the morning at a kind of reception on a small scale, which was held by Miss Aldclyffe of her namesake only.

Here she read her letters before the glass, whilst undergoing the operation of being brushed and dressed.

'What woman can this be, I wonder?' she said on the morning succeeding that of the last section. '"London, N.!" It is the first time in my life I ever had a letter from that outlandish place, the North side of London.'

Cytherea had just come into her presence to learn if there was anything for herself; and on being thus addressed, walked up to Miss

Aldclyffe's corner of the room to look at the curiosity which had raised such an exclamation. But the lady, having opened the envelope and read a few lines, put it quickly in her pocket, before Cytherea could reach her side.

'O, 'tis nothing,' she said. She proceeded to make general remarks in a noticeably forced tone of *sang-froid*, from which she soon lapsed into silence. Not another word was said about the letter: she seemed very anxious to get her dressing done, and the room cleared. Thereupon Cytherea went away to the other window, and a few minutes later left the room to follow her own pursuits.

It was late when Miss Aldclyffe descended to the breakfast-table and then she seemed there to no purpose; tea, coffee, eggs, cutlets, and all their accessories, were left absolutely untasted. The next that was seen of her was when walking up and down the south terrace, and round the flower-beds; her face was pale, and her tread was fitful, and she crumpled a letter in her hand.

Dinner-time came round as usual; she did not speak ten words, or indeed seem conscious of the meal; for all that Miss Aldclyffe did in the way of eating, dinner might have been taken out as intact as it was taken in.

In her own private apartment Miss Aldclyffe again pulled out the letter of the morning. One passage in it ran thus:—

242

Of course, being his wife, I could publish the fact, and compel him to acknowledge me at any moment, notwithstanding his threats, and reasonings that it will be better to wait. I have waited, and waited again, and the time for such acknowledgment seems no nearer than at first. To show you how patiently I have waited I can tell you that not till a fortnight ago, when by stress of circumstances I had been driven to new lodgings, have I ever assumed my married name, solely on account of its having been his request all along that I should not do it. This writing to you, madam, is my first disobedience, and I am justified in it. A woman who is driven to visit her husband like a thief in the night and then sent away like a street dog—left to get up, unbolt, unbar, and find her way out of the house as she best may—is justified in doing anything.

But should I demand of him a restitution of rights, there would be involved a publicity which I could not endure, and a noisy scandal flinging my name the length and breadth of the country.

What I still prefer to any such violent means is that you reason with him privately, and compel him to bring me home to your parish in a decent and careful manner, in the way that would be adopted by any respectable man, whose wife had been living away from him for some time, by reason, say, of peculiar family circumstances which had caused disunion, but not enmity, and who at length was enabled to reinstate her in his house.

You will, I know, oblige me in this, especially as knowledge of a peculiar transaction of your own, which took place some years ago, has lately come to me in a singular way. I will not at present trouble you by describing how. It is enough, that I alone, of all people living, know *all the sides of the story*, those from whom I collected it having each only a partial knowledge which confuses them and points to nothing. One person knows of your early engagement and its sudden termination; another, of the reason of those strange meetings at inns and coffee-houses; another, of what was sufficient to cause all this, and so on. I know what fits one and all the circumstances like a key, and shows them to be the natural outcrop of a rational (though rather rash) line of conduct for a young lady. You will at once perceive how it was that some at least of these things were revealed to me.

This knowledge then, common to, and

secretly treasured by us both, is the ground upon which I beg for your friendship and help, with a feeling that you will be too generous to refuse it to me.

I may add that, as yet, my husband knows nothing of this, neither need he if you remember my request.

'A threat—a flat stinging threat! as delicately wrapped up in words as the woman could do it; a threat from a miserable unknown creature to an Aldclyffe, and not the least proud member of the family either! A threat on his account—O, O! shall it be?'

Presently this humour of defiance vanished, and the members of her body became supple again, her proceedings proving that it was absolutely necessary to give way, Aldclyffe as she was. She wrote a short answer to Mrs. Manston, saying civilly that Mr. Manston's possession of such a near relation was a fact quite new to herself, and that she would see what could be done in such an unfortunate affair.

6. NOVEMBER THE TWENTY-FIRST

Manston received a message the next day requesting his attendance at the House punctually at eight o'clock the ensuing evening. Miss Aldclyffe was brave and imperious, but with the purpose she had in view she could not look him in the face whilst daylight shone upon her.

The steward was shown into the library. On entering it, he was immediately struck with the unusual gloom which pervaded the apartment. The fire was dead and dull, one lamp, and that a comparatively small one, was burning at the extreme end, leaving the main proportion of the lofty and sombre room in an artificial twilight, scarcely powerful enough to render visible the titles of the folio and quarto volumes which were jammed into the lower tiers of the bookshelves.

After keeping him waiting for more than twenty minutes (Miss Aldclyffe knew that excellent recipe for taking the stiffness out of human flesh, and for extracting all pre-arrangement from human speech) she entered the room.

Manston sought her eye directly. The hue of her features was not discernible, but the calm glance she flung at him, from which all attempt at returning his scrutiny was absent, awoke him to the perception that probably his secret was by some means or other known to her; how it had become known he could not tell.

She drew forth the letter, unfolded it, and held it up to him, letting it hang by one corner from between her finger and thumb, so that the light from the lamp, though remote, fell directly upon its surface.

'You know whose writing this is?' she said.

He saw the strokes plainly, instantly resolving to burn his ships and hazard all on an advance.

'My wife's,' he said calmly.

His quiet answer threw her off her balance. She had no more expected an answer than does a preacher when he exclaims from the pulpit, 'Do you feel your sin?' She had clearly expected a sudden alarm.

'And why all this concealment?' she said again, her voice rising, as she vainly endeavoured to control her feelings, whatever they were.

'It doesn't follow that, because a man is married, he must tell every stranger of it, madam,' he answered, just as calmly as before.

'Stranger! well, perhaps not; but, Mr. Manston, why did you choose to conceal it, I ask again? I have a perfect right to ask this question, as you will perceive, if you consider the terms of my advertisement.'

'I will tell you. There were two simple reasons. The first was this practical one; you advertised for an unmarried man, if you remember?'

'Of course I remember.'

'Well, an incident suggested to me that I should try for the situation. I was married; but, knowing that in getting an office where there is a restriction of this kind, leaving one's wife

247

behind is always accepted as a fulfilment of the condition, I left her behind for awhile. The other reason is, that these terms of yours afforded me a plausible excuse for escaping (for a short time) the company of a woman I had been mistaken in marrying.'

'Mistaken! what was she?' the lady inquired.

'A third-rate actress, whom I met with during my stay in Liverpool last summer, where I had gone to fulfil a short engagement with an architect.'

'Where did she come from?'

'She is an American by birth, and I grew to dislike her when we had been married a week.'

'She was ugly, I imagine?'

'She is not an ugly woman by any means.'

'Up to the ordinary standard?'

'Quite up to the ordinary standard—indeed, handsome. After a while we quarrelled and separated.'

'You did not ill-use her, of course?' said Miss Aldclyffe, with a little sarcasm.

'I did not.'

'But at any rate, you got thoroughly tired of her.'

Manston looked as if he began to think her questions out of place; however, he said quietly, 'I did get tired of her. I never told her so, but we separated; I to come here, bringing her with me as far as London and leaving her there in perfectly comfortable quarters; and though your advertisement expressed a single man, I have always intended to tell you the whole truth; and this was when I was going to tell it, when your satisfaction with my careful management of your affairs should have proved the risk to be a safe one to run.'

She bowed.

'Then I saw that you were good enough to be interested in my welfare to a greater extent than I could have anticipated or hoped, judging you by the frigidity of other employers, and this caused me to hesitate. I was vexed at the complication of affairs. So matters stood till three nights ago; I was then walking home from the pottery, and came up to the railway. The down-train came along close to me, and there, sitting at a carriage window, I saw my wife: she had found out my address, and had thereupon determined to follow me here. I had not been home many minutes before she came in. Next morning early she left again—'

'Because you treated her so cavalierly?'

'And as I suppose, wrote to you directly. That's the whole story of her, madam.' Whatever were Manston's real feelings towards the lady who had received his explanation in these supercilious tones, they remained locked within him as within a casket of steel.

'Did your friends know of your marriage, Mr. Manston?' she continued.

'Nobody at all; we kept it a secret for various reasons.'

'It is true then that, as your wife tells me in this letter, she has not passed as Mrs. Manston till within these last few days?'

'It is quite true; I was in receipt of a very small and uncertain income when we married; and so she continued playing at the theatre as before our marriage, and in her maiden name.'

'Has she any friends?'

'I have never heard that she has any in England. She came over here on some theatrical speculation, as one of a company who were going to do much, but who never did anything; and here she has remained.'

A pause ensued, which was terminated by Miss Aldclyffe.

'I understand,' she said. 'Now, though I have no direct right to concern myself with your private affairs (beyond those which arise from your misleading me and getting the office you hold)—'

'As to that, madam,' he interrupted, rather hotly, 'as to coming here, I am vexed as much as you. Somebody, a member of the Institute of Architects—who, I could never tell—sent to my old address in London your advertisement cut from the paper; it was forwarded to me; I wanted to get away from Liverpool, and it seemed as if this was put in my way on purpose, by some old friend or other. I answered the advertisement certainly, but I was not particularly anxious to come here, nor am I anxious to stay.'

250

Miss Aldclyffe descended from haughty superiority to womanly persuasion with a haste which was almost ludicrous. Indeed, the *Quos ego* of the whole lecture had been less the genuine menace of the imperious ruler of Knapwater than an artificial utterance to hide a failing heart.

'Now, now, Mr. Manston, you wrong me; don't suppose I wish to be overbearing, or anything of the kind; and you will allow me to say this much, at any rate, that I have become interested in your wife, as well as in yourself.'

'Certainly, madam,' he said, slowly, like a man feeling his way in the dark. Manston was utterly at fault now. His previous experience of the effect of his form and features upon womankind en masse, had taught him to flatter himself that he could account by the same law of natural selection for the extraordinary interest Miss Aldclyffe had hitherto taken in him, as an unmarried man; an interest he did not at all object to, seeing that it kept him near Cytherea, and enabled him, a man of no wealth, to rule on the estate as if he were its lawful owner. Like Curius at his Sabine farm, he had counted it his glory not to possess gold himself, but to have power over her who did. But at this hint of the lady's wish to take his wife under her wing also, he was perplexed: could she have any sinister motive in doing so? But he did not allow himself to be troubled with these doubts, which only concerned his wife's happiness.

'She tells me,' continued Miss Aldclyffe, 'how utterly alone in the world she stands, and that is an additional reason why I should sympathize with her. Instead, then, of requesting the favour of your retirement from the post, and dismissing your interests altogether, I will retain you as my steward still, on condition that you bring home your wife, and live with her respectably, in short, as if you loved her; you understand. I *wish* you to stay here if you grant that everything shall flow smoothly between yourself and her.'

The breast and shoulders of the steward rose, as if an expression of defiance was about to be poured forth; before it took form, he controlled himself and said, in his natural voice—

'My part of the performance shall be carried out, madam.'

'And her anxiety to obtain a standing in the world ensures that hers will,' replied Miss Aldclyffe. 'That will be satisfactory, then.'

After a few additional remarks, she gently signified that she wished to put an end to the interview. The steward took the hint and retired.

He felt vexed and mortified; yet in walking homeward he was convinced that telling the whole truth as he had done, with the single exception of his love for Cytherea (which he tried to hide even from himself), had never served him in better stead than it had done that night.

Manston went to his desk and thought of Cytherea's beauty with the bitterest, wildest regret. After the lapse of a few minutes he calmed himself by a stoical effort, and wrote the subjoined letter to his wife:—

KNAPWATER,
November 21, 1864.

DEAR EUNICE,—I hope you reached London safely after your flighty visit to me.

As I promised, I have thought over our conversation that night, and your wish that your coming here should be no longer delayed. After all, it was perfectly natural that you should have spoken unkindly as you did, ignorant as you were of the circumstances which bound me.

So I have made arrangements to fetch you home at once. It is hardly worth while for you to attempt to bring with you any luggage you may have gathered about you (beyond mere clothing). Dispose of superfluous things at a broker's; your bringing them would only make a talk in this parish, and lead people to believe we had long been keeping house separately.

Will next Monday suit you for coming? You have nothing to do that can occupy you for more than a day or two, as far as I can see, and the remainder of this week will afford ample time. I can be in London the night before, and we will come down together by the mid-day train—Your very affectionate husband,

ÆNEAS MANSTON.

Now, of course, I shall no longer write to you as Mrs. Rondley.

The address on the envelope was—

MRS. MANSTON,
    41 CHARLES SQUARE,
        HOXTON,
            LONDON, N.

He took the letter to the House, and it being too late for the country post, sent one of the stablemen with it to Casterbridge, instead of troubling to go to Budmouth with it himself as heretofore. He had no longer any necessity to keep his condition a secret.

7. FROM THE TWENTY-SECOND TO THE TWENTY-SEVENTH OF NOVEMBER

But the next morning Manston found that he had been forgetful of another matter, in naming the following Monday to his wife for the journey.

The fact was this. A letter had just come, reminding him that he had left the whole of the succeeding week open for an important business engagement with a neighbouring land-agent, at that gentleman's residence thirteen miles off. The particular day he had suggested to his wife, had, in the interim, been appropriated by his correspondent. The meeting could not now be put off.

So he wrote again to his wife, stating that business, which could not be postponed, called him away from home on Monday, and would entirely prevent him coming all the way to fetch her on Sunday night as he had intended, but that he would meet her at the Carriford Road Station with a conveyance when she arrived there in the evening.

The next day came his wife's answer to his first letter, in which she said that she would be ready to be fetched at the time named. Having already written his second letter, which was by that time in her hands, he made no further reply.

The week passed away. The steward had, in the meantime, let it become generally known in the village that he was a married man, and by a little judicious management, sound family reasons for his past secrecy upon the subject, which were floated as adjuncts to the story, were placidly received; they seemed so natural and justifiable to the unsophisticated minds of nine-tenths of his neighbours, that curiosity in

255

the matter, beyond a strong curiosity to see the lady's face, was well-nigh extinguished.

X.

THE EVENTS OF A DAY AND NIGHT

1. NOVEMBER THE TWENTY-EIGHTH. UNTIL TEN P.M.

Monday came, the day named for Mrs. Manston's journey from London to her husband's house; a day of singular and great events, influencing the present and future of nearly all the personages whose actions in a complex drama form the subject of this record.

The proceedings of the steward demand the first notice. Whilst taking his breakfast on this particular morning, the clock pointing to eight, the horse-and-gig that was to take him to Chettlewood waiting ready at the door, Manston hurriedly cast his eyes down the column of *Bradshaw* which showed the details and duration of the selected train's journey.

The inspection was carelessly made, the leaf being kept open by the aid of one hand, whilst the other still held his cup of coffee; much more carelessly than would have been the case had the expected new-comer been Cytherea Graye, instead of his lawful wife.

He did not perceive, branching from the column down which his finger ran, a small twist, called a shunting-line, inserted at a particular place, to imply that at that point the train was divided into two. By this oversight he understood that the arrival of his wife at Carriford Road Station would not be till late in the evening: by the second half of the train, containing the third-class passengers, and passing two hours and three-quarters later than the previous one, by which the lady, as a second-class passenger, would really be brought.

He then considered that there would be plenty of time for him to return from his day's engagement to meet this train. He finished his breakfast, gave proper and precise directions to his servant on the preparations that were to be made for the lady's reception, jumped into his gig, and drove off to Lord Claydonfield's, at Chettlewood.

He went along by the front of Knapwater House. He could not help turning to look at what he knew to be the window of Cytherea's room. Whilst he looked, a hopeless expression of passionate love and sensuous anguish came upon his face and lingered there for a few seconds; then, as on previous occasions, it was resolutely repressed, and he trotted along the smooth white road, again endeavouring to banish all thought of the young girl whose beauty and grace had so enslaved him.

Thus it was that when, in the evening of the same day, Mrs. Manston reached Carriford Road Station, her husband was still at Chettlewood, ignorant of her arrival, and on looking up and down the platform, dreary with autumn gloom and wind, she could see no sign that any preparation whatever had been made for her reception and conduct home.

The train went on. She waited, fidgeted with the handle of her umbrella, walked about, strained her eyes into the gloom of the chilly night, listened for wheels, tapped with her foot, and showed all the usual signs of annoyance and irritation: she was the more irritated in that this seemed a second and culminating instance of her husband's neglect—the first having been shown in his not fetching her.

Reflecting awhile upon the course it would be best to take, in order to secure a passage to Knapwater, she decided to leave all her luggage, except a dressing-bag, in the cloak-room, and walk to her husband's house, as she had done on her first visit. She asked one of the porters if he could find a lad to go with her and carry her bag: he offered to do it himself.

The porter was a good-tempered, shallow-minded, ignorant man. Mrs. Manston, being apparently in very gloomy spirits, would probably have preferred walking beside him without saying a word: but her companion would not allow silence to continue between them for a longer period than two or three minutes together.

He had volunteered several remarks upon her arrival, chiefly to the effect that it was very unfortunate Mr. Manston had not come to the station for her, when she suddenly asked him concerning the inhabitants of the parish.

He told her categorically the names of the chief—first the chief possessors of property; then of brains; then of good looks. As first among the latter he mentioned Miss Cytherea Graye.

After getting him to describe her appearance as completely as lay in his power, she wormed out of him the statement that everybody had been saying—before Mrs. Manston's existence was heard of—how well the handsome Mr. Manston and the beautiful Miss Graye were suited for each other as man and wife, and that Miss Aldclyffe was the only one in the parish who took no interest in bringing about the match.

'He rather liked her you think?'

The porter began to think he had been too explicit, and hastened to correct the error.

'O no, he don't care a bit about her, ma'am,' he said solemnly.

'Not more than he does about me?'

'Not a bit.'

'Then that must be little indeed,' Mrs. Manston murmured. She stood still, as if reflecting upon the painful neglect her words had recalled to her mind; then, with a sudden impulse, turned round, and walked petulantly a few steps back again in the direction of the station.

The porter stood still and looked surprised.

'I'll go back again; yes, indeed, I'll go back again!' she said plaintively. Then she paused and looked anxiously up and down the deserted road.

'No, I mustn't go back now,' she continued, in a tone of resignation. Seeing that the porter was watching her, she turned about and came on as before, giving vent to a slight laugh.

It was a laugh full of character; the low forced laugh which seeks to hide the painful perception of a humiliating position under the mask of indifference.

Altogether her conduct had shown her to be what in fact she was, a weak, though a calculating woman, one clever to conceive, weak to execute: one whose best-laid schemes were for ever liable to be frustrated by the ineradicable blight of vacillation at the critical hour of action.

'O, if I had only known that all this was going to happen!' she murmured again, as they paced along upon the rustling leaves.

'What did you say, ma'am?' said the porter.

'O, nothing particular; we are getting near the old manor-house by this time, I imagine?'

'Very near now, ma'am.'

They soon reached Manston's residence, round which the wind blew mournfully and chill.

Passing under the detached gateway, they entered the porch. The porter stepped forward, knocked heavily and waited.

Nobody came.

Mrs. Manston then advanced to the door and gave a different series of rappings—less forcible, but more sustained.

There was not a movement of any kind inside, not a ray of light visible; nothing but the echo of her own knocks through the passages, and the dry scratching of the withered leaves blown about her feet upon the floor of the porch.

The steward, of course, was not at home. Mrs. Crickett, not expecting that anybody would arrive till the time of the later train, had set the place in order, laid the supper-table, and then locked the door, to go into the village and converse with her friends.

'Is there an inn in the village?' said Mrs. Manston, after the fourth and loudest rapping upon the iron-studded old door had resulted only in the fourth and loudest echo from the passages inside.

'Yes, ma'am.'

'Who keeps it?'

'Farmer Springrove.'

'I will go there to-night,' she said decisively. 'It is too cold, and altogether too bad, for a woman to wait in the open road on anybody's account, gentle or simple.'

They went down the park and through the gate, into the village of Carriford. By the time they reached the Three Tranters, it was verging upon ten o'clock. There, on the spot where two months earlier in the season the sunny and lively group of villagers making cider under the trees had greeted Cytherea's eyes, was nothing now intelligible but a vast cloak of darkness, from which came the low sough of the elms, and the occasional creak of the swinging sign.

They went to the door, Mrs. Manston shivering; but less from the cold, than from the dreariness of her emotions. Neglect is the coldest of winter winds.

It so happened that Edward Springrove was expected to arrive from London either on that evening or the next, and at the sound of voices his father came to the door fully expecting to see him. A picture of disappointment seldom witnessed in a man's face was visible in old Mr. Springrove's, when he saw that the comer was a stranger.

Mrs. Manston asked for a room, and one that had been prepared for Edward was immediately named as being ready for her, another being adaptable for Edward, should he come in.

Without taking any refreshment, or entering any room downstairs, or even lifting her veil, she walked straight along the passage and up to her apartment, the chambermaid preceding her.

'If Mr. Manston comes to-night,' she said, sitting on the bed as she had come in, and addressing the woman, 'tell him I cannot see him.'

'Yes, ma'am.'

The woman left the room, and Mrs. Manston locked the door. Before the servant had gone down more than two or three stairs, Mrs. Manston unfastened the door again, and held it ajar.

'Bring me some brandy,' she said.

The chambermaid went down to the bar and brought up the spirit in a tumbler. When she came into the room, Mrs. Manston had not removed a single article of apparel, and was walking up and down, as if still quite undecided upon the course it was best to adopt.

Outside the door, when it was closed upon her, the maid paused to listen for an instant. She heard Mrs. Manston talking to herself.

'This is welcome home!' she said.

2. FROM TEN TO HALF-PAST ELEVEN P.M.

A strange concurrence of phenomena now confronts us.

During the autumn in which the past scenes were enacted, Mr. Springrove had ploughed, harrowed, and cleaned a narrow and shaded

263

piece of ground, lying at the back of his house, which for many years had been looked upon as irreclaimable waste.

The couch-grass extracted from the soil had been left to wither in the sun; afterwards it was raked together, lighted in the customary way, and now lay smouldering in a large heap in the middle of the plot.

It had been kindled three days previous to Mrs. Manston's arrival, and one or two villagers, of a more cautious and less sanguine temperament than Springrove, had suggested that the fire was almost too near the back of the house for its continuance to be unattended with risk; for though no danger could be apprehended whilst the air remained moderately still, a brisk breeze blowing towards the house might possibly carry a spark across.

'Ay, that's true enough,' said Springrove. 'I must look round before going to bed and see that everything's safe; but to tell the truth I am anxious to get the rubbish burnt up before the rain comes to wash it into ground again. As to carrying the couch into the back field to burn, and bringing it back again, why, 'tis more than the ashes would be worth.'

'Well, that's very true,' said the neighbours, and passed on.

Two or three times during the first evening after the heap was lit, he went to the back door to take a survey. Before bolting and barring up for the night, he made a final and more careful examination. The slowly-smoking pile showed not the slightest signs of activity. Springrove's perfectly sound conclusion was, that as long as the heap was not stirred, and the wind continued in the quarter it blew from then, the couch would not flame, and that there could be no shadow of danger to anything, even a combustible substance, though it were no more than a yard off.

The next morning the burning couch was discovered in precisely the same state as when he had gone to bed the preceding night. The heap smoked in the same manner the whole of that day: at bed-time the farmer looked towards it, but less carefully than on the first night.

The morning and the whole of the third day still saw the heap in its old smouldering condition; indeed, the smoke was less, and there seemed a probability that it might have to be re-kindled on the morrow.

After admitting Mrs. Manston to his house in the evening, and hearing her retire, Mr. Springrove returned to the front door to listen for a sound of his son, and inquired concerning him of the railway-porter, who sat for a while in the kitchen. The porter had not noticed young Mr. Springrove get out of the train, at which intelligence the old man concluded that he would probably not see his son till the next day, as Edward had hitherto made a point of coming by the train which had brought Mrs. Manston.

Half-an-hour later the porter left the inn, Springrove at the same time going to the door to listen again an instant, then he walked round and in at the back of the house.

The farmer glanced at the heap casually and indifferently in passing; two nights of safety seemed to ensure the third; and he was about to bolt and bar as usual, when the idea struck him that there was just a possibility of his son's return by the latest train, unlikely as it was that he would be so delayed. The old man thereupon left the door unfastened, looked to his usual matters indoors, and went to bed, it being then half-past ten o'clock.

Farmers and horticulturists well know that it is in the nature of a heap of couch-grass, when kindled in calm weather, to smoulder for many days, and even weeks, until the whole mass is reduced to a powdery charcoal ash, displaying the while scarcely a sign of combustion beyond the volcano-like smoke from its summit; but the continuance of this quiet process is throughout its length at the mercy of one particular whim of Nature: that is, a sudden breeze, by which the heap is liable to be fanned into a flame so brisk as to consume the whole in an hour or two.

Had the farmer narrowly watched the pile when he went to close the door, he would have seen, besides the familiar twine of smoke from its summit, a quivering of the air around the mass, showing that a considerable heat had arisen inside.

As the railway-porter turned the corner of the row of houses adjoining the Three Tranters, a brisk new wind greeted his face, and spread past him into the village. He walked along the high-road till he came to a gate, about three hundred yards from the inn. Over the gate could be discerned the situation of the building he had just quitted. He carelessly turned his head in passing, and saw behind him a clear red glow indicating the position of the couch-heap: a glow without a flame, increasing and diminishing in brightness as the breeze quickened or fell, like the coal of a newly lighted cigar. If those cottages had been his, he thought, he should not care to have a fire so near them as that—and the wind rising. But the cottages not being his, he went on his way to the station, where he was about to resume duty for the night. The road was now quite deserted: till four o'clock the next morning, when the carters would go by to the stables there was little probability of any human being passing the Three Tranters Inn.

By eleven, everybody in the house was asleep. It truly seemed as if the treacherous element knew there had arisen a grand opportunity for devastation.

At a quarter past eleven a slight stealthy crackle made itself heard amid the increasing moans of the night wind; the heap glowed brighter still, and burst into a flame; the flame sank, another breeze entered it, sustained it, and it grew to be first continuous and weak, then continuous and strong.

At twenty minutes past eleven a blast of wind carried an airy bit of ignited fern several yards forward, in a direction parallel to the houses and inn, and there deposited it on the ground.

Five minutes later another puff of wind carried a similar piece to a distance of five-and-twenty yards, where it also was dropped softly on the ground.

Still the wind did not blow in the direction of the houses, and even now to a casual observer they would have appeared safe. But Nature does few things directly. A minute later yet, an ignited fragment fell upon the straw covering of a long thatched heap or 'grave' of mangel-wurzel, lying in a direction at right angles to the house, and down toward the hedge. There the fragment faded to darkness.

A short time subsequent to this, after many intermediate deposits and seemingly baffled attempts, another fragment fell on the mangel-wurzel grave, and continued to glow; the glow was increased by the wind; the straw caught fire and burst into flame. It was inevitable that the flame should run along the ridge of the thatch towards a piggery at the end. Yet had the piggery been tiled, the time-honoured hostel would even now at this last moment have been safe; but it was constructed as piggeries are mostly constructed, of wood and thatch. The hurdles and straw roof of the frail erection became ignited in their turn, and abutting as the shed did on the back of the inn, flamed up to the eaves of the main roof in less than thirty seconds.

3. HALF-PAST ELEVEN TO TWELVE P.M.

A hazardous length of time elapsed before the inmates of the Three Tranters knew of their danger. When at length the discovery was made, the rush was a rush for bare life.

A man's voice calling, then screams, then loud stamping and shouts were heard.

Mr. Springrove ran out first. Two minutes later appeared the ostler and chambermaid, who were man and wife. The inn, as has been stated, was a quaint old building, and as inflammable as a bee-hive; it overhung the base at the level of the first floor, and again overhung at the eaves, which were finished with heavy oak barge-boards; every atom in its substance, every feature in its construction, favoured the fire.

The forked flames, lurid and smoky, became nearly lost to view, bursting forth again with a bound and loud crackle, increased tenfold in power and brightness. The crackling grew sharper. Long quivering shadows began to be flung from the stately trees at the end of the house; the square outline of the church tower, on the other side of the way, which had hitherto been a dark mass against a sky comparatively light, now began to appear as a light object against a sky of darkness; and even the narrow surface of the flag-staff at the top could be seen in its dark surrounding, brought out from its obscurity by the rays from the dancing light.

Shouts and other noises increased in loudness and frequency. The lapse of ten minutes brought most of the inhabitants of that end of the village into the street, followed in a short time by the rector, Mr. Raunham.

Casting a hasty glance up and down, he beckoned to one or two of the men, and vanished again. In a short time wheels were heard, and Mr. Raunham and the men reappeared, with the garden engine, the only one in the village, except that at Knapwater House. After some little trouble the hose was connected with a tank in the old stable-yard, and the puny instrument began to play.

Several seemed paralyzed at first, and stood transfixed, their rigid faces looking like red-hot iron in the glaring light. In the confusion a woman cried, 'Ring the bells backwards!' and three or four of the old and superstitious entered the belfry and jangled them indescribably. Some were only half dressed,

270

and, to add to the horror, among them was Clerk Crickett, running up and down with a face streaming with blood, ghastly and pitiful to see, his excitement being so great that he had not the slightest conception of how, when, or where he came by the wound.

The crowd was now busy at work, and tried to save a little of the furniture of the inn. The only room they could enter was the parlour, from which they managed to bring out the bureau, a few chairs, some old silver candlesticks, and half-a-dozen light articles; but these were all.

Fiery mats of thatch slid off the roof and fell into the road with a deadened thud, whilst white flakes of straw and wood-ash were flying in the wind like feathers. At the same time two of the cottages adjoining, upon which a little water had been brought to play from the rector's engine, were seen to be on fire. The attenuated spirt of water was as nothing upon the heated and dry surface of the thatched roof; the fire prevailed without a minute's hindrance, and dived through to the rafters.

Suddenly arose a cry, 'Where's Mr. Springrove?'

He had vanished from the spot by the churchyard wall, where he had been standing a few minutes earlier.

'I fancy he's gone inside,' said a voice.

'Madness and folly! what can he save?' said another. 'Good God, find him! Help here!'

A wild rush was made at the door, which had fallen to, and in defiance of the scorching flame that burst forth, three men forced themselves through it. Immediately inside the threshold they found the object of their search lying senseless on the floor of the passage.

To bring him out and lay him on a bank was the work of an instant; a basin of cold water was dashed in his face, and he began to recover consciousness, but very slowly. He had been saved by a miracle. No sooner were his preservers out of the building than the window-frames lit up as if by magic with deep and waving fringes of flames. Simultaneously, the joints of the boards forming the front door started into view as glowing bars of fire: a star of red light penetrated the centre, gradually increasing in size till the flames rushed forth.

Then the staircase fell.

'Everybody is out safe,' said a voice.

'Yes, thank God!' said three or four others.

'O, we forgot that a stranger came! I think she is safe.'

'I hope she is,' said the weak voice of some one coming up from behind. It was the chambermaid's.

Springrove at that moment aroused himself; he staggered to his feet, and threw his hands up wildly.

'Everybody, no! no! The lady who came by train, Mrs. Manston! I tried to fetch her out, but I fell.'

An exclamation of horror burst from the crowd; it was caused partly by this disclosure of Springrove, more by the added perception which followed his words.

An average interval of about three minutes had elapsed between one intensely fierce gust of wind and the next, and now another poured over them; the roof swayed, and a moment afterwards fell in with a crash, pulling the gable after it, and thrusting outwards the front wall of wood-work, which fell into the road with a rumbling echo; a cloud of black dust, myriads of sparks, and a great outburst of flame followed the uproar of the fall.

'Who is she? what is she?' burst from every lip again and again, incoherently, and without leaving a sufficient pause for a reply, had a reply been volunteered.

The autumn wind, tameless, and swift, and proud, still blew upon the dying old house, which was constructed so entirely of combustible materials that it burnt almost as fiercely as a corn-rick. The heat in the road increased, and now for an instant at the height of the conflagration all stood still, and gazed silently, awestruck and helpless, in the presence of so irresistible an enemy. Then, with minds full of the tragedy unfolded to them, they rushed forward again with the obtuse directness of waves, to their labour of saving goods from the houses adjoining, which it was evident were all doomed to destruction.

The minutes passed by. The Three Tranters Inn sank into a mere heap of red-hot charcoal: the fire pushed its way down the row as the church clock opposite slowly struck the hour of midnight, and the bewildered chimes, scarcely heard amid the crackling of the flames, wandered through the wayward air of the Old Hundred-and-Thirteenth Psalm.

4. NINE TO ELEVEN P.M.

Manston mounted his gig and set out from Chettlewood that evening in no very enviable frame of mind. The thought of domestic life in Knapwater Old House, with the now eclipsed wife of the past, was more than disagreeable, was positively distasteful to him.

Yet he knew that the influential position, which, from whatever fortunate cause, he held on Miss Aldclyffe's manor, would never again fall to his lot on any other, and he tacitly assented to this dilemma, hoping that some consolation or other would soon suggest itself to him; married as he was, he was near Cytherea.

He occasionally looked at his watch as he drove along the lanes, timing the pace of his horse by the hour, that he might reach Carriford Road Station just soon enough to meet the last London train.

He soon began to notice in the sky a slight

yellow halo, near the horizon. It rapidly increased; it changed colour, and grew redder; then the glare visibly brightened and dimmed at intervals, showing that its origin was affected by the strong wind prevailing.

Manston reined in his horse on the summit of a hill, and considered.

'It is a rick-yard on fire,' he thought; 'no house could produce such a raging flame so suddenly.'

He trotted on again, attempting to particularize the local features in the neighbourhood of the fire; but this it was too dark to do, and the excessive winding of the roads misled him as to its direction, not being an old inhabitant of the district, or a countryman used to forming such judgments; whilst the brilliancy of the light shortened its real remoteness to an apparent distance of not more than half: it seemed so near that he again stopped his horse, this time to listen; but he could hear no sound.

Entering now a narrow valley, the sides of which obscured the sky to an angle of perhaps thirty or forty degrees above the mathematical horizon, he was obliged to suspend his judgment till he was in possession of further knowledge, having however assumed in the interim, that the fire was somewhere between Carriford Road Station and the village.

The self-same glare had just arrested the eyes of another man. He was at that minute gliding along several miles to the east of the steward's position, but nearing the same point as that to which Manston tended. The younger Edward Springrove was returning from London to his father's house by the identical train which the steward was expecting to bring his wife, the truth being that Edward's lateness was owing to the simplest of all causes, his temporary want of money, which led him to make a slow journey for the sake of travelling at third-class fare.

Springrove had received Cytherea's bitter and admonitory letter, and he was clearly awakened to a perception of the false position in which he had placed himself, by keeping silence at Budmouth on his long engagement. An increasing reluctance to put an end to those few days of ecstasy with Cytherea had overruled his conscience, and tied his tongue till speaking was too late.

'Why did I do it? how could I dream of loving her?' he asked himself as he walked by day, as he tossed on his bed by night: 'miserable folly!'

An impressionable heart had for years—perhaps as many as six or seven years—been distracting him, by unconsciously setting itself to yearn for somebody wanting, he scarcely knew whom. Echoes of himself, though rarely, he now and then found. Sometimes they were men, sometimes women, his cousin Adelaide being one of these; for in spite of a fashion which pervades the whole community at the present day—the habit of exclaiming that woman is not undeveloped man, but diverse, the fact remains that, after all, women are Mankind, and that in many of the sentiments of life the difference of sex is but a difference of degree.

But the indefinable helpmate to the remoter sides of himself still continued invisible. He grew older, and concluded that the ideas, or rather emotions, which possessed him on the subject, were probably too unreal ever to be found embodied in the flesh of a woman. Thereupon, he developed a plan of satisfying his dreams by wandering away to the heroines of poetical imagination, and took no further thought on the earthly realization of his formless desire, in more homely matters satisfying himself with his cousin.

Cytherea appeared in the sky: his heart started up and spoke:

'Tis She, and here
Lo! I unclothe and clear
My wishes' cloudy character.'

Some women kindle emotion so rapidly in a man's heart that the judgment cannot keep pace with its rise, and finds, on comprehending the situation, that faithfulness to the old love is already treachery to the new. Such women are not necessarily the greatest of their sex, but there are very few of them. Cytherea was one.

On receiving the letter from her he had taken to thinking over these things, and had not answered it at all. But 'hungry generations' soon tread down the muser in a city. At length he thought of the strong necessity of living. After a dreary search, the negligence of which was ultimately overcome by mere conscientiousness, he obtained a situation as assistant to an architect in the neighbourhood of Charing Cross: the duties would not begin till after the lapse of a month.

He could not at first decide whither he should go to spend the intervening time; but in the midst of his reasonings he found himself on the road homeward, impelled by a secret and unowned hope of getting a last glimpse of Cytherea there.

5. MIDNIGHT

It was a quarter to twelve when Manston drove into the station-yard. The train was punctual, and the bell, announcing its arrival, rang as he crossed the booking-office to go out upon the platform.

The porter who had accompanied Mrs. Manston to Carriford, and had returned to the station on his night duty, recognized the steward as he entered, and immediately came towards him.

'Mrs. Manston came by the nine o'clock train, sir,' he said.

The steward gave vent to an expression of vexation.

'Her luggage is here, sir,' the porter said.

'Put it up behind me in the gig if it is not too much,' said Manston.

'Directly this train is in and gone, sir.'

The man vanished and crossed the line to meet the entering train.

'Where is that fire?' Manston said to the booking-clerk.

Before the clerk could speak, another man ran in and answered the question without having heard it.

'Half Carriford is burnt down, or will be!' he exclaimed. 'You can't see the flames from this station on account of the trees, but step on the bridge—'tis tremendous!'

He also crossed the line to assist at the entry of the train, which came in the next minute.

The steward stood in the office. One passenger alighted, gave up his ticket, and crossed the room in front of Manston: a young man with a black bag and umbrella in his hand. He passed out of the door, down the steps, and struck out into the darkness.

'Who was that young man?' said Manston, when the porter had returned. The young man, by a kind of magnetism, had drawn the steward's thoughts after him.

'He's an architect.'

'My own old profession. I could have sworn it by the cut of him,' Manston murmured. 'What's his name?' he said again.

'Springrove—Farmer Springrove's son, Edward.'

'Farmer Springrove's son, Edward,' the steward repeated to himself, and considered a matter to which the words had painfully recalled his mind.

The matter was Miss Aldclyffe's mention of the young man as Cytherea's lover, which, indeed, had scarcely ever been absent from his thoughts.

'But for the existence of my wife that man might have been my rival,' he pondered, following the porter, who had now come back to him, into the luggage-room. And whilst the man was carrying out and putting in one box, which was sufficiently portable for the gig, Manston still thought, as his eyes watched the process—

'But for my wife, Springrove might have been my rival.'

He examined the lamps of his gig, carefully laid out the reins, mounted the seat and drove along the turnpike-road towards Knapwater Park.

The exact locality of the fire was plain to him as he neared home. He soon could hear the shout of men, the flapping of the flames, the crackling of burning wood, and could smell the smoke from the conflagration.

Of a sudden, a few yards ahead, within the compass of the rays from the right-hand lamp, burst forward the figure of a man. Having been walking in darkness the newcomer raised his hands to his eyes, on approaching nearer, to screen them from the glare of the reflector.

Manston saw that he was one of the villagers: a small farmer originally, who had drunk himself down to a day-labourer and reputed poacher.

'Hoy!' cried Manston, aloud, that the man might step aside out of the way.

'Is that Mr. Manston?' said the man.

'Yes.'

'Somebody ha' come to Carriford: and the rest of it may concern you, sir.'

'Well, well.'

'Did you expect Mrs. Manston to-night, sir?'

'Yes, unfortunately she's come, I know, and asleep long before this time, I suppose.'

The labourer leant his elbow upon the shaft of the gig and turned his face, pale and sweating from his late work at the fire, up to Manston's.

'Yes, she did come,' he said . . . 'I beg pardon, sir, but I should be glad of—of—'

'What?'

'Glad of a trifle for bringen ye the news.'

'Not a farthing! I didn't want your news, I knew she was come.'

'Won't you give me a shillen, sir?'

'Certainly not.'

'Then will you lend me a shillen, sir? I be tired out, and don't know what to do. If I don't pay you back some day I'll be d—d.'

'The devil is so cheated that perdition isn't worth a penny as a security.'

'Oh!'

'Let me go on,' said Manston.

'Thy wife is *dead*; that's the rest o' the news,' said the labourer slowly. He waited for a reply; none came.

'She went to the Three Tranters, because she couldn't get into thy house, the burnen roof fell in upon her before she could be called up, and she's a cinder, as thou'lt be some day.'

'That will do, let me drive on,' said the steward calmly.

Expectation of a concussion may be so intense that its failure strikes the brain with more force than its fulfilment. The labourer sank back into the ditch. Such a Cushi could not realize the possibility of such an unmoved David as this.

Manston drove hastily to the turning of the road, tied his horse, and ran on foot to the site of the fire.

The stagnation caused by the awful accident had been passed through, and all hands were helping to remove from the remaining cottage what furniture they could lay hold of; the thatch of the roofs being already on fire. The Knapwater fire-engine had arrived on the spot, but it was small, and ineffectual. A group was collected round the rector, who in a coat which had become bespattered, scorched, and torn in his exertions, was directing on one hand the proceedings relative to the removal of goods into the church, and with the other was pointing out the spot on which it was most desirable that the puny engines at their disposal should be made to play. Every tongue was instantly silent at the sight of Manston's pale and clear countenance, which contrasted strangely with the grimy and streaming faces of the toiling villagers.

'Was she burnt?' he said in a firm though husky voice, and stepping into the illuminated area. The rector came to him, and took him aside. 'Is she burnt?' repeated Manston.

'She is dead: but thank God, she was spared the horrid agony of burning,' the rector said solemnly; 'the roof and gable fell in upon her, and crushed her. Instant death must have followed.'

'Why was she here?' said Manston.

'From what we can hurriedly collect, it seems that she found the door of your house locked, and concluded that you had retired, the fact being that your servant, Mrs. Crickett, had gone out to supper. She then came back to the inn and went to bed.'

'Where's the landlord?' said Manston.

Mr. Springrove came up, walking feebly, and wrapped in a cloak, and corroborated the evidence given by the rector.

'Did she look ill, or annoyed, when she came?' said the steward.

'I can't say. I didn't see; but I think—'

'What do you think?'

'She was much put out about something.'

'My not meeting her, naturally,' murmured the other, lost in reverie. He turned his back on Springrove and the rector, and retired from the shining light.

Everything had been done that could be done with the limited means at their disposal. The whole row of houses was destroyed, and each presented itself as one stage of a series, progressing from smoking ruins at the end where the inn had stood, to a partly flaming mass—glowing as none but wood embers will glow—at the other.

A feature in the decline of town fires was noticeably absent here—steam. There was present what is not observable in towns—incandescence.

The heat, and the smarting effect upon their eyes of the strong smoke from the burning oak and deal, had at last driven the villagers back from the road in front of the houses, and they now stood in groups in the churchyard, the surface of which, raised by the interments of generations, stood four or five feet above the level of the road, and almost even with the top of the low wall dividing one from the other.

The headstones stood forth whitely against the dark grass and yews, their brightness being repeated on the white smock-frocks of some of the labourers, and in a mellower, ruddier form on their faces and hands, on those of the grinning gargoyles, and on other salient stonework of the weather-beaten church in the background.

The rector had decided that, under the distressing circumstances of the case, there would be no sacrilege in placing in the church, for the night, the pieces of furniture and utensils which had been saved from the several houses. There was no other place of safety for them, and they accordingly were gathered there.

6. HALF-PAST TWELVE TO ONE A.M.

Manston, when he retired to meditate, had walked round the churchyard, and now entered the opened door of the building.

He mechanically pursued his way round the piers into his own seat in the north aisle. The lower atmosphere of this spot was shaded by its own wall from the shine which streamed in over the window-sills on the same side. The only light burning inside the church was a small tallow candle, standing in the font, in the opposite aisle of the building to that in which Manston had sat down, and near where the furniture was piled. The candle's mild rays were overpowered by the ruddier light from the ruins, making the weak flame to appear like the moon by day.

Sitting there he saw Farmer Springrove enter the door, followed by his son Edward, still carrying his travelling-bag in his hand. They were speaking of the sad death of Mrs. Manston, but the subject was relinquished for that of the houses burnt.

This row of houses, running from the inn eastward, had been built under the following circumstances:—

Fifty years before this date, the spot upon which the cottages afterwards stood was a blank strip, along the side of the village street, difficult to cultivate, on account of the outcrop thereon of a large bed of flints called locally a 'lanch' or 'lanchet.'

The Aldclyffe then in possession of the estate conceived the idea that a row of cottages would be an improvement to the spot, and accordingly granted leases of portions to several respectable inhabitants. Each lessee was to be subject to the payment of a merely nominal rent for the whole term of lives, on condition that he built his own cottage, and delivered it up intact at the end of the term.

Those who had built had, one by one, relinquished their indentures, either by sale or barter, to Farmer Springrove's father. New lives were added in some cases, by payment of a sum to the lord of the manor, etc., and all the leases were now held by the farmer himself, as one of the chief provisions for his old age.

The steward had become interested in the following conversation:—

'Try not to be so depressed, father; they are all insured.'

The words came from Edward in an anxious tone.

'You mistake, Edward; they are not insured,' returned the old man gloomily.

'Not?' the son asked.

'Not one!' said the farmer.

'In the Helmet Fire Office, surely?'

'They were insured there every one. Six months ago the office, which had been raising the premiums on thatched premises higher for some years, gave up insuring them altogether, as two or three other fire-offices had done previously, on account, they said, of the uncertainty and greatness of the risk of thatch undetached. Ever since then I have been continually intending to go to another office, but have never gone. Who expects a fire?'

'Do you remember the terms of the leases?' said Edward, still more uneasily.

'No, not particularly,' said his father absently.

'Where are they?'

'In the bureau there; that's why I tried to save it first, among other things.'

'Well, we must see to that at once.'

'What do you want?'

'The key.'

They went into the south aisle, took the candle from the font, and then proceeded to open the bureau, which had been placed in a corner under the gallery. Both leant over upon the flap; Edward holding the candle, whilst his father took the pieces of parchment from one of the drawers, and spread the first out before him.

'You read it, Ted. I can't see without my glasses. This one will be sufficient. The terms of all are the same.'

Edward took the parchment, and read quickly and indistinctly for some time; then aloud and slowly as follows:—

And *the said John Springrove for himself his heirs executors and administrators doth covenant and agree with the said Gerald Fellcourt Aldclyffe his heirs and assigns that he the said John Springrove his heirs and assigns during the said term shall pay unto the said Gerald Fellcourt Aldclyffe his heirs and assigns the clear yearly rent of ten shillings and sixpence . . . at the several times hereinbefore appointed for the payment thereof respectively. And also shall and at all times during the said term well and sufficiently repair and keep the said Cottage or Dwelling-house and all other the premises and all houses or buildings erected or to be erected thereupon in good and proper repair in every respect without exception and the said premises in such good repair upon the determination of this demise shall yield up unto the said Gerald Fellcourt Aldclyffe his heirs and assigns.*

They closed the bureau and turned towards the door of the church without speaking.

Manston also had come forward out of the gloom. Notwithstanding the farmer's own troubles, an instinctive respect and generous sense of sympathy with the steward for his awful loss caused the old man to step aside, that Manston might pass out without speaking to them if he chose to do so.

'Who is he?' whispered Edward to his father, as Manston approached.

'Mr. Manston, the steward.'

Manston came near, and passed down the aisle on the side of the younger man. Their faces came almost close together: one large flame, which still lingered upon the ruins outside, threw long dancing shadows of each across the nave till they bent upwards against the aisle wall, and also illuminated their eyes, as each met those of the other. Edward had learnt, by a letter from home, of the steward's passion for Cytherea, and his mysterious repression of it, afterwards explained by his marriage. That marriage was now nought. Edward realized the man's newly acquired freedom, and felt an instinctive enmity towards him—he would hardly own to himself why. The steward, too, knew Cytherea's attachment to Edward, and looked keenly and inscrutably at him.

7. ONE TO TWO A.M.

Manston went homeward alone, his heart full of strange emotions. Entering the house, and dismissing the woman to her own home, he at once proceeded upstairs to his bedroom.

Reasoning worldliness, especially when allied with sensuousness, cannot repress on some extreme occasions the human instinct to pour out the soul to some Being or Personality, who in frigid moments is dismissed with the title of Chance, or at most Law. Manston was selfishly and inhumanly, but honestly and unutterably, thankful for the recent catastrophe. Beside his bed, for that first time during a period of nearly twenty years, he fell down upon his knees in a passionate outburst of feeling.

Many minutes passed before he arose. He walked to the window, and then seemed to remember for the first time that some action on his part was necessary in connection with the sad circumstance of the night.

Leaving the house at once, he went to the scene of the fire, arriving there in time to hear the rector making an arrangement with a certain number of men to watch the spot till morning. The ashes were still red-hot and flaming. Manston found that nothing could be done towards searching them at that hour of the night. He turned homeward again, in the company of the rector, who had considerately persuaded him to retire from the scene for a while, and promised that as soon as a man could live amid the embers of the Three Tranters Inn, they should be carefully searched for the remains of his unfortunate wife.

Manston then went indoors, to wait for morning.

XI.

THE EVENTS OF FIVE DAYS

1. NOVEMBER THE TWENTY-NINTH

The search began at dawn, but a quarter past nine o'clock came without bringing any result. Manston ate a little breakfast, and crossed the hollow of the park which intervened between the old and modern manor-houses, to ask for an interview with Miss Aldclyffe.

He met her midway. She was about to pay him a visit of condolence, and to place every man on the estate at his disposal, that the search for any relic of his dead and destroyed wife might not be delayed an instant.

He accompanied her back to the house. At first they conversed as if the death of the poor woman was an event which the husband must of necessity deeply lament; and when all under this head that social form seemed to require had been uttered, they spoke of the material damage done, and of the steps which had better be taken to remedy it.

It was not till both were shut inside her private room that she spoke to him in her blunt and cynical manner. A certain newness of bearing in him, peculiar to the present morning, had hitherto forbidden her this tone: the demeanour of the subject of her favouritism had altered, she could not tell in what way. He was entirely a changed man.

'Are you really sorry for your poor wife, Mr. Manston?' she said.

'Well, I am,' he answered shortly.

'But only as for any human being who has met with a violent death?'

He confessed it—'For she was not a good woman,' he added.

'I should be sorry to say such a thing now the poor creature is dead,' Miss Aldclyffe returned reproachfully.

'Why?' he asked. 'Why should I praise her if she doesn't deserve it? I say exactly what I have often admired Sterne for saying in one of his letters—that neither reason nor Scripture asks us to speak nothing but good of the dead.

And now, madam,' he continued, after a short interval of thought, 'I may, perhaps, hope that you will assist me, or rather not thwart me, in endeavouring to win the love of a young lady living about you, one in whom I am much interested already.'

'Cytherea!'

'Yes, Cytherea.'

'You have been loving Cytherea all the while?'

'Yes.'

Surprise was a preface to much agitation in her, which caused her to rise from her seat, and pace to the side of the room. The steward quietly looked on and added, 'I have been loving and still love her.'

She came close up to him, wistfully contemplating his face, one hand moving indecisively at her side.

'And your secret marriage was, then, the true and only reason for that backwardness regarding the courtship of Cytherea, which, they tell me, has been the talk of the village; not your indifference to her attractions.' Her voice had a tone of conviction in it, as well as of inquiry; but none of jealousy.

'Yes,' he said; 'and not a dishonourable one. What held me back was just that one thing—a sense of morality that perhaps, madam, you did not give me credit for.' The latter words were spoken with a mien and tone of pride.

Miss Aldclyffe preserved silence.

'And now,' he went on, 'I may as well say a word in vindication of my conduct lately, at the risk, too, of offending you. My actual motive in submitting to your order that I should send for my late wife, and live with her, was not the mercenary policy of wishing to retain an office which brings me greater comforts than any I have enjoyed before, but this unquenchable passion for Cytherea. Though I saw the weakness, folly, and even wickedness of it continually, it still forced me to try to continue near her, even as the husband of another woman.'

He waited for her to speak: she did not.

'There's a great obstacle to my making any way in winning Miss Graye's love,' he went on.

'Yes, Edward Springrove,' she said quietly. 'I know it, I did once want to see them married; they have had a slight quarrel, and it will soon be made up again, unless—' she spoke as if she had only half attended to Manston's last statement.

'He is already engaged to be married to somebody else,' said the steward.

'Pooh!' said she, 'you mean to his cousin at Peakhill; that's nothing to help us; he's now come home to break it off.'

'He must not break it off,' said Manston, firmly and calmly.

His tone attracted her, startled her. Recovering herself, she said haughtily, 'Well, that's your affair, not mine. Though my wish

294

has been to see her your wife, I can't do anything dishonourable to bring about such a result.'

'But it must be *made* your affair,' he said in a hard, steady voice, looking into her eyes, as if he saw there the whole panorama of her past.

One of the most difficult things to portray by written words is that peculiar mixture of moods expressed in a woman's countenance when, after having been sedulously engaged in establishing another's position, she suddenly suspects him of undermining her own. It was thus that Miss Aldclyffe looked at the steward.

'You—know—something—of me?' she faltered.

'I know all,' he said.

'Then curse that wife of yours! She wrote and said she wouldn't tell you!' she burst out. 'Couldn't she keep her word for a day?' She reflected and then said, but no more as to a stranger, 'I will not yield. I have committed no crime. I yielded to her threats in a moment of weakness, though I felt inclined to defy her at the time: it was chiefly because I was mystified as to how she got to know of it. Pooh! I will put up with threats no more. O, can you threaten me?' she added softly, as if she had for the moment forgotten to whom she had been speaking.

'My love must be made your affair,' he repeated, without taking his eyes from her.

An agony, which was not the agony of being

discovered in a secret, obstructed her utterance for a time. 'How can you turn upon me so when I schemed to get you here— schemed that you might win her till I found you were married. O, how can you! O! ... O!' She wept; and the weeping of such a nature was as harrowing as the weeping of a man.

'Your getting me here was bad policy as to your secret—the most absurd thing in the world,' he said, not heeding her distress. 'I knew all, except the identity of the individual, long ago. Directly I found that my coming here was a contrived thing, and not a matter of chance, it fixed my attention upon you at once. All that was required was the mere spark of life, to make of a bundle of perceptions an organic whole.'

'Policy, how can you talk of policy? Think, do think! And how can you threaten me when you know—you know—that I would befriend you readily without a threat!'

'Yes, yes, I think you would,' he said more kindly; 'but your indifference for so many, many years has made me doubt it.'

'No, not indifference—'twas enforced silence. My father lived.'

He took her hand, and held it gently.

*   *   *

'Now listen,' he said, more quietly and humanly, when she had become calmer:

'Springrove must marry the woman he's engaged to. You may make him, but only in one way.'

'Well: but don't speak sternly, Æneas!'

'Do you know that his father has not been particularly thriving for the last two or three years?'

'I have heard something of it, once or twice, though his rents have been promptly paid, haven't they?'

'O yes; and do you know the terms of the leases of the houses which are burnt?' he said, explaining to her that by those terms she might compel him even to rebuild every house. 'The case is the clearest case of fire by negligence that I have ever known, in addition to that,' he continued.

'I don't want them rebuilt; you know it was intended by my father, directly they fell in, to clear the site for a new entrance to the park?'

'Yes, but that doesn't affect the position, which is that Farmer Springrove is in your power to an extent which is very serious for him.'

'I won't do it—'tis a conspiracy.'

'Won't you for me?' he said eagerly.

Miss Aldclyffe changed colour.

'I don't threaten now, I implore,' he said.

'Because you might threaten if you chose,' she mournfully answered. 'But why be so— when your marriage with her was my own pet idea long before it was yours? What must I do?'

'Scarcely anything: simply this. When I have seen old Mr. Springrove, which I shall do in a day or two, and told him that he will be expected to rebuild the houses, do you see the young man. See him yourself, in order that the proposals made may not appear to be anything more than an impulse of your own. You or he will bring up the subject of the houses. To rebuild them would be a matter of at least six hundred pounds, and he will almost surely say that we are hard in insisting upon the extreme letter of the leases. Then tell him that scarcely can you yourself think of compelling an old tenant like his father to any such painful extreme—there shall be no compulsion to build, simply a surrender of the leases. Then speak feelingly of his cousin, as a woman whom you respect and love, and whose secret you have learnt to be that she is heart-sick with hope deferred. Beg him to marry her, his betrothed and your friend, as some return for your consideration towards his father. Don't suggest too early a day for their marriage, or he will suspect you of some motive beyond womanly sympathy. Coax him to make a promise to her that she shall be his wife at the end of a twelvemonth, and get him, on assenting to this, to write to Cytherea, entirely renouncing her.'

'She has already asked him to do that.'

'So much the better—and telling her, too,

that he is about to fulfil his long-standing promise to marry his cousin. If you think it worth while, you may say Cytherea was not indisposed to think of me before she knew I was married. I have at home a note she wrote me the first evening I saw her, which looks rather warm, and which I could show you. Trust me, he will give her up. When he is married to Adelaide Hinton, Cytherea will be induced to marry me—perhaps before; a woman's pride is soon wounded.'

'And hadn't I better write to Mr. Nyttleton, and inquire more particularly what's the law upon the houses?'

'O no, there's no hurry for that. We know well enough how the case stands—quite well enough to talk in general terms about it. And I want the pressure to be put upon young Springrove before he goes away from home again.'

She looked at him furtively, long, and sadly, as after speaking he became lost in thought, his eyes listlessly tracing the pattern of the carpet. 'Yes, yes, she will be mine,' he whispered, careless of Cytherea Aldclyffe's presence. At last he raised his eyes inquiringly.

'I will do my best, Æneas,' she answered.

Talibus incusat. Manston then left the house, and again went towards the blackened ruins, where men were still raking and probing.

2. FROM NOVEMBER THE TWENTY-NINTH TO DECEMBER THE SECOND

The smouldering remnants of the Three Tranters Inn seemed to promise that, even when the searchers should light upon the remains of the unfortunate Mrs. Manston, very little would be discoverable.

Consisting so largely of the charcoal and ashes of hard dry oak and chestnut, intermingled with thatch, the interior of the heap was one glowing mass of embers, which, on being stirred about, emitted sparks and flame long after it was dead and black on the outside. It was persistently hoped, however, that some traces of the body would survive the effect of the hot coals, and after a search pursued uninterruptedly for thirty hours, under the direction of Manston himself, enough was found to set at rest any doubts of her fate.

The melancholy gleanings consisted of her watch, bunch of keys, a few coins, and two charred and blackened bones.

Two days later the official inquiry into the cause of her death was held at the Rising Sun Inn, before Mr. Floy, the coroner, and a jury of the chief inhabitants of the district. The little tavern—the only remaining one in the village—was crowded to excess by the neighbouring peasantry as well as their richer employers: all who could by any possibility obtain an hour's release from their duties being present as listeners.

The jury viewed the sad and infinitesimal remains, which were folded in a white cambric cloth, and laid in the middle of a well-finished coffin lined with white silk (by Manston's order), which stood in an adjoining room, the bulk of the coffin being completely filled in with carefully arranged flowers and evergreens—also the steward's own doing.

Abraham Brown, of Hoxton, London—an old white-headed man, without the ruddiness which makes white hairs so pleasing—was sworn, and deposed that he kept a lodging-house at an address he named. On a Saturday evening less than a month before the fire, a lady came to him, with very little luggage, and took the front room on the second floor. He did not inquire where she came from, as she paid a week in advance, but she gave her name as Mrs. Manston, referring him, if he wished for any guarantee of her respectability, to Mr. Manston, Knapwater Park. Here she lived for three weeks, rarely going out. She slept away from her lodgings one night during the time. At the end of that time, on the twenty-eighth of November, she left his house in a four-wheeled cab, about twelve o'clock in the day, telling the driver to take her to the Waterloo Station. She paid all her lodging expenses, and not having given notice the full week previous to her going away, offered to pay for the next, but he only took half. She wore a thick black veil, and grey waterproof cloak, when she left him, and her luggage was two boxes, one of plain deal, with black japanned clamps, the other sewn up in canvas.

Joseph Chinney, porter at the Carriford Road Station, deposed that he saw Mrs. Manston, dressed as the last witness had described, get out of a second-class carriage on the night of the twenty-eighth. She stood beside him whilst her luggage was taken from the van. The luggage, consisting of the clamped deal box and another covered with canvas, was placed in the cloak-room. She seemed at a loss at finding nobody there to meet her. She asked him for some person to accompany her, and carry her bag to Mr. Manston's house, Knapwater Park. He was just off duty at that time, and offered to go himself. The witness here repeated the conversation he had had with Mrs. Manston during their walk, and testified to having left her at the door of the Three Tranters Inn, Mr. Manston's house being closed.

Next, Farmer Springrove was called. A murmur of surprise and commiseration passed round the crowded room when he stepped forward.

The events of the few preceding days had so worked upon his nervously thoughtful nature that the blue orbits of his eyes, and the mere spot of scarlet to which the ruddiness of his cheeks had contracted, seemed the result of a heavy sickness. A perfect silence pervaded the assembly when he spoke.

His statement was that he received Mrs. Manston at the threshold, and asked her to enter the parlour. She would not do so, and stood in the passage whilst the maid went upstairs to see that the room was in order. The maid came down to the middle landing of the staircase, when Mrs. Manston followed her up to the room. He did not speak ten words with her altogether.

Afterwards, whilst he was standing at the door listening for his son Edward's return, he saw her light extinguished, having first caught sight of her shadow moving about the room.

The Coroner: 'Did her shadow appear to be that of a woman undressing?'

Springrove: 'I cannot say, as I didn't take particular notice. It moved backwards and forwards; she might have been undressing or merely pacing up and down the room.'

Mrs. Fitler, the ostler's wife and chambermaid, said that she preceded Mrs. Manston into the room, put down the candle, and went out. Mrs. Manston scarcely spoke to her, except to ask her to bring a little brandy. Witness went and fetched it from the bar, brought it up, and put it on the dressing-table.

The Coroner: 'Had Mrs. Manston begun to undress, when you came back?'

'No, sir; she was sitting on the bed, with

everything on, as when she came in.'

'Did she begin to undress before you left?'

'Not exactly before I had left; but when I had closed the door, and was on the landing I heard her boot drop on the floor, as it does sometimes when pulled off.'

'Had her face appeared worn and sleepy?'

'I cannot say, as her bonnet and veil were still on when I left, for she seemed rather shy and ashamed to be seen at the Three Tranters at all.'

'And did you hear or see any more of her?'

'No more, sir.'

Mrs. Crickett, temporary servant to Mr. Manston, said that in accordance with Mr. Manston's orders, everything had been made comfortable in the house for Mrs. Manston's expected return on Monday night. Mr. Manston told her that himself and Mrs. Manston would be home late, not till between eleven and twelve o'clock, and that supper was to be ready. Not expecting Mrs. Manston so early, she had gone out on a very important errand to Mrs. Leat the postmistress.

Mr. Manston deposed that in looking down the columns of *Bradshaw* he had mistaken the time of the train's arrival, and hence was not at the station when she came. The broken watch produced was his wife's—he knew it by a scratch on the inner plate, and by other signs. The bunch of keys belonged to her: two of them fitted the locks of her two boxes.

Mr. Flooks, agent to Lord Claydonfield at Chettlewood, said that Mr. Manston had pleaded as his excuse for leaving him rather early in the evening after their day's business had been settled, that he was going to meet his wife at Carriford Road Station, where she was coming by the last train that night.

The surgeon said that the remains were those of a human being. The small fragment seemed a portion of one of the lumbar vertebrae—the other the head of the os femoris—but they were both so far gone that it was impossible to say definitely whether they belonged to the body of a male or female. There was no moral doubt that they were a woman's. He did not believe that death resulted from burning by fire. He thought she was crushed by the fall of the west gable, which being of wood, as well as the floor, burnt after it had fallen, and consumed the body with it.

Two or three additional witnesses gave unimportant testimony.

The coroner summed up, and the jury without hesitation found that the deceased Mrs. Manston came by her death accidentally through the burning of the Three Tranters Inn.

When Mr. Springrove came from the door of the Rising Sun at the end of the inquiry, Manston walked by his side as far as the stile to the park, a distance of about a stone's-throw.

'Ah, Mr. Springrove, this is a sad affair for everybody concerned.'

'Everybody,' said the old farmer, with deep sadness, ' 'tis quite a misery to me. I hardly know how I shall live through each day as it breaks. I think of the words, "In the morning thou shalt say, Would God it were even! and at even thou shalt say, Would God it were morning! for the fear of thine heart wherewith thou shalt fear, and for the sight of thine eyes which thou shalt see."' His voice became broken.

'Ah—true. I read Deuteronomy myself,' said Manston.

'But my loss is as nothing to yours,' the farmer continued.

'Nothing; but I can commiserate you. I should be worse than unfeeling if I didn't, although my own affliction is of so sad and solemn a kind. Indeed my own loss makes me more keenly alive to yours, different in nature as it is.'

'What sum do you think would be required of me to put the houses in place again?'

'I have roughly thought six or seven hundred pounds.'

'If the letter of the law is to be acted up to,' said the old man, with more agitation in his voice.

'Yes, exactly.'

'Do you know enough of Miss Aldclyffe's mind to give me an idea of how she means to treat me?'

'Well, I am afraid I must tell you that though I know very little of her mind as a rule, in this matter I believe she will be rather peremptory; she might share to the extent of a sixth or an eighth perhaps, in consideration of her getting new lamps for old, but I should hardly think more.'

The steward stepped upon the stile, and Mr. Springrove went along the road with a bowed head and heavy footsteps towards his niece's cottage, in which, rather against the wish of Edward, they had temporarily taken refuge.

The additional weight of this knowledge soon made itself perceptible. Though indoors with Edward or Adelaide nearly the whole of the afternoon, nothing more than monosyllabic replies could be drawn from him. Edward continually discovered him looking fixedly at the wall or floor, quite unconscious of another's presence. At supper he ate just as usual, but quite mechanically, and with the same abstraction.

4. DECEMBER THE THIRD

The next morning he was in no better spirits. Afternoon came: his son was alarmed, and managed to draw from him an account of the conversation with the steward.

'Nonsense; he knows nothing about it,' said Edward vehemently. 'I'll see Miss Aldclyffe myself. Now promise me, father, that you'll not believe till I come back, and tell you to believe it, that Miss Aldclyffe will do any such unjust thing.'

Edward started at once for Knapwater House. He strode rapidly along the high-road, till he reached a wicket where a footpath allowed of a short cut to the mansion. Here he leant down upon the bars for a few minutes, meditating as to the best manner of opening his speech, and surveying the scene before him in that absent mood which takes cognizance of little things without being conscious of them at the time, though they appear in the eye afterwards as vivid impressions. It was a yellow, lustrous, late autumn day, one of those days of the quarter when morning and evening seem to meet together without the intervention of a noon. The clear yellow sunlight had tempted forth Miss Aldclyffe herself, who was at this same time taking a walk in the direction of the village. As Springrove lingered he heard behind the plantation a woman's dress brushing along amid the prickly husks and leaves which had fallen into the path from the boughs of the chestnut trees. In another minute she stood in front of him.

He answered her casual greeting respectfully, and was about to request a few minutes' conversation with her, when she directly addressed him on the subject of the fire. 'It is a sad misfortune for your father,' she said, 'and I hear that he has lately let his insurances expire?'

'He has, madam, and you are probably aware that either by the general terms of his holding, or the same coupled with the origin of the fire, the disaster may involve the necessity of his rebuilding the whole row of houses, or else of becoming a debtor to the estate, to the extent of some hundreds of pounds?'

She assented. 'I have been thinking of it,' she went on, and then repeated in substance the words put into her mouth by the steward.

Some disturbance of thought might have been fancied as taking place in Springrove's mind during her statement, but before she had reached the end, his eyes were clear, and directed upon her.

'I don't accept your conditions of release,' he said.

'They are not conditions exactly.'

'Well, whatever they are not, they are very uncalled-for remarks.'

'Not at all—the houses have been burnt by

your family's negligence.'

'I don't refer to the houses—you have of course the best of all rights to speak of that matter; but you, a stranger to me comparatively, have no right at all to volunteer opinions and wishes upon a very delicate subject, which concerns no living beings but Miss Graye, Miss Hinton, and myself.'

Miss Aldclyffe, like a good many others in her position, had plainly not realized that a son of her tenant and inferior could have become an educated man, who had learnt to feel his individuality, to view society from a Bohemian standpoint, far outside the farming grade in Carriford parish, and that hence he had all a developed man's unorthodox opinion about the subordination of classes. And fully conscious of the labyrinth into which he had wandered between his wish to behave honourably in the dilemma of his engagement to his cousin Adelaide and the intensity of his love for Cytherea, Springrove was additionally sensitive to any allusion to the case. He had spoken to Miss Aldclyffe with considerable warmth.

And Miss Aldclyffe was not a woman likely to be far behind any second person in warming to a mood of defiance. It seemed as if she were prepared to put up with a cold refusal, but that her haughtiness resented a criticism of her conduct ending in a rebuke. By this, Manston's discreditable object, which had been made

310

hers by compulsion only, was now adopted by choice. She flung herself into the work.

A fiery man in such a case would have relinquished persuasion and tried palpable force. A fiery woman added unscrupulousness and evolved daring strategy; and in her obstinacy, and to sustain herself as mistress, she descended to an action the meanness of which haunted her conscience to her dying hour.

'I don't quite see, Mr. Springrove,' she said, 'that I am altogether what you are pleased to call a stranger. I have known your family, at any rate, for a good many years, and I know Miss Graye particularly well, and her state of mind with regard to this matter.'

Perplexed love makes us credulous and curious as old women. Edward was willing, he owned it to himself, to get at Cytherea's state of mind, even through so dangerous a medium.

'A letter I received from her,' he said, with assumed coldness, 'tells me clearly enough what Miss Graye's mind is.'

'You think she still loves you? O yes, of course you do—all men are like that.'

'I have reason to.' He could feign no further than the first speech.

'I should be interested in knowing what reason?' she said, with sarcastic archness.

Edward felt he was allowing her to do, in fractional parts, what he rebelled against when regarding it as a whole; but the fact that his

311

antagonist had the presence of a queen, and features only in the early evening of their beauty, was not without its influence upon a keenly conscious man. Her bearing had charmed him into toleration, as Mary Stuart's charmed the indignant Puritan visitors. He again answered her honestly.

'The best of reasons—the tone of her letter.'

'Pooh, Mr. Springrove!'

'Not at all, Miss Aldclyffe! Miss Graye desired that we should be strangers to each other for the simple practical reason that intimacy could only make wretched complications worse, not from lack of love—love is only suppressed.'

'Don't you know yet, that in thus putting aside a man, a woman's pity for the pain she inflicts gives her a kindness of tone which is often mistaken for suppressed love?' said Miss Aldclyffe, with soft insidiousness.

This was a translation of the ambiguity of Cytherea's tone which he had certainly never thought of; and he was too ingenuous not to own it.

'I had never thought of it,' he said.

'And don't believe it?'

'Not unless there was some other evidence to support the view.'

She paused a minute and then began hesitatingly—

'My intention was—what I did not dream of owning to you—my intention was to try to

312

induce you to fulfil your promise to Miss Hinton not solely on her account and yours (though partly). I love Cytherea Graye with all my soul, and I want to see her happy even more than I do you. I did not mean to drag her name into the affair at all, but I am driven to say that she wrote that letter of dismissal to you—for it was a most pronounced dismissal—not on account of your engagement. She is old enough to know that engagements can be broken as easily as they can be made. She wrote it because she loved another man; very suddenly, and not with any idea or hope of marrying him, but none the less deeply.'

'Who?'

'Mr. Manston.'

'Good—! I can't listen to you for an instant, madam; why, she hadn't seen him!'

'She had; he came here the day before she wrote to you; and I could prove to you, if it were worth while, that on that day she went voluntarily to his house, though not artfully or blamably; stayed for two hours playing and singing; that no sooner did she leave him than she went straight home, and wrote the letter saying she should not see you again, entirely because she had seen him and fallen desperately in love with him—a perfectly natural thing for a young girl to do, considering that he's the handsomest man in the county. Why else should she not have written to you before?'

'Because I was such a—because she did not know of the connection between me and my cousin until then.'

'I must think she did.'

'On what ground?'

'On the strong ground of my having told her so, distinctly, the very first day she came to live with me.'

'Well, what do you seek to impress upon me after all? This—that the day Miss Graye wrote to me, saying it was better that we should part, coincided with the day she had seen a certain man—'

'A remarkably handsome and talented man.'

'Yes, I admit that.'

'And that it coincided with the hour just subsequent to her seeing him.'

'Yes, just when she had seen him.'

'And been to his house alone with him.'

'It is nothing.'

'And stayed there playing and singing with him.'

'Admit that, too,' he said; 'an accident might have caused it.'

'And at the same instant that she wrote your dismissal she wrote a letter referring to a secret appointment with him.'

'Never, by God, madam! never!'

'What do you say, sir?'

'Never.'

She sneered.

'There's no accounting for beliefs, and the

314

whole history is a very trivial matter; but I am resolved to prove that a lady's word is truthful, though upon a matter which concerns neither you nor herself. You shall learn that she *did* write him a letter concerning an assignation— that is, if Mr. Manston still has it, and will be considerate enough to lend it me.'

'But besides,' continued Edward, 'a married man to do what would cause a young girl to write a note of the kind you mention!'

She flushed a little.

'That I don't know anything about,' she stammered. 'But Cytherea didn't, of course, dream any more than I did, or others in the parish, that he was married.'

'Of course she didn't.'

'And I have reason to believe that he told her of the fact directly afterwards, that she might not compromise herself, or allow him to. It is notorious that he struggled honestly and hard against her attractions, and succeeded in hiding his feelings, if not in quenching them.'

'We'll hope that he did.'

'But circumstances are changed now.'

'Very greatly changed,' he murmured abstractedly.

'You must remember,' she added more suasively, 'that Miss Graye has a perfect right to do what she likes with her own—her heart, that is to say.'

Her descent from irritation was caused by perceiving that Edward's faith was really

315

disturbed by her strong assertions, and it gratified her.

Edward's thoughts flew to his father, and the object of his interview with her. Tongue-fencing was utterly distasteful to him.

'I will not trouble you by remaining longer, madam,' he remarked, gloomily; 'our conversation has ended sadly for me.'

'Don't think so,' she said, 'and don't be mistaken. I am older than you are, many years older, and I know many things.'

* * *

Full of miserable doubt, and bitterly regretting that he had raised his father's expectations by anticipations impossible of fulfilment, Edward slowly went his way into the village, and approached his cousin's house. The farmer was at the door looking eagerly for him. He had been waiting there for more than half-an-hour. His eye kindled quickly.

'Well, Ted, what does she say?' he asked, in the intensely sanguine tones which fall sadly upon a listener's ear, because, antecedently, they raise pictures of inevitable disappointment for the speaker, in some direction or another.

'Nothing for us to be alarmed at,' said Edward, with a forced cheerfulness.

'But must we rebuild?'

'It seems we must, father.'

316

The old man's eyes swept the horizon, then he turned to go in, without making another observation. All light seemed extinguished in him again. When Edward went in he found his father with the bureau open, unfolding the leases with a shaking hand, folding them up again without reading them, then putting them in their niche only to remove them again.

Adelaide was in the room. She said thoughtfully to Edward, as she watched the farmer—

'I hope it won't kill poor uncle, Edward. What should we do if anything were to happen to him? He is the only near relative you and I have in the world.' It was perfectly true, and somehow Edward felt more bound up with her after that remark.

She continued: 'And he was only saying so hopefully the day before the fire, that he wouldn't for the world let any one else give me away to you when we are married.'

For the first time a conscientious doubt arose in Edward's mind as to the justice of the course he was pursuing in resolving to refuse the alternative offered by Miss Aldclyffe. Could it be selfishness as well as independence? How much he had thought of his own heart, how little he had thought of his father's peace of mind!

The old man did not speak again till supper-time, when he began asking his son an endless number of hypothetical questions on what

317

might induce Miss Aldclyffe to listen to kinder terms; speaking of her now not as an unfair woman, but as a Lachesis or Fate whose course it behoved nobody to condemn. In his earnestness he once turned his eyes on Edward's face: their expression was woful: the pupils were dilated and strange in aspect.

'If she will only agree to that!' he reiterated for the hundredth time, increasing the sadness of his listeners.

An aristocratic knocking came to the door, and Jane entered with a letter, addressed—

'MR. EDWARD SPRINGROVE, Junior.'

'Charles from Knapwater House brought it,' she said.

'Miss Aldclyffe's writing,' said Mr. Springrove, before Edward had recognized it himself. 'Now 'tis all right; she's going to make an offer; she doesn't want the houses there, not she; they are going to make that the way into the park.'

Edward opened the seal and glanced at the inside. He said, with a supreme effort of self-command—

'It is only directed by Miss Aldclyffe, and refers to nothing connected with the fire. I wonder at her taking the trouble to send it to-night.'

His father looked absently at him and turned away again. Shortly afterwards they

318

retired for the night. Alone in his bedroom Edward opened and read what he had not dared to refer to in their presence.

The envelope contained another envelope in Cytherea's handwriting, addressed to '—— Manston, Esq., Old Manor House.' Inside this was the note she had written to the steward after her detention in his house by the thunderstorm—

KNAPWATER HOUSE,
September 20th.

I find I cannot meet you at seven o'clock by the waterfall as I promised. The emotion I felt made me forgetful of realities.

C. GRAYE.

Miss Aldclyffe had not written a line, and, by the unvarying rule observable when words are not an absolute necessity, her silence seemed ten times as convincing as any expression of opinion could have been.

He then, step by step, recalled all the conversation on the subject of Cytherea's feelings that had passed between himself and Miss Aldclyffe in the afternoon, and by a confusion of thought, natural enough under the trying experience, concluded that because the lady was truthful in her portraiture of effects, she must necessarily be right in her assumption of causes. That is, he was convinced that Cytherea—the hitherto-believed faithful Cytherea—had, at any rate, looked with something more than indifference upon the extremely handsome face and form of Manston.

Did he blame her, as guilty of the impropriety of allowing herself to love the newcomer in the face of his not being free to return her love? No; never for a moment did he doubt that all had occurred in her old, innocent, impulsive way; that her heart was gone before she knew it—before she knew anything, beyond his existence, of the man to whom it had flown. Perhaps the very note enclosed to him was the result of first reflection. Manston he would unhesitatingly have called a scoundrel, but for one strikingly redeeming fact. It had been patent to the whole parish, and had come to Edward's own knowledge by that indirect channel, that Manston, as a married man, conscientiously avoided Cytherea after those first few days of his arrival during which her irresistibly beautiful and fatal glances had rested upon him—his upon her.

Taking from his coat a creased and pocket-worn envelope containing Cytherea's letter to himself, Springrove opened it and read it through. He was upbraided therein, and he was dismissed. It bore the date of the letter sent to Manston, and by containing within it the phrase, 'All the day long I have been thinking,' afforded justifiable ground for assuming that it was written subsequently to the other (and in Edward's sight far sweeter one) to the steward.

But though he accused her of fickleness, he would not doubt the genuineness, in its kind, of her partiality for him at Budmouth. It was a short and shallow feeling—not perfect love:

> Love is not love
> Which alters when it alteration finds.

But it was not flirtation; a feeling had been born in her and had died. It would be well for his peace of mind if his love for her could flit away so softly, and leave so few traces behind.

Miss Aldclyffe had shown herself desperately concerned in the whole matter by the alacrity with which she had obtained the letter from Manston, and her labours to induce himself to marry his cousin. Taken in connection with her apparent interest in, if not love for, Cytherea, her eagerness, too, could only be accounted for on the ground that Cytherea indeed loved the steward.

5. DECEMBER THE FOURTH

Edward passed the night he scarcely knew how, tossing feverishly from side to side, the blood throbbing in his temples, and singing in his ears.

Before the day began to break he dressed himself. On going out upon the landing he found his father's bedroom door already open. Edward concluded that the old man had risen softly, as was his wont, and gone out into the fields to start the labourers.

But neither of the outer doors was unfastened. He entered the front room, and found it empty. Then animated by a new idea, he went round to the little back parlour, in which the few wrecks saved from the fire were deposited, and looked in at the door. Here, near the window, the shutters of which had been opened half way, he saw his father leaning on the bureau, his elbows resting on the flap, his body nearly doubled, his hands clasping his forehead. Beside him were ghostly-looking square folds of parchment—the leases of the houses destroyed.

His father looked up when Edward entered, and wearily spoke to the young man as his face came into the faint light.

'Edward, why did you get up so early?'

'I was uneasy, and could not sleep.'

The farmer turned again to the leases on the bureau, and seemed to become lost in reflection. In a minute or two, without lifting his eyes, he said—

'This is more than we can bear, Ted—more than we can bear! Ted, this will kill me. Not the loss only—the sense of my neglect about the insurance and everything. Borrow I never will. 'Tis all misery now. God help us—all misery now!'

Edward did not answer, continuing to look fixedly at the dreary daylight outside.

'Ted,' the farmer went on, 'this upset of beën burnt out o' home makes me very nervous and doubtful about everything. There's this troubles me besides—our liven here with your cousin, and fillen up her house. It must be very awkward for her. But she says she doesn't mind. Have you said anything to her lately about when you are going to marry her?'

'Nothing at all lately.'

'Well, perhaps you may as well, now we are so mixed in together. You know, no time has ever been mentioned to her at all, first or last, and I think it right that now, since she has waited so patiently and so long—you are almost called upon to say you are ready. It would simplify matters very much, if you were to walk up to church wi' her one of these mornings, get the thing done, and go on liven here as we are. If you don't I must get a house all the sooner. It would lighten my mind, too, about the two little freeholds over the hill— not a morsel a-piece, divided as they were between her mother and me, but a tidy bit tied together again. Just think about it, will ye, Ted?'

He stopped from exhaustion produced by

the intense concentration of his mind upon the weary subject, and looked anxiously at his son.

'Yes, I will,' said Edward.

'But I am going to see her of the Great House this morning,' the farmer went on, his thoughts reverting to the old subject. 'I must know the rights of the matter, the when and the where. I don't like seeing her, but I'd rather talk to her than the steward. I wonder what she'll say to me.'

The younger man knew exactly what she would say. If his father asked her what he was to do, and when, she would simply refer him to Manston: her character was not that of a woman who shrank from a proposition she had once laid down. If his father were to say to her that his son had at last resolved to marry his cousin within the year, and had given her a promise to that effect, she would say, 'Mr. Springrove, the houses are burnt: we'll let them go: trouble no more about them.'

His mind was already made up. He said calmly, 'Father, when you are talking to Miss Aldclyffe, mention to her that I have asked Adelaide if she is willing to marry me next Christmas. She is interested in my union with Adelaide, and the news will be welcome to her.'

'And yet she can be iron with reference to me and her property,' the farmer murmured. 'Very well, Ted, I'll tell her.'

6. DECEMBER THE FIFTH

Of the many contradictory particulars constituting a woman's heart, two had shown their vigorous contrast in Cytherea's bosom just at this time.

It was a dark morning, the morning after old Mr. Springrove's visit to Miss Aldclyffe, which had terminated as Edward had intended. Having risen an hour earlier than was usual with her, Cytherea sat at the window of an elegant little sitting-room on the ground floor, which had been appropriated to her by the kindness or whim of Miss Aldclyffe, that she might not be driven into that lady's presence against her will. She leant with her face on her hand, looking out into the gloomy grey air. A yellow glimmer from the flapping flame of the newly-lit fire fluttered on one side of her face and neck like a butterfly about to settle there, contrasting warmly with the other side of the same fair face, which received from the window the faint cold morning light, so weak that her shadow from the fire had a distinct outline on the window-shutter in spite of it. There the shadow danced like a demon, blue and grim.

The contradiction alluded to was that in spite of the decisive mood which two months earlier in the year had caused her to write a peremptory and final letter to Edward, she was now hoping for some answer other than the only possible one a man who, as she held, did not love her wildly, could send to such a communication. For a lover who did love wildly, she had left one little loophole in her otherwise straightforward epistle. Why she expected the letter on some morning of this particular week was, that hearing of his return to Carriford, she fondly assumed that he meant to ask for an interview before he left. Hence it was, too, that for the last few days, she had not been able to keep in bed later than the time of the postman's arrival.

The clock pointed to half-past seven. She saw the postman emerge from beneath the bare boughs of the park trees, come through the wicket, dive through the shrubbery, reappear on the lawn, stalk across it without reference to paths—as country postmen do—and come to the porch. She heard him fling the bag down on the seat, and turn away towards the village, without hindering himself for a single pace.

Then the butler opened the door, took up the bag, brought it in, and carried it up the staircase to place it on the slab by Miss Aldclyffe's dressing-room door. The whole proceeding had been depicted by sounds.

She had a presentiment that her letter was in the bag at last. She thought then in diminishing pulsations of confidence, 'He asks to see me! Perhaps he asks to see me: I hope he asks to see me.'

A quarter to eight: Miss Aldclyffe's bell—rather earlier than usual. 'She must have heard the post-bag brought,' said the maiden, as, tired of the chilly prospect outside, she turned to the fire, and drew imaginative pictures of her future therein.

A tap came to the door, and the lady's-maid entered.

'Miss Aldclyffe is awake,' she said; 'and she asked if you were moving yet, miss.'

'I'll run up to her,' said Cytherea, and flitted off with the utterance of the words. 'Very fortunate this,' she thought; 'I shall see what is in the bag this morning all the sooner.'

She took it up from the side table, went into Miss Aldclyffe's bedroom, pulled up the blinds, and looked round upon the lady in bed, calculating the minutes that must elapse before she looked at her letters.

'Well, darling, how are you? I am glad you have come in to see me,' said Miss Aldclyffe. 'You can unlock the bag this morning, child, if you like,' she continued, yawning factitiously.

'Strange!' Cytherea thought; 'it seems as if she knew there was likely to be a letter for me.'

From her bed Miss Aldclyffe watched the girl's face as she tremblingly opened the post-bag and found there an envelope addressed to her in Edward's handwriting; one he had written the day before, after the decision he had come to on an impartial, and on that account torturing, survey of his own, his father's, his cousin Adelaide's, and what he believed to be Cytherea's, position.

The haughty mistress's soul sickened remorsefully within her when she saw suddenly appear upon the speaking countenance of the young lady before her a wan desolate look of agony.

The master-sentences of Edward's letter were these: 'You speak truly. That we never meet again is the wisest and only proper course. That I regret the past as much as you do yourself, it is hardly necessary for me to say.'

XII.

THE EVENTS OF TEN MONTHS

1. DECEMBER TO APRIL

Week after week, month after month, the time had flown by. Christmas had passed; dreary winter with dark evenings had given place to more dreary winter with light evenings. Thaws had ended in rain, rain in wind, wind in dust. Showery days had come—the period of pink dawns and white sunsets; with the third week in April the cuckoo had appeared, with the fourth, the nightingale.

Edward Springrove was in London, attending to the duties of his new office, and it had become known throughout the neighbourhood of Carriford that the engagement between himself and Miss Adelaide Hinton would terminate in marriage at the end of the year.

The only occasion on which her lover of the idle delicious days at Budmouth watering-place had been seen by Cytherea after the time of the decisive correspondence, was once in church, when he sat in front of her, and beside Miss Hinton.

The rencounter was quite an accident. Springrove had come there in the full belief that Cytherea was away from home with Miss Aldclyffe; and he continued ignorant of her presence throughout the service.

It is at such moments as these, when a sensitive nature writhes under the conception that its most cherished emotions have been treated with contumely, that the sphere-descended Maid, Music, friend of Pleasure at other times, becomes a positive enemy—racking, bewildering, unrelenting. The congregation sang the first Psalm and came to the verse—

Like some fair tree which, fed by streams,
With timely fruit doth bend,
He still shall flourish, and success
All his designs attend.

Cytherea's lips did not move, nor did any sound escape her; but could she help singing the words in the depths of her being, although the man to whom she applied them sat at her rival's side?

Perhaps the moral compensation for all a woman's petty cleverness under thriving conditions is the real nobility that lies in her extreme foolishness at these other times; her sheer inability to be simply just, her exercise of an illogical power entirely denied to men in general—the power not only of kissing, but of delighting to kiss the rod by a punctilious observance of the self-immolating doctrines in the Sermon on the Mount.

As for Edward—a little like other men of his temperament, to whom, it is somewhat humiliating to think, the aberrancy of a given love is in itself a recommendation—his sentiment, as he looked over his cousin's book, was of a lower rank, Horatian rather than Psalmodic—

O, what hast thou of her, of her
Whose every look did love inspire;
Whose every breathing fanned my fire,
And stole me from myself away!

Then, without letting him see her, Cytherea slipt out of church early, and went home, the tones of the organ still lingering in her ears as she tried bravely to kill a jealous thought that would nevertheless live: 'My nature is one capable of more, far more, intense feeling than hers! She can't appreciate all the sides of him—she never will! He is more tangible to me even now, as a thought, than his presence itself is to her!' She was less noble then.

But she continually repressed her misery and bitterness of heart till the effort to do so showed signs of lessening. At length she even tried to hope that her lost lover and her rival would love one another very dearly.

The scene and the sentiment dropped into the past. Meanwhile, Manston continued visibly before her. He, though quiet and subdued in his bearing for a long time after the calamity of November, had not simulated a grief that he did not feel. At first his loss seemed so to absorb him—though as a startling change rather than as a heavy sorrow—that he paid Cytherea no attention whatever. His conduct was uniformly kind and respectful, but little more. Then, as the date of the catastrophe grew remoter, he began to wear a different aspect towards her. He always contrived to obliterate by his manner all recollection on her side that she was comparatively more dependent than himself— making much of her womanhood, nothing of her situation. Prompt to aid her whenever occasion offered, and full of delightful *petits soins* at all times, he was not officious. In this way he irresistibly won for himself a position as her friend, and the more easily in that he allowed not the faintest symptom of the old love to be apparent.

Matters stood thus in the middle of the spring when the next move on his behalf was made by Miss Aldclyffe.

2. THE THIRD OF MAY

She led Cytherea to a summer-house called the Fane, built in the private grounds about the mansion in the form of a Grecian temple; it overlooked the lake, the island on it, the trees, and their undisturbed reflection in the smooth still water. Here the old and young maid halted; here they stood, side by side, mentally imbibing the scene.

The month was May—the time, morning. Cuckoos, thrushes, blackbirds, and sparrows gave forth a perfect confusion of song and twitter. The road was spotted white with the fallen leaves of apple-blossoms, and the sparkling grey dew still lingered on the grass and flowers. Two swans floated into view in front of the women, and then crossed the water towards them.

'They seem to come to us without any will of their own—quite involuntarily—don't they?' said Cytherea, looking at the birds' graceful advance.

'Yes, but if you look narrowly you can see their hips just beneath the water, working with the greatest energy.'

'I'd rather not see that, it spoils the idea of proud indifference to direction which we associate with a swan.'

'It does; we'll have "involuntarily." Ah, now this reminds me of something.'

'Of what?'

'Of a human being who involuntarily comes towards yourself.'

Cytherea looked into Miss Aldclyffe's face; her eyes grew round as circles, and lines of wonderment came visibly upon her countenance. She had not once regarded Manston as a lover since his wife's sudden appearance and subsequent death. The death of a wife, and such a death, was an overwhelming matter in her ideas of things.

'Is it a man or woman?' she said, quite innocently.

'Mr. Manston,' said Miss Aldclyffe quietly.

'Mr. Manston attracted by me *now*?' said Cytherea, standing at gaze.

'Didn't you know it?'

'Certainly I did not. Why, his poor wife has only been dead six months.'

'Of course he knows that. But loving is not done by months, or method, or rule, or nobody would ever have invented such a phrase as "falling in love." He does not want his love to be observed just yet, on the very account you

333

mention; but conceal it as he may from himself and us, it exists definitely—and very intensely, I assure you.'

'I suppose then, that if he can't help it, it is no harm of him,' said Cytherea naively, and beginning to ponder.

'Of course it isn't—you know that well enough. She was a great burden and trouble to him. This may become a great good to you both.'

A rush of feeling at remembering that the same woman, before Manston's arrival, had just as frankly advocated Edward's claims, checked Cytherea's utterance for a while.

'There, don't look at me like that, for Heaven's sake!' said Miss Aldclyffe. 'You could almost kill a person by the force of reproach you can put into those eyes of yours, I verily believe.'

Edward once in the young lady's thoughts, there was no getting rid of him. She wanted to be alone.

'Do you want me here?' she said.

'Now there, there; you want to be off, and have a good cry,' said Miss Aldclyffe, taking her hand. 'But you mustn't, my dear. There's nothing in the past for you to regret. Compare Mr. Manston's honourable conduct towards his wife and yourself, with Springrove towards his betrothed and yourself, and then see which appears the more worthy of your thoughts.'

3. FROM THE FOURTH OF MAY TO THE TWENTY-FIRST OF JUNE

The next stage in Manston's advances towards her hand was a clearly defined courtship. She was sadly perplexed, and some contrivance was necessary on his part in order to meet with her. But it is next to impossible for an appreciative woman to have a positive repugnance towards an unusually handsome and gifted man, even though she may not be inclined to love him. Hence Cytherea was not so alarmed at the sight of him as to render a meeting and conversation with her more than a matter of difficulty.

Coming and going from church was his grand opportunity. Manston was very religious now. It is commonly said that no man was ever converted by argument, but there is a single one which will make any Laodicean in England, let him be once love-sick, wear prayer-books and become a zealous Episcopalian—the argument that his sweetheart can be seen from his pew.

Manston introduced into his method a system of bewitching flattery, everywhere pervasive, yet, too, so transitory and intangible, that, as in the case of the poet Wordsworth and the Wandering Voice, though she felt it present, she could never find it. As a foil to heighten its effect, he occasionally spoke philosophically of the evanescence of female beauty—the worthlessness of mere appearance. 'Handsome is that handsome does' he considered a proverb which should be written on the looking-glass of every woman in the land. 'Your form, your motions, your heart have won me,' he said, in a tone of playful sadness. 'They are beautiful. But I see these things, and it comes into my mind that they are doomed, they are gliding to nothing as I look. Poor eyes, poor mouth, poor face, poor maiden! "Where will her glories be in twenty years?" I say. "Where will all of her be in a hundred?" Then I think it is cruel that you should bloom a day, and fade for ever and ever. It seems hard and sad that you will die as ordinarily as I, and be buried; be food for roots and worms, be forgotten and come to earth, and grow up a mere blade of churchyard-grass and an ivy leaf. Then, Miss Graye, when I see you are a Lovely Nothing, I pity you, and the love I feel then is better and sounder, larger and more lasting than that I felt at the beginning.' Again an ardent flash of his handsome eyes.

It was by this route that he ventured on an indirect declaration and offer of his hand.

She implied in the same indirect manner that she did not love him enough to accept it.

An actual refusal was more than he had expected. Cursing himself for what he called his egregious folly in making himself the slave of a mere lady's attendant, and for having given the parish, should they know of her refusal, a chance of sneering at him—certainly a ground for thinking less of his standing than before—he went home to the Old House, and walked indecisively up and down his back-yard. Turning aside, he leant his arms upon the edge of the rain-water-butt standing in the corner, and looked into it. The reflection from the smooth stagnant surface tinged his face with the greenish shades of Correggio's nudes.

Staves of sunlight slanted down through the still pool, lighting it up with wonderful distinctness. Hundreds of thousands of minute living creatures sported and tumbled in its depth with every contortion that gaiety could suggest; perfectly happy, though consisting only of a head, or a tail, or at most a head and a tail, and all doomed to die within the twenty-four hours.

'Damn my position! Why shouldn't I be happy through my little day too? Let the parish sneer at my repulses, let it. I'll get her, if I move heaven and earth to do it!'

Indeed, the inexperienced Cytherea had, towards Edward in the first place, and Manston afterwards, unconsciously adopted bearings that would have been the very tactics of a professional fisher of men who wished to have them each successively dangling at her heels. For if any rule at all can be laid down in a matter which, for men collectively, is notoriously beyond regulation, it is that to snub a petted man, and to pet a snubbed man, is the way to win in suits of both kinds. Manston with Springrove's encouragement would have become indifferent. Edward with Manston's repulses would have sheered off at the outset, as he did afterwards. Her supreme indifference added fuel to Manston's ardour— it completely disarmed his pride. The invulnerable Nobody seemed greater to him than a susceptible Princess.

4. FROM THE TWENTY-FIRST OF JUNE TO THE END OF JULY

Cytherea had in the meantime received the following letter from her brother. It was the first definite notification of the enlargement of that cloud no bigger than a man's hand which had for nearly a twelvemonth hung before them in the distance, and which was soon to give a colour to their whole sky from horizon to horizon.

BUDMOUTH REGIS,
Saturday.

DARLING SIS,—I have delayed telling you for a long time of a little matter which, though not one to be seriously alarmed about, is sufficiently vexing, and it would be unfair in me to keep it from

338

you any longer. It is that for some time past I have again been distressed by that lameness which I first distinctly felt when we went to Lulstead Cove, and again when I left Knapwater that morning early. It is an unusual pain in my left leg, between the knee and the ankle. I had just found fresh symptoms of it when you were here for that half-hour about a month ago—when you said in fun that I began to move like an old man. I had a good mind to tell you then, but fancying it would go off in a few days, I thought it was not worth while. Since that time it has increased, but I am still able to work in the office, sitting on the stool. My great fear is that Mr. G. will have some out-door measuring work for me to do soon, and that I shall be obliged to decline it.

However, we will hope for the best. How it came, what was its origin, or what it tends to, I cannot think. You shall hear again in a day or two, if it is no better . . . —Your loving brother,   OWEN.'

This she answered, begging to know the worst, which she could bear, but suspense and anxiety never. In two days came another letter from him, of which the subjoined paragraph is a portion:—

I had quite decided to let you know the

worst, and to assure you that it was the worst, before you wrote to ask it. And again I give you my word that I will conceal nothing—so that there will be no excuse whatever for your wearing yourself out with fears that I am worse than I say. This morning then, for the first time, I have been obliged to stay away from the office. Don't be frightened at this, dear Cytherea. Rest is all that is wanted, and by nursing myself now for a week, I may avoid an illness of six months.

After a visit from her he wrote again:—

Dr. Chestman has seen me. He said that the ailment was some sort of rheumatism, and I am now undergoing proper treatment for its cure. My leg and foot have been placed in hot bran, liniments have been applied, and also severe friction with a pad. He says I shall be as right as ever in a very short time. Directly I am I shall run up by the train to see you. Don't trouble to come to me if Miss Aldclyffe grumbles again about your being away, for I am going on capitally . . . You shall hear again at the end of the week.

At the time mentioned came the following:—

'I am sorry to tell you, because I know it will be so disheartening after my last letter, that I am not so well as I was then, and that there has been a sort of hitch in the proceedings. After I had been treated for rheumatism a few days longer (in which treatment they pricked the place with a long needle several times,) I saw that Dr. Chestman was in doubt about something, and I requested that he would call in a brother professional man to see me as well. They consulted together and then told me that rheumatism was not the disease after all, but erysipelas. They then began treating it differently, as became a different matter. Blisters, flour, and starch, seem to be the order of the day now—medicine, of course, besides.

Mr. Gradfield has been in to inquire about me. He says he has been obliged to get a designer in my place, which grieves me very much, though, of course, it could not be avoided.

A month passed away; throughout this period, Cytherea visited him as often as the limited time at her command would allow, and wore as cheerful a countenance as the womanly determination to do nothing which might depress him could enable her to wear. Another letter from him then told her these additional facts:—

The doctors find they are again on the wrong tack. They cannot make out what the disease is. O Cytherea! how I wish they knew! This suspense is wearing me out. Could not Miss Aldclyffe spare you for a day? Do come to me. We will talk about the best course then. I am sorry to complain, but I am worn out.

Cytherea went to Miss Aldclyffe, and told her of the melancholy turn her brother's illness had taken. Miss Aldclyffe at once said that Cytherea might go, and offered to do anything to assist her which lay in her power. Cytherea's eyes beamed gratitude as she turned to leave the room, and hasten to the station.

'O, Cytherea,' said Miss Aldclyffe, calling her back; 'just one word. Has Mr. Manston spoken to you lately?'

'Yes,' said Cytherea, blushing timorously.

'He proposed?'

'Yes.'

'And you refused him?'

'Yes.'

'Tt, tt! Now listen to my advice,' said Miss Aldclyffe emphatically, 'and accept him before he changes his mind. The chance which he offers you of settling in life is one that may possibly, probably, not occur again. His position is good and secure, and the life of his

342

wife would be a happy one. You may not be sure that you love him madly; but suppose you are not sure? My father used to say to me as a child when he was teaching me whist, "When in doubt win the trick!" That advice is ten times as valuable to a woman on the subject of matrimony. In refusing a man there is always the risk that you may never get another offer.'

'Why didn't you win the trick when you were a girl?' said Cytherea.

'Come, my lady Pert; I'm not the text,' said Miss Aldclyffe, her face glowing like fire.

Cytherea laughed stealthily.

'I was about to say,' resumed Miss Aldclyffe severely, 'that here is Mr. Manston waiting with the tenderest solicitude for you, and you overlooking it, as if it were altogether beneath you. Think how you might benefit your sick brother if you were Mrs. Manston. You will please me *very much* by giving him some encouragement. You understand me, Cythie dear?'

Cytherea was silent.

'And,' said Miss Aldclyffe, still more emphatically, 'on your promising that you will accept him some time this year, I will take especial care of your brother. You are listening, Cytherea?'

'Yes,' she whispered, leaving the room.

She went to Budmouth, passed the day with her brother, and returned to Knapwater wretched and full of foreboding. Owen had looked startlingly thin and pale—thinner and paler than ever she had seen him before. The brother and sister had that day decided that notwithstanding the drain upon their slender resources, another surgeon should see him. Time was everything.

Owen told her the result in his next letter:—

The three practitioners between them have at last hit the nail on the head, I hope. They probed the place, and discovered that the secret lay in the bone. I underwent an operation for its removal three days ago (after taking chloroform) ... Thank God it is over. Though I am so weak, my spirits are rather better. I wonder when I shall be at work again? I asked the surgeons how long it would be first. I said a month? They shook their heads. A year? I said. Not so long, they said. Six months? I inquired. They would not, or could not, tell me. But never mind.

Run down, when you have half a day to spare, for the hours drag on so drearily. O Cytherea, you can't think how drearily!'

She went. Immediately on her departure Miss Aldclyffe sent a note to the Old House, to Manston. On the maiden's return, tired and sick at heart as usual, she found Manston at the station awaiting her. He asked politely if he might accompany her to Knapwater. She tacitly acquiesced.

During their walk he inquired the particulars of her brother's illness, and with an irresistible desire to pour out her trouble to some one, she told him of the length of time which must elapse before he could be strong again, and of the lack of comfort in lodgings.

Manston was silent awhile. Then he said impetuously: 'Miss Graye, I will not mince matters—I love you—you know it. Stratagem they say is fair in love, and I am compelled to adopt it now. Forgive me, for I cannot help it. Consent to be my wife at any time that may suit you—any remote day you may name will satisfy me—and you shall find him well provided for.'

For the first time in her life she truly dreaded the handsome man at her side who pleaded thus selfishly, and shrank from the hot voluptuous nature of his passion for her, which, disguise it as he might under a quiet and polished exterior, at times radiated forth with a scorching white heat. She perceived how animal was the love which bargained.

'I do not love you, Mr. Manston,' she replied coldly.

5. FROM THE FIRST TO THE TWENTY-SEVENTH OF AUGUST

The long sunny days of the later summer-time brought only the same dreary accounts from Budmouth, and saw Cytherea paying the same sad visits.

She grew perceptibly weaker, in body and mind. Manston still persisted in his suit, but with more of his former indirectness, now that he saw how unexpectedly well she stood an open attack. His was the system of Dares at the Sicilian games—

> He, like a captain who beleaguers round
> Some strong-built castle on a rising ground,
> Views all the approaches with observing eyes,
> This and that other part again he tries,
> And more on industry than force relies.

Miss Aldclyffe made it appear more clearly than ever that aid to Owen from herself depended entirely upon Cytherea's acceptance of her steward. Hemmed in and distressed, Cytherea's answers to his importunities grew less uniform; they were firm, or wavering, as Owen's malady fluctuated. Had a register of her pitiful oscillations been kept, it would have rivalled in pathos the diary wherein De Quincey tabulates his combat with Opium— perhaps as noticeable an instance as any in which a thrilling dramatic power has been

346

given to mere numerals. Thus she wearily and monotonously lived through the month, listening on Sundays to the well-known round of chapters narrating the history of Elijah and Elisha in famine and drought; on week-days to buzzing flies in hot sunny rooms. 'So like, so very like, was day to day.' Extreme lassitude seemed all that the world could show her.

Her state was in this wise, when one afternoon, having been with her brother, she met the surgeon, and begged him to tell the actual truth concerning Owen's condition.

The reply was that he feared that the first operation had not been thorough; that although the wound had healed, another attempt might still be necessary, unless nature were left to effect her own cure. But the time such a self-healing proceeding would occupy might be ruinous.

'How long would it be?' she said.

'It is impossible to say. A year or two, more or less.'

'And suppose he submitted to another artificial extraction?'

'Then he might be well in four or six months.'

Now the remainder of his and her possessions, together with a sum he had borrowed, would not provide him with necessary comforts for half that time. To combat the misfortune, there were two courses open—her becoming betrothed to Manston, or

347

the sending Owen to the County Hospital.

Thus terrified, driven into a corner, panting and fluttering about for some loophole of escape, yet still shrinking from the idea of being Manston's wife, the poor little bird endeavoured to find out from Miss Aldclyffe whether it was likely Owen would be well treated in the hospital.

'County Hospital!' said Miss Aldclyffe; 'why, it is only another name for slaughter-house—in surgical cases at any rate. Certainly if anything about your body is snapt in two they do join you together in a fashion, but 'tis so askew and ugly, that you may as well be apart again.' Then she terrified the inquiring and anxious maiden by relating horrid stories of how the legs and arms of poor people were cut off at a moment's notice, especially in cases where the restorative treatment was likely to be long and tedious.

'You know how willing I am to help you, Cytherea,' she added reproachfully. 'You know it. Why are you so obstinate then? Why do you selfishly bar the clear, honourable, and only sisterly path which leads out of this difficulty? I cannot, on my conscience, countenance you; no, I cannot.'

Manston once more repeated his offer; and once more she refused, but this time weakly, and with signs of an internal struggle. Manston's eye sparkled; he saw for the hundredth time in his life, that perseverance, if only systematic, was irresistible by womankind.

6. THE TWENTY-SEVENTH OF AUGUST

On going to Budmouth three days later, she found to her surprise that the steward had been there, had introduced himself, and had seen her brother. A few delicacies had been brought him also by the same hand. Owen spoke in warm terms of Manston and his free and unceremonious call, as he could not have refrained from doing of any person, of any kind, whose presence had served to help away the tedious hours of a long day, and who had, moreover, shown that sort of consideration for him which the accompanying basket implied— antecedent consideration, so telling upon all invalids—and which he so seldom experienced except from the hands of his sister.

How should he perceive, amid this tithe-paying of mint, and anise, and cummin, the weightier matters which were left undone?

Again the steward met her at Carriford Road Station on her return journey. Instead of being frigid as at the former meeting at the same place, she was embarrassed by a strife of thought, and murmured brokenly her thanks for what he had done. The same request that he might see her home was made.

He had perceived his error in making his kindness to Owen a conditional kindness, and had hastened to efface all recollection of it. 'Though I let my offer on her brother's—my friend's—behalf, seem dependent on my lady's graciousness to me,' he whispered wooingly in the course of their walk, 'I could not conscientiously adhere to my statement; it was said with all the impulsive selfishness of love. Whether you choose to have me, or whether you don't, I love you too devotedly to be anything but kind to your brother . . . Miss Graye, Cytherea, I will do anything,' he continued earnestly, 'to give you pleasure—indeed I will.'

She saw on the one hand her poor and much-loved Owen recovering from his illness and troubles by the disinterested kindness of the man beside her, on the other she drew him dying, wholly by reason of her self-enforced poverty. To marry this man was obviously the course of common sense, to refuse him was impolitic temerity. There was reason in this. But there was more behind than a hundred reasons—a woman's gratitude and her impulse to be kind.

The wavering of her mind was visible in her tell-tale face. He noticed it, and caught at the opportunity.

They were standing by the ruinous foundations of an old mill in the midst of a meadow. Between grey and half-overgrown stonework—the only signs of masonry remaining—the water gurgled down from the old millpond to a lower level, under the cloak of rank broad leaves—the sensuous natures of the vegetable world. On the right hand the sun, resting on the horizon-line, streamed across the ground from below copper-coloured and lilac clouds, stretched out in flats beneath a sky of pale soft green. All dark objects on the earth that lay towards the sun were overspread by a purple haze, against which a swarm of wailing gnats shone forth luminously, rising upward and floating away like sparks of fire.

The stillness oppressed and reduced her to mere passivity. The only wish the humidity of the place left in her was to stand motionless. The helpless flatness of the landscape gave her, as it gives all such temperaments, a sense of bare equality with, and no superiority to, a single entity under the sky.

He came so close that their clothes touched. 'Will you try to love me? Do try to love me!' he said, in a whisper, taking her hand. He had never taken it before. She could feel his hand trembling exceedingly as it held hers in its clasp.

Considering his kindness to her brother, his love for herself, and Edward's fickleness, ought she to forbid him to do this? How truly pitiful it was to feel his hand tremble so—all for her! Should she withdraw her hand? She would think whether she would. Thinking, and hesitating, she looked as far as the autumnal haze on the marshy ground would allow her to see distinctly. There was the fragment of a hedge—all that remained of a 'wet old garden'—standing in the middle of the mead, without a definite beginning or ending, purposeless and valueless. It was overgrown, and choked with mandrakes, and she could almost fancy she heard their shrieks . . . Should she withdraw her hand? No, she could not withdraw it now; it was too late, the act would not imply refusal. She felt as one in a boat without oars, drifting with closed eyes down a river—she knew not whither.

He gave her hand a gentle pressure, and relinquished it.

Then it seemed as if he were coming to the point again. No, he was not going to urge his suit that evening. Another respite.

7. THE EARLY PART OF SEPTEMBER

Saturday came, and she went on some trivial errand to the village post-office. It was a little grey cottage with a luxuriant jasmine encircling the doorway, and before going in Cytherea paused to admire this pleasing feature of the exterior. Hearing a step on the gravel behind the corner of the house, she resigned the jasmine and entered. Nobody was in the room. She could hear Mrs. Leat, the widow who acted as postmistress, walking about over her head. Cytherea was going to the foot of the stairs to call Mrs. Leat, but before she had accomplished her object, another form stood at the half-open door. Manston came in.

'Both on the same errand,' he said gracefully.

'I will call her,' said Cytherea, moving in haste to the foot of the stairs.

'One moment.' He glided to her side. 'Don't call her for a moment,' he repeated.

But she had said, 'Mrs. Leat!'

He seized Cytherea's hand, kissed it tenderly, and carefully replaced it by her side.

She had that morning determined to check his further advances, until she had thoroughly considered her position. The remonstrance was now on her tongue, but as accident would have it, before the word could be spoken Mrs. Leat was stepping from the last stair to the floor, and no remonstrance came.

With the subtlety which characterized him in all his dealings with her, he quickly concluded his own errand, bade her a good-bye, in the tones of which love was so garnished with pure politeness that it only showed its presence to herself, and left the house—putting it out of her power to refuse him her companionship homeward, or to object to his late action of kissing her hand.

The Friday of the next week brought another letter from her brother. In this he informed her that, in absolute grief lest he should distress her unnecessarily, he had some

353

time earlier borrowed a few pounds. A week ago, he said, his creditor became importunate, but that on the day on which he wrote, the creditor had told him there was no hurry for a settlement, that 'his *sister's suitor* had guaranteed the sum.' 'Is he Mr. Manston? tell me, Cytherea,' said Owen.

He also mentioned that a wheeled chair had been anonymously hired for his especial use, though as yet he was hardly far enough advanced towards convalescence to avail himself of the luxury. 'Is this Mr. Manston's doing?' he inquired.

She could dally with her perplexity, evade it, trust to time for guidance, no longer. The matter had come to a crisis: she must once and for all choose between the dictates of her understanding and those of her heart. She longed, till her soul seemed nigh to bursting, for her lost mother's return to earth, but for one minute, that she might have tender counsel to guide her through this, her great difficulty.

As for her heart, she half fancied that it was not Edward's to quite the extent that it once had been; she thought him cruel in conducting himself towards her as he did at Budmouth, cruel afterwards in making so light of her. She knew he had stifled his love for her—was utterly lost to her. But for all that she could not help indulging in a woman's pleasure of recreating defunct agonies, and lacerating herself with them now and then.

'If I were rich,' she thought, 'I would give way to the luxury of being morbidly faithful to him for ever without his knowledge.'

But she considered; in the first place she was a homeless dependent; and what did practical wisdom tell her to do under such desperate circumstances? To provide herself with some place of refuge from poverty, and with means to aid her brother Owen. This was to be Mr. Manston's wife.

She did not love him.

But what was love without a home? Misery. What was a home without love? Alas, not much; but still a kind of home.

'Yes,' she thought, 'I am urged by my common sense to marry Mr. Manston.'

Did anything nobler in her say so too?

With the death (to her) of Edward her heart's occupation was gone. Was it necessary or even right for her to tend it and take care of it as she used to in the old time, when it was still a capable minister?

By a slight sacrifice here she could give happiness to at least two hearts whose emotional activities were still unwounded. She would do good to two men whose lives were far more important than hers.

'Yes,' she said again, 'even Christianity urges me to marry Mr. Manston.'

Directly Cytherea had persuaded herself that a kind of heroic self-abnegation had to do with the matter, she became much more content in the consideration of it. A wilful indifference to the future was what really prevailed in her, ill and worn out, as she was, by the perpetual harassments of her sad fortune, and she regarded this indifference, as gushing natures will do under such circumstances, as genuine resignation and devotedness.

Manston met her again the following day: indeed, there was no escaping him now. At the end of a short conversation between them, which took place in the hollow of the park by the waterfall, obscured on the outer side by the low hanging branches of the limes, she tacitly assented to his assumption of a privilege greater than any that had preceded it. He stooped and kissed her brow.

Before going to bed she wrote to Owen explaining the whole matter. It was too late in the evening for the postman's visit, and she placed the letter on the mantelpiece to send it the next day.

The morning (Sunday) brought a hurried postscript to Owen's letter of the day before:—

September 9, 1865.
DEAR CYTHEREA,—I have received a frank and friendly letter from Mr. Manston explaining the position in which he stands now, and also that in which he hopes to stand towards you. Can't you

love him? Why not? Try, for he is a good, and not only that, but a cultured man. Think of the weary and laborious future that awaits you if you continue for life in your present position, and do you see any way of escape from it except by marriage? I don't. Don't go against your heart, Cytherea, but be wise.—Ever affectionately yours,

OWEN.

She thought that probably he had replied to Mr. Manston in the same favouring mood. She had a conviction that that day would settle her doom. Yet

So true a fool is love,

that even now she nourished a half-hope that something would happen at the last moment to thwart her deliberately-formed intentions, and favour the old emotion she was using all her strength to thrust down.

8. THE TENTH OF SEPTEMBER

The Sunday was the thirteenth after Trinity, and the afternoon service at Carriford was nearly over. The people were singing the Evening Hymn.

Manston was at church as usual in his

accustomed place two seats forward from the large square pew occupied by Miss Aldclyffe and Cytherea.

The ordinary sadness of an autumnal evening-service seemed, in Cytherea's eyes, to be doubled on this particular occasion. She looked at all the people as they stood and sang, waving backwards and forwards like a forest of pines swayed by a gentle breeze; then at the village children singing too, their heads inclined to one side, their eyes listlessly tracing some crack in the old walls, or following the movement of a distant bough or bird with features petrified almost to painfulness. Then she looked at Manston; he was already regarding her with some purpose in his glance.

'It is coming this evening,' she said in her mind. A minute later, at the end of the hymn, when the congregation began to move out, Manston came down the aisle. He was opposite the end of her seat as she stepped from it, the remainder of their progress to the door being in contact with each other. Miss Aldclyffe had lingered behind.

'Don't let's hurry,' he said, when Cytherea was about to enter the private path to the House as usual. 'Would you mind turning down this way for a minute till Miss Aldclyffe has passed?'

She could not very well refuse now. They turned into a secluded path on their left, leading round through a thicket of laurels to the other gate of the church-yard, walking very slowly. By the time the further gate was reached, the church was closed. They met the sexton with the keys in his hand.

'We are going inside for a minute,' said Manston to him, taking the keys unceremoniously. 'I will bring them to you when we return.'

The sexton nodded his assent, and Cytherea and Manston walked into the porch, and up the nave.

They did not speak a word during their progress, or in any way interfere with the stillness and silence that prevailed everywhere around them. Everything in the place was the embodiment of decay: the fading red glare from the setting sun, which came in at the west window, emphasizing the end of the day and all its cheerful doings, the mildewed walls, the uneven paving-stones, the wormy pews, the sense of recent occupation, and the dank air of death which had gathered with the evening, would have made grave a lighter mood than Cytherea's was then.

'What sensations does the place impress you with?' she said at last, very sadly.

'I feel imperatively called upon to be honest, from very despair of achieving anything by stratagem in a world where the materials are such as these.' He, too, spoke in a depressed voice, purposely or otherwise.

'I feel as if I were almost ashamed to be

seen walking such a world,' she murmured; 'that's the effect it has upon me; but it does not induce me to be honest particularly.'

He took her hand in both his, and looked down upon the lids of her eyes.

'I pity you sometimes,' he said more emphatically.

'I am pitiable, perhaps; so are many people. Why do you pity me?'

'I think that you make yourself needlessly sad.'

'Not needlessly.'

'Yes, needlessly. Why should you be separated from your brother so much, when you might have him to stay with you till he is well?'

'That can't be,' she said, turning away.

He went on, 'I think the real and only good thing that can be done for him is to get him away from Budmouth a while; and I have been wondering whether it could not be managed for him to come to my house to live for a few weeks. Only a quarter of a mile from you. How pleasant it would be!'

'It would.'

He moved himself round immediately to the front of her, and held her hand more firmly, as he continued, 'Cytherea, why do you say "It would," so entirely in the tone of abstract supposition? I want him there: I want him to be my brother, too. Then make him so, and be my wife! I cannot live without you. O

Cytherea, my darling, my love, come and be my wife!'

His face bent closer and closer to hers, and the last words sank to a whisper as weak as the emotion inspiring it was strong.

She said firmly and distinctly, 'Yes, I will.'

'Next month?' he said on the instant, before taking breath.

'No; not next month.'

'The next?'

'No.'

'December? Christmas Day, say?'

'I don't mind.'

'O, you darling!' He was about to imprint a kiss upon her pale, cold mouth, but she hastily covered it with her hand.

'Don't kiss me—at least where we are now!' she whispered imploringly.

'Why?'

'We are too near God.'

He gave a sudden start, and his face flushed. She had spoken so emphatically that the words 'Near God' echoed back again through the hollow building from the far end of the chancel.

'What a thing to say!' he exclaimed; 'surely a pure kiss is not inappropriate to the place!'

'No,' she replied, with a swelling heart; 'I don't know why I burst out so—I can't tell what has come over me! Will you forgive me?'

'How shall I say "Yes" without judging you? How shall I say "No" without losing the

361

pleasure of saying "Yes?"' He was himself again.

'I don't know,' she absently murmured.

'I'll say "Yes,"' he answered daintily. 'It is sweeter to fancy we are forgiven, than to think we have not sinned; and you shall have the sweetness without the need.'

She did not reply, and they moved away. The church was nearly dark now, and melancholy in the extreme. She stood beside him while he locked the door, then took the arm he gave her, and wound her way out of the churchyard with him. Then they walked to the house together, but the great matter having been set at rest, she persisted in talking only on indifferent subjects.

'Christmas Day, then,' he said, as they were parting at the end of the shrubbery.

'I meant Old Christmas Day,' she said evasively.

'H'm, people do not usually attach that meaning to the words.'

'No; but I should like it best if it could not be till then?' It seemed to be still her instinct to delay the marriage to the utmost.

'Very well, love,' he said gently. ' 'Tis a fortnight longer still; but never mind. Old Christmas Day.'

9. THE ELEVENTH OF SEPTEMBER

'There. It will be on a Friday!'

She sat upon a little footstool gazing intently into the fire. It was the afternoon of the day following that of the steward's successful solicitation of her hand.

'I wonder if it would be proper in me to run across the park and tell him it is a Friday?' she said to herself, rising to her feet, looking at her hat lying near, and then out of the window towards the Old House. Proper or not, she felt that she must at all hazards remove the disagreeable, though, as she herself owned, unfounded impression the coincidence had occasioned. She left the house directly, and went to search for him.

Manston was in the timber-yard, looking at the sawyers as they worked. Cytherea came up to him hesitatingly. Till within a distance of a few yards she had hurried forward with alacrity—now that the practical expression of his face became visible she wished almost she had never sought him on such an errand; in his business-mood he was perhaps very stern.

'It will be on a Friday,' she said confusedly, and without any preface.

'Come this way!' said Manston, in the tone he used for workmen, not being able to alter at an instant's notice. He gave her his arm and led her back into the avenue, by which time he was lover again. 'On a Friday, will it, dearest?

You do not mind Fridays, surely? That's nonsense.'

'Not seriously mind them, exactly—but if it could be any other day?'

'Well, let us say Old Christmas Eve, then. Shall it be Old Christmas Eve?'

'Yes, Old Christmas Eve.'

'Your word is solemn, and irrevocable now?'

'Certainly, I have solemnly pledged my word; I should not have promised to marry you if I had not meant it. Don't think I should.' She spoke the words with a dignified impressiveness.

'You must not be vexed at my remark, dearest. Can you think the worse of an ardent man, Cytherea, for showing some anxiety in love?'

'No, no.' She could not say more. She was always ill at ease when he spoke of himself as a piece of human nature in that analytical way, and wanted to be out of his presence. The time of day, and the proximity of the house, afforded her a means of escape. 'I must be with Miss Aldclyffe now—will you excuse my hasty coming and going?' she said prettily. Before he had replied she had parted from him.

'Cytherea, was it Mr. Manston I saw you scudding away from in the avenue just now?' said Miss Aldclyffe, when Cytherea joined her.

'Yes.'

'"Yes." Come, why don't you say more than that? I hate those taciturn "Yess"es of yours. I tell you everything, and yet you are as close as wax with me.'

'I parted from him because I wanted to come in.'

'What a novel and important announcement! Well, is the day fixed?'

'Yes.'

Miss Aldclyffe's face kindled into intense interest at once. 'Is it indeed? When is it to be?'

'On Old Christmas Eve.'

'Old Christmas Eve.' Miss Aldclyffe drew Cytherea round to her front, and took a hand in each of her own. 'And then you will be a bride!' she said slowly, looking with critical thoughtfulness upon the maiden's delicately rounded cheeks.

The normal area of the colour upon each of them decreased perceptibly after that slow and emphatic utterance by the elder lady.

Miss Aldclyffe continued impressively, 'You did not say "Old Christmas Eve" as a fiancée should have said the words: and you don't receive my remark with the warm excitement that foreshadows a bright future . . . How many weeks are there to the time?'

'I have not reckoned them.'

'Not? Fancy a girl not counting the weeks! I find I must take the lead in this matter—you are so childish, or frightened, or stupid, or something, about it. Bring me my diary, and we will count them at once.'

Cytherea silently fetched the book.

Miss Aldclyffe opened the diary at the page containing the almanac, and counted sixteen weeks, which brought her to the thirty-first of December—a Sunday. Cytherea stood by, looking on as if she had no appetite for the scene.

'Sixteen to the thirty-first. Then let me see, Monday will be the first of January, Tuesday the second, Wednesday third, Thursday fourth, Friday fifth—you have chosen a Friday, as I declare!'

'A Thursday, surely?' said Cytherea.

'No: Old Christmas Day comes on a Saturday.'

The perturbed little brain had reckoned wrong. 'Well, it must be a Friday,' she murmured in a reverie.

'No: have it altered, of course,' said Miss Aldclyffe cheerfully.

'There's nothing bad in Friday, but such a creature as you will be thinking about its being unlucky—in fact, I wouldn't choose a Friday myself to be married on, since all the other days are equally available.'

'I shall not have it altered,' said Cytherea firmly; 'it has been altered once already: I shall let it be.'

XIII.

THE EVENTS OF ONE DAY

1. THE FIFTH OF JANUARY. BEFORE DAWN

We pass over the intervening weeks. The time of the story is thus advanced more than a quarter of a year.

On the midnight preceding the morning which would make her the wife of a man whose presence fascinated her into involuntariness of bearing, and whom in absence she almost dreaded, Cytherea lay in her little bed, vainly endeavouring to sleep.

She had been looking back amid the years of her short though varied past, and thinking of the threshold upon which she stood. Days and months had dimmed the form of Edward Springrove like the gauzes of a vanishing stage-scene, but his dying voice could still be heard faintly behind. That a soft small chord in her still vibrated true to his memory, she would not admit: that she did not approach Manston with feelings which could by any stretch of words be called hymeneal, she calmly owned.

'Why do I marry him?' she said to herself. 'Because Owen, dear Owen my brother, wishes me to marry him. Because Mr. Manston is, and has been, uniformly kind to Owen, and to me.

367

"Act in obedience to the dictates of common-sense," Owen said, "and dread the sharp sting of poverty. How many thousands of women like you marry every year for the same reason, to secure a home, and mere ordinary, material comforts, which after all go far to make life endurable, even if not supremely happy."

' 'Tis right, I suppose, for him to say that. O, if people only knew what a timidity and melancholy upon the subject of her future grows up in the heart of a friendless woman who is blown about like a reed shaken with the wind, as I am, they would not call this resignation of one's self by the name of scheming to get a husband. Scheme to marry? I'd rather scheme to die! I know I am not pleasing my heart; I know that if I only were concerned, I should like risking a single future. But why should I please my useless self overmuch, when by doing otherwise I please those who are more valuable than I?'

In the midst of desultory reflections like these, which alternated with surmises as to the inexplicable connection that appeared to exist between her intended husband and Miss Aldclyffe, she heard dull noises outside the walls of the house, which she could not quite fancy to be caused by the wind. She seemed doomed to such disturbances at critical periods of her existence. 'It is strange,' she pondered, 'that this my last night in Knapwater House should be disturbed precisely as my first was, no occurrence of the kind having intervened.'

As the minutes glided by the noise increased, sounding as if some one were beating the wall below her window with a bunch of switches. She would gladly have left her room and gone to stay with one of the maids, but they were without doubt all asleep.

The only person in the house likely to be awake, or who would have brains enough to comprehend her nervousness, was Miss Aldclyffe, but Cytherea never cared to go to Miss Aldclyffe's room, though she was always welcome there, and was often almost compelled to go against her will.

The oft-repeated noise of switches grew heavier upon the wall, and was now intermingled with creaks, and a rattling like the rattling of dice. The wind blew stronger; there came first a snapping, then a crash, and some portion of the mystery was revealed. It was the breaking off and fall of a branch from one of the large trees outside. The smacking against the wall, and the intermediate rattling, ceased from that time.

Well, it was the tree which had caused the noises. The unexplained matter was that neither of the trees ever touched the walls of the house during the highest wind, and that trees could not rattle like a man playing castanets or shaking dice.

She thought, 'Is it the intention of Fate that something connected with these noises shall influence my future as in the last case of the kind?'

During the dilemma she fell into a troubled sleep, and dreamt that she was being whipped with dry bones suspended on strings, which rattled at every blow like those of a malefactor on a gibbet; that she shifted and shrank and avoided every blow, and they fell then upon the wall to which she was tied. She could not see the face of the executioner for his mask, but his form was like Manston's.

'Thank Heaven!' she said, when she awoke and saw a faint light struggling through her blind. 'Now what were those noises?' To settle that question seemed more to her than the event of the day.

She pulled the blind aside and looked out. All was plain. The evening previous had closed in with a grey drizzle, borne upon a piercing air from the north, and now its effects were visible. The hoary drizzle still continued; but the trees and shrubs were laden with icicles to an extent such as she had never before witnessed. A shoot of the diameter of a pin's head was iced as thick as her finger; all the boughs in the park were bent almost to the earth with the immense weight of the glistening incumbrance; the walks were like a looking-glass. Many boughs had snapped beneath their burden, and lay in heaps upon the icy grass. Opposite her eye, on the nearest tree, was a fresh yellow scar, showing where the branch that had terrified her had been splintered from the trunk.

'I never could have believed it possible,' she thought, surveying the bowed-down branches, 'that trees would bend so far out of their true positions without breaking.' By watching a twig she could see a drop collect upon it from the hoary fog, sink to the lowest point, and there become coagulated as the others had done.

'Or that I could so exactly have imitated them,' she continued. 'On this morning I am to be married—unless this is a scheme of the great Mother to hinder a union of which she does not approve. Is it possible for my wedding to take place in the face of such weather as this?'

2. MORNING

Her brother Owen was staying with Manston at the Old House. Contrary to the opinion of the doctors, the wound had healed after the first surgical operation, and his leg was gradually acquiring strength, though he could only as yet get about on crutches, or ride, or be dragged in a chair.

Miss Aldclyffe had arranged that Cytherea should be married from Knapwater House, and not from her brother's lodgings at Budmouth, which was Cytherea's first idea. Owen, too, seemed to prefer the plan. The capricious old maid had latterly taken to the contemplation of the wedding with even greater warmth than had at first inspired her, and appeared determined to do everything in her power, consistent with her dignity, to render the adjuncts of the ceremony pleasing and complete.

But the weather seemed in flat contradiction of the whole proceeding. At eight o'clock the coachman crept up to the House almost upon his hands and knees, entered the kitchen, and stood with his back to the fire, panting from his exertions in pedestrianism.

The kitchen was by far the pleasantest apartment in Knapwater House on such a morning as this. The vast fire was the centre of the whole system, like a sun, and threw its warm rays upon the figures of the domestics, wheeling about it in true planetary style. A nervously-feeble imitation of its flicker was continually attempted by a family of polished metallic utensils standing in rows and groups against the walls opposite, the whole collection of shines nearly annihilating the weak daylight from outside. A step further in, and the nostrils were greeted by the scent of green herbs just gathered, and the eye by the plump form of the cook, wholesome, white-aproned, and floury—looking as edible as the food she manipulated—her movements being supported and assisted by her satellites, the kitchen and scullery maids. Minute recurrent sounds prevailed—the click of the smoke-jack, the flap of the flames, and the light touches of the women's slippers upon the stone floor.

The coachman hemmed, spread his feet more firmly upon the hearthstone, and looked hard at a small plate in the extreme corner of the dresser.

'No wedden this mornen—that's my opinion. In fact, there can't be,' he said abruptly, as if the words were the mere torso of a many-membered thought that had existed complete in his head.

The kitchen-maid was toasting a slice of bread at the end of a very long toasting-fork, which she held at arm's length towards the unapproachable fire, travestying the flanconade in fencing.

'Bad out of doors, isn't it?' she said, with a look of commiseration for things in general.

'Bad? Not even a liven soul, gentle or simple, can stand on level ground. As to getten up hill to the church, 'tis perfect lunacy. And I speak of foot-passengers. As to horses and carriage, 'tis murder to think of 'em. I am going to send straight as a line into the breakfast-room, and say 'tis a closer . . . Hullo—here's Clerk Crickett and John Day a-comen! Now just look at 'em and picture a wedden if you can.'

All eyes were turned to the window, from which the clerk and gardener were seen crossing the court, bowed and stooping like Bel and Nebo.

'You'll have to go if it breaks all the horses' legs in the county,' said the cook, turning from the spectacle, knocking open the oven-door with the tongs, glancing critically in, and slamming it together with a clang.

'O, O; why shall I?' asked the coachman, including in his auditory by a glance the clerk and gardener who had just entered.

'Because Mr. Manston is in the business. Did you ever know him to give up for weather of any kind, or for any other mortal thing in heaven or earth?'

'—Mornen so's—such as it is!' interrupted Mr. Crickett cheerily, coming forward to the blaze and warming one hand without looking at the fire. 'Mr. Manston gie up for anything in heaven or earth, did you say? You might ha' cut it short by sayen "to Miss Aldclyffe," and leaven out heaven and earth as trifles. But it might be put off; putten off a thing isn't getten rid of a thing, if that thing is a woman. O no, no!'

The coachman and gardener now naturally subsided into secondaries. The cook went on rather sharply, as she dribbled milk into the exact centre of a little crater of flour in a platter—

'It might be in this case; she's so indifferent.'

'Dang my old sides! and so it might be. I have a bit of news—I thought there was

374

something upon my tongue; but 'tis a secret; not a word, mind, not a word. Why, Miss Hinton took a holiday yesterday.'

'Yes?' inquired the cook, looking up with perplexed curiosity.

'D'ye think that's all?'

'Don't be so three-cunning—if it is all, deliver you from the evil of raising a woman's expectations wrongfully; I'll skimmer your pate as sure as you cry Amen!'

'Well, it isn't all. When I got home last night my wife said, "Miss Adelaide took a holiday this mornen," says she (my wife, that is); "walked over to Nether Mynton, met the comen man, and got married!" says she.'

'Got married! what, Lord-a-mercy, did Springrove come?'

'Springrove, no—no—Springrove's nothen to do wi' it—'twas Farmer Bollens. They've been playing bo-peep for these two or three months seemingly. Whilst Master Teddy Springrove has been daddlen, and hawken, and spetten about having her, she's quietly left him all forsook. Serve him right. I don't blame the little woman a bit.'

'Farmer Bollens is old enough to be her father!'

'Ay, quite; and rich enough to be ten fathers. They say he's so rich that he has business in every bank, and measures his money in half-pint cups.'

'Lord, I wish it was me, don't I wish 'twas

me!' said the scullery-maid.

'Yes, 'twas as neat a bit of stitching as ever I heard of,' continued the clerk, with a fixed eye, as if he were watching the process from a distance. 'Not a soul knew anything about it, and my wife is the only one in our parish who knows it yet. Miss Hinton came back from the wedden, went to Mr. Manston, puffed herself out large, and said she was Mrs. Bollens, but that if he wished, she had no objection to keep on the house till the regular time of giving notice had expired, or till he could get another tenant.'

'Just like her independence,' said the cook.

'Well, independent or no, she's Mrs. Bollens now. Ah, I shall never forget once when I went by Farmer Bollens's garden—years ago now—years, when he was taking up ashleaf taties. A merry feller I was at that time, a very merry feller—for 'twas before I took holy orders, and it didn't prick my conscience as 'twould now. "Farmer," says I, "little taties seem to turn out small this year, don't em?" "O no, Crickett," says he, "some be fair-sized." He's a dull man—Farmer Bollens is—he always was. However, that's neither here nor there; he's a-married to a sharp woman, and if I don't make a mistake she'll bring him a pretty good family, gie her time.'

'Well, it don't matter; there's a Providence in it,' said the scullery-maid. 'God A'mighty always sends bread as well as children.'

'But 'tis the bread to one house and the children to another very often. However, I think I can see my lady Hinton's reason for chosen yesterday to sickness-or-health-it. Your young miss, and that one, had crossed one another's path in regard to young Master Springrove; and I expect that when Addy Hinton found Miss Graye wasn't caren to have en, she thought she'd be beforehand with her old enemy in marrying somebody else too. That's maids' logic all over, and maids' malice likewise.'

Women who are bad enough to divide against themselves under a man's partiality are good enough to instantly unite in a common cause against his attack. 'I'll just tell you one thing then,' said the cook, shaking out her words to the time of a whisk she was beating eggs with. 'Whatever maids' logic is and maids' malice too, if Cytherea Graye even now knows that young Springrove is free again, she'll fling over the steward as soon as look at him.'

'No, no: not now,' the coachman broke in like a moderator. 'There's honour in that maid, if ever there was in one. No Miss Hinton's tricks in her. She'll stick to Manston.'

'Pifh!'

'Don't let a word be said till the wedden is over, for Heaven's sake,' the clerk continued. 'Miss Aldclyffe would fairly hang and quarter me, if my news broke off that there wedden at a last minute like this.'

'Then you had better get your wife to bolt you in the closet for an hour or two, for you'll chatter it yourself to the whole boiling parish if she don't! 'Tis a poor womanly feller!'

'You shouldn't ha' begun it, clerk. I knew how 'twould be,' said the gardener soothingly, in a whisper to the clerk's mangled remains.

The clerk turned and smiled at the fire, and warmed his other hand.

3. NOON

The weather gave way. In half-an-hour there began a rapid thaw. By ten o'clock the roads, though still dangerous, were practicable to the extent of the half-mile required by the people of Knapwater Park. One mass of heavy leaden cloud spread over the whole sky; the air began to feel damp and mild out of doors, though still cold and frosty within.

They reached the church and passed up the nave, the deep-coloured glass of the narrow windows rendering the gloom of the morning almost night itself inside the building. Then the ceremony began. The only warmth or spirit imported into it came from the bridegroom, who retained a vigorous—even Spenserian—bridal-mood throughout the morning.

Cytherea was as firm as he at this critical moment, but as cold as the air surrounding her. The few persons forming the wedding-party were constrained in movement and tone, and from the nave of the church came occasional coughs, emitted by those who, in spite of the weather, had assembled to see the termination of Cytherea's existence as a single woman. Many poor people loved her. They pitied her success, why, they could not tell, except that it was because she seemed to stand more like a statue than Cytherea Graye.

Yet she was prettily and carefully dressed; a strange contradiction in a man's idea of things—a saddening, perplexing contradiction. Are there any points in which a difference of sex amounts to a difference of nature? Then this is surely one. Not so much, as it is commonly put, in regard to the amount of consideration given, but in the conception of the thing considered. A man emasculated by coxcombry may spend more time upon the arrangement of his clothes than any woman, but even then there is no fetichism in his idea of them—they are still only a covering he uses for a time. But here was Cytherea, in the bottom of her heart almost indifferent to life, yet possessing an instinct with which her heart had nothing to do, the instinct to be particularly regardful of those sorry trifles, her robe, her flowers, her veil, and her gloves.

The irrevocable words were soon spoken— the indelible writing soon written—and they came out of the vestry. Candles had been necessary here to enable them to sign their names, and on their return to the church the light from the candles streamed from the small open door, and across the chancel to a black chestnut screen on the south side, dividing it from a small chapel or chantry, erected for the soul's peace of some Aldclyffe of the past. Through the open-work of this screen could now be seen illuminated, inside the chantry, the reclining figures of cross-legged knights, damp and green with age, and above them a huge classic monument, also inscribed to the Aldclyffe family, heavily sculptured in cadaverous marble.

Leaning here—almost hanging to the monument—was Edward Springrove, or his spirit.

The weak daylight would never have revealed him, shaded as he was by the screen; but the unexpected rays of candle-light in the front showed him forth in startling relief to any and all of those whose eyes wandered in that direction. The sight was a sad one—sad beyond all description. His eyes were wild, their orbits leaden. His face was of a sickly paleness, his hair dry and disordered, his lips parted as if he could get no breath. His figure was spectre-thin. His actions seemed beyond his own control.

Manston did not see him; Cytherea did. The healing effect upon her heart of a year's silence—a year and a half's separation—was undone in an instant. One of those strange revivals of passion by mere sight—commoner in women than in men, and in oppressed women commonest of all—had taken place in her—so transcendently, that even to herself it seemed more like a new creation than a revival.

Marrying for a home—what a mockery it was!

It may be said that the means most potent for rekindling old love in a maiden's heart are, to see her lover in laughter and good spirits in her despite when the breach has been owing to a slight from herself; when owing to a slight from him, to see him suffering for his own fault. If he is happy in a clear conscience, she blames him; if he is miserable because deeply to blame, she blames herself. The latter was Cytherea's case now.

First, an agony of face told of the suppressed misery within her, which presently could be suppressed no longer. When they were coming out of the porch, there broke from her in a low plaintive scream the words, 'He's dying—dying! O God, save us!' She began to sink down, and would have fallen had not Manston caught her. The chief bridesmaid applied her vinaigrette.

'What did she say?' inquired Manston.

Owen was the only one to whom the words were intelligible, and he was far too deeply impressed, or rather alarmed, to reply. She did not faint, and soon began to recover her self-command. Owen took advantage of the hindrance to step back to where the apparition had been seen. He was enraged with Springrove for what he considered an unwarrantable intrusion.

But Edward was not in the chantry. As he had come, so he had gone, nobody could tell how or whither.

4. AFTERNOON

It might almost have been believed that a transmutation had taken place in Cytherea's idiosyncrasy, that her moral nature had fled.

The wedding-party returned to the house. As soon as he could find an opportunity, Owen took his sister aside to speak privately with her on what had happened. The expression of her face was hard, wild, and unreal—an expression he had never seen there before, and it disturbed him. He spoke to her severely and sadly.

'Cytherea,' he said, 'I know the cause of this emotion of yours. But remember this, there was no excuse for it. You should have been woman enough to control yourself. Remember whose wife you are, and don't think anything more of a mean-spirited fellow like Springrove; he had no business to come there as he did. You are altogether wrong, Cytherea, and I am vexed with you more than I can say—

382

very vexed.'

'Say ashamed of me at once,' she bitterly answered.

'I am ashamed of you,' he retorted angrily; 'the mood has not left you yet, then?'

'Owen,' she said, and paused. Her lip trembled; her eye told of sensations too deep for tears. 'No, Owen, it has not left me; and I will be honest. I own now to you, without any disguise of words, what last night I did not own to myself, because I hardly knew of it. I love Edward Springrove with all my strength, and heart, and soul. You call me a wanton for it, don't you? I don't care; I have gone beyond caring for anything!' She looked stonily into his face and made the speech calmly.

'Well, poor Cytherea, don't talk like that!' he said, alarmed at her manner.

'I thought that I did not love him at all,' she went on hysterically. 'A year and a half had passed since we met. I could go by the gate of his garden without thinking of him—look at his seat in church and not care. But I saw him this morning—dying because he loves me so— I know it is that! Can I help loving him too? No, I cannot, and I will love him, and I don't care! We have been separated somehow by some contrivance—I know we have. O, if I could only die!'

He held her in his arms. 'Many a woman has gone to ruin herself,' he said, 'and brought those who love her into disgrace, by acting upon such impulses as possess you now. I have a reputation to lose as well as you. It seems that do what I will by way of remedying the stains which fell upon us, it is all doomed to be undone again.' His voice grew husky as he made the reply.

The right and only effective chord had been touched. Since she had seen Edward, she had thought only of herself and him. Owen—her name—position—future—had been as if they did not exist.

'I won't give way and become a disgrace to you, at any rate,' she said.

'Besides, your duty to society, and those about you, requires that you should live with (at any rate) all the appearance of a good wife, and try to love your husband.'

'Yes—my duty to society,' she murmured. 'But ah, Owen, it is difficult to adjust our outer and inner life with perfect honesty to all! Though it may be right to care more for the benefit of the many than for the indulgence of your own single self, when you consider that the many, and duty to them, only exist to you through your own existence, what can be said? What do our own acquaintances care about us? Not much. I think of mine. Mine will now (do they learn all the wicked frailty of my heart in this affair) look at me, smile sickly, and condemn me. And perhaps, far in time to come, when I am dead and gone, some other's accent, or some other's song, or thought, like an old one of mine, will carry them back to what I used to say, and hurt their hearts a little that they blamed me so soon. And they will pause just for an instant, and give a sigh to me, and think, "Poor girl!" believing they do great justice to my memory by this. But they will never, never realize that it was my single opportunity of existence, as well as of doing my duty, which they are regarding; they will not feel that what to them is but a thought, easily held in those two words of pity, "Poor girl!" was a whole life to me; as full of hours, minutes, and peculiar minutes, of hopes and dreads, smiles, whisperings, tears, as theirs: that it was my world, what is to them their world, and they in that life of mine, however much I cared for them, only as the thought I seem to them to be. Nobody can enter into another's nature truly, that's what is so grievous.'

'Well, it cannot be helped,' said Owen.

'But we must not stay here,' she continued, starting up and going. 'We shall be missed. I'll do my best, Owen—I will, indeed.'

It had been decided that on account of the wretched state of the roads, the newly-married pair should not drive to the station till the latest hour in the afternoon at which they could get a train to take them to Southampton (their destination that night) by a reasonable time in the evening. They intended the next morning to cross to Havre, and thence to

Paris—a place Cytherea had never visited—for their wedding tour.

The afternoon drew on. The packing was done. Cytherea was so restless that she could stay still nowhere. Miss Aldclyffe, who, though she took little part in the day's proceedings, was, as it were, instinctively conscious of all their movements, put down her charge's agitation for once as the natural result of the novel event, and Manston himself was as indulgent as could be wished.

At length Cytherea wandered alone into the conservatory. When in it, she thought she would run across to the hot-house in the outer garden, having in her heart a whimsical desire that she should also like to take a last look at the familiar flowers and luxuriant leaves collected there. She pulled on a pair of overshoes, and thither she went. Not a soul was in or around the place. The gardener was making merry on Manston's and her account.

The happiness that a generous spirit derives from the belief that it exists in others is often greater than the primary happiness itself. The gardener thought 'How happy they are!' and the thought made him happier than they.

Coming out of the forcing-house again, she was on the point of returning indoors, when a feeling that these moments of solitude would be her last of freedom induced her to prolong them a little, and she stood still, unheeding the wintry aspect of the curly-leaved plants, the straw-covered beds, and the bare fruit-trees around her. The garden, no part of which was visible from the house, sloped down to a narrow river at the foot, dividing it from the meadows without.

A man was lingering along the public path on the other side of the river; she fancied she knew the form. Her resolutions, taken in the presence of Owen, did not fail her now. She hoped and prayed that it might not be one who had stolen her heart away, and still kept it. Why should he have reappeared at all, when he had declared that he went out of her sight for ever?

She hastily hid herself, in the lowest corner of the garden close to the river. A large dead tree, thickly robed in ivy, had been considerably depressed by its icy load of the morning, and hung low over the stream, which here ran slow and deep. The tree screened her from the eyes of any passer on the other side.

She waited timidly, and her timidity increased. She would not allow herself to see him—she would hear him pass, and then look to see if it had been Edward.

But, before she heard anything, she became aware of an object reflected in the water from under the tree which hung over the river in such a way that, though hiding the actual path, and objects upon it, it permitted their reflected images to pass beneath its boughs. The reflected form was that of the man she had seen further off, but being inverted, she could not definitely characterize him.

He was looking at the upper windows of the House—at hers—was it Edward, indeed? If so, he was probably thinking he would like to say one parting word. He came closer, gazed into the stream, and walked very slowly. She was almost certain that it was Edward. She kept more safely hidden. Conscience told her that she ought not to see him. But she suddenly asked herself a question: 'Can it be possible that he sees my reflected image, as I see his? Of course he does!'

He was looking at her in the water.

She could not help herself now. She stepped forward just as he emerged from the other side of the tree and appeared erect before her. It was Edward Springrove—till the inverted vision met his eye, dreaming no more of seeing his Cytherea there than of seeing the dead themselves.

'Cytherea!'

'Mr. Springrove,' she returned, in a low voice, across the stream.

He was the first to speak again.

'Since we have met, I want to tell you something, before we become quite as strangers to each other.'

'No—not now—I did not mean to speak—it is not right, Edward.' She spoke hurriedly and turned away from him, beating the air with her hand.

'Not one common word of explanation?' he implored. 'Don't think I am bad enough to try to lead you astray. Well, go—it is better.'

Their eyes met again. She was nearly choked. O, how she longed—and dreaded—to hear his explanation!

'What is it?' she said desperately.

'It is that I did not come to the church this morning in order to distress you: I did not, Cytherea. It was to try to speak to you before you were—married.'

He stepped closer, and went on, 'You know what has taken place? Surely you do?—my cousin is married, and I am free.'

'Married—and not to you?' Cytherea faltered, in a weak whisper.

'Yes, she was married yesterday! A rich man had appeared, and she jilted me. She said she never would have jilted a stranger, but that by jilting me, she only exercised the right everybody has of snubbing their own relations. But that's nothing now. I came to you to ask once more if . . . But I was too late.'

'But, Edward, what's that, what's that!' she cried, in an agony of reproach. 'Why did you leave me to return to her? Why did you write me that cruel, cruel letter that nearly killed me!'

'Cytherea! Why, you had grown to love—like—Mr. Manston, and how could you be anything to me—or care for me? Surely I acted naturally?'

'O no—never! I loved you—only you—not him—always you!—till lately . . . I try to love him now.'

'But that can't be correct! Miss Aldclyffe told me that you wanted to hear no more of me—proved it to me!' said Edward.

'Never! she couldn't.'

'She did, Cytherea. And she sent me a letter—a love-letter, you wrote to Mr. Manston.'

'A love-letter I wrote?'

'Yes, a love-letter—you could not meet him just then, you said you were sorry, but the emotion you had felt with him made you forgetful of realities.'

The strife of thought in the unhappy girl who listened to this distortion of her meaning could find no vent in words. And then there followed the slow revelation in return, bringing with it all the misery of an explanation which comes too late. The question whether Miss Aldclyffe were schemer or dupe was almost passed over by Cytherea, under the immediate oppressiveness of her despair in the sense that her position was irretrievable.

Not so Springrove. He saw through all the cunning half-misrepresentations—worse than downright lies—which had just been sufficient to turn the scale both with him and with her; and from the bottom of his soul he cursed the woman and man who had brought all this agony upon him and his Love. But he could not add more misery to the future of the poor child by revealing too much. The whole scheme she should never know.

'I was indifferent to my own future,' Edward said, 'and was urged to promise adherence to my engagement with my cousin Adelaide by Miss Aldclyffe: now you are married I cannot tell you how, but it was on account of my father. Being forbidden to think of you, what did I care about anything? My new thought that you still loved me was first raised by what my father said in the letter announcing my cousin's marriage. He said that although you were to be married on Old Christmas Day— that is to-morrow—he had noticed your appearance with pity: he thought you loved me still. It was enough for me—I came down by the earliest morning train, thinking I could see you some time to-day, the day, as I thought, before your marriage, hoping, but hardly daring to hope, that you might be induced to marry me. I hurried from the station; when I reached the village I saw idlers about the church, and the private gate leading to the House open. I ran into the church by the small door and saw you come out of the vestry; I was too late. I have now told you. I was compelled to tell you. O, my lost darling, now I shall live content—or die content!'

'I am to blame, Edward, I am,' she said mournfully; 'I was taught to dread pauperism; my nights were made sleepless; there was continually reiterated in my ears till I believed it—

    'The world and its ways have a certain
        worth,
    And to press a point where these oppose
    Were a simple policy.

'But I will say nothing about who influenced—who persuaded. The act is mine, after all. Edward, I married to escape dependence for my bread upon the whim of Miss Aldclyffe, or others like her. It was clearly represented to me that dependence is bearable if we have another place which we can call home; but to be a dependent and to have no other spot for the heart to anchor upon—O, it is mournful and harassing! . . . But that without which all persuasion would have been as air, was added by my miserable conviction that you were false; that did it, that turned me! You were to be considered as nobody to me, and Mr. Manston was invariably kind. Well, the deed is done—I must abide by it. I shall never let him know that I do not love him—never. If things had only remained as they seemed to be, if you had really forgotten me and married another woman, I could have borne it better. I wish I did not know the truth as I know it now! But our life, what is it? Let us be brave, Edward, and live out our few remaining years with dignity. They will not be long. O, I hope they will not be long! . . . Now, good-bye, good-bye!'

'I wish I could be near and touch you once, just once,' said Springrove, in a voice which he vainly endeavoured to keep firm and clear.

They looked at the river, then into it; a shoal of minnows was floating over the sandy bottom, like the black dashes on miniver; though narrow, the stream was deep, and there was no bridge.

'Cytherea, reach out your hand that I may just touch it with mine.'

She stepped to the brink and stretched out her hand and fingers towards his, but not into them. The river was too wide.

'Never mind,' said Cytherea, her voice broken by agitation, 'I must be going. God bless and keep you, my Edward! God bless you!'

'I must touch you, I must press your hand,' he said.

They came near—nearer—nearer still— their fingers met. There was a long firm clasp, so close and still that each hand could feel the other's pulse throbbing beside its own.

'My Cytherea! my stolen pet lamb!'

She glanced a mute farewell from her large perturbed eyes, turned, and ran up the garden without looking back. All was over between them. The river flowed on as quietly and obtusely as ever, and the minnows gathered again in their favourite spot as if they had never been disturbed.

Nobody indoors guessed from her countenance and bearing that her heart was near to breaking with the intensity of the misery which gnawed there. At these times a woman does not faint, or weep, or scream, as she will in the moment of sudden shocks. When lanced by a mental agony of such refined and special torture that it is indescribable by men's words, she moves among her acquaintances much as before, and contrives so to cast her actions in the old moulds that she is only considered to be rather duller than usual.

5. HALF-PAST TWO TO FIVE O'CLOCK P.M.

Owen accompanied the newly-married couple to the railway-station, and in his anxiety to see the last of his sister, left the brougham and stood upon his crutches whilst the train was starting.

When the husband and wife were about to enter the railway-carriage they saw one of the porters looking frequently and furtively at them. He was pale, and apparently very ill.

'Look at that poor sick man,' said Cytherea compassionately, 'surely he ought not to be here.'

'He's been very queer to-day, madam, very queer,' another porter answered. 'He do hardly hear when he's spoken to, and d' seem giddy, or as if something was on his mind. He's been like it for this month past, but nothing so bad as he is to-day.'

'Poor thing.'

She could not resist an innate desire to do some just thing on this most deceitful and wretched day of her life. Going up to him she gave him money, and told him to send to the old manor-house for wine or whatever he wanted.

The train moved off as the trembling man was murmuring his incoherent thanks. Owen waved his hand; Cytherea smiled back to him as if it were unknown to her that she wept all the while.

Owen was driven back to the Old House. But he could not rest in the lonely place. His conscience began to reproach him for having forced on the marriage of his sister with a little too much peremptoriness. Taking up his crutches he went out of doors and wandered about the muddy roads with no object in view save that of getting rid of time.

The clouds which had hung so low and densely during the day cleared from the west just now as the sun was setting, calling forth a weakly twitter from a few small birds. Owen crawled down the path to the waterfall, and lingered thereabout till the solitude of the place oppressed him, when he turned back and into the road to the village. He was sad; he said to himself—

'If there is ever any meaning in those heavy feelings which are called presentiments—and I don't believe there is—there will be in mine to-day . . . Poor little Cytherea!'

At that moment the last low rays of the sun touched the head and shoulders of a man who was approaching, and showed him up to Owen's view. It was old Mr. Springrove. They had grown familiar with each other by reason of Owen's visits to Knapwater during the past year. The farmer inquired how Owen's foot was progressing, and was glad to see him so nimble again.

'How is your son?' said Owen mechanically.

'He is at home, sitting by the fire,' said the farmer, in a sad voice. 'This morning he slipped indoors from God knows where, and there he sits and mopes, and thinks, and thinks, and presses his head so hard, that I can't help feeling for him.'

'Is he married?' said Owen. Cytherea had feared to tell him of the interview in the garden.

'No. I can't quite understand how the matter rests . . . Ah! Edward, too, who started with such promise; that he should now have become such a careless fellow—not a month in one place. There, Mr. Graye, I know what it is mainly owing to. If it hadn't been for that heart affair, he might have done—but the less said about him the better. I don't know what we should have done if Miss Aldclyffe had insisted

396

upon the conditions of the leases. Your brother-in-law, the steward, had a hand in making it light for us, I know, and I heartily thank him for it.' He ceased speaking, and looked round at the sky.

'Have you heard o' what's happened?' he said suddenly; 'I was just coming out to learn about it.'

'I haven't heard of anything.'

'It is something very serious, though I don't know what. All I know is what I heard a man call out bynow—that it very much concerns somebody who lives in the parish.'

It seems singular enough, even to minds who have no dim beliefs in adumbration and presentiment, that at that moment not the shadow of a thought crossed Owen's mind that the somebody whom the matter concerned might be himself, or any belonging to him. The event about to transpire was as portentous to the woman whose welfare was more dear to him than his own, as any, short of death itself, could possibly be; and ever afterwards, when he considered the effect of the knowledge the next half-hour conveyed to his brain, even his practical good sense could not refrain from wonder that he should have walked toward the village after hearing those words of the farmer, in so leisurely and unconcerned a way. 'How unutterably mean must my intelligence have appeared to the eye of a foreseeing God,' he frequently said in after-time. 'Columbus on the eve of his discovery of a world was not so contemptibly unaware.'

After a few additional words of commonplace the farmer left him, and, as has been said, Owen proceeded slowly and indifferently towards the village.

The labouring men had just left work, and passed the park gate, which opened into the street as Owen came down towards it. They went along in a drift, earnestly talking, and were finally about to turn in at their respective doorways. But upon seeing him they looked significantly at one another, and paused. He came into the road, on that side of the village-green which was opposite the row of cottages, and turned round to the right. When Owen turned, all eyes turned; one or two men went hurriedly indoors, and afterwards appeared at the doorstep with their wives, who also contemplated him, talking as they looked. They seemed uncertain how to act in some matter.

'If they want me, surely they will call me,' he thought, wondering more and more. He could no longer doubt that he was connected with the subject of their discourse.

The first who approached him was a boy.

'What has occurred?' said Owen.

'O, a man ha' got crazy-religious, and sent for the pa'son.'

'Is that all?'

'Yes, sir. He wished he was dead, he said,

and he's almost out of his mind wi' wishen it so much. That was before Mr. Raunham came.'

'Who is he?' said Owen.

'Joseph Chinney, one of the railway-porters; he used to be night-porter.'

'Ah—the man who was ill this afternoon; by the way, he was told to come to the Old House for something, but he hasn't been. But has anything else happened—anything that concerns the wedding to-day?'

'No, sir.'

Concluding that the connection which had seemed to be traced between himself and the event must in some way have arisen from Cytherea's friendliness towards the man, Owen turned about and went homewards in a much quieter frame of mind—yet scarcely satisfied with the solution. The route he had chosen led through the dairy-yard, and he opened the gate.

Five minutes before this point of time, Edward Springrove was looking over one of his father's fields at an outlying hamlet of three or four cottages some mile and a half distant. A turnpike-gate was close by the gate of the field.

The carrier to Casterbridge came up as Edward stepped into the road, and jumped down from the van to pay toll. He recognized Springrove. 'This is a pretty set-to in your place, sir,' he said. 'You don't know about it, I suppose?'

'What?' said Springrove.

The carrier paid his dues, came up to Edward, and spoke ten words in a confidential whisper: then sprang upon the shafts of his vehicle, gave a clinching nod of significance to Springrove, and rattled away.

Edward turned pale with the intelligence. His first thought was, 'Bring her home!'

The next—did Owen Graye know what had been discovered? He probably did by that time, but no risks of probability must be run by a woman he loved dearer than all the world besides. He would at any rate make perfectly sure that her brother was in possession of the knowledge, by telling it him with his own lips.

Off he ran in the direction of the old manor-house.

The path was across arable land, and was ploughed up with the rest of the field every autumn, after which it was trodden out afresh. The thaw had so loosened the soft earth, that lumps of stiff mud were lifted by his feet at every leap he took, and flung against him by his rapid motion, as it were doggedly impeding him, and increasing tenfold the customary effort of running.

But he ran on—uphill, and downhill, the same pace alike—like the shadow of a cloud. His nearest direction, too, like Owen's, was through the dairy-barton, and as Owen entered it he saw the figure of Edward rapidly descending the opposite hill, at a distance of two or three hundred yards. Owen advanced amid the cows.

The dairyman, who had hitherto been talking loudly on some absorbing subject to the maids and men milking around him, turned his face towards the head of the cow when Owen passed, and ceased speaking.

Owen approached him and said—

'A singular thing has happened, I hear. The man is not insane, I suppose?'

'Not he—he's sensible enough,' said the dairyman, and paused. He was a man noisy with his associates—stolid and taciturn with strangers.

'Is it true that he is Chinney, the railway-porter?'

'That's the man, sir.' The maids and men sitting under the cows were all attentively listening to this discourse, milking irregularly, and softly directing the jets against the sides of the pail.

Owen could contain himself no longer, much as his mind dreaded anything of the nature of ridicule. 'The people all seem to look at me, as if something seriously concerned me; is it this stupid matter, or what is it?'

'Surely, sir, you know better than anybody else if such a strange thing concerns you.'

'What strange thing?'

'Don't you know! His confessing to Parson Raunham.'

'What did he confess? Tell me.'

'If you really ha'n't heard, 'tis this. He was as

usual on duty at the station on the night of the fire last year, otherwise he wouldn't ha' known it.'

'Known what? For God's sake tell, man!'

But at this instant the two opposite gates of the dairy-yard, one on the east, the other on the west side, slammed almost simultaneously.

The rector from one, Springrove from the other, came striding across the barton.

Edward was nearest, and spoke first. He said in a low voice: 'Your sister is not legally married! His first wife is still living! How it comes out I don't know!'

'O, here you are at last, Mr. Graye, thank Heaven!' said the rector breathlessly. 'I have been to the Old House, and then to Miss Aldclyffe's looking for you—something very extraordinary.' He beckoned to Owen, afterwards included Springrove in his glance, and the three stepped aside together.

'A porter at the station. He was a curious nervous man. He had been in a strange state all day, but he wouldn't go home. Your sister was kind to him, it seems, this afternoon. When she and her husband had gone, he went on with his work, shifting luggage-vans. Well, he got in the way, as if he were quite lost to what was going on, and they sent him home at last. Then he wished to see me. I went directly. There was something on his mind, he said, and told it. About the time when the fire of last November twelvemonth was got under, whilst

402

he was by himself in the porter's room, almost asleep, somebody came to the station and tried to open the door. He went out and found the person to be the lady he had accompanied to Carriford earlier in the evening, Mrs. Manston. She asked, when would be another train to London? The first the next morning, he told her, was at a quarter-past six o'clock from Budmouth, but that it was express, and didn't stop at Carriford Road—it didn't stop till it got to Anglebury. "How far is it to Anglebury?" she said. He told her, and she thanked him, and went away up the line. In a short time she ran back and took out her purse. "Don't on any account say a word in the village or anywhere that I have been here, or a single breath about me—I'm ashamed ever to have come." He promised; she took out two sovereigns. "Swear it on the Testament in the waiting-room," she said, "and I'll pay you these." He got the book, took an oath upon it, received the money, and she left him. He was off duty at half-past five. He has kept silence all through the intervening time till now, but lately the knowledge he possessed weighed heavily upon his conscience and weak mind. Yet the nearer came the wedding-day, the more he feared to tell. The actual marriage filled him with remorse. He says your sister's kindness afterwards was like a knife going through his heart. He thought he had ruined her.'

'But whatever can be done? Why didn't he speak sooner?' cried Owen.

'He actually called at my house twice yesterday,' the rector continued, 'resolved, it seems, to unburden his mind. I was out both times—he left no message, and, they say, he looked relieved that his object was defeated. Then he says he resolved to come to you at the Old House last night—started, reached the door, and dreaded to knock—and then went home again.'

'Here will be a tale for the newsmongers of the county,' said Owen bitterly. 'The idea of his not opening his mouth sooner—the criminality of the thing!'

'Ah, that's the inconsistency of a weak nature. But now that it is put to us in this way, how much more probable it seems that she should have escaped than have been burnt—'

'You will, of course, go straight to Mr. Manston, and ask him what it all means?' Edward interrupted.

'Of course I shall! Manston has no right to carry off my sister unless he's her husband,' said Owen. 'I shall go and separate them.'

'Certainly you will,' said the rector.

'Where's the man?'

'In his cottage.'

' 'Tis no use going to him, either. I must go off at once and overtake them—lay the case before Manston, and ask him for additional and certain proofs of his first wife's death. An up-train passes soon, I think.'

'Where have they gone?' said Edward.

'To Paris—as far as Southampton this afternoon, to proceed to-morrow morning.'

'Where in Southampton?'

'I really don't know—some hotel. I only have their Paris address. But I shall find them by making a few inquiries.'

The rector had in the meantime been taking out his pocket-book, and now opened it at the first page, whereon it was his custom every month to gum a small railway time-table—cut from the local newspaper.

'The afternoon express is just gone,' he said, holding open the page, 'and the next train to Southampton passes at ten minutes to six o'clock. Now it wants—let me see—five-and-forty minutes to that time. Mr. Graye, my advice is that you come with me to the porter's cottage, where I will shortly write out the substance of what he has said, and get him to sign it. You will then have far better grounds for interfering between Mr. and Mrs. Manston than if you went to them with a mere hearsay story.'

The suggestion seemed a good one. 'Yes, there will be time before the train starts,' said Owen.

Edward had been musing restlessly.

'Let me go to Southampton in your place, on account of your lameness?' he said suddenly to Graye.

'I am much obliged to you, but I think I can scarcely accept the offer,' returned Owen coldly. 'Mr. Manston is an honourable man, and I had much better see him myself.'

'There is no doubt,' said Mr. Raunham, 'that the death of his wife was fully believed in by himself.'

'None whatever,' said Owen; 'and the news must be broken to him, and the question of other proofs asked, in a friendly way. It would not do for Mr. Springrove to appear in the case at all.' He still spoke rather coldly; the recollection of the attachment between his sister and Edward was not a pleasant one to him.

'You will never find them,' said Edward. 'You have never been to Southampton, and I know every house there.'

'That makes little difference,' said the rector; 'he will have a cab. Certainly Mr. Graye is the proper man to go on the errand.'

'Stay; I'll telegraph to ask them to meet me when I arrive at the terminus,' said Owen; 'that is, if their train has not already arrived.'

Mr. Raunham pulled out his pocket-book again. 'The two-thirty train reached Southampton a quarter of an hour ago,' he said.

It was too late to catch them at the station. Nevertheless, the rector suggested that it would be worth while to direct a message to 'all the respectable hotels in Southampton,' on

406

the chance of its finding them, and thus saving a deal of personal labour to Owen in searching about the place.

'I'll go and telegraph, whilst you return to the man,' said Edward—an offer which was accepted. Graye and the rector then turned off in the direction of the porter's cottage.

Edward, to despatch the message at once, hurriedly followed the road towards the station, still restlessly thinking. All Owen's proceedings were based on the assumption, natural under the circumstances, of Manston's good faith, and that he would readily acquiesce in any arrangement which should clear up the mystery. 'But,' thought Edward, 'suppose— and Heaven forgive me, I cannot help supposing it—that Manston is not that honourable man, what will a young and inexperienced fellow like Owen do? Will he not be hoodwinked by some specious story or another, framed to last till Manston gets tired of poor Cytherea? And then the disclosure of the truth will ruin and blacken both their futures irremediably.'

However, he proceeded to execute his commission. This he put in the form of a simple request from Owen to Manston, that Manston would come to the Southampton platform, and wait for Owen's arrival, as he valued his reputation. The message was directed as the rector had suggested, Edward guaranteeing to the clerk who sent it off that every expense connected with the search would be paid.

No sooner had the telegram been despatched than his heart sank within him at the want of foresight shown in sending it. Had Manston, all the time, a knowledge that his first wife lived, the telegram would be a forewarning which might enable him to defeat Owen still more signally.

Whilst the machine was still giving off its multitudinous series of raps, Edward heard a powerful rush under the shed outside, followed by a long sonorous creak. It was a train of some sort, stealing softly into the station, and it was an up-train. There was the ring of a bell. It was certainly a passenger train.

Yet the booking-office window was closed.

'Ho, ho, John, seventeen minutes after time and only three stations up the line. The incline again?' The voice was the stationmaster's, and the reply seemed to come from the guard.

'Yes, the other side of the cutting. The thaw has made it all in a perfect cloud of fog, and the rails are as slippery as glass. We had to bring them through the cutting at twice.'

'Anybody else for the four-forty-five express?' the voice continued. The few passengers, having crossed over to the other side long before this time, had taken their places at once.

A conviction suddenly broke in upon Edward's mind; then a wish overwhelmed him.

The conviction—as startling as it was sudden—was that Manston was a villain, who at some earlier time had discovered that his wife lived, and had bribed her to keep out of sight, that he might possess Cytherea. The wish was—to proceed at once by this very train that was starting, find Manston before he would expect from the words of the telegram (if he got it) that anybody from Carriford could be with him—charge him boldly with the crime, and trust to his consequent confusion (if he were guilty) for a solution of the extraordinary riddle, and the release of Cytherea!

The ticket-office had been locked up at the expiration of the time at which the train was due. Rushing out as the guard blew his whistle, Edward opened the door of a carriage and leapt in. The train moved along, and he was soon out of sight.

Springrove had long since passed that peculiar line which lies across the course of falling in love—if, indeed, it may not be called the initial itself of the complete passion—a longing to cherish; when the woman is shifted in a man's mind from the region of mere admiration to the region of warm fellowship. At this assumption of her nature, she changes to him in tone, hue, and expression. All about the loved one that said 'She' before, says 'We' now. Eyes that were to be subdued become eyes to be feared for: a brain that was to be probed by cynicism becomes a brain that is to be tenderly assisted; feet that were to be tested in the dance become feet that are not to be distressed; the once-criticized accent, manner, and dress, become the clients of a special pleader.

6. FIVE TO EIGHT O'CLOCK P.M.

Now that he was fairly on the track, and had begun to cool down, Edward remembered that he had nothing to show—no legal authority whatever to question Manston or interfere between him and Cytherea as husband and wife. He now saw the wisdom of the rector in obtaining a signed confession from the porter. The document would not be a death-bed confession—perhaps not worth anything legally—but it would be held by Owen; and he alone, as Cytherea's natural guardian, could separate them on the mere ground of an unproved probability, or what might perhaps be called the hallucination of an idiot. Edward himself, however, was as firmly convinced as the rector had been of the truth of the man's story, and paced backward and forward the solitary compartment as the train wound through the dark heathery plains, the mazy woods, and moaning coppices, as resolved as ever to pounce on Manston, and charge him with the crime during the critical interval

410

between the reception of the telegram and the hour at which Owen's train would arrive—trusting to circumstances for what he should say and do afterwards, but making up his mind to be a ready second to Owen in any emergency that might arise.

At thirty-three minutes past seven he stood on the platform of the station at Southampton—a clear hour before the train containing Owen could possibly arrive.

Making a few inquiries here, but too impatient to pursue his investigation carefully and inductively, he went into the town.

At the expiration of another half-hour he had visited seven hotels and inns, large and small, asking the same questions at each, and always receiving the same reply—nobody of that name, or answering to that description, had been there. A boy from the telegraph-office had called, asking for the same persons, if they recollected rightly.

He reflected awhile, struck again by a painful thought that they might possibly have decided to cross the Channel by the night-boat. Then he hastened off to another quarter of the town to pursue his inquiries among hotels of the more old-fashioned and quiet class. His stained and weary appearance obtained for him but a modicum of civility, wherever he went, which made his task yet more difficult. He called at three several houses in this neighbourhood, with the same result as before.

He entered the door of the fourth house whilst the clock of the nearest church was striking eight.

'Have a tall gentleman named Manston, and a young wife arrived here this evening?' he asked again, in words which had grown odd to his ears from very familiarity.

'A new-married couple, did you say?'

'They are, though I didn't say so.'

'They have taken a sitting-room and bedroom, number thirteen.'

'Are they indoors?'

'I don't know. Eliza!'

'Yes, m'm.'

'See if number thirteen is in—that gentleman and his wife.'

'Yes, m'm.'

'Has any telegram come for them?' said Edward, when the maid had gone on her errand.

'No—nothing that I know of.'

'Somebody did come and ask if a Mr. and Mrs. Masters, or some such name, were here this evening,' said another voice from the back of the bar-parlour.

'And did they get the message?'

'Of course they did not—they were not here—they didn't come till half-an-hour after that. The man who made inquiries left no message. I told them when they came that they, or a name something like theirs, had been asked for, but they didn't seem to understand why it should be, and so the matter dropped.'

The chambermaid came back. 'The gentleman is not in, but the lady is. Who shall I say?'

'Nobody,' said Edward. For it now became necessary to reflect upon his method of proceeding. His object in finding their whereabouts—apart from the wish to assist Owen—had been to see Manston, ask him flatly for an explanation, and confirm the request of the message in the presence of Cytherea—so as to prevent the possibility of the steward's palming off a story upon Cytherea, or eluding her brother when he came. But here were two important modifications of the expected condition of affairs. The telegram had not been received, and Cytherea was in the house alone.

He hesitated as to the propriety of intruding upon her in Manston's absence. Besides, the women at the bottom of the stairs would see him—his intrusion would seem odd—and Manston might return at any moment. He certainly might call, and wait for Manston with the accusation upon his tongue, as he had intended. But it was a doubtful course. That idea had been based upon the assumption that Cytherea was not married. If the first wife were really dead after all—and he felt sick at the thought—Cytherea as the steward's wife might in after-years—perhaps, at once—be subjected

413

to indignity and cruelty on account of an old lover's interference now.

Yes, perhaps the announcement would come most properly and safely for her from her brother Owen, the time of whose arrival had almost expired.

But, on turning round, he saw that the staircase and passage were quite deserted. He and his errand had as completely died from the minds of the attendants as if they had never been. There was absolutely nothing between him and Cytherea's presence. Reason was powerless now; he must see her—right or wrong, fair or unfair to Manston—offensive to her brother or no. His lips must be the first to tell the alarming story to her. Who loved her as he! He went back lightly through the hall, up the stairs, two at a time, and followed the corridor till he came to the door numbered thirteen.

He knocked softly: nobody answered.

There was no time to lose if he would speak to Cytherea before Manston came. He turned the handle of the door and looked in. The lamp on the table burned low, and showed writing materials open beside it; the chief light came from the fire, the direct rays of which were obscured by a sweet familiar outline of head and shoulders—still as precious to him as ever.

7. A QUARTER-PAST EIGHT O'CLOCK P.M.

There is an attitude—approximatively called pensive—in which the soul of a human being, and especially of a woman, dominates outwardly and expresses its presence so strongly, that the intangible essence seems more apparent than the body itself. This was Cytherea's expression now. What old days and sunny eves at Budmouth Bay was she picturing? Her reverie had caused her not to notice his knock.

'Cytherea!' he said softly.

She let drop her hand, and turned her head, evidently thinking that her visitor could be no other than Manston, yet puzzled at the voice.

There was no preface on Springrove's tongue; he forgot his position—hers—that he had come to ask quietly if Manston had other proofs of being a widower—everything—and jumped to a conclusion.

'You are not his wife, Cytherea—come away, he has a wife living!' he cried in an agitated whisper. 'Owen will be here directly.'

She started up, recognized the tidings first, the bearer of them afterwards. 'Not his wife? O, what is it—what—who is living?' She awoke by degrees. 'What must I do? Edward, it is you! Why did you come? Where is Owen?'

'What has Manston shown you in proof of the death of his other wife? Tell me quick.'

'Nothing—we have never spoken of the subject. Where is my brother Owen? I want him, I want him!'

'He is coming by-and-by. Come to the station to meet him—do,' implored Springrove. 'If Mr. Manston comes, he will keep you from me: I am nobody,' he added bitterly, feeling the reproach her words had faintly shadowed forth.

'Mr. Manston is only gone out to post a letter he has just written,' she said, and without being distinctly cognizant of the action, she wildly looked for her bonnet and cloak, and began putting them on, but in the act of fastening them uttered a spasmodic cry.

'No, I'll not go out with you,' she said, flinging the articles down again. Running to the door she flitted along the passage, and downstairs.

'Give me a private room—quite private,' she said breathlessly to some one below.

'Number twelve is a single room, madam, and unoccupied,' said some tongue in astonishment.

Without waiting for any person to show her into it, Cytherea hurried upstairs again, brushed through the corridor, entered the room specified, and closed the door. Edward heard her sob out—

'Nobody but Owen shall speak to me—nobody!'

'He will be here directly,' said Springrove,

close against the panel, and then went towards the stairs. He had seen her; it was enough.

He descended, stepped into the street, and hastened to meet Owen at the railway-station.

As for the poor maiden who had received the news, she knew not what to think. She listened till the echo of Edward's footsteps had died away, then bowed her face upon the bed. Her sudden impulse had been to escape from sight. Her weariness after the unwonted strain, mental and bodily, which had been put upon her by the scenes she had passed through during the long day, rendered her much more timid and shaken by her position than she would naturally have been. She thought and thought of that single fact which had been told her—that the first Mrs. Manston was still living—till her brain seemed ready to burst its confinement with excess of throbbing. It was only natural that she should, by degrees, be unable to separate the discovery, which was matter of fact, from the suspicion of treachery on her husband's part, which was only matter of inference. And thus there arose in her a personal fear of him.

'Suppose he should come in now and seize me!' This at first mere frenzied supposition grew by degrees to a definite horror of his presence, and especially of his intense gaze. Thus she raised herself to a heat of excitement, which was none the less real for being vented in no cry of any kind. No; she could not meet

Manston's eye alone, she would only see him in her brother's company.

Almost delirious with this idea, she ran and locked the door to prevent all possibility of her intentions being nullified, or a look or word being flung at her by anybody whilst she knew not what she was.

8. HALF-PAST EIGHT O'CLOCK P.M.

Then Cytherea felt her way amid the darkness of the room till she came to the head of the bed, where she searched for the bell-rope and gave it a pull. Her summons was speedily answered by the landlady herself, whose curiosity to know the meaning of these strange proceedings knew no bounds. The landlady attempted to turn the handle of the door. Cytherea kept the door locked. 'Please tell Mr. Manston when he comes that I am ill,' she said from the inside, 'and that I cannot see him.'

'Certainly I will, madam,' said the landlady. 'Won't you have a fire?'

'No, thank you.'

'Nor a light?'

'I don't want one, thank you.'

'Nor anything?'

'Nothing.'

The landlady withdrew, thinking her visitor half insane.

Manston came in about five minutes later, and went at once up to the sitting-room, fully expecting to find his wife there. He looked round, rang, and was told the words Cytherea had said, that she was too ill to be seen.

'She is in number twelve room,' added the maid.

Manston was alarmed, and knocked at the door. 'Cytherea!'

'I am unwell, I cannot see you,' she said.

'Are you seriously ill, dearest? Surely not.'

'No, not seriously.'

'Let me come in; I will get a doctor.'

'No, he can't see me either.'

'She won't open the door, sir, not to nobody at all!' said the chambermaid, with wonder-waiting eyes.

'Hold your tongue, and be off!' said Manston with a snap.

The maid vanished.

'Come, Cytherea, this is foolish—indeed it is—not opening the door . . . I cannot comprehend what can be the matter with you. Nor can a doctor either, unless he sees you.'

Her voice had trembled more and more at each answer she gave, but nothing could induce her to come out and confront him. Hating scenes, Manston went back to the sitting-room, greatly irritated and perplexed.

And there Cytherea from the adjoining room could hear him pacing up and down. She thought, 'Suppose he insists upon seeing me—

419

he probably may—and will burst open the door!' This notion increased, and she sank into a corner in a half-somnolent state, but with ears alive to the slightest sound. Reason could not overthrow the delirious fancy that outside her door stood Manston and all the people in the hotel, waiting to laugh her to scorn.

9. HALF-PAST EIGHT TO ELEVEN P.M.

In the meantime, Springrove was pacing up and down the arrival platform of the railway-station.

Half-past eight o'clock—the time at which Owen's train was due—had come, and passed, but no train appeared.

'When will the eight-thirty train be in?' he asked of a man who was sweeping the mud from the steps.

'She is not expected yet this hour.'

'How is that?'

'Christmas-time, you see, 'tis always so. People are running about to see their friends. The trains have been like it ever since Christmas Eve, and will be for another week yet.'

Edward again went on walking and waiting under the draughty roof. He found it utterly impossible to leave the spot. His mind was so intent upon the importance of meeting with Owen, and informing him of Cytherea's whereabouts, that he could not but fancy Owen might leave the station unobserved if he turned his back, and become lost to him in the streets of the town.

The hour expired. Ten o'clock struck. 'When will the train be in?' said Edward to the telegraph clerk.

'In five-and-thirty minutes. She's now at L——. They have extra passengers, and the rails are bad to-day.'

At last, at a quarter to eleven, the train came in.

The first to alight from it was Owen, looking pale and cold. He casually glanced round upon the nearly deserted platform, and was hurrying to the outlet, when his eyes fell upon Edward. At sight of his friend he was quite bewildered, and could not speak.

'Here I am, Mr. Graye,' said Edward cheerfully. 'I have seen Cytherea, and she has been waiting for you these two or three hours.'

Owen took Edward's hand, pressed it, and looked at him in silence. Such was the concentration of his mind, that not till many minutes after did he think of inquiring how Springrove had contrived to be there before him.

10. ELEVEN O'CLOCK P.M.

On their arrival at the door of the hotel, it was

421

arranged between Springrove and Graye that the latter only should enter, Edward waiting outside. Owen had remembered continually what his friend had frequently overlooked, that there was yet a possibility of his sister being Manston's wife, and the recollection taught him to avoid any rashness in his proceedings which might lead to bitterness hereafter.

Entering the room, he found Manston sitting in the chair which had been occupied by Cytherea on Edward's visit, three hours earlier. Before Owen had spoken, Manston arose, and stepping past him closed the door. His face appeared harassed—much more troubled than the slight circumstance which had as yet come to his knowledge seemed to account for.

Manston could form no reason for Owen's presence, but intuitively linked it with Cytherea's seclusion. 'Altogether this is most unseemly,' he said, 'whatever it may mean.'

'Don't think there is meant anything unfriendly by my coming here,' said Owen earnestly; 'but listen to this, and think if I could do otherwise than come.'

He took from his pocket the confession of Chinney the porter, as hastily written out by the vicar, and read it aloud. The aspects of Manston's face whilst he listened to the opening words were strange, dark, and mysterious enough to have justified suspicions that no deceit could be too complicated for the possessor of such impulses, had there not overridden them all, as the reading went on, a new and irrepressible expression—one unmistakably honest. It was that of unqualified amazement in the steward's mind at the news he heard. Owen looked up and saw it. The sight only confirmed him in the belief he had held throughout, in antagonism to Edward's suspicions.

There could no longer be a shadow of doubt that if the first Mrs. Manston lived, her husband was ignorant of the fact. What he could have feared by his ghastly look at first, and now have ceased to fear, it was quite futile to conjecture.

'Now I do not for a moment doubt your complete ignorance of the whole matter; you cannot suppose for an instant that I do,' said Owen when he had finished reading. 'But is it not best for both that Cytherea should come back with me till the matter is cleared up? In fact, under the circumstances, no other course is left open to me than to request it.'

Whatever Manston's original feelings had been, all in him now gave way to irritation, and irritation to rage. He paced up and down the room till he had mastered it; then said in ordinary tones—

'Certainly, I know no more than you and others know—it was a gratuitous unpleasantness in you to say you did not doubt me. Why should you, or anybody, have doubted me?'

'Well, where is my sister?' said Owen.

'Locked in the next room.'

His own answer reminded Manston that Cytherea must, by some inscrutable means, have had an inkling of the event.

Owen had gone to the door of Cytherea's room. 'Cytherea, darling—'tis Owen,' he said, outside the door. A rustling of clothes, soft footsteps, and a voice saying from the inside, 'Is it really you, Owen,—is it really?'

'It is.'

'O, will you take care of me?'

'Always.'

She unlocked the door, and retreated again. Manston came forward from the other room with a candle in his hand, as Owen pushed open the door.

Her frightened eyes were unnaturally large, and shone like stars in the darkness of the background, as the light fell upon them. She leapt up to Owen in one bound, her small taper fingers extended like the leaves of a lupine. Then she clasped her cold and trembling hands round his neck and shivered.

The sight of her again kindled all Manston's passions into activity. 'She shall not go with you,' he said firmly, and stepping a pace or two closer, 'unless you prove that she is not my wife; and you can't do it!'

'This is proof,' said Owen, holding up the paper.

'No proof at all,' said Manston hotly. ' 'Tis not a death-bed confession, and those are the only things of the kind held as good evidence.'

'Send for a lawyer,' Owen returned, 'and let him tell us the proper course to adopt.'

'Never mind the law—let me go with Owen!' cried Cytherea, still holding on to him. 'You will let me go with him, won't you, sir?' she said, turning appealingly to Manston.

'We'll have it all right and square,' said Manston, with more quietness. 'I have no objection to your brother sending for a lawyer, if he wants to.'

It was getting on for twelve o'clock, but the proprietor of the hotel had not yet gone to bed on account of the mystery on the first floor, which was an occurrence unusual in the quiet family lodging. Owen looked over the banisters, and saw him standing in the hall. It struck Graye that the wisest course would be to take the landlord to a certain extent into their confidence, appeal to his honour as a gentleman, and so on, in order to acquire the information he wanted, and also to prevent the episode of the evening from becoming a public piece of news. He called the landlord up to where they stood, and told him the main facts of the story.

The landlord was fortunately a quiet, prejudiced man, and a meditative smoker.

'I know the very man you want to see—the very man,' he said, looking at the general

425

features of the candle-flame. 'Sharp as a needle, and not over-rich. Timms will put you all straight in no time—trust Timms for that.'

'He's in bed by this time for certain,' said Owen.

'Never mind that—Timms knows me, I know him. He'll oblige me as a personal favour. Wait here a bit. Perhaps, too, he's up at some party or another—he's a nice, jovial fellow, sharp as a needle, too; mind you, sharp as a needle, too.'

He went downstairs, put on his overcoat, and left the house, the three persons most concerned entering the room, and standing motionless, awkward, and silent in the midst of it. Cytherea pictured to herself the long weary minutes she would have to stand there, whilst a sleepy man could be prepared for consultation, till the constraint between them seemed unendurable to her—she could never last out the time. Owen was annoyed that Manston had not quietly arranged with him at once; Manston at Owen's homeliness of idea in proposing to send for an attorney, as if he would be a touchstone of infallible proof.

Reflection was cut short by the approach of footsteps, and in a few moments the proprietor of the hotel entered, introducing his friend. 'Mr. Timms has not been in bed,' he said; 'he had just returned from dining with a few friends, so there's no trouble given. To save time I explained the matter as we came along.'

426

It occurred to Owen and Manston both that they might get a misty exposition of the law from Mr. Timms at that moment of concluding dinner with a few friends.

'As far as I can see,' said the lawyer, yawning, and turning his vision inward by main force, 'it is quite a matter for private arrangement between the parties, whoever the parties are—at least at present. I speak more as a father than as a lawyer, it is true, but, let the young lady stay with her father, or guardian, safe out of shame's way, until the mystery is sifted, whatever the mystery is. Should the evidence prove to be false, or trumped up by anybody to get her away from you, her husband, you may sue them for the damages accruing from the delay.'

'Yes, yes,' said Manston, who had completely recovered his self-possession and common-sense; 'let it all be settled by herself.'

Turning to Cytherea he whispered so softly that Owen did not hear the words—

'Do you wish to go back with your brother, dearest, and leave me here miserable, and lonely, or will you stay with me, your own husband.'

'I'll go back with Owen.'

'Very well.' He relinquished his coaxing tone, and went on sternly: 'And remember this, Cytherea, I am as innocent of deception in this thing as you are yourself. Do you believe me?'

'I do,' she said.

'I had no shadow of suspicion that my first wife lived. I don't think she does even now. Do you believe me?'

'I believe you,' she said.

'And now, good-evening,' he continued, opening the door and politely intimating to the three men standing by that there was no further necessity for their remaining in his room. 'In three days I shall claim her.'

The lawyer and the hotel-keeper retired first. Owen, gathering up as much of his sister's clothing as lay about the room, took her upon his arm, and followed them. Edward, to whom she owed everything, who had been left standing in the street like a dog without a home, was utterly forgotten. Owen paid the landlord and the lawyer for the trouble he had occasioned them, looked to the packing, and went to the door.

A fly, which somewhat unaccountably was seen lingering in front of the house, was called up, and Cytherea's luggage put upon it.

'Do you know of any hotel near the station that is open for night arrivals?' Owen inquired of the driver.

'A place has been bespoke for you, sir, at the White Unicorn—and the gentleman wished me to give you this.'

'Bespoken by Springrove, who ordered the fly, of course,' said Owen to himself. By the light of the street-lamp he read these lines, hurriedly traced in pencil:—

I have gone home by the mail-train. It is better for all parties that I should be out of the way. Tell Cytherea that I apologize for having caused her such unnecessary pain, as it seems I did—but it cannot be helped now.   E.S.

Owen handed his sister into the vehicle, and told the flyman to drive on.

'Poor Springrove—I think we have served him rather badly,' he said to Cytherea, repeating the words of the note to her.

A thrill of pleasure passed through her bosom as she listened to them. They were the genuine reproach of a lover to his mistress; the trifling coldness of her answer to him would have been noticed by no man who was only a friend. But, in entertaining that sweet thought, she had forgotten herself, and her position for the instant.

Was she still Manston's wife—that was the terrible supposition, and her future seemed still a possible misery to her. For, on account of the late jarring accident, a life with Manston which would otherwise have been only a sadness, must become a burden of unutterable sorrow.

Then she thought of the misrepresentation and scandal that would ensue if she were no wife. One cause for thankfulness accompanied the reflection; Edward knew the truth.

They soon reached the quiet old inn, which had been selected for them by the forethought of the man who loved her well. Here they installed themselves for the night, arranging to go to Budmouth by the first train the next day.

At this hour Edward Springrove was fast approaching his native county on the wheels of the night-mail.

XIV.

THE EVENTS OF FIVE WEEKS

1. FROM THE SIXTH TO THE THIRTEENTH OF JANUARY

Manston had evidently resolved to do nothing in a hurry.

This much was plain, that his earnest desire and intention was to raise in Cytherea's bosom no feelings of permanent aversion to him. The instant after the first burst of disappointment had escaped him in the hotel at Southampton, he had seen how far better it would be to lose her presence for a week than her respect for ever.

'She shall be mine; I will claim the young thing yet,' he insisted. And then he seemed to reason over methods for compassing that object, which, to all those who were in any

430

degree acquainted with the recent event, appeared the least likely of possible contingencies.

He returned to Knapwater late the next day, and was preparing to call on Miss Aldclyffe, when the conclusion forced itself upon him that nothing would be gained by such a step. No; every action of his should be done openly—even religiously. At least, he called on the rector, and stated this to be his resolve.

'Certainly,' said Mr. Raunham, 'it is best to proceed candidly and fairly, or undue suspicion may fall on you. You should, in my opinion, take active steps at once.'

'I will do the utmost that lies in my power to clear up the mystery, and silence the hubbub of gossip that has been set going about me. But what can I do? They say that the man who comes first in the chain of inquiry is not to be found—I mean the porter.'

'I am sorry to say that he is not. When I returned from the station last night, after seeing Owen Graye off, I went again to the cottage where he has been lodging, to get more intelligence, as I thought. He was not there. He had gone out at dusk, saying he would be back soon. But he has not come back yet.'

'I rather doubt if we shall see him again.'

'Had I known of this, I would have done what in my flurry I did not think of doing—set a watch upon him. But why not advertise for your missing wife as a preliminary, consulting your solicitor in the meantime?'

'Advertise. I'll think about it,' said Manston, lingering on the word as he pronounced it. 'Yes, that seems a right thing—quite a right thing.'

He went home and remained moodily indoors all the next day and the next—for nearly a week, in short. Then, one evening at dusk, he went out with an uncertain air as to the direction of his walk, which resulted, however, in leading him again to the rectory.

He saw Mr. Raunham. 'Have you done anything yet?' the rector inquired.

'No—I have not,' said Manston absently. 'But I am going to set about it.' He hesitated, as if ashamed of some weakness he was about to betray. 'My object in calling was to ask if you had heard any tidings from Budmouth of my— Cytherea. You used to speak of her as one you were interested in.'

There was, at any rate, real sadness in Manston's tone now, and the rector paused to weigh his words ere he replied.

'I have not heard directly from her,' he said gently. 'But her brother has communicated with some people in the parish—'

'The Springroves, I suppose,' said Manston gloomily.

'Yes; and they tell me that she is very ill, and I am sorry to say, likely to be for some days.'

'Surely, surely, I must go and see her!' Manston cried.

'I would advise you not to go,' said Raunham. 'But do this instead—be as quick as you can in making a movement towards ascertaining the truth as regards the existence of your wife. You see, Mr. Manston, an out-step place like this is not like a city, and there is nobody to busy himself for the good of the community; whilst poor Cytherea and her brother are socially too dependent to be able to make much stir in the matter, which is a greater reason still why you should be disinterestedly prompt.'

The steward murmured an assent. Still there was the same indecision!—not the indecision of weakness—the indecision of conscious perplexity.

On Manston's return from this interview at the rectory, he passed the door of the Rising Sun Inn. Finding he had no light for his cigar, and it being three-quarters of a mile to his residence in the park, he entered the tavern to get one. Nobody was in the outer portion of the front room where Manston stood, but a space round the fire was screened off from the remainder, and inside the high oak settle, forming a part of the screen, he heard voices conversing. The speakers had not noticed his footsteps, and continued their discourse.

One of the two he recognized as a well-known night-poacher, the man who had met him with tidings of his wife's death on the evening of the conflagration. The other

433

seemed to be a stranger following the same mode of life. The conversation was carried on in the emphatic and confidential tone of men who are slightly intoxicated, its subject being an unaccountable experience that one of them had had on the night of the fire.

What the steward heard was enough, and more than enough, to lead him to forget or to renounce his motive in entering. The effect upon him was strange and strong. His first object seemed to be to escape from the house again without being seen or heard.

Having accomplished this, he went in at the park gate, and strode off under the trees to the Old House. There sitting down by the fire, and burying himself in reflection, he allowed the minutes to pass by unheeded. First the candle burnt down in its socket and stunk: he did not notice it. Then the fire went out: he did not see it. His feet grew cold; still he thought on.

It may be remarked that a lady, a year and a quarter before this time, had, under the same conditions—an unrestricted mental absorption —shown nearly the same peculiarities as this man evinced now. The lady was Miss Aldclyffe.

It was half-past twelve when Manston moved, as if he had come to a determination.

The first thing he did the next morning was to call at Knapwater House; where he found that Miss Aldclyffe was not well enough to see him.

She had been ailing from slight internal

haemorrhage ever since the confession of the porter Chinney. Apparently not much aggrieved at the denial, he shortly afterwards went to the railway-station and took his departure for London, leaving a letter for Miss Aldclyffe, stating the reason of his journey thither—to recover traces of his missing wife.

During the remainder of the week paragraphs appeared in the local and other newspapers, drawing attention to the facts of this singular case. The writers, with scarcely an exception, dwelt forcibly upon a feature which had at first escaped the observation of the villagers, including Mr. Raunham—that if the announcement of the man Chinney were true, it seemed extremely probable that Mrs. Manston left her watch and keys behind on purpose to blind people as to her escape; and that therefore she would not now let herself be discovered, unless a strong pressure were put upon her. The writers added that the police were on the track of the porter, who very possibly had absconded in the fear that his reticence was criminal, and that Mr. Manston, the husband, was, with praiseworthy energy, making every effort to clear the whole matter up.

2. FROM THE EIGHTEENTH TO THE END OF JANUARY

Five days from the time of his departure, Manston returned from London and Liverpool, looking very fatigued and thoughtful. He explained to the rector and other of his acquaintance that all the inquiries he had made at his wife's old lodgings and his own had been totally barren of results.

But he seemed inclined to push the affair to a clear conclusion now that he had commenced. After the lapse of another day or two he proceeded to fulfil his promise to the rector, and advertised for the missing woman in three of the London papers. The advertisement was a carefully considered and even attractive effusion, calculated to win the heart, or at least the understanding, of any woman who had a spark of her own nature left in her.

There was no answer.

Three days later he repeated the experiment; with the same result as before.

'I cannot try any further,' said Manston speciously to the rector, his sole auditor throughout the proceedings. 'Mr. Raunham, I'll tell you the truth plainly: I don't love her; I do love Cytherea, and the whole of this business of searching for the other woman goes altogether against me. I hope to God I shall never see her again.'

'But you will do your duty at least?' said Mr. Raunham.

'I have done it,' said Manston. 'If ever a man on the face of this earth has done his duty towards an absent wife, I have towards her—living or dead—at least,' he added, correcting himself, 'since I have lived at Knapwater. I neglected her before that time—I own that, as I have owned it before.'

'I should, if I were you, adopt other means to get tidings of her if advertising fails, in spite of my feelings,' said the rector emphatically. 'But at any rate, try advertising once more. There's a satisfaction in having made any attempt three several times.'

When Manston had left the study, the rector stood looking at the fire for a considerable length of time, lost in profound reflection. He went to his private diary, and after many pauses, which he varied only by dipping his pen, letting it dry, wiping it on his sleeve, and then dipping it again, he took the following note of events:—

January 25.—Mr. Manston has just seen me for the third time on the subject of his lost wife. There have been these peculiarities attending the three interviews:—

The first. My visitor, whilst expressing by words his great anxiety to do everything for her recovery, showed plainly by his bearing that he was convinced he should never see her again.

The second. He had left off feigning anxiety to do rightly by his first wife, and honestly asked after Cytherea's welfare.

The third (and most remarkable). He seemed to have lost all consistency. Whilst expressing his love for Cytherea (which certainly is strong) and evincing the usual indifference to the first Mrs. Manston's fate, he was unable to conceal the intensity of his eagerness for me to advise him to advertise *again* for her.

A week after the second, the third advertisement was inserted. A paragraph was attached, which stated that this would be the last time the announcement would appear.

3. THE FIRST OF FEBRUARY

At this, the eleventh hour, the postman brought a letter for Manston, directed in a woman's hand.

A bachelor friend of the steward's, Mr. Dickson by name, who was somewhat of a chatterer—*plenus rimarum*—and who boasted of an endless string of acquaintances, had come over from Casterbridge the preceding day by invitation—an invitation which had been a pleasant surprise to Dickson himself, insomuch that Manston, as a rule, voted him a bore almost to his face. He had stayed over the night, and was sitting at breakfast with his host when the important missive arrived.

Manston did not attempt to conceal the subject of the letter, or the name of the writer. First glancing the pages through, he read aloud as follows:—

'MY HUSBAND,—I implore your forgiveness.

'During the last thirteen months I have repeated to myself a hundred times that you should never discover what I voluntarily tell you now, namely, that I am alive and in perfect health.

'I have seen all your advertisements. Nothing but your persistence has won me round. Surely, I thought, he must love me still. Why else should he try to win back a woman who, faithful unto death as she will be, can, in a social sense, aid him towards acquiring nothing?—rather the reverse, indeed.

'You yourself state my own mind—that the only grounds upon which we can meet and live together, with a reasonable hope of happiness, must be a mutual consent to bury in oblivion all past differences. I heartily and willingly forget everything— and forgive everything. You will do the same, as your actions show.

439

'There will be plenty of opportunity for me to explain the few facts relating to my escape on the night of the fire. I will only give the heads in this hurried note. I was grieved at your not coming to fetch me, more grieved at your absence from the station, most of all by your absence from home. On my journey to the inn I writhed under a passionate sense of wrong done me. When I had been shown to my room I waited and hoped for you till the landlord had gone upstairs to bed. I still found that you did not come, and then I finally made up my mind to leave. I had half undressed, but I put on my things again, forgetting my watch (and I suppose dropping my keys, though I am not sure where) in my hurry, and slipped out of the house. The—'

'Well, that's a rum story,' said Mr. Dickson, interrupting.

'What's a rum story?' said Manston hastily, and flushing in the face.

'Forgetting her watch and dropping her keys in her hurry.'

'I don't see anything particularly wonderful in it. Any woman might do such a thing.'

'Any woman might if escaping from fire or shipwreck, or any such immediate danger. But it seems incomprehensible to me that any woman in her senses, who quietly decides to leave a house, should be so forgetful.'

'All that is required to reconcile your seeming with her facts is to assume that she was not in her senses, for that's what she did plainly, or how could the things have been found there? Besides, she's truthful enough.' He spoke eagerly and peremptorily.

'Yes, yes, I know that. I merely meant that it seemed rather odd.'

'O yes.' Manston read on:—

'—and slipped out of the house. The rubbish-heap was burning up brightly, but the thought that the house was in danger did not strike me; I did not consider that it might be thatched.

'I idled in the lane behind the wood till the last down-train had come in, not being in a mood to face strangers. Whilst I was there the fire broke out, and this perplexed me still more. However, I was still determined not to stay in the place. I went to the railway-station, which was now quiet, and inquired of the solitary man on duty there concerning the trains. It was not till I had left the man that I saw the effect the fire might have on my history. I considered also, though not in any detailed manner, that the event, by attracting the attention of the village to my former abode, might set people on my track should they doubt my death, and a sudden dread of having to go back again to Knapwater—a place which had seemed inimical to me from first to last— prompted me to run back and bribe the porter to secrecy. I then walked on to Anglebury, lingering about the outskirts of the town till the morning train came in, when I proceeded by it to London, and then took these lodgings, where I have been supporting myself ever since by needlework, endeavouring to save enough money to pay my passage home to America, but making melancholy progress in my attempt. However, all that is changed—can I be otherwise than happy at it? Of course not. I am happy. Tell me what I am to do, and believe me still to be your faithful wife,

EUNICE.

'My name here is (as before)

'MRS. RONDLEY, and my address,

79 ADDINGTON STREET,

LAMBETH.'

The name and address were written on a separate slip of paper.

'So it's to be all right at last then,' said Manston's friend. 'But after all there's another woman in the case. You don't seem very sorry for the little thing who is put to such distress by this turn of affairs? I wonder you can let her go so coolly.'

442

The speaker was looking out between the mullions of the window—noticing that some of the lights were glazed in lozenges, some in squares—as he said the words, otherwise he would have seen the passionate expression of agonized hopelessness that flitted across the steward's countenance when the remark was made. He did not see it, and Manston answered after a short interval. The way in which he spoke of the young girl who had believed herself his wife, whom, a few short days ago, he had openly idolized, and whom, in his secret heart, he idolized still, as far as such a form of love was compatible with his nature, showed that from policy or otherwise, he meant to act up to the requirements of the position into which fate appeared determined to drive him.

'That's neither here nor there,' he said; 'it is a point of honour to do as I am doing, and there's an end of it.'

'Yes. Only I thought you used not to care overmuch about your first bargain.'

'I certainly did not at one time. One is apt to feel rather weary of wives when they are so devilish civil under all aspects, as she used to be. But anything for a change—Abigail is lost, but Michal is recovered. You would hardly believe it, but she seems in fancy to be quite another bride—in fact, almost as if she had really risen from the dead, instead of having only done so virtually.'

'You let the young pink one know that the other has come or is coming?'

'*Cui bono*?' The steward meditated critically, showing a portion of his intensely wide and regular teeth within the ruby lips.

'I cannot say anything to her that will do any good,' he resumed. 'It would be awkward—either seeing or communicating with her again. The best plan to adopt will be to let matters take their course—she'll find it all out soon enough.'

Manston found himself alone a few minutes later. He buried his face in his hands, and murmured, 'O my lost one! O my Cytherea! That it should come to this is hard for me! 'Tis now all darkness—"a land of darkness as darkness itself; and of the shadow of death without any order, and where the light is as darkness."'

Yes, the artificial bearing which this extraordinary man had adopted before strangers ever since he had overheard the conversation at the inn, left him now, and he mourned for Cytherea aloud.

4. THE TWELFTH OF FEBRUARY

Knapwater Park is the picture—at eleven o'clock on a muddy, quiet, hazy, but bright morning—a morning without any blue sky, and without any shadows, the earth being enlivened and lit up rather by the spirit of an invisible sun than by its bodily presence.

The local Hunt had met for the day's sport on the open space of ground immediately in front of the steward's residence—called in the list of appointments, 'Old House, Knapwater'—the meet being here once every season, for the pleasure of Miss Aldclyffe and her friends.

Leaning out from one of the first-floor windows, and surveying with the keenest interest the lively picture of pink and black coats, rich-coloured horses, and sparkling bits and spurs, was the returned and long-lost woman, Mrs. Manston.

The eyes of those forming the brilliant group were occasionally turned towards her, showing plainly that her adventures were the subject of conversation equally with or more than the chances of the coming day. She did not flush beneath their scrutiny; on the contrary, she seemed rather to enjoy it, her eyes being kindled with a light of contented exultation, subdued to square with the circumstances of her matronly position.

She was, at the distance from which they surveyed her, an attractive woman—comely as the tents of Kedar. But to a close observer it was palpable enough that God did not do all the picture. Appearing at least seven years older than Cytherea, she was probably her senior by double the number, the artificial means employed to heighten the natural good appearance of her face being very cleverly applied. Her form was full and round, its voluptuous maturity standing out in strong contrast to the memory of Cytherea's lissom girlishness.

It seems to be an almost universal rule that a woman who once has courted, or who eventually will court, the society of men on terms dangerous to her honour cannot refrain from flinging the meaning glance whenever the moment arrives in which the glance is strongly asked for, even if her life and whole future depended upon that moment's abstinence.

Had a cautious, uxorious husband seen in his wife's countenance what might now have been seen in this dark-eyed woman's as she caught a stray glance of flirtation from one or other of the red-coated gallants outside, he would have passed many days in an agony of restless jealousy and doubt. But Manston was not such a husband, and he was, moreover, calmly attending to his business at the other end of the manor.

The steward had fetched home his wife in the most matter-of-fact way a few days earlier, walking round the village with her the very next morning—at once putting an end, by this simple solution, to all the riddling inquiries and surmises that were rank in the village and its neighbourhood. Some men said that this woman was as far inferior to Cytherea as earth

446

to heaven; others, older and sager, thought Manston better off with such a wife than he would have been with one of Cytherea's youthful impulses, and inexperience in household management. All felt their curiosity dying out of them. It was the same in Carriford as in other parts of the world—immediately circumstantial evidence became exchanged for direct, the loungers in court yawned, gave a final survey, and turned away to a subject which would afford more scope for speculation.

XV.

THE EVENTS OF THREE WEEKS

1. FROM THE TWELFTH OF FEBRUARY TO THE SECOND OF MARCH

Owen Graye's recovery from the illness that had incapacitated him for so long a time was, professionally, the dawn of a brighter prospect for him in every direction, though the change was at first very gradual, and his movements and efforts were little more than mechanical. With the lengthening of the days, and the revival of building operations for the forthcoming season, he saw himself, for the first time, on a road which, pursued with care, would probably lead to a comfortable income at some future day. But he was still very low down the hill as yet.

The first undertaking entrusted to him in the new year began about a month after his return from Southampton. Mr. Gradfield had come back to him in the wake of his restored health, and offered him the superintendence, as clerk of works, of a church which was to be nearly rebuilt at the village of Tolchurch, fifteen or sixteen miles from Budmouth, and about half that distance from Carriford.

'I am now being paid at the rate of a hundred and fifty pounds a year,' he said to his sister in a burst of thankfulness, 'and you shall never, Cytherea, be at any tyrannous lady's beck and call again as long as I live. Never pine or think about what has happened, dear; it's no disgrace to you. Cheer up; you'll be somebody's happy wife yet.'

He did not say Edward Springrove's, for, greatly to his disappointment, a report had reached his ears that the friend to whom Cytherea owed so much had been about to pack up his things and sail for Australia. However, this was before the uncertainty concerning Mrs. Manston's existence had been dispersed by her return, a phenomenon that altered the cloudy relationship in which Cytherea had lately been standing towards her old lover, to one of distinctness; which result would have been delightful but for circumstances about to be mentioned.

Cytherea was still pale from her recent illness, and still greatly dejected. Until the news of Mrs. Manston's return had reached them, she had kept herself closely shut up during the day-time, never venturing forth except at night. Sleeping and waking she had been in perpetual dread lest she should still be claimed by a man whom, only a few weeks earlier, she had regarded in the light of a future husband with quiet assent, not unmixed with cheerfulness.

But the removal of the uneasiness in this direction—by Mrs. Manston's arrival, and her own consequent freedom—had been the imposition of pain in another. Utterly fictitious details of the finding of Cytherea and Manston had been invented and circulated, unavoidably reaching her ears in the course of time. Thus the freedom brought no happiness, and it seemed well-nigh impossible that she could ever again show herself the sparkling creature she once had been—

Apt to entice a deity.

On this account, and for the first time in his life, Owen made a point of concealing from her the real state of his feelings with regard to the unhappy transaction. He writhed in secret under the humiliation to which they had been subjected, till the resentment it gave rise to,

449

and for which there was no vent, was sometimes beyond endurance; it induced a mood that did serious damage to the material and plodding perseverance necessary if he would secure permanently the comforts of a home for them.

They gave up their lodgings at Budmouth, and went to Tolchurch as soon as the work commenced.

Here they were domiciled in one half of an old farmhouse, standing not far from the ivy-covered church tower (which was all that was to remain of the original structure). The long steep roof of this picturesque dwelling sloped nearly down to the ground, the old tiles that covered it being overgrown with rich olive-hued moss. New red tiles in twos and threes had been used for patching the holes wrought by decay, lighting up the whole harmonious surface with dots of brilliant scarlet.

The chief internal features of this snug abode were a wide fireplace, enormous cupboards, a brown settle, and several sketches on the wood mantel, done in outline with the point of a hot poker—the subjects mainly consisting of old men walking painfully erect, with a curly-tailed dog behind.

After a week or two of residence in Tolchurch, and rambles amid the quaint scenery circumscribing it, a tranquillity began to spread itself through the mind of the maiden, which Graye hoped would be a preface to her complete restoration. She felt ready and willing to live the whole remainder of her days in the retirement of their present quarters: she began to sing about the house in low tremulous snatches—

'—I said, if there's peace to be found in the
    world,
A heart that is humble may hope for it
    here.'

2. THE THIRD OF MARCH

Her convalescence had arrived at this point on a certain evening towards the end of the winter, when Owen had come in from the building hard by, and was changing his muddy boots for slippers, previously to sitting down to toast and tea.

A prolonged though quiet knocking came to the door.

The only person who ever knocked at their door in that way was the new vicar, the prime mover in the church-building. But he was that evening dining with the Squire.

Cytherea was uneasy at the sound—she did not know why, unless it was because her nerves were weakened by the sickness she had undergone. Instead of opening the door she ran out of the room, and upstairs.

'What nonsense, Cytherea!' said her

brother, going to the door.

Edward Springrove stood in the grey light outside.

'Capital—not gone to Australia, and not going, of course!' cried Owen. 'What's the use of going to such a place as that?—I never believed that you would.'

'I am going back to London again to-morrow,' said Springrove, 'and I called to say a word before going. Where is . . . ?'

'She has just run upstairs. Come in—never mind scraping your shoes—we are regular cottagers now; stone floor, yawning chimney-corner, and all, you see.'

'Mrs. Manston came,' said Edward awkwardly, when he had sat down in the chimney-corner by preference.

'Yes.' At mention of one of his skeletons Owen lost his blitheness at once, and fell into a reverie.

'The history of her escape is very simple.'

'Very.'

'You know I always had wondered, when my father was telling any of the circumstances of the fire to me, how it could be that a woman could sleep so soundly as to be unaware of her horrid position till it was too late even to give shout or sound of any kind.'

'Well, I think that would have been possible, considering her long wearisome journey. People have often been suffocated in their beds before they awoke. But it was hardly

452

likely a body would be completely burnt to ashes as this was assumed to be, though nobody seemed to see it at the time. And how positive the surgeon was too, about those bits of bone! Why he should have been so, nobody can tell. I cannot help saying that if it has ever been possible to find pure stupidity incarnate, it was in that jury of Carriford. There existed in the mass the stupidity of twelve and not the penetration of one.'

'Is she quite well?' said Springrove.

'Who?—O, my sister, Cytherea. Thank you, nearly well, now. I'll call her.'

'Wait one minute. I have a word to say to you.'

Owen sat down again.

'You know, without my saying it, that I love Cytherea as dearly as ever . . . I think she loves me too,—does she really?'

There was in Owen enough of that worldly policy on the subject of matchmaking which naturally resides in the breasts of parents and guardians, to give him a certain caution in replying, and, younger as he was by five years than Edward, it had an odd effect.

'Well, she may possibly love you still,' he said, as if rather in doubt as to the truth of his words.

Springrove's countenance instantly saddened; he had expected a simple 'Yes,' at the very least. He continued in a tone of greater depression—

'Supposing she does love me, would it be fair to you and to her if I made her an offer of marriage, with these dreary conditions attached—that we lived for a few years on the narrowest system, till a great debt, which all honour and duty require me to pay off, shall be paid? My father, by reason of the misfortune that befell him, is under a great obligation to Miss Aldclyffe. He is getting old, and losing his energies. I am attempting to work free of the burden. This makes my prospects gloomy enough at present.

'But consider again,' he went on. 'Cytherea has been left in a nameless and unsatisfactory, though innocent state, by this unfortunate, and now void, marriage with Manston. A marriage with me, though under the—materially— untoward conditions I have mentioned, would make us happy; it would give her a *locus standi*. If she wished to be out of the sound of her misfortunes we would go to another part of England—emigrate—do anything.'

'I'll call Cytherea,' said Owen. 'It is a matter which she alone can settle.' He did not speak warmly. His pride could not endure the pity which Edward's visit and errand tacitly implied. Yet, in the other affair, his heart went with Edward; he was on the same beat for paying off old debts himself.

'Cythie, Mr. Springrove is here,' he said, at the foot of the staircase.

His sister descended the creaking old steps

454

with a faltering tread, and stood in the firelight from the hearth. She extended her hand to Springrove, welcoming him by a mere motion of the lip, her eyes averted—a habit which had engendered itself in her since the beginning of her illness and defamation. Owen opened the door and went out—leaving the lovers alone. It was the first time they had met since the memorable night at Southampton.

'I will get a light,' she said, with a little embarrassment.

'No—don't, please, Cytherea,' said Edward softly, 'Come and sit down with me.'

'O yes. I ought to have asked *you* to,' she returned timidly. 'Everybody sits in the chimney-corner in this parish. You sit on that side. I'll sit here.'

Two recesses—one on the right, one on the left hand—were cut in the inside of the fireplace, and here they sat down facing each other, on benches fitted to the recesses, the fire glowing on the hearth between their feet. Its ruddy light shone on the underslopes of their faces, and spread out over the floor of the room with the low horizontality of the setting sun, giving to every grain of sand and tumour in the paving a long shadow towards the door.

Edward looked at his pale love through the thin azure twines of smoke that went up like ringlets between them, and invested her, as seen through its medium, with the shadowy appearance of a phantom. Nothing is so potent for coaxing back the lost eyes of a woman as a discreet silence in the man who has so lost them—and thus the patient Edward coaxed hers. After lingering on the hearth for half a minute, waiting in vain for another word from him, they were lifted into his face.

He was ready primed to receive them. 'Cytherea, will you marry me?' he said.

He could not wait in his original position till the answer came. Stepping across the front of the fire to her own side of the chimney corner, he reclined at her feet, and searched for her hand. She continued in silence awhile.

'Edward, I can never be anybody's wife,' she then said sadly, and with firmness.

'Think of it in every light,' he pleaded; 'the light of love, first. Then, when you have done that, see how wise a step it would be. I can only offer you poverty as yet, but I want—I do so long to secure you from the intrusion of that unpleasant past, which will often and always be thrust before you as long as you live the shrinking solitary life you do now—a life which purity chooses, it may be; but to the outside world it appears like the enforced loneliness of neglect and scorn—and tongues are busy inventing a reason for it which does not exist.'

'I know all about it,' she said hastily; 'and those are the grounds of my refusal. You and Owen know the whole truth—the two I love best on earth—and I am content. But the scandal will be continually repeated, and I can never give any one the opportunity of saying to you—that—your wife . . .' She utterly broke down and wept.

'Don't, my own darling!' he entreated. 'Don't, Cytherea!'

'Please to leave me—we will be friends, Edward—but don't press me—my mind is made up—I cannot—I will not marry you or any man under the present ambiguous circumstances—never will I—I have said it: never!'

They were both silent. He listlessly regarded the illuminated blackness overhead, where long flakes of soot floated from the sides and bars of the chimney-throat like tattered banners in ancient aisles; whilst through the square opening in the midst one or two bright stars looked down upon them from the grey March sky. The sight seemed to cheer him.

'At any rate you will love me?' he murmured to her.

'Yes—always—for ever and for ever!'

He kissed her once, twice, three times, and arose to his feet, slowly withdrawing himself from her side towards the door. Cytherea remained with her gaze fixed on the fire. Edward went out grieving, but hope was not extinguished even now.

He smelt the fragrance of a cigar, and immediately afterwards saw a small red star of fire against the darkness of the hedge. Graye was pacing up and down the lane, smoking as he walked. Springrove told him the result of the interview.

'You are a good fellow, Edward,' he said; 'but I think my sister is right.'

'I wish you would believe Manston a villain, as I do,' said Springrove.

'It would be absurd of me to say that I like him now—family feeling prevents it, but I cannot in honesty say deliberately that he is a bad man.'

Edward could keep the secret of Manston's coercion of Miss Aldclyffe in the matter of the houses a secret no longer. He told Owen the whole story.

'That's one thing,' he continued, 'but not all. What do you think of this—I have discovered that he went to Budmouth post-office for a letter the day before the first advertisement for his wife appeared in the papers. One was there for him, and it was directed in his wife's handwriting, as I can prove. This was not till after the marriage with Cytherea, it is true, but if (as it seems to show) the advertising was a farce, there is a strong presumption that the rest of the piece was.'

Owen was too astounded to speak. He dropped his cigar, and fixed his eyes upon his companion.

'Collusion!'

'Yes.'

'With his first wife?'

'Yes—with his wife. I am firmly persuaded

of it.'

'What did you discover?'

'That he fetched from the post-office at Budmouth a letter from her the day *before* the first advertisement appeared.'

Graye was lost in a long consideration. 'Ah!' he said, 'it would be difficult to prove anything of that sort now. The writing could not be sworn to, and if he is guilty the letter is destroyed.'

'I have other suspicions—'

'Yes—as you said,' interrupted Owen, who had not till now been able to form the complicated set of ideas necessary for picturing the position. 'Yes, there is this to be remembered—Cytherea had been taken from him before that letter came—and his knowledge of his wife's existence could not have originated till after the wedding. I could have sworn he believed her dead then. His manner was unmistakable.'

'Well, I have other suspicions,' repeated Edward; 'and if I only had the right—if I were her husband or brother, he should be convicted of bigamy yet.'

'The reproof was not needed,' said Owen, with a little bitterness. 'What can I do—a man with neither money nor friends—whilst Manston has Miss Aldclyffe and all her fortune to back him up? God only knows what lies between the mistress and her steward, but since this has transpired—if it is true—I can believe the connection to be even an unworthy one—a thing I certainly never so much as owned to myself before.'

3. THE FIFTH OF MARCH

Edward's disclosure had the effect of directing Owen Graye's thoughts into an entirely new and uncommon channel.

On the Monday after Springrove's visit, Owen had walked to the top of a hill in the neighbourhood of Tolchurch—a wild hill that had no name, beside a barren down where it never looked like summer. In the intensity of his meditations on the ever-present subject, he sat down on a weather-beaten boundary-stone gazing towards the distant valleys—seeing only Manston's imagined form.

Had his defenceless sister been trifled with? that was the question which affected him. Her refusal of Edward as a husband was, he knew, dictated solely by a humiliated sense of inadequacy to him in repute, and had not been formed till since the slanderous tale accounting for her seclusion had been circulated. Was it not true, as Edward had hinted, that he, her brother, was neglecting his duty towards her in allowing Manston to thrive unquestioned, whilst she was hiding her head for no fault at all?

Was it possible that Manston was sensuous

villain enough to have contemplated, at any moment before the marriage with Cytherea, the return of his first wife, when he should have grown weary of his new toy? Had he believed that, by a skilful manipulation of such circumstances as chance would throw in his way, he could escape all suspicion of having known that she lived? Only one fact within his own direct knowledge afforded the least ground for such a supposition. It was that, possessed by a woman only in the humble and unprotected station of a lady's hired companion, his sister's beauty might scarcely have been sufficient to induce a selfish man like Manston to make her his wife, unless he had foreseen the possibility of getting rid of her again.

'But for that stratagem of Manston's in relation to the Springroves,' Owen thought, 'Cythie might now have been the happy wife of Edward. True, that he influenced Miss Aldclyffe only rests on Edward's suspicions, but the grounds are good—the probability is strong.'

He went indoors and questioned Cytherea.

'On the night of the fire, who first said that Mrs. Manston was burnt?' he asked.

'I don't know who started the report.'

'Was it Manston?'

'It was certainly not he. All doubt on the subject was removed before he came to the spot—that I am certain of. Everybody knew that she did not escape *after* the house was on fire, and thus all overlooked the fact that she might have left before—of course that would have seemed such an improbable thing for anybody to do.'

'Yes, until the porter's story of her irritation and doubt as to her course made it natural.'

'What settled the matter at the inquest,' said Cytherea, 'was Mr. Manston's evidence that the watch was his wife's.'

'He was sure of that, wasn't he?'

'I believe he said he was certain of it.'

'It might have been hers—left behind in her perturbation, as they say it was—impossible as that seems at first sight. Yes—on the whole, he might have believed in her death.'

'I know by several proofs that then, and at least for some time after, he had no other thought than that she was dead. I now think that before the porter's confession he knew something about her—though not that she lived.'

'Why do you?'

'From what he said to me on the evening of the wedding-day, when I had fastened myself in the room at the hotel, after Edward's visit. He must have suspected that I knew something, for he was irritated, and in a passion of uneasy doubt. He said, "You don't suppose my first wife is come to light again, madam, surely?" Directly he had let the remark slip out, he seemed anxious to

462

withdraw it.'

'That's odd,' said Owen.

'I thought it very odd.'

'Still we must remember he might only have hit upon the thought by accident, in doubt as to your motive. Yes, the great point to discover remains the same as ever—did he doubt his first impression of her death *before* he married you. I can't help thinking he did, although he was so astounded at our news that night. Edward swears he did.'

'It was perhaps only a short time before,' said Cytherea; 'when he could hardly recede from having me.'

'Seasoning justice with mercy as usual, Cytherea. 'Tis unfair to yourself to talk like that. If I could only bring him to ruin as a bigamist—supposing him to be one—I should die happy. That's what we must find out by fair means or foul—was he a wilful bigamist?'

'It is no use trying, Owen. You would have to employ a solicitor, and how can you do that?'

'I can't at all—I know that very well. But neither do I altogether wish to at present—a lawyer must have a case—facts to go upon, that means. Now they are scarce at present—as scarce as money is with us, and till we have found more money there is no hurry for a lawyer. Perhaps by the time we have the facts we shall have the money. The only thing we lose in working alone in this way, is time—not the issue: for the fruit that one mind matures in a twelvemonth forms a more perfectly organized whole than that of twelve minds in one month, especially if the interests of the single one are vitally concerned, and those of the twelve are only hired. But there is not only my mind available—you are a shrewd woman, Cythie, and Edward is an earnest ally. Then, if we really get a sure footing for a criminal prosecution, the Crown will take up the case.'

'I don't much care to press on in the matter,' she murmured. 'What good can it do us, Owen, after all?'

'Selfishly speaking, it will do this good—that all the facts of your journey to Southampton will become known, and the scandal will die. Besides, Manston will have to suffer—it's an act of justice to you and to other women, and to Edward Springrove.'

He now thought it necessary to tell her of the real nature of the Springroves' obligation to Miss Aldclyffe—and their nearly certain knowledge that Manston was the prime mover in effecting their embarrassment. Her face flushed as she listened.

'And now,' he said, 'our first undertaking is to find out where Mrs. Manston lived during the separation; next, when the first communications passed between them after the fire.'

'If we only had Miss Aldclyffe's countenance and assistance as I used to have them,'

Cytherea returned, 'how strong we should be! O, what power is it that he exercises over her, swaying her just as he wishes! She loves me now. Mrs. Morris in her letter said that Miss Aldclyffe prayed for me—yes, she heard her praying for me, and crying. Miss Aldclyffe did not mind an old friend like Mrs. Morris knowing it, either. Yet in opposition to this, notice her dead silence and inaction throughout this proceeding.'

'It is a mystery; but never mind that now,' said Owen impressively. 'About where Mrs. Manston has been living. We must get this part of it first—learn the place of her stay in the early stage of their separation, during the period of Manston's arrival here, and so on, for that was where she was first communicated with on the subject of coming to Knapwater, before the fire; and that address, too, was her point of departure when she came to her husband by stealth in the night—you know—the time I visited you in the evening and went home early in the morning, and it was found that he had been visited too. Ah! couldn't we inquire of Mrs. Leat, who keeps the post-office at Carriford, if she remembers where the letters to Mrs. Manston were directed?'

'He never posted his letters to her in the parish—it was remarked at the time. I was thinking if something relating to her address might not be found in the report of the inquest in the *Casterbridge Chronicle* of the date. Some facts about the inquest were given in the papers to a certainty.'

Her brother caught eagerly at the suggestion. 'Who has a file of the *Chronicles*?' he said.

'Mr. Raunham used to file them,' said Cytherea. 'He was rather friendly-disposed towards me, too.'

Owen could not, on any consideration, escape from his attendance at the church-building till Saturday evening; and thus it became necessary, unless they actually wasted time, that Cytherea herself should assist 'I act under your orders, Owen,' she said.

XVI.

THE EVENTS OF ONE WEEK

1. MARCH THE SIXTH

The next morning the opening move of the game was made. Cytherea, under cover of a thick veil, hired a conveyance and drove to within a mile or so of Carriford. It was with a renewed sense of depression that she saw again the objects which had become familiar to her eye during her sojourn under Miss Aldclyffe's roof—the outline of the hills, the meadow streams, the old park trees. She hastened by a lonely path to the rectory-house, and asked if Mr. Raunham was at home.

Now the rector, though a solitary bachelor, was as gallant and courteous to womankind as an ancient Iberian; and, moreover, he was Cytherea's friend in particular, to an extent far greater than she had ever surmised. Rarely visiting his relative, Miss Aldclyffe, except on parish matters, more rarely still being called upon by Miss Aldclyffe, Cytherea had learnt very little of him whilst she lived at Knapwater. The relationship was on the impecunious paternal side, and for this branch of her family the lady of the estate had never evinced much sympathy. In looking back upon our line of descent it is an instinct with us to feel that all our vitality was drawn from the richer party to any unequal marriage in the chain.

Since the death of the old captain, the rector's bearing in Knapwater House had been almost that of a stranger, a circumstance which he himself was the last man in the world to regret. This polite indifference was so frigid on both sides that the rector did not concern himself to preach at her, which was a great deal in a rector; and she did not take the trouble to think his sermons poor stuff, which in a cynical woman was a great deal more.

Though barely fifty years of age, his hair was as white as snow, contrasting strangely with the redness of his skin, which was as fresh and healthy as a lad's. Cytherea's bright eyes, mutely and demurely glancing up at him Sunday after Sunday, had been the means of driving away many of the saturnine humours that creep into an empty heart during the hours of a solitary life; in this case, however, to supplant them, when she left his parish, by those others of a more aching nature which accompany an over-full one. In short, he had been on the verge of feeling towards her that passion to which his dignified self-respect would not give its true name, even in the privacy of his own thought.

He received her kindly; but she was not disposed to be frank with him. He saw her wish to be reserved, and with genuine good taste and good nature made no comment whatever upon her request to be allowed to see the *Chronicle* for the year before the last. He placed the papers before her on his study table, with a timidity as great as her own, and then left her entirely to herself.

She turned them over till she came to the first heading connected with the subject of her search—'Disastrous Fire and Loss of Life at Carriford.'

The sight, and its calamitous bearing upon her own life, made her so dizzy that she could, for a while, hardly decipher the letters. Stifling recollection by an effort she nerved herself to her work, and carefully read the column. The account reminded her of no other fact than was remembered already.

468

She turned on to the following week's report of the inquest. After a miserable perusal she could find no more pertaining to Mrs. Manston's address than this:—

ABRAHAM BROWN, of Hoxton, London, at whose house the deceased woman had been living, deposed, &c.

Nobody else from London had attended the inquest.

She arose to depart, first sending a message of thanks to Mr. Raunham, who was out of doors gardening.

He stuck his spade into the ground, and accompanied her to the gate.

'Can I help you in anything, Cytherea?' he said, using her Christian name by an intuition that unpleasant memories might be revived if he called her Miss Graye after wishing her good-bye as Mrs. Manston at the wedding. Cytherea saw the motive and appreciated it, nevertheless replying evasively—

'I only guess and fear.'

He earnestly looked at her again.

'Promise me that if you want assistance, and you think I can give it, you will come to me.'

'I will,' she said.

The gate closed between them.

'You don't want me to help you in anything now, Cytherea?' he repeated.

If he had spoken what he felt, 'I want very

much to help you, Cytherea, and have been watching Manston on your account,' she would gladly have accepted his offer. As it was, she was perplexed, and raised her eyes to his, not so fearlessly as before her trouble, but as modestly, and with still enough brightness in them to do fearful execution as she said over the gate—

'No, thank you.'

She returned to Tolchurch weary with her day's work. Owen's greeting was anxious—

'Well, Cytherea?'

She gave him the words from the report of the inquest, pencilled on a slip of paper.

'Now to find out the name of the street and number,' Owen remarked.

'Owen,' she said, 'will you forgive me for what I am going to say? I don't think I can—indeed I don't think I can—take any further steps towards disentangling the mystery. I still think it a useless task, and it does not seem any duty of mine to be revenged upon Mr. Manston in any way.' She added more gravely, 'It is beneath my dignity as a woman to labour for this; I have felt it so all day.'

'Very well,' he said, somewhat shortly; 'I shall work without you then. There's dignity in justice.' He caught sight of her pale tired face, and the dilated eye which always appeared in her with weariness. 'Darling,' he continued warmly, and kissing her, 'you shall not work so hard again—you are worn out quite. But you

470

must let me do as I like.'

2. MARCH THE TENTH

On Saturday evening Graye hurried off to Casterbridge, and called at the house of the reporter to the *Chronicle*. The reporter was at home, and came out to Graye in the passage. Owen explained who and what he was, and asked the man if he would oblige him by turning to his notes of the inquest at Carriford in the December of the year preceding the last—just adding that a family entanglement, of which the reporter probably knew something, made him anxious to ascertain some additional details of the event, if any existed.

'Certainly,' said the other, without hesitation; 'though I am afraid I haven't much beyond what we printed at the time. Let me see—my old note-books are in my drawer at the office of the paper: if you will come with me I can refer to them there.' His wife and family were at tea inside the room, and with the timidity of decent poverty everywhere he seemed glad to get a stranger out of his domestic groove.

They crossed the street, entered the office, and went thence to an inner room. Here, after a short search, was found the book required. The precise address, not given in the condensed report that was printed, but written down by the reporter, was as follows:—

ABRAHAM BROWN,
      LODGING-HOUSE KEEPER,
            41 CHARLES SQUARE,
                HOXTON.

Owen copied it, and gave the reporter a small fee. 'I want to keep this inquiry private for the present,' he said hesitatingly. 'You will perhaps understand why, and oblige me.'

The reporter promised. 'News is shop with me,' he said, 'and to escape from handling it is my greatest social enjoyment.'

It was evening, and the outer room of the publishing-office was lighted up with flaring jets of gas. After making the above remark, the reporter came out from the inner apartment in Graye's company, answering an expression of obligation from Owen with the words that it was no trouble. At the moment of his speech, he closed behind him the door between the two rooms, still holding his note-book in his hand.

Before the counter of the front room stood a tall man, who was also speaking, when they emerged. He said to the youth in attendance, 'I will take my paper for this week now I am here, so that you needn't post it to me.'

The stranger then slightly turned his head, saw Owen, and recognized him. Owen passed

472

out without recognizing the other as Manston.

Manston then looked at the reporter, who, after walking to the door with Owen, had come back again to lock up his books. Manston did not need to be told that the shabby marble-covered book which he held in his hand, opening endways and interleaved with blotting-paper, was an old reporting-book. He raised his eyes to the reporter's face, whose experience had not so schooled his features but that they betrayed a consciousness, to one half initiated as the other was, that his late proceeding had been connected with events in the life of the steward. Manston said no more, but, taking his newspaper, followed Owen from the office, and disappeared in the gloom of the street.

Edward Springrove was now in London again, and on this same evening, before leaving Casterbridge, Owen wrote a careful letter to him, stating therein all the facts that had come to his knowledge, and begging him, as he valued Cytherea, to make cautious inquiries. A tall man was standing under the lamp-post, about half-a-dozen yards above the post-office, when he dropped the letter into the box.

That same night, too, for a reason connected with the rencounter with Owen Graye, the steward entertained the idea of rushing off suddenly to London by the mail-train, which left Casterbridge at ten o'clock. But remembering that letters posted after the hour at which Owen had obtained his information—whatever that was—could not be delivered in London till Monday morning, he changed his mind and went home to Knapwater. Making a confidential explanation to his wife, arrangements were set on foot for his departure by the mail on Sunday night.

3. MARCH THE ELEVENTH

Starting for church the next morning several minutes earlier than was usual with him, the steward intentionally loitered along the road from the village till old Mr. Springrove overtook him. Manston spoke very civilly of the morning, and of the weather, asking how the farmer's barometer stood, and when it was probable that the wind might change. It was not in Mr. Springrove's nature—going to church as he was, too—to return anything but a civil answer to such civil questions, however his feelings might have been biassed by late events. The conversation was continued on terms of greater friendliness.

'You must be feeling settled again by this time, Mr. Springrove, after the rough turn-out you had on that terrible night in November.'

'Ay, but I don't know about feeling settled, either, Mr. Manston. The old window in the chimney-corner of the old house I shall never forget. No window in the chimney-corner where I am now, and I had been used to it for more than fifty years. Ted says 'tis a great loss to me, and he knows exactly what I feel.'

'Your son is again in a good situation, I believe?' said Manston, imitating that inquisitiveness into the private affairs of the natives which passes for high breeding in country villages.

'Yes, sir. I hope he'll keep it, or do something else and stick to it.'

' 'Tis to be hoped he'll be steady now.'

'He's always been that, I assure 'ee,' said the old man tartly.

'Yes—yes—I mean intellectually steady. Intellectual wild oats will thrive in a soil of the strictest morality.'

'Intellectual gingerbread! Ted's steady enough—that's all I know about it.'

'Of course—of course. Has he respectable lodgings? My own experience has shown me that that's a great thing to a young man living alone in London.'

'Warwick Street, Charing Cross—that's where he is.'

'Well, to be sure—strange! A very dear friend of mine used to live at number fifty-two in that very same street.'

'Edward lives at number forty-nine—how very near being the same house!' said the old farmer, pleased in spite of himself.

'Very,' said Manston. 'Well, I suppose we had better step along a little quicker, Mr.

Springrove; the parson's bell has just begun.'
'Number forty-nine,' he murmured.

4. MARCH THE TWELFTH

Edward received Owen's letter in due time, but on account of his daily engagements he could not attend to any request till the clock had struck five in the afternoon. Rushing then from his office in Westminster, he called a hansom and proceeded to Hoxton. A few minutes later he knocked at the door of number forty-one, Charles Square, the old lodging of Mrs. Manston.

A tall man who would have looked extremely handsome had he not been clumsily and closely wrapped up in garments that were much too elderly in style for his years, stood at the corner of the quiet square at the same instant, having, too, alighted from a cab, that had been driven along Old Street in Edward's rear. He smiled confidently when Springrove knocked.

Nobody came to the door. Springrove knocked again.

This brought out two people—one at the door he had been knocking upon, the other from the next on the right.

'Is Mr. Brown at home?' said Springrove.

'No, sir.'

'When will he be in?'

'Quite uncertain.'

'Can you tell me where I may find him?'

'No. O, here he is coming, sir. That's Mr. Brown.'

Edward looked down the pavement in the direction pointed out by the woman, and saw a man approaching. He proceeded a few steps to meet him.

Edward was impatient, and to a certain extent still a countryman, who had not, after the manner of city men, subdued the natural impulse to speak out the ruling thought without preface. He said in a quiet tone to the stranger, 'One word with you—do you remember a lady lodger of yours of the name of Mrs. Manston?'

Mr. Brown half closed his eyes at Springrove, somewhat as if he were looking into a telescope at the wrong end.

'I have never let lodgings in my life,' he said, after his survey.

'Didn't you attend an inquest a year and a half ago, at Carriford?'

'Never knew there was such a place in the world, sir; and as to lodgings, I have taken acres first and last during the last thirty years, but I have never let an inch.'

'I suppose there is some mistake,' Edward murmured, and turned away. He and Mr. Brown were now opposite the door next to the one he had knocked at. The woman who was still standing there had heard the inquiry and the result of it.

'I expect it is the other Mr. Brown, who used to live there, that you want, sir,' she said. 'The Mr. Brown that was inquired for the other day?'

'Very likely that is the man,' said Edward, his interest reawakening.

'He couldn't make a do of lodging-letting here, and at last he went to Cornwall, where he came from, and where his brother still lived, who had often asked him to come home again. But there was little luck in the change; for after London they say he couldn't stand the rainy west winds they get there, and he died in the December following. Will you step into the passage?'

'That's unfortunate,' said Edward, going in. 'But perhaps you remember a Mrs. Manston living next door to you?'

'O yes,' said the landlady, closing the door. 'The lady who was supposed to have met with such a horrible fate, and was alive all the time. I saw her the other day.'

'Since the fire at Carriford?'

'Yes. Her husband came to ask if Mr. Brown was still living here—just as you might. He seemed anxious about it; and then one evening, a week or fortnight afterwards, when he came again to make further inquiries, she was with him. But I did not speak to her—she stood back, as if she were shy. I was interested, however, for old Mr. Brown had told me all

478

about her when he came back from the inquest.'

'Did you know Mrs. Manston before she called the other day?'

'No. You see she was only Mr. Brown's lodger for two or three weeks, and I didn't know she was living there till she was near upon leaving again—we don't notice next-door people much here in London. I much regretted I had not known her when I heard what had happened. It led me and Mr. Brown to talk about her a great deal afterwards. I little thought I should see her alive after all.'

'And when do you say they came here together?'

'I don't exactly remember the day—though I remember a very beautiful dream I had that same night—ah, I shall never forget it! Shoals of lodgers coming along the square with angels' wings and bright golden sovereigns in their hands wanting apartments at West End prices. They would not give any less; no, not if you—'

'Yes. Did Mrs. Manston leave anything, such as papers, when she left these lodgings originally?' said Edward, though his heart sank as he asked. He felt that he was outwitted. Manston and his wife had been there before him, clearing the ground of all traces.

'I have always said "No" hitherto,' replied the woman, 'considering I could say no more if put upon my oath, as I expected to be. But

479

speaking in a common everyday way now the occurrence is past, I believe a few things of some kind (though I doubt if they were papers) were left in a workbox she had, because she talked about it to Mr. Brown, and was rather angry at what occurred—you see, she had a temper by all account, and so I didn't like to remind the lady of this workbox when she came the other day with her husband.'

'And about the workbox?'

'Well, from what was casually dropped, I think Mrs. Manston had a few articles of furniture she didn't want, and when she was leaving they were put in a sale just by. Amongst her things were two workboxes very much alike. One of these she intended to sell, the other she didn't, and Mr. Brown, who collected the things together, took the wrong one to the sale.'

'What was in it?'

'O, nothing in particular, or of any value— some accounts, and her usual sewing materials I think—nothing more. She didn't take much trouble to get it back—she said the bills were worth nothing to her or anybody else, but that she should have liked to keep the box because her husband gave it her when they were first married, and if he found she had parted with it, he would be vexed.'

'Did Mrs. Manston, when she called recently with her husband, allude to this, or inquire for it, or did Mr. Manston?'

'No—and I rather wondered at it. But she seemed to have forgotten it—indeed, she didn't make any inquiry at all, only standing behind him, listening to his; and he probably had never been told anything about it.'

'Whose sale were these articles of hers taken to?'

'Who was the auctioneer? Mr. Halway. His place is the third turning from the end of that street you see there. Anybody will tell you the shop—his name is written up.'

Edward went off to follow up his clue with a promptness which was dictated more by a dogged will to do his utmost than by a hope of doing much. When he was out of sight, the tall and cloaked man, who had watched him, came up to the woman's door, with an appearance of being in breathless haste.

'Has a gentleman been here inquiring about Mrs. Manston?'

'Yes; he's just gone.'

'Dear me! I want him.'

'He's gone to Mr. Halway's.'

'I think I can give him some information upon the subject. Does he pay pretty liberally?'

'He gave me half-a-crown.'

'That scale will do. I'm a poor man, and will see what my little contribution to his knowledge will fetch. But, by the way, perhaps you told him all I know—where she lived before coming to live here?'

'I didn't know where she lived before

coming here. O no—I only said what Mr. Brown had told me. He seemed a nice, gentle young man, or I shouldn't have been so open as I was.'

'I shall now about catch him at Mr. Halway's,' said the man, and went away as hastily as he had come.

Edward in the meantime had reached the auction-room. He found some difficulty, on account of the inertness of those whose only inducement to an action is a mere wish from another, in getting the information he stood in need of, but it was at last accorded him. The auctioneer's book gave the name of Mrs. Higgins, 3 Canley Passage, as the purchaser of the lot which had included Mrs. Manston's workbox.

Thither Edward went, followed by the man. Four bell pulls, one above the other like waistcoat-buttons, appeared on the door-post. Edward seized the first he came to.

'Who did you woant?' said a thin voice from somewhere.

Edward looked above and around him; nobody was visible.

'Who did you woant?' said the thin voice again.

He found now that the sound proceeded from below the grating covering the basement window. He dropped his glance through the bars, and saw a child's white face.

'Who did you woant?' said the voice the

third time, with precisely the same languid inflection.

'Mrs. Higgins,' said Edward.

'Third bell up,' said the face, and disappeared.

He pulled the third bell from the bottom, and was admitted by another child, the daughter of the woman he was in search of. He gave the little thing sixpence, and asked for her mamma. The child led him upstairs.

Mrs. Higgins was the wife of a carpenter who from want of employment one winter had decided to marry. Afterwards they both took to drink, and sank into desperate circumstances. A few chairs and a table were the chief articles of furniture in the third-floor back room which they occupied. A roll of baby-linen lay on the floor; beside it a pap-clogged spoon and an overturned tin pap-cup. Against the wall a Dutch clock was fixed out of level, and ticked wildly in longs and shorts, its entrails hanging down beneath its white face and wiry hands, like the faeces of a Harpy ('foedissima ventris proluvies, uncaeque manus, et pallida semper ora'). A baby was crying against every chair-leg, the whole family of six or seven being small enough to be covered by a washing-tub. Mrs. Higgins sat helpless, clothed in a dress which had hooks and eyes in plenty, but never one opposite the other, thereby rendering the dress almost useless as a screen to the bosom. No workbox was visible anywhere.

It was a depressing picture of married life among the very poor of a city. Only for one short hour in the whole twenty-four did husband and wife taste genuine happiness. It was in the evening, when, after the sale of some necessary article of furniture, they were under the influence of a quartern of gin.

Of all the ingenious and cruel satires that from the beginning till now have been stuck like knives into womankind, surely there is not one so lacerating to them, and to us who love them, as the trite old fact, that the most wretched of men can, in the twinkling of an eye, find a wife ready to be more wretched still for the sake of his company.

Edward hastened to despatch his errand.

Mrs. Higgins had lately pawned the workbox with other useless articles of lumber, she said. Edward bought the duplicate of her, and went downstairs to the pawnbroker's.

In the back division of a musty shop, amid the heterogeneous collection of articles and odours invariably crowding such places, he produced his ticket, and with a sense of satisfaction out of all proportion to the probable worth of his acquisition, took the box and carried it off under his arm. He attempted to lift the cover as he walked, but found it locked.

It was dusk when Springrove reached his lodging. Entering his small sitting-room, the front apartment on the ground floor, he struck a light, and proceeded to learn if any scrap or mark within or upon his purchase rendered it of moment to the business in hand. Breaking open the cover with a small chisel, and lifting the tray, he glanced eagerly beneath, and found—nothing.

He next discovered that a pocket or portfolio was formed on the underside of the cover. This he unfastened, and slipping his hand within, found that it really contained some substance. First he pulled out about a dozen tangled silk and cotton threads. Under them were a short household account, a dry moss-rosebud, and an old pair of carte-de-visite photographs. One of these was a likeness of Mrs. Manston—'Eunice' being written under it in ink—the other of Manston himself.

He sat down dispirited. This was all the fruit of his task—not a single letter, date, or address of any kind to help him—and was it likely there would be?

However, thinking he would send the fragments, such as they were, to Graye, in order to satisfy him that he had done his best so far, he scribbled a line, and put all except the silk and cotton into an envelope. Looking at his watch, he found it was then twenty minutes to seven; by affixing an extra stamp he would be enabled to despatch them by that evening's post. He hastily directed the packet, and ran with it at once to the post-office at

Charing Cross.

On his return he took up the workbox again to examine it more leisurely.

He then found there was also a small cavity in the tray under the pincushion, which was movable by a bit of ribbon. Lifting this he uncovered a flattened sprig of myrtle, and a small scrap of crumpled paper. The paper contained a verse or two in a man's handwriting. He recognized it as Manston's, having seen notes and bills from him at his father's house. The stanza was of a complimentary character, descriptive of the lady who was now Manston's wife.

EUNICE

Whoso for hours or lengthy days
Shall catch her aspect's changeful rays,
Then turn away, can none recall
Beyond a galaxy of all
        In hazy portraiture;
Lit by the light of azure eyes
Like summer days by summer skies:
Her sweet transitions seem to be
A kind of pictured melody,
        And not a set contour.
             'Æ. M.

To shake, pull, and ransack the box till he had almost destroyed it was now his natural action. But it contained absolutely nothing more.

'Disappointed again,' he said, flinging down the box, the bit of paper, and the withered twig that had lain with it.

Yet valueless as the new acquisition was, on second thoughts he considered that it would be worth while to make good the statement in his late note to Graye—that he had sent everything the box contained except the sewing-thread. Thereupon he enclosed the verse and myrtle-twig in another envelope, with a remark that he had overlooked them in his first search, and put it on the table for the next day's post.

In his hurry and concentration upon the matter that occupied him, Springrove, on entering his lodging and obtaining a light, had not waited to pull down the blind or close the shutters. Consequently all that he had done had been visible from the street. But as on an average not one person a minute passed along the quiet pavement at this time of the evening, the discovery of the omission did not much concern his mind.

But the real state of the case was that a tall man had stood against the opposite wall and watched the whole of his proceeding. When Edward came out and went to the Charing Cross post-office, the man followed him and saw him drop the letter into the box. The stranger did not further trouble himself to follow Springrove back to his lodging again.

Manston now knew that there had been photographs of some kind in his wife's workbox, and though he had not been near enough to see them, he guessed whose they were. The least reflection told him to whom they had been sent.

He paused a minute under the portico of the post-office, looking at the two or three omnibuses stopping and starting in front of him. Then he rushed along the Strand, through Holywell Street, and on to Old Boswell Court. Kicking aside the shoeblacks who began to importune him as he passed under the colonnade, he turned up the narrow passage to the publishing-office of the Post-Office Directory. He begged to be allowed to see the Directory of the south-west counties of England for a moment.

The shopman immediately handed down the volume from a shelf, and Manston retired with it to the window-bench. He turned to the county, and then to the parish of Tolchurch. At the end of the historical and topographical description of the village he read:—

Postmistress—Mrs. Hurston. Letters received at 6.30 A.M. by foot-post from Anglebury.

Returning his thanks, he handed back the book and quitted the office, thence pursuing his way to an obscure coffee-house by the

Strand, where he now partook of a light dinner. But rest seemed impossible with him Some absorbing intention kept his body continually on the move. He paid his bill, took his bag in his hand, and went out to idle about the streets and over the river till the time should have arrived at which the night-mail left the Waterloo Station, by which train he intended to return homeward.

There exists, as it were, an outer chamber to the mind, in which, when a man is occupied centrally with the most momentous question of his life, casual and trifling thoughts are just allowed to wander softly for an interval, before being banished altogether. Thus, amid his concentration did Manston receive perceptions of the individuals about him in the lively thoroughfare of the Strand; tall men looking insignificant; little men looking great and profound; lost women of miserable repute looking as happy as the days are long; wives, happy by assumption, looking careworn and miserable. Each and all were alike in this one respect, that they followed a solitary trail like the inwoven threads which form a banner, and all were equally unconscious of the significant whole they collectively showed forth.

At ten o'clock he turned into Lancaster Place, crossed the river, and entered the railway-station, where he took his seat in the down mail-train, which bore him, and Edward Springrove's letter to Graye, far away from

489

London.

XVII.

THE EVENTS OF ONE DAY

1. MARCH THE THIRTEENTH. THREE TO SIX O'CLOCK A.M.

They entered Anglebury Station in the dead, still time of early morning, the clock over the booking-office pointing to twenty-five minutes to three. Manston lingered on the platform and saw the mail-bags brought out, noticing, as a pertinent pastime, the many shabby blotches of wax from innumerable seals that had been set upon their mouths. The guard took them into a fly, and was driven down the road to the post-office.

It was a raw, damp, uncomfortable morning, though, as yet, little rain was falling. Manston drank a mouthful from his flask and walked at once away from the station, pursuing his way through the gloom till he stood on the side of the town adjoining, at a distance from the last house in the street of about two hundred yards.

The station road was also the turnpike-road into the country, the first part of its course being across a heath. Having surveyed the highway up and down to make sure of its bearing, Manston methodically set himself to walk backwards and forwards a stone's throw in each direction. Although the spring was temperate, the time of day, and the condition of suspense in which the steward found himself, caused a sensation of chilliness to pervade his frame in spite of the overcoat he wore. The drizzling rain increased, and drops from the trees at the wayside fell noisily upon the hard road beneath them, which reflected from its glassy surface the faint halo of light hanging over the lamps of the adjacent town.

Here he walked and lingered for two hours, without seeing or hearing a living soul. Then he heard the market-house clock strike five, and soon afterwards, quick hard footsteps smote upon the pavement of the street leading towards him. They were those of the postman for the Tolchurch beat. He reached the bottom of the street, gave his bags a final hitch-up, stepped off the pavement, and struck out for the country with a brisk shuffle.

Manston then turned his back upon the town, and walked slowly on. In two minutes a flickering light shone upon his form, and the postman overtook him.

The new-comer was a short, stooping individual of above five-and-forty, laden on both sides with leather bags large and small, and carrying a little lantern strapped to his breast, which cast a tiny patch of light upon the road ahead.

'A tryen mornen for travellers!' the postman cried, in a cheerful voice, without turning his head or slackening his trot.

'It is, indeed,' said Manston, stepping out abreast of him. 'You have a long walk every day.'

'Yes—a long walk—for though the distance is only sixteen miles on the straight—that is, eight to the furthest place and eight back, what with the ins and outs to the gentlemen's houses, it makes two-and-twenty for my legs. Two-and-twenty miles a day, how many a year? I used to reckon it, but I never do now. I don't care to think o' my wear and tear, now it do begin to tell upon me.'

Thus the conversation was begun, and the postman proceeded to narrate the different strange events that marked his experience. Manston grew very friendly.

'Postman, I don't know what your custom is,' he said, after a while; 'but between you and me, I always carry a drop of something warm in my pocket when I am out on such a morning as this. Try it.' He handed the bottle of brandy.

'If you'll excuse me, please. I haven't took no stimmilents these five years.'

' 'Tis never too late to mend.'

'Against the regulations, I be afraid.'

'Who'll know it?'

'That's true—nobody will know it. Still, honesty's the best policy.'

'Ah—it is certainly. But, thank God, I've

been able to get on without it yet. You'll surely drink with me?'

'Really, 'tis a'most too early for that sort o' thing—however, to oblige a friend, I don't object to the faintest shadder of a drop.' The postman drank, and Manston did the same to a very slight degree. Five minutes later, when they came to a gate, the flask was pulled out again.

'Well done!' said the postman, beginning to feel its effect; 'but guide my soul, I be afraid 'twill hardly do!'

'Not unless 'tis well followed, like any other line you take up,' said Manston. 'Besides, there's a way of liking a drop of liquor, and of being good—even religious—at the same time.'

'Ay, for some thimble-and-button in-an-out fellers; but I could never get into the knack o' it; not I.'

'Well, you needn't be troubled; it isn't necessary for the higher class of mind to be religious—they have so much common-sense that they can risk playing with fire.'

'That hits me exactly.'

'In fact, a man I know, who always had no other god but "Me;" and devoutly loved his neighbour's wife, says now that believing is a mistake.'

'Well, to be sure! However, believing in God is a mistake made by very few people, after all.'

'A true remark.'

'Not one Christian in our parish would walk half a mile in a rain like this to know whether the Scripture had concluded him under sin or grace.'

'Nor in mine.'

'Ah, you may depend upon it they'll do away wi' Goda'mity altogether before long, although we've had him over us so many years.'

'There's no knowing.'

'And I suppose the Queen 'ill be done away wi' then. A pretty concern that'll be! Nobody's head to put on your letters; and then your honest man who do pay his penny will never be known from your scamp who don't. O, 'tis a nation!'

'Warm the cockles of your heart, however. Here's the bottle waiting.'

'I'll oblige you, my friend.'

The drinking was repeated. The postman grew livelier as he went on, and at length favoured the steward with a song, Manston himself joining in the chorus.

He flung his mallet against the wall,
Said, 'The Lord make churches and
    chapels to fall,
And there'll be work for tradesmen all!'
    When Joan's ale was new,
        My boys,
    When Joan's ale was new.

'You understand, friend,' the postman

494

added, 'I was originally a mason by trade: no offence to you if you be a parson?'

'None at all,' said Manston.

The rain now came down heavily, but they pursued their path with alacrity, the produce of the several fields between which the lane wound its way being indicated by the peculiar character of the sound emitted by the falling drops. Sometimes a soaking hiss proclaimed that they were passing by a pasture, then a patter would show that the rain fell upon some large-leafed root crop, then a paddling plash announced the naked arable, the low sound of the wind in their ears rising and falling with each pace they took.

Besides the small private bags of the county families, which were all locked, the postman bore the large general budget for the remaining inhabitants along his beat. At each village or hamlet they came to, the postman searched for the packet of letters destined for that place, and thrust it into an ordinary letter-hole cut in the door of the receiver's cottage— the village post-offices being mostly kept by old women who had not yet risen, though lights moving in other cottage windows showed that such people as carters, woodmen, and stablemen had long been stirring.

The postman had by this time become markedly unsteady, but he still continued to be too conscious of his duties to suffer the steward to search the bag. Manston was perplexed, and at lonely points in the road cast his eyes keenly upon the short bowed figure of the man trotting through the mud by his side, as if he were half inclined to run a very great risk indeed.

It frequently happened that the houses of farmers, clergymen, &c., lay a short distance up or down a lane or path branching from the direct track of the postman's journey. To save time and distance, at the point of junction of some of these paths with the main road, the gate-post was hollowed out to form a letter-box, in which the postman deposited his missives in the morning, looking in the box again in the evening to collect those placed there for the return post. Tolchurch Dairy and Farmstead, lying back from the village street, were served on this principle. This fact the steward now learnt by conversing with the postman, and the discovery relieved Manston greatly, making his intentions much clearer to himself than they had been in the earlier stages of his journey.

They had reached the outskirts of the village. Manston insisted upon the flask being emptied before they proceeded further. This was done, and they approached the lane to the dairy, and the farmhouse in which Owen and Cytherea were living.

The postman paused, fumbled in his bag, took out by the light of his lantern some half-dozen letters, and tried to sort them. He could not perform the task.

'We be crippled disciples a b'lieve,' he said, with a sigh and a stagger.

'Not drunk, but market-merry,' said Manston cheerfully.

'Well done! If I bain't so weak that I can't see the clouds—much less letters. Guide my soul, if so be anybody should tell the Queen's postmaster-general of me! The whole story will have to go through Parliament House, and I shall be high-treasoned—as safe as houses—and be fined, and who'll pay for a poor martel! O, 'tis a world!'

'Trust in the Lord—he'll pay.'

'He pay a b'lieve! why should he when he didn't drink the drink? He pay a b'lieve! D'ye think the man's a fool?'

'Well, well, I had no intention of hurting your feelings—but how was I to know you were so sensitive?'

'True—you were not to know I was so sensitive. Here's a caddle wi' these letters! Guide my soul, what will Billy do!'

Manston offered his services.

'They are to be divided,' the man said.

'How?' said Manston.

'These, for the village, to be carried on into it: any for the vicarage or vicarage farm must be left in the box of the gate-post just here. There's none for the vicarage-house this mornen, but I saw when I started there was one for the clerk o' works at the new church.

This is it, isn't it?'

He held up a large envelope, directed in Edward Springrove's handwriting:—

MR. OWEN GRAYE,
    CLERK OF WORKS,
        TOLCHURCH,
            NEAR ANGLEBURY.

The letter-box was scooped in an oak gate-post about a foot square. There was no slit for inserting the letters, by reason of the opportunity such a lonely spot would have afforded mischievous peasant-boys of doing damage had such been the case; but at the side was a small iron door, kept close by an iron reversible strap locked across it. One side of this strap was painted black, the other white, and white or black outwards implied respectively that there were letters inside, or none.

The postman had taken the key from his pocket and was attempting to insert it in the keyhole of the box. He touched one side, the other, above, below, but never made a straight hit.

'Let me unlock it,' said Manston, taking the key from the postman. He opened the box and reached out with his other hand for Owen's letter.

'No, no. O no—no,' the postman said. 'As one of—Majesty's servants—care—Majesty's mails—duty—put letters—own hands.' He slowly and solemnly placed the letter in the small cavity.

'Now lock it,' he said, closing the door.

The steward placed the bar across, with the black side outwards, signifying 'empty,' and turned the key.

'You've put the wrong side outwards!' said the postman. ' 'Tisn't empty.'

'And dropped the key in the mud, so that I can't alter it,' said the steward, letting something fall.

'What an awkward thing!'

'It is an awkward thing.'

They both went searching in the mud, which their own trampling had reduced to the consistency of pap, the postman unstrapping his little lantern from his breast, and thrusting it about, close to the ground, the rain still drizzling down, and the dawn so tardy on account of the heavy clouds that daylight seemed delayed indefinitely. The rays of the lantern were rendered individually visible upon the thick mist, and seemed almost tangible as they passed off into it, after illuminating the faces and knees of the two stooping figures dripping with wet; the postman's cape and private bags, and the steward's valise, glistening as if they had been varnished.

'It fell on the grass,' said the postman.

'No; it fell in the mud,' said Manston. They

searched again.

'I'm afraid we shan't find it by this light,' said the steward at length, washing his muddy fingers in the wet grass of the bank.

'I'm afraid we shan't,' said the other, standing up.

'I'll tell you what we had better do,' said Manston. 'I shall be back this way in an hour or so, and since it was all my fault, I'll look again, and shall be sure to find it in the daylight. And I'll hide the key here for you.' He pointed to a spot behind the post. 'It will be too late to turn the index then, as the people will have been here, so that the box had better stay as it is. The letter will only be delayed a day, and that will not be noticed; if it is, you can say you placed the iron the wrong way without knowing it, and all will be well.'

This was agreed to by the postman as the best thing to be done under the circumstances, and the pair went on. They had passed the village and come to a crossroad, when the steward, telling his companion that their paths now diverged, turned off to the left towards Carriford.

No sooner was the postman out of sight and hearing than Manston stalked back to the vicarage letter-box by keeping inside a fence, and thus avoiding the village; arrived here, he took the key from his pocket, where it had been concealed all the time, and abstracted Owen's letter. This done, he turned towards home, by the help of what he carried in his valise adjusting himself to his ordinary appearance as he neared the quarter in which he was known.

An hour and half's sharp walking brought him to his own door in Knapwater Park.

2. EIGHT O'CLOCK A.M.

Seated in his private office he wetted the flap of the stolen letter, and waited patiently till the adhesive gum could be loosened. He took out Edward's note, the accounts, the rosebud, and the photographs, regarding them with the keenest interest and anxiety.

The note, the accounts, the rosebud, and his own photograph, he restored to their places again. The other photograph he took between his finger and thumb, and held it towards the bars of the grate. There he held it for half-a-minute or more, meditating.

'It is a great risk to run, even for such an end,' he muttered.

Suddenly, impregnated with a bright idea, he jumped up and left the office for the front parlour. Taking up an album of portraits, which lay on the table, he searched for three or four likenesses of the lady who had so lately displaced Cytherea, which were interspersed among the rest of the collection, and carefully regarded them. They were taken in different attitudes and styles, and he compared each singly with that he held in his hand. One of them, the one most resembling that abstracted from the letter in general tone, size, and attitude, he selected from the rest, and returned with it to his office.

Pouring some water into a plate, he set the two portraits afloat upon it, and sitting down tried to read.

At the end of a quarter of an hour, after several ineffectual attempts, he found that each photograph would peel from the card on which it was mounted. This done, he threw into the fire the original likeness and the recent card, stuck upon the original card the recent likeness from the album, dried it before the fire, and placed it in the envelope with the other scraps.

The result he had obtained, then, was this: in the envelope were now two photographs, both having the same photographer's name on the back and consecutive numbers attached. At the bottom of the one which showed his own likeness, his own name was written down; on the other his wife's name was written; whilst the central feature, and whole matter to which this latter card and writing referred, the likeness of a lady mounted upon it, had been changed.

Mrs. Manston entered the room, and begged him to come to breakfast. He followed her and they sat down. During the meal he told her what he had done, with scrupulous regard to every detail, and showed her the result.

'It is indeed a great risk to run,' she said, sipping her tea.

'But it would be a greater not to do it.'

'Yes.'

The envelope was again fastened up as before, and Manston put it in his pocket and went out. Shortly afterwards he was seen, on horseback, riding in a direction towards Tolchurch. Keeping to the fields, as well as he could, for the greater part of the way, he dropped into the road by the vicarage letter-box, and looking carefully about, to ascertain that no person was near, he restored the letter to its nook, placed the key in its hiding-place, as he had promised the postman, and again rode homewards by a roundabout way.

3. AFTERNOON

The letter was brought to Owen Graye, the same afternoon, by one of the vicar's servants who had been to the box with a duplicate key, as usual, to leave letters for the evening post. The man found that the index had told falsely that morning for the first time within his recollection; but no particular attention was paid to the mistake, as it was considered. The contents of the envelope were scrutinized by Owen and flung aside as useless.

The next morning brought Springrove's second letter, the existence of which was unknown to Manston. The sight of Edward's handwriting again raised the expectations of brother and sister, till Owen had opened the envelope and pulled out the twig and verse.

'Nothing that's of the slightest use, after all,' he said to her; 'we are as far as ever from the merest shadow of legal proof that would convict him of what I am morally certain he did, marry you, suspecting, if not knowing, her to be alive all the time.'

'What has Edward sent?' said Cytherea.

'An old amatory verse in Manston's writing. Fancy,' he said bitterly, 'this is the strain he addressed her in when they were courting—as he did you, I suppose.'

He handed her the verse and she read—

EUNICE.

Whoso for hours or lengthy days
Shall catch her aspect's changeful rays,
Then turn away, can none recall
Beyond a galaxy of all
    In hazy portraiture;
Lit by the light of azure eyes
Like summer days by summer skies:
Her sweet transitions seem to be
A kind of pictured melody,
    And not a set contour.

'Æ. M.'

504

A strange expression had overspread Cytherea's countenance. It rapidly increased to the most death-like anguish. She flung down the paper, seized Owen's hand tremblingly, and covered her face.

'Cytherea! What is it, for Heaven's sake?'

'Owen—suppose—O, you don't know what I think.'

'What?'

'*"The light of azure eyes,"*' she repeated with ashy lips.

'Well, "the light of azure eyes"?' he said, astounded at her manner.

'Mrs. Morris said in her letter to me that her eyes are *black*!'

'H'm. Mrs. Morris must have made a mistake—nothing likelier.'

'She didn't.'

'They might be either in this photograph,' said Owen, looking at the card bearing Mrs. Manston's name.

'Blue eyes would scarcely photograph so deep in tone as that,' said Cytherea. 'No, they seem black here, certainly.'

'Well, then, Manston must have blundered in writing his verses.'

'But could he? Say a man in love may forget his own name, but not that he forgets the colour of his mistress's eyes. Besides she would have seen the mistake when she read them, and have had it corrected.'

'That's true, she would,' mused Owen. 'Then, Cytherea, it comes to this—you must have been misinformed by Mrs. Morris, since there is no other alternative.'

'I suppose I must.'

Her looks belied her words.

'What makes you so strange—ill?' said Owen again.

'I can't believe Mrs. Morris wrong.'

'But look at this, Cytherea. If it is clear to us that the woman had blue eyes two years ago, she must have blue eyes now, whatever Mrs. Morris or anybody else may fancy. Any one would think that Manston could change the colour of a woman's eyes to hear you.'

'Yes,' she said, and paused.

'You say yes, as if he could,' said Owen impatiently.

'By changing the woman herself,' she exclaimed. 'Owen, don't you see the horrid—what I dread?—that the woman he lives with is not Mrs. Manston—that she was burnt after all—and that I am HIS WIFE!'

She tried to support a stoicism under the weight of this new trouble, but no! The unexpected revulsion of ideas was so overwhelming that she crept to him and leant against his breast.

Before reflecting any further upon the subject Graye led her upstairs and got her to lie down. Then he went to the window and stared out of it up the lane, vainly endeavouring to come to some conclusion upon the fantastic enigma that confronted him. Cytherea's new view seemed incredible, yet it had such a hold upon her that it would be necessary to clear it away by positive proof before contemplation of her fear should have preyed too deeply upon her.

'Cytherea,' he said, 'this will not do. You must stay here alone all the afternoon whilst I go to Carriford. I shall know all when I return.'

'No, no, don't go!' she implored.

'Soon, then, not directly.' He saw her subtle reasoning—that it was folly to be wise.

Reflection still convinced him that good would come of persevering in his intention and dispelling his sister's idle fears. Anything was better than this absurd doubt in her mind. But he resolved to wait till Sunday, the first day on which he might reckon upon seeing Mrs. Manston without suspicion. In the meantime he wrote to Edward Springrove, requesting him to go again to Mrs. Manston's former lodgings.

XVIII.

THE EVENTS OF THREE DAYS

1. MARCH THE EIGHTEENTH

Sunday morning had come, and Owen was trudging over the six miles of hill and dale that lay between Tolchurch and Carriford.

Edward Springrove's answer to the last letter, after expressing his amazement at the strange contradiction between the verses and Mrs. Morris's letter, had been to the effect that he had again visited the neighbour of the dead Mr. Brown, and had received as near a description of Mrs. Manston as it was possible to get at second-hand, and by hearsay. She was a tall woman, wide at the shoulders, and full-chested, and she had a straight and rather large nose. The colour of her eyes the informant did not know, for she had only seen the lady in the street as she went in or out. This confusing remark was added. The woman had almost recognized Mrs. Manston when she had called with her husband lately, but she had kept her veil down. Her residence, before she came to Hoxton, was quite unknown to this next-door neighbour, and Edward could get no manner of clue to it from any other source.

Owen reached the church-door a few

minutes before the bells began chiming. Nobody was yet in the church, and he walked round the aisles. From Cytherea's frequent description of how and where herself and others used to sit, he knew where to look for Manston's seat; and after two or three errors of examination he took up a prayer-book in which was written 'Eunice Manston.' The book was nearly new, and the date of the writing about a month earlier. One point was at any rate established: that the woman living with Manston was presented to the world as no other than his lawful wife.

The quiet villagers of Carriford required no pew-opener in their place of worship: natives and in-dwellers had their own seats, and strangers sat where they could. Graye took a seat in the nave, on the north side, close behind a pillar dividing it from the north aisle, which was completely allotted to Miss Aldclyffe, her farmers, and her retainers, Manston's pew being in the midst of them. Owen's position on the other side of the passage was a little in advance of Manston's seat, and so situated that by leaning forward he could look directly into the face of any person sitting there, though, if he sat upright, he was wholly hidden from such a one by the intervening pillar.

Aiming to keep his presence unknown to Manston if possible, Owen sat, without once turning his head, during the entrance of the congregation. A rustling of silk round by the north passage and into Manston's seat, told him that some woman had entered there, and as it seemed from the accompaniment of heavier footsteps, Manston was with her.

Immediately upon rising up, he looked intently in that direction, and saw a lady standing at the end of the seat nearest himself. Portions of Manston's figure appeared on the other side of her. In two glances Graye read thus many of her characteristics, and in the following order:—

She was a tall woman.

She was broad at the shoulders.

She was full-bosomed.

She was easily recognizable from the photograph but nothing could be discerned of the colour of her eyes.

With a preoccupied mind he withdrew into his nook, and heard the service continued— only conscious of the fact that in opposition to the suspicion which one odd circumstance had bred in his sister concerning this woman, all ostensible and ordinary proofs and probabilities tended to the opposite conclusion. There sat the genuine original of the portrait—could he wish for more? Cytherea wished for more. Eunice Manston's eyes were blue, and it was necessary that this woman's eyes should be blue also.

Unskilled labour wastes in beating against the bars ten times the energy exerted by the practised hand in the effective direction. Owen felt this to be the case in his own and Edward's attempts to follow up the clue afforded them. Think as he might, he could not think of a crucial test in the matter absorbing him, which should possess the indispensable attribute—a capability of being applied privately; that in the event of its proving the lady to be the rightful owner of the name she used, he might recede without obloquy from an untenable position.

But to see Mrs. Manston's eyes from where he sat was impossible, and he could do nothing in the shape of a direct examination at present. Miss Aldclyffe had possibly recognized him, but Manston had not, and feeling that it was indispensable to keep the purport of his visit a secret from the steward, he thought it would be as well, too, to keep his presence in the village a secret from him; at any rate, till the day was over.

At the first opening of the doors, Graye left the church and wandered away into the fields to ponder on another scheme. He could not call on Farmer Springrove, as he had intended, until this matter was set at rest. Two hours intervened between the morning and afternoon services.

This time had nearly expired before Owen had struck out any method of proceeding, or could decide to run the risk of calling at the Old House and asking to see Mrs. Manston point-blank. But he had drawn near the place, and was standing still in the public path, from which a partial view of the front of the building could be obtained, when the bells began chiming for afternoon service. Whilst Graye paused, two persons came from the front door of the half-hidden dwelling whom he presently saw to be Manston and his wife. Manston was wearing his old garden-hat, and carried one of the monthly magazines under his arm. Immediately they had passed the gateway he branched off and went over the hill in a direction away from the church, evidently intending to ramble along, and read as the humour moved him. The lady meanwhile turned in the other direction, and went into the church path.

Owen resolved to make something of this opportunity. He hurried along towards the church, doubled round a sharp angle, and came back upon the other path, by which Mrs. Manston must arrive.

In about three minutes she appeared in sight without a veil. He discovered, as she drew nearer, a difficulty which had not struck him at first—that it is not an easy matter to particularize the colour of a stranger's eyes in a merely casual encounter on a path out of doors. That Mrs. Manston must be brought close to him, and not only so, but to look closely at him, if his purpose were to be accomplished.

He shaped a plan. It might by chance be

effectual; if otherwise, it would not reveal his intention to her. When Mrs. Manston was within speaking distance, he went up to her and said—

'Will you kindly tell me which turning will take me to Casterbridge?'

'The second on the right,' said Mrs. Manston.

Owen put on a blank look: he held his hand to his ear—conveying to the lady the idea that he was deaf.

She came closer and said more distinctly—

'The second turning on the right.'

Owen flushed a little. He fancied he had beheld the revelation he was in search of. But had his eyes deceived him?

Once more he used the ruse, still drawing nearer and intimating by a glance that the trouble he gave her was very distressing to him.

'How very deaf!' she murmured. She exclaimed loudly—

'The second turning to the right.'

She had advanced her face to within a foot of his own, and in speaking mouthed very emphatically, fixing her eyes intently upon his. And now his first suspicion was indubitably confirmed. Her eyes were as black as midnight.

All this feigning was most distasteful to Graye. The riddle having been solved, he unconsciously assumed his natural look before she had withdrawn her face. She found him to be peering at her as if he would read her very

513

soul—expressing with his eyes the notification of which, apart from emotion, the eyes are more capable than any other—inquiry.

Her face changed its expression—then its colour. The natural tint of the lighter portions sank to an ashy gray; the pink of her cheeks grew purpler. It was the precise result which would remain after blood had left the face of one whose skin was dark, and artificially coated with pearl-powder and carmine.

She turned her head and moved away, murmuring a hasty reply to Owen's farewell remark of 'Good-day,' and with a kind of nervous twitch lifting her hand and smoothing her hair, which was of a light-brown colour.

'She wears false hair,' he thought, 'or has changed its colour artificially. Her true hair matched her eyes.'

And now, in spite of what Mr. Brown's neighbours had said about nearly recognizing Mrs. Manston on her recent visit—which might have meant anything or nothing; in spite of the photograph, and in spite of his previous incredulity; in consequence of the verse, of her silence and backwardness at the visit to Hoxton with Manston, and of her appearance and distress at the present moment, Graye had a conviction that the woman was an impostor.

What could be Manston's reason for such an astounding trick he could by no stretch of imagination divine.

He changed his direction as soon as the

514

woman was out of sight, and plodded along the lanes homeward to Tolchurch.

One new idea was suggested to him by his desire to allay Cytherea's dread of being claimed, and by the difficulty of believing that the first Mrs. Manston lost her life as supposed, notwithstanding the inquest and verdict. Was it possible that the real Mrs. Manston, who was known to be a Philadelphian by birth, had returned by the train to London, as the porter had said, and then left the country under an assumed name, to escape that worst kind of widowhood—the misery of being wedded to a fickle, faithless, and truant husband?

*   *   *

In her complicated distress at the news brought by her brother, Cytherea's thoughts at length reverted to her friend, the Rector of Carriford. She told Owen of Mr. Raunham's warm-hearted behaviour towards herself, and of his strongly expressed wish to aid her.

'He is not only a good, but a sensible man. We seem to want an old head on our side.'

'And he is a magistrate,' said Owen in a tone of concurrence. He thought, too, that no harm could come of confiding in the rector, but there was a difficulty in bringing about the confidence. He wished that his sister and himself might both be present at an interview with Mr. Raunham, yet it would be unwise for them to call on him together, in the sight of all the servants and parish of Carriford.

There could be no objection to their writing him a letter.

No sooner was the thought born than it was carried out. They wrote to him at once, asking him to have the goodness to give them some advice they sadly needed, and begging that he would accept their assurance that there was a real justification for the additional request they made—that instead of their calling upon him, he would any evening of the week come to their cottage at Tolchurch.

2. MARCH THE TWENTIETH. SIX TO NINE O'CLOCK P.M.

Two evenings later, to the total disarrangement of his dinner-hour, Mr. Raunham appeared at Owen's door. His arrival was hailed with genuine gratitude. The horse was tied to the palings, and the rector ushered indoors and put into the easy-chair.

Then Graye told him the whole story, reminding him that their first suspicions had been of a totally different nature, and that in endeavouring to obtain proof of their truth they had stumbled upon marks which had surprised them into these new uncertainties, thrice as marvellous as the first, yet more

516

prominent.

Cytherea's heart was so full of anxiety that it superinduced a manner of confidence which was a death-blow to all formality. Mr. Raunham took her hand pityingly.

'It is a serious charge,' he said, as a sort of original twig on which his thoughts might precipitate themselves.

'Assuming for a moment that such a substitution was rendered an easy matter by fortuitous events,' he continued, 'there is this consideration to be placed beside it—what earthly motive can Mr. Manston have had which would be sufficiently powerful to lead him to run such a very great risk? The most abandoned *roué* could not, at that particular crisis, have taken such a reckless step for the mere pleasure of a new companion.'

Owen had seen that difficulty about the motive; Cytherea had not.

'Unfortunately for us,' the rector resumed, 'no more evidence is to be obtained from the porter, Chinney. I suppose you know what became of him? He got to Liverpool and embarked, intending to work his way to America, but on the passage he fell overboard and was drowned. But there is no doubt of the truth of his confession—in fact, his conduct tends to prove it true—and no moral doubt of the fact that the real Mrs. Manston left here to go back by that morning's train. This being the case, then, why, if this woman is not she, did

517

she take no notice of the advertisement—I mean not necessarily a friendly notice, but from the information it afforded her have rendered it impossible that she should be personified without her own connivance?'

'I think that argument is overthrown,' Graye said, 'by my earliest assumption of her hatred of him, weariness of the chain which bound her to him, and a resolve to begin the world anew. Let's suppose she has married another man—somewhere abroad, say; she would be silent for her own sake.'

'You've hit the only genuine possibility,' said Mr. Raunham, tapping his finger upon his knee. 'That would decidedly dispose of the second difficulty. But his motive would be as mysterious as ever.'

Cytherea's pictured dreads would not allow her mind to follow their conversation. 'She's burnt,' she said. 'O yes; I fear—I fear she is!'

'I don't think we can seriously believe that now, after what has happened,' said the rector.

Still straining her thought towards the worst, 'Then, perhaps, the first Mrs. Manston was not his wife,' she returned; 'and then I should be his wife just the same, shouldn't I?'

'They were married safely enough,' said Owen. 'There is abundance of circumstantial evidence to prove that.'

'Upon the whole,' said Mr. Raunham, 'I should advise your asking in a straightforward way for legal proof from the steward that the present woman is really his original wife—a thing which, to my mind, you should have done at the outset.' He turned to Cytherea kindly, and asked her what made her give up her husband so unceremoniously.

She could not tell the rector of her aversion to Manston, and of her unquenched love for Edward.

'Your terrified state no doubt,' he said, answering for her, in the manner of those accustomed to the pulpit. 'But into such a solemn compact as marriage, all-important considerations, both legally and morally, enter; it was your duty to have seen everything clearly proved. Doubtless Mr. Manston is prepared with proofs, but as it concerns nobody but yourself that her identity should be publicly established (and by your absenteeism you act as if you were satisfied) he has not troubled to exhibit them. Nobody else has taken the trouble to prove what does not affect them in the least—that's the way of the world always. You, who should have required all things to be made clear, ran away.'

'That was partly my doing,' said Owen.

The same explanation—her want of love for Manston—applied here too, but she shunned the revelation.

'But never mind,' added the rector, 'it was all the greater credit to your womanhood, perhaps. I say, then, get your brother to write a line to Mr. Manston, saying you wish to be satisfied that all is legally clear (in case you should want to marry again, for instance), and I have no doubt that you will be. Or, if you would rather, I'll write myself?'

'O no, sir, no,' pleaded Cytherea, beginning to blanch, and breathing quickly. 'Please don't say anything. Let me live here with Owen. I am so afraid it will turn out that I shall have to go to Knapwater and be his wife, and I don't want to go. Do conceal what we have told you. Let him continue his deception—it is much the best for me.'

Mr. Raunham at length divined that her love for Manston, if it had ever existed, had transmuted itself into a very different feeling now.

'At any rate,' he said, as he took his leave and mounted his mare, 'I will see about it. Rest content, Miss Graye, and depend upon it that I will not lead you into difficulty.'

'Conceal it,' she still pleaded.

'We'll see—but of course I must do my duty.'

'No—don't do your duty!' She looked up at him through the gloom, illuminating her own face and eyes with the candle she held.

'I will consider, then,' said Mr. Raunham, sensibly moved. He turned his horse's head, bade them a warm adieu, and left the door.

The rector of Carriford trotted homewards under the cold and clear March sky, its countless stars fluttering like bright birds. He

520

was unconscious of the scene. Recovering from the effect of Cytherea's voice and glance of entreaty, he laid the subject of the interview clearly before himself.

The suspicions of Cytherea and Owen were honest, and had foundation—that he must own. Was he—a clergyman, magistrate, and conscientious man—justified in yielding to Cytherea's importunities to keep silence, because she dreaded the possibility of a return to Manston? Was she wise in her request? Holding her present belief, and with no definite evidence either way, she could, for one thing, never conscientiously marry any one else. Suppose that Cytherea were Manston's wife—*i.e.*, that the first wife was really burnt? The adultery of Manston would be proved, and, Mr. Raunham thought, cruelty sufficient to bring the case within the meaning of the statute. Suppose the new woman was, as stated, Mr. Manston's restored wife? Cytherea was perfectly safe as a single woman whose marriage had been void. And if it turned out that, though this woman was not Manston's wife, his wife was still living, as Owen had suggested, in America or elsewhere, Cytherea was safe.

The first supposition opened up the worst contingency. Was she really safe as Manston's wife? Doubtful. But, however that might be, the gentle, defenceless girl, whom it seemed nobody's business to help or defend, should be put in a track to proceed against this man. She had but one life, and the superciliousness with which all the world now regarded her should be compensated in some measure by the man whose carelessness—to set him in the best light—had caused it.

Mr. Raunham felt more and more positively that his duty must be done. An inquiry must be made into the matter. Immediately on reaching home, he sat down and wrote a plain and friendly letter to Mr. Manston, and despatched it at once to him by hand. Then he flung himself back in his chair, and went on with his meditation. Was there anything in the suspicion? There could be nothing, surely. Nothing is done by a clever man without a motive, and what conceivable motive could Manston have for such abnormal conduct? Corinthian that he might be, who had preyed on virginity like St. George's dragon, he would never have been absurd enough to venture on such a course for the possession alone of the woman—there was no reason for it—she was inferior to Cytherea in every respect, physical and mental.

On the other hand, it seemed rather odd, when he analyzed the action, that a woman who deliberately hid herself from her husband for more than a twelvemonth should be brought back by a mere advertisement. In fact, the whole business had worked almost too smoothly and effectually for unpremeditated sequence. It was too much like the indiscriminate righting of everything at the end of an old play. And there was that curious business of the keys and watch. Her way of accounting for their being left behind by forgetfulness had always seemed to him rather forced. The only unforced explanation was that suggested by the newspaper writers—that she left them behind on purpose to blind people as to her escape, a motive which would have clashed with the possibility of her being fished back by an advertisement, as the present woman had been. Again, there were the two charred bones. He shuffled the books and papers in his study, and walked about the room, restlessly musing on the same subject. The parlour-maid entered.

'Can young Mr. Springrove from London see you to-night, sir?'

'Young Mr. Springrove?' said the rector, surprised.

'Yes, sir.'

'Yes, of course he can see me. Tell him to come in.'

Edward came so impatiently into the room, as to show that the few short moments his announcement had occupied had been irksome to him. He stood in the doorway with the same black bag in his hand, and the same old gray cloak on his shoulders, that he had worn fifteen months earlier when returning on the night of the fire. This appearance of his conveyed a true impression; he had become a stagnant man. But he was excited now.

'I have this moment come from London,' he said, as the door was closed behind him.

The prophetic insight, which so strangely accompanies critical experiences, prompted Mr. Raunham's reply.

'About the Grayes and Manston?'

'Yes. That woman is not Mrs. Manston.'

'Prove it.'

'I can prove that she is somebody else—that her name is Anne Seaway.'

'And are their suspicions true indeed!'

'And I can do what's more to the purpose at present.'

'Suggest Manston's motive?'

'Only suggest it, remember. But my assumption fits so perfectly with the facts that have been secretly unearthed and conveyed to me, that I can hardly conceive of another.'

There was in Edward's bearing that entire unconsciousness of himself which, natural to wild animals, only prevails in a sensitive man at moments of extreme intentness. The rector saw that he had no trivial story to communicate, whatever the story was.

'Sit down,' said Mr. Raunham. 'My mind has been on the stretch all the evening to form the slightest guess at such an object, and all to no purpose—entirely to no purpose. Have you said anything to Owen Graye?'

'Nothing—nor to anybody. I could not trust

to the effect a letter might have upon yourself, either; the intricacy of the case brings me to this interview.'

Whilst Springrove had been speaking the two had sat down together. The conversation, hitherto distinct to every corner of the room, was carried on now in tones so low as to be scarcely audible to the interlocutors, and in phrases which hesitated to complete themselves. Three-quarters of an hour passed. Then Edward arose, came out of the rector's study and again flung his cloak around him. Instead of going thence homeward, he went first to the Carriford Road Station with a telegram, having despatched which he proceeded to his father's house for the first time since his arrival in the village.

3. FROM NINE TO TEN O'CLOCK P.M.

The next presentation is the interior of the Old House on the evening of the preceding section. The steward was sitting by his parlour fire, and had been reading the letter arrived from the rectory. Opposite to him sat the woman known to the village and neighbourhood as Mrs. Manston.

'Things are looking desperate with us,' he said gloomily. His gloom was not that of the hypochondriac, but the legitimate gloom which has its origin in a syllogism. As he uttered the words he handed the letter to her.

'I almost expected some such news as this,' she replied, in a tone of much greater indifference. 'I knew suspicion lurked in the eyes of that young man who stared at me so in the church path: I could have sworn it.'

Manston did not answer for some time. His face was worn and haggard; latterly his head had not been carried so uprightly as of old. 'If they prove you to be—who you are . . . Yes, if they do,' he murmured.

'They must not find that out,' she said, in a positive voice, and looking at him. 'But supposing they do, the trick does not seem to me to be so serious as to justify that wretched, miserable, horrible look of yours. It makes my flesh creep; it is perfectly deathlike.'

He did not reply, and she continued, 'If they say and prove that Eunice is indeed living— and dear, you know she is—she is sure to come back.'

This remark seemed to awaken and irritate him to speech. Again, as he had done a hundred times during their residence together, he categorized the events connected with the fire at the Three Tranters. He dwelt on every incident of that night's history, and endeavoured, with an anxiety which was extraordinary in the apparent circumstances, to prove that his wife must, by the very nature of things, have perished in the flames. She arose from her seat, crossed the hearthrug, and

526

set herself to soothe him; then she whispered that she was still as unbelieving as ever. 'Come, supposing she escaped—just supposing she escaped—where is she?' coaxed the lady.

'Why are you so curious continually?' said Manston.

'Because I am a woman and want to know. Now where is she?'

'In the Flying Isle of San Borandan.'

'Witty cruelty is the cruellest of any. Ah, well—if she is in England, she will come back.'

'She is not in England.'

'But she will come back?'

'No, she won't . . . Come, madam,' he said, arousing himself, 'I shall not answer any more questions.'

'Ah—ah—ah—she is not dead,' the woman murmured again poutingly.

'She is, I tell you.'

'I don't think so, love.'

'She was burnt, I tell you!' he exclaimed.

'Now to please me, admit the bare possibility of her being alive—just the possibility.'

'O yes—to please you I will admit that,' he said quickly. 'Yes, I admit the possibility of her being alive, to please you.'

She looked at him in utter perplexity. The words could only have been said in jest, and yet they seemed to savour of a tone the furthest remove from jesting. There was his face plain to her eyes, but no information of any kind was to be read there.

'It is only natural that I should be curious,' she murmured pettishly, 'if I resemble her as much as you say I do.'

'You are handsomer,' he said, 'though you are about her own height and size. But don't worry yourself. You must know that you are body and soul united with me, though you are but my housekeeper.'

She bridled a little at the remark. 'Wife,' she said, 'most certainly wife, since you cannot dismiss me without losing your character and position, and incurring heavy penalties.'

'I own it—it was well said, though mistakenly—very mistakenly.'

'Don't riddle to me about mistakenly and such dark things. Now what was your motive, dearest, in running the risk of having me here?'

'Your beauty,' he said.

'She thanks you much for the compliment, but will not take it. Come, what was your motive?'

'Your wit.'

'No, no; not my wit. Wit would have made a wife of me by this time instead of what I am.'

'Your virtue.'

'Or virtue either.'

'I tell you it was your beauty—really.'

'But I cannot help seeing and hearing, and if what people say is true, I am not nearly so good-looking as Cytherea, and several years older.'

The aspect of Manston's face at these words from her was so confirmatory of her hint, that his forced reply of 'O no,' tended to develop her chagrin.

'Mere liking or love for me,' she resumed, 'would not have sprung up all of a sudden, as your pretended passion did. You had been to London several times between the time of the fire and your marriage with Cytherea—you had never visited me or thought of my existence or cared that I was out of a situation and poor. But the week after you married her and were separated from her, off you rush to make love to me—not first to me either, for you went to several places—'

'No, not several places.'

'Yes, you told me so yourself—that you went first to the only lodging in which your wife had been known as Mrs. Manston, and when you found that the lodging-house-keeper had gone away and died, and that nobody else in the street had any definite ideas as to your wife's personal appearance, and came and proposed the arrangement we carried out—that I should personate her. Your taking all this trouble shows that something more serious than love had to do with the matter.'

'Humbug—what trouble after all did I take? When I found Cytherea would not stay with me after the wedding I was much put out at being left alone again. Was that unnatural?'

'No.'

'And those favouring accidents you mention—that nobody knew my first wife—seemed an arrangement of Providence for our mutual benefit, and merely perfected a half-formed impulse—that I should call you my first wife to escape the scandal that would have arisen if you had come here as anything else.'

'My love, that story won't do. If Mrs. Manston was burnt, Cytherea, whom you love better than me, could have been compelled to live with you as your lawful wife. If she was not burnt, why should you run the risk of her turning up again at any moment and exposing your substitution of me, and ruining your name and prospects?'

'Why—because I might have loved you well enough to run the risk (assuming her not to be burnt, which I deny).'

'No—you would have run the risk the other way. You would rather have risked her finding you with Cytherea as a second wife, than with me as a personator of herself—the first one.'

'You came easiest to hand—remember that.'

'Not so very easy either, considering the labour you took to teach me your first wife's history. All about how she was a native of Philadelphia. Then making me read up the guide-book to Philadelphia, and details of American life and manners, in case the birthplace and history of your wife, Eunice, should ever become known in this

530

neighbourhood—unlikely as it was. Ah! and then about the handwriting of hers that I had to imitate, and the dying my hair, and rouging, to make the transformation complete? You mean to say that that was taking less trouble than there would have been in arranging events to make Cytherea believe herself your wife, and live with you?'

'You were a needy adventuress, who would dare anything for a new pleasure and an easy life—and I was fool enough to give in to you—'

'Good heavens above!—did I ask you to insert those advertisements for your old wife, and to make me answer it as if I was she? Did I ask you to send me the letter for me to copy and send back to you when the third advertisement appeared—purporting to come from the long-lost wife, and giving a detailed history of her escape and subsequent life—all which you had invented yourself? You deluded me into loving you, and then enticed me here! Ah, and this is another thing. How did you know the real wife wouldn't answer it, and upset all your plans?'

'Because I knew she was burnt.'

'Why didn't you force Cytherea to come back, then? Now, my love, I have caught you, and you may just as well tell first as last, *what was your motive in having me here as your first wife?*'

'Silence!' he exclaimed.

She was silent for the space of two minutes, and then persisted in going on to mutter, 'And why was it that Miss Aldclyffe allowed her favourite young lady, Cythie, to be overthrown and supplanted without an expostulation or any show of sympathy? Do you know I often think you exercise a secret power over Miss Aldclyffe. And she always shuns me as if I shared the power. A poor, ill-used creature like me sharing power, indeed!'

'She thinks you are Mrs. Manston.'

'That wouldn't make her avoid me.'

'Yes it would,' he exclaimed impatiently. 'I wish I was dead—dead!'

He had jumped up from his seat in uttering the words, and now walked wearily to the end of the room. Coming back more decisively, he looked in her face.

'We must leave this place if Raunham suspects what I think he does,' he said. 'The request of Cytherea and her brother may simply be for a satisfactory proof, to make her feel legally free—but it may mean more.'

'What may it mean?'

'How should I know?'

'Well, well, never mind, old boy,' she said, approaching him to make up the quarrel. 'Don't be so alarmed—anybody would think that you were the woman and I the man. Suppose they do find out what I am—we can go away from here and keep house as usual. People will say of you, "His first wife was burnt

532

to death" (or "ran away to the Colonies," as the case may be); "he married a second, and deserted her for Anne Seaway." A very everyday case—nothing so horrible, after all.'

He made an impatient movement. 'Whichever way we do it, *nobody must know that you are not my wife Eunice.* And now I must think about arranging matters.'

Manston then retired to his office, and shut himself up for the remainder of the evening.

XIX.

THE EVENTS OF A DAY AND NIGHT

1. MARCH THE TWENTY-FIRST. MORNING

Next morning the steward went out as usual. He shortly told his companion, Anne, that he had almost matured their scheme, and that they would enter upon the details of it when he came home at night. The fortunate fact that the rector's letter did not require an immediate answer would give him time to consider.

Anne Seaway then began her duties in the house. Besides daily superintending the cook and housemaid one of these duties was, at rare intervals, to dust Manston's office with her own hands, a servant being supposed to disturb the books and papers unnecessarily. She softly wandered from table to shelf with the duster in her hand, afterwards standing in the middle of the room, and glancing around to discover if any noteworthy collection of dust had still escaped her.

Her eye fell upon a faint layer which rested upon the ledge of an old-fashioned chestnut cabinet of French Renaissance workmanship, placed in a recess by the fireplace. At a height of about four feet from the floor the upper portion of the front receded, forming the ledge alluded to, on which opened at each end two small doors, the centre space between them being filled out by a panel of similar size, making the third of three squares. The dust on the ledge was nearly on a level with the woman's eye, and, though insignificant in quantity, showed itself distinctly on account of this obliquity of vision. Now opposite the central panel, concentric quarter-circles were traced in the deposited film, expressing to her that this panel, too, was a door like the others; that it had lately been opened, and had skimmed the dust with its lower edge.

At last, then, her curiosity was slightly rewarded. For the right of the matter was that Anne had been incited to this exploration of Manston's office rather by a wish to know the reason of his long seclusion here, after the arrival of the rector's letter, and their subsequent discourse, than by any immediate desire for cleanliness. Still, there would have been nothing remarkable to Anne in this sight but for one recollection. Manston had once casually told her that each of the two side-lockers included half the middle space, the panel of which did not open, and was only put in for symmetry. It was possible that he had opened this compartment by candlelight the preceding night, or he would have seen the marks in the dust, and effaced them, that he might not be proved guilty of telling her an untruth. She balanced herself on one foot and stood pondering. She considered that it was very vexing and unfair in him to refuse her all knowledge of his remaining secrets, under the peculiar circumstances of her connection with him. She went close to the cabinet. As there was no keyhole, the door must be capable of being opened by the unassisted hand. The circles in the dust told her at which edge to apply her force. Here she pulled with the tips of her fingers, but the panel would not come forward. She fetched a chair and looked over the top of the cabinet, but no bolt, knob, or spring was to be seen.

'O, never mind,' she said, with indifference; 'I'll ask him about it, and he will tell me.' Down she came and turned away. Then looking back again she thought it was absurd such a trifle should puzzle her. She retraced her steps, and opened a drawer beneath the ledge of the cabinet, pushing in her hand and feeling about on the underside of the board.

Here she found a small round sinking, and pressed her finger into it. Nothing came of the pressure. She withdrew her hand and looked at the tip of her finger: it was marked with the impress of the circle, and, in addition, a line ran across it diametrically.

'How stupid of me; it is the head of a screw.' Whatever mysterious contrivance had originally existed for opening the puny cupboard of the cabinet, it had at some time been broken, and this rough substitute provided. Stimulated curiosity would not allow her to recede now. She fetched a screwdriver, withdrew the screw, pulled the door open with a penknife, and found inside a cavity about ten inches square. The cavity contained—

Letters from different women, with unknown signatures, Christian names only (surnames being despised in Paphos). Letters from his wife Eunice. Letters from Anne herself, including that she wrote in answer to his advertisement. A small pocket-book. Sundry scraps of paper.

The letters from the strange women with pet names she glanced carelessly through, and then put them aside. They were too similar to her own regretted delusion, and curiosity requires contrast to excite it.

The letters from his wife were next examined. They were dated back as far as Eunice's first meeting with Manston, and the early ones before their marriage contained the usual pretty effusions of women at such a period of their existence. Some little time after he had made her his wife, and when he had come to Knapwater, the series began again, and now their contents arrested her attention more forcibly. She closed the cabinet, carried the letters into the parlour, reclined herself on the sofa, and carefully perused them in the order of their dates.

JOHN STREET,
October 17, 1864.

MY DEAREST HUSBAND,—I received your hurried line of yesterday, and was of course content with it. But why don't you tell me your exact address instead of that 'Post-Office, Budmouth?' This matter is all a mystery to me, and I ought to be told every detail. I cannot fancy it is the same kind of occupation you have been used to hitherto. Your command that I am to stay here awhile until you can 'see how things look' and can arrange to send for me, I must necessarily abide by. But if, as you say, a married man would have been rejected by the person who engaged you, and that hence my existence must be kept a secret until you have secured your position, why did you think of going at all?

The truth is, this keeping our marriage a secret is troublesome, vexing, and wearisome to me. I see the poorest woman in the street bearing her husband's name openly—living with him in the most matter-of-fact ease, and why shouldn't I? I wish I was back again in Liverpool.

To-day I bought a grey waterproof cloak. I think it is a little too long for me, but it was cheap for one of such a quality. The weather is gusty and dreary, and till this morning I had hardly set foot outside the door since you left. Please do tell me when I am to come.—Very affectionately yours,

EUNICE.

JOHN STREET,
October 25, 1864.

MY DEAR HUSBAND,—Why don't you write? Do you hate me? I have not had the heart to do anything this last week. That I, your wife, should be in this strait, and my husband well to do! I have been obliged to leave my first lodging for debt—among other things, they charged me for a lot of brandy which I am quite sure I did not taste. Then I went to Camberwell and was found out by them. I went away privately from thence, and changed my name the second time. I am now Mrs. Rondley. But the new lodging was the wretchedest and dearest I ever set foot in, and I left it after being there only a day. I am now at No. 20 in the same street that you left me in originally. All last night the sash of my window rattled so dreadfully that I could not sleep, but I had not energy enough to get out of bed to stop it. This morning I have been walking—I don't know how far—but far enough to make my feet ache. I have been looking at the outside of two or three of the theatres, but they seem forbidding if I regard them with the eye of an actress in search of an engagement. Though you said I was to think no more of the stage, I believe you would not care if you found me there. But I am not an actress by nature, and art will never make me one. I am too timid and retiring; I was intended for a cottager's wife. I certainly shall not try to go on the boards again whilst I am in this strange place. The idea of being brought on as far as London and then left here alone! Why didn't you leave me in Liverpool? Perhaps you thought I might have told somebody that my real name was Mrs. Manston. As if I had a living friend to whom I could impart it—no such good fortune! In fact, my nearest friend is no nearer than what most people would call a stranger. But perhaps I ought to tell you that a week before I wrote my last letter to you, after wishing that my uncle and aunt in Philadelphia (the only near relatives I had) were still alive, I suddenly resolved to send a line to my cousin James, who, I believe, is still living in that neighbourhood. He has never seen me since we were babies together. I did not tell him of my marriage, because I thought you might not like it, and I gave my real maiden name, and an address at the post-office here. But God knows if the letter will ever reach him.

Do write me an answer, and send something.—Your affectionate wife,

EUNICE.

FRIDAY, *October 28.*
MY DEAR HUSBAND,—The order for ten pounds has just come, and I am truly glad to get it. But why will you write so bitterly? Ah—well, if I had only had the money I should have been on my way to America by this time, so don't think I want to bore you of my own free-will. Who can you have met with at that new place? Remember I say this in no malignant tone, but certainly the facts go

to prove that you have deserted me! You are inconstant—I know it. O, why are you so? Now I have lost you, I love you in spite of your neglect. I am weakly fond— that's my nature. I fear that upon the whole my life has been wasted. I know there is another woman supplanting me in your heart—yes, I know it. Come to me—do come.

EUNICE.

41 CHARLES SQUARE, HOXTON,
November 19.
DEAR ÆNEAS,—Here I am back again after my visit. Why should you have been so enraged at my finding your exact address? Any woman would have tried to do it—you know she would have. And no woman would have lived under assumed names so long as I did. I repeat that I did not call myself Mrs. Manston until I came to this lodging at the beginning of this month—what could you expect?

A helpless creature I, had not fortune favoured me unexpectedly. Banished as I was from your house at dawn, I did not suppose the indignity was about to lead to important results. But in crossing the park I overheard the conversation of a young man and woman who had also risen early. I believe her to be the girl who has won you away from me. Well, their conversation concerned you and Miss Aldclyffe, very peculiarly. The remarkable thing is that you yourself, without knowing it, told me of what, added to their conversation, completely reveals a secret to me that neither of you understand. Two negatives never made such a telling positive before. One clue more, and you would see it. A single consideration prevents my revealing it— just one doubt as to whether your ignorance was real, and was not feigned to deceive me. Civility now, please.

EUNICE.

41 CHARLES SQUARE,
Tuesday, November 22.

MY DARLING HUSBAND,—Monday will suit me excellently for coming. I have acted exactly up to your instructions, and have sold my rubbish at the broker's in the next street. All this movement and bustle is delightful to me after the weeks of monotony I have endured. It is a relief to wish the place good-bye—London always has seemed so much more foreign to me than Liverpool. The mid-day train on Monday will do nicely for me. I shall be anxiously looking out for you on

Sunday night.

I hope so much that you are not angry with me for writing to Miss Aldclyffe. You are not, dear, are you? Forgive me.— Your loving wife,

EUNICE.

This was the last of the letters from the wife to the husband. One other, in Mrs. Manston's handwriting, and in the same packet, was differently addressed.

THREE TRANTERS INN,
CARRIFORD,
November 28, 1864.

DEAR COUSIN JAMES,—Thank you indeed for answering my letter so promptly. When I called at the post-office yesterday I did not in the least think there would be one. But I must leave this subject. I write again at once under the strangest and saddest conditions it is possible to conceive.

I did not tell you in my last that I was a married woman. Don't blame me—it was my husband's influence. I hardly know where to begin my story. I had been living apart from him for a time—then he sent for me (this was last week) and I was glad to go to him. Then this is what he did. He promised to fetch me, and did not—leaving me to do the journey alone. He promised to meet me at the station here—he did not. I went on through the darkness to his house, and found his door locked and himself away from home. I have been obliged to come here, and I write to you in a strange room in a strange village inn! I choose the present moment to write to drive away my misery. Sorrow seems a sort of pleasure when you detail it on paper—poor pleasure though.

But this is what I want to know—and I am ashamed to tell it. I would gladly do as you say, and come to you as a housekeeper, but I have not the money even for a steerage passage. James, do you want me badly enough—do you pity me enough to send it? I could manage to subsist in London upon the proceeds of my sale for another month or six weeks. Will you send it to the same address at the post-office? But how do I know that you . . .

Thus the letter ended. From creases in the paper it was plain that the writer, having got so far, had become dissatisfied with her production, and had crumpled it in her hand. Was it to write another, or not to write at all?

The next thing Anne Seaway perceived was that the fragmentary story she had coaxed out of Manston, to the effect that his wife had left England for America, might be truthful, according to two of these letters, corroborated by the evidence of the railway-porter. And yet, at first, he had sworn in a passion that his wife was most certainly consumed in the fire.

If she had been burnt, this letter, written in her bedroom, and probably thrust into her pocket when she relinquished it, would have been burnt with her. Nothing was surer than that. Why, then, did he say she was burnt, and never show Anne herself this letter?

The question suddenly raised a new and much stranger one—kindling a burst of amazement in her. How did Manston become possessed of this letter?

That fact of possession was certainly the most remarkable revelation of all in connection with this epistle, and perhaps had something to do with his reason for never showing it to her.

She knew by several proofs, that before his marriage with Cytherea, and up to the time of the porter's confession, Manston believed— honestly believed—that Cytherea would be his lawful wife, and hence, of course, that his wife Eunice was dead. So that no communication could possibly have passed between his wife and himself from the first moment that he believed her dead on the night of the fire, to the day of his wedding. And yet he had that letter. How soon afterwards could they have communicated with each other?

The existence of the letter—as much as, or more than its contents—implying that Mrs. Manston was not burnt, his belief in that calamity must have terminated at the moment he obtained possession of the letter, if no earlier. Was, then, the only solution to the riddle that Anne could discern, the true one?—that he had communicated with his wife somewhere about the commencement of Anne's residence with him, or at any time since?

It was the most unlikely thing on earth that a woman who had forsaken her husband should countenance his scheme to personify her—whether she were in America, in London, or in the neighbourhood of Knapwater.

Then came the old and harassing question, what was Manston's real motive in risking his name on the deception he was practising as regarded Anne. It could not be, as he had always pretended, mere passion. Her thoughts had reverted to Mr. Raunham's letter, asking for proofs of her identity with the original Mrs. Manston. She could see no loophole of escape for the man who supported her. True, in her own estimation, his worst alternative was not so very bad after all—the getting the name of libertine, a possible appearance in the divorce or some other court of law, and a question of damages. Such an exposure might hinder his worldly progress for some time. Yet to him this alternative was, apparently, terrible as death itself.

She restored the letters to their hiding-place, scanned anew the other letters and memoranda, from which she could gain no fresh information, fastened up the cabinet, and left everything in its former condition.

Her mind was ill at ease. More than ever she wished that she had never seen Manston. Where the person suspected of mysterious moral obliquity is the possessor of great physical and intellectual attractions, the mere sense of incongruity adds an extra shudder to dread. The man's strange bearing terrified Anne as it had terrified Cytherea; for with all the woman Anne's faults, she had not descended to such depths of depravity as to willingly participate in crime. She had not even known that a living wife was being displaced till her arrival at Knapwater put retreat out of the question, and had looked upon personation simply as a mode of subsistence a degree better than toiling in poverty and alone, after a bustling and somewhat pampered life as housekeeper in a gay mansion.

Non illa colo calathisve Minervae
Foemineas assueta manus.

547

2. AFTERNOON

Mr. Raunham and Edward Springrove had by this time set in motion a machinery which they hoped to find working out important results.

The rector was restless and full of meditation all the following morning. It was plain, even to the servants about him, that Springrove's communication wore a deeper complexion than any that had been made to the old magistrate for many months or years past. The fact was that, having arrived at the stage of existence in which the difficult intellectual feat of suspending one's judgment becomes possible, he was now putting it in practice, though not without the penalty of watchful effort.

It was not till the afternoon that he determined to call on his relative, Miss Aldclyffe, and cautiously probe her knowledge of the subject occupying him so thoroughly. Cytherea, he knew, was still beloved by this solitary woman. Miss Aldclyffe had made several private inquiries concerning her former companion, and there was ever a sadness in her tone when the young lady's name was mentioned, which showed that from whatever cause the elder Cytherea's renunciation of her favourite and namesake proceeded, it was not from indifference to her fate.

'Have you ever had any reason for supposing your steward anything but an upright man?' he said to the lady.

'Never the slightest. Have you?' said she reservedly.

'Well—I have.'

'What is it?'

'I can say nothing plainly, because nothing is proved. But my suspicions are very strong.'

'Do you mean that he was rather cool towards his wife when they were first married, and that it was unfair in him to leave her? I know he was; but I think his recent conduct towards her has amply atoned for the neglect.'

He looked Miss Aldclyffe full in the face. It was plain that she spoke honestly. She had not the slightest notion that the woman who lived with the steward might be other than Mrs. Manston—much less that a greater matter might be behind.

'That's not it—I wish it was no more. My suspicion is, first, that the woman living at the Old House is not Mr. Manston's wife.'

'Not—Mr. Manston's wife?'

'That is it.'

Miss Aldclyffe looked blankly at the rector. 'Not Mr. Manston's wife—who else can she be?' she said simply.

'An improper woman of the name of Anne Seaway.'

Mr. Raunham had, in common with other people, noticed the extraordinary interest of Miss Aldclyffe in the well-being of her steward, and had endeavoured to account for it in various ways. The extent to which she was shaken by his information, whilst it proved that the understanding between herself and Manston did not make her a sharer of his secrets, also showed that the tie which bound her to him was still unbroken. Mr. Raunham had lately begun to doubt the latter fact, and now, on finding himself mistaken, regretted that he had not kept his own counsel in the matter. This it was too late to do, and he pushed on with his proofs. He gave Miss Aldclyffe in detail the grounds of his belief.

Before he had done, she recovered the cloak of reserve that she had adopted on his opening the subject.

'I might possibly be convinced that you were in the right, after such an elaborate argument,' she replied, 'were it not for one fact, which bears in the contrary direction so pointedly, that nothing but absolute proof can turn it. It is that there is no conceivable motive which could induce any sane man—leaving alone a man of Mr. Manston's clear-headedness and integrity—to venture upon such an extraordinary course of conduct—no motive on earth.'

'That was my own opinion till after the visit of a friend last night—a friend of mine and poor little Cytherea's.'

'Ah—and Cytherea,' said Miss Aldclyffe, catching at the idea raised by the name. 'That he loved Cytherea—yes and loves her now, wildly and devotedly, I am as positive as that I breathe. Cytherea is years younger than Mrs. Manston—as I shall call her—twice as sweet in disposition, three times as beautiful. Would he have given her up quietly and suddenly for a common. Mr. Raunham, your story is monstrous, and I don't believe it!' She glowed in her earnestness.

The rector might now have advanced his second proposition—the possible motive—but for reasons of his own he did not.

'Very well, madam. I only hope that facts will sustain you in your belief. Ask him the question to his face, whether the woman is his wife or no, and see how he receives it.'

'I will to-morrow, most certainly,' she said. 'I always let these things die of wholesome ventilation, as every fungus does.'

But no sooner had the rector left her presence, than the grain of mustard-seed he had sown grew to a tree. Her impatience to set her mind at rest could not brook a night's delay. It was with the utmost difficulty that she could wait till evening arrived to screen her movements. Immediately the sun had dropped behind the horizon, and before it was quite dark, she wrapped her cloak around her, softly left the house, and walked erect through the gloomy park in the direction of the old manor-house.

The same minute saw two persons sit down in the rectory-house to share the rector's usually solitary dinner. One was a man of official appearance, commonplace in all except his eyes. The other was Edward Springrove.

*   *   *

The discovery of the carefully-concealed letters rankled in the mind of Anne Seaway. Her woman's nature insisted that Manston had no right to keep all matters connected with his lost wife a secret from herself. Perplexity had bred vexation; vexation, resentment; curiosity had been continuous. The whole morning this resentment and curiosity increased.

The steward said very little to his companion during their luncheon at mid-day. He seemed reckless of appearances—almost indifferent to whatever fate awaited him. All his actions betrayed that something portentous was impending, and still he explained nothing. By carefully observing every trifling action, as only a woman can observe them, the thought at length dawned upon her that he was going to run away secretly. She feared for herself; her knowledge of law and justice was vague, and she fancied she might in some way be made responsible for him.

In the afternoon he went out of the house again, and she watched him drive away in the direction of the county-town. She felt a desire to go there herself, and, after an interval of half-an-hour, followed him on foot notwithstanding the distance—ostensibly to do some shopping.

One among her several trivial errands was to make a small purchase at the druggist's. Near the druggist's stood the County Bank. Looking out of the shop window, between the coloured bottles, she saw Manston come down the steps of the bank, in the act of withdrawing his hand from his pocket, and pulling his coat close over its mouth.

It is an almost universal habit with people, when leaving a bank, to be carefully adjusting their pockets if they have been receiving money; if they have been paying it in, their hands swing laxly. The steward had in all likelihood been taking money—possibly on Miss Aldclyffe's account—that was continual with him. And he might have been removing his own, as a man would do who was intending to leave the country.

3. FROM FIVE TO EIGHT O'CLOCK P.M.

Anne reached home again in time to preside over preparations for dinner. Manston came in half-an-hour later. The lamp was lighted, the shutters were closed, and they sat down together. He was pale and worn—almost haggard.

The meal passed off in almost unbroken silence. When preoccupation withstands the influence of a social meal with one pleasant companion, the mental scene must be surpassingly vivid. Just as she was rising a tap came to the door.

Before a maid could attend to the knock, Manston crossed the room and answered it himself. The visitor was Miss Aldclyffe.

Manston instantly came back and spoke to Anne in an undertone. 'I should be glad if you could retire to your room for a short time.'

'It is a dry, starlight evening,' she replied. 'I will go for a little walk if your object is merely a private conversation with Miss Aldclyffe.'

'Very well, do; there's no accounting for tastes,' he said. A few commonplaces then passed between her and Miss Aldclyffe, and Anne went upstairs to bonnet and cloak herself. She came down, opened the front door, and went out.

She looked around to realize the night. It was dark, mournful, and quiet. Then she stood still. From the moment that Manston had requested her absence, a strong and burning desire had prevailed in her to know the subject of Miss Aldclyffe's conversation with him. Simple curiosity was not entirely what inspired her. Her suspicions had been thoroughly aroused by the discovery of the morning. A conviction that her future depended on her power to combat a man who, in desperate circumstances, would be far from a friend to her, prompted a strategic movement to acquire

554

the important secret that was in handling now. The woman thought and thought, and regarded the dull dark trees, anxiously debating how the thing could be done.

Stealthily re-opening the front door she entered the hall, and advancing and pausing alternately, came close to the door of the room in which Miss Aldclyffe and Manston conversed. Nothing could be heard through the keyhole or panels. At a great risk she softly turned the knob and opened the door to a width of about half-an-inch, performing the act so delicately that three minutes, at least, were occupied in completing it. At that instant Miss Aldclyffe said—

'There's a draught somewhere. The door is ajar, I think.'

Anne glided back under the staircase. Manston came forward and closed the door. This chance was now cut off, and she considered again. The parlour, or sitting-room, in which the conference took place, had the window-shutters fixed on the outside of the window, as is usual in the back portions of old country-houses. The shutters were hinged one on each side of the opening, and met in the middle, where they were fastened by a bolt passing continuously through them and the wood mullion within, the bolt being secured on the inside by a pin, which was seldom inserted till Manston and herself were about to retire for the night; sometimes not at all.

If she returned to the door of the room she might be discovered at any moment, but could she listen at the window, which overlooked a part of the garden never visited after nightfall, she would be safe from disturbance. The idea was worth a trial.

She glided round to the window, took the head of the bolt between her finger and thumb, and softly screwed it round until it was entirely withdrawn from its position. The shutters remained as before, whilst, where the bolt had come out, was now a shining hole three-quarters of an inch in diameter, through which one might see into the middle of the room. She applied her eye to the orifice.

Miss Aldclyffe and Manston were both standing; Manston with his back to the window, his companion facing it. The lady's demeanour was severe, condemnatory, and haughty. No more was to be seen; Anne then turned sideways, leant with her shoulder against the shutters and placed her ear upon the hole.

'You know where,' said Miss Aldclyffe. 'And how could you, a man, act a double deceit like this?'

'Men do strange things sometimes.'

'What was your reason—come?'

'A mere whim.'

'I might even believe that, if the woman were handsomer than Cytherea, or if you had been married some time to Cytherea and had grown tired of her.'

'And can't you believe it, too, under these conditions; that I married Cytherea, gave her up because I heard that my wife was alive, found that my wife would not come to live with me, and then, not to let any woman I love so well as Cytherea run any risk of being displaced and ruined in reputation, should my wife ever think fit to return, induced this woman to come to me, as being better than no companion at all?'

'I cannot believe it. Your love for Cytherea was not of such a kind as that excuse would imply. It was Cytherea or nobody with you. As an object of passion, you did not desire the company of this Anne Seaway at all, and certainly not so much as to madly risk your reputation by bringing her here in the way you have done. I am sure you didn't, Æneas.'

'So am I,' he said bluntly.

Miss Aldclyffe uttered an exclamation of astonishment; the confession was like a blow in its suddenness. She began to reproach him bitterly, and with tears.

'How could you overthrow my plans, disgrace the only girl I ever had any respect for, by such inexplicable doings! . . . That woman must leave this place—the country perhaps. Heavens! the truth will leak out in a day or two!'

'She must do no such thing, and the truth must be stifled somehow—nobody knows how.

If I stay here, or on any spot of the civilized globe, as Æneas Manston, this woman must live with me as my wife, or I am damned past redemption!'

'I will not countenance your keeping her, whatever your motive may be.'

'You must do something,' he murmured. 'You must. Yes, you must.'

'I never will,' she said. 'It is a criminal act.'

He looked at her earnestly. 'Will you not support me through this deception if my very life depends upon it? Will you not?'

'Nonsense! Life! It will be a scandal to you, but she must leave this place. It will out sooner or later, and the exposure had better come now.'

Manston repeated gloomily the same words. 'My life depends upon your supporting me—my very life.'

He then came close to her, and spoke into her ear. Whilst he spoke he held her head to his mouth with both his hands. Strange expressions came over her face; the workings of her mouth were painful to observe. Still he held her and whispered on.

The only words that could be caught by Anne Seaway, confused as her hearing frequently was by the moan of the wind and the waterfall in her outer ear, were these of Miss Aldclyffe, in tones which absolutely quivered: 'They have no money. What can they prove?'

The listener tasked herself to the utmost to catch his answer, but it was in vain. Of the remainder of the colloquy one fact alone was plain to Anne, and that only inductively—that Miss Aldclyffe, from what he had revealed to her, was going to scheme body and soul on Manston's behalf.

Miss Aldclyffe seemed now to have no further reason for remaining, yet she lingered awhile as if loth to leave him. When, finally, the crestfallen and agitated lady made preparations for departure, Anne quickly inserted the bolt, ran round to the entrance archway, and down the steps into the park. Here she stood close to the trunk of a huge lime-tree, which absorbed her dark outline into its own.

In a few minutes she saw Manston, with Miss Aldclyffe leaning on his arm, cross the glade before her and proceed in the direction of the house. She watched them ascend the rise and advance, as two black spots, towards the mansion. The appearance of an oblong space of light in the dark mass of walls denoted that the door was opened. Miss Aldclyffe's outline became visible upon it; the door shut her in, and all was darkness again. The form of Manston returning alone arose from the gloom, and passed by Anne in her hiding-place.

Waiting outside a quarter of an hour longer, that no suspicion of any kind might be excited,

Anne returned to the old manor-house.

4. FROM EIGHT TO ELEVEN O'CLOCK P.M.

Manston was very friendly that evening. It was evident to her, now that she was behind the scenes, that he was making desperate efforts to disguise the real state of his mind.

Her terror of him did not decrease. They sat down to supper, Manston still talking cheerfully. But what is keener than the eye of a mistrustful woman? A man's cunning is to it as was the armour of Sisera to the thin tent-nail. She found, in spite of his adroitness, that he was attempting something more than a disguise of his feeling. He was trying to distract her attention, that he might be unobserved in some special movement of his hands.

What a moment it was for her then! The whole surface of her body became attentive. She allowed him no chance whatever. We know the duplicated condition at such times—when the existence divides itself into two, and the ostensibly innocent chatterer stands in front, like another person, to hide the timorous spy.

Manston played the same game, but more palpably. The meal was nearly over when he seemed possessed of a new idea of how his object might be accomplished. He tilted back his chair with a reflective air, and looked

560

steadily at the clock standing against the wall opposite to him. He said sententiously, 'Few faces are capable of expressing more by dumb show than the face of a clock. You may see in it every variety of incentive—from the softest seductions to negligence to the strongest hints for action.'

'Well, in what way?' she inquired. His drift was, as yet, quite unintelligible to her.

'Why, for instance: look at the cold, methodical, unromantic, business-like air of all the right-angled positions of the hands. They make a man set about work in spite of himself. Then look at the piquant shyness of its face when the two hands are over each other. Several attitudes imply "Make ready." The "make ready" of ten minutes to one differs from the "make ready" of ten minutes to twelve, as youth differs from age. "Upward and onward" says twenty-five minutes to eleven. Mid-day or midnight expresses distinctly "It is done." You surely have noticed that?'

'Yes, I have.'

He continued with affected quaintness:—

'The easy dash of ten minutes past seven, the rakish recklessness of a quarter past, the drooping weariness of twenty-five minutes past, must have been observed by everybody.'

'Whatever amount of truth there may be, there is a good deal of imagination in your fancy,' she said.

He still contemplated the clock.

'Then, again, the general finish of the face has a great effect upon the eye. This old-fashioned brass-faced one we have here, with its arched top, half-moon slit for the day of the month, and ship rocking at the upper part, impresses me with the notion of its being an old cynic, elevating his brows, whose thoughts can be seen wavering between good and evil.'

A thought now enlightened her: the clock was behind her, and he wanted to get her back turned. She dreaded turning, yet, not to excite his suspicion, she was on her guard; she quickly looked behind her at the clock as he spoke, recovering her old position again instantly. The time had not been long enough for any action whatever on his part.

'Ah,' he casually remarked, and at the same minute began to pour her out a glass of wine. 'Speaking of the clock has reminded me that it must nearly want winding up. Remember that it is wound to-night. Suppose you do it at once, my dear.'

There was no possible way of evading the act. She resolutely turned to perform the operation: anything was better than that he should suspect her. It was an old-fashioned eight-day clock, of workmanship suited to the rest of the antique furniture that Manston had collected there, and ground heavily during winding.

Anne had given up all idea of being able to watch him during the interval, and the noise of the wheels prevented her learning anything by her ears. But, as she wound, she caught sight of his shadow on the wall at her right hand.

What was he doing? He was in the very act of pouring something into her glass of wine.

He had completed the manoeuvre before she had done winding. She methodically closed the clock-case and turned round again. When she faced him he was sitting in his chair as before she had risen.

In a familiar scene which has hitherto been pleasant it is difficult to realize that an added condition, which does not alter its aspect, can have made it terrible. The woman thought that his action must have been prompted by no other intent than that of poisoning her, and yet she could not instantly put on a fear of her position.

And before she had grasped these consequences, another supposition served to make her regard the first as unlikely, if not absurd. It was the act of a madman to take her life in a manner so easy of discovery, unless there were far more reason for the crime than any that Manston could possibly have.

Was it not merely his intention, in tampering with her wine, to make her sleep soundly that night? This was in harmony with her original suspicion, that he intended secretly to abscond. At any rate, he was going to set about some stealthy proceeding, as to which she was to be kept in utter darkness. The difficulty now was to avoid drinking the wine.

By means of one pretext and another she put off taking her glass for nearly five minutes, but he eyed her too frequently to allow her to throw the potion under the grate. It became necessary to take one sip. This she did, and found an opportunity of absorbing it in her handkerchief.

Plainly he had no idea of her countermoves. The scheme seemed to him in proper train, and he turned to poke out the fire. She instantly seized the glass, and poured its contents down her bosom. When he faced round again she was holding the glass to her lips, empty.

In due course he locked the doors and saw that the shutters were fastened. She attended to a few closing details of housewifery, and a few minutes later they retired for the night.

5. FROM ELEVEN O'CLOCK TO MIDNIGHT

When Manston was persuaded, by the feigned heaviness of her breathing, that Anne Seaway was asleep, he softly arose, and dressed himself in the gloom. With ears strained to their utmost she heard him complete this operation; then he took something from his pocket, put it in the drawer of the dressing-table, went to the door, and down the stairs. She glided out of bed and looked in the drawer. He had only restored to its place a small phial she had seen there before. It was labelled 'Battley's Solution of Opium.' She felt relieved that her life had not been attempted. That was to have been her sleeping-draught. No time was to be lost if she meant to be a match for him. She followed him in her nightdress. When she reached the foot of the staircase he was in the office and had closed the door, under which a faint gleam showed that he had obtained a light. She crept to the door, but could not venture to open it, however slightly. Placing her ear to the panel, she could hear him tearing up papers of some sort, and a brighter and quivering ray of light coming from the threshold an instant later, implied that he was burning them. By the slight noise of his footsteps on the uncarpeted floor, she at length imagined that he was approaching the door. She flitted upstairs again and crept into bed.

Manston returned to the bedroom close upon her heels, and entered it—again without a light. Standing motionless for an instant to assure himself that she still slept, he went to the drawer in which their ready-money was kept, and removed the casket that contained it. Anne's ear distinctly caught the rustle of notes, and the chink of the gold as he handled it. Some he placed in his pocket, some he returned to its place. He stood thinking, as it were weighing a possibility. While lingering thus, he noticed the reflected image of his own face in the glass—pale and spectre-like in its indistinctness. The sight seemed to be the feather which turned the balance of indecision: he drew a heavy breath, retired from the room, and passed downstairs. She heard him unbar the back-door, and go out into the yard.

Feeling safe in a conclusion that he did not intend to return to the bedroom again, she arose, and hastily dressed herself. On going to the door of the apartment she found that he had locked it behind him. 'A precaution—it can be no more,' she muttered. Yet she was all the more perplexed and excited on this account. Had he been going to leave home immediately, he would scarcely have taken the trouble to lock her in, holding the belief that she was in a drugged sleep. The lock shot into a mortice, so that there was no possibility of her pushing back the bolt. How should she follow him? Easily. An inner closet opened from the bedroom: it was large, and had some time heretofore been used as a dressing or bath room, but had been found inconvenient from having no other outlet to the landing. The window of this little room looked out upon the roof of the porch, which was flat and covered with lead. Anne took a pillow from the bed, gently opened the casement of the inner room and stepped forth on the flat. There, leaning over the edge of the small parapet that ornamented the porch, she dropped the pillow upon the gravel path, and let herself down over the parapet by her hands till her toes swung about two feet from the ground. From this position she adroitly alighted upon the pillow, and stood in the path.

Since she had come indoors from her walk in the early part of the evening the moon had risen. But the thick clouds overspreading the whole landscape rendered the dim light pervasive and grey: it appeared as an attribute of the air. Anne crept round to the back of the house, listening intently. The steward had had at least ten minutes' start of her. She had waited here whilst one might count fifty, when she heard a movement in the outhouse—a fragment once attached to the main building. This outhouse was partitioned into an outer and an inner room, which had been a kitchen and a scullery before the connecting erections were pulled down, but they were now used respectively as a brewhouse and workshop, the only means of access to the latter being through the brewhouse. The outer door of this first apartment was usually fastened by a padlock on the exterior. It was now closed, but not fastened. Manston was evidently in the outhouse.

She slightly moved the door. The interior of the brewhouse was wrapped in gloom, but a streak of light fell towards her in a line across the floor from the inner or workshop door, which was not quite closed. This light was unexpected, none having been visible through hole or crevice. Glancing in, the woman found that he had placed cloths and mats at the various apertures, and hung a sack at the window to prevent the egress of a single ray. She could also perceive from where she stood that the bar of light fell across the brewing-copper just outside the inner door, and that upon it lay the key of her bedroom. The illuminated interior of the workshop was also partly visible from her position through the two half-open doors. Manston was engaged in emptying a large cupboard of the tools, gallipots, and old iron it contained. When it was quite cleared he took a chisel, and with it began to withdraw the hooks and shoulder-nails holding the cupboard to the wall. All these being loosened, he extended his arms, lifted the cupboard bodily from the brackets under it, and deposited it on the floor beside him.

That portion of the wall which had been screened by the cupboard was now laid bare. This, it appeared, had been plastered more recently than the bulk of the outhouse. Manston loosened the plaster with some kind of tool, flinging the pieces into a basket as they fell. Having now stripped clear about two feet area of wall, he inserted a crowbar between the joints of the bricks beneath, softly wriggling it until several were loosened. There was now disclosed the mouth of an old oven, which was apparently contrived in the thickness of the wall, and having fallen into disuse, had been closed up with bricks in this manner. It was formed after the simple old-fashioned plan of oven-building—a mere oblate cavity without a flue.

Manston now stretched his arm into the oven, dragged forth a heavy weight of great bulk, and let it slide to the ground. The woman who watched him could see the object plainly. It was a common corn-sack, nearly full, and was tied at the mouth in the usual way.

The steward had once or twice started up, as if he had heard sounds, and his motions now became more cat-like still. On a sudden he put out the light. Anne had made no noise, yet a foreign noise of some kind had certainly been made in the intervening portion of the house. She heard it. 'One of the rats,' she thought.

He seemed soon to recover from his alarm, but changed his tactics completely. He did not light his candle—going on with his work in the dark. She had only sounds to go by now, and, judging as well as she could from these, he was piling up the bricks which closed the oven's mouth as they had been before he disturbed them. The query that had not left her brain all the interval of her inspection—how should she get back into her bedroom again?—now received a solution. Whilst he was replacing the cupboard, she would glide across the brewhouse, take the key from the top of the copper, run upstairs, unlock the door, and bring back the key again: if he returned to bed, which was unlikely, he would think the lock had failed to catch in the staple. This thought and intention, occupying such length of words, flashed upon her in an instant, and hardly disturbed her strong curiosity to stay and learn the meaning of his actions in the workshop.

Slipping sideways through the first door and closing it behind her, she advanced into the darkness towards the second, making every individual footfall with the greatest care, lest the fragments of rubbish on the floor should crackle beneath her tread. She soon stood close by the copper, and not more than a foot from the door of the room occupied by Manston himself, from which position she could distinctly hear him breathe between each exertion, although it was far too dark to discern anything of him.

To secure the key of her chamber was her first anxiety, and accordingly she cautiously reached out with her hand to where it lay. Instead of touching it, her fingers came in contact with the boot of a human being.

She drooped faint in a cold sweat. It was the foot either of a man or woman, standing on the brewing-copper where the key had lain. A warm foot, covered with a polished boot.

The startling discovery so terrified her that she could hardly repress a sound. She withdrew her hand with a motion like the flight of an arrow. Her touch was so light that the leather seemed to have been thick enough to keep the owner of the foot in entire ignorance of it, and the noise of Manston's scraping might have been quite sufficient to drown the slight rustle of her dress.

The person was obviously not the steward: he was still busy. It was somebody who, since the light had been extinguished, had taken advantage of the gloom, to come from some dark recess in the brewhouse and stand upon the brickwork of the copper. The fear which had at first paralyzed her lessened with the birth of a sense that fear now was utter failure: she was in a desperate position and must abide by the consequences. The motionless person on the copper was, equally with Manston, quite unconscious of her proximity, and she ventured to advance her hand again, feeling behind the feet, till she found the key. On its return to her side, her finger-tip skimmed the lower verge of a trousers-leg.

It was a man, then, who stood there. To go to the door just at this time was impolitic, and she shrank back into an inner corner to wait. The comparative security from discovery that her new position ensured resuscitated reason a little, and empowered her to form some logical inferences:—

1.   The man who stood on the copper had taken advantage of the darkness to get there, as she had to enter.

2.   The man must have been hidden in the

outhouse before she had reached the door.

3.   He must be watching Manston with much calculation and system, and for purposes of his own.

She could now tell by the noises that Manston had completed his re-erection of the cupboard. She heard him replacing the articles it had contained—bottle by bottle, tool by tool—after which he came into the brewhouse, went to the window, and pulled down the cloths covering it; but the window being rather small, this unveiling scarcely relieved the darkness of the interior. He returned to the workshop, hoisted something to his back by a jerk, and felt about the room for some other article. Having found it, he emerged from the inner door, crossed the brewhouse, and went into the yard. Directly he stepped out she could see his outline by the light of the clouded and weakly moon. The sack was slung at his back, and in his hand he carried a spade.

Anne now waited in her corner in breathless suspense for the proceedings of the other man. In about half-a-minute she heard him descend from the copper, and then the square opening of the doorway showed the outline of this other watcher passing through it likewise. The form was that of a broad-shouldered man enveloped in a long coat. He vanished after the steward.

The woman vented a sigh of relief, and moved forward to follow. Simultaneously, she discovered that the watcher whose foot she had touched was, in his turn, watched and followed also.

It was by one of her own sex. Anne Seaway shrank backward again. The unknown woman came forward from the further side of the yard, and pondered awhile in hesitation. Tall, dark, and closely wrapped, she stood up from the earth like a cypress. She moved, crossed the yard without producing the slightest disturbance by her footsteps, and went in the direction the others had taken.

Anne waited yet another minute—then in her turn noiselessly followed the last woman.

But so impressed was she with the sensation of people in hiding, that in coming out of the yard she turned her head to see if any person were following her, in the same way. Nobody was visible, but she discerned, standing behind the angle of the stable, Manston's horse and gig, ready harnessed.

He did intend to fly after all, then, she thought. He must have placed the horse in readiness, in the interval between his leaving the house and her exit by the window. However, there was not time to weigh this branch of the night's events. She turned about again, and continued on the trail of the other three.

6. FROM MIDNIGHT TO
HALF-PAST ONE A.M.

Intentness pervaded everything; Night herself seemed to have become a watcher.

The four persons proceeded across the glade, and into the park plantation, at equi-distances of about seventy yards. Here the ground, completely overhung by the foliage, was coated with a thick moss which was as soft as velvet beneath their feet. The first watcher, that is, the man walking immediately behind Manston, now fell back, when Manston's housekeeper, knowing the ground pretty well, dived circuitously among the trees and got directly behind the steward, who, encumbered with his load, had proceeded but slowly. The other woman seemed now to be about opposite to Anne, or a little in advance, but on Manston's other hand.

He reached a pit, midway between the waterfall and the engine-house. There he stopped, wiped his face, and listened.

Into this pit had drifted uncounted generations of withered leaves, half filling it. Oak, beech, and chestnut, rotten and brown alike, mingled themselves in one fibrous mass. Manston descended into the midst of them, placed his sack on the ground, and raking the leaves aside into a large heap, began digging. Anne softly drew nearer, crept into a bush, and turning her head to survey the rest, missed the man who had dropped behind, and whom we have called the first watcher. Concluding that he, too, had hidden himself, she turned her attention to the second watcher, the other woman, who had meanwhile advanced near to where Anne lay in hiding, and now seated herself behind a tree, still closer to the steward than was Anne Seaway.

Here and thus Anne remained concealed. The crunch of the steward's spade, as it cut into the soft vegetable mould, was plainly perceptible to her ears when the periodic cessations between the creaks of the engine concurred with a lull in the breeze, which otherwise brought the subdued roar of the cascade from the further side of the bank that screened it. A large hole—some four or five feet deep—had been excavated by Manston in about twenty minutes. Into this he immediately placed the sack, and then began filling in the earth, and treading it down. Lastly he carefully raked the whole mass of dead and dry leaves into the middle of the pit, burying the ground with them as they had buried it before.

For a hiding-place the spot was unequalled. The thick accumulation of leaves, which had not been disturbed for centuries, might not be disturbed again for centuries to come, whilst their lower layers still decayed and added to the mould beneath.

By the time this work was ended the sky had grown clearer, and Anne could now see

575

distinctly the face of the other woman, stretching from behind the tree, seemingly forgetful of her position in her intense contemplation of the actions of the steward. Her countenance was white and motionless.

It was impossible that Manston should not soon notice her. At the completion of his labour he turned, and did so.

'Ho—you here!' he exclaimed.

'Don't think I am a spy upon you,' she said, in an imploring whisper.

Anne recognized the voice as Miss Aldclyffe's.

The trembling lady added hastily another remark, which was drowned in the recurring creak of the engine close at hand. The first watcher, if he had come no nearer than his original position, was too far off to hear any part of this dialogue, on account of the roar of the falling water, which could reach him unimpeded by the bank.

The remark of Miss Aldclyffe to Manston had plainly been concerning the first watcher, for Manston, with his spade in his hand, instantly rushed to where the man was concealed, and, before the latter could disengage himself from the boughs, the steward struck him on the head with the blade of the instrument. The man fell to the ground.

'Fly!' said Miss Aldclyffe to Manston. Manston vanished amidst the trees. Miss Aldclyffe went off in a contrary direction.

Anne Seaway was about to run away likewise, when she turned and looked at the fallen man. He lay on his face, motionless.

Many of these women who own to no moral code show considerable magnanimity when they see people in trouble. To act right simply because it is one's duty is proper; but a good action which is the result of no law of reflection shines more than any. She went up to him and gently turned him over, upon which he began to show signs of life. By her assistance he was soon able to stand upright.

He looked about him with a bewildered air, endeavouring to collect his ideas. 'Who are you?' he said to the woman, mechanically.

It was bad policy now to attempt disguise. 'I am the supposed Mrs. Manston,' she said. 'Who are you?'

'I am the officer employed by Mr. Raunham to sift this mystery—which may be criminal.' He stretched his limbs, pressed his head, and seemed gradually to awake to a sense of having been incautious in his utterance. 'Never you mind who I am,' he continued. 'Well, it doesn't matter now, either—it will no longer be a secret.'

He stooped for his hat and ran in the direction the steward had taken—coming back again after the lapse of a minute.

'It's only an aggravated assault, after all,' he said hastily, 'until we have found out for certain what's buried here. It may be only a bag of building rubbish; but it may be more. Come and help me dig.' He seized the spade with the awkwardness of a town man, and went into the pit, continuing a muttered discourse. 'It's no use my running after him single-handed,' he said. 'He's ever so far off by this time. The best step is to see what is here.'

It was far easier for the detective to re-open the hole than it had been for Manston to form it. The leaves were raked away, the loam thrown out, and the sack dragged forth.

'Hold this,' he said to Anne, whose curiosity still kept her standing near. He turned on the light of a dark lantern he had brought, and gave it into her hand.

The string which bound the mouth of the sack was now cut. The officer laid the bag on its side, seized it by the bottom, and jerked forth the contents. A large package was disclosed, carefully wrapped up in impervious tarpaulin, also well tied. He was on the point of pulling open the folds at one end, when a light coloured thread of something, hanging on the outside, arrested his eye. He put his hand upon it; it felt stringy, and adhered to his fingers. 'Hold the light close,' he said.

She held it close. He raised his hand to the glass, and they both peered at an almost intangible filament he held between his finger and thumb.

It was a long hair; the hair of a woman.

'God! I couldn't believe it—no, I couldn't

578

believe it!' the detective whispered, horror-struck. 'And I have lost the man for the present through my unbelief. Let's get into a sheltered place . . . Now wait a minute whilst I prove it.'

He thrust his hand into his waistcoat pocket, and withdrew thence a minute packet of brown paper. Spreading it out he disclosed, coiled in the middle, another long hair. It was the hair the clerk's wife had found on Manston's pillow nine days before the Carriford fire. He held the two hairs to the light: they were both of a pale-brown hue. He laid them parallel and stretched out his arms: they were of the same length to a nicety. The detective turned to Anne.

'It is the body of his first wife,' he said quietly. 'He murdered her, as Mr. Springrove and the rector suspected—but how and when, God only knows.'

'And I!' exclaimed Anne Seaway, a probable and natural sequence of events and motives explanatory of the whole crime—events and motives shadowed forth by the letter, Manston's possession of it, his renunciation of Cytherea, and instalment of herself—flashing upon her mind with the rapidity of lightning.

'Ah—I see,' said the detective, standing unusually close to her: and a handcuff was on her wrist. 'You must come with me, madam. Knowing as much about a secret murder as God knows is a very suspicious thing: it doesn't make you a goddess—far from it.' He directed the bull's-eye into her face.

'Pooh—lead on,' she said scornfully, 'and don't lose your principal actor for the sake of torturing a poor subordinate like me.'

He loosened her hand, gave her his arm, and dragged her out of the grove—making her run beside him till they had reached the rectory. A light was burning here, and an auxiliary of the detective's awaiting him: a horse ready harnessed to a spring-cart was standing outside.

'You have come—I wish I had known that,' the detective said to his assistant, hurriedly and angrily. 'Well, we've blundered—he's gone— you should have been here, as I said! I was sold by that woman, Miss Aldclyffe—she watched me.' He hastily gave directions in an undertone to this man. The concluding words were, 'Go in to the rector—he's up. Detain Miss Aldclyffe. I, in the meantime, am driving to Casterbridge with this one, and for help. We shall be sure to have him when it gets light.'

He assisted Anne into the vehicle, and drove off with her. As they went, the clear, dry road showed before them, between the grassy quarters at each side, like a white riband, and made their progress easy. They came to a spot where the highway was overhung by dense firs for some distance on both sides. It was totally dark here.

There was a smash; and a rude shock. In the very midst of its length, at the point where the road began to drop down a hill, the detective drove against something with a jerk which nearly flung them both to the ground.

The man recovered himself, placed Anne on the seat, and reached out his hand. He found that the off-wheel of his gig was locked in that of another conveyance of some kind.

'Hoy!' said the officer.

Nobody answered.

'Hoy, you man asleep there!' he said again.

No reply.

'Well, that's odd—this comes of the folly of travelling without gig-lamps because you expect the dawn.' He jumped to the ground and turned on his lantern.

There was the gig which had obstructed him, standing in the middle of the road; a jaded horse harnessed to it, but no human being in or near the vehicle.

'Do you know whose gig this is?' he said to the woman.

'No,' she said sullenly. But she did recognize it as the steward's.

'I'll swear it's Manston's! Come, I can hear it by your tone. However, you needn't say anything which may criminate you. What forethought the man must have had—how carefully he must have considered possible contingencies! Why, he must have got the horse and gig ready before he began shifting the body.'

He listened for a sound among the trees.

581

None was to be heard but the occasional scamper of a rabbit over the withered leaves. He threw the light of his lantern through a gap in the hedge, but could see nothing beyond an impenetrable thicket. It was clear that Manston was not many yards off, but the question was how to find him. Nothing could be done by the detective just then, encumbered as he was by the horse and Anne. If he had entered the thicket on a search unaided, Manston might have stepped unobserved from behind a bush and murdered him with the greatest ease. Indeed, there were such strong reasons for the exploit in Manston's circumstances at that moment that without showing cowardice, his pursuer felt it hazardous to remain any longer where he stood.

He hastily tied the head of Manston's horse to the back of his own vehicle, that the steward might be deprived of the use of any means of escape other than his own legs, and drove on thus with his prisoner to the county-town. Arrived there, he lodged her in the police-station, and then took immediate steps for the capture of Manston.

XX.

THE EVENTS OF THREE HOURS

1. MARCH THE TWENTY-THIRD. MIDDAY

Thirty-six hours had elapsed since Manston's escape.

It was market-day at the county-town. The farmers outside and inside the corn-exchange looked at their samples of wheat, and poured them critically as usual from one palm to another, but they thought and spoke of Manston. Grocers serving behind their counters, instead of using their constant phrase, 'The next article, please?' substituted, 'Have you heard if he's caught?' Dairymen and drovers standing beside the sheep and cattle pens, spread their legs firmly, readjusted their hats, thrust their hands into the lowest depths of their pockets, regarded the animals with the utmost keenness of which the eye was capable, and said, 'Ay, ay, so's: they'll have him avore night.'

Later in the day Edward Springrove passed along the street hurriedly and anxiously. 'Well, have you heard any more?' he said to an acquaintance who accosted him.

'They tracked him in this way,' said the other young man. 'A vagrant first told them that Manston had passed a rick at daybreak, under which this man was lying. They followed the track he pointed out and ultimately came to a stile. On the other side was a heap of half-hardened mud, scraped from the road. On the surface of the heap, where it had been smoothed by the shovel, was distinctly imprinted the form of a man's hand, the buttons of his waistcoat, and his watch-chain, showing that he had stumbled in hurrying over the stile, and fallen there. The pattern of the chain proved the man to have been Manston. They followed on till they reached a ford crossed by stepping-stones—on the further bank were the same footmarks that had shown themselves beside the stile. The whole of this course had been in the direction of Budmouth. On they went, and the next clue was furnished them by a shepherd. He said that wherever a clear space three or four yards wide ran in a line through a flock of sheep lying about a ewe-lease, it was a proof that somebody had passed there not more than half-an-hour earlier. At twelve o'clock that day he had noticed such a feature in his flock. Nothing more could be heard of him, and they got into Budmouth. The steam-packet to the Channel Islands was to start at eleven last night, and they at once concluded that his hope was to get to France by way of Jersey and St. Malo—his only chance, all the railway-stations being watched.

'Well, they went to the boat: he was not on board then. They went again at half-past ten: he had not come. Two men now placed themselves under the lamp immediately beside the gangway. Another stayed by the office door, and one or two more up Mary Street—the straight cut to the quay. At a quarter to eleven the mail-bags were put on board. Whilst the attention of the idlers was directed to the mails, down Mary Street came a man as boldly as possible. The gait was Manston's, but not the clothes. He passed over to the shaded part of the street: heads were turned. I suppose this warned him, for he never emerged from the shadow.

They watched and waited, but the steward did not reappear. The alarm was raised—they searched the town high and low—no Manston. All this morning they have been searching, but there's not a sign of him anywhere. However, he has lost his last chance of getting across the Channel. It is reported that he has since changed clothes with a labourer.'

During this narration, Edward, lost in thought, had let his eyes follow a shabby man in a smock-frock, but wearing light boots—who was stalking down the street under a bundle of straw which overhung and concealed his head. It was a very ordinary circumstance for a man with a bundle of straw on his shoulders and overhanging his head, to go down the High Street. Edward saw him cross the bridge which divided the town from the country, place his shaggy encumbrance by the side of the road, and leave it there.

Springrove now parted from his acquaintance, and went also in the direction of the bridge, and some way beyond it. As far as he could see stretched the turnpike road, and, while he was looking, he noticed a man to leap from the hedge at a point two hundred, or two hundred and fifty yards ahead, cross the road, and go through a wicket on the other side. This figure seemed like that of the man who had been carrying the bundle of straw. He looked at the straw: it still stood alone.

The subjoined facts sprang, as it were, into juxtaposition in his brain:—

Manston had been seen wearing the clothes of a labouring man—a brown smock-frock. So had this man, who seemed other than a labourer, on second thoughts: and he had concealed his face by his bundle of straw with the greatest ease and naturalness.

The path the man had taken led, among other places, to Tolchurch, where Cytherea was living.

If Mrs. Manston was murdered, as some said, on the night of the fire, Cytherea was the steward's lawful wife. Manston at bay, and reckless of results, might rush to his wife and harm her.

It was a horrible supposition for a man who loved Cytherea to entertain; but Springrove could not resist its influence. He started off for Tolchurch.

2. ONE TO TWO O'CLOCK P.M.

On that self-same mid-day, whilst Edward was proceeding to Tolchurch by the footpath across the fields, Owen Graye had left the village and was riding along the turnpike road to the county-town, that he might ascertain the exact truth of the strange rumour which had reached him concerning Manston. Not to disquiet his sister, he had said nothing to her of the matter.

She sat by the window reading. From her position she could see up the lane for a distance of at least a hundred yards. Passers-by were so rare in this retired nook, that the eyes of those who dwelt by the wayside were invariably lifted to every one on the road, great and small, as to a novelty.

A man in a brown smock-frock turned the corner and came towards the house. It being market-day at Casterbridge, the village was nearly deserted, and more than this, the old farm-house in which Owen and his sister were staying, stood, as has been stated, apart from the body of cottages. The man did not look respectable; Cytherea arose and bolted the door.

Unfortunately he was near enough to see

her cross the room. He advanced to the door, knocked, and, receiving no answer, came to the window; he next pressed his face against the glass, peering in.

Cytherea's experience at that moment was probably as trying a one as ever fell to the lot of a gentlewoman to endure. She recognized in the peering face that of the man she had married.

But not a movement was made by her, not a sound escaped her. Her fear was great; but had she known the truth—that the man outside, feeling he had nothing on earth to lose by any act, was in the last stage of recklessness, terrified nature must have given way.

'Cytherea,' he said, 'let me come in: I am your husband.'

'No,' she replied, still not realizing the magnitude of her peril. 'If you want to speak to us, wait till my brother comes.'

'O, he's not at home? Cytherea, I can't live without you! All my sin has been because I love you so! Will you fly with me? I have money enough for us both—only come with me.'

'Not now—not now.'

'I am your husband, I tell you, and I must come in.'

'You cannot,' she said faintly. His words began to terrify her.

'I will, I say!' he exclaimed. 'Will you let me in, I ask once more?'

'No—I will not,' said Cytherea.

'Then I will let myself in!' he answered resolutely. 'I will, if I die for it!'

The windows were glazed in lattice panes of leadwork, hung in casements. He broke one of the panes with a stone, thrust his hand through the hole, unfastened the latch which held the casement close, and began opening the window.

Instantly the shutters flew together with a slam, and were barred with desperate quickness by Cytherea on the inside.

'Damn you!' he exclaimed.

He ran round to the back of the house. His impatience was greater now: he thrust his fist through the pantry window at one blow, and opened it in the same way as the former one had been opened, before the terror-stricken girl was aware that he had gone round. In an instant he stood in the pantry, advanced to the front room where she was, flung back the shutters, and held out his arms to embrace her.

In extremely trying moments of bodily or mental pain, Cytherea either flushed hot or faded pale, according to the state of her constitution at the moment. Now she burned like fire from head to foot, and this preserved her consciousness.

Never before had the poor child's natural agility served her in such good stead as now. A heavy oblong table stood in the middle of the room. Round this table she flew, keeping it between herself and Manston, her large eyes wide open with terror, their dilated pupils constantly fixed upon Manston's, to read by his expression whether his next intention was to dart to the right or the left.

Even he, at that heated moment, could not endure the expression of unutterable agony which shone from that extraordinary gaze of hers. It had surely been given her by God as a means of defence. Manston continued his pursuit with a lowered eye.

The panting and maddened desperado— blind to everything but the capture of his wife—went with a rush under the table: she went over it like a bird. He went heavily over it: she flew under it, and was out at the other side.

> One on her youth and pliant limbs relies,
> One on his sinews and his giant size.

But his superior strength was sure to tire her down in the long-run. She felt her weakness increasing with the quickness of her breath; she uttered a wild scream, which in its heartrending intensity seemed to echo for miles.

At the same juncture her hair became unfastened, and rolled down about her shoulders. The least accident at such critical periods is sufficient to confuse the overwrought intelligence. She lost sight of his intended direction for one instant, and he immediately outmanoeuvred her.

'At last! my Cytherea!' he cried, overturning the table, springing over it, seizing one of the long brown tresses, pulling her towards him, and clasping her round. She writhed downwards between his arms and breast, and fell fainting on the floor. For the first time his action was leisurely. He lifted her upon the sofa, exclaiming, 'Rest there for a while, my frightened little bird!'

And then there was an end of his triumph. He felt himself clutched by the collar, and whizzed backwards with the force of a battering-ram against the fireplace. Springrove, wild, red, and breathless, had sprung in at the open window, and stood once more between man and wife.

Manston was on his legs again in an instant. A fiery glance on the one side, a glance of pitiless justice on the other, passed between them. It was again the meeting in the vineyard of Naboth the Jezreelite: 'Hast thou found me, O mine enemy? And he answered, I have found thee: because thou hast sold thyself to work evil in the sight of the Lord.'

A desperate wrestle now began between the two men. Manston was the taller, but there was in Edward much hard tough muscle which the delicate flesh of the steward lacked. They flew together like the jaws of a gin. In a minute they were both on the floor, rolling over and over, locked in each other's grasp as tightly as if they had been one organic being at war with itself—Edward trying to secure Manston's arms with a small thong he had drawn from his pocket, Manston trying to reach his knife.

Two characteristic noises pervaded the apartment through this momentous space of time. One was the sharp panting of the two combatants, so similar in each as to be undistinguishable; the other was the stroke of their heels and toes, as they smote the floor at every contortion of body or limbs.

Cytherea had not lost consciousness for more than half-a-minute. She had then leapt up without recognizing that Edward was her deliverer, unfastened the door, and rushed out, screaming wildly, 'Come! Help! O, help!'

Three men stood not twenty yards off, looking perplexed. They dashed forward at her words. 'Have you seen a shabby man with a smock-frock on lately?' they inquired. She pointed to the door, and ran on the same as before.

Manston, who had just loosened himself from Edward's grasp, seemed at this moment to renounce his intention of pushing the conflict to a desperate end. 'I give it all up for life—dear life!' he cried, with a hoarse laugh. 'A reckless man has a dozen lives—see how I'll baffle you all yet!'

He rushed out of the house, but no further. The boast was his last. In one half-minute more he was helpless in the hands of his pursuers.

*   *   *

Edward staggered to his feet, and paused to recover breath. His thoughts had never forsaken Cytherea, and his first act now was to hasten up the lane after her. She had not gone far. He found her leaning upon a bank by the roadside, where she had flung herself down in sheer exhaustion. He ran up and lifted her in his arms, and thus aided she was enabled to stand upright—clinging to him. What would Springrove have given to imprint a kiss upon her lips then!

They walked slowly towards the house. The distressing sensation of whose wife she was could not entirely quench the resuscitated pleasure he felt at her grateful recognition of him, and her confiding seizure of his arm for support. He conveyed her carefully into the house.

A quarter of an hour later, whilst she was sitting in a partially recovered, half-dozing state in an arm-chair, Edward beside her waiting anxiously till Graye should arrive, they saw a spring-cart pass the door. Old and dry mud-splashes from long-forgotten rains disfigured its wheels and sides; the varnish and paint had been scratched and dimmed; ornament had long been forgotten in a restless

593

contemplation of use. Three men sat on the seat, the middle one being Manston. His hands were bound in front of him, his eyes were set directly forward, his countenance pallid, hard, and fixed.

Springrove had told Cytherea of Manston's crime in a few short words. He now said solemnly, 'He is to die.'

'And I cannot mourn for him,' she replied with a shudder, leaning back and covering her face with her hands.

In the silence that followed the two short remarks, Springrove watched the cart round the corner, and heard the rattle of its wheels gradually dying away as it rolled in the direction of the county-town.

XXI.

THE EVENTS OF EIGHTEEN HOURS

1. MARCH THE TWENTY-NINTH. NOON

Exactly seven days after Edward Springrove had seen the man with the bundle of straw walking down the streets of Casterbridge, old Farmer Springrove was standing on the edge of the same pavement, talking to his friend, Farmer Baker.

There was a pause in their discourse. Mr.

Springrove was looking down the street at some object which had attracted his attention. 'Ah, 'tis what we shall all come to!' he murmured.

The other looked in the same direction. 'True, neighbour Springrove; true.'

Two men, advancing one behind the other in the middle of the road, were what the farmers referred to. They were carpenters, and bore on their shoulders an empty coffin, covered by a thin black cloth.

'I always feel a satisfaction at being breasted by such a sight as that,' said Springrove, still regarding the men's sad burden. 'I call it a sort of medicine.'

'And it is medicine . . . I have not heard of any body being ill up this way lately? D'seem as if the person died suddenly.'

'May be so. Ah, Baker, we say sudden death, don't we? But there's no difference in their nature between sudden death and death of any other sort. There's no such thing as a random snapping off of what was laid down to last longer. We only suddenly light upon an end— thoughtfully formed as any other—which has been existing at that very same point from the beginning, though unseen by us to be so soon.'

'It is just a discovery to your own mind, and not an alteration in the Lord's.'

'That's it. Unexpected is not as to the thing, but as to our sight.'

'Now you'll hardly believe me, neighbour,

but this little scene in front of us makes me feel less anxious about pushing on wi' that threshing and winnowing next week, that I was speaking about. Why should we not stand still, says I to myself, and fling a quiet eye upon the Whys and the Wherefores, before the end o' it all, and we go down into the mouldering-place, and are forgotten?'

' 'Tis a feeling that will come. But 'twont bear looking into. There's a back'ard current in the world, and we must do our utmost to advance in order just to bide where we be. But, Baker, they are turning in here with the coffin, look.'

The two carpenters had borne their load into a narrow way close at hand. The farmers, in common with others, turned and watched them along the way.

' 'Tis a man's coffin, and a tall man's, too,' continued Farmer Springrove. 'His was a fine frame, whoever he was.'

'A very plain box for the poor soul—just the rough elm, you see.' The corner of the cloth had blown aside.

'Yes, for a very poor man. Well, death's all the less insult to him. I have often thought how much smaller the richer class are made to look than the poor at last pinches like this. Perhaps the greatest of all the reconcilers of a thoughtful man to poverty—and I speak from experience—is the grand quiet it fills him with when the uncertainty of his life shows itself more than usual.'

As Springrove finished speaking, the bearers of the coffin went across a gravelled square facing the two men and approached a grim and heavy archway. They paused beneath it, rang a bell, and waited.

Over the archway was written in Egyptian capitals,

'COUNTY GAOL.'

The small rectangular wicket, which was constructed in one of the two iron-studded doors, was opened from the inside. The men severally stepped over the threshold, the coffin dragged its melancholy length through the aperture, and both entered the court, and were covered from sight.

'Somebody in the gaol, then?'

'Yes, one of the prisoners,' said a boy, scudding by at the moment, who passed on whistling.

'Do you know the name of the man who is dead?' inquired Baker of a third bystander.

'Yes, 'tis all over town—surely you know, Mr. Springrove? Why, Manston, Miss Aldclyffe's steward. He was found dead the first thing this morning. He had hung himself behind the door of his cell, in some way, by a handkerchief and some strips of his clothes. The turnkey says his features were scarcely changed, as he looked at 'em with the early sun a-shining in at the grating upon him. He has left a full account of the murder, and all that led to it. So there's an end of him.'

* * *

It was perfectly true: Manston was dead.

The previous day he had been allowed the use of writing-materials, and had occupied himself for nearly seven hours in preparing the following confession:—

LAST WORDS.

Having found man's life to be a wretchedly conceived scheme, I renounce it, and, to cause no further trouble, I write down the facts connected with my past proceedings.

After thanking God, on first entering my house, on the night of the fire at Carriford, for my release from bondage to a woman I detested, I went, a second time, to the scene of the disaster, and, finding that nothing could be done by remaining there, shortly afterwards I returned home again in the company of Mr. Raunham.

He parted from me at the steps of my porch, and went back towards the rectory. Whilst I still stood at the door, musing on my strange deliverance, I saw a figure advance from beneath the shadow of the park trees. It was the figure of a woman.

When she came near, the twilight was sufficient to show me her attire: it was a cloak reaching to the bottom of her dress, and a thick veil covering her face. These features, together with her size and gait, aided also by a flash of perception as to the chain of events which had saved her life, told me that she was my wife Eunice.

I gnashed my teeth in a frenzy of despair; I had lost Cytherea; I had gained one whose beauty had departed, whose utterance was complaint, whose mind was shallow, and who drank brandy every day. The revulsion of feeling was terrible. Providence, whom I had just thanked, seemed a mocking tormentor laughing at me. I felt like a madman.

She came close—started at seeing me outside—then spoke to me. Her first words were reproof for what I had unintentionally done, and sounded as an earnest of what I was to be cursed with as long as we both lived. I answered angrily; this tone of mine changed her complaints to irritation. She taunted me with a secret she had discovered, which concerned Miss Aldclyffe and myself. I was surprised to learn it—more surprised that she knew it, but concealed my feeling.

'How could you serve me so?' she said,

her breath smelling of spirits even then. 'You love another woman—yes, you do. See how you drive me about! I have been to the station, intending to leave you for ever, and yet I come to try you once more.'

An indescribable exasperation had sprung up in me as she talked—rage and regret were all in all. Scarcely knowing what I did, I furiously raised my hand and swung it round with my whole force to strike her. She turned quickly—and it was the poor creature's end. By her movement my hand came edgewise exactly in the nape of the neck—as men strike a hare to kill it. The effect staggered me with amazement. The blow must have disturbed the vertebrae; she fell at my feet, made a few movements, and uttered one low sound.

I ran indoors for water and some wine, I came out and lanced her arm with my penknife. But she lay still, and I found that she was dead.

It was a long time before I could realize my horrible position. For several minutes I had no idea of attempting to escape the consequences of my deed. Then a light broke upon me. Had anybody seen her since she left the Three Tranters? Had they not, she was already believed by the parishioners to be dust and ashes. I should never be found out.

Upon this I acted.

The first question was how to dispose of the body. The impulse of the moment was to bury her at once in the pit between the engine-house and waterfall; but it struck me that I should not have time. It was now four o'clock, and the working-men would soon be stirring about the place. I would put off burying her till the next night. I carried her indoors.

In turning the outhouse into a workshop, earlier in the season, I found, when driving a nail into the wall for fixing a cupboard, that the wall sounded hollow. I examined it, and discovered behind the plaster an old oven which had long been disused, and was bricked up when the house was prepared for me.

To unfix this cupboard and pull out the bricks was the work of a few minutes. Then, bearing in mind that I should have to remove the body again the next night, I placed it in a sack, pushed it into the oven, packed in the bricks, and replaced the cupboard.

I then went to bed. In bed, I thought whether there were any very remote possibilities that might lead to the supposition that my wife was not consumed by the flames of the burning house. The thing which struck me most forcibly was this, that the searchers might think it odd that no remains whatever should be found.

The clinching and triumphant deed would be to take the body and place it among the ruins of the destroyed house. But I could not do this, on account of the men who were watching against an outbreak of the fire. One remedy remained.

I arose again, dressed myself, and went down to the outhouse. I must take down the cupboard again. I did take it down. I pulled out the bricks, pulled out the sack, pulled out the corpse, and took her keys from her pocket and the watch from her side.

I then replaced everything as before.

With these articles in my pocket I went out of the yard, and took my way through the withy copse to the churchyard, entering it from the back. Here I felt my way carefully along till I came to the nook where pieces of bones from newly-dug graves are sometimes piled behind the laurel-bushes. I had been earnestly hoping to find a skull among these old bones; but though I had frequently seen one or two in the rubbish here, there was not one now. I then groped in the other corner with the same result—nowhere could I find a skull. Three or four fragments of leg and back-bones were all I could collect, and with these I was forced to be content.

Taking them in my hand, I crossed the road, and got round behind the inn, where the couch heap was still smouldering. Keeping behind the hedge, I could see the heads of the three or four men who watched the spot.

Standing in this place I took the bones, and threw them one by one over the hedge and over the men's heads into the smoking embers. When the bones had all been thrown, I threw the keys; last of all I threw the watch.

I then returned home as I had gone, and went to bed once more, just as the dawn began to break. I exulted— 'Cytherea is mine again!'

At breakfast-time I thought, 'Suppose the cupboard should by some unlikely chance get moved to-day!'

I went to the mason's yard hard by, while the men were at breakfast, and brought away a shovelful of mortar. I took it into the outhouse, again shifted the cupboard, and plastered over the mouth of the oven behind. Simply pushing the cupboard back into its place, I waited for the next night that I might bury the body, though upon the whole it was in a tolerably safe hiding-place.

When the night came, my nerves were in some way weaker than they had been on the previous night. I felt reluctant to touch the body. I went to the outhouse, but instead of opening the oven, I firmly drove in the shoulder-nails that held the cupboard to the wall. 'I will bury her to-morrow night, however,' I thought.

But the next night I was still more reluctant to touch her. And my reluctance increased, and there the body remained. The oven was, after all, never likely to be opened in my time.

I married Cytherea Graye, and never did a bridegroom leave the church with a heart more full of love and happiness, and a brain more fixed on good intentions, than I did on that morning.

When Cytherea's brother made his appearance at the hotel in Southampton, bearing his strange evidence of the porter's disclosure, I was staggered beyond expression. I thought they had found the body. 'Am I to be apprehended and to lose her even now?' I mourned. I saw my error, and instantly saw, too, that I must act externally like an honourable man. So at his request I yielded her up to him, and meditated on several schemes for enabling me to claim the woman I had a legal right to claim as my wife, without disclosing the reason why I knew myself to have it.

I went home to Knapwater the next day, and for nearly a week lived in a state of indecision. I could not hit upon a scheme for proving my wife dead without compromising myself.

Mr. Raunham hinted that I should take steps to discover her whereabouts by advertising. I had no energy for the farce. But one evening I chanced to enter the Rising Sun Inn. Two notorious poachers were sitting in the settle, which screened my entrance. They were half drunk— their conversation was carried on in the solemn and emphatic tone common to that stage of intoxication, and I myself was the subject of it.

The following was the substance of their disjointed remarks: On the night of the great fire at Carriford, one of them was sent to meet me, and break the news of the death of my wife to me. This he did; but because I would not pay him for his news, he left me in a mood of vindictiveness. When the fire was over, he joined his comrade. The favourable hour of the night suggested to them the possibility of some unlawful gain before daylight came. My fowl-house stood in a tempting position, and still resenting his repulse during the evening, one of them proposed to operate upon my birds. I was believed to have gone to the rectory with Mr. Raunham. The other was disinclined to go, and the first went off alone.

It was now about three o'clock. He had advanced as far as the shrubbery, which grows near the north wall of the house, when he fancied he heard, above the rush of the waterfall, noises on the other side of the building. He described them in these words, 'The ghost of a wife nagging her man—then a fall—then a groan— then the rush of the water and creak of the engine as before.' Only one explanation occurred to him; the house was haunted. And, whether those of the living or the dead, voices of any kind were inimical to one who had come on such an errand. He stealthily crept home.

His unlawful purpose in being behind the house led him to conceal his adventure. No suspicion of the truth entered his mind till the railway-porter had startled everybody by his strange announcement. Then he asked himself, had the horrifying sounds of that night been really an enactment in the flesh between me and my wife?

The words of the other man were:

'Why don't he try to find her if she's alive?'

'True,' said the first. 'Well, I don't forget what I heard, and if she don't turn up alive my mind will be as sure as a Bible upon her murder, and the parson shall know it, though I do get six months on the treadmill for being where I was.

'And if she should turn up alive?'

'Then I shall know that I am wrong, and believing myself a fool as well as a rogue, hold my tongue.'

I glided out of the house in a cold sweat. The only pressure in heaven or earth which could have forced me to renounce Cytherea was now put upon me—the dread of a death upon the gallows.

I sat all that night weaving strategy of various kinds. The only effectual remedy for my hazardous standing that I could see was a simple one. It was to substitute another woman for my wife before the suspicions of that one easily-hoodwinked man extended further.

The only difficulty was to find a practicable substitute.

The one woman at all available for the purpose was a friendless, innocent creature, named Anne Seaway, whom I had known in my youth, and who had for some time been the housekeeper of a lady in London. On account of this lady's sudden death, Anne stood in rather a precarious position, as regarded her future subsistence. She was not the best kind of woman for the scheme; but there was no alternative. One quality of hers was valuable; she was not a talker. I went to London the very next day, called at the Hoxton lodging of my wife (the only place at which she had been known as Mrs. Manston), and found that no great difficulties stood in the way of a personation. And thus favouring circumstances determined my course. I visited Anne Seaway, made love to her, and propounded my plan.

* * *

We lived quietly enough until the Sunday before my apprehension. Anne came home from church that morning, and told me of the suspicious way in which a young man had looked at her there. Nothing could be done beyond waiting the issue of events. Then the letter came from Raunham. For the first time in my life I was half indifferent as to what fate awaited me. During the succeeding day I thought once or twice of running away, but could not quite make up my mind. At any rate it would be best to bury the body of my wife, I thought, for the oven might be opened at any time. I went to Casterbridge and made some arrangements. In the evening Miss Aldclyffe (who is united to me by a common secret which I have no right or wish to disclose) came to my house, and alarmed me still more. She said that she could tell by Mr. Raunham's manner that evening, that he kept back from her a suspicion of more importance even than the one he spoke of, and that strangers were in his house even then.

I guessed what this further suspicion was, and resolved to enlighten her to a certain extent, and so secure her assistance. I said that I killed my wife by an accident on the night of the fire, dwelling upon the advantage to her of the death of the only woman who knew her secret.

Her terror, and fears for my fate, led her to watch the rectory that evening. She saw the detective leave it, and followed him to my residence. This she told me hurriedly when I perceived her after digging my wife's grave in the plantation. She did not suspect what the sack contained.

I am now about to enter on my normal condition. For people are almost always in their graves. When we survey the long race of men, it is strange and still more strange to find that they are mainly dead men, who have scarcely ever been otherwise.

ÆNEAS MANSTON.

The steward's confession, aided by circumstantial evidence of various kinds, was the means of freeing both Anne Seaway and Miss Aldclyffe from all suspicion of complicity with the murderer.

2. SIX O'CLOCK P.M.

It was evening—just at sunset—on the day of Manston's death.

In the cottage at Tolchurch was gathered a group consisting of Cytherea, her brother, Edward Springrove, and his father. They sat by the window conversing of the strange events which had just taken place. In Cytherea's eye there beamed a hopeful ray, though her face was as white as a lily.

Whilst they talked, looking out at the yellow evening light that coated the hedges, trees, and church tower, a brougham rolled round the corner of the lane, and came in full view. It reflected the rays of the sun in a flash from its polished panels as it turned the angle, the spokes of the wheels bristling in the same light like bayonets. The vehicle came nearer, and arrived opposite Owen's door, when the driver pulled the rein and gave a shout, and the panting and sweating horses stopped.

'Miss Aldclyffe's carriage!' they all exclaimed.

Owen went out. 'Is Miss Graye at home?' said the man. 'A note for her, and I am to wait for an answer.'

Cytherea read in the handwriting of the Rector of Carriford:—

DEAR MISS GRAYE,—Miss Aldclyffe is ill, though not dangerously. She continually repeats your name, and now wishes very much to see you. If you possibly can, come in the carriage.—Very sincerely yours,

JOHN RAUNHAM.

'How comes she ill?' Owen inquired of the coachman.

'She caught a violent cold by standing out of doors in the damp, on the night the steward ran away. Ever since, till this morning, she complained of fulness and heat in the chest. This morning the maid ran in and told her suddenly that Manston had killed himself in gaol—she shrieked—broke a blood-vessel—and fell upon the floor. Severe internal haemorrhage continued for some time and then stopped. They say she is sure to get over it; but she herself says no. She has suffered from it before.'

Cytherea was ready in a few moments, and entered the carriage.

3. SEVEN O'CLOCK P.M.

Soft as was Cytherea's motion along the corridors of Knapwater House, the preternaturally keen intelligence of the suffering woman caught the maiden's well-known footfall. She entered the sick-chamber with suspended breath.

In the room everything was so still, and sensation was as it were so rarefied by solicitude, that thinking seemed acting, and the lady's weak act of trying to live a silent wrestling with all the powers of the universe. Nobody was present but Mr. Raunham, the nurse having left the room on Cytherea's entry, and the physician and surgeon being engaged in a whispered conversation in a side-chamber. Their patient had been pronounced out of danger.

Cytherea went to the bedside, and was instantly recognized. O, what a change—Miss Aldclyffe dependent upon pillows! And yet not a forbidding change. With weakness had come softness of aspect: the haughtiness was extracted from the frail thin countenance, and a sweeter mild placidity had taken its place.

Miss Aldclyffe signified to Mr. Raunham that she would like to be alone with Cytherea.

'Cytherea?' she faintly whispered the instant the door was closed.

Cytherea clasped the lady's weak hand, and sank beside her.

Miss Aldclyffe whispered again. 'They say I am certain to live; but I know that I am certainly going to die.'

'They know, I think and hope.'

'I know best, but we'll leave that. Cytherea—O Cytherea, can you forgive me!'

Her companion pressed her hand.

'But you don't know yet—you don't know yet,' the invalid murmured. 'It is forgiveness for that misrepresentation to Edward Springrove that I implore, and for putting such force upon him—that which caused all the train of your innumerable ills!'

'I know all—all. And I do forgive you. Not in a hasty impulse that is revoked when coolness comes, but deliberately and sincerely: as I myself hope to be forgiven, I accord you my forgiveness now.'

Tears streamed from Miss Aldclyffe's eyes, and mingled with those of her young companion, who could not restrain hers for sympathy. Expressions of strong attachment, interrupted by emotion, burst again and again from the broken-spirited woman.

'But you don't know my motive. O, if you only knew it, how you would pity me then!'

Cytherea did not break the pause which ensued, and the elder woman appeared now to nerve herself by a superhuman effort. She spoke on in a voice weak as a summer breeze, and full of intermission, and yet there pervaded it a steadiness of intention that seemed to demand firm tones to bear it out worthily.

'Cytherea,' she said, 'listen to me before I die.

'A long time ago—more than thirty years ago—a young girl of seventeen was cruelly betrayed by her cousin, a wild officer of six-and-twenty. He went to India, and died.

'One night when that miserable girl had just arrived home with her parents from Germany, where her baby had been born, she took all the money she possessed, pinned it on her infant's bosom, together with a letter, stating, among other things, what she wished the child's Christian name to be; wrapped up the little thing, and walked with it to Clapham. Here, in a retired street, she selected a house. She placed the child on the doorstep and knocked at the door, then ran away and watched. They took it up and carried it indoors.

'Now that her poor baby was gone, the girl blamed herself bitterly for cruelty towards it, and wished she had adopted her parents' counsel to secretly hire a nurse. She longed to see it. She didn't know what to do. She wrote in an assumed name to the woman who had taken it in, and asked her to meet the writer with the infant at certain places she named. These were hotels or coffee-houses in Chelsea, Pimlico, or Hammersmith. The woman, being well paid, always came, and asked no questions. At one meeting—at an inn in

Hammersmith—she made her appearance without the child, and told the girl it was so ill that it would not live through the night. The news, and fatigue, brought on a fainting-fit . . .'

Miss Aldclyffe's sobs choked her utterance, and she became painfully agitated. Cytherea, pale and amazed at what she heard, wept for her, bent over her, and begged her not to go on speaking.

'Yes—I must,' she cried, between her sobs. 'I will—I must go on! And I must tell yet more plainly! . . . you must hear it before I am gone, Cytherea.' The sympathizing and astonished girl sat down again.

'The name of the woman who had taken the child was *Manston*. She was the widow of a schoolmaster. She said she had adopted the child of a relation.

'Only one man ever found out who the mother was. He was the keeper of the inn in which she fainted, and his silence she has purchased ever since.

'A twelvemonth passed—fifteen months— and the saddened girl met a man at her father's house named Graye—your father, Cytherea, then unmarried. Ah, such a man! Inexperience now perceived what it was to be loved in spirit and in truth! But it was too late. Had he known her secret he would have cast her out. She withdrew from him by an effort, and pined.

'Years and years afterwards, when she

became mistress of a fortune and estates by her father's death, she formed the weak scheme of having near her the son whom, in her father's life-time, she had been forbidden to recognize. Cytherea, you know who that weak woman is.

*   *   *

'By such toilsome labour as this I got him here as my steward. And I wanted to see him *your husband*, Cytherea!—the husband of my true lover's child. It was a sweet dream to me . . . Pity me—O, pity me! To die unloved is more than I can bear! I loved your father, and I love him now.'

That was the burden of Cytherea Aldclyffe.

'I suppose you must leave me again—you always leave me,' she said, after holding the young woman's hand a long while in silence.

'No—indeed I'll stay always. Do you like me to stay?'

Miss Aldclyffe in the jaws of death was Miss Aldclyffe still, though the old fire had degenerated to mere phosphorescence now. 'But you are your brother's housekeeper?'

'Yes.'

'Well, of course you cannot stay with me on a sudden like this . . . Go home, or he will be at a loss for things. And to-morrow morning come again, won't you, dearest, come again— we'll fetch you. But you mustn't stay now, and

616

put Owen out. O no—it would be absurd.' The absorbing concern about trifles of daily routine, which is so often seen in very sick people, was present here.

Cytherea promised to go home, and come the next morning to stay continuously.

'Stay till I die then, will you not? Yes, till I die—I shan't die till to-morrow.'

'We hope for your recovery—all of us.'

'I know best. Come at six o'clock, darling.'

'As soon as ever I can,' returned Cytherea tenderly.

'But six is too early—you will have to think of your brother's breakfast. Leave Tolchurch at eight, will you?'

Cytherea consented to this. Miss Aldclyffe would never have known had her companion stayed in the house all night; but the honesty of Cytherea's nature rebelled against even the friendly deceit which such a proceeding would have involved.

An arrangement was come to whereby she was to be taken home in the pony-carriage instead of the brougham that fetched her; the carriage to put up at Tolchurch farm for the night, and on that account to be in readiness to bring her back earlier.

MARCH THE THIRTIETH. DAYBREAK

The third and last instance of Cytherea's

subjection to those periodic terrors of the night which had emphasized her connection with the Aldclyffe name and blood occurred at the present date.

It was about four o'clock in the morning when Cytherea, though most probably dreaming, seemed to awake—and instantly was transfixed by a sort of spell, that had in it more of awe than of affright. At the foot of her bed, looking her in the face with an expression of entreaty beyond the power of words to portray, was the form of Miss Aldclyffe—wan and distinct. No motion was perceptible in her; but longing—earnest longing—was written in every feature.

Cytherea believed she exercised her waking judgment as usual in thinking, without a shadow of doubt, that Miss Aldclyffe stood before her in flesh and blood. Reason was not sufficiently alert to lead Cytherea to ask herself how such a thing could have occurred.

'I would have remained with you—why would you not allow me to stay!' Cytherea exclaimed. The spell was broken: she became broadly awake; and the figure vanished.

It was in the grey time of dawn. She trembled in a sweat of disquiet, and not being able to endure the thought of her brother being asleep, she went and tapped at his door.

'Owen!'

He was not a heavy sleeper, and it was verging upon his time to rise.

'What do you want, Cytherea?'

'I ought not to have left Knapwater last night. I wish I had not. I really think I will start at once. She wants me, I know.'

'What time is it?'

'A few minutes past four.'

'You had better not. Keep to the time agreed upon. Consider, we should have such a trouble in rousing the driver, and other things.'

Upon the whole it seemed wiser not to act on a mere fancy. She went to bed again.

An hour later, when Owen was thinking of getting up, a knocking came to the front door. The next minute something touched the glass of Owen's window. He waited—the noise was repeated. A little gravel had been thrown against it to arouse him.

He crossed the room, pulled up the blind, and looked out. A solemn white face was gazing upwards from the road, expectantly straining to catch the first glimpse of a person within the panes. It was the face of a Knapwater man sitting on horseback.

Owen saw his errand. There is an unmistakable look in the face of every man who brings tidings of death. Graye opened the window.

'Miss Aldclyffe . . .' said the messenger, and paused.

'Ah—dead?'

'Yes—she is dead.'

'When did she die?'

619

'At ten minutes past four, after another effusion. She knew best, you see, sir. I started directly, by the rector's orders.'

SEQUEL

Fifteen months have passed, and we are brought on to Midsummer Night, 1867.

The picture presented is the interior of the old belfry of Carriford Church, at ten o'clock in the evening.

Six Carriford men and one stranger are gathered there, beneath the light of a flaring candle stuck on a piece of wood against the wall. The six Carriford men are the well-known ringers of the fine-toned old bells in the key of F, which have been music to the ears of Carriford parish and the outlying districts for the last four hundred years. The stranger is an assistant, who has appeared from nobody knows where.

The six natives—in their shirt-sleeves, and without hats—pull and catch frantically at the dancing bellropes, the locks of their hair waving in the breeze created by their quick motions; the stranger, who has the treble bell, does likewise, but in his right mind and coat. Their ever-changing shadows mingle on the wall in an endless variety of kaleidoscopic forms, and the eyes of all the seven are religiously fixed on a diagram like a large addition sum, which is chalked on the floor.

Vividly contrasting with the yellow light of the candle upon the four unplastered walls of the tower, and upon the faces and clothes of the men, is the scene discernible through the screen beneath the tower archway. At the extremity of the long mysterious avenue of the nave and chancel can be seen shafts of moonlight streaming in at the east window of the church—blue, phosphoric, and ghostly.

A thorough renovation of the bell-ringing machinery and accessories had taken place in anticipation of an interesting event. New ropes had been provided; every bell had been carefully shifted from its carriage, and the pivots lubricated. Bright red 'sallies' of woollen texture—soft to the hands and easily caught— glowed on the ropes in place of the old ragged knots, all of which newness in small details only rendered more evident the irrepressible aspect of age in the mass surrounding them.

The triple-bob-major was ended, and the ringers wiped their faces and rolled down their shirt-sleeves, previously to tucking away the ropes and leaving the place for the night.

'Piph—h—h—h! A good forty minutes,' said a man with a streaming face, and blowing out his breath—one of the pair who had taken the tenor bell.

'Our friend here pulled proper well—that 'a did—seeing he's but a stranger,' said Clerk Crickett, who had just resigned the second rope, and addressing the man in the black coat.

' 'A did,' said the rest.

'I enjoyed it much,' said the man modestly.

'What we should ha' done without you words can't tell. The man that belongs by rights to that there bell is ill o' two gallons of old cider.'

'And now so's,' remarked the fifth ringer, as pertaining to the last allusion, 'we'll finish this drop o' cider and metheglin, and every man home-along straight as a line.'

'Wi' all my heart,' Clerk Crickett replied. 'And the Lord send if I ha'n't done my duty by Master Teddy Springrove—that I have so.'

'And the rest of us,' they said, as the cup was handed round.

'Ay, ay—in ringen—but I was spaken in a spiritual sense o' this mornen's business o' mine up by the chancel rails there. 'Twas very convenient to lug her here and marry her instead o' doen it at that twopenny-halfpenny town o' Budm'th. Very convenient.'

'Very. There was a little fee for Master Crickett.'

'Ah—well. Money's money—very much so— very—I always have said it. But 'twas a pretty sight for the nation. He coloured up like any maid, that he did.'

'Well enough 'a mid colour up. 'Tis no small matter for a man to play wi' fire.'

'Whatever it may be to a woman,' said the clerk absently.

'Thou'rt thinken o' thy wife, clerk,' said Gad Weedy. 'She'll play wi'it again when thou hast got mildewed.'

'Well—let her, God bless her; for I'm but a poor third man, I. The Lord have mercy upon the fourth! . . . Ay, Teddy's got his own at last. What little white ears that maid has, to be sure! Choose your wife as you choose your pig—a small ear and a small tale—that was always my joke when I was a merry feller, ah—years agone now! But Teddy's got her. Poor chap, he was getten as thin as a hermit wi' grief—so was she.'

'Maybe she'll fill out now.'

'True—'tis nater's law, which no man shall gainsay. Ah, well do I bear in mind what I said to Pa'son Raunham, about thy mother's family o' seven, Gad, the very first week of his coming here, when I was just in my prime. "And how many daughters has that poor Weedy got, clerk?" he says. "Six, sir," says I, "and every one of 'em has a brother!" "Poor woman," says he, "a dozen children!—give her this half-sovereign from me, clerk." 'A laughed a good five minutes afterwards, when he found out my merry nater—'a did. But there, 'tis over wi' me now. Enteren the Church is the ruin of a man's wit, for wit's nothen without a faint shaddow o' sin.'

'If so be Teddy and the lady had been kept apart for life, they'd both have died,' said Gad emphatically.

'But now instead o' death there'll be increase o' life,' answered the clerk.

'It all went proper well,' said the fifth bell-ringer. 'They didn't flee off to Babylonish places—not they.' He struck up an attitude—'Here's Master Springrove standen so: here's the married woman standen likewise; here they d'walk across to Knapwater House; and there they bide in the chimley corner, hard and fast.'

'Yes, 'twas a pretty wedden, and well attended,' added the clerk. 'Here was my lady herself—red as scarlet: here was Master Springrove, looken as if he half wished he'd never a-come—ah, poor souls!—the men always do! The women do stand it best—the maid was in her glory. Though she was so shy the glory shone plain through that shy skin.'

'Ay,' said Gad, 'and there was Tim Stroodin and his five journeymen carpenters, standen on tiptoe and peepen in at the chancel winders. There was Dairyman Dodman waiten in his new spring-cart to see 'em come out—whip in hand—that 'a was. Then up comes two master tailors. Then there was Christopher Runt with his pickaxe and shovel. There was women-folk and there was men-folk traypsen up and down church'ard till they wore a path wi' traypsen so—letten the squalling children slip down through their arms and nearly skinning o' em. And these were all over and above the gentry and Sunday-clothes folk inside. Well, I seed Mr. Owen Graye at last dressed up quite the dand. "Well, Mr. Graye," says I from the top o' church'ard wall, "how's yerself?" Mr. Owen Graye never spoke—he'd prided away his hearen. Seize the man, I didn' want en to speak. Teddy hears it, and turns round: "All right, Gad!" says he, and laughed like a boy. There's more in Teddy.'

'Well,' said Clerk Crickett, turning to the man in black, 'now you've been among us so long, and know us so well, won't ye tell us what ye've come here for, and what your trade is?'

'I am no trade,' said the thin man, smiling, 'and I came to see the wickedness of the land.'

'I said thou wast one o' the devil's brood wi' thy black clothes,' replied a sturdy ringer, who had not spoken before.

'No, the truth is,' said the thin man, retracting at this horrible translation, 'I came for a walk because it is a fine evening.'

'Now let's be off, neighbours,' the clerk interrupted.

The candle was inverted in the socket, and the whole party stepped out into the churchyard. The moon was shining within a day or two of full, and just overlooked the three or four vast yews that stood on the south-east side of the church, and rose in unvaried and flat darkness against the illuminated atmosphere behind them.

'Good-night,' the clerk said to his comrades, when the door was locked. 'My nearest way is through the park.'

'I suppose mine is too?' said the stranger. 'I am going to the railway-station.'

'Of course—come on.'

626

The two men went over a stile to the west, the remainder of the party going into the road on the opposite side.

'And so the romance has ended well,' the clerk's companion remarked, as they brushed along through the grass. 'But what is the truth of the story about the property?'

'Now look here, neighbour,' said Clerk Crickett, 'if so be you'll tell me what your line o' life is, and your purpose in coming here to-day, I'll tell you the truth about the wedden particulars.'

'Very well—I will when you have done,' said the other man.

' 'Tis a bargain; and this is the right o' the story. When Miss Aldclyffe's will was opened, it was found to have been drawn up on the very day that Manston (her love-child) married Miss Cytherea Graye. And this is what that deep woman did. Deep? she was as deep as the North Star. She bequeathed all her property, real and personal, to *the wife of Æneas Manston* (with one exception): failen her life, to her husband: failen his life to the heirs of his head—body I would say: failen them to her absolutely and her heirs for ever: failen these to Pa'son Raunham, and so on to the end o' the human race. Now do you see the depth of her scheme? Why, although upon the surface it appeared her whole property was for Miss Cytherea, by the word *"wife"* being used, and not Cytherea's name, whoever was the wife o'

Manston would come in for't. Wasn't that real depth? It was done, of course, that her son Æneas, under any circumstances, should be master o' the property, without folk knowen it was her son or suspecting anything, as they would if it had been left to him straightway.'

'A clever arrangement! And what was the exception?'

'The payment of a legacy to her relative, Pa'son Raunham.'

'And Miss Cytherea was now Manston's widow and only relative, and inherited all absolutely.'

'True, she did. "Well," says she, "I shan't have it" (she didn't like the notion o' getten anything through Manston, naturally enough, pretty dear). She waived her right in favour o' Mr. Raunham. Now, if there's a man in the world that cares nothen about land—I don't say there is, but *if* there is—'tis our pa'son. He's like a snail. He's a-growed so to the shape o' that there rectory that 'a wouldn' think o' leaven it even in name. "'Tis yours, Miss Graye," says he. "No, 'tis yours," says she. "'Tis'n' mine," says he. The Crown had cast his eyes upon the case, thinken o' forfeiture by felony—but 'twas no such thing, and the Crown gied it up, too. Did you ever hear such a tale?—three people, a man and a woman, and a Crown—neither o' 'em in a madhouse— flinging an estate backwards and forwards like an apple or nut? Well, it ended in this way.

Mr. Raunham took it: young Springrove was had as agent and steward, and put to live in Knapwater House, close here at hand—just as if 'twas his own. He does just what he'd like—Mr. Raunham never interferen—and hither to-day he's brought his new wife, Cytherea. And a settlement ha' been drawn up this very day, whereby their children, heirs, and cetrer, are to inherit after Mr. Raunham's death. Good fortune came at last. Her brother, too, is doing well. He came in first man in some architectural competition, and is about to move to London. Here's the house, look. Stap out from these bushes, and you'll get a clear sight o't.'

They emerged from the shrubbery, breaking off towards the lake, and down the south slope. When they arrived exactly opposite the centre of the mansion, they halted.

It was a magnificent picture of the English country-house. The whole of the severe regular front, with its pilasters and cornices, was built of a white smoothly-faced freestone, which appeared in the rays of the moon as pure as Pentelic marble. The sole objects in the scene rivalling the fairness of the façade were a dozen swans floating upon the lake.

At this moment the central door at the top of the steps was opened, and two figures advanced into the light. Two contrasting figures were they. A young lithe woman in an airy fairy dress—Cytherea Springrove: a young man in black stereotype raiment—Edward, her husband.

They stood at the top of the steps together, looking at the moon, the water, and the general loveliness of the prospect.

'That's the married man and wife—there, I've illustrated my story by real liven specimens,' the clerk whispered.

'To be sure, how close together they do stand! You couldn' slip a penny-piece between 'em—that you couldn'! Beautiful to see it, isn't it—beautiful! . . . But this is a private path, and we won't let 'em see us, as all the ringers are going there to a supper and dance to-morrow night.'

The speaker and his companion softly moved on, passed through the wicket, and into the coach-road. Arrived at the clerk's house at the further boundary of the park, they paused to part.

'Now for your half o' the bargain,' said Clerk Crickett. 'What's your line o' life, and what d'ye come here for?'

'I'm the reporter to the *Casterbridge Chronicle*, and I come to pick up the news. Good-night.'

*   *   *

Meanwhile Edward and Cytherea, after lingering on the steps for several minutes, slowly descended the slope to the lake. The skiff was lying alongside.

'O, Edward,' said Cytherea, 'you must do something that has just come into my head!'

'Well, dearest—I know.'

'Yes—give me one half-minute's row on the lake here now, just as you did on Budmouth Bay three years ago.'

He handed her into the boat, and almost noiselessly pulled off from shore. When they were half-way between the two margins of the lake, he paused and looked at her.

'Ah, darling, I remember exactly how I kissed you that first time,' said Springrove. 'You were there as you are now. I unshipped the sculls in this way. Then I turned round and sat beside you—in this way. Then I put my hand on the other side of your little neck—'

'I think it was just on my cheek, in this way.'

'Ah, so it was. Then you moved that soft red mouth round to mine—'

'But, dearest—you pressed it round if you remember; and of course I couldn't then help letting it come to your mouth without being unkind to you, and I wouldn't be that.'

'And then I put my cheek against that cheek, and turned my two lips round upon those two lips, and kissed them—so.'

Like a Bird

a novel

Fariha Róisín

The Unnamed Press
Los Angeles, CA

To every survivor. I wrote this for us.

The way of love is not
a subtle argument.

The door there
is devastation.

Birds make great sky-circles
of their freedom.
How do they learn it?

They fall, and falling,
they're given wings.
—Rumi

I don't imagine your death
but it is here, setting my hands on fire.
—Ilya Kaminsky

What I most regretted were my silences.
Of what had I *ever* been afraid?
—Audre Lorde

Like a Bird

1.

To be a person was a great mystery to me; even at a young age I felt heavy with the weight of dissatisfaction. Like a frog in warming water, I had spent much of my early years feeling as if I were slowly simmering toward my own demise. As if I were sedately, on a low setting, boiling to death. And yet, I was nothing if not quietly ambitious. I didn't know how to locate my compass, but I knew I had one; looking back, maybe that's what eventually saved me. My desperation to survive, even if I didn't know if I really could.

Because, since childhood, forlorn and fast-eyed, the most abstract of all emotions to me was happiness. How did one get it? I wanted to own it, to have it in my possession, beaming out, because I, Taylia (*Tay-lee-uh*) Chatterjee (*Cha-taar-gee*), had never been happy. It's something that I had never fully understood, either, as I had two parents who hated themselves and, together, passed down their own qualities of self-loathing on to me.

2.

Our building jutted out with perfectly aligned alabaster columns that stood like ivory trunks, recalling the miniature jewel-encrypted elephants Baba brought back from India once. The orange blossoms were arranged neatly in the yard, shaping the crisp exterior. The whiteness of our home, a beaming Taj Mahal on the Upper West Side, was gaudy. Like the way immigrants who desperately want to be white were all Gap-wearing and "Howdy," all Wonder bread and capitalism, incapable of knowing who they

really were, like my father and his feelings of inadequacy, a constant lump in his throat. This is what it meant to assimilate.

Baba was a closeted law-abiding coconut. I always assumed that Indians, to Baba, were mosquito-ravaged infidels. But I'd see him sometimes miss the motherland. I would catch him lingering before the ghee at the supermarket, or taking a second glance at the DVD section dedicated to Bollywood films in a Blockbuster we used to frequent. I once overheard him telling Mama that he could still taste the faint sulfite burning in the back of his throat, the memory of his tonsils brushing against the arid heat of dry cinnamon. India was home—but the United States was the future, his star-spangled American dream. But it was complicated; I knew his feelings for America, for white people, were confused. I could see how he knew he was in a country of wolves, but I wondered if he believed in a real escape or just an imagined one.

Mama was an American Jew, Ivy League educated, and a woebegone liberal fighting for immigrant rights at dinner parties, where her faux-Marxist friends digested full-bodied côtes du rhônes and discussed the lack of American health care and Philip Roth. Her face was intoxicating, and her hair was either worn in twisted milkmaid braids or free-flowing and thick, bouncing silently as she sang. Her voice was rapturous and silky, rounding *r*'s like a Canadian. My sister, Alyssa, was such a portrait of our mother, right down to the flushed cheeks, easily reddened to a perfect blush.

My parents met accidentally, inside a bodega. She was buying Tylenol for an impending cold; her face pale, a trickle of slime slowly oozing through her nasal cavity, she smiled at the handsome Indian as he slid past her to buy a soda. His voice had a transatlantic twang, the charm of a man who was begging to be taken seriously. "I love pop," he said, the incongruence of *pop* striking a strange subtlety, Mama recalled. He paid, gulping down his purchased goods. Perhaps fevered by the secret twenty-three flavors of Dr Pepper, they began talking. She explained

her flu-like symptoms, and Baba commiserated, suggesting a concoction of lemon, honey, garlic, and ginger instead of pills. *A naturalist with a love for soda*, thought Mama, as she focused on the peach-fuzz beard Baba had managed to grow, paired with the Dr Pepper that dribbled at the corner of his lip. She decided right then and there that she liked him, and that was that.

They were both students at Columbia: Mama, an art history major; Baba, prelaw. In her mind, Mama had it figured out. The '80s, like the few decades before it, were about experimentation, and he, her soon-to-be husband, was the most exciting and masculine thing she had ever laid eyes on. Their blooming love was inevitable, their future impossibly quaint. They were smart, they were beautiful, and they were an aberration to tradition.

In the months before their marriage, she scoured his dorm for *Playboys* and dirt. She found nothing, Baba was clean. Avoiding all things that could possibly distract him from his wholesome American future, he sublimated his desire for pussy by eating ice-cream sandwiches and slurping Popsicles, growing fond of encyclopedias, old almanacs, and the tattered pages of American classics. Naturally suspicious of narrative literature (but equally committed to safeguarding his pop-cultural knowledge), he resigned himself to mulling over the tomes of *Moby-Dick* and *The Adventures of Huckleberry Finn*—a preventative measure for the off chance he was ever quizzed on what it meant to be a true American, comme Melville, Hawthorne, and the rest.

Like many white girls, even Jewish ones, Mama wanted to cause her Ashkenazi parents deep distress. She watched *Guess Who's Coming to Dinner* with a sadistic reverie and preached to her friends that the racial divide was the true abomination in American society. Ignorant to the fact that her white-girl utopian idealism was a privilege in and of itself, she considered herself a savior and thought her protests were enough, an Angela Davis type wanting to be the target of police, not knowing that pretty white redheads were rarely seen in handcuffs. But she tried. And she fought. And she married Baba.

3.

Alyssa and I enjoyed competing against each other, just like any two sisters would. We constantly tried to best the other, usually in the form of proving to our father that we were something, *anything*. As a wannabe intellectual, my heart insisted on his approval, though it was hardly ever won. I related to him, I even looked more like him and felt Indian in a way Alyssa didn't. So, I guess you could say my love for him was more complex. Or maybe being Indian gave me a sense of purpose, in a way, that it didn't give Alyssa. For me, it became my very own lighthouse: a reflection of my being, or the possibility of who I could be and what I could become. It gave me a reference.

Warm nights always ignited conversation at the Chatterjee residence. Monomaniacal by nature, Baba was a militant grammarian, obsessively monitoring our usage and syntax, turning it into a game. His English had an archaic diligence birthed from a deep fascination with etymology. "What does *nadir* mean? And what is its direct antonym?"

Alyssa and I grew fond of dictionaries.

"It means 'the lowest point of any given thing,'" I would say, quickly looking at Alyssa as a buffer. "The antonym is *zenith*."

I would usually stay focused on her, my hands sticky with perspiration, and as if through a chain reaction, she'd turn to watch our father. If we were right, he would sometimes nod, replying with "good." More often than not, he would simply say nothing. If we were wrong, he would clear his throat with a *hmm*, dismissing us entirely.

Baba wasn't cold, he was austere. He never learned the beauty or value of gesture, of kind words. Mama would say it was because men from India were socialized in such ways, but I disagreed. Baba was different. His austerity was rooted in a disinterest in

small talk. He hated hyperbole and despised social niceties—he deemed them unnecessary. "There's nothing wrong with silence," he would say, muttering like a croaky parrot.

Through the years, his reluctance to show affection became manageable; it was accepted as one of his many idiosyncrasies. In some ways, I almost admired it. Still, I yearned to see a glimmer of familiarity shine through his face whenever I answered correctly. That look that would speak: *Good, I have taught them well.*

Alyssa, next to me, was a complete juxtaposition. People were drawn to her beauty and energy, and for that I was always jealous. In those days, I couldn't finish a glass of water without sighing. My mind, filled with deliberations, pulled at my interiors like a harness. There was a restlessness inside me, gnawing to be sated. I was no good at it. I wanted to be like her, and it crept through me like a disease. I sometimes felt like I was stalking her, obsessed with her languid, nymphlike mannerisms; with her face, the way her skin was pucker-free, not a pore in sight, dewy like dulce de leche. She was like Rani Mukerji in *Kuch Kuch Hota Hai*: divine, light eyed (almost), and brown haired. Every girl at every family gathering *ever* wanted to be like her, inching toward her like she was Mother Mary. Her tiny waist in her lehenga, the way she made it cute that she didn't hardly know any Bengali. All the girls fawned, and all the boys watched with wide eyes.

We sat at the dinner table, Alyssa groaning with despair about something school related, and our parents (especially Mama) gathered around her like lovers from commedia dell'arte. We were in our early teens, when Alyssa still had the verve, the steeped innocence, that she wielded so mysteriously. I remember the moon being swollen, like a wheel of cheese—*when the moon hits your eye like a big pizza pie*—a big hunk of brie, peering in and hitting us at the dining room table. The bones of the fish we ate glistened on our plates, and the mashed sweet potato that I abandoned still on mine, golden under the moon's hues.

"Ms. O'Neil is such a *bitch*, though, Ma!" She had grown cocky, swearing more to see how much she could get away with.

"Lyse, please..."

"It's true—Tay, back me up!"

Sometimes, I felt cuckolded by my sister. Drawn into her dance. I surrendered. "I mean... she's annoying, but she's all right."

"Tay. Don't... She's a goddamn paleolithic cr-creature."

"Lyse, don't talk about women like that."

"Maaaaa, you're not listening to me! I'm not talking about women any kinda way, I'm jus' saying that she's annoying as fu—!" She clicked her tongue to fill the sound of *fuck*.

Mama laughed, defusing Alyssa's strange current, the way, even when she was whining, she made you feel like she was revealing an important secret only *to you*. That was Lyse's strongest skill: her ability to feign intimacy. The two of them went about whispering, and I got up to clear the mood, returning to my own internal dance, where I was paid attention to.

Baba was prone to smoking a fat, dark cigar at the dining table after dinner, ashing into a beautiful crystal midcentury modern ashtray that Mama bought in an estate sale. He looked so out of place, a Brown, skinny Indian smoking a thick knob, resembling anything other than a Mob boss. Certainly not Tony Soprano, whom he was not-so-secretly emulating, given his recent and uncharacteristic obsession with *The Sopranos*. I returned to the table, sitting opposite him, lost in my thoughts about Ms. O'Neil, a pretty white woman who looked like a nun. She had introduced me to Toni Morrison, and I felt indebted to her for that. I related so much to Pecola, the protagonist of *The Bluest Eye*. As I watched Alyssa in full form, heady with confidence, I thought of how odd it was that two girls with the same parents, one white and the other Brown, could feel so differently about existing in this world. How that impacted their cellular constructs in such a way that navigating life was so distinctly dissimilar. I thought of how much I longed to be seen and how I could count the people who had made me feel special on one hand.

Alyssa was beautiful in a way I'd never been, fair skinned and rapturous, the way that girls you can't place are normally

exotified. The light-eyed/light-skinned cocktail. I was darker skinned and darker eyed, which made all the difference. Baba would talk about Alyssa like a specimen of grand genetics—"An almost Kashmiri!" he'd say, slightly proud. A rare compliment from a Hindu Indian, and the absence of one directed at me hit like a flood. Today I was merely observing the grace that Alyssa exuded, Mama fully locked in to her story like an avid audience member, and I felt the darkness in my center of not being enough, even for my own family.

After her story about Ms. O'Neil, we sat still, lapsed into the night's quiet fortress. The silence beckoning us into our separate slumbers. Nobody said another word, as we all in unison stood to help Mama clean up. That night even Baba helped.

4.

I covered the sadness of being invisible to my family in many ways. I treated my ability to hide and remain unseen like a sport. Besides, I told myself, I hated that the glare of attention made my body convulse in shame and nervousness, which made it impossible to casually interact with people. So, to avoid such atrocities, I'd blanch myself with unappeal, never wearing makeup, allowing my figure to be subsumed by toting a massive JanSport backpack at all times. Longish loungewear that Mama bought me from Bloomingdale's was my preferred method of clothing. I liked the way a basic smock could stretch and sling over my body like a compact hammock, erasing my physicality that had become such a burden.

Mama had a friend named Zeina. She was Mama's closest friend—the isomorphic auntie, an Eastern beauty—who was obsessed with telling me that I *could* be beautiful if only I didn't

crouch all the time, frown all the time—if only, *only*, I smiled more. But I was disgusted by my own presence, and I wasn't sure how to cope while being in somebody else's. I had been whipped into thinking a certain way, and I was forsaken into that loneliness for what felt like an eternity. The pain festered in volumes.

Herself Muslim Iranian, Zeina had married an Ashkenazi doctor. She and Mama had met at Columbia, after Mama had admired her emerald-green peacoat. Zeina still wore it years later, the coat the color of fresh-packed succulents, with big floating arms and a hefty bow at the neck.

Mama was obsessed with Zeina's beauty: her cowlicked eyeliner, the pale peach lipstick she'd wear—Mama never missed an opportunity to make us acutely aware of the power such beauty possessed. Of how Zeina would always have the best velvet bell-bottoms, curving over her ass, flowering out after her calves. Or her strappy sandals, matched with tailored white blazers. She was like Bianca Jagger, making Mama exotic by mere association. Once, recalling with embarrassment, Mama confessed her reliance on Pond's Cold Cream, Elizabeth Arden, and tacky drugstore perfumes—until she met Zeina, "the cultured one."

"I made your mother cool, you know!" Zeina had once told Alyssa and me as she obliterated a hamburger in just a few bites (after dressing it with half a jar of Dijon mustard).

I watched Zeina laugh, her face youthful, eyes brightly amused. She had a voice that was sweet and faraway, the timbre of the notes carrying through the house like diffractions of a lighthouse. She drank her cosmopolitans without spilling a drop, a clove cigarette or a Camel lodged between her right index and forefinger as she held the glass by its stem. She'd suggest polo, sudoku parties, and wear pantsuits with deep bare backs. Her hair was short like Mia Farrow's in the summer, then long and black like Cher's in the '70s just in time for fall. She was as elegant as a flamingo and flamboyant in the way Pakistani aunties are, vivacious, lively, and rapturous.

She owned an eponymous boutique in the Lower East Side, consigning the coolest brands from Sweden and Denmark, imprinting her fashionable quirks on the fabric of American style. She encouraged Lyse and me to come down for a visit and to bring our friends. Lyse would sometimes go. She even worked for her one summer as an intern. I passed by but never went in. Everything looked magical, if heaven was furnished with ergonomic lounges and heavy, wall-sized art. Every edge of Zeina's body smelled fragrant, as if wrapped in a robe of smoke and coriander. When I walked past, I could smell her from the curb, too.

One afternoon Zeina was over for tea, and her and Mama's voices reverberated through the dining room and into the rest of the apartment. It was Mama's favorite place to sit, overlooking the vines of ivy that laced the old walls of our back fence, the daffodils abloom with tiny petals of yellow.

"How's Alyssa?"

"Oh, she's great." Mama's voice was bursting with pride. "Wait, did I tell you she has a boyfriend?"

"No, you didn't! I can't wait to meet him. I bet he's handsome, or I hope he is, because she's so beautiful!"

The way in which Zeina said "she's so beautiful" was a fact, a summation. I could sense my mother's face light up from the kitchen.

"Oh, he's great. Ryan. He goes to the Dwight School, too. Plus he's Black."

Mama loved telling people this.

"Have you met him yet?"

"I haven't met him! It's agonizing! But she's been telling me about him... He sounds kind of perfect for her," my mother almost screamed.

They both laughed. "Kathryn, please!"

"Ugh, you know they always say this, but it's true—kids really grow up so fast, *too* fast."

Zeina started humming and laughing, maybe to dissolve the momentary sadness that lingered in my mother's voice. I sat on the staircase, listening, feeling the sudden grief usurp me.

"God, I don't know what I'll do when she leaves."

Mama loved art. An art history major, she'd take us to exhibits or on day trips to MoMA. I enjoyed the great expanse of museums and art galleries. The way people, full with ideas, interacted in galleries was intoxicating, gathered in reverent luminosity over the Carrie Mae Weemses and Kerry James Marshalls. Their measured footsteps like sleepwalkers'.

One time at the Brooklyn Museum, Mama looked at a line portrait by Kiki Smith and stated with an insipid arrogance (classically snooty, a perfect New Yorker), "All portraits of people are just portraits of Mona Lisa." Alyssa and I stood behind her, snorting with the infiniteness you experience when you're young—a rampant sense of possibility, especially in those diurnal art settings where rogue thoughts were fostered and encouraged. Well, at least from snooty, of-a-certain-class white women.

Mama introduced us to artists like Ryan Trecartin and Ryan McGinley, proving to us teens that art could be created from angst. They felt like rare moments when she was directing us, providing Alyssa and me with the tools for creation. I loved McGinley and Trecartin because sin attracted me. The sin of being alive, with the gangly bodies of McGinley's world, ripe like fruit, nudes that were supple and grotesquely white; with Trecartin's combustive colors, the agonizing breadth of his Sodom-and-Gomorrah-like panels. I was consumed by these things that I never had access to—that's when I felt most alive. When I could see the possibility of what was outside of myself.

On a Saturday afternoon we went to Walter de Maria's *Earth Room*. It was a terrifying place, the darkness of the soil contrasting against the lightness of the white, the sterility of the walls stark against the hard-packed earth, 140 tons of it. It made me feel small, as if I were standing at the edge of the ocean. In the stillness of that moment I thought of death. I thought of my body, sunken into the soil, in the very depths of being *no more*. Mama turned

to me, witnessing the color drain from my face. Soon after, we walked out.

"What did you think, T?"

I couldn't stop thinking about being underground, in a casket, locked beneath the soil with no hope of coming out. I wanted to tell her that I felt Dadi-ma, my father's dead mother, deep in my chest, giving me a sign—ghosts, ghosts, ghosts, swishing through me like carp, guileless in a shallow pond. But, instead, I murmured inaudibly, pushing those imaginations as far from myself as I could.

We stopped for lunch at Mama's favorite restaurant, Souen (she liked it because she heard Fran Lebowitz ate there, too), and as I began to emerge from the dark place I had been, something shifted. Suddenly, a spirit of the dead began to materialize right in front of me. Mama and Lyse sat across from me, chatting about nothing, and I just sat, dumbfounded, before turning to the figure who had appeared to my right. Her neck was wrinkled, and she was wearing a shadha saree. Dadi-ma was sitting at the table. I could see her body moving like a ripple of water, and I could feel her hazy warmth surround me as I stared at the empty chair next to mine. Mama, in an attempt to break me from my daze, reiterated her question regarding my thoughts on the exhibit.

I breathed: "It felt like death."

"Do you want to explain 'it felt like death'?" She said it with air quotes, exaggerating the last bit through her teeth.

I shook my head.

She scowled, immediately turning to Alyssa. "How about you?"

Alyssa went on a tangent, but at a distance of a thousand miles away. I sat transfixed on Dadi-ma. Her moon-shaped smile lingering for just a moment, and then she was gone. I felt calmer, and suddenly, words didn't matter so much.

Alyssa would often recite Austen—"I declare after all there is no enjoyment like reading! How much sooner one tires of anything

than of a book!"—her favorite *Pride and Prejudice* bit to whip out at times of social lethargy. Her faux-English accent, liquid and charming, wooed our guests and her friends; waxing lyrical of nineteenth-century realism, she'd educate us on Austen's history. "She suffered from Addison's disease, just like JFK! Did you know?" I didn't know. "She never married. Can you imagine never marrying, T?" I definitely could.

When she was young, my sister's waking life was spent dreaming of the moors and green pastures, the idyll of bluish clouds and grand Gothic castles of Great Britain. I'd sometimes find her watching BBC renditions of Austen on her MacBook, paused on swathes of fine linen (or was it silk?) and Elizabeth Bennet pondering the caustic nature of Mr. Darcy.

Her book collection told a story in and of itself: a candy-cane-pink copy of Nabokov's *Lolita* sat perched on the middle shelf, where everyone could see. Every young neo-feminist needed to understand the complexities of infantile sexual desire and the phenomenology of disgraceful, horny old men. She collected the classics, from a 1958 edition of *1984* to a battered copy of *Brave New World*. Books excited her, because there in the pages—indelible in blue—would be her distinctive scrawl, paragraphs blotted with ink and peppered with annotations. I had once picked up a copy of *Wuthering Heights* and read her inscriptions:

> *To love is to hurt... to sacrifice... to persevere for the other and for your own happiness. Torment is desirable and often required in order to fully appreciate life and love.*

She was such a Scorpio.

5.

I met Simon for the first time at maybe nine or ten. He was a couple of years older than Alyssa and me. It was at a family gathering in the fall. I remember because the air in New York is different in the fall—there's a crispness to the pavement, the sun-bleached sidewalks are no longer glistening with wavy heat. We enter a new realm of the psyche in the fall, fatigue setting in for the impending winter.

Alyssa seemed overly familiar with Simon. They always happened to find themselves next to each other at parties, and when she was near him, she'd oscillate a fold of hair to one side of her head, massaging the tendrils with the tips of her fingers as she smiled at him. Constantly. I knew this because I watched them both. Not in a creepy way, but out of curiosity and, later, with envy. Most boys would leave the girls behind, playing video games, gossiping in some unsuspecting bedroom, but I always noticed that Simon lingered. He talked to the mothers, welcoming their tedious questions about school, life, and so on, thoroughly enjoying how they fawned over him. And then, after a certain point, he always found Alyssa.

I wondered what he was like in his locked room, when he wasn't focused on keeping up appearances. His mind seemed brilliant but dark. I always got the sense that Simon would have loved to watch a beautiful house burn down in a magical, haunting way. Even still, I felt myself be open with him. I wanted him to decide that I was worth looking at, like how I imagined some people look at wolvish dogs: boldly, without thinking it might eat you—or maybe, more accurately, in spite of the thought.

Simon's father, Rakesh, wore thick-framed black Ray-Bans—the same style I'd see the politicians on billboards back in India wear. He was a handsome Indian, like Baba. He seemed impatient, the veins at his temple pulsating like the lines of a Matisse. We

would see him occasionally, the once-upon-a-time Marxist now head neurologist at the Mount Sinai Hospital in East Harlem. As an avid walker, every working day he would march with diligence through the rain and mud, under the caved arches of Central Park. Alyssa and I would sometimes watch him, gossiping freely, as he vigorously walked past the edge of our block with a navy umbrella in one hand, always decked in pin-striped pants and crisp white shirts treated with Reckitt's Crown Blue. I once overheard that he had experienced racism similar to Baba. Patients telling him (to his face!) that they wanted the "best guy for the job," when what they really meant was "Get me someone white, or get me outta here!" Even still, he desperately wanted to be accepted by white people.

"Adi, please." Rakesh rocked his head back and forth. "Not this again."

"You can't possibly believe there's any oil in Iraq, eh."

"I don't have to know. That's not my job—"

"You don't think it's a ploy?"

"Ploy for whom*st*, old friend?"

"Eesh." Baba sat back on his tanned leather recliner and took a puff of his cigar, disappointed.

I overheard them debating ideology one afternoon, their voices carrying through the house.

From time to time the whole family would come over, Simon sidling behind his parents. His mother, Marissa, was a white woman type from Georgia, fragile and southern. She was small and mousy, kind but strange, and always slightly removed from the conversation. She had none of the personality that Mama had, who wore her Eileen Fisher jumpsuits and Ralph Lauren all whites next to Marissa, always in dowdy, almost hideous Chanel.

Simon was an only child and wore it with pride, as if it were an achievement. Puckering like broody men do, a semi–"blue

steel," he'd sit with his parents, scanning our home like a thief. Alyssa would sometimes lock eyes with him, giggling dramatically. What they'd discuss in those half glances I'd never know. But they could never be anything more than silly flirts, because by then Alyssa was dating Ryan.

Ryan was of the "right class" and of the "right privilege," and even though he was Black (both Mama and Baba would never be outwardly racist, but instead just make a lot of racist assumptions), he looked implacable, like Alyssa, and therefore was just right. I'd watch as Mama and Alyssa would talk in secret: their hushed tones as Alyssa dried the plates that Mama washed; the excited whispers as Mama watered her gardenias and Alyssa stood dramatically, her animated hands moving fast as she relayed life and love in drastic gyration. I liked how Ryan treated Alyssa, the way he'd linger like a puppy, smiling and chatting or listening with admiration. I wanted someone to look at me like that, like I was wanted.

Any night was a good time for Baba to whip out his tin of cigars and his amber bottle of single malt Scotch. I'd watch as he would sit in his leather beast of an armchair, a generous sliver of Laphroaig perched in his left hand. He liked Ryan, so he would engage with him. In many ways, Baba was a male cliché: he loved talking about politics and economics, but wouldn't readily discuss either with Alyssa and me. In his mind, they were gendered topics—I guess our pussies couldn't handle it. I resented him for his sometimes subaltern weaknesses—you know, where they exaggerated gender like the bubonic plague. I always felt as if Baba fancied a boy and was secretly upset when both of his children turned out to be girls, something he took out subconsciously on me. Alyssa could be overlooked because she was the firstborn. But me? I was the familial force majeure. I was an immediate failure.

Ryan was sweet but not as charming as Alyssa. He always came to our home bearing gifts. Sometimes it was a geographically bright bottle of sauvignon blanc that his father had brought back

on a business trip; other times it was a bouquet from the flower shop Mama loved on Amsterdam Avenue. We had a great big dining room that housed a table Mama had spent countless hours searching for, heavy and glazed with promises. Mama would arrange our meal on one-of-a-kind plates from a ceramicist near our summer home in the Catskills. She had two sets of dinnerware, one for her fancy (rude) Waspy neighbors, the other for herself that she used with us and people like Zeina and her husband, Karl, who had taste.

One night we sat down and began eating, and as usual, Mama started asking questions. She was a self-proclaimed cool mom, despicably nosy but in the most well-meaning way. "So what do you know about Simon, Ryan?"

"Simon?" Ryan asked, a look of surprise flooding his face.

At that exact moment I could feel Alyssa's body decelerate, her heart beating palpably slower. My body suddenly mirrored hers, tense in its inquisitiveness.

"You know, Simon..." It was a statement, as if Simon were like Prince or Madonna.

"Oh, Simon Sharma?" Ryan laughed. He knew Simon through school, both Dwight School seniors. "Oh man, I hear..."

He stopped midsentence and looked at my mother, her face smiling, her red hair in a loose braid.

"...oh, I dunno." He shrugged.

Mama looked disappointed.

"Why do you ask?" This time it was Alyssa. There was often unsaid communication between the two of them, but tonight I watched her gape at Mama and find nothing.

"I don't know, he's such an interesting character."

Ryan seemed unconvinced. "Frankly, Simon is a little obnoxious."

Alyssa froze again. I could feel the energy between us shift, the force field I had attuned myself to. Her index finger slowly tapping on the side of her fork buzzed mine like a puppeteer's claw.

"Oh, I wouldn't say that, Ryan," Mama said. "He's just ambitious."

"No offense, Kathryn, I know guys like him—men who've had the world handed to them."

This was the first time Baba's ears perked up, suddenly he was out of his academic fog. "Who are you talking about?" he asked.

"Simon. Rakesh's son," Mama explained.

Baba took a second. "Oh."

That was his vote of confidence. Baba would watch cricket with Simon and Rakesh, rooting for different teams, but maybe it was because of this competitiveness with Rakesh, and how Baba saw Simon as an equal, a fellow adult, that Baba never considered Simon as a choice for Alyssa to date. Or maybe secretly Baba was scared of him, too.

Alyssa's nerves were dancing off of her now, the sleeves of her dress creasing at the elbows as she pushed the hair back up behind her ears, pulling and un-pulling a single piece back and forth, listening intently. She was so fucking beautiful.

"Anyway, it isn't important," Mama concluded. "He's just a boy."

And he was.

A week later, Mama took us downtown to shop. Generally we stayed just around the strip of Broadway-Lafayette, where we were allowed to fraternize with the loud, fat Americans, as she liked to think of them.

We were on Prince Street, near the bookstore on Mulberry, when we saw Simon, wearing a black baseball cap back-to-front, gray pin-striped pants, and a Black Flag T-shirt, ambling toward us. He stopped to talk but looked out of breath, his eyes sunken and hollow. I bypassed the conversation, lingering only on the redness of his lips. I ignored what was said, entranced by how stunning he was.

"This one doesn't talk too much, does she?" Simon jeered.

All eyes were on me. Alyssa looked amused, Mama concerned. Simon's eyes were gray and insipid, but I was floating in them.

"She's not as outgoing as *me*," I heard Alyssa say, my cheeks flushing over immediately. I hated being the center of attention. My breasts were blooming, and I hadn't yet figured out how to stand to obscure my nipples from perking outward like little meerkats in the sand. Nothing seemed as horrifying as my nipples being visible through my shirt.

Mama agreed with Alyssa, but I felt Simon's gaze lingering. In my mind, I was hoping it was because he thought I was unstoppably attractive, that he saw past the merging pimples on my T-zone and my baggy, ill-fitted denim. I hoped that he recognized that I was a person, that I was pretty, that I was *enough*. When I looked up at him again, seconds later, he was still staring at me, just as he had been before, but he didn't seem moved. Alyssa grabbed his attention again, activating her sweetness. In a strangely rushed, perfunctory way, he asked her if she'd like to go have dinner sometime. Radiant, I knew she was about to say yes, when Mama interrupted.

"Alyssa is dating Ryan. You know him, right, Simon?"

I watched Alyssa roll her eyes as Mama detailed how much she herself liked Ryan. She managed to insert that he was Black, as if to impress Simon, though of course he knew. It was entertaining in its shamelessness. As Simon walked away, turning around to smile back at us, his dimples uncharacteristically boyish, Mama beamed in the afterglow of a man's undivided attention and declared, "What a terrifyingly handsome young man."

6.

A few weeks later, it was Sunday, a supposed day of tranquil, but at home nothing ever felt like rest. I was both surveilled and

forgotten by my parents, as if they caught me only in moments of clumsiness or stupidity, which had a chain effect: the torment of being met with perpetual eye rolls from them both. Mama's were more dramatic, always followed with a deep groan: "Taylia!" Then there was "Taaaaaaylia...," an exaggerated huff of boredom at my ineptitude. *"Taylia!"* was sharp, it was fast, the annoyance like a whip.

I had taken the morning to read by my bedroom window. The sun felt like a flood of nourishment, a vitamin D zing. Over time, I had learned how to like being alone. I trained myself to embrace it, to kiss the sun and let the big chunks of light baptize me. Each week, a new beginning. I spent a lot of time in my room; socializing felt like a burden. Baba also had weird expectations that he let Alyssa thwart, but I would be judged and questioned if I ever wanted to have fun. As if I wasn't deserving.

If I went out, it was rarely to meet friends, but more to walk in the city's blind spots. To find New York unfolding on the neighborhood streets. Kids who are raised in the city are just different, too. Unruly. Or at least, the proximity to strangeness is so ubiquitous, you become fearless. But at times, especially alone, it felt cold. Topsy-turvy. The city had dark parts, too. Sometimes it was hard to look away. After these walks, I'd return home. But I longed for sanctuary, for someone to cradle my head. So, my room became a cocoon. After time, I trained myself to accept that this was a kind of care. At least I had a home, as many in the streets didn't. I imagined myself in their place, using it to humble myself. I may not have had the love that I deeply craved from my parents, but at least I had my imagination. My dreams became a portal to my survival.

This Sunday, Mama, in a bid to not feel isolated from her husband's roots, was hosting a bunch of Indians for dinner. She didn't dare cook, but had the entire event catered by a chic young Indian chef, Shriya Rao, whom she had met downtown at a New Museum mixer. Mama wanted to show (desperately prove) that she had perspective, that she wasn't just another balmy white

woman, incapable of showing depth. She knew she had it, and she relied on her faith, to a certain degree.

Like most young Jewish New Yorkers, she had a relatively positive experience with Judaism; she went to temple, had a Bat Mitzvah, and was raised with the teachings in an intellectual way. She didn't agree with everything (least of all her parents, whom she found stuffy and incongruently racist), but she found respite in the Torah, in her people, in the struggle for justice. She read Susan Sontag and Vivian Gornick avidly and looked to them as a certain class of intellectual mentorship she longed for. She wanted to show these Indians that she understood the violence of white supremacy. Because, on some level, she did.

Baba and she had a shared sense of winning. They saw their marriage as a component to strengthen themselves, separately and together. An Indian and a Jew unite to make a better future for each other and their children. It was romantic, we (as a family, a unit) became a political statement. Except neither of them had the verve to carry this on with much intentionality. It was easier to pretend than to become. I witnessed this, in the ways they held their friends accountable for standards they were too lazy to unlearn. They slid in and out of political radicality, but for the most part, they got lost in the fumes of a desire for a good life. Because, in more ways than one, they both wanted proximity to whiteness. Which is why their self-hating qualities were so egregious and strong. Besides, when wealth became palpable, both from an inheritance for my mother (which included, among a lot of money, a brownstone in the Upper West Side) and their joint income as tenured professors at Columbia University (Mama was also a curator), they became upper middle class in a stealth way. They hated the idea of the rich, without acknowledging they themselves had joined the ranks of the class they hated so much. It went against their principles—oh, how garish and pompous were the wealthy!

They loved each other, which is why they could put up with this farce together. Both each other's protectors, comrades,

partners in an innocent crime. It didn't seem so bad to be fake, to not stand behind your values in a total way. They were human, they were allowed to have faults—everybody had a black hole of foibles. In order to keep up with the charade, it was important to have someone to rely on, someone who would reflect only the most shiny parts of yourself back to you. So they needed the other. It was a weird, mild obsession. I knew it was rare to witness this kind of love from parents, and in that regard, I was lucky.

But, still, I personally felt like an add-on. I began to understand the dissonance of my being in this family in my early teens. But at that point, what was I to do? I knew they shared a love and devotion with Alyssa, but not with me. Not for a lack of trying, but I just wasn't like her. I was made with more mistakes. She was Michelangelo's *David*, marble bodied and toned. I was an Uffizi's *David*, a mere replica. Without distinction of my own, I was doomed to a life of comparison. It sounds dramatic, and it was. In so many ways not being like Alyssa haunted me.

Mama had warned Alyssa and me ahead of time that we were responsible for cleaning up the house before the Sunday dinner. She said, "Don't test me!" with a grave look I suppose every mother had a variation of. To me, it felt a task both reasonable and valuable, two things I liked. So I agreed.

I came downstairs, out of my private sun-time read, to help. Alyssa was on the couch, her headphones sucking her ears in. Her legs across the leather or the headrest like a slope. I tried to get her attention, but she was in her own world, so I skulked around Mama, awaiting instruction. A little anxious, I hated not knowing where to stand. Mama, slightly caustic, sighed passed me and I stayed silent, waiting for a signal. When she had her head in the pantry, I made my move.

"Ma, I'm here." Sometimes, even English, or language itself, felt foreign to me.

"I can see that Taylia."

"What can I do?"

"Hang on a second." Her tone was already annoyed.

I looked toward Alyssa, legs still sprawled across the sofa like a fan, chewing gum. I bit the inside of my cheek, a rubbery sole. Inhaling shortly, to minimize crying, I exhaled fast. "Okay, Mama."

Eventually she told me diligently, as if I were applying for a job. I ended up doing everything (cleaning the downstairs family room and the guest bathroom, vacuuming all the floors), as Alyssa had helped for roughly only ten minutes, feigned an excuse, and left. When I eventually told Mama all had been done, she looked at me and said matter-of-factly, "Please don't wear anything tight today, you're looking a bit lumpy right now." In response I didn't say anything, maybe in shock, and walked away.

I always wondered what it was about me that felt so abstracted next to my sister. I understood I was pretty, to a certain degree, but maybe it felt blurry next to Alyssa's definitions. My parents didn't help in that regard, either. In many ways, I was voluptuous in a way Alyssa wasn't. I had tits and an ass, I had form. I knew that was seemingly attractive on others, but on me it felt like an excess. I didn't wear it well. Mama would add to this by watching my body with a glaring awareness that pivoted to perpetual critique. As if all I needed to do was embrace x, y, and z—and I would be beautiful. "Just lose a bit of the baby fat," or "Don't walk so heavily on the stairs," or "Eat less at night." Mama became a weight checker and reprimander. Alyssa seemed to have perfect form, the kind of metabolism models have. Thinness felt like another passport I didn't have.

In her own ways, Alyssa tried to confront this, using her tools of persuasion against our parents. She wasn't the type of person who enjoyed being put on a pedestal. It annoyed her, and in that shared frustration, we formed an alliance. Things changed in our relationship when she decided to protect me. It was subtle, but we both knew. Sisters can be the worst, but with a shared goal, we could be powerful.

Zeina, though not Indian, was a perfect pawn in Mama's night for hosting the Indians. I watched her as she elegantly entertained

a crowd of captivated women. Simon's parents, Rakesh and Marissa, were in attendance, including a few others who had teen kids who didn't come. Unsurprisingly, Simon had. Since I had cried earlier from Mama's comments, my focus that night was a bit blurry, though I do remember Alyssa and Simon walking in from outside looking sedated, eyes glazed, a frightening strung-out look of glee stuck on their faces like clown paint. They looked suspicious, but that night I didn't really care. I watched Zeina with mild reverie, the way she walked around the house, a giraffe, head to toe in a perfect brown beige, hair sleek. Mama looked like she was having fun, talking to Shriya, her pixie-cut-having, boy-band-member-hot chef friend. Shriya had served modern-style French-Indian cooking like crab curry bouillabaisse and chicken tikka masala mousse. Everyone seemed to enjoy the pretentiousness, including me, and Mama loved collecting cool Brown tokens, proof that she was more evolved than her own parents, at the very least. Baba looked bored for most of the pleasantries, like he gave about no fucks to begin with. But then, in a quick second, he'd look mildly alive—fired up like a birthday sparkler—as he debated Rakesh, the way best friends who were bitter rivals did.

Later, everyone but Zeina had gone. Baba, a splendid brat as usual, had left the dishes to the women, and Mama acquiesced because she loved him. She found humor in his latent, and arguably lazy, misogyny. A habit, and advantage, of being the only son. It's not as if his mother, Dadi-ma, had spoiled him, but his culture definitely did. It propped up his intelligence above any woman's, and like many unspectacular men, he believed in the bullshit to save his ego.

Alyssa was eating ice cream, Ben and Jerry's Half Baked, right out of the tub. I could tell Zeina was enamored by Alyssa's elegance, as so many were. It was her eyes, but also her entire demeanor: slightly coquettish, yet composed, with wisdom. It was less seductive and more alluring.

"My God, honey, you really are a beauty," Zeina exclaimed, a New Jersey accent emerging from the depths.

Ma sighed, taken, suddenly, by her eldest daughter's beauty, a sincerely perfect combination of hers and Baba's. Alyssa looked uncomfortable, shuddering at the attention. She sucked on her last spoonful of ice cream.

"Honestly," she muttered after a few moments, gulping down the last slime of cream, "Tay's the most beautiful person I've ever seen."

Up until then I had been staring at Zeina's perfect moon-shaped cuticles, wondering why mine didn't look the same. Pulled out of this thought, I was launched into the center of attention. One I hadn't asked for and, yet, I was moved by. Both Mama and Zeina were staring at me, smiling in the fake indulgent way people smile at you sometimes. Alyssa repeated herself, but this time to me: "You're the most beautiful person I've ever seen." Thing is, I believed her. Maybe that's why I loved her, she saw me. She validated me, even knowing I had hair on my lower back and bumps on my legs and arms that I had recently found out was keratosis pilaris.

Mama and Zeina smiled and carried on, moving through the weirdness of conversation, but a little drunk. Alyssa was dancing, tapping her toes on the Persian runner in the hallway as Alice Coltrane's *Reflection on Creation and Space* played, and we all, in our ways, languidly cleaned up the mess of the night's unravelings.

7.

Baba had been acting more erratic these days. His anger—once a collected fire that had limits, that knew its own terrain—was now a thick bloom of smoke, billowing over. Months after the loss of Alyssa, he was forgetting words (which made him angrier), stumbling on details. Phone numbers he once could recall with

an impressive fastness he now no longer remembered. Simultaneously he forgot the names of friends back in India, of the colleges he went to, and the stores he used to love to peruse. His memories were fading, maybe as a protective measure, for all the pain he couldn't quite grasp anymore. But it scared him, and it scared Mama, too.

I saw her begin to worry, to shiver with subservience. She had never been a subservient wife, just a loving one. Still, she had during our childhoods put up with his mood swings, the fresh spark of his sometimes megalomaniacal anger that would eventually cool with time. Now, it was a different, more reserved kind of anger, and she was visibly gaunt from the stress, from the pressures of sadness. I could see that her emotions tugged at the idea that she and her husband would get through this together. That they could reconstruct their past, that their home should not be a tomb. At times, I saw her be strong for the both of them, but it frustrated me that she didn't understand that Baba was a broken trolley with an inclination to steer only toward what he deemed right. He never liked asking for advice, especially not now.

Since taking a break from college, I'd been spending hours in my room alone, remembering, revisiting, thinking what else I could have done or seen in advance. Suddenly, my mother knocked at the door. She never knocked, never beckoned, never called my name anymore. It's as if knocking was acknowledging the absence of Alyssa. I cracked the door open, but only just.

"There's a phone call," she whispered. "It's Simon Sharma."

"For me?"

She nodded. There was a lightness to her I hadn't seen in months. I took the phone from her hand and cumbersomely brought it to my ear.

"Hello?"

I watched my mother as he said hello back. We were both frowning, wearing the same expression of nervousness. He

asked if he could see me. I said yes. He asked when. I said any time: "I'm always free." I knew that it echoed desperation, but I had never had a man call me at home before and I was hungry for that kind of love, for Mama to see me receive it. But I also felt silly thinking Simon Sharma could love me. He wanted to get drinks, "possibly dinner. Tonight?" I said of course. Of course I said of course. He gave me a time and I said sure, then with determination he hung up. I still held the phone to my ear, listening to the sound of an empty line. I looked Mama in the eye and she smiled. It was the first smile I had seen in months.

After what happened to Alyssa, I knew I had to do something, *anything*. It wasn't like me to watch my mother deteriorate. I had so many memories of them together—her pride of Alyssa blazed through her like beams of light, and Alyssa's filial piety shone like its beacon. Through the two of them, I was able to conceptualize the real strength of maternal love.

Simon picked me up at eight o'clock sharp in an Uber. Mama loved a punctual man. He stood and charmed her outside as I leaned against the base of the stairs, entirely nervous. Lately everything had been stunted, dimmed. At last, despite the nerves, I felt the air around me sharpening, the colors changing into brighter hues. I could smell the liveliness and I became excited, having forgotten entirely that I had the ability to feel that still.

We careened through the Friday night traffic with nothing much to talk about. Music, curated by the Uber driver, played to fill in the gaps of conversation, but I didn't mind. I was always more fond of conversational silence than I was of actual conversing. The air inside the car was stale and climatized, and my legs were cold inside my clothes. Another chill rose as I felt his hand on my biceps. "How are you doing over there, Ms. Always in My Head?"

"Oh, I'm fine," I said, reacting fast, laughing it off. I was uncomfortable by the tease, but angry at my uneasiness. I brushed it off and didn't indulge him with more of an answer. Instead, I watched as the tiny bulbs of city light moved across and around

me. I was so captivated by the rhythm of my surroundings that the sound of a car door opening startled me as I realized we had arrived. Bracing myself, I took a few moments to open my own side, but by the time I reached over he had already come and opened it for me. Again, I felt uncomfortable, but I let it go, not knowing how to dissect the feeling in real time. I imagined I was just being dramatic, or a wuss. We walked into a wood-fired pizza place and it was crowded. I felt myself recoiling from the eyes on us, but I also wanted to stop the mental gymnastics of anxiety, so focused on shutting my mind down. I wanted to enjoy this, I reminded myself. Shifting my focus to Simon, I immediately noticed the glances from women nearby and the waiters at his feet.

As we were finally ushered to a table, I sat down and looked around meekly, feeling, for the most part, undeserving of his time.

"You're wondering why I asked you here, aren't you?"

"I can't say I haven't thought about that..." My smile was crooked. Grateful for the chance to be transparent.

He smiled back, saying nothing. After a break in the conversation, he changed the tone, abruptly, intently: "I am sorry about your sister."

"Oh."

"I really liked her."

I stared down at the fork lingering in my hand.

"I did it for Alyssa."

"For Alyssa?"

Today marked the second anniversary of her death. Did he know? Did he remember? He didn't answer me, but smiled.

"You always act so embarrassed," Alyssa admonished me days after seeing Simon on the street downtown. I was baking, attempting to make a flourless chocolate cake. She sat opposite, slurping on a tart cherry Popsicle, chastising me.

"I do?" I asked, already embarrassed.

"Girl, you know you do."

"I'm sorry," I muttered, greasing the cake pan with butter.

She leaned over the counter and flicked me on the side of my left shoulder, right near the bone. "Stop apologizing for everything."

"Okay, first, ow. Second, what the fuck else am I supposed to do?" I didn't know all the answers like her, I didn't have all the answers like her.

"You act like you don't know shit."

I didn't know how to tell her that I didn't know shit. "I'm not like you, okay? I don't have fancy good taste. I'm not confident..."

I paused and looked up. I felt like I was lying, like I was playing a role that had been assigned to me; subconsciously I had deemed Alyssa superior to me, and I felt like I served her at times. It's as if I baited her to feel sorry for me, to take pity. But I also wanted her to feel powerful, and I was feeding her. I was feeding her ego. I almost apologized again, but before I could she stopped me. "Yes, maybe you're right. Maybe I do have it easier..."

"I mean, just a little." I didn't want to enumerate all the ways she really did have it easier. I also didn't want to burden her with all the ways in which she benefited from her access to whiteness. So instead I just made a cake, pouring the batter diligently into the circular tin. I passed her the blue speckled bowl that had all the leftover batter, to dip our fingers into like Dadi-ma when she cooked, edging her pointed, fat finger, using it as a spatula to taste. We shared the moment, with batter in between, staring into the divide of our beings, all the things that separated us. These were moments that stuck out to me, when she tried to understand me. Nobody had ever tried to do that before.

Simon was evocative in the strangest way. There was an unnerving quality to his handsomeness, like a shrill, penetrating hostility. His eyes were shrewd and discerning, and an inexplicable sen-

sation lingered in my gut every time I saw him looking my way. They were so gray, and at moments near the light, I saw them flicker with an emotion I couldn't place.

"Is there something wrong with your food?" he asked doubt-fully.

"No, no." I was mumbling, chewing on a slice of a Margherita.

"Good. Good."

He took a swig from his beer, watching me as he drank.

"You ever been on a date before?"

This was a date? I wanted to gag.

"Um, no," I said, and laughed. "Not really."

"Yeah, Alyssa was more of the dating type."

"Heh." And I was more of the loser type.

"So, you enjoying college?"

I was thankful for him trying to start a conversation, even though I could have just sat, glumly eating my food, feeling like an undatable loser. But maybe some part of me was trying to be bolder, and I felt like this was my ticket.

I lied—I hadn't been to school in months. "Yeah, it's great."

"What do you do again?"

"History and comparative English."

"Oh yeah, that's it, I remember."

I could tell that he couldn't remember.

"Where?"

"Columbia." He didn't need to know that I had almost failed and that my professors hated me.

"Ah, right, like Uncle. Good girl."

I wanted to tell him it was like Alyssa and Mama, too, both of whom had also went to Columbia. I hated the way he said it, arrogantly, as if to feign intimacy, but I still nodded, awkwardly smiling, wanting to cringe. I didn't want to offend, so I didn't.

"What do you want to do?"

I looked at him fully. I wasn't sure yet, and it seemed like such an impossible, gnawing question. "I want to be a lawyer." I paused dramatically. "I think."

"You think?"

My tongue felt like a big useless object in my mouth, so I shrugged. I hated how condescending he was, but I kept being polite.

"Do you think you'd enjoy it?"

"Law? Does anybody?"

He took another swig. I felt like I was annoying him. Maybe it was the fact that I wasn't more like Alyssa. I wasn't flirty or seductive; I wasn't even a good conversationalist.

"It's a big plan for somebody that's not sure."

I agreed, laughing again, not wanting to anger him, but immediately I saw him look away. At that moment I resented how boring I was, embarrassed that I was wasting his time. There was a long silence until he returned to my face, taking me in with a deep, guttural sigh.

"You know, you have a lot going for you. Honestly, you're really pretty."

I stared at some red shoes at the bar, looking past him. Unable to raise my head any higher, I felt weighed down by my simultaneous shock and excitement.

"It's true."

The stern tone of his voice resonated through the small bubble within which we were sitting in, like an oracle.

"Some of my friends have seen you around. They like the way you look."

I nodded my head, deflecting. "Hmm."

"You want another drink?"

"Sure," I replied, fiddling with my napkin.

I looked around briefly. The restaurant was even fuller than when we first entered it. From top to bottom, the ceilings, walls, and floor were wooden. It looked like an old, repurposed barn, the edges of the walls and bar gilded with a strange rusted patina. The furnishings were kitschy, with the characteristic Brooklyn aesthetic of steel, wood, and ferns perched on shelves that lined the entire interior. The pies were soft-crusted, the cheese perfectly

stringy, and the drinks strong, the smell of whiskey and yeast leaking everywhere.

"I guess I've been interested in real estate for a while. They say Brooklyn is the new Manhattan, but Manhattan will always be fucking Manhattan, you know?"

He droned on and on. He was once so handsome, but now he looked lifeless. His cheeks were ruddy and red, like a toddler's.

"I could have played professional cricket. I have dual citizenship, which is quite uncommon, you know? I used to play when I was younger and I was really, really good. Then I started growing an interest in medicine and I thought it'd be more meaningful if I pursued that."

"Also like your dad?" I tried to relate. "Do you think that will make you happy?"

"Some people just can't be happy, and that's why there's money, Taylia."

I saw him clink his pint of IPA with someone nearby, and the foam oozed out like a volcano as they both laughed. I looked over at the person, a white face that looked oddly familiar, but before I could process, Simon turned back and smirked at me, slightly annoyed. It was as if my challenge of happiness angered him. For the first time, in that moment, I felt an honesty shine through. No pretense, just Simon. From the back, I suddenly saw another familiar face. It belonged to Vijay, whom I recognized. Simon was always loitering with these two boys, and the three of them looked like a pack of dogs. Vijay was a distant family friend, also Bengali. His face was forever lined with a mild frown, bored, chewing gum like he was fighting nicotine. He was at the bar, talking to the white guy, which I found odd. But I decided to look away and pretended not to see him. I didn't want to start anything; I wanted this night to be easy.

I was not used to "going out." I didn't have the verve for it. I rarely enjoyed meeting new people unless they shared my oddly specific taste in film ('80s cult classic *Manhunter*). At Columbia, it was hard to make friends for this very reason. I was a strange being,

I knew this. I'd never been able to mesh with a group or belong to a clique. Consumed, instead, by books. In the absence of Alyssa, home felt like a different kind of reprieve—one removed from the social obligations of adulthood that I wasn't ready to face. I had lost the friends I used to have, and now I didn't know where, or how, to begin to retrieve myself. As I sat opposite Simon, maybe I hoped to be absolved of this burden.

"You know that I went out with Alyssa, right?"

I felt my senses, which were being blurred and thinned by the alcohol, suddenly kick in. "She never told me that." That was the truth. She had never told me that. Looking back, one could assume. I guess I could've tried to look at what was right before me.

"Really?"

"Did you guys go out for a long time?"

"Yeah, awhile. I'd say I made some big changes in her life."

None of this new information made sense to me. She was with Ryan up until she died. All of a sudden, I felt as if I was hallucinating, because I could hear somebody laugh and I recognized the voice. "Big changes"? My heart froze for a split second and a coldness engulfed me. Ignoring the feeling, instead, I raised my glass and sent my drink swishing past my tonsils. I continued to laugh to maintain my intentional blindness.

8.

"Tay, you weirdo!" Alyssa laughs.

I stick out my tongue and the March wind freezes my taste buds. We had jogged out into an empty field in the Catskills.

"I'm getting tired, Tay, can you stop?"

"What's the magic word?"

"If you don't stop I'll punch your face in?"

"Funny."

I stop and fall to the ground, and then we lie parallel.

"We should do this more often."

She agrees in hums.

"Anything to get away from everything."

Alyssa remains quiet. I've started to notice her eyes never look at me anymore, the irises don't face mine. I used to be able to look into my sister's eyes and know how she was doing, what she was wrestling with. I could rupture a feeling just by seeing her, by taking her in. Now she avoids my gaze, looking around my face—nose, freckle on my cheek, the line on my forehead—splitting her stare into two different eyeballs. Thing is, maybe I don't really want to know what's going on.

"I wish this is where I could live. Just here." I say it to fill in the gap. It's not the truth. I want to ask her how she is, but I'm lying. I'm trying to buy time.

I am faced with her silence again. After a few moments, she asks me a question.

"What do you define as freedom?" Cryptic. I take in that she's been philosophical recently, pondering life's mysteries.

I pause: "Something with no boundaries, I guess."

Alyssa nods her head. "Like a bird."

Ryan was often at our home, knees to his chest, sitting on an armchair with a shearling shawl swung over the top. The first time it happened I remembered it so clearly, because he looked as if he sat on a cloud, radiating a sadness that loomed over us all. He would come just to sit in the house, like a statue, always the first thing I saw when I came home for the weekends. I could not face the buzzing social world of university. We all felt so purposeless. The unhappiness was so alive. It had taken over the big bright void that Alyssa left behind.

I began to cook for the family and sometimes Ryan, who had become our family. I was helping by doing something tangible.

I learned how to cook soups and stews like minestrone or turkey chili. Sometimes I'd make a paella in a cast-iron pan or *my* version of a chicken curry, the way that Dadi-ma had once taught me. The trick was all in the sautéed tomatoes mixed in with the curry powder and garam masala. You had to mix it right at the beginning of the dish to give the curry the extra kick, the depth of spice.

The first time I made it, ad-libbing the ingredients from memory, I was nervous to have Baba taste it. Not a cook himself, I wondered if he would be disappointed by the dish. I cooked basmati rice as well, and in a medium-sized mason jar we had some of Dadi-ma's mango pickles, sticky and fermented, from years ago that I clawed out with a fork, placing them on a shallow dish next to the chicken. We ate in silence.

The steam from the heat of the dish felt like a cleanse, absolving us of our internal torture. I watched everyone quietly take more. Then, as Baba inhaled some achar with the cooked rice, a tear emerged.

"Taylia, this is very, very good. How did you learn to cook this?"

I briefly paused. "Dadi-ma taught me, Baba."

He was shocked. "She taught you? When?"

Everyone was looking at me.

"Remember, they were very close, Adi," Mama said. "But your father is right, Tay. This is so tasty."

Ryan agreed, and it was a moment of serenity in a time when there was none.

Later, as Ryan and Baba cleaned the dishes, I fit the rest of the food into glass containers. There was a pathetic grace in how they moved: swiftly at times, then—mimicking the other—racked by sadness again.

Perhaps this, this pain, was a shared intimacy that the other took solace in. In many ways, Ryan, like Simon, had become the son that Baba never had. And though I knew some part of him did wish we were boys, we had achieved so many of those genderless milestones.

In those ways and others, Dad was a feminist. He liked that Mama was assured, robust in her beliefs and patience. Ironically, the one

thing he didn't like was that she'd sometimes wear things that were just *slightly* revealing—the only times they ever fought. I remember, clear as day: they'd be heading out to a dinner party, or we'd all be nearly out the door, and if Baba saw something he didn't like on Mama, he would sit on a little ottoman by the door, looking toward the floor, silent. Like a bratty child. It was a sign of disapproval, but maybe worse: embarrassment. At first, when we were young but able to comprehend, Mama would resist. She'd yell, "My body, my choice, Adi!" Slamming doors until she calmed. For years, it was a fight. A declaration of independence. Baba would condescendingly claim that he had no desire to thwart her, that he was *merely suggesting she look more proper.* It's where I could see what a schmuck he truly was. But, slowly, she amended herself. I witnessed it. How, through the ages, Baba began to slowly change the way Mama dressed. It was a series of small requests or concerns, mostly cleavage based (truthfully, Mama had great tits), but the classic Indian pashmina move became a habit Ma embraced, generally making it look all kinds of Georgia O'Keeffe chic.

Through time, Baba slowly turned his gaze to Alyssa and me. His was different from Mama's survey; this was purely a sexuality critique. Offhandedly, he'd make odd comments about how our pants were too tight in places, how he could see a bra strap peek from behind the edges of our clothes or the shadow of underwear revealing itself from underneath, like an imprint. I began to feel disgusted by myself, now again burdened by my own body. Alyssa, on the other hand, never cared. She'd mock Baba's sensibilities in a jovial way, creating zero tension with her charming comebacks, always knowing the boundaries of every situation. She knew how to temper them both and get her way.

"Eh, two daughters, it's a hard life, nah?" Rakesh spoke, and Baba cocked his head. A pink smear revealed itself in the sky, as the sun set far into the distance.

"Don't tell me you're a misogynist, Rakesh." Baba's teeth gleamed.

"Arré! Come on, man, you know what I'm saying."

I was home from Columbia for winter break reading *Sleepless Nights*, by Elizabeth Hardwick, in a nook near my father, far enough for the two friends to be quaintly coarse with each other without being worried that their disdain would reveal itself.

"I'm just saying, eh, I wouldn't want daughters. Simon is hard enough."

"Do you mean Sly Si?"

Rakesh guffawed. "Eesh, is that what your daughters are calling him?"

"He looks shady, nah?"

"Adi, don't be rude."

Baba changed tone. "Having daughters is not hard..."

"You think having daughters isn't hard? Have you met any boys recently? Arré, didn't you hear about what happened in Delhi? She was with her fiancé on a bus..."

"Absolutely reprehensible."

"They don't teach them manners, no common decency. Completely uncivilized, filthy, so filthy. Actual dogs, *kutha*." Rakesh spat the word out.

"What was she doing? You know, when it happened?"

"Who knows what kids do these days. What nonsense they get into. Girls wear short skirts..."

"And boys are what?"

Rakesh was silent, and Baba didn't probe.

Nonsense. The word struck me, it felt so clinical, given the context. From what I gathered, they were talking about Jyoti Singh Pandey. I'd read about her rape in the news. I remember it vividly, it was the last time Lyse and I would both be together for winter break.

"Things like that never happened to girls we knew. This world has changed."

"There was this girl, Dolly... medical student, more of a lothario than all the men in the *entireeeee* department."

I could hear Baba shirk at the very idea. "Sex, pex... nobody has any self-decency anymore. Kids these days don't respect themselves."

"Adi, you sound like a Muslim... so repugnant."

"I'm serious! Women like that deserve to be raped, eh-nah?"

Rakesh growled, laughing. "Mate, the New World hasn't made you more liberal."

"No, I'm serious, it's not about liberalism. Women should be admonished if they aren't more careful with their bodies."

"What would Kathryn say if she heard it? Isn't she a *feminist*?"

"She would agree. I'm sure of it. We used to laugh at girls in our college days, wearing short skirts in the dead of winter, freezing their skinny white legs off. What are they trying to prove? Besides, she was always the meanest, tearing them apart. It would enrage her. I've always liked her because she never wanted to be like that, you know? *That kind of woman.*"

Jyoti's death made me want to learn more about what it meant to be Indian. I saw her as an emblem for the feminine that was under attack. I wanted to understand the culture Baba came from even more, because I needed to know how men became like this. I didn't know that there would never be an answer.

Yet, here we all were again, cleaning the dishes, chanting mantras to calm our hearts. Ryan, disassociated; Baba, darkened into an uncomfortable quietude; Mama, catatonic and bipolar; me, assailable, broken in misery. Here we all were, unabsolved by Alyssa's sacrifice.

9.

We'd go to our house in the Catskills as often as we could. I loved that we had a home in nature; the trees, the cabins of iridescent

design around us, were all beckoning with a life that I wanted to lead. Whenever we were up north, I felt for a time that I was sincerely alive, and it was there that I understood what infinity really was. I would look at the stars and dream of the impossibility of the universe, of the cosmos. On one of those trips I became obsessed with Carl Sagan and asked Baba to find me books about string theory and quantum physics. He complied with my request. I felt there was so much beyond me, without much to lose. In those moments, I felt purposeful.

I can recall sitting at the edges of our patio, hanging from the timber like a stretching cat; I would find corners, lost sections, places I could carve as my very own, and read for hours, turning pages with fingers or the nub of my nose. We owned a great big wooden house and everything was insanely symmetrical, lined and traced with the blades of the tree bark on the sides of the wall—a reminder that this world was theirs before it was ours.

I heard Baba come up behind me, but we rarely talked, so I ignored him.

"I have something for you," he said.

I was stunned, but I didn't turn around.

"It's a book."

I quickly looked at him, and it was true—in his hand he had a small paperback, black with bright light blue swirls on the cover. It read *The Elegant Universe*. I sometimes felt Baba to be a man in the military. So composed, showing little to no emotion. Sometimes he'd pat me on the head, but today he smiled.

"I had a look inside. You know, it's very interesting." Over the years he had developed a more American-esque transatlantic accent, and I liked hearing it.

He gestured for me to come along, and we began walking down the steps toward the lake that was just a few yards south of our place. We were silent as we walked, but I cherished this time with him. We stopped at a bench, and he sat down and looked at me, his eyes telling me to do the same. Baba communicated so much without words. I sat down as he spoke.

"I'm very scared of deep things, Taylia, of deep, unknown spaces."

I didn't ask why—I always knew that if he wanted to tell me something, he would.

"The ocean. Space. These things terrify me."

I was amazed. My father never shared emotional anecdotes with us.

"Maybe it's because I don't know what's out there."

I let that sit with me. I didn't know what was out there, either, but I wanted to believe that whatever it was, it was something worthwhile.

"Life is cruel, Taylia. You have to get used to knowing that. If you're prepared for that, then you're prepared for the worst." He looked at the ground. The lake was so still, a dark navy smudge like ink, a mystery. "I sacrificed a great deal to get here, Taylia. We were not a rich family. Your Dadi-ma and Dadi-ji didn't have a lot of money, but they made do. They sent me to America to have a better life, because that's what people in our culture do. They give their sons and daughters opportunities for a better life. But they sacrificed a lot to get me here. And I owe them everything."

I wondered if he was talking to me anymore.

"Nothing is as important as honor, Taylia. I owe my parents everything, and I will never forget that." This time he almost whispered it: "Nothing is as important as honor."

He didn't embrace me, but instead left it there—that statement— to hang in the air, fragile and explosive in its honesty.

As he said it, I'd remembered that the year previously he'd uttered the same words. We were in a taxi van in Malaysia, on our way to India, Alyssa holding on to Mama as we swerved to the airport. Earlier that day I saw a man with no eyes, hollowed out like ice-cream scoops. I was still ruminating over the way his waxy hands gripped on to my shirt as I walked by, begging for money. Baba looked at us but also past us, declaring one thing only: "Don't plan your lives, girls. Don't ever plan your lives."

He and I would eventually return to the house, after our talk by the lake, where Mama was smoking a brisket, greasy in a cerulean-blue Le Creuset dutch oven. Alyssa was barbecuing corn, next to a pyramid of sweet potato latkes and a wooden salad bowl of creamy cabbage slaw. A smorgasbord of options, all feast-worthy. I watched as Mama and Alyssa sang ballads together, perhaps lovers in a past life. Baba drank Scotch, and I laughed, too distracted to grieve being an outsider. There were moments like this, when there was a semblance of normalcy. When we felt like a family.

It didn't last long when it happened, maybe for a night, sometimes cascading into the next morning, and often it came to an end with a remark from one parent about my body, my gait, the way I opened and closed cabinet doors ("They're *teak*, Taylia."). To that, Alyssa would defend me with a spitting verve and eloquence I had been denied, speaking for me like a justice-loving saint. I knew I could defend myself, but I deferred to her because maybe it felt like love. It felt more like love than anything I'd ever experienced. My parents, much like Alyssa, loved a good debate—and they were on their own team, fortified by their adult intelligence.

"Lyse, it's great you love your sister, but, honey, I'm just giving some advice."

"Ma, can't you see you always attack her?"

"Lyse, honey, every critique comes from my heart. And, look, Tay isn't saying anything!"

Neither would even look at me, to glean my truth.

"That's because she's probably upset!"

At a certain point I'd walk away, my mood already ruptured. I wanted to belong to something. To a unit. I wanted to have something to rely on. My birth family never felt like that. I was somehow always labeled "overly sensitive" because I was quiet. If only they would see the strange and adorable parts that were emerging in me. If only they looked up and saw what was in front of them.

50

Instead, they haunted me like a mystery. Even still, there was a voice, deep down, that felt I must've been born into this family for a reason. I remember having this conversation with Liza, Vijay's sister, years ago. I heard she had left her family house at eighteen to live with her then girlfriend. A taboo act, unlike any other, especially within a conservative, wealthy group of Indians like Baba's friends. Liza's parents were both architects and owned a firm in the Financial District. But, behind the guise of modernity and approachability, they still had their Pandora's box of dos and don'ts. The remnants of caste based standards. It's what no parent, especially those who consider themselves fair or liberal, wanted to admit. It's another one of those tiny hypocrisies they dare not unlearn, otherwise the entire Jenga monument would fall. So, instead, they pretended in public and admonished in secret. She was a few years older than us all, but I saw her at a gathering of families, her hair chopped into an *Amélie* bob, wearing all white—a band T-shirt with no logo and white Dickies.

I made eye contact with her for a split second, enraptured by the oddity of seeing a girl who didn't care what she looked like, yet who remained still so beautiful. She came toward me, maybe witnessing solidarity. As she sat next to me, she smelled like jasmine and rose. She was irreverent; the tattoos across her arms were scattered like constellations.

"Hey, Taylia. Right?" she asked, her voice a little deep.

"Yeah, hey... Liza. Right?" The awkward dance.

"That's right." She smiled.

"I like your tattoos..." I drifted off, getting lost in them. She had a star on her hand and a moon on her wrist. I wanted to touch them, I wanted to lick her skin.

"You think you'll ever get any?"

I laughed. "No, no way."

"Alyssa's your sister, yeah? I think my baby bro is in love with her." She laughed, but I didn't want Alyssa to derail me in this conversation, so I just nodded. After a few beats, I spoke.

"Sometimes I feel like I wasn't supposed to be in this family."
I don't know what emboldened me—maybe knowing she could
relate. Or maybe because I wanted her to take me seriously, to
know I understood in words of recognition.

"Oof, well, don't I know the feeling."

"How'd you work through that?... The feeling, I mean."

She paused. "Huh. Well, I guess just time, really. Sounds like
a cliché, but I find life kind of is. Like, time just sort of heals
things, you know? Besides, my friend Frankie says that we're
always born into the family we are supposed to. Like, it's karmic.
Which is mad Hindu, right?"

I laughed.

A year later I'd hear that Liza was disowned by her family for
wanting to marry her girlfriend. That her parents would rather
die from shame than allow it. Feeling sentimental, I asked Alyssa
what she knew of her. "I heard she went to Tisch to become a
director or something." There seemed to be a sense of awe in
Alyssa, too, that she was astounded that people could choose
themselves. Those days, I guess, we were both learning how to
be outside of ourselves. I know I was longing for it more, for a
handbook, for an example. I craved understanding myself more
clearly. Maybe I was also beginning to *want to* understand why I
was in this family. Thing is, I was beginning to feel like there was
no reason. Just a sad twist of pathetic fate.

10.

I felt a tingle alight my senses. As I came to, I noticed the weight
of a medium-sized hand on my back. It was a rough hand that
felt strong and caustic against me, callused with slight indents
across the tops of the fingers. The pressure of the hand sent an

eerie sensation through me. Something felt off. It felt peculiar. Unnatural.

I knew I'd been sleeping for a while: the dryness of my face pinched as my eyes flickered against what little light existed in the room. I was silent, trying to identify my surroundings. Underneath a curtain of my own hair I gathered that it was a small room. Like an attic. There was a strange draft coming in, and the shadows of the clouds on the hardwood floor made it clear that we were high up, above somewhere.

I was still lying down, rawness enveloping me, my ass to the sky. I lightly brushed my tongue against what was beneath me; it was *salty*. The floor tasted *salty*. The hand on my back now moved toward my shoulders, as if massaging me, then pushed down toward the small of my back with one quick motion. This hand did not plan to treat me right. I remained still for as long as I could, until he suddenly spoke.

"I know you're awake."

My heart pounded rapidly and I knew I was in danger. I didn't speak.

"Do you know how I know you're awake?"

Simon paused, as if wanting to allow me to answer. I didn't.

"I know, because *I* like bodies when they're lifeless. Wait, no—that's too morbid, let me start again—there's a beauty to a woman's body when she doesn't fight back, when there's no hesitation. That only happens when you're asleep or dead."

I felt his face look up, the acoustics of his voice changing slightly. I couldn't help thinking he sounded sociopathic.

"Get up, Taylia, I want to tell you a story."

My mind jumped from one plan to the next. *Should I run?* But I didn't and instead sat on my feet. I'm not sure if it was my inert body or fear that kept me there. I slowly lifted my torso up, my hair still a cloud around my face, refusing to look Simon in the eye.

"God, can you hurry? You are so fucking annoying."

I was distracted by the ambient sounds outside; I wanted to know where I could possibly be.

"You are even more annoying than *Alyssa*."

I was back inside of myself again—she always brought me right back.

"Alyssa and her fucking tight pussy. Jesus. What a girl." He sighed. "I loved Alyssa. I think I really did love her. She was needy, like you, but you're not hot like her. What's wrong with you? God!" He laughed. "What a fucking disappointment you must be."

I gritted my teeth, fearing this was true.

"I see it. I see what a loser you are. I saw how Alyssa would look at you, the way she'd talk about you, as if you were a burden. You *are* a burden. But you know that already." He paused. "And I'm a nice guy, Taylia. I'm generous. I have influence, and I wanted to use that in kindness. I wanted to give them some hope about you. It's been two years, it's time to move on. The way your mom walks around constantly on the clock, hoping you'll get a life, it's pathetic. So I asked you out on a date, Taylia. As a favor. No harm, no foul, right?"

A man of idioms, what a relief. I looked to the ground. My eyes were glassy as I took in what I could within my perimeter: everything was wooden, it looked and felt like an attic. The draft was persistent. I needed to fucking get out of here.

"You know she was a nympho? God. *A fucking nympho*. She wanted it everywhere. Once we fucked outside of your house! Did she ever tell you?"

I heaved a sudden shake. Thinking of her alive pained me. How could I have let myself get into this much danger? I felt ashamed. It came from the very depths inside of me, and before I knew it, my whole body pulled against myself as I shook. He noticed nothing.

"A cock-loving skank who wanted to be caught red-handed, with my dick right up her ass. Don't you get it, Taylia? Can't you see how desperate your sister really was?"

I started to cry. I didn't know what was happening, but I knew none of this was good.

"Do you like it up the ass, Taylia?"

His voice was not condescending—he was sincerely asking. He continued: "No, you're not a whore like your sister, are you, Taylia?" This time he was silent for a longer time. Waiting for me to answer.

"Alyssa wasn't a whore." It was all I managed to say.

He moved even closer and sat down with his legs crossed. He pushed my chin up with one finger and brushed my hair to the side. I looked at his lips. They were still red but no longer desirable. Now, those lips were ready to eat me, and all I wanted was to run.

But I didn't.

I looked at his shirt; he was still wearing the crisp blue oxford from dinner. I wondered if it was the next morning or if I'd been here for days. I quickly glanced around me. The room was empty, and I had been right—it was small. There was an old wooden chair, its cream shellac flaking, in the corner of the room underneath a row of white hooks.

He moved my head back to his face with his right hand, squeezing me with just enough pressure to frighten me. "I want to know if you're a whore, Taylia."

I looked him in the eye, but my face remained expressionless. I didn't want to fight—not for this, not for anything. I couldn't handle this life anymore, and maybe this moment was my way out. He came toward me and kissed me violently, sucking on my bottom lip before he pulled away.

"Are you a good little whore?" he asked as his hands began to separate my shaking legs.

I complied; I wanted to suffer. He pushed his fingers inside of me with a quickness, crawling.

"I'm asking you a question, Taylia, and you're being very rude."

"I'm not a whore." My head nodded as I said it, I was so ashamed.

"Of course you're not. Who'd want to fuck you?"

Nobody, I thought. Absolutely nobody.

"But I'm feeling generous today. I'm going to fuck you, Taylia. I'm gonna do you a favor."

Without warning, he pulled my body against him and then to the floor, slamming me against the ground. I lay crumpled and disgusted by myself. Just as quickly, he lunged inside my thighs and began to take it all away. The dryness built up a natural wall, but he pushed his way through, tearing me open. My eyes glazed over as I lay there, again, no longer in control of my own senses. The searing bluntness moved through me in waves, and with it the knowledge that I might die on this shard of hell. So I let myself drift, to remove myself. His heaving echoed through me, reverberating within the hollow of my chest, the floor groaning underneath the full weight of his body, and me, me—was I a me anymore?

Detached but still cognizant, I noticed a darkened shape, or two, coming toward us. I couldn't see their faces, only the blackened, threatening shape of them. One looked like Vijay; the other, I realized, the white guy at the bar, was Alton, a rich Italian. Both were Simon's boys. But I couldn't look, I couldn't take it in. If this was going to happen, I didn't want to know anything. I felt Simon pull out of me, and my eyes burned as I shut them tight, and then another, maybe Vijay (he smelled like fresh coffee and cinnamon), entered me. Simon sat beside us, watching, his eyes venom and burning through me. The girth of this man was different, and he kept repeating *"good pussy, good pussy, fuck, fuck, fuck."*

Somewhere I passed out.

"Baba told Mama to give me *the talk*."

Alyssa was eating grapes from a bowl, slicing each piece in half with her teeth before swallowing one part and examining the other.

"Grapes are so juicy," she muttered to herself. A charm of hers.

"What do you mean 'the talk'?" I asked, my eyebrows slightly arched.

"The talk talk, like sex talk."

"Huh?" Sometimes I acted dumb, I don't know why.

"Mama told *me* that Baba told *her* that she oughta give me the sex talk. He doesn't want me to have sex. He told Mama to tell me that I can't have sex."

"With Ryan?"

"Yes. God, Taylia, why can you never get things faster?"

I shrugged, feeling suddenly hurt that my charade backfired.

"I'm sorry. That sounded mean. Anyway, isn't that hilarious?"

"Why would he tell her to tell you that, though? Baba never talks about boys."

"Right? That's what I told Mama. But she said it's because sex is a big thing to him and he's really weird about it because it's 'cultural' or something. As if Indians don't have sex! I mean, they invented the Kama Sutra, come the fuck on, man!"

I had read that South Asian culture was super sex conservative in *Newsweek* once. There was an entire article about boycotts and riots when a Canadian-Indian director released a film that was deemed "sexually deviant." To me, it made sense that Baba was protective about this, of all things. It seemed in line with his beliefs about the sanctity of a woman's virginity. I was sure that's why he fell in love with Mama—there was something so angelic about her.

"Are you going to listen to them?" I asked.

"You mean am I not going to have sex?"

I nodded.

"Well, it'd be too late to do that now, wouldn't it?"

She seemed amused, or pleased, or both, and I was reminded again of how Alyssa contained multitudes. I hid my surprise—I didn't want to give her the satisfaction. "So what are you going to tell them, then?"

"Taylia. There's only one option, and it's the best option: deny, deny, deny."

Baba was, for all intents and purposes, a cliché. As a young socialist, I learned, his nickname was "Lenin" in school. His politics were radical, because he believed in Bengali liberation, the future outside of Pakistan. Dadi-ma had indicated as much to me when we were in India, taking me to a dank corner of the study where all of Baba's notebooks and Penguin handbooks on socialism still lay, dusty in a sad pile. I read through the diaries mainly, but a lot of them were in Bangla, a language I had never mastered but was one that was integral to Baba's identity as an intellectual. He was obsessed with the poetry of Rabindranath Tagore and the films of Satyajit Ray and Ritwik Ghatak. And like many other young Bengalis, he had very intense political views. There was still a faded, yet oddly indelible, poster of Mao Zedong hanging, the colors bright, a smiling kaleidoscope.

Sometimes I wanted to ask Baba what happened, what changed. It's not that he was completely lacking in politick, but the father I knew was lazy. He seemed to have had passion, a drive to make this world better, as a young boy. It's something I felt Mama once had, too. But they both enabled the other in their bad habits, both neutered the other of self-possession, as if it was easier to fit a mold of a person rather than to be one. I wondered why he'd never worked in Brown liberation in America, supporting the Black Panthers, creating programs that facilitated conversations about actual revolution. I wondered why they both stopped caring.

As much as I know he loved Mama, I wondered if he had jumped to go back to India when Dadi-ma was sick as a way to engineer a possible return for us all. He never voiced it, but he secretly hated America. On top of knowing he was a hypocrite, living in a country like America, I knew he must have experienced racism so unfettered that the only way to not combust was to marry a white woman and assimilate into society rather than confront all the parts of a life that made no space for him. No nuance. In the United States he was an Apu, a caricature of a person, broken and slimy, who became a token no matter where

he went. Always an immigrant, the other. From servers mimicking a head nod behind his back to cashiers commenting on the thickness of his accent (which was, for what it's worth, untrue), Baba was in a perpetual state of embarrassment. That's what it meant to be Indian in America.

Maybe that's what gave them permission—the fact that they were both unwanted, so why not steal from the system and have a good life? The United States is a racist country and also an anti-Semitic one. They both instilled in Alyssa and me an understanding of that. That our identities would always be different. Yet, all their unconscious actions, all their biases, reeked of wanting to be white. As in more white, as in normal. They were tired of fighting, and finally, in each other, they found redemption. They also found a mirroring of needs, a holy thing indeed.

Once I heard Rakesh, my father, and my mother in the living room. There we had a big old bookcase that lined the entire living space, floor to ceiling. When I was a child I'd pretend that we had a ladder, and in my private moments, when nobody was watching, I'd pretend I was Belle in *Beauty and the Beast*. I'd swing from book to book over our Persian carpets, thick with bloodred wool and intricate, geometric Muslim details, padding my steps deftly as I pranced.

I don't know why Rakesh and Baba spent so much time together when they so clearly despised each other, like mortal enemies. Their entire relationship was antagonistic, and yet, within that insufferable, toxic bond, they seemed to find reprieve. That day, Mama was in the mix, a strange but appropriate addition. She was just the right bit of incisive, but still intellectually flirty, which Baba loved, because it was something that both Rakesh and he could admire. It was also a quiet way to be petty, to show who had the smarter, cooler American wife. After all these years, I didn't know much about Marissa or her marriage to Rakesh, though I could tell she wasn't happy. She always seemed abandoned, as if her spirit had been dimmed.

"You cannot possibly compare Partition to the Holocaust!" Mama shrieked. That's what caught my attention. I could just imagine Baba's face, shocked at his wife's lack of holistic understanding. I'm sure this pained him.

Rakesh cut in. "Americans always think—"

"Are you not American?" Mama mocked.

"Let me finish," Rakesh spat, annoyed. "Americans"—by which I knew he meant to say "white Americans," but because he was partially talking to a white American, and was married to a white American, he coded it in generalizations (this was when many, especially those of Baba and Rakesh's generation of Indian Americans, felt that they had to be delicate with white folks)— "use the Holocaust as the be all end all of barbarism and genocide, which is a limited belief. It is simply not true."

"Ask any country that confronted colonialism—"

"We're also talking about complete displaced chaos where you were taught to mistrust your neighbor if they were a different religion." I still saw this in Baba and Rakesh, especially the latter, the way he contrasted himself against Muslims after 9/11. There was something to be said about the Brahmanical order of Hinduism.

"The English destroyed us for centuries, taking our lands, our gems, looting us and putting our property in the Victoria and Albert Museum, exploiting us, raping our women, killing our children. Partition was just the boiling point. But what they really wanted was to make sure that Indians would never be united, so that we could never collapse the British Empire and take what was taken from us." I sighed shivers as Baba finished that sentence.

"Partition was an orchestration of sectarian violence."

"Yes, but also savage sexual violence, too," Baba uttered, which surprised us all, even me. I was sitting in my favorite place to read and listen to family gossip, the stairs.

"I actually heard that women were mutilated..."

"Arré, women's breasts were hacked off with machetes, pregnant women were stabbed in the stomach, babies were roasted alive.

Then what happened in Bangladesh in 1971 is the worst account of genocidal rape in the history of the world." There was almost a sense of thrill in his voice, a sense of palpable excitement at retelling this shocking gore. There was a short pause until my father's mild voice erupted. "Kathryn, it's not useful to use the Holocaust as a litmus test, because there has been so much genocide that has not been reported, and many of those are not white people's deaths."

My mother scoffed. "Adi, that's insensitive."

"But it's also the truth."

"One is not worse, all death is death, it's all bad," Rakesh chimed in.

Everyone was silent again.

Alyssa had not yet died, so the gravity of this conversation remained hypothetical, rooted in the past, but one day they would realize that all death was death. Even rape, as an act of death. And it was all bad. Nothing was truer.

For Mama, the Holocaust had been sort of an abstraction most of her life. It was so terrifying, so noxious, so cruel, that it was easier to accept that it had been bad, but to not let herself be beholden to the memory or the trauma. I could tell she admired being Jewish in a way ancestral lineage gives you a purpose and direction. She imparted that wisdom to us. I didn't feel Jewish because I wasn't white, and that isolated me, but the older I got, I saw how it defined me. How it, maybe, also gave me a sense of purpose.

In more ways than one, Mama enjoyed the Jewish identity of Bernie Sanders, of revolutionaries like Emma Goldman, of thinkers like Freud, Noam Chomsky, Hannah Arendt, Max Brod, Judith Butler, and Kafka. She looked at the inclusive, future-thinking Jewish parts. That's what she passed down to me and Alyssa in her small ways.

I felt her spark, I felt her need for change, but I also saw her complacency. How she had gotten used to a certain kind of life—

of fancy cocktails, of spring galas and board meetings with art investors. She got used to the thrill of her Maria Cornejo splurges and expensive candles with bold labels and collapsing letters. She masked the slight shame she felt, but I saw how she changed after Alyssa. Some part of her let go, sinking into a depression that at times consumed her. I felt she was weighed down by the loss because it fed into an ancestral fear. Like a curse, a deep voice in her soul, that, despite all her might, she never truly silenced. One that was dark, like a small demon: *How could* you *ever be happy? You don't get nice things.* I could sense this feeling, as I could locate it in my own body. It tasted like sulfur, the voice emerging from a tiny cave, questioning your validity to be alive. I think Mama was always expecting tragedy. It was historic, this feeling. And when it escaped it was like a dark crescendo. After Alyssa's death I saw Mama fight with the fear that she'd never have a good life.

Mama's parents, my grandparents, whom I had never met, I knew had had the same fear, but I also understood that their lives had been harder. Mama would always remind us of that. In her own way, she still showed respect.

Her parents, Marty and Den (short for Denise), had grown up during more rampant anti-Semitism, which they both battled within their respective fields, which galvanized their singular investment in a good life. Marty was a psychiatrist, and Den was a CEO of a womens wear brand similar to Spanx, but with clothes made in the old-fashioned style of ugly cream nylon. Den was a Gloria Steinem feminist, but she was also extremely, sycophantically obsessed with being the best wife to Marty that she could be.

Both were born in New York, and both were the first generation that started to pull their families out of poverty. Raised in the Lower East Side tenements, they dreamed of a better life, of having money, power, a nice house, and a family of their own. They both had that desire in common, so in many ways were ideal for each other. They worked hard to pull themselves out

of a tough situation, and they both believed it was their trust in God. So they felt entitled to success, to a good life. Because they were people chosen by God.

Marty hardened in his old age, and his desire for a better life poisoned his ability to enjoy the moment, which only made him even crankier. He loved Den, she was a wonderful wife. He even loved his strange daughter, Kathryn. He admired her quiet tenacity. But the moment she brought home an Indian? It was too much. He had worked too hard to be betrayed like this by his own daughter.

That shift in her father, I believe, was the catalyst that turned Mama against him. She saw it as a betrayal and as being politicized in ways she felt motivated by. She'd been the best daughter she could be, but she chose Adi. She would always choose Adi.

11.

I hate Simon. I hate him in a maddening way. In my dreams he has a mercurial disposition, like death. His natural evasiveness, the smug way he holds himself, chokes me. The tortured viscera of my body makes me want to scream, *AH, AH, AH!* I want to scream endlessly across canyons and valleys, to feel the torment of my internal self play out in front of me with a destructive force.

I want to kill him.

In one dream, I'm in the desert and he's following me. *Am I weak?* I ask myself this question again and again. I turn, and he's brazen, the sun shadowing across us and the great expanse of mustard-colored soil. I stumble in fear, and as I do so, I fall onto a cactus, the needles cutting into me with decisive stings. One just misses my heart and I pull out the rest, plucking out the

spines, watching as my blood spools like gold. Then something else pours out of me: "I believe in myself like a religion." I whisper it out of nowhere, like a prayer I once forgot. "I believe in myself like a religion." I repeat it.

As I stare at the same rounded eyes I've known all my life—all mine—I feel a kind of love that I've never experienced before. *The early stages of change may mimic deterioration.* I read that once, somewhere, and now I hear it everywhere around me like a Buddhist mandala that rings around, and around, and around, pushing us into our uncomfortable center.

I look back at Simon; he's no longer there. I'm alone in the desert, but the holes from the splinters shine like rubies on my body, glinting red in the heat. I am alone. *Loneliness is an abstraction.*

I opened my eyes the next morning, remembering who I was, what I was, where I was—in my room—and that I wasn't dead. Not yet. I felt momentarily safe, but then felt the sudden thud of my vagina's soreness, and that's when the deluge of memories flooded in. My mind was desperate to fill in the gaps left by the preventative efforts of traumatic shock. It was as if subconsciously, I didn't want to disappear into that moment in time, like a portal. But his body's imprint was still on top of me like a skin-crawling sensation of numbness. He was still there, his hand around my throat.

I looked around my shrine, this room. Books littered the ground near my bed, the most recently read novel on top of the pile: *The God of Small Things*, by Arundhati Roy. I scanned the rest of the corners: my perfume station, with its various types of incense and dried roses in mason jars. The curtains were slightly ajar, and the light filled the top triangle of my bed. I played around with my fingers but they were heavy; I felt groggy and out of sync. I couldn't stop having short, sudden flashes of the night before, and as each moment flew into my mind, I knew that life would never be the same again. This was my event horizon. I

placed my fingers on my cracked lips and slid my tongue across the remnants of the blood that had dried over. Every muscle in my body ached unbearably. I began to cry, the tears stinging the small cuts on my face, followed by a wave of dread. Every thought was swirling, like a gnawing fog, crashing into my impaired self.

The house felt still, more quiet than I remembered it to be, which brought me some respite. I was hungry, I needed to eat. I needed to forget.

After a few tries, I successfully gathered myself into a big ball, my comforter a styled heap, a soft bulwark between me and the world. With that buffer, I opened my door slightly to hear the sounds of Mama and Baba, but I couldn't hear them. No sounds of a Beethoven concerto, no loud voices on MSNBC or NPR to fill the gap of silence. I went to my window to see if Mama was in the garden; she wasn't.

All of a sudden, I felt safe. Ever since I was a child, I craved an empty home. I loved the feeling of walking around unobserved, finally free. Where were they? It didn't matter. For a few moments I could be still and I could be alone. I could be in this room, a quiet sanctuary, and comfort my entire being, something I had become quite good at since the loss of Alyssa. I would just go into another world—I guess you could call it dreaming.

I began to think about life, about safety. Without directly thinking about what had happened to me the night before, I wondered where women were truly safe, when some of us weren't even safe in our own homes. Where could we rest? Outside of these prisms of expectation. Of violence. Of fear. Where could I lay my head and not feel coldness usurp me? In that moment, I was grateful to have a bed, to have a home I could return to— even if it wasn't ideal, even if I didn't have love, at least I had that.

But a beat skipped, and all of a sudden I was concerned about my parents. How would they react? What would they say? Something felt dangerous. My insides sat like a knotted pretzel. I

gently coerced myself out of it; I knew I couldn't linger on these thoughts. Not now.

Eventually, I made my way downstairs and still found no trace of my parents. Maybe they went out, which was strange, they usually let me know. Something felt wrong, deeply wrong, but I breathed through it. As I walked into the kitchen, I suddenly became voraciously hungry. Scavenging for food, I found some cold roasted chicken that I picked apart, piling it on a plate with a piece of toast sloppily dressed with mayonnaise. I ate watching the leaves outside fall and rest on our patio. Mama would complain about them dusting about later, fixating on the smallest interruptions as a sign of impending doom. I understood why she did it. She was filling in the gaps of Alyssa's absence, which hung on to her life, a ghost.

After washing the dish, I went upstairs and slowly began to unfurl from my cocoon. The food had helped me return to my humanity, or what was left of it. My body didn't feel like my body anymore, it felt like an outlier to my system. I wanted a spaceship, a body that was mine and mine only to control. I closed my eyes. I wanted to disappear. I couldn't keep still, and my mind was suddenly erratic. It wanted to go to the pain, the lingering one just south of my belly, but I wasn't ready to face it.

I must have fallen asleep because I awoke to a knock on the door. It slowly opened soon after, and my mother stood, staring down at me. She had been crying, there were streaks underneath her eyes that lined her skin. She looked broken, like she did soon after we lost Alyssa. Over the last couple years, she'd been making a slow recovery, as Baba's health was now dissolving. Maybe that's what kicked her into action, the idea of mothering someone she wanted to save. She looked past me now, as my father came in behind her, his hands on her shoulders. They were like a sad human centipede. As they stood for a few moments, the feeling of knots returned to my stomach. After years of practice, I had memorized every facial expression of my father's. I counted to

three in my head. *One.* He is looking down. *Two.* He is looking down. *Three.* He is still looking down. I was in for bad news.

"Taylia," my father croaked. His focus was entirely on his shoes, as if suddenly finding interest in their manicured leather. The air in the room was stale and bent, and a singing began in my ears to deafen the blow that I knew was to come. *Because*—of course I knew. I knew how it would look to them. Me, Taylia Chatterjee, a deep blundering mess. I knew because I had listened to Baba, I had heard him loud and clear: *Don't ever plan your life, Taylia. Don't you dare get used to this. This. All of this. You can't have it, it's not yours, Taylia.*

They must have gone out to discuss their plan to throw me out.

I could imagine the smarmy look on Simon's dumb face. *She just got too out of hand. She was at my place, but I'm sorry—she was so out of control.*

Mama would believe him because she wanted to believe men and their lies, and Baba would believe him because he was trained to not plan his life.

After losing Alyssa, nothing mattered.

"Taylia."

He paused for an eternity. I heard it in a daze.

"Taylia   your mother
                              and I have

                              decided

that it is b e s t

you no l o n g e r stay with

u s

or are c o n n e c t e d

with this family."

I looked at my mother; she was witnessing something she
didn't have the stomach for. We stared at the deafening quiet together. I wanted to scream at her, scream at him. A black question
mark hovered before me: *Did neither of you plan your lives, so this
is easy?* My mother, now brittle, ugly in her betrayal, certainly
not as defiant as she once was when her roots were thick and
she stood with a power that announced itself. I remember the
menace in her eyes when Baba and she would sometimes fight,
her eyes spitting venom. *Don't you dare tell me what to wear,
Aaditya.* Now, she was ravaged by weakness, ravaged by loss.
She couldn't lose Baba, too. I knew that, but I hated her for it. I
knew that she was protecting him. I was just always the last one
to save.

"Please, take what you need and... get out."

"What did he say? What did he tell you?" I stumbled, lost.

"It's not important now..."

"No, it is." I was filled with rage.

My hands went to the back of my head, like a tic. I felt the
spidery matted hair behind my ears that I had a sudden desire

to play with as I prayed in front of my parents for mercy. There were so many inconsistencies in my appearance, how could they refuse to see the damage done to *me*? As I swallowed I felt the chemical aftertaste of blood in my mouth—the cum and saliva—it was the taste of iron(y). I looked over at my mother again, imagining her hands between her knees, jittery and swollen after she'd been fucked by an army of men. Was I being strong, sitting there, still alive? I wasn't sure anymore.

My father's voice croaked. "Simon explained that your decorum was..."

"Was *what*?"

"Disgusting."

"How?" I was defiant, still. I would be till the very end. They couldn't throw me out this quickly.

"Because, Taylia"—his voice leveled up, strained—"you threw yourself at him. You made a mess. He told us everything. Do you have no shame? Didn't I, or your mother, teach you to be better? And you repay us like this? Rakesh is my friend of more than twenty years, how will I show my face to him again? Huh? Taylia, this is incomprehensible."

"So you're throwing me out? For something *he* told you?"

"Why would Simon lie?"

"So what did he tell you, *exactly*?" I asked instead, wanting my own clarifications.

There was no response.

"Baba?" I asked. I craved closeness. Now more than ever, I wanted my father's care. "Baba, please." This was a nightmare, and I felt myself release a beg. "It's not what it looks like, I promise."

"He said you couldn't stop drinking, that you became so sloppy that you began to come on to everyone at the bar, like a dog. That you started to take your clothes off in front of them all, being a *slut*... This is so far from what we ever expected from you. How could you do this to me? To us? To your *mother*." He hissed the last part.

I tried to remember the real events of the night before, at least knowing that Simon was lying, and was momentarily confused. Had I, at all, acted inappropriately? Had I allowed this to happen to me? My truth was too far and too clouded to reach. So I stayed quiet and kept listening, hoping for a breakthrough, for a clear memory that was my own. Simon was pathetic. I was right, he was sociopathic. This was a different level of deranged pettiness. I suddenly remembered Vijay's face, bored, as he loomed over me. *Good pussy, good pussy, fuck, fuck, fuck.* Now, all of a sudden, I wanted to look him in the eye.

"He said you made his friends feel deeply uncomfortable. He said he'd never seen a young woman act so poorly. He was embarrassed *for* you. Can you imagine what you put him through last night? After he had reached out, acted like a gentleman, and you disrespect him, me, your mother, your family name and legacy..." He stumbled. "We can't have this kind of behavior, Taylia. This is unacceptable. I have no patience for this kind of thing. You always knew that, and I will not be the one to remind you of that again. You want to be a... a... slut? You can do that on your own dime. This won't take place under *my* roof." The *my* had a poetic vengeance. He was competing for an American life even against his own daughter.

Nothing is as important as honor was ringing in my ears. *Nothing.* It was as if all the years of advice had led me to this point. Had he always wanted to throw me out? And did she always want to let him? I didn't care about his mind anymore, the way it broke my spirit to see him stumble on the easiest pronunciations or the small, tempered shake his hands were now rhythmed with. I didn't care. My grief knew no limits, too, yet now it was being yanked like a weed out of the topsoil.

As I began to move about my room—*their* room now—my mother wheezed into the wall opposite from me. She was kneeling over the floor, sobbing, contesting, her body writhing with sorrow. I felt sick watching her cry. There was no room inside of me for sympathy. I fumbled and found my wallet, walked to

my wardrobe, grabbed a jacket, and put it on. From the depths of my closet I pulled out my raggedy JanSport bag, having the intelligence to pack some underwear, a hairbrush, jeans, a sweatshirt, and a few Uniqlo tees. I was grateful for my beautiful noise-canceling headphones, which I put around my neck. I would drown myself in music. I would survive this. I thought of Vijay's sister, Liza, and how she had been disowned, too. I would be okay, I repeated to myself. I could walk away and survive. The coldness of the moment enveloped me. The warm jacket didn't take away the chill, goose bumps visible as I moved. As I walked away from my room, I took a quick glance at myself in the mirror— I didn't look *that* bad; I knew what had happened to me, and that was much worse. I paused for a moment, my back to my parents. I would be okay, I would be okay. I believed in myself like a religion.

How do you pack all the memories you have and contain them? I thought that over and over again. How much I wanted to start again. How I wanted a different life. Not this, *not this.* Not this fucking pain. I felt simultaneously lost and virulent—my rage a shield against the agony of starting again, alone. Alone. *Here you are again, fucking alone, Taylia. Can you do anything right? What is wrong with you? You've done it again, you've fucked everything up, you dumb, dumb bitch.* I wanted to scream, I wanted to vomit. I wanted a hug. I pushed through that feeling and returned to rage, a sudden numbness enveloping me. I pushed my needs down with the puke. I didn't want to die. I knew that. Not now. I wanted to survive in the face of this injustice. I had to. I had nothing else to lose.

I turned to look at them. My mother's face, with her soft skin, milky, soaked with tears. Her red hair ruffling to the rhythm of her shivering body. My father stood there with his eyes unfocused, staring out the window as the leaves fell to the floor of Mama's perfect garden. Their names felt foreign in my mind: *baba* and *mama.* Had I ever known such things?

Moving quickly, I walked out of my room, looking at the floor as I passed my father. I leaped down the stairs, embarrassed by

my body, the weight of it and what it represented: shame. I spun around in circles taking it all in. *My house. My life.* All this that is, all this that was, all of it that was now being taken away from me. I pasted the picture of it all in my mind's eye. The life that could have worked. If only. *If only.* I let my eyes scan everything thoroughly, making sure I'd be able to close them and see Alyssa.

Alyssa sitting at the window.

Alyssa coming home from school.

Alyssa brushing her hair in front of the hallway mirror.

Alyssa smiling.

The smile that made you feel a surge of elation, no matter what mood you were in.

These are the last memories. I suddenly remembered a word I had learned only a few days earlier.

atomization
(noun)
The process of separating something into fine particles; to reduce to atoms

I opened the front door, allowing a gust of wind to wash over me. I looked over at my parents on the top level and nodded my head in a last goodbye and walked out—just like that. I heard my mother howl. But I didn't look back. I couldn't. The sun shone in my eyes. My mother screamed. I walked on.

12.

"What's rape?"

Alyssa stopped outlining and put down her pencil. "Where did you hear that word?"

I shrugged.

"Tay?"

"There was an interview with a woman on television."

"About?"

"She'd been raped."

"What did she say?"

"She's Pakistani. She's trying to bring justice to herself."

Pause.

"Is Baba Pakistani?"

"No, he's Indian, Tay."

"She dressed like Dadi-ma."

"Who?"

"The raped woman."

"Don't call her that."

"Sorry."

Alyssa picked up her pencil again, twirling it in between her middle and forefinger.

"So, what does it mean?"

"I'm trying to think of an appropriate way to explain it to you."

"Just explain it to me however."

"It's not that easy."

I felt uncomfortable, like I was prying into business that didn't involve me.

"Do you know what sex is yet?"

I shrugged. When you're young you think you know it all, even if you're insecure about everything to do with yourself.

"Well, rape is when someone wants to have sex with another person and forces it on to them."

I immediately understood. One of the things I had always hated was when others forced me to do something. It generally involved eating the food at my parents' friends' houses, brandishing me with dishes like it was a competitive sport. I sat down on Alyssa's bed, hoping for more information.

"I've read awful stories. Sometimes men are so vicious that they cut you open with knives and sticks for no reason. Then

those women get stoned to death because society is siiiiiiiickk and they think the women were 'asking for it.'"

"'Asking for it'?"

"Men are gross. They want to punish women because they think it's their fault that they want to fuck them."

I didn't know what *fuck* meant yet, but it sounded ominous. I wondered if it was an onomatopoeia, *fuckfuckfuckfuckfuckfuck*. Alyssa's face lit up when she said it, rolling it off her tongue like a prayer, her cheeks flushed over and her eyes widened. I watched her, entranced, chewing my nails in fear.

I never used to understand the importance of believing in oneself. I knew I lacked self-esteem, but I never saw how that affected anybody but myself. I didn't know a life without that lack. It felt like how people have allergies their whole lives and become accustomed to the chronic uncomfort of it all: the phlegm caught in the throat, the constant pull of a sneeze lodged against the chest. That was me, the ache of dissatisfaction had become a common thread in my existence.

A few times when I was younger, my parents—out of fear, maybe—sent me to a child psychologist. She was a haughty woman in her mid-fifties who looked eerily similar to Gertrude Stein. She had no patience for my sadness and would often become frustrated with me. I would feel the urge to tell her that she was in the wrong profession if she had no tolerance for despair. But I lacked the chutzpah. So, instead, there I was— nine years old, silently suffering from depression.

We get so lost in our own universes, unaware of the troubles that surround us with every heartbeat. Not a soul in the world has a life devoid of pain. I tried to focus on that as I felt the misery overwhelm me in the days following leaving my parents. I knew the only way to push out of the grief inside my heart was to look to the sky. I wanted to look up and see twilight, the beams of a blue sky and the green, green trees. I wanted to see growth and cycles and *change*. I wanted to focus on my future.

I remember walking around the streets after 9/11. The city felt vacant, as if entire swathes of people had uprooted and left. That palpability of anxiety, of loss, of traumatic fear—they were left in those streets, mellowing out the anger, burying the loneliness under their ash. I felt them, even as a kid. There was a very poignant smell to that loss, to that sadness: a dank, unfettered human smell, musty and unkempt. When people mourn such massive tragedies they tend to forget to look after themselves— they revert to a more primal state, forgetting what a toothbrush feels like. They forget who they are, bound by pain and pain alone.

Alyssa and I went out with Mama maybe two, three weeks after it all happened. At first, Mama pretended as if it were just any normal trip downtown. We took the subway to Battery Park, maybe as a ruse, an excuse to see what the city smelled like now, what the fabric of the air felt like against our skin, so close to where it happened. We didn't do anything once we got out. Mama didn't do or say anything—she just *walked*. We sulked past the Staten Island Ferry and she paused. "Are you okay?" asked Alyssa. Mama stayed quiet. There was something different in the air—you could feel the absence, you could feel the hurt festering around us. Everything about the city felt dark, cloudy. We stood next to the railing by the water and held Mama's hands, one on each side, as she cried muted, soft tears that floated down to her chin. She looked out past the skyline—way, way past.

As I watched the water move around this city, I thought of how many people had died in the history of the making of this country: Black people who built this nation under enslavement, the Native Americans robbed of the land that was theirs, and now innocent people caught in the cross fire of political ambition and white supremacy.

After 9/11, everyone had become an unknown patriot. Even then, I wondered how the United States could have a finger in every pie and not know that it would backfire. I said that to Mama over dinner a few nights after our trip downtown and she

screamed at me. "Do you know how many people died, Taylia? How could you possibly be so heartless?"

Alyssa looked at her food, glum, but Baba glared at Mama, as if to challenge her. There was a flicker, a moment, and though Baba spoke no words, I knew he was thinking the exact same thing. Maybe Mama sensed it, too, because she never said anything like that again.

I understood that I could both love this country but still see people like Baba—Brown people—and Black people and people like me, the in-betweeners: people unloved for what they represented, even with all the benefits of class privilege; who were neglected and then chastised for being mad. Baba didn't say anything because I knew he still wanted to be an American, but it was clear: he knew that he never would be. Especially in the aftermath of such hate. In the days, months, years post-9/11, things changed for him. Alyssa never had any trouble, but I felt the stares in school, and I caught wind of the rumor that Baba had family back home in India who were terrorists. Alyssa didn't care, but I did. I felt the weight of the shame. I wore it for all of us.

Living and going to school on the Upper West Side meant that I was irrevocably cut off from a large part of the New York experience. I had heard that other kids, other kids not like me, roamed the city—farther than I had gone—to the edges of its greatness and its vast expanses, its corners like museums, those blind spots. Reaching out, sprawling, advancing as they got older to other sections. Using the streets in the same way kids growing up in the country used rivers, forests, large rocks, and caves, mapping their world out completely.

I hardly ever spent much time below Sixty-Third Street. I walked, but New York never excited me that much, so I was happy to live in a bubble. Surprising to some, maybe, but I craved consistency. When we were in India, I was confused by my relatives and their obsession with New York. I couldn't imagine the thrill it brought others, how to them, their imagination spoke

great wonders. My reference point for super, super downtown the last few years had been the Whole Foods on Broadway and Fourteenth, the Staples—everything else was a bit of a blur. As for the Lower East Side, I was a complete fool. I remotely knew the few places I had been to in the East Village during my high school days, when my friends and I would sneak out and shop at Trash and Vaudeville. St. Marks and the dirtiness of the East Village seemed worlds apart from my New York, that of pristine brownstones and greenery on the Upper West Side.

I tried shoplifting in the Lower East Side once. There was a bodega, around the corner from this Indian place called the Punjab Grocery and Deli, on East Houston that my high school friends and I would go to. Once I tried stealing a Gatorade at the bodega but chickened out at the last moment. I wondered if it was still there or if it had also been caught in the gross gentrification of the LES. My friend Carolyn was with me when I attempted to steal a Gatorade of all things, a hasty decision on my part. I wanted to impress her, as I always wanted to impress girls my age; besides she had hair like Kate Moss's. It framed her face in perfect angles. She laughed when I couldn't do it and said it was fine that I *couldn't* steal. I felt thankful for her laugh, it felt like a commiseration. Afterward, she jokingly lamented the absence of the Gatorade to all our other friends, who were sitting outside on the curb: "Taylia pussied out!" She shouted it, her punishment. I was so shocked, a tingly reservation came over me as my spine rounded over and my shoulders began to slump. This was a memorable moment of friend betrayal for me. You know, when those Shakespearean moments in your life happen.

Luckily now, years later, I still had the Punjab Grocery and Deli, which was mine (a thing I could rarely claim), and it became an LES haven for me, cheap food for my lonely days. It had really good samosas and pakoras, things that I missed about India. Delicious, fragrant street food wasn't such a novelty in India, costing close to nothing. On the streets, Mama would sometimes let us buy things, but very often would redirect us to packaged

foods for "our own safety," and Alyssa and I would resent her for it. I used to love these chips, which were shrimp flavored and crunchy like a Cheeto. But I craved the hot foods, the sizzling fried pakoras. Even Baba held back when it came to the devouring of jhalmuri or jalebi—supposed favorites of yore. He would incongruently pat his tummy and tell us that his stomach had grown weary from the time and space away. He never referred to India as home, which always surprised me. I felt bloated with a blue love for India.

In the Deli I experienced a certain kind of solidarity. The servers were kind, talkative. One or two had asked me where I was from in a direct and nosy way, with a familiarity that spans borders. Whenever I mentioned that I was half Indian they would beam—"Indian! *Yoo-aare-Indiaan???*" It would become one phrase linked together like a stringed banner, the words mashed up and fast. I would imagine many question marks as they stood suspended in motion, some with tea-colored eyes, others with skin dark and waxy and with teeth black from paan—a chewing tobacco made from betel leaf—lining the gaps around their gums like caves. Their grins comical in their extended friendliness. Halfness didn't matter to them; I was one of them and they accepted me. They could see me.

In my expansion of learning about New York, which was really just a way to fill my days, I started off with the Highline. I knew it was a sign of a gentrifying New York, and as a New Yorker, I felt I was betraying my city—but still, I didn't care what people said about it, it was beautiful: a refurbished train track with a view of the Hudson River, a cascading cement dream. The first time I came here was soon after it officially opened—when it was still closed off past Thirtieth Street. I came with Mama and Alyssa on a brisk early spring day. Everything felt magical, alive. Alyssa wore a black puffy vest and a bright red hat, her hair trapped like silk in her clothes. Smothered with warmth, we caught the subway to Fourteenth Street and walked to Chelsea Market, bought some snacks, and made our way to the Highline. Mama

was overjoyed, cooing at every corner, pointing out every buried weed and fragile flower. Alyssa and I laughed, throwing salted peanuts into each other's mouths, taking pictures on the bridge, and dreaming about the West Village and Chelsea apartments with their rooftop gardens and cascading vines. She was so much fun. *That's it.* She was so much fun.

The days kept arriving, even if I didn't want them to. No matter how far I ran, I couldn't escape the perpetual tide of time. Luckily New York City provided a form of catharsis. The momentum of the streets kept me awake, kept me from completely succumbing to my pain. I don't think I ever walked as much as I did on the day I was disowned. It was like a meditation. I didn't have an objective or a destination. I just walked.

For the first couple of days after, I would go to the Highline, returning each day between roving from diner to diner. The memory of Alyssa attached me to this place, and it put things into perspective. As I sat on those postmodern benches overlooking the Hudson, or on that lawn facing the West Side skyline, I'd be reminded of her. Napping in the sun, I'd lose myself. In the rogue flowers and the sultriness of the earth and grass I'd see Mama. Of course positive thoughts were fleeting and transitory, lasting but a few moments throughout the day, though they were enough to keep my stamina up and running. To keep going.

I scurried around from place to place like a rat. For a city like New York that's so overexposed, there are a lot of hidden corners. But I couldn't sleep; my body felt like it was in overdrive. I felt tense, like I was locked in anxiety, so I closed my eyes intermittently and went to another realm instead. I couldn't fathom it ever being different, but I knew I had no choice but to keep going. I didn't want to die, I kept telling myself. I remembered Dadi-ma, I remembered Alyssa, and knew that they would guide me; I knew I would know where to stop to rest.

Walking through the West Village and the Meatpacking District reminded me of the beautiful juxtaposition of the city. The grit near the glamour, the seediness cut open by the Jeffrey boutique. I decided to pay Magnolia Bakery a visit, remembering that Alyssa used to love buying desserts there because of *Sex and the City*. She was a Carrie; I was a Miranda. I liked being a Miranda, because she was the bluntest. I wanted to be that blunt, that real, in my own life. Upon reentering the bakery, without Alyssa, I felt tattered and dissociative. I focused on the interiors. It reminded me of 1950s glitz, the employees buzzing with alacrity, and the subdued softness highlighted my inadequacy. I felt as if I were insulting its innocence, so I ordered quickly and sat outside, enjoying my treat while watching the people go by. I can't explain what I wanted. I needed normalcy, comfort. I wanted a home. I watched a couple in love and felt my mind slip and wander to the pain in my womb, instantly transported back to that night. I clenched my jaw and stopped myself from going any further. Breathing heavily, I looked down at my cupcake and was saddened by what I saw. I no longer felt hungry. I sighed and threw it away.

The day had made me feel annoyed. Whenever I remembered the pain of my body, with a quick assaulting flash, I really just felt betrayed by it. I didn't want to feel the sting of the tiny tears on my vagina rub against the unruly cotton blend of my ugly underwear. Everything felt insulting, as if it were mocking me.

So I took brief moments of gratitude for my music, for the wondrous sounds that shielded me from the world like a buffer, and began to walk toward NYU. Although I had heard quite a few complaints from my parents' friends about its desire to colonize Lower Manhattan, I quite liked it. I felt it gave New York a new character, and that's essentially what made New York what it was: diverging characters. As I walked up West Fourth Street, on one side of me there was Washington Square Park, a true New York icon, but I had entirely forgotten its existence. How many movies had I watched that panned over its

stone exterior? I walked across the park and peered at the many different faces that had congregated there. I watched as a few kids played near the fountain, which served its part as a modern-day watering hole. After a few moments of admiring the Arc de Triomphe–like figure in the middle, I walked farther north, toward a tree that stood on the corner. It was a beautiful, majestic tree, and as I got closer, I saw Dadi-ma resting, meditating, with her eyes closed. I knew she would tell me when it was safe. Getting her signal, I felt steady. I plunked down in front of her, deciding that this would be *my tree*. I christened it with the name Cillian, an homage to Alyssa's favorite actor, Cillian Murphy. We both fell in love with him when we rented *Disco Pigs*. Alyssa always thought he was hot, but in a "murdery kind of way." I even had a crush on a boy once *because* he looked like him, following my faux Cillian from school to the gates of his place. I thought he was so handsome, so quintessentially cheekboned and Irish.

As I sat down underneath Cillian, pulled out of my trance, I slowly allowed myself to recall what I had been through in the past few days. I was still wearing the same clothes, and they stuck uncomfortably to the sweat and grime that had built up around me, like a protective wall. Suddenly embarrassed, I sat wondering what a vision I must have been on the streets, walking aimlessly, like a forlorn wilding. I was alone. I was completely alone.

I looked around, searching for answers, but all I saw was the city's arrogance. Now that I wasn't in motion, finally still, the blurriness began to form distinct pictures in my mind. Suddenly I was angered by the cars, by the people with their venti lattes, expensive textbooks, and by the stupid and domineering Bobst Library with its shapeless blood exterior. I felt like shouting, so I did, a loud bellow. A few looked around, but mostly everyone went about their business. We were New Yorkers, we understood the natural law of the universe. *Sometimes everyone has shit—doesn't mean you have to stop and stare.* I looked around, humored by the lack of judgment. I sat back against Cillian, resting my head in

my exhaustion. Does it matter whether the weight of living is overwhelming?

It felt strange to be so close to a school, when my own hopes of schooling had been so altered by the shocking loss of Alyssa. I felt like my once intense ambition had been abducted and replaced by a pathetic, mercurial dullness. I felt robbed of all hope, like a toddler who had heard too many no's for one lifetime. It had once felt special to commemorate Mama and Baba through the intensity of fierce education, to walk the halls of Columbia like them, like a poem or a sweet hymn, but I had no desire to do that anymore. I was no longer tied to that coiling archipelago of what it means to have generational legacy. That terrible myth of blood family, as if that meant anything.

When I dropped out, it felt shameful. I had missed too many French literature classes, and my haughty professor had no desire to give me any leeway. "This is Columbia," she would say, her face a mask of white paint, like a Venetian doll's. Her eyeliner was always a pencil-dotted streak under her eyes, kohl the color of blue china, and her hair, a coiled wig. She looked about ninety, the bones in her fingers like tiny birds that jutted out of the skin. "At Columbia, we don't make excuses."

Had none of these people heard of depression, or did they just not care? After Alyssa passed, I perpetually felt as if there were no air left inside of me. All human interaction felt heavy and charged. In all honesty, I didn't feel safe anywhere I went. She had left me feeling like an empty vault, but one in constant search for some warmth. It felt disarming to lose the only ally I felt I had. What little life I had was sapped out of me, and I dropped out a few months after she died.

Though, sometimes, before I left home, when the sky was tangerine pink, I felt the longing surround me like a faint air— like the smell of the oily couches creased with age that sat in the halls of Columbia's vast libraries. Temporarily, I clung to that feeling—of wanting so badly to be held, to be cocooned, by an institution, a legacy. What was I without it? I had, in many, tragic

ways, bought into my parents' thinking. Like them, I craved validation. I tried, after Alyssa, to return to ambition, but it was too hard. I couldn't focus, I didn't have it in me to live for something anymore. When I left school, Baba wouldn't look me in the eyes for weeks, only saying, "My daughters are failures," while walking, in a huff, to his study. He couldn't stand it, he felt like I was betraying him. Like Alyssa had.

I sighed, looking far into the distance, and noticed a small café. It looked so warm, I could practically smell the fresh croissants, the chemistry of the yeast and flour, the golden edges browning over the curves of its hump. I wondered what it would be like to eat, to live, to survive as Taylia now. I had never *really* felt like a Chatterjee—and now the feeling of distance and confusion was thoroughly intensified. I felt removed from the identity that had been carved out for me. It was the feeling of endlessly swimming, a buoy amid so many promises, so many aspirations. The whiplash of loneliness struck me, beating against my bones, my spine hinged against all the dissatisfaction—but I sat there, the smell of baked goods evoking some kind of earthly nostalgia inside of me. It was not something that I remembered Mama cooking, but it felt like home. A home that I had built in my mind—maybe one we all built, about the lives that we felt we deserved.

I inhaled the wind, the smell of fresh bread. Maybe I could do this, I thought. I knew what I needed: security, money, a place to live *permanently*. I remembered some Dutch foreign exchange students who had told me about a youth hostel they'd be staying at in the interim as they waited for Columbia lodging. I realized I could do this, there were options for nomads like me. But I would need a job. That's what brought me to Kat Armand.

13.

Kat was short for Khadijah. Khadijah with a K. That's how Kat introduced herself, preemptively knowing the beats in conversation, the rhythms of the *heys* and *hows*. She knew how predictable people were when they'd ask how to spell her name, their faces simultaneously showing they didn't really care, their expressions droopy, the corners of their lips dancing with a twitch. I really liked that about Kat; she didn't seem surprised by people's bullshit. It wasn't good or bad, it was just data to her.

Kat had grown up in Brooklyn and been in New York her whole life—like me. She had bony hands and skinny legs but a wide, luscious chest and generous upper body that she adorned with cotton-blend T-shirts she bought from Uniqlo over cool black slacks that were "all Lemaire, baby." She told me that last bit with such panache.

When I met Kat she was wearing all black and her hair was natural and short. It was more red than brown, like a burnt auburn, suntanned and warm. She had on several silver rings that she wore even despite having to take them off when she worked. The one on her ring finger wrapped like a clasp over an entwined lemony-yellow citrine crystal. Kat said she wore the citrine because it strengthened the "crown chakra and heightened intuitive perception." She said this matter-of-factly, without loftiness. She was stylish, boyishly tailored, and together. *Together in a real way.* She wore Nike sneakers with high insoles that elongated her thin-like-straps ankles and curved calves. I was enraptured by the way Kat moved, she seemed stately, assured; she was like Alyssa. She told me her love for Eartha Kitt and how they shared the same birthday. This was all in the first ten minutes of meeting.

Feeling connected to her, via her food and energy, I had been visiting Kat's café and bakery for a daily treat all week, usually ordering

a chocolate croissant (or sometimes even an apple Danish, or a slice of pumpkin bread, or a salted caramel Rice Krispies treat—always with a small almond milk latte). But that day, as I sat under Cillian and felt protected by the tree—a caryatid, like the mother figure I never had to protect me—I had an idea. Maybe like Siddhartha under the tree, Dadi-ma, my oracle for safety, had brought me here and I was listening to my visions, or intuition, more ardently. And something was drawing me to Kat. I had been reading a book about astrophysics that I had picked up from the discount trolley outside of the Strand, and I thought of how her café, Milk Thistle, was my desperate daily reminder of self-care. In the days right after leaving, it was agonizingly lonely. I longed for direction and asked the stars to give me something, anything. Kat was always personable, always welcoming me into her sacred space, and being around her were moments of the day I took solace in. This felt like a connection worth investigating, even if it didn't lead to anything more substantial.

I took showers every day at the Blink around the corner; I had decided to join after I heard it had decent facilities, and for twenty-six dollars a month, I figured it was a necessary purchase. One thing I had always feared, ever since I was a child, was being laughed at because of my smell. I think that was part of the Indian shame—smelling badly—and something I had picked up from Baba. He loved eating fish but was always scared of the way his hands would stink after. The reaction was exaggerated, almost traumatic. I'd watch as he'd obsessively wash his hands and smell his fingers, grossly inhaling as if he were in that movie *Superstar*. Now that I no longer had my perfume corner, I was devolving a little, and I wanted to feel clean and smell good. I also needed a job to keep up my pastry habit, acquire some scents, and all the other expenses that spilled over.

"Hello." I greeted Kat with an openmouthed grin as I walked in. The smile stretched from ear to ear, an eccentric Taylia smear on my face. I felt like I looked like the Cheshire cat.

She squinted up at me, a smile slowly appearing on her face. "Hi."

I knew she could sense my hesitance.

"How's your day been?" I said, almost breathless, bopping on my toes like I needed to pee. The café was almost empty, which I knew it would be. Kat would close up shop in an hour, and I knew it would be the safest time for me to stumble, to be earnest. She leaned onto the counter. "Not bad." She paused. "You've been coming in pretty often lately."

I nodded, fake enthusiastically, already way too nervous for my impending rejection, slight and jittery. "Yeah." I coughed a croak away. "Every day."

"Are you okay? It's Taylia, right?"

I breathed and toppled right in, oddly fearless: "I'm looking for a job. Do you know anyone nearby that's hiring?"

Kat took a minute and then suddenly burst out laughing, like I had told a joke. I followed suit, my chuckle racking my nerves, overly fast.

"Just to be clear, you're asking me for a job, right, Taylia?"

My laugh stopped short. "Yes. That's what I'm attempting to do."

She smiled and then softly pouted. "Tell me, why do you want a job?" Her tone had now morphed into something serious. In the little while since I'd been coming into Milk Thistle, with its prime real estate by bustling NYU (and its equally entitled students), I had witnessed Kat's way with people. It was something that I envied, like I had envied Alyssa or Zeina. Women who knew how to be, without question or pause. Women who had no puff of anxiety breaching every interaction. Kat was gregarious in a way that was inspiring.

I stumbled, as I always did. "I... like you, and I like this place... and well, frankly, I need the money."

She was short, direct: "Have you ever worked in the service industry before?"

"Yeah... I mean, I worked at the Body Shop near my house in the summers." It took me years to get on cash duty. Those registers

were complicated and seductive, with their wads of cash just floating in a plastic tray.

"But you've never worked in food service before?"

I paused, marking my words in my head.

"I only ask because it's not easy. You have to put up with a lot of personalities."

I nodded, profusely embarrassed that I had taken so much of her time already.

"Buuuuuut, it's funny you came in... Kind of magical, actually. I've been looking for somebody for a while to help me with shifts. I was even planning on putting a sign out there. But I haven't because I knew it'd eff with the vibe. Believe it or not, I wanted to hire someone organically."

I pursed my lips, wondering if this was organic *enough*.

"This"—she giggled—"is pretty organic, though."

"Yeah?" I asked, slightly desperate.

"You have an endearing frankness to you, Taylia."

I smiled weakly, already afraid of the job I hadn't yet started.

My first shift was early in the morning the next day. As I polished silverware, Kat prepped scones for the oven. It was close quarters, so we quickly became acquainted, and I admired her openness. She was a divorced thirty-seven-year-old mother of two. She had a joviality to her, like people with higher frequencies who just buzz different.

"Man, the Body Shop, you remember when it was *all* the rage?"

"Yeah, I mean, I bought those body butters in bulk."

"Hmm... Mango..." we both muttered, shaking our heads simultaneously, looking at each other in glee. "Throwback!"

Smiling, she made us some coffees, showing me how to do it a few times, allowing me a couple of tries as well, before we officially opened. We were leaning toward each other drinking perfect milky coconut lattes, zero foam, all cream.

"What's your situation like?" She hesitated, I could tell not wanting to pry. "As in, where do you live?"

I hadn't been confronted with this question yet. My tongue rolled like a sardine trapped in a can. Finally, I blurted out, "I left school, so I'm between places. It's temporary."

"Well, I'll need an address for work purposes..." She paused, slowing her words down to enunciate her thoughts. "You know, for taxes and your paycheck. But we can see how we get on for now and go from there..."

She was cut off by a bulky white woman who stormed in with a bad mood, despite the sign on the door still saying CLOSED.

"I fucking just saw some dude that looked like fucking Bill O'Reilly! Bill ugly fucking O'Reilly. I really think it was him!"

"Oh, wow, um." Kat was a bit dumbfounded but took it in stride.

"As if we needed to see another fucking Republican around here, am I right? Are your cupcakes vegan?"

Neither Kat nor I thought it necessary to say anything else. I was used to compartmentalizing white entitlement. After the woman left, Kat and I burst into laughter.

"Get used to that right there. Also, watch out for the NYU brats. Jesus. Some of them are entitled little..." She made a face. "But... a lot of them love pastries, so... ?" She said this next part seriously, though: "Also, never, *ever* call the cops. No matter what. If there's a problem with any of the customers and I'm not here, call me. I'll always guide you through it. But just never call the cops."

I nodded my head, taking it in fully.

There was an intimacy we had with each other that was unnerving to me. Maybe because of how fluid it was, how easy. I felt safe around Kat in a way I didn't with most people. She didn't make me feel anxious; she made me feel heard. We talked about real things. Or, rather, she talked about real things, and I listened.

I was still too shell-shocked, maybe, to let it all out, but I enjoyed her trust in me. It made me feel worthy of being talked to. I found out that Kat had started seeing someone relatively recently, but she didn't know where it was going. She didn't know if *she* wanted it to go anywhere. She wanted to be in the throes of it, the throes of love and whatever it came with. I couldn't help agreeing and, somewhere in the distance, wanting the same for myself. Not that I knew what that looked like for me.

"Taylia, I'm a romantic."

The café was closed and we were cleaning up. The soles of my feet felt brittle, like I might collapse, but my spirits were high.

"I used to think it was so easy. Just find the right person and fall in love. But there's no right person. These days I think love is nothin' *but* holding on. If you have two people that can hold on, then you got yourself that *sustainable* kind of love. But then you gotta remember not to hold on too tight. We all gotta die one day, so don't hold on too tight, but hold on just *enough*."

The lady Kat was seeing was a professor of literature at NYU named Claudia Pierre. She'd come in regularly at the café, and then one day, she asked Kat out. They had gone on two dates, and Claudia had paid for both of them, Kat told me as she showed me how to pull espresso again, even though we had already cleaned up the machines, because she wanted the "coffee perfection of Australians." There was a determination in her that I admired—it was motivating. On their first date Claudia took Kat to a nice little West Village restaurant where they shared smoked hen-of-the-woods mushrooms and preserved lemon on a duck breast, accompanied by a silky piece of white fish ("It was a delicious, buttery hake!") with pickled fennel.

"She's quite something, though. She knew I was a foodie and she took me to this place that I had heard of but didn't realize it'd be so damn special. She pursued me, Taylia. I can't tell you what it means to be pursued, for someone to be romantic. To show up and want to impress you. To want to make you come alive. I've never felt that way with a man before. *Khallas*." She crossed her

heart with the tip of her right pointer finger, like a crossbones, *cross my heart, hope to die.*

They hadn't slept together yet, and Kat seemed happy to take her time. "I can't do what I used to do in my twenties. Sometimes it's good to wait! Before Voldemort—that's what I call my ex"— she smirked at her statement—"before him, I didn't know what it meant to wait. Then we met and we waited. He left my ass anyway. But with women, it's different. With women, waiting is fun. Means all the juices get a little time to settle and develop."

She tapped her tongue on the right side of her lip seductively. We laughed—and I felt a blush come over me.

Although ultimately I knew I had had "sex," it didn't feel like sex. It hadn't felt like sex at the time, either. It just felt like something that I had to do in order to survive. Like a level on a video game I needed to pass to move on, except if I didn't do it I'd die. And also it was a terrible thing to survive. I still didn't have words for it, it's as if everything about my body was blurred. The baby cuts on my vagina from the dryness were the worst part, because I had to walk around like I wasn't carrying several open wounds daily. I hadn't even touched myself near there since it happened. Even when I went to the bathroom I avoided touching, brushing past the padding of hair, grateful for its existence. Mirrors became things I avoided, and car windows, too—or windows in general: reflective buildings, big huge revolving doors. I didn't want to see myself. I couldn't bear to look at what I had become.

Kat and I spent hours together those first few days. I liked the routine: I finally had a bed in a hostel where I could leave everything but my phone, and I would get up, go to Blink for a shower (the ones in the hostel were unisex and therefore felt unsafe), and then walk to her café for my shift. One day we ate stale olive oil cake and almond croissants on the floor of beautifully symmetrical white tiles at the end of the shift. She had great ambitions about her "tiny home," which was just a little bigger than a hole in the wall. She wanted it to become a part

of people's lives, an important New York outpost. She felt as though she had created something special—and she wanted to share that with others. She had the right personality for it, too. She was ambitious and unabashedly so. "I make good shit, Taylia. I know that's not what gets you far all the time, but I actually make *good* shit. So help me God, nobody's gonna stop me from making what I wanna be making."

She told me she came from a lineage of folks who were entrepreneurs. In the '80s, her aunt Sydney had become a realtor in New York, encouraging all her sisters (she had three, including Kat's mother, Oriah) to buy property. They listened. Oriah and her husband, Franklin (an Afro-Panamanian art collector), bought three properties across Brooklyn, all brownstones: one on Carlton and Dekalb, one on Bedford and Putnam, and the last one a block down from the first one, right across from Fort Greene Park on Willoughby Avenue and Washington Park. Over the years, their accrued familial wealth had generated more interest in properties. So, when the hot little pocket of NYC real estate became available, right near NYU and Washington Square Park, Oriah found out through Sydney and then told Kat, who would ask her mother for a loan to build her tiny café dream. It was this determination to not just pay back her mother but also succeed like her that encouraged Kat to be ambitious, *and* to make the best product. No surprises there, she was a Capricorn.

We were both smart, but Alyssa had been tenacious. She was good at getting what she wanted, but she liked to fight for it, too. It's strange how we individually processed how to fight. Alyssa and I had learned the same things, and yet our styles were so completely different.

Each night at the hostel, I was afraid of the noises that'd wake me, afraid of men banging on the door, of touching me in my sleep. I made myself invisible, which had always been a survival tactic. I had to be aware of factors that I didn't necessarily have

the energy for, but I had accepted that this was my new life. Just as I was thinking this, Kat started talking. It had been about ten days straight that I had shadow-worked with her. The day was coming to an end, and I was beginning to stare into the distance, completely fatigued by the physicality of the labor involved in manning a café.

"Taylia. In all honesty," she started, "and please don't take this the wrong way, but I know you stay at that hostel on Bond Street." She bit her lip. "I saw you walk out once, even before you came in and asked about the job. You have a memorable face. Those strong eyebrows! So I recognized you from coming into the café. When you asked for a job, I was intrigued, and you've been really great so far..." She paused dramatically, and a lifetime of fear built up until she spoke again. "I hired you because I like your energy, which these days is everything to me. A lot of people talk the talk, but not a lotta people walk the walk. There's something about you that's very honest. Sure, you're a lot more private than I was expecting, but I respect that."

She was so insanely transparent. I stayed silent, not daring to interrupt what I felt like I knew was coming.

"So, listen, this isn't something I'd normally offer someone I don't know very well, but until you have enough money saved, you *could* stay with me. I told you I have space, and the boys would love a houseguest."

I was shocked, though not entirely surprised. I had clocked Kat as much as she had clocked me: we were people of the same ilk. "What do you mean by that?"

"I mean, we'd figure out a system. And this wouldn't be a handout as much as it would be a push up—"

I cut her off. "You can't possibly be serious."

She smiled slyly. "This isn't a favor. I'm gonna make you work for it. You know that I will. I just want you to know that I see you."

With a long exhale, I started crying, covering my face with the palms of both my hands. For the first time in a long time I felt dumb lucky. I felt hopeful. She didn't come over and embrace me,

but just let me cry until I composed myself, and I was grateful. I was full of emotion, maybe because I had been subconsciously praying for something, somebody, to reach out and show me I wasn't alone. This statement from Kat felt like a lifeline, one I hadn't been afforded since Alyssa's death.

Later, I explained to Kat that I did have *some* money, so that I *would* pay rent, but that I could do with *more* money. She acquiesced, confused as to why I'd live in a hostel if I had *some* money, telling me that was some "white people shit." I couldn't yet explain, to anyone, the rough shapes of my past and how they haunted me. How I had grown tired of expectation, so I meekly expected nothing, offering myself nothing.

I realized I had never known what it was like to choose oneself, having always bitterly deferred to someone else. Watching Kat, I wondered if anyone had ever told her that she had to fight for herself or if that was an inherent understanding. I felt tired of not knowing *how to fight*, but knew I soon must. Maybe when I walked out of my parents' house that day, I was trying to redirect my narrative. I was tired of being a victim.

That night, at Kat's, I took a hot shower and tried to look at myself in the foggy mirror. I wanted to become my own witness. I had visions of Dadi-ma as I washed and grasped at my old talisman, my chain with two rings on it that I always wore around my neck. I thought back to when she had gotten very ill. She lived in Kolkata, and Baba, full with filial piety, insisted that we move to give her moral support in her last days. So we relocated to India for a few months during the summer holidays in my early teens, leaving our Upper West Side brownstone for a home in bustling West Bengal.

It's strange how death was such a sly interloper of feelings. At the announcement of impending mortality, Baba's sense of duty was suddenly forced into motion with a fortitude of longing and soured regrets: regrets of not being physically closer, regrets of

leaving his mother and father. Perhaps, also, the misgivings of marrying a white woman and not being able to bear sons—nothing to continue our name or his and his parents' culture.

I was soon enchanted by India. Growing up in New York often provides you with the conceit that no other city is worth venturing to. The busy streets of India were, unlike New York, filled with an unnameable exuberance and a strong, dreamy energy. The rickshaws, the cars, even the raucous fumes, felt like home. I grew fond of seeing lakes, cement, and sloping green trees (the secret Mughal gardens) with a readied excitement. Outpacing the chase, what resided in the streets of Kolkata was also a kindred resilience. The people were friendly and cared for you, and that was the strangest part of it all. Dadi-ma, someone I had never met before in my life, cared about me. Her love was so thick I could feel it, slick and stretched out, floating past me even when I was away from her.

The first night I was there, she sat me down and combed my hair, lovingly caressing my temples to my roots, slathering my hair with coconut oil. The light through the venetian blinds traced our bodies as I sat at her feet, my torso enveloped in her shadha saree. She smelled of burnt cinnamon and her hands were soft and rubbery, like a toy—comforting, as she drew me to her. Gold bands lined her delicate wrists, hanging off her body's ancient tapestry, clicking and clinking every time she moved. Every night after that, she'd kiss me good night and call me her puuthul. She never fretted over the fact that I wasn't like Alyssa; she loved me unconditionally for *who I was*. I meant something to her. And that meant everything to me.

Within the cracks of my childhood, my relationship with my dadi-ma was the tangible kintsugi to my healing. Like gold glue, the veins of a leaf, she filled me with an intense, overwhelming serenity, but more—she initiated a healing of sorts. There was something powerful in being seen by her—the theme of my life. The need for my body to be seen in all of its varying dimensions was like a drug I was hooked on; it gave me permission to like

myself, too. A diminutive me, Dadi-ma and I even had the same thick, fuzzy brows, the same button nose, the same petal-shaped lips. She spoke mainly in Bangla (not because she couldn't speak English, but because she didn't want to) and would argue with Baba for not teaching me and Alyssa the language. "You must read Rokeya Sakhawat Hossain, Taylia." That was one of the few things she ever said to me in English, both a suggestion and a command.

I also liked the way she clearly loved me more than Alyssa. Possibly the only person where that was the case. I had never needed to prove my worthiness of love to my dadi-ma as a faulty Alyssa, a less exceptional, diluted version of her. To Dadi-ma, I was me, in all my clumsy glory, and in days where we napped, lined by milky mosquito nets, I remembered that I was loved.

She passed away five weeks into our visit. Although I knew it would happen, I never believed it really could. Here was a strong woman, never submitting to the demands society put on her sex. She went to school when women weren't allowed to; she raised a son and sent him to America despite growing up relatively middle class. She was strong-willed in every sense of the word and had a great understanding of herself and what she wanted to contribute to the world.

I remember, because I understood there was something violent in her. I could see it in the way she went walking with me through the woods, the ways in which she could still cut the throat of a chicken and pluck it for dinner. She was fearless, but she was also wise. She wasn't petty. Baba's cousins were brats, and their children, Alyssa's and my second cousins, were living nightmares who had no interest in us, the foreigners. Alyssa's charms wouldn't win them over, and she resented them for that. Despite the hardness of the family around her, Dadi-ma was just. She rarely raised her voice, her sternness was all in the looks. She seemed so incapable of deteriorating. I was determined to believe that she would prove everyone wrong and live an eternal life of forthrightness and certitude, equipped only with her

chewable vitamin C tablets and four golden churis, two on each wrist.

A few weeks before she died, she gave me a necklace grooved with indents, her fingers lacing the chain around my neck—from hers to mine—spooling the golden strand underneath my hair. There were two rings: one yellow and the other silver. When she showed me the former, she pointed to me and said, "You." Then she indicated the silver one—a twine of longing—and said, "Husband." I understood her and nodded, my breath catching up to the excitement of knowing that somebody cared. There were pockets of her that would always be mysterious to me— invisible, yet still somehow tangible in a ghostlike way. I could sense her even when I couldn't see her. She taught me her Jedi tricks, she picked up on my psychic-ness.

She took me under her wing and taught me to meditate, to do yoga—training me, simultaneously, to feel her pulse move through the airtight corners, to feel the friction of space and time, to see the void but know that she was watching me, my skin goose-bumped and blue, my calf muscles flexed, knowing that death was not the end. In those long afternoons with her, it's hard to explain—but it was the first time I witnessed magic. We communicated with nonwords so much, my attunement began to exponentially radiate.

The night before she died, she spoke to me again about love. Her hair was out of its braids, the mosaic of silver strands spar-kling, splayed across her red cashmere sweater. She wiped away my tears and told me things would change. I rested my head against her fleshy waist, her belly exposed only slightly. I knew that she understood my pain—she could see it in my eyes as we lay there underneath the layers of tulle like bandages, protecting our wounds against the outside world.

The day she died, a storm of mosquitos rose from beneath her bed as I felt her take her last breath. The last soft whoosh passed through her with a melodic hum; I was lying next to her, watching with my eyes wide as it happened. I peeped

through the sheets and saw Baba crying silently, his head in his hands, and my mother on the floor at his feet, snot dribbling as she clutched at her salwar. There was no stranger malady, I assumed, than watching a parent die, metamorphosizing, shifting from this world to another. The maids stood crying, too, their lilac- and rose-colored sarees strangling their emotions as they whispered prayers. I remember the smell of her charred body, the bright flames burning, licking through her body on the pyre, devouring like a cruel animal. Turned into ash, emerging as a jewel, she had left me—and this world—allowing me to feel hopeful.

14.

I craved stability but continued to fear the dependence that came with finding it in someone else. I admired Kat and could feel the good emanate through her skin, undulating with kindness and morality; but our friendship made me nervous. The conversational intimacy, the brutal candor—things that come so effortlessly to some—felt like a bone stuck in my throat. I knew that if I could speak like the Alyssas and Kats of the world, it would obviate the chance of confusion, miscommunication, hurt feelings (on both sides), and my general embarrassment—but I had never been able to compel those gears into motion. I had never found myself interesting enough. But with Kat, it *was* different. I was still the same, but she somehow accepted me. It felt exploitative, to feel this organic human connection, a synchronicity so uncommon that it felt forced, fraudulent. Next to her candidness, I stood filled with reservations, my tightly locked box of secrets clutched so desperately to my heart, and yet she made space for that, never once using it against me. I accepted this new dynamic,

this new friend. In fact, I welcomed it, because I was hungry for real love.

When I woke up, it was my second week at Kat's—early— before Kat and her children, Luc and Isaac (whom I was beginning to care for deeply), rose. I felt an itch. Thankfully, it was a weekend, which meant the café was closed. As I began to scratch, I felt it rise right into my ass, into that raw, cavernous hole. Shifting like a diffraction, the itch moved through me, showing no signs of slowing down. I fell back against the unhelpful comfort of my pillows. I wanted to cut myself out. *Scratch, scratch, scratch.*

Kat had emerged. "Babe, are you okay?" She had heard a commotion, knocked, and opened the door to find me defeated, my eyes pale with pent-up tears. I began explaining to her my bodily dysfunctions. She half laughed and said it in one way: "Sounds like a yeast infection, baby."

"I thought I had had them before... but this feels really, *really* bad."

She had a habit of researching things on Google and explaining to the boys, so she began reading off her iPhone. "Yeast infections are caused by the fungus *Candida*. This fungus is associated with intense itching, irritation... blah blah blah..."

I stopped listening, in pain, and instantly began to think of that night again. Fingers, slimy groping fingers. Those diseased hands. I was going to die. I mopped my wet brow as she read, squeezing the place between my legs as if I were a human-sized tweezer pushing down on the multiple ticks that were pulsing through me. It started burning, but I kept pushing with sweaty urgency. I was drifting. *Don't think of that night, Taylia.* Everything tasted sour.

"Your eyes look like white disks. Are you okay?"

Her voice sounded distant, her tonsils jiggling as she coughed. "Taylia?"

Tell her, Taylia. Tell her what? *Tell her about that night.* No.

My eyes were zeroing out and I could feel the life pumping, the blood flowing like a beat, in my down there. It felt like a

boom box, bouncing pulses of sound and goop. I needed to get out. I felt like I was about to suffocate.

"What do I do?" I asked her.

Kat suggested medication, carefully giving me instructions to the nearest pharmacy. I could sense she wanted to volunteer getting it, but I was profusely wanting to prove that I was fine, so she patted me on the back with a kindness that she wanted me to feel, and I walked out. Outside, the city felt like glass and light, the windows high. The air made a sizzling noise as I walked on the pavement, and everything felt fuel-shimmered and smoky, hot to the touch. I walked into a Duane Reade on Dekalb Avenue and bought Monistat, skipping out like Wile E. Coyote. I wanted to pull my pants down right there, but instead I waited until I got home. Kat cooed outside the bathroom as I plied open myself and layered on swathes of the cooling cream. It reminded me of when I had had a burn as a child; Mama had run swiftly to the garden, cutting open the flesh of her robust aloe vera plant. She came back with such grace, holding it in her left hand, floppy with juice, and gently placing the transparent lobster-like flesh on my gibbous burn. The crustaceany aloe felt so cool, so right, on my bony little arm. I remembered her vividly for a brief moment, then cried by the chlorine-stained toilet seat.

Later that day, momentarily cured, I found books on the tarot in Kat's bookshelf, which I wanted to look into. I was impressed by her ability to juggle life so effortlessly. At the current moment, she was in the backyard with her friend Crystal, who also had a young boy about Isaac's age. I could hear them both roaring through the ecosystem, the boys playing with plastic lightsabers, doing the *zhoom-zhoom* sound as they waved them around like batons. Kat made me feel welcome. It's the ethos she had with the café, too, of allowing people to come and create a haven against the harsh city. She'd seen the way the city could make you feel unwanted, she understood the perils. I think she longed for a community she could rely on, which is why she made her home an offering as well.

Our friendship was quite fortuitous simply because she trusted me and trusted that I could handle things for her in the absence of her ex, if need be. I was always good at filling in the gaps for other people. We came to an agreement that I would pay cheapish rent (since Kat's family owned the place) for my room and that I would get paid an hourly wage for my three-month apprenticeship. If things worked out, I would get on the payroll, maybe even become a manager. We were both open to possibilities.

I felt grateful that, although I had left in haste, I had a small, sober inheritance that Dadi-ma had left me when she passed. Thank God I was naturally frugal—except for my apparently new pastry addiction. The inheritance from Dadi-ma of $15,000 had seemed negligible when I first received it. I had turned snooty after time with wealthy peers. But now, it was a godsend, and some part of me was relieved it didn't come from my parents. There was a part of me that wanted to start anew. Dadi-ma must have known that I would need it one day. All of this made me feel that I had struck a good deal with the universe.

When I hurt, I let it hurt, but I tried—with Kat's suggestion— to take my ego out of it as much as I could. And it was paying off: I didn't know why, but the city was making me feel things were possible; it was reviving me. To make something of myself, on my own, and by my own definition, when I previously (just a few weeks ago) had felt like I was nothing. I knew investing in myself was a worthy pursuit.

Kat and I started a nightly ritual. We would smoke hash when the boys went to bed and Kat would read our tarot, teaching me the energetic science of it all. One night, as we sat at her back porch with a beautiful Oriental-style blue-and-white pipe, she asked me what my question was for the night. Up until then, my conversations with the higher forces had been naive, unformed, but tonight I was tender. I asked, "When will I find love?"

Kat cocked her eyebrow, teasing. "You mean like a *boyfriend*?"

I snorted the Bloody Mary I was drinking right out of my nose, the gin firing through me with fusillade precision. *"Noooooo!!!!!"* I had not thought of men in an eternity. I shivered.

"Why'd you just shiver?"

"I didn't."

"Uh-huh, yeah, you did."

She stared at me, and I felt my cheeks begin to burn with memories.

"Taylia."

"It's nothing."

"Hmm..."

I sighed. "I don't know if you've ever realized that I'm not good... with men?"

"Is anyone good with men, honey?"

"My sister—" I stopped. I hadn't even realized what I was saying when it came out.

"Oh... You have a sister?"

I didn't know how to answer that. "Hmm... But men are awful. They're scary!" I said, changing the subject.

She laughed, by now fluent in my conversational swerves. "Ugh, women are scary, too."

I felt the question rise through me like a wave; I wanted to know. "Kat, have you ever been in love? If so, can you tell me about it?"

I rarely caught her off guard, but here she was, suddenly silent. There were many pauses before she finally started to talk, hesitant.

"Yeah. I think... If I'm going to be frank... as much as Elijah is a major S.O.B...." She looked toward the boys' room to see if the door was closed; it was. "We were massively in love. Hell, maybe that's why it hurts so much. Even if you love somebody it doesn't always work out." She paused. "He was good when he was good, you know? *Like good.* And it doesn't make any sense why he left me with two kids, scurrying off like an effing rat... and you know now that Claudia and I are getting more serious, or I don't know... more intense or whatever... I find myself thinking about love again, but with fear. So much fear." She had started

crying. "And I hate that he took my faith away in love, Taylia. What if it doesn't work out again? I hate being scared."

She cried silently, composed. Her huffs like rhythms as she gently rocked herself back and forth. I went to her knees and pressed them gently, laying my head at her thighs. That was the beginning of our enduring connection.

I didn't really know if I had the capacity to fully love, if I really had that ability to let go. My heart felt gutted out, concaved, yet at the same time I was tired of my grief. At this point, I was almost bored of it. I wanted so much to say something to her—to say that I understood, that I knew what it was like to have someone leave you with no remorse. To wake up one day and find that what loved you yesterday was no longer there. That the perversely banal life that you led was outshadowed by the one person who cared for you so supremely, but who had also abandoned you. I could never have fathomed the pain Alyssa would leave me in; I could never have imagined how her absence would make me feel.

Kat cried, and we sat together, cradled, watching the moon.

As I entered work the next day, trash bags swelled with decay near the back door. Kat must've forgotten, which was unlike her. The smell was so pungent that I felt temporarily hit by its tenacity. The dry heave of puke almost made it to my mouth, but I stopped it just in time. I had a whole day's work ahead of me, I couldn't afford momentary nausea.

Kat was off getting emerald-green polish on her toes and watching a movie at the Film Forum with her friend Frank, which she kept trying to back out of, and I—well, I was paying my necessary dues. She assured me I would do fine without her, and sincerely, I was managing. I was never good with people, but I had always been curious of others. I was trying to lean into this quality, into the thrill of new experiences. There were people coming in and out on the regular, and for the most part it was

stimulating. Tracking the gentle back and forth of old customers who loved Kat and newcomers who were impressed by the place was enjoyable. My answers were always short, tamed, rehearsed, and yet still so stickily uncomposed. I didn't have the conversational lucidity of Khadijah with a K. I took a breath and told myself, in my head, to have some compassion for myself. It's the first time that ever happened.

Around eleven I was in the store's back area, taking a quick break after the morning rush, when I heard a voice.

"Hello?"

Caught off guard, I ran to greet the person.

I got to the cash register and faced her. Her hair was dark and ponytailed, eyes round and cat shaped with eyelashes that were elegant and delicate. Her lips were pasted with freshly applied lip gloss, probably fruit flavored. I wondered if it was one of those sweet ones you could lick off.

"Hi." I smiled. "Sorry, I was just—"

She cut me off. "I'm here to pick up a special order."

Kat hadn't told me about this. "Ah, sure, what's your name?"

"Jade Leung."

I was buying time. "What was your order?"

"A baked Italian cheesecake with a raspberry coulis." She paused. "Wait, isn't Kat here?"

I frowned, buying time. "You ordered it with Kat?"

"Yes," she replied, "I ordered it with Kat."

I turned around and made a face, mimicking her now imperfect-lipped drawl. I walked to the fridge and took a peek inside: nothing. As I started freaking out I heard a commotion in the front of the shop. It sounded like another person had entered and I could hear that Jade was squealing. I rolled my eyes and felt frustrated. As I reentered I saw that there was a man talking to her, and as I came closer he looked up and smiled. I didn't smile back. The man was tall and was wearing a brown jacket and pale denim. His hair was the color of dark, unmilked coffee. Long and matted at the sides. As he looked at me again, I noticed his eyes were a strange hue, and even

from a distance I could see their peculiarly green-brown-colored gaze. He smiled at me, now for the second time, and I looked down quickly, pretending to not have been eyeing him.

"Did you find our cake?" Jade asked, milder now.

"No, I—I'm sorry..."

"Can't you just call Kat?"

"Yeah..."

"Because she said today, and I'm not coming back again."

"Okay. Yeah. I'm sure everything is fine." I said it with a little too much reservation.

"Yeah, I'm sure it is, too," she said curtly.

I called Kat desperately on her cell. *Dinnnnngggggggggggg.* It kept ringing, but she wasn't picking up. They were both eagerly waiting.

"So?"

"She isn't picking up..."

"Ugh, I take a chance on a local place—"

Just as she said that Kat walked through the door, a paper box in her left arm. "Hello, darlings!"

My heart pounded.

"Taylia, I hope you have been entertaining."

I smiled a weak, thin line. I wanted to punch Jade in the face.

"She's been great," the man chimed in, looking back at me, smiling.

"So, here you go. All as requested. Raspberry coulis made, like, a minute ago."

Sometimes Kat was like a magician—wasn't she supposed to be at the movies? I watched her astounded but inspired.

Jade squealed again. "Roman is going to love this!"

"This is for Roman?" Kat asked. "You didn't tell me that. He was my favorite regular, but I haven't seen him in weeks."

"*We know!* He's been on this huge case, so he's been in another zone, working nonstop. But this is why we asked for this cake from you. He just loves this place so much, and he's been missing his daily dose. We're actually going to go surprise him now! It's

his birthday and we're so happy we could get this cake from you! Thank you."

"Oh, what a sweetheart. Well, tell him happy birthday!"

As Jade and Kat talked, the man came up to me. "Hey, I'm Ky."

I stared at his hand for seconds; the cuticles were well trimmed, and the moon-shaped part of his nail was pronounced, almost like Zeina. His hands were slightly tanned and laced with veins. There was even a tattoo in between his thumb and forefinger that looked like two bows and arrows crossed over each other. I looked back up at him, momentarily shocked by the giddy feeling that moved through me. He seemed unfazed, but his stare was intense. Like he was taking me in in a noncreepy way.

"Taylia."

"Taylia? Cool name."

I shrugged inelegantly.

In the background, Kat worked her charm—that's why people flocked to her. She was genuine.

"How's your day been, Taylia?"

I had not done this in so long. "My day has been fine."

"How do you mean?"

I shrugged again.

"Your eyes tell secrets, Taylia."

I assumed someone as empirically handsome as Ky would say this to women and they would feel understood and flattered by his observation, and even though I knew that, I felt that he really meant what he had said to me. Still, my guard was up. "Hmm, maybe."

A loop went through my stomach, multiplying into a figure eight. I suddenly felt so immeasurably happy.

"Ky." Jade broke the spell.

I felt embarrassed by my hypnotized state, like a deer caught in headlights. I felt seen again, an anomaly in this city. But that was it: I felt seen.

He turned to them both.

"Ky, you should start coming by more!" Kat cooed.

"Oh, I definitely shall."

I heard them giggle and chatter, but my mind had gone, drifting in ethereal blackness, in a black hole; I felt like a star spinning through it all with such languid ease.

A few weeks later we were sitting inside the café, picking at an olive oil cake and sipping on a shared iced cappuccino. I was about to head out for a break when I felt compelled to ask.

"Kat, be honest, do you think I've put on weight?"

"What?" Truly astonished, she just stared.

"I feel so—so..."

"*Fat?*"

"Lethargic," I corrected her.

"Why?"

"I don't know. I always feel out of breath, I think I'm getting sick..."

"You should maybe go see a doctor, my li'l principessa. Is there anyone you can go see?"

"Yeah, I'll think about it." I hadn't even begun to comprehend what health insurance and accessing doctors would be like now that I no longer talked to my parents. But I also didn't want to think about it, so I put it to the side.

"Well, honey, here's the thing—if you think you're fat, maybe you are and that's okay. You gotta rejig that thinking and look around you. You are beautiful! I promise. Don't let the man tell you otherwise." She winked her left eye and blew a kiss. I laughed, rolled my eyes, tempering her mildly, and walked out.

Moving toward the park, I eventually sat down next to Cillian. The warmth under him, like in those first few days after I left, filled me with an immeasurable spirit. Now, he felt like the steadiness of family, like grounding; I felt connected to the earth through the roots of him. The first real spiritual experiences I had were through the narratives of Indian culture with Dadi-ma. Tales by Kālidāsa and *Shesher Kabita* by Tagore, the rhymes and

wordplay like stringed songs she'd sing, fluid poetry that was a gilded part of Bengali culture. Being under Cillian reminded me of India, the trees and nature such a part of its loamy terrain. Dadi-ma and I would often sit by big jackfruit and mango trees near the house, guarded by a small pukur filled with fresh, gulpy fish. The trees such a bright lime green, the tall palms bending across the waters in prostrated salutations.

Dadi-ma had a rounded knife with a cherry-red handle that she'd pull out of the belt of her petticoat to swiftly cut apples into halves and halves again, eight times in total. I'd count *one, two, three* every time. She put a slice in her mouth and then spit out the seeds through the whistle of her lips. Then she'd pass a slice to me, clucking with joy. In her presence, I learned that small, beautiful things could be treasured, too. There, I began my love for sitting on uneven grassy plains, the ants and soil-colored bugs crawling past my chubby limbs. We'd never talk, but she'd recite to me dramatic verses, her words resonant and voweled. Intermittently she'd smile and pinch the middle of my cheek with two clipped fingers, cackling at the annoyed faces I'd make in return. I started to learn broken Bangla: আমি ভাল. তুমি কিমন আছ? She'd give me a thumbs-up for good, thumbs-down for poor, her bangles *clank clank clank*ing as she laughed her haughty, rapturous guffaw. The trees near the deep lakes, the water dusty and a lukewarm brown, made me think of death. Even in moments of bliss, it haunted me. Maybe it was the realization that this woman—in so many ways a soul mate—would soon be gone. I liked everything about her, even how much she despised us being American, rolling her eyes whenever we spoke English or said "wow." She found English to be so unuseful, so unromantic, unfeeling, and callous. She felt like a role model, someone in opposition to Alyssa, and felt maybe more aligned with the person I wanted to be. That made me both joyous and sad. There'd be moments I'd stare into the infiniteness of the pukur and wonder what it would feel like to suffocate in its muddy, opaque waters. Living without her felt impossible.

Yesterday the light was heavy from the moon. Today, as I looked at the sky, again under Cillian, almost dusk, I thought of the solar system. The spinning plates of Saturn, the braille exterior of Pluto—so, *so* far—the lip of the galactic system, mystical orbs in a continuous loop in the blackness. I used to hate touching *National Geographic* pictures of space (Baba had stacks of them in his study). The onyx glossiness of the page, like freshly potted dark soil, terrorized me. I felt that if I touched the deep space, I'd suck myself in like an apparition, every picture my personal portkey. I was absolutely terrified of space, but I loved the mystery of it. There was a full-sized poster of Uranus on the walls of my school that I'd walk by silently, sometimes only darting quick looks at its mountains drafting shadows onto my fear-based theories of life and death, my eyes dizzying. But now, under Cillian, I felt so calm.

"Who's Cillian?" Kat asked me a day later.

I gave her a widemouthed smile. "How on earth would you know of him?"

She passed me a poem that I had offhandedly scribbled on a shift as I waited, evidently bored. Small love hearts framed his bolded name.

"So, who is he?"

"He's not what you think."

"What is he then?"

"He's a tree."

She looked at me strangely. It was one of those slow Tuesdays, an hour before close, when the lull of foot traffic felt frustratingly slow. Days like these, Kat and I clinged to each other, sharing stories of our youth, of our dreams. I mainly listened to Kat's glorious retelling of growing up in Brooklyn in the '80s, of the perils of Fort Greene Park, with health-conscious parents who forced wheatgrass down her throat and made her take French class because of her Martinique ancestry. She told me her father

wanted her to read Frantz Fanon, Aimé Césaire, and Édouard Glissant to understand her roots, to understand radicality in the context of the Afro-Carribean diaspora. It was something that was coming up with Claudia, too, who was Haitian. At the reminder of Claudia, Kat zeroed in on me. I knew she was about to ask me about romance. I sensed the poem about Cillian had made her feel sorry for me, so all day she had been figuring out a way to broach the conversation on how to date in the city. There was a cupid trapped inside of her, and I needed to leave.

"So, any cuties been catching your eye recently?"

It was so funny because it was so sincere. If I wasn't so embarrassed by the question, I'd find it endearing. "And that's my cue to leave."

"No! Where are you going? Don't leave me!"

"Don't know, window-shopping or something." Today I felt like I had to move, like there was energy trapped inside of me. I swung my bag over my shoulders.

"I'll see you back at home! I'll probably go to all the shops the cool kids go to, you know, like ABC Carpet and Home for a sec."

Her eyes narrowed on me, like she knew I was being avoidant, but she merely said, "Hmm."

We both knew it really wasn't where the cool kids went, but I craved a home of my own, and I wanted to be lost in the place that housed the most beautiful home decor I had ever seen. I also wanted to see if I could afford a nice perfume treat.

"Okay, whatever makes you happy!" she said, a bit glum.

I liked feeling needed by her, I liked knowing I added value to her life. I also knew Claudia was scheduled to pick Kat up later, and I was avoiding our inevitable meeting. Maybe because I was embarrassed. I wasn't sure she'd like me. What did I have to offer anyone besides my sometimes thoughtful (but mainly cursory) tidbits? I felt ill equipped to talk to a professor, fearing she'd remind me of my parents.

"Do you want anything while I'm out?"

Smiling, she said, "Nope. But have fun gloating at what rich white people buy!"

As I walked closer to ABC Carpet and Home, there was a rabid dog barking, cowering, its leash almost in shreds. I tried walking around it but tripped on the leash, almost plunging headfirst onto the sidewalk. Bleary-eyed, I shuffled away, my heart beating fast like a vibrating plate. I felt distracted as I pulled at the door, walked inside, and let the rush of this place silence my thoughts.

ABC Carpet and Home. Sigh. I don't know why I liked it so much; maybe it felt nostalgic to come here, like I was closer to Mama. She'd bring us here to buy goods for home (not ironically; she loved the corner filled with "Indian" goods that was always manned by brutish white women), and the cascading chandeliers, the panels of silk and crystal, and the chic homeware cocooned me in safety. Big doors shielding the opulence inside. Rows and rows of unique one-off pieces the price of average New York City rent or facials from Goop.

Expensive things felt nice to be around. Sometimes.

From a young age I was engaged by smell. My aesthetic praxis, through the controlled tenderness I'd show myself (albeit rarely), was in pursuit of smell. I'd walk around after school to those small Tibetan hubs, or to natural health food stores with their wall dedicated to my dizzying fetish, and pick out perfumes: jasmine, sandalwood, lavender. My favorite spot was in the West Village, just near Bleecker Street. It was unassuming, yet bright. The outside was always decorated with Himalayan threads, triangular patterns of calm design. The colors evoked vibrations of the streets of Kolkata—alight, colorful, and alive. The store, like Punjab Grocery and Deli, reminded me of the nebulous, hollow scabs that patched me, reminders tethering me so tightly to India.

My mantelpiece, back at my parents', housed my many trinkets, filled with sweet and oily perfumes I'd scavenged over the years. I loved the fragile glass bottles with thick gold etchings, ones that looked like miniature Russian castles, the colors diluted.

My morning ritual consisted of creating my own scent, my fingers sticky from the bottles. Like drawing blood from a vial, I placed the teardrop of oil across my body, a sign of the cross in my own private ceremony. I gravitated toward a certain smell intuitively each morning, and it became my earthly companion, heightening my state of euphoria throughout the day.

I began to read about Muslim perfumery, how it was extracted through steam distillation. I read about Jābir ibn Hayyān and Al-Kindi, who established the perfume industry in the golden age of Islam. I even tirelessly looked into how to collect the mysterious odor of plants and flowers, wanting to make my own salves and perfumes. It was fascinating to read about resins and wood; about the sacredness of perfume in the Arab world, which brought the art of perfumes to Europe; about the way that Muslims used smells and incense at mosques, how elevating fragrance was a way of dedication to one's exterior body but also to God. I noticed how women in abayas, stunning and statuesque, bodies erect in majesty, always smelled so mellifluously sweet, a fragile muskiness pervading their path—*swish, swish*—as they moved.

There, within the wonderland of ABC, I again remembered the sudden rush of jubilation my morning creations would give me. I wondered, with a stab, what had happened to my perfume corner after I had left. I blinked at the objects near me repetitively to stop my eyes from welling up and caught them on a dainty, crooked piece, standing right in my sight line. I picked up the glass-like wonder and immediately lusted over its curves and crushed edges. I was transfixed by its splendor, until I could sense a hand reaching toward me. Like clockwork, my heart jumped, and I felt dread wash over me. I spun around quickly to see who it was and the bottle fell and smashed on the floor.

"Oh, shit," I whimpered.

"Ugh, sorry."

He leaned down to help me pick up the shards of glass. I didn't look at the man. I was crying. I was crying over something

so menial. He got out a *New York Times* from his bag and brushed all the pieces onto it with a natural swerve. All I could see were his hands. They were brown, with fingers that were elegant and well-cut circular cuticles. A tattoo. Momentarily fixed on them, I felt a strange, ethereal surge push through me, past the tears, and suddenly the hands were up my leg. I stopped myself from dreaming and pulled back. The man with the hands was turned away from me and talking to someone behind him. I slumped, feeling humiliated. Getting up slowly, cautiously, drowning my-self with a heavy head, I looked up at him. He was broad shoul-dered with a toned back, and as I watched him the sensation moved through me again. My desire, although transitory—and uncommon—pulled me into a blissful tension between my legs, a slow and easy tightness lingering like a mild sedative. Even though it subsided within moments, I felt so uneasy by this sudden lack of control. I mean, I was attracted to *his back*.

I was so lost inside my mind's conversation that I hardly heard my name being called.

"Taylia," the man said, coming toward me.

I pulled my head up with a jolt, suddenly overwrought. I slowly and reluctantly focused on his face. It was familiar, I knew him. He was the guy from Kat's bakery last week or so.

"Hey, how are you?" Ky paused. "Are you okay?"

I wiped the tears that I hadn't noticed were still on my face. "Er, I'm okay," I answered, concentrating on his jawline. He had stubble growing around and on his chin. I looked up at his eyes and noticed they weren't as green today.

"Upset about the prices, huh?"

I looked at him, confused but smiling. "No."

"That was a joke."

"Okay."

"I followed you here, kind of."

I felt my body go cold.

"That's creepy. I mean I went by Kat's and was hoping you'd be there, but she said that you might be here. So..."

"Kat told you I was here?"

"Yeah, I even got a coffee and we talked about you."

I felt my face physically frown.

"We didn't talk *about* you... Okay, wow, I don't usually make so many failed jokes in one conversation, but, wait, let's go outside... ?"

I didn't want to go outside, and my body felt like it was slowly crumbling in the heat of this man's unwarranted attention. "No..."

"Only just it's getting crowded."

I looked around; he was right. "Okay, wait. I think I have to pay for that stupid bottle."

"S'all good, I got it."

I looked at him in the light that was coming in acute bright angles through the store window and nodded. We walked outside and stood near the left-hand corner of the entrance, me on the ramp, arms tightly wrapped around my body; him on the street, leaning toward me.

"I didn't get to talk to you much the other day."

"Okay."

He laughed. "I..." He stopped. "Hmm, this is going to sound so unrehearsed and like such a weird request, considering we don't know each other, but I just want to get to know you..."

I was sure my face was the shocked emoji.

As if he heard me: "I—I can't explain it, Taylia. I... all I want is to be your friend, obviously, that's it. I, um, don't even really know why, but I was pulled to go back to the café to go see you and that kind of thing doesn't really happen. Like, I don't do those things, normally."

"Like, you're not a stalker. Normally," I said coldly.

He chuckled nervously. "Yeah, exactly. I'm not a stalker. Thanks for clarifying..."

He looked at me, his face sharp. A wave of goose bumps moved past my body. He was silent for eons until he said it.

"I feel like we could be friends."

No.

I was going to puke. The acid of my stomach, like a tongue whipping at my insides, curled with dissatisfaction. I broke my stance and leaned against the railing, suddenly incapable of standing.

"Whoa," Ky said, coming toward me, his hands reaching out.

"Don't touch me! Don't touch me!" I whispered.

"Okay, I'm not touching you. Taylia, are you okay?"

I could feel the winds changing and the energy shifting. My body swayed.

"Taylia. Are you okay?"

No.

"Taylia, should I take you somewhere else?"

No.

I leaned against the cool stone wall, shaking my head no, wishing away this feeling of unkempt, vibrating nausea.

"Ma'am, are you okay?" The security guard was behind me, and the thudding in my head began. A ticking beat. I felt the slimy hands, the visions bringing me back. The white chair, the line of hooks. The rancid taste in my mouth, and that bleating hangover. I felt Simon's fingers inside of me again and again and again. At the roots of my hair I felt him pulling me across fire and earth, along pointed grainy stalactite; his body was pinning me against all the pains of the world.

"Fuck no. Fuck no. Fuck, fuck, fuck." I leaned my body toward Ky and whispered, "Take me somewhere *safe*." I hissed the *safe*.

As if taking orders, he immediately wrapped his left arm around my waist and pulled my weight onto him. We lean-walked down a few blocks and then he put me in an Uber, which I hadn't even known he'd ordered, coming around the other side.

The beats of my heart were spaced far apart, spread out and bumpy. I felt my physical limpness ease as I now sat. The cars moving, Ky not saying a word. The ghosts were still there, strident, but my body no longer felt like trembling goop. I was getting

back my definitions. The limbo of existing was intoxicating. I realized how much more work I still had to do.

15.

We moved over the Williamsburg Bridge and I watched the waters of the East River shiver beneath us. I wondered what it would be like to drown in that water and thought of the muddy pukur, of Dadi-ma afloat. I hadn't felt her presence in a few days. I imagined the river was quite filthy and, at the same time, filled with mysteries. Bones patterned with verdigris, blood staining the moss-lined cobbled walls. The toxicity of greed and untimely deaths. All those lost, lost souls. As we came over the bridge and entered Brooklyn, the driver took a few turns before he came to a complete halt.

Ky got out and came to my door, fidgeting his fingers before he opened it and took me out with patient delicacy. "Come on," he said, his hands gently pulsing at the corners of my back, a loose grip. He held my right hand as we walked to the front door, stopping only to take out his keys. With one hand he opened it and with the other he brought me in. I could feel his left palm gently pressing against my lower back, and in that moment I felt an irrevocable sense of solace. There was something undeniably comforting about a body against your own. A firm touch; a lighthouse.

We walked in, piles of books lying on the floor greeting us. The organized chaos gave the house an unassuming, open vibe. There was a lot of wood, a lot of steel, and a lot of greenery. The last was surprising. As I stood, mouth gaping, I looked across the wall closest to me. There was exposed brick and a large, dilapidated wooden mirror hung across it, the glass shattered

with age. I took in the image that was staring at me from within. Her eyes were bloodshot; her skin splotchy, exposed with open pores, swelling with an inflamed pinkness that looked like an impending rash. I felt embarrassed. Had I looked like this the whole time? Ky came behind me and asked me to sit anywhere, and I did, collapsing onto a nearby bourbon-colored leather sofa, with a slump.

Ky went into the kitchen. I watched him gliding around through a crack. He came back out and handed me a glass of water and a big block of Lindt (sea salt, my favorite). "My mother says chocolate usually helps with most things."

I sat up properly, looking around. I sensed him staring at me, searching. Suddenly bold, my eye contact was direct. I was challenging him to speak, to probe the beast.

"The sadness is real."

I suddenly retracted, knowing full well I wasn't ready to be challenged. *I think you should shut the fuck up* is what I thought.

"I don't think you're normally this quiet."

You think a lot of things, don't you?

"I think you're probably a little wild. First to get drunk, last one to leave?"

I lied: "I don't drink."

"Drugs?"

I shook my head, annoyed.

"Rock and roll?"

I shrugged jokingly.

His eyes leveled with mine. "I don't want to sound arrogant..."

"But you're going to power through it anyway, right?"

He smiled a small smile. "I think you want someone to talk to."

I didn't answer.

"So, what's your story, then? Are you an orphaned wizard? A fox on a mission to undermine some humans?"

"Why am I even here?"

Now he shrugged. "Maybe you just needed someone to ask how you're doing."

"You assume a lot."

We both snickered a little, but then the room was met with silence again.

"Or we can just sit he—"

"I don't have anything to say." I realized, then, that I wanted to tell him.

"One thing I keep learning, Taylia, is that every person on earth has a story."

"So then, what's the point?" I was suddenly defiant. "What's the point? If all of us hurt, what's the fucking point? Why do we go on?"

I had been thinking this for months. In moments of stillness, despite how far I'd come, I felt myself drifting, plunging into that dark, unforgiving hole: the wretched wrath of self-pity. I hadn't forgotten or absolved anyone of their sins, but I was focused on moving forward, and yet it wasn't that easy of a fix. At this moment, I didn't need Ky to answer anything for me, but I felt calm knowing that my misery could be felt by anyone. My story wasn't exceptional, and there was something undeniably liberating about accepting that—but also terrifying. Everybody wanted their pain to be hagiographic, perched up, anthologized. So, how to carry on when human pain was so universal? How to feel, when the only option was to push through and not fester? Still, the pent-up energy lay coiled around my throat, like a weed springing to life, wrapping around my esophagus; I wanted to speak.

I looked up at him. His eyes were a hazy nebula, stringing me together as we watched each other, silent, the moment pulsating with thick nerves. I wanted to speak to him and be heard. Fiercely, and ardently, I wanted him to know me. I wanted him to feel close to me, to embrace me. To be let in like no other human before. Suddenly, as if a light went on inside of me, like the strums of an orchestra, I wanted to share myself like a lover. To be open, close—for an eternity, or even a moment. I wanted to be loved by this man. But I remained quiet, unmoving.

He persisted. "Taylia?"

I didn't answer.

"Taylia? What's going on?"

I inhaled deeply. "I..." I started again. "I..."

My breath felt like a bloody tightrope. How much *is too much* to share with a stranger? Each mouthful that I would begin to stutter was a recognition that there was no way back. Each sweaty syllable was a deep acceptance of my death. Living really was a manual on learning how to die, and I was about to forgo my facade to an outsider. Once what was said *was said*—I would not be able to crawl out of its black and blue depths. All the bluish hues of pain, the bruises of life that sink us into a deeper melancholy, I would not be able to escape. Like a blow that builds the bruise, the words I was about to utter would enter us both into a steep plunge of intimacy. Yet, I was still afraid. Afraid of that commitment, afraid of the responsibility that came with closeness, or more: the expectation that resided, on both parts, in its aftermath. What if it was rejection? Dismissal? I didn't want to be pitied, I wanted to be *seen*. Seen for all that I was, trepidatious out of necessity.

"I'm sorry..."

"Whatever you need to say, want to say, don't worry. Just say it. It doesn't need to be coherent."

He looked so earnest. It made me want to kiss and slap him at the same time.

"Okay, fine... I was..." I paused. "Fuccckkkkk."

I paused again, unable to quite form the words. I dug my nails into my right hand to stop it from happening, but the tides could not be stopped, I began to cry. My bottom lip trembled and I bit it, embarrassed. My tears slurred the words. Why the fuck did I want to tell him?

"I got kicked out of my parents' house."

He was silent, but his eyes asked why.

The ultimate question that defined me in other people's eyes.

"I..." I stopped and started a few times. "I was r-raped."

I didn't say anything for a few seconds. It came out like a statement, not a question—which is how it had sat in my mind, coiled around my amygdala. Right now, I felt everything: I wanted to barf, I wanted to cry, I wanted to kiss him, I wanted him to touch me, to ravage me. I wanted to run. I wanted to disappear, like lost time. I wanted to be invisible, so I stayed silent.

He broke it.

"And your parents kicked you out?"

He waited for an answer. He didn't get one.

He mumbled, "What the fuck is wrong with them?"

Theoretically, I thought it'd make me feel better. To tell somebody. But it didn't. I remained silent for the next few minutes, but in truth we were both quiet for a huge chunk of time. After the combination of our mixed awkwardness, I understood that to stay any longer would be too emotionally imposing. I felt that the words spoken had a gravity that I had not anticipated, a reality that, perhaps, I had been avoiding. Its tumultuous weight felt unavoidable, and yet... I'd come so far these many months without even stringing the words together. I'd avoided all feelings of this because what lay beneath the surface seemed incorrigible. Buried, the memories of the night my life fucking changed were suddenly resurfacing—like an earthquake, a ten on the Richter scale. They began to move through me like waves, and so I let them, I let them flow, with no judgment.

He gently placed his hand on my shoulder.

    1. *He's touching me.*

    2. *He's touching me.*

    3. *I'm okay.*

I was altogether ready to go. Maybe Ky's purpose was purely to allow a safe space to unfold, so that I could put words to the brash pain that still lingered, gloating.

"No one really wants to listen to other people's pain." I stood up, but, like a chain reaction, his fallen hand grabbed hold of my right trembling paw, securing it with his.

"Stay, please."

"Taylia." He had been calling my name for a while.

I returned to the moment. He was standing over me as I lay on the couch.

"You're here," he said quietly, smiling.

My mind was filled with a song and its humming. I wanted to suddenly laugh, raucously. "I'm here," I said.

He'd made linguini from scratch, drinking a beer as he cooked, and I obliged. As I ate the food I felt the emptiness inside me buzz with warmth. We were sitting and watching the light become dark outside in his garden. David Bowie's cover of "Sorrow" played, mildly, on the fuzzy speakers inside. It was a beautiful scene: potted plants all around, a large array of vivid green cacti and herbs. I recognized thyme, rosemary, and a wild card: thai basil, pulpy and pungently purple. Mulberry leaves leaned over the back fence, while aloe vera spilled out of mason jars and pale-colored succulents bloomed in tiny little tin cans, corrugated on the sides. Flowers in colors of aubergine, fuschia, and rose hung in fitted hanging pots, and lightbulbs laced the enclave in a full circle, beckoning me to stay. My full attention, however, was on the continuous stars, a string of them, the black sky and its godly pearls. In a hungry way, I watched them. How to drift into that endless tar pond? My exploration was always through the pulsating vacuum of space.

Ky told me his mother was an architect and that his parents had bought this town house for $250,000 in the early aughts; now it was worth a few million. Ky's agreement was that he paid off their mortgage. I thought of what it would be like to have parents who cared for you, who looked after you. Ky, a bit tipsy, interrupted the silence with a maelstrom.

"Taylia, w-w-what if you stayed here with me?"

My eyes favored the stars. I was unable to move. "What?" I asked distantly.

"I've been looking for another roommate..."

"What do you do again?" I was being coy, but also wanted to embarrass him with my bluntness.

"Um, oh. I'm a writer."

"Oh."

"So? Is that a yes? Or do you have something against writers?"

"I can't afford this place." The sounds of fear rang across my mind.

"That's a nonissue."

There was something so annoying about him, and yet I was enamored by his arrogance. I needed an excuse. I started running through a gamut of excuses but decided to tell the truth. "Look, Ky, think about it, you don't *know* me, and living with Kat has been truly healing and maybe what I most need right now."

"Taylia, I know you must feel uncomfortable. You've had a difficult past, and I am a man and a stranger asking you to stay with me. You don't want to get yourself into another bad situation, I get that..." His voice trailed off. He wasn't looking over at me anymore, but as I watched him from the corners of my eyes, I wondered if he had a savior complex: his generosity was on the brink of absurd. I looked fondly over at the white bulb in the sky, the now blurry stars, and asked for holy guidance.

He mumbled with sedated solemnity: "I don't know why, but I want to help you."

I didn't look at him. I didn't know how to answer him. Not believing him, I sat with my heart full, lighting up as he continued to speak. But still, I knew he saw me, the weak Taylia, and he, for whatever reason, accepted me for this. I looked up steeply, toward where the moon lit the power lines, and felt a calm wash over. Each muscle of mine felt fluorescent, tendered in kindness, suddenly, with a sadistic urge, trusting this man.

"You can just pay whatever you were paying Kat. As long as she's okay with that, by the way. I want Kat to be my friend forever."

It was the earnestness that got me. And besides, I had been feeling like I was taking up too much of Kat's space and kindness. Maybe this would be a welcome break for her?

"Well, do you even have a room for me?"

He looked at me again, surprised and elated, nodding a wrinkled yes.

There was not a lot to do or say at that moment. Happiness had won. We sat there as the penumbra lingered over us, descending into the invisible, washing the bitterness away.

16.

That night I slept without waking up in the middle of the night for the first time, tragically, since my rape. Alyssa was back, and I felt her there, in the dream plane. She'd found me, as Dadi-ma had found me by Cillian. As I fell asleep, fidgeting, my pulsing, red-veined eyes finally staying closed, I still held on to some doubt that this feeling of satisfaction would last. Ky's energy, his outlook on life, certainly gave me hope, but I still wasn't totally sure about him. In all honesty, I wasn't sure if I'd ever feel safe around men ever again, at least not fully. It was too soon to tell. Though I still stayed the night, maybe because I wanted to feel free.

"Tay? Tay, wake up. There was an interview with a woman on television."

"About?"

"She'd been raped."

"What did she say?"

"She's Pakistani. She's trying to bring justice to herself."

It was a conversation we once had.

"So, what does it mean?"

The next morning, I woke up thinking about how Alyssa was back, in my dreams, but I wanted to know if she'd appear before

me in real life as well. I looked around the room. It was eight A.M. Only half awake, I was already searching for her. The room was bland with striped linen sheets, like how spare bedrooms are often set up. As an east-facing room, there was ample sunlight. A giant monstera sat like a king near the window, but otherwise it had no character.

"Psst, Lyse. Are you there?"

There was nothing. But I felt a humming, a resolve. She would appear soon. Maybe she was trying to tell me something.

Though blanketed by warmth, there was an anxiety that festered within me, not yet ready to greet the day. With a jolt I remembered: *Fuck, Kat.* I needed to tell Kat where I was. I looked at my phone, and a little calendar reminder for work popped up, as if I had known I'd need to be reminded. As well as seven missed calls from her. I knew I owed Kat so much, and I didn't want to disappoint her. She had high standards because she was offering me more than anyone would. So I was indebted, and I carried that responsibility. I got up, hastily rewore my clothes from the night before, and waddled to Ky's room.

A few knocks later he stood at his door, shadowed in blue, a soft red light against all that felt sad and weird about this world. He leaned into the doorframe.

"Hi," I muttered, nausea usurping me.

"Hey. Did you sleep well?"

"Hmm."

"Okay?"

I felt lost. I needed to get to Kat. *What is even the address here?* I needed to learn to navigate my life now from this compass, and Ky's place felt too abrupt. How was I supposed to accept this? I didn't know this man. Feeling disgusted with myself, I was ashamed of wanting his attention.

"I need to get to work. What's the best way out of here?"

"Oh, wait, I'll head out with you then."

I did the math: Did that mean we'd have to talk to each other? The entire time? The thought of it gave me more anxiety.

"Of course," I said instead, and he followed me downstairs. As I slowly maneuvered myself into the kitchen, I was met with a man in gray pajamas.

"Hello! I'm your roommate."

"Oh." I looked at Ky, aghast, and mouthed, *Roommate?* I had sensed he lived alone. Ky nodded and mentioned Emi was a semipermanent resident as well, as if he'd been recruiting roommates into this giant space. Maybe he was just lonely. I felt embarrassed to think I was special to this man. All of a sudden, I felt a strangeness engulf me. Could I share space with two men? I didn't even know if I could trust Ky, let alone whoever this was. I felt all of this, but also found myself wanting to drown the voice of hesitancy. I just wanted to rest somewhere.

We made small talk with this roommate called Emi after a quick introduction. He seemed nice enough, jovial, almost annoyingly so. Like a puppy. Even though there was a sadness present, too. He was in between places after his girlfriend cheated on him. He looked like a schmuck, all doe-eyed and pathetic. It was beautiful. Maybe that added to my acceptance of the situation, too. I knew I must not have had the best intuition, since, in one way or another, it was hard not to blame myself for trusting Simon. I had had every reason to listen to my gut about the sliminess I knew lingered inside of him, but instead I listened to what others thought. I let Alyssa override me. But since that night, I had been trying to change. To listen. So that's what I did. With Emi and Ky I listened, and I would keep listening.

Ky finally looked at me, ushering us to get a move on. I nodded sedately, but yelled *on y va* in my mind. He was meeting his agent in Manhattan, so we shared an Uber into the city. He told me he was working on a novel but that he also worked at a huge tech company, brainstorming creative projects. From the sounds of it, he was paid very well, which I weirdly resented. It didn't sound like he deserved it. He dropped me off first, and as I got out of the car to face Kat, there was a song playing in the distance. Was it Patsy Cline playing on repeat? "She's Got You,"

that's it. Faint through the wind past the loud snoring sounds of the city heat, the percussion of the traffic, the bus pounding rhythms mundane. As the city roared on, Patsy played like a David Lynch dream, languid and cool, smooth across the rooftop of Ms. Cline's mouth. Moving closer toward the café, my face met Kat's, and I braced myself as we made eye contact through the glass before I even entered. Like a small animal cowering in a ruckus, the tic in my anxiety was as evident as her annoyance. I walked inside and she waited until Arnold, a local actor, left. Then, through gritted teeth, the question came out in one string: "Where-have-you-been?"

I smiled at her, but her response was dull. "I can't even imagine how to tell you."

"Well. Imagine!" The curtness came out shrill.

"Look, Kat, I'm so *sorrrrry*."

"Okay, but, where were you?"

"Ky's." I said it with an embarrassing assuredness; maybe I knew she'd like the gossip.

"Ky?" She was shocked. "Okay, *woof*."

She grinned a big toothy snarl. I had known she'd want to know every detail—that's something I loved about Kat, she was present. She watched me as she clipped the sides of her short nails (which she had to keep short for the baking, she hated it) with her teeth, and then she shrieked as it hit her: "Wait, did you... ?" She just stared at me, without asking further. What could I tell her? I didn't even know what it was that I felt. He had a girlfriend, so clearly there was no reason to assume there was a hint of romance between Ky and me, and truthfully, I didn't know if I *even* wanted that. I mean, what about Jade?

I sat down in front of her, looking for approval. I felt frustrated by how much I didn't know how to be a person. As in, how to talk about lust in an intangible way. Crushes had never been a possibility for me before, I felt so unworthy of attention. Now, I was aware of my body, of my tender parts. It's as if a scratch had turned bold: I was yearning for something. I had never really had

the experience of feeling my heart quiver, so I was suspicious of even the idea of love, even though I wanted it. But, much like my new perspective on Ky (despite how I *was* beginning to feel about him romantically) and Emi, I was beginning to pay attention to myself, even in the smallest ways, to the signals in my body. Surely that's how you started to build intuition.

"Macchiato?" Kat asked to fill the void. I must have dozed off into my dream reality.

"Please."

"Next time—text me, let me know you're all right."

"I will."

She started buzzing around. "Okay, so, tell me—if you weren't *ahem*-ing Mr. Ky, then"—she said it languidly, like she was reciting Shakespeare—"what the eff were you doing there?"

I admired the way Kat would occasionally PG rate her swear words, a habit she had picked up for the boys.

"He, um, wants me to move in with him?"

She was dumbstruck. "Huh?"

"You heard right the first time."

"Wait, Ky..."

"Yes."

"...wants you, Taylia..."

"Yes."

"...someone he doesn't know..."

"Correct."

"...to move in with him?"

"That's it."

She cocked her eyebrows again. "And y'all wanna tell me you ain't fucking? Tay, please..." She looked upset.

"Kat," I assured her with the labored emphasis of my hands. "*T-r-u-s-t meeeee*. I'm not hiding anything."

Her eyes went small, the pupils hardly visible, and she gruffed. "Okay then, what does he want from you?" I liked how she enjoyed a sense of drama as much as I did. Besides, I had been asking myself that very same question.

Kat had written out a poem on a piece of ripped yellow legal pad paper:

To keep up a
passionate courtship
with a tree
one must be mad.

I found it on the way back to hers and laughed. That night I decided I would sleep at Kat's. I wasn't ready to face what an offer like staying at Ky's would mean, and I was trying to give my intuition time to work. I texted him about giving myself some time to think it through, and he replied that he understood.

After work a few days later, I sat underneath Cillian, daring myself not to touch any of my baked goods, and I let my mind wander. I had decided that I would start dipping my toe and feel out living with Ky. Kat and I had discussed it, and I explained to her that it felt important for me to see how it would feel to explore something unknown. At first, she voiced judgment, but, over time, I was able to convince her that something was calling me there. To Ky. I think because she was romantic, she got it.

Dadi-ma used to practice meditation under the teachings of a guru Saraswati. So I had always been interested in the mysticism of meditation and its effects on the human body. Especially after witnessing the effects it had on her. In just five weeks she was able to convince me so thoroughly of her living standards, providing inspiration, that almost a decade later I still remembered her in day-to-day life, like Scripture. Nobody occupied my life like that. She was so agile, so sprightly; her senses were so keen—right up until she died. I admired her ability, her strength. Through her, I was able to understand God existed. I went back to these memories as I began to track my instincts; it was as if I were relearning old magic. So there I sat, under Cillian, meditat-

ing, trying to remember how to conjure the data she had passed down on to me.

I longed for family, I always had. But I don't know if I ever really believed that I'd get it from my parents. So, at a certain point, I let go of trying. Also their trusting of Simon over me, their own daughter, felt like the worst blow yet. So I let go even more. In the last moments, as I had accepted my rape, I also accepted my fate-to-come without real resistance. Otherwise I wouldn't have survived. What my parents decided felt like an actual betrayal. And maybe that's what made me stand up for myself, made me leave and follow Dadi-ma, and Alyssa, in the stars. I needed them to really hurt me, and they delivered.

All in all, I know I had it lucky. Others had given their lives to this. I thought of Jyoti Singh Pandey. *Jyoti, Jyoti, Jyoti,* I heard myself ringing. I couldn't sleep the first time I had heard what happened, like I felt it in my body. Like it had happened to me, and the many versions of me before. It's hard to explain what I felt. It's as if the agony of all women had seeped into me and that I screamed their pain in vengeance. Gutted out with a steel pipe, *Jyoti, Jyoti, Jyoti, my sister.* I still remember overhearing, like it was yesterday, the conversation between Baba and Rakesh, two Indian men with such little compassion. Women were not believed, were hunted and killed, and I had survived. I would do something of this life, I would make it mine. I had to learn how to do that, at the very least.

And with that, all of a sudden, under Cillian, I started crying, unstoppable. It was the first time since the rape that I had felt it again. The burden of what had happened to my body. I wanted to forgive myself, but I couldn't yet. I felt I had betrayed myself as well. Maybe that was the hardest truth to face. I felt I had let what happened to me happen to me. Even though I could theorize that it was more complex, right now I still only had myself to blame.

My body was burning. Thinking of Jyoti, then myself, I felt a dull ache of resistance as my bones started vibrating. I felt as if I owed Jyoti something for surviving. I resented myself for living and breathed in, shrouding myself in my misery. It was okay, I told myself. I had to carry on, I had no other choice.

I didn't understand why I felt that now that I was *trying* to pay attention, to listen for instructions. But I knew I was being directed to Ky's. So, with Kat's blessing, I moved into his place with all my belongings that still fit into my old JanSport bag—a few books, a sweater, two dresses, one pair of jeans, and under-wear—and placed them on the striped linen bed. I was excited to make something of this space, to carve out a home. With the boys, I secretly felt I was always in Kat's way. She never made me feel it, but I knew I was. I felt irresponsible that I had let her help me, but I had taken it, selfishly. At Ky's I felt like there was an equal exchange, or at least I could make sure there would be.

I placed my belongings in their relative places, and after a half hour of lying on the bed, I decided to make myself something to eat and claim the home further. Being in another space was exciting: there was such a nice layout to this home, different from Kat's, whose was more chic, almost French; Ky's was like a millennial's take on midcentury modern. I guess Ky's mom had converted the inside of the triplex after buying the entire building. The interiors were clean and linear, the ideal vision of adulthood in your twenties. I felt, again, a bit spiteful. Some people's privileges astounded me, and this was coming from me. As I walked down to the kitchen, I brainstormed ideas for the room. I'd get a hanging plant from the farmers' market, maybe go down to Brooklyn Flea to find some nice keepsakes. Building a room was a metaphor for all the ways you had to rebuild your-self, and it was daunting. I felt out of breath. Still excited, but my nerves were getting the best of me. And then when I got into the kitchen I realized I wasn't alone.

"Hello," a voice whispered out of the corner. I looked over cautiously: it was Emilio.

"Oh, hi," I said with relief.

He smiled, his fingers sticky from Triscuits smeared with purple grape jelly. His mouth was full. "You're seeing me at my worst."

"Oh, no judgment, seriously."

"You hungry?"

I nodded a half nod.

"Let me cook us something real," he said, gesturing.

I nodded my head because I wanted to be a woman who could accept care from a man. I sat down on a nearby stool, lightly combing my hair with my fingers. He stood, mildly ashamed, licking his fingers one by one, hastily finishing off his ritual by sucking on the webbed side of his palm. Swiftly, he reached down to his pants, rubbing his fingers against the denim three times before he started. There was something on the stove, and as I inhaled, the sweet smell of coconut milk wafted through me and memories of India floated through the room. The busy streets and the air filled with humidity and spices; the acid reek of petrol and random rot that smelled like garbage, mixed in with the aromatic bliss of cooking cardamom. It filled me with an intense nostalgia. In that instant Dadi-ma's face drifted in and around my soul, and in mere moments she was there with me, sitting clear eyed, the lines on her face tracing upward to her smile. The hem of her saree brushed against my right forearm, and as we watched each other, her eyes gelatinous, everything felt resplendent for a moment. With her presence, again, I was beginning to trust myself to the situation I had found myself in. Her pale wrinkled left hand, spotted with a solar system of smudgy dots, lingered near my right, and the calmness emanated, *at last—at last.*

The three of us sat in our silence for a while.

"I'm making a coconut chai rice pudding."

"Okay, wow."

"I may be a mess, but I can cook."

"That's usually an impressive quality."

He laughed. "Usually."

There was a pause.

"Are you okay?"

"Yeah..." He seemed unsure. "I've just been filling my days with my work. I'm a graphic designer, so I can basically be lazy and have flashes of inspiration, then be lazy again. It's a nice cycle of productivity."

I laughed, I related. It had always been hard to inspire me, but there'd be moments when I would feel it, and it would pay off. I knew I had talents; I just needed to learn how to harness them.

"Ky went out with Jade, they'll be back later."

Ugh. I looked at Dadi-ma. She looked regrettably unfazed.

"It's her birthday," he added.

"When did they go?"

"A while ago."

I sat silently, wondering why Dadi-ma was here, placid.

"So tell me about yourself, Taylia! This is exciting, new friends."

I came back to myself, biting the left corner of my lip. "Oh."

"Let's start with when is *your* birthday? LOL. What's your sign?"

Birthday? I forgot I even had one.

"June twenty-seventh... I'm a Cancer." I coughed, drawing the awkwardness out. "Are Jade and Ky serious... you think?" I cringed at my abruptness.

"Oh... I think you'll have to ask him that," Emi answered blankly.

I wondered why he said it like that.

Jealousy came over me. I let myself steep in the pettiness that was coming up. I bet Jade was one of those girls who would say Ky's full name to establish intimacy, to establish a past, to establish a history that nobody else knew of. I imagined her begging, *Eat my pussy, Kynan, baby, please.*

"Girlfriends are... tricky?"

I came back to myself again, feeling uncontained. "Oh?"

"After this last breakup, I'm just not sure if I could do it again."

"Date, you mean?"

"Yeah. I mean, I loved her and she just fucking..." His voice began to break.

I was stunned, so I observed him in his softness, in this moment of delicacy. From the corners of my eyes I saw Dadi-ma's force field fading around me. "I'm sorry."

"It's okay."

He reached his wet palm to mine, swollen with sadness. He reached for comfort, but it was too fast a movement and my body reacted in a convulsed outrage, jolting back into my seat. His look was generous despite my outbreak.

"I'm sorry, Taylia, I didn't mean to startle you..."

The absence of saliva was making my throat dry. I sighed through the words: "I just don't like people touching me... all of a sudden. You know?" I wasn't really asking, but it came out that way.

"Of course." A stream of sweat passed through the side of his face. "I mean, that makes sense."

It was how he said it: it was suggestive.

"What do you mean?" An unbearable acidity began to rise in my cotton-dry mouth, suddenly raspy.

"Because..." He looked at me fully this time, "...of what happened."

We made eye contact, and in the connection I felt extreme rage. I felt like the wind had been knocked out of me. There was no refuge here. Feeling the blood move through my face, I wanted to scream. I wanted to run.

He was judging me, I knew it. I could feel it. I knew in the back of his mind he was looking at me with disgust, wondering what Simon had seen in me. I could see him talking but nothing was registering. I slowly pulled myself out of it and looked at him again, tremulous and sick. My mind rolled with one thought:

That son of a bitch, Ky. My senses were dilated and I wanted to run from this internal heaviness. *It's your own fault nobody likes you, Taylia. You dumb bitch, you thought you could trust these men? Huh. Nobody loves you, especially not Ky.*

Dadi-ma flickered with an eerie velocity, becoming transparent, until she disappeared.

"I gotta go, I can't be here."

Endowed with a composure I forgot I had, I walked out.

17.

A car pulled up, "Raspberry Beret" blaring, and Alyssa sashayed over from across the street. She swayed, moving to the beat like a clock ticking to time. Her face was a myriad of baroque expressions that transported us to a stage.

"Tay..."

I looked up at her, my face full of questions. "Yes?"

"Do you think we were raised with class awareness as a construct, but we were just never told we benefited from class privilege?... I've been thinking about it a lot. About this farce we've been born into."

I stayed silent.

"You know what Mama is like with money, and, well, Baba..." She trailed off. "It's about so much more." She paused. "Don't you think? So much more than what we've been allowed to see."

She was looking over at me. Her eyes were bloodshot and her face was strained. She looked tired and lethargic, her eyes a bit sunken in. I very rarely saw my sister looking so weak and lifeless. I was afraid. Something had recently changed in her.

"I've been feeling so, so disillusioned."

My breathing was slowing down.

"I'm beginning to realize how much I don't know."

I was starting to feel faint.

"How much I didn't get to learn."

We were both silent after that. We both wallowed in our own pain, our hearts searing with disappointment. I knew what I was too afraid to say out loud: Alyssa had become tired of life, and now it was too late.

I was beginning to see myself as someone who had no one, cared for only by women who were dead, besides Kat. I decided to go back to Ky's, but to maintain a quietly hostile demeanor when I returned. I knew I was being a brat, a little passive aggressive, but I also didn't care. I wanted to be a person who owned her feelings. I had to stay alert; I no longer felt comforted by his kindness or his and Emi's feigned concerns. For a second right after Emi told me, I thought I'd go back to Kat, but welcomed the free months of rent Ky offered, as a means of repair, and I felt some kind of justice taking it. I knew that my silence was confusing for him, but I also didn't really care. I wanted to stand by what was coming up for me. I was tired of accepting disrespect.

A week later, I caught the A train down to the beach at Jacob Riis. I felt empty as I sat on the subway, people-watching and daydreaming. When I finally arrived at the beach there was a cold sting in the wind, a black surf in the distance. The fear of drowning enchanted me. There was so much destruction attached to the waves. The water was smooth and cunning; its seduction could pull you, hold you down, and kill you. In two hours Ky would come home and maybe knock on the door, perhaps say sorry yet again. I sat and watched the water.

You'll like it.

The blood drained from my face like sand in an hourglass.

You'll like it.

The images were vivid. Recollections of that night flashed in front of me. I felt the hands searching me again, their insipid

cocks living vicariously through their fingers. I closed my eyes and thought of something good. I needed to transport myself to happiness. But there was nothing. The feeling was too strong. These bad memories were indelible. I lay down, submerging myself into the sinking sand, splaying out across its majestic vastness. As I parted my arms like an angel, I hit something along the way. A piece of glass scratched my hand lightly. I picked it up and eyed the crystal-like object closely as it reflected the sunlight. I turned the glass at an angle and then sliced it down onto my arm without skipping a beat. The divine pain was my gateway drug; blood poured out next to me as I saw stars.

This was it: the sweet spot. I had entered the red room, I had entered actual melancholia. To wallow in it sedated me in those nanoseconds. I looked up again toward the stars, through the sun, the clear skies, trying to concentrate on a bird. I longed to be free; I longed to forgive myself and let it all go. I moved to my side so now I faced the water. Out in front of me was a small boat, the cruel waves slowly crashing against its hull. I focused on the sea. The persistent tide gradually mesmerized me, the subsisting force awoke a hunger inside of me. I fell into the hypnotism of the never-ending waters that stirred the small boat. It floated in the middle of nowhere, abandoned by mankind, neglected of its purpose. There, in the middle of the water, that's where I was in my life.

I recalled Valéry, *"The Sea, the sea, perpetually renewed."*

I took off my clothes and the necklace with the rings that Dadi-ma had given me and placed them on the sand. I walked to the edge of the water, completely bare, offering myself to this power. Hoping to be renewed. I cleaned myself, rubbed away the grime from my skin. Blinking in fury, I resigned myself to this moment. I didn't care who was around me, I was one with the moment. The water had a judgmental sharpness to it, as if it sensed my weakness. It remembered me, it consoled me. *You are strong,* it told me. *No, I'm not,* I screamed back. The cut along my arm burned senselessly, the salt in the water piercing deeper,

but I meditated on that pain. *Please don't get infected.* I screamed, wanting to self-destruct.

The moon was low as I cleaned the blood off the shard of glass and brought it to my hair and chopped, chopped, crunched it off. My hair was thick, but I got to the end of it. I needed it gone, it lingered from that night. The memory of their hands still groped me in the silence, it still mauled me on this empty beach. The cut was uneven. There was hair peeking out at all different hesitant lengths. But mostly, it hung below my ears in a do akin to a bob, but not quite. For now it would suffice. What was done was done. *Khallas,* as Kat would sometimes say. I was entering a new beginning. I realized that my parents would never know my story. I hated them for not caring enough to find out what really happened. Here, on this beach, I felt bitter and hard, and even as my eyes scanned the horizon, the savage twilight failed to soothe me.

Hatred was much better. It gave me resolve to move forward.

"Last Goodbye," by Jeff Buckley, played in my ear—*Taylia, you have to go home, you have to go back to Ky*—

I awoke abruptly. The sharp wind was on my face. Immediately, I stared out onto the water, monumental, opaque, like a sweeping ghost, and the depth and breadth of it stared back at me. The blackness of the crepuscular ocean, like thick tar, no longer enchanted me. A hypnotic fear rose up inside as I heard myself say I didn't want to die. As I ran from the beach I only faintly remembered why I awoke so quickly. I'd had a dream, and Alyssa was in it. She had spoken to me, she was there, along the constellations. I ran from the night, this time in search of warmth, wanting a home so badly.

I couldn't find my keys, so I knocked on the door. Ky opened it. The muscles in his jaw bunched up when he saw that it was me. I felt a fleeting sense of elation wash over me, gleefully

malicious, as if I enjoyed that I had an effect on him. He ushered me in, closing the door behind.

"Where have you been?" he asked gravely. There was a tinge of anger in his voice.

I glared at him.

"Taylia, where were you?" He paused. "And what happened to your hair?"

I turned around and started to make my way up the stairs, enjoying the drama of it all, but he grabbed me by the hand with a measured tightness, holding me back.

"Taylia?"

"Let go," I whispered, and tore my hand from underneath his. He again pulled at me, this time along the now crusty cut on my arm. I cried out, enraged.

He looked down, the tension of the unknown building up in his body. "What is that?"

It looked gruesome, not infected, but pulsing. His voice was stern, like an army general demanding answers. I didn't like his tone, but some part of me also did.

"Tay?"

"What? Just let go of me."

"What is that on your arm?"

"What does it fucking look like?"

He continued, alert and impatient: "What the fuck... You did that to yourself?"

I stayed silent. I didn't know what I wanted at that moment, maybe a shared grief. Maybe sympathy. Maybe I just wanted to be taken care of, but I didn't know how to articulate that.

"You did this to yourself?"

"Yes."

"Why?" He sounded broken.

"Because I felt like it."

"You can't do this to yourself. This isn't right."

"Ky." I paused, tired. "You can't begin to imagine what I'm going through."

"If you shut me out, then I never will."

"Shut you out? I opened up to you and you fucking betrayed me!" It came out like a deluge; all of a sudden, I wanted to punish him. He inhaled deeply as I just gawked, waiting for an apology.

"Life isn't a fucking John Green novel or whatever the fuck, Taylia. I didn't betray you. I told Emi—yes. Should I have asked you? Yes. And I'm sorry. But I wanted him to understand the situation. I wanted him to understand *your* situation. I care about you, that's why I did it."

He watched me solemnly and I felt mute. My emotions lay jumbled. Despite how much he annoyed me, I felt connected to him, I felt close to him. I felt the sadness of not getting what I wanted usurp me, and the inevitability of what was to come sank into me like an etching. I would get hurt, there was no doubt about it. But I felt open to him, more open than I had felt in years.

He took my silence as anger, which it both was and wasn't.

"Taylia?"

Besides, what could I say? Could I even dare to feel this way about him?

"Taylia?"

I had read about the path of the lovers' discourse. Love was tinged with sadness, it bled with uncertainty, and I had always been too weak for love. Fuck, I sounded like Alyssa. But I liked it, I wanted to be more like her.

"Taylia?"

He put his hands on my shoulders, knocking me out of it. I looked up at him. I wanted him to think I was powerful. That I didn't need him.

"Go to hell." I didn't shout it, I whispered it with spying eyes.

The next few days felt excessively aimless for me, and I hardly knew how to interact with him anymore. I didn't know where this intensity of feeling had emerged from. I felt stuck. In love. In this horrendous feeling. Each day, he did his part to be nice, as if he were paying his dues. Every morning I'd hear him breath-

ing through the door, post-run, pre-shower. I had memorized his schedule defiantly, believing that if I mirrored his actions in my mind I would somehow be there—not just in spirit, but with him at any given or precise moment. I would feel his thumping heartbeat and it would be as if we shared an experience together; his shadows began to define my reality. I'd imagine how it would feel to have his flickering breath linger on my face, how his eyes would hold mine in conversation. How maybe he'd laugh and put his hand on my shoulder and then brush my blood-warmed cheeks with his fingers and stroke the happiness that radiated through me. The ache I felt was tangible. I could feel it wail and grow stronger in its disobedience.

I had heard quite a bit about Ky's darling brother, Roman. Even after hearing both Emi and Ky (and sometimes even Jade) bring him up like he was a hero, I was suspicious. I wondered how sincerely admirable this man, or *any man* (Ky included), could possibly be. At the café, the few times I'd had a glimpse of him, he seemed completely normal. Was it merely an exaggeration they had all accepted?

"Taylia, you grew up in New York, too, I hear."

It was a Sunday, and the leaves were bright like tree frogs, glossy like them, too. Ky and Emi had invited Roman over for dinner. I was also invited. Jade was supposed to attend but was caught up with work, so it was just the four of us.

I was in charge of making the potatoes, Emi was doing the chicken, and Ky was doing the salads—we had two: beets with goat cheese, dill, and mint, as well as a kale and walnut Caesar. I began prepping before Roman came, and by the time he was at the house, the chicken was already in the oven, roasting; the potatoes were in a cast iron, toasting; and all the salads needed were their respective dressings. We were good to go. Now, we were sitting, waiting for things to cook and bloat with tenderness. Roman and I were sipping on a biodynamic Riesling (that's what

he called it) he brought; the other two were sipping rum, El Dorado 12, also a gift from Roman.

"I mean... I sure as hell didn't have the excitement you all had." I laughed my awkwardness off, but he seemed calm in my response.

"We really did have an exceptional childhood. This city in the early nineties was daaaank!" Roman looked toward Ky, then Emi. "Our parents kind of let us run amok, right?"

"I mean, y'all's parents let y'all run amok... My Catholic immigrant mom didn't want none of that shit," chimed in Emi.

"Oh, fuck off!" Ky shouted.

The three of them laughed.

"You were a brat dude..." Ky added.

Roman interjected. "I mean, Emi's kinda right. Mom and Dad let us do a lot of things. Remember Mr. G?"

"Holy shit! Mr. G. We were so mean to him."

"See, perfect example. I never joined in on your bullying escapades."

"Emi, I don't know what dutiful choir boy charade you're trying to pull, man, it's not working."

"Listen, my moms wouldn't let me do shit!"

"She was pretty judgmental of us..." Ky added.

"Nah, that's not true... she was just... she was busy, she was sad. She was lonely, man." Emi paused. "It's crazy how you begin to understand them years later."

He looked at me and briefly smiled. I looked away, training my eyes unnaturally on the food not yet on the table, a hallucination. My voice was suddenly gorged inside my throat like a scratch.

"You know, for years I thought she was angry, but nah, man. She was just mad sad, dude. She was just scared, too. Can you imagine coming to this country and being so damn poor with kids, and then no matter where you go you're a dirty fucking immigrant and nobody wants to give you shit and resents you for *everythiiiiing*. It makes me angry. All the things I never had

to even think about because I'm American straight off the bat, or whatever."

I wanted to say it was because he was a man, too, but I didn't. Because some part of what he was saying was true. We were all children of immigrants.

"The ridiculous thing is, we don't understand all the unconscious bias there is against us. We think because we're born here it's different..." Roman trailed off. "But it's really not. This country is fucked at its foundation. Only rich white people have true, unadulterated access. All the rest of us beg. Tahsin..." He paused, then looked at me to explain whom he was talking about. "My wife, Tahsin, and I were recently talking about the sort of sacrifices both our parents made. She's Lebanese, and her family came here after the civil war... Though a lot of her family is back there, in Beirut, which, you know, has been under siege for so long. So, it's this wild juxtaposition where you're split, always longing for a home that you can never return to, but being here and never being fully accepted. She's Muslim as well, so that just adds an entirely new dimension of racism on to her experience."

We were silent, grappling with our individual experiences.

"Yeah, I mean, the kind of racism she's had to overcome, man. That shit is real, that shit is deep," Emi added.

"Tahsin is always randomly selected for extra screening... you know, shit like that, and now with Sufjan, our kid," he said, turning to me again, "we're like, 'What's good, America?'"

"You're just like, 'What's good, Ameriiccaaaa?'" Ky asked.

"At the airport, 'What's good, bitch?!'" Emi added.

Ky started laughing. "You're so stupid."

They all laughed, brothers. In this moment, I deeply missed Alyssa.

"Where's Tahsin?" I asked, hoping for a comrade of my own.

"She's with her sister, who is her best homie, no kidding."

"Oh, how's the sis?" asked Ky, and I felt a pang of jealousy at his sudden interest.

"I think she's good, we should all hang out, she's super dope. Maybe I'll bring her by next time."

I smiled fakely alongside the other two.

"How about you, Taylia... what's your story?" Roman met my eyes, asking me directly.

I didn't move. Clearing out my throat with a tick, I bided my time. "Um, well, what exactly about me?"

"About your parents." People were always curious to know where I was from. I looked South Asian but ethnically unplaceable. Maybe it also had to do a lot with people not knowing much about the history of South Asia, me included. The bare minimum was what exotified us, but in many ways we were still seen as subhuman because we were so easily erased.

"Oh..." I cleared my throat again. "Well... my dad is Indian, from India. Kolkata to be exact. So he's actually technically Bengali... though not from Bangladesh. It's this weird thing where the Hindu Bengalis stayed in India and the Muslims stayed in Bangladesh." I gauged the room, and they all seemed interested, so I went on. "See, India was split up by religious lines during Partition, so Bangladesh was known as 'East Pakistan.' It was literally considered Pakistan's property even though it's, like, a completely different country, literally on the other side of India from Pakistan, like thousands and thousands of miles away, so it was completely unfair and unjustified to separate the country like that." I paused again. "So yeah, my dad's from there. And my mom is white, well, she's Jewish. She grew up in New York, on the Upper West Side actually. Which is where I was raised. Her parents kinda hated my dad, my sister, and me. They weren't ever outrightly racist, but we were raised knowing that they didn't want our mother to marry my father. So I guess she was protecting us because we never met them. Which kinda sucks..." I trailed off.

Concerned, Roman asked, "Where are your parents now?"

I couldn't face Ky, not entirely, but I felt his glare as he cut in. "Before Taylia answers that, we should set the table, food is going to be ready soon."

I cherished his interjection, knowing he had done so intentionally. I couldn't acknowledge it, so I kept my head down. Ky got up immediately, and I followed, aching a few feet behind him. He passed me the plates in silence, and by the time I got to the table, Emi and Roman were already on to something else. My heart skipped a beat knowing that Ky had saved me from this moment.

Later Jade joined us. The evening had moved into the backyard again, and as the stars sprawled I lingered on how strange the last few months had been. Emi and Roman were smoking a thin joint, and Jade was eating a plate of dinner while Ky massaged her shoulders. I watched them, frustrated but also, I noticed, more open than I had been in a while.

For so many years, I presumed I was unlikable, maybe even unsociable. Living with Alyssa, I guess, had made me feel dispirited, like I'd never be good enough, so why try? But nothing had changed, I was still me, and yet people found me interesting, maybe even charming. Emi passed me the roach, and I inhaled, taking comfort, but was soon sideswept a few seconds after the puff, perhaps regaining my tiny levels of unconscious anxiety. Suddenly, I could tell Jade was suspicious of my presence, and I was annoyed by that and by her. She was so beautiful, her skin so plump and glowing. Like a moonbeam. She had freckles like Lucy Liu, and she was beautiful in a way I could never be. There was a small part of me that wanted to hurt her, but of course, I resisted. I knew my feelings toward her were unfair, because I was really just comparing myself and feeling unworthy. I didn't want to be this simple-minded. Which frustrated me, the feeling like a loop. I let out a shallow sigh and made eye contact with Roman. He smiled at me, and suddenly I felt relieved, temporarily acquitted of the sprawling judgmental thoughts of my brain.

Maybe because of my latent envy of Jade, I realized I needed to avoid Ky at all costs. What I was feeling for him was a seizing of

fierce, concentrated passion, an ever-present throbbing of constant distress. Especially in my vagina, an area I still refused to touch or even really acknowledge. When I wasn't around Ky I felt a yearning—a nostalgia for the infinite, for him. But a part of me also wondered: Did he deserve this? Did he deserve my pining?

When I was in my early teens, just coming into my anxiety, Alyssa would often point out how intense I was. Her inflection would reek of disapproval. I knew it was her way of telling me to change, as if my attributes were malleable to her whim. I think, as a result, my intensity was deeply foreign to me.

"I feel grotesque, my limbs are all tangled."

Alyssa was sitting on my bed in Ky's place. We were always so dramatic with each other, cosplaying Yeats and Lord Byron.

"Taylia, why?"

"I don't know how to let this feeling settle."

"God, I wish someone had said this to me: *enjoy it!*"

I pleaded, "Untie me. Will you untie this knot?"

"Between me and you, or Ky and you?"

"Both."

She howled; I sneered.

"Listen closely, my little Taylia: there is nothing else quite like the horrors that love blooms."

Wide-eyed, I gulped and then watched her evaporate. She had said that to me once before when we were living in India. Both Alyssa and I would read incessantly, sometimes competing with each other, sometimes sharing the books or the family Kindle. We were building a tiny library in Dadi-ma's home, and though Mama thought it was a waste, when we could be exploring the city with her, Baba thought it was encouraging. "Let them live a little," he'd tell her. Of course he thought reading literature was akin to really "enjoying life." It was during this period that I saw Alyssa become a little more melancholy than I'd ever seen her before. Ma, especially, overcompensated. When we weren't reading, she'd take Alyssa out on day trips to the Marble Palace,

the Victoria Memorial, or the Kalighat Kali Temple, while I preferred to stay home with Dadi-ma. Alyssa did not take to life in India, it made her feel claustrophobic and watched, two things she hated. With all that reading, perhaps she lived in a second universe; the pages became her new home, closer to the life she'd grown so fond of having in New York.

One day, when I was sad at the prospect of Dadi-ma dying, an ever-looming reality, I shared this with Alyssa, hoping for a detailed summary of how I'd be fine or, at the very least, for some compassion. Dadi-ma, outside of my sister, had been the only person in the world I had felt genuinely close to. She'd been reading *Tender Is the Night*, and her tone was mildly incredulous in response to my sadness. She simply said, "There is nothing else quite like the horrors that love blooms," plumping her lips into a heart shape.

About two weeks after the first dinner gathering where I met Roman, I walked home to Ky's from Milk Thistle. I had, since my beachside incident, with Kat's guidance, received a haircut akin to a short bob, less triangular than Amélie's but a similar style. I briefly thought of Liza in admiration, wondering where she was these days. Personally, I liked the way the wind wept on the nape of my neck, a cathartic whisper. For a few months now, I'd also been wearing some of Kat's old clothes she was going to donate to Beacon's Closet. Some of it was perfect—formless, genderless, but also chic. The way my body swayed in Kat's extra Pleats Please (ones she let me borrow; she really knew how to live), along with my white Stan Smiths, made me feel like I was finally carving out who I was. With every new day, I was coming closer to the person I envisioned myself being. This Taylia preferred walking, maybe because it allowed my body to feel like it had agency and direction. I also didn't like the closed spaces of the subway. The forced intimacy of the carriages made me feel disorientated, the meandering eyes of the passengers and the self-imposed awkward body dances at every jerk of the track struck a strong discord deep within me. So, instead, I enjoyed the

walk through the history of New York's streets, particularly the vivid and welcoming buzz of the Lower East Side: the cascaded blocks, the young basketballers—even the grime of Delancey Street was charming. Walking over the East River each day reminded me of my mortality; I knew that with the slightest of pulls, I could be dead, drowning from asphyxiation. But as I walked over it I felt alive. I felt like I was beginning my life.

I approached the front door and noticed that it was open. I breathed in relief, knowing that it meant a quick and jolted escape to my still almost empty room. Yet in these last few weeks it had become my sanctuary. I crept up the stairs and crossed the hall-way. As I placed my hand on my door I heard faint, eerie crying from Ky's room. It felt familiar, like a moment trapped in time: the dark room in the corner where a deep pain resided. I put my ear to the door, pulled by the cry—the utmost bloodcurdling sound of human exhaustion, the ferocity of loss. Frustrated, I edged closer to the door, wanting so desperately to know what had happened. My senses were in overdrive; the replay of life quietly taunted me.

"So you heard," a voice standing next to me whispered.

As I turned sharply to face Emi, I realized he had been crying too. "What's wrong?" I said, afraid, wanting answers quick.

His eyes were peaked with tears as he detailed the events of the night before. As I listened I stood horrified, my feet glued to the floor and completely unable to process any form of movement.

"He's so fucked up right now."

I watched him pause. The short intake of breath, the excess of saliva, the subterfuge of the tongue, and the impulses of the body, releasing under the stress of misery. I wanted to hold him, Emi, but I hardly knew what to do after. Instead I communicated with my eyes, staring with my full intensity, hoping—in some small way— to communicate my condolences.

Emi left to get some air, so I walked downstairs.

The quiet was deafening, the silence usurping this sleepy cavern. I watched the stillness drift past for minutes, hours. It was so strange how we fear and yet still anticipate death, in some ways

believing that for us, and that for our loved ones, it will be different. Despite these preparations it's never what we thought it would be. The air in this apartment had shifted, the energy of this place responded to the loss of Roman. The house grieved, as we all did. Though Ky's crying had stopped, the residue of the wretchedness lingered. I knew, because I could feel it like tree sap dripping all around me.

Just yesterday, Roman had come over for a minute bearing gifts. As the eldest brother, I could tell he was a caretaker of sorts. Or, at least, the responsible one. He and his wife, Tahsin, had gone to Sahadi's, a giant Arab grocery store, picking up delicacies like juicy, taffy-like dates, salty labneh, and über-green za'atar. After dropping off Tahsin (who had their son) at home in Park Slope, he came to Ky's to say hi and offered everything from squeezable harissa to fresh, smoky baba ghanoush to a fat packet of lemony Marcona almonds.

Emi had known Roman and Ky since they were kids, as they all grew up together near a housing estate on Avenue C speaking Spanish. Despite the common language, Emi's religious Venezuelan mother was skeptical of Roman and Ky's liberal parents: a Peruvian and Japanese couple who had left cosmopolitan Lima to test their fates in the New York art scene.

I hadn't had many moments with Roman, but I could see a generosity emanate from him that I had rarely seen in men. It had not been an exaggeration: he was the brilliant, gregarious big brother invested in his baby sibling's life—and I had grown to feel guilty of my earlier cynicism. For Emi, I could see how he looked up to Roman all his life, with no filial obligation or sibling defiance, so the love was pure and unfiltered. It was a love of someone you idolize, who has the life you want, but you're free from jealousy because you genuinely admire him. Perhaps it's easier, too, if he isn't *really* your sibling. Ky was less forthcoming with his adoration, but you could tell that he relied on Roman for all manner of things, as a stabilizing force, as a brother, and now he was gone.

The next day I walked upstairs toward Ky, my hands laden with a freshly baked (that day!) olive oil cake that I brought home from work. I sensed how he must be feeling toward this immeasurable loss. I paused at his door, inhaling strength. I knew that my past experience would allow me to have some perspective. I could help him with my wisdom. I almost laughed at myself. *My wisdom?* Jesus.

I knocked lightly on the door and entered, I didn't expect him to open it. It was dark inside, the curtains firmly drawn together. My eyes adjusted to the darkness as I searched for him. There was a dim light on at one corner, but no sign of Ky. I peeked around his room. Taking in the art that hung beautifully from the walls, I noticed a large unframed canvas that rested on the wall to my right, the colors raw and fleshy, like fresh salmon. I wondered if he had painted it, but remembered Jade was an artist, so it was most likely hers, and suddenly wanted to groan in annoyance. I again resisted. The rest of his room was neatly put together. It was spacious, and even under the circumstances, it looked beautiful. There was a door on the other side; as I looked toward it, it opened and Ky came out. Light stubble tinted his jaw, making him appear disheveled, and his eyes were tired— the usual warmth had subsided, the bright green now a warm hazel. Surprise struck him as he noticed me; at first he faltered, but eventually—reluctantly—he came out.

"Hi," I said awkwardly.

He stayed silent, walked to his bed and sat on the covers.

"How are you feeling?"

I staggered up to him and halted, keeping a respectable distance. My hands were shaking, but I extended the plate toward him. We hadn't talked directly to each other since the night I told him to go to hell.

"I brought this from the café today." I paused for him to answer. He didn't, so I continued. "Olive oil cake is kind of Kat's thing." She often served it with fresh whipped heavy cream and wild strawberry compote; it was delicious.

He glared up at me dangerously, but didn't answer.

"You should eat."

"That's an odd request."

I made a face of confusion.

"You've avoided me for weeks, but now you want me to eat?"

"Ky, come on..."

He shrugged sluggishly, pouty.

"Ky, I'm sorry. I just haven't been in a good mood." I paused. "Look, I know I'm tough to be around—"

"You're actually not."

I was almost certain he'd agree with me. "I'm not?"

"No."

I was excited. "I..."

He sat waiting for me to finish my sentence, but I stopped myself, quickly changing tone.

"I'm sorry about Roman."

I felt like a fraud. I hardly cared about Roman right now. He was insignificant to me. In this moment all that mattered was that after all I had done to Ky, he still didn't think I was crazy. Life felt promising. I wanted to smile, I wanted to embrace him and tell him how much I appreciated his facial hair and how handsome he looked even when he was completely unkempt and melancholy.

He sighed, exhaling with a "How's your arm?"

His voice pulled me out of my daydream.

"My arm?"

Slumping onto his bed, he pointed to his arm. "Your little... indiscretion."

That was a very tempered way of saying *your self-harm*. I smiled, fully knowing how inappropriate my timing was. But I didn't really care. The fact that he remembered filled me with happiness. I shook myself out of it. "Do you want to talk, Ky?"

He looked down at his hands, completely hopeless. "Is it worth it?"

I played with the dry skin on the sides of my nails. "Depends."

"On?"

"Whether or not you want to allow yourself to be okay with whatever comes out."

I could sense him watching me. I knew I had moved him; I could feel his warmth respond to me.

He sighed again. "I don't know what I want."

I knew how he felt. "I think talking will help sift through those feelings."

"I guess I am afraid of what might come out."

I peered at his shirt, thinking it was a happy medium between his face and the floor. "Maybe those things need to be said."

"Maybe, Taylia." He paused and then sang: *"Maybe it's because I don't know you at all."*

I was struck with familiarity. "Jeff Buckley."

"'Last Goodbye.'"

The regret of the unsaid.

"What a face." Ashamed, I realized I had said that out loud.

Ky seemed amused. "Unfortunately I concentrated more on his songwriting skills. And that falsetto..."

I salvaged the moment, smiling crookedly: "Your loss."

Ky gave out one loud bellow. There was a long pause. "Roman used to love Buckley."

Ironically, Baba had introduced me (and Alyssa) to his music, through Nusrat Fateh Ali Khan. As I thought of that, with a pang, momentarily, Ky grabbed hold of my hand. I noticed how tight his grip was and realized he was also crying.

"Fuck, it's past tense. Taylia, it's fucking past tense... He's in the past. His life is history. Fuck, fuck, fuck. Taylia, fuck..."

I held on tightly.

"Roman..."

He jerked his hands out of mine, pulling at his hair. I fumbled with my hands to give myself something to do.

"What the fuck. Oh God, what do I do now? The last time he was on the phone he said, 'I love you, Ky,' and I scoffed. I'm such a piece of shit."

He had collapsed onto his palms.

We were quiet. After a while I decided it was time.

"The pain might not subside, but the absence is easier to bear after a while."

He seemed unconvinced.

"I know because when I was nineteen, Alyssa, my sister, committed suicide." I breathed in. "She was the only person that I think ever came close to loving me, you know, like how I wanted to be loved. Or maybe... something like that. These days I'm not sure of that, either."

He looked up at me, tears rolling down his face. I watched them stop just at the curve of his jawline and trickle down just below his neck.

"You lost your sister?"

I wanted to say that I had lost a lot of things. I had lost, in the past few years: my sister, my virginity, my dignity, both of my parents... and, potentially, also my mind.

I got up. "You'd better eat that cake. It's super fresh."

"Don't go," he said unexpectedly.

I was surprised but thrilled. "Don't worry. I'm just getting you some water."

I remember waking up to the sound of my mother crying. Something was definitely wrong—my mother never cried, not like this. I tried to think of what day it was. *The twenty-sixth of October,* the day after Alyssa's birthday. I sat silently for a while, replaying the dream I'd had the night before. Alyssa had been in it, wearing a white dress. As I replayed the dream I could hear her voice, but nothing she was saying was audible. Screeching wheels, shattering glass—the dream was filled with sounds that struck you painfully, on repeat.

I pulled myself out of the warm refuge of my bed and went to where I could hear the crying. The door was locked, so I slithered onto the floor. But all I could hear was anguish floating from under the crack of my parents' bedroom door. My mother's

senseless huffing and puffing, her expressions of devastation, resonated. I was stuck in her pulse, and her heartbeat moved through, shaking me into an involuntary convulsion. I was drifting in her screams as they gnawed like parasites. What was wrong? Mama wouldn't have been crying like this for her parents, and Dadi-ma and Dadi-ji (my father's father) were both dead. Then the horrible thought entered my head: something had happened to Alyssa.

Suddenly and without warning, she seemed incredibly far away to me; I couldn't feel her smiling face, I couldn't feel *her*. As I moved slowly back to my room, I was flooded with questions, so I opened the door to hers and crept in. Hope swelled inside of me, *she's there, she's there*. I moved over her covers, but they were empty and the room was lifeless, I could feel nothing. And suddenly I knew—how sisters knew—that Alyssa was dead. I looked around her room; the previous day it had been filled with people, and today it was empty. On the floor I saw the box I had packaged her present in. It had been a white dress, like I saw in my dream. I bent down toward the box and looked inside. It was empty. I went around her room, searching like an outsider. The space was a complete void, the gaping kind of immediacy that absence brings.

I cried until I had nothing left in me.

Every object in her room was a sign. Had she left a message in the way she opened her curtains? Was half open a half mast? She couldn't have left without saying something significant. Seized by the hope that there was something more, I moved my shaking hands through everything. I trolled through her carefully selected jewelry box, her table, the notebook on the side of her bed, her bookshelf. I picked up the book she had been reading by her window just a few days earlier.

"What are you reading?"

"*Kafka on the Shore*."

She was distant.

I was bored. So, I walked out.

I walked out. I walked out. I walked out.

Before I left, which would turn out to be the last time I'd lay foot in her room, I went to her wardrobe and touched her clothes like they were a living organ. Her life was pulsing through their veins. They still lingered with the smell of her. She had been alive in these clothes. She had bled in these clothes, laughed in these clothes, cried in these clothes. They were the only tangible part of her that was left. I looked outside her gloomy window and watched the leaves fall to the ground for moments, hours, gone by. It was finally beginning to feel like fall; the garden ground was covered with leaves as if they, too, had been mourning her.

Mama's pain was insurmountable. In those days, weeks, months after Alyssa's death, it felt like a burden, a dark cloud whenever I was near her, spilling over onto me, the emotionally susceptible one. She slept for days at a time. Baba rarely disrupted her, instead choosing to sit in a fog of cigar and ash in the private confines of his office. The loneliness was stifling, compounding the feeling of loss even more intensely. In my grief, perhaps in the only way I knew how to grieve, I learned to take care of my parents. I cooked, I cleaned, and I cared for them in remembrance of Alyssa. But nobody looked after me.

One day, a few weeks after her death, I went to my parents' bedroom. No one answered when I knocked, so I opened the door to a hollowed silence, almost a void. Like the hum of *om* during meditation, the silence was unnerving. The curtains weren't drawn, and inside the cavern sat Mama, like a pallid *Flaming June*—eyes closed, in a sleepy repose. I walked in, close enough to smell her, although she didn't wear her perfume—a mix of saffron and musk—instead she lay still, heavy lidded, almost dead.

"Mama?" I whispered.

Nothing.

"Mama?" I whispered again.

I don't know what I wanted, maybe to be seen. To be looked at and remembered as the other daughter. The one who was still

there. I touched her gently and she shrank from my touch so rapidly that I felt like I had committed a sin.

"I'm sorry—"

"Taylia. Not now, just go away. Please, I beg of you."

I shuffled away, and by the time I was back in my room, the door sealed, tears had begun to stream. I plummeted to my own bed. Looking for ways to ease the pain, I screamed into my pillowcase.

Zeina was over, and Mama was lying on her lap, cracking her toe knuckles against the side of the sofa. She seemed both depressed and mad, her body on fire, emanating heat; I could feel her as I sat and listened on the stairs. They both couldn't see me, and I preferred it that way.

"All my weaknesses were distilled into her. She was my Trojan horse. I don't have anything to live for anymore. I have nothing."

Zeina just told her to hush gently. In lulling Mama out of her sadness, she threw in my name, like a lifeboat. But I couldn't help but feel the venom in Mama's silence, which made me believe some part of her wished it was I who had died.

"Do you think Dadi-ma was burned alive?" Alyssa asked me on the staircase.

"How could you even think of that?"

"Could you feel her breathing stop?"

"Lyse..."

"Don't you sometimes wonder what happens in the moments after? When life leaves you, when you've finally surrendered? Don't you think it's such a beautiful thing to leave a body, a space, that can no longer hold you?"

"Um, no. That's fucking weird."

"It's just, don't you ever wonder how odd it is that she died in our presence, like on cue?" I felt an anger rise up inside of me.

"I'm not sure I know what you're trying to say."

154

"You always pretend as if you don't get it, T... but you always do."

I filled a glass with water and took it back upstairs. Ky had gotten out of bed. Still sitting down, now he was leaning over his knees, sobbing softly into his hands as if to muffle the sound. Someone else's pain is always so much harder to bear than your own, and I felt the pang settle in my lungs, smothering me as I breathed. I crept down in front of him.

"Ky, have some water."

He took the glass, putting it to his lips and tilting his head backward as he swallowed in big, spaced gulps. He put the glass down and collapsed into his hands again.

"How do you get over it?"

My attention was on him again. "You don't, unless you throw yourself into things. People say time mends it, but I'm not sure if it does. I mean, while time goes by, when you think about it again the same feelings always come rushing back. It never really fades."

He sighed heavily. I watched him, surprised and delighted by his emotion. My father was the only other man I had known closely—maybe not intimately, but enough—and he was completely devoid of feeling at all times. After Alyssa's death I often stared at him, hoping to see a sign, a revelation, but nothing. He just wallowed in his empty cavity, playing the heroic lead. As I currently examined Ky, it was heartwarming to see how moved he was.

Something came over me. "It's okay."

I cupped my hands around his jaw. I always assumed that my touch repulsed others, but here I was, touching someone. I felt surprise exude through my very fingertips. Ky responded to my kindness eagerly, craving assurance. A small part of my caged self let go.

"It's okay, I'm here," I whispered.

He drew back and looked at me, his eyes moved and slowly focused on mine. With precision, his fingers brushed my face and he reached out toward me, clasping his hands over my neck, slowly touching his lips with mine. And I responded. I responded with no fear of rejection. He tasted different, in a foreign but comforting way. I remember wondering if this was a moment that I would remember for the rest of my life. People always say that about these kinds of things, but I wondered if it was true. He moved one hand to my cheek, and I wanted to fall into him. I wanted to disappear in his lips, into the folds of his tongue and the crevices of his mouth.

His perfect face was all of a sudden frozen in my mind: his high cheekbones and that skin that looked like bright toffee, his dark hair bleached mildly from the sun. He had a surfer aesthetic to him that added to his coolness, his hair always long and shaggy. He was so beautiful, I wanted to cry.

He has a girlfriend, Taylia.

Remembering, I pushed him off me. He stumbled as if in a trance. I sensed him pulling back toward me and I felt wanted, I felt safe.

I had nothing to say: no words could explain my elation and simultaneous fear. I finally moved, avoiding all possible contact when I got up. I didn't see his face, but I could feel his eyes on me, burning my skin. I ran reluctantly down the stairs and adrenaline shot through me like traveling light. I rushed to the back door and released myself. Making sure I was clear of hearing distance, I let out a primal scream, hoping to free the aggression that had been cooped up inside of me. I felt ready to combust, a speeding force that needed to hit the ground and shatter into a million fragments. I sat on the concrete hoping that what I felt had been a reality. I couldn't bear it if this was a dream. I pinched myself, savoring the pain for a few moments. I felt the wind on my face and the dew of the grass wet my knees. I knew that the best of dreams, even among some of the most vivid ones, were never colored with this much mundane yet beautiful detail.

18.

I woke up that morning feeling unresolved. Happy, in a state of wild bliss, but like a thread of loose yarn I was being yanked. I couldn't believe what had actually happened the day before. *Had I truly kissed Ky? Could it be real?* I bobbed my head up to look at my empty, cavernous room. A new beginning. I wanted to feel settled, I wanted to feel embraced. I yearned to make this room a home, this home a home. But now I had gone and kissed Ky, and everything felt both meaningful and *too* loaded. The light was coming in from my window, the trees like guides, a star constellation that ushered me in to my higher self. I lay with the shattering feeling of remorse, or maybe more shame, which overcame me. I knew I had to tell Jade. So I called her. She had given me her number offhandedly, in a spooked way, as if to keep tabs on me. I felt angry at both myself and her for knowing.

"Hello?"

"Hey, um, Jade?"

"Yes?"

"This is Taylia."

"Who?"

"Uh, Taylia."

"Oh right. Ky's roommate."

I took an unacceptable pause.

"Taylia, I'm sorry, but I'm on another call with a client, I thought you were somebody else so I picked up. Is everything okay?"

She annoyed me so much.

"Uh, Ky's not doing too well."

"What do you mean?"

She still didn't know.

"Roman died."

"What? Are you serious? The fuck... Oh my God... How... the fuck?"

"I—"

"When did it happen?! How did this happen?"

"To be honest, I'm not so sure."

"Tell Ky I'll be right over."

He kissed me. He kissed me!

"Okay."

I heard her fidget on the other side.

"Poor baby." She was sniffling.

I winced. Her romantic vernacular seemed so forced.

"Thanks for calling me, Tahlia."

"Taylia."

I heard the irritation in her voice. "Sorry, Taylia. I'll be there soon. Let him know that, won't you?"

But I wouldn't.

What if I was sidelined by her? What if what had happened in his bedroom was just a reaction? What if it was just his way of numbing the pain? What if he had mistaken me for Jade, hoping to lose himself in me, not caring who or what I may be, only craving the satisfaction of blanking out for a few seconds so that the trauma could be overwritten by nonparalyzing mistakes? I didn't want that to be me. For once I so desperately wanted to be a positive choice.

Jade stayed over that night. I wondered if she fucked him. I thought about that until I finally allowed myself to fall asleep. I waited for sounds of moaning, my ears turned to the door, red with impatience. I watched the stairs, but I was confronted by silence. I imagined Jade in bed. I wondered if she moved sinuously like actors in the movies. Did she ask for more, did she get on her hands and knees and get him to fuck her hard? I couldn't picture her talking dirty and I couldn't imagine her coming, her face contorted into forms of passion; everything about her seemed so wooden, almost mechanical. An image kept playing in my mind. I thought of her on the bed, hands trembling as she clenched on to the old Pendleton blanket in front of her, Ky's cock bruising her beautifully. I replayed the image of him sweaty

and broken, fucking her to ease the pain. I felt the wandering lust savage me. The image was no longer Jade. I was now in front of him, knees to the floor, waiting for him to devour me.

I woke up.

I felt wetness between my legs. I hadn't had a feeling down there that was pleasant since it happened. The wetness felt viscous and sticky, the heaviness weighing down my panties. I got up and fast-tracked myself to the bathroom, closing the door behind me. There was a warmth between my legs and I felt a gravitational pull toward it. Mouth ajar, I placed my hand to see if that comforted it at all; it didn't. I needed something harder. I placed myself against the bathroom sink and rubbed myself up and down against it, and after a little while there was a release, a sigh passing through me. Afterward, I sat myself down next to the toilet. With my lips twisted, I pulled off my underwear and put my fingers to the wetness. I hadn't touched myself in so long, but right now, it felt so good. I moved against my own flesh, circling the ridge, so tiny and yet so overwhelming, feeling the undulations move through to my chest and head. I kept playing with it, this time picturing Ky. I felt him entering me, I watched him move in and out of me. Focused, he was hovering like a hologram above me. His hazel-green, now almost orange, eyes sunk into me like teeth. Tears scattering past my flushed cheeks, I felt the tides move through my skin, lifting me off the ground into serenity. I sighed a big, greedy sigh and sat for a few seconds in awe that I could be transported like this. I looked down at my fingers, spliced with come. I could smell it on me. It was a very human stench and lasted even after I washed my hands of it. I got up, feeling lighter than usual.

After getting ready, I went downstairs to prepare breakfast, smelling my hands, again and again, as I rushed, happily transported to the bathroom tiles. Hoping to avoid the early-morning traffic of an overnight guest, I planned to beeline for the fridge, but when I got to the kitchen my view was suddenly blockaded by an indecent amount of exposure. I felt my body shrink and

my heart sink. Jealousy riddled its way into me. Her hands were awkwardly placed on his body. He was holding her gently, his lips even more beautiful when they moved against skin. I couldn't look away. I stared unconsciously for a while when someone said something.

"Oh. Hi, Taylia."

I was back in that moment. "Oh, hey." I rushed the words quickly out of my mouth,

They both stared at me. I made eye contact with only one of them.

"I'm sorry, I have to go."

"Won't you have breakfast?" he asked.

"Not that hungry."

I charged to the front door and walked to the bakery. I was back in my head, the most solitary place to be.

After work, I took an extra-long route through SoHo, exploring the cobbled streets and the expensive boutiques. New York, on my own terms, had an incredible effect on me. The streets were always so healing. I thought of the other lost souls who had walked through these passages, hoping to be saved by this city's enduring charm. I was soothed by its sibilant sounds, knowing things would be okay. This was a new feeling, one of home. Even if I lost everything, I would still have the city. I would pick myself up and reemerge again.

As I walked into the house, instantly glum, remembering the details of the morning, a voice interrupted my depressing meditation.

"Hey."

I gazed up. It was him.

"Hi."

I knew my voice was a few octaves higher than usual.

"Did you just get back from work?"

"Uh, yeah."

"That was a long shift."

"No, I actually went walking around the city."

"Find anything interesting?"

"Yeah." I smiled a thin line. "The city's secrets."

He smiled. "You seem like you're getting comfortable here."

I rested one hand on the skinny banister. "Uh, yeah, I am."

"Good. I'm glad that you're here."

Please don't do this to me.

I stayed silent.

"About yesterday..."

I nodded my head profusely. "It's whatever. Don't worry about it."

He was piercing through me.

"It was nice of you to call Jade."

I nodded my head again.

"I can tell you don't like her."

"She's whatever. It's whatever. I thought you just needed some, you know, love."

"Yeah."

"I'm sorry, I was there on the bed. You probably thought I was Jade, I mean you were so emotional and—"

"I didn't think you were Jade."

"Oh." I let it out without realizing.

"I knew it was you, Taylia. And you don't have to apologize. You didn't do anything wrong. I was in the wrong. It was inappropriate of me to do—"

"Where's Jade?"

"She's out somewhere. She said she was going to get me a surprise."

"That's exciting."

He smiled. "Do you want to hang out? I don't know when she'll get here, but we have some time to just hang out. If you want."

I paused. "I actually have a lot of reading to do."

He smiled again. "Oh, reading."

"No, I do. I have a lot of reading."

"I'm sure."

I laughed. He followed.

"How are you feeling today?"

"I'm..." He paused. "...numb...You know how it is."

I nodded, I did.

"What is it that you're reading, Taylia, that you can't make time?"

I stuttered. "I—I am reading Jhumpa Lahiri's *The Namesake*."

"Oh."

"So..."

"Too busy, huh?"

His brother just died, you bitch!

"Seems like it."

I could feel him staring into me. But I knew it would be problematic for me to stay, to linger, to want more. Jade wasn't so bad, and it was unfair that I hated her.

"I can't tempt you with a movie?"

He walked toward me and brought his hands to my cheeks. I watched his hands move to my face in slow motion. He rubbed them softly, brushing the redness away. I was transported to the smell on my hands earlier that morning as I thought of him.

"You're warm."

"I know."

He laughed. There was a long pause.

"*The Namesake* is calling me..." I was still looking down.

"Okay."

His hands were still on my face.

"Okay."

I moved away swiftly and his hands fell to his sides. I felt him watch me walk up the stairs. I wanted him so badly that I was afraid I would keel over from the desire moving through me like fire. I closed the door behind me, and my body shook against the beat of my fast-moving heart.

19.

I was lying on her floor, among her clothes, leaning on a plush hoodie as an armrest. She was applying a red Chanel lacquer to her toenails. Mama hated the color because she thought "red nail polish is tacky," but Alyssa didn't seem to care. She had recently bought pumps, knockoff Louboutins, where her toes peeked out, and it was for an occasion. The occasion of looking good. I watched her, then broke the silence.

"How does it feel to be in love?" I asked.

She lingered on her baby toe. "It's just that, a feeling..."

"A feeling?" This didn't seem right.

"It's a state of mind, I guess."

"Does that mean that people have a choice to not be in love?"

"Oh no, of course not. The whole idea of love is that even if it hurts, you can't help it."

"That doesn't make any sense."

I watched her moisturize her hands. She seemed frustrated by my questions.

"Tay, you're young, okay? You don't get these things. When you're my age you'll know."

"Know what?"

"What love is. Gosh, Taylia. Why the twenty-one questions?"

I paused, giving her space to breathe. "Do you love Ryan?" They had been dating for a few months. I watched her closely: she was resisting the urge to chew her bottom lip.

She shrugged. "Sometimes."

It sounded like a choice to me. "Well, how do you know when you're in love?"

"You just know. It's like when you're with the one person, you're whole... you're complete. That's just when you just know. Capisce?"

It sounded awful. I was scared at the idea that I would never be complete. How did it feel to be fragments of a person? Only half

whole? I wanted to ask her what the feeling was between two siblings. Was that the same love? I wasn't sure. After Alyssa killed herself, I tried to convince myself that it would have to be enough, but I felt weary and insatiable.

I had always had crushes. Those schoolgirl obsessions with teachers, like Ms. O'Neil, my history teacher. Alyssa hated her, but I loved the way she smelled—like crisp cinnamon. She had short hair that parted to the side like bleached grass, so she looked like Nick Carter. I always had crushes on older women when I was younger, and perhaps that stunted and confused me. I knew I liked men, but they seemed so unattainable, so my misery felt like a more reliable companion. In many ways, I hadn't changed.

I walked to the bathroom, sensing that someone was inside. I looked in and saw Emi washing his hands, using water frugally, fingers slight and swollen.

"Hello, lovely Taylia!" He was all smiles.

We still hadn't properly talked since the incident, and it was a few days later, I managed to smile back.

"We never really talked after..."

"Oh, I know."

"I'm sorry about it all, Taylia. Maybe I've been too self-involved."

"No way! How?"

"I don't know... I've been so nonexistent, I'm sorry. I've just been binge-watching *The Wire*, working on my work projects, and crying..." He chuckled. "I haven't even properly spent time with Ky. I'm being an asshole, I know I should be more attentive to him since Roman, but I've been going through it, too, you know? I'm sorry."

For the first time I saw Emi as a person outside of Ky. I'd been so focused on what I could get out of him, as a proxy for Ky, but now I took him in completely. Contracting my eyes, I pulled back. He was handsome and round-faced with large brown eyes that tilted down at the sides, almost drooping, like Goofy's, but

it gave him a charm, a warm absurdity to his looks. I stared at him, head to one side, noticing his calm tenderness that seeped through every lopsided grin. An expression of purity shone through him.

"Earth to Taylia."

"Oh! Shit. Sorry, I disappear sometimes."

"I just said that Ky told me to say hello. He couldn't catch you before he left."

Left? My heart sunk a little. "Oh?"

"He was going to say goodbye but you weren't awake yet."

"Where did he go?"

Emi paused. "To make all the funeral arrangements for Roman. He decided to go take some time with his family. His parents live upstate now, so he's there for a few days."

I nodded my head.

"We should have dinner. I wanna know how you're doing."

It sank even further. "He's gone for that long?"

"He didn't tell you he was leaving?"

"No."

"That's strange."

I nodded my head in cautious agreement.

"He must've forgotten."

My innocence was suddenly exposed. "Hmm..." My smile was faulty, I could feel the edges quiver against their will. I knew Jade must've gone with him, and that maddened me. I caught my breath mid-sigh, and Emi moved past me, speaking. Feigning tiredness, I warded him off, and he seemed keen to get back to work, or *The Wire*, anyway. He walked away and I heard the dialogue of the TV show start again. I stood still, my pulse at my tonsils, beating like a splaying frog. The salty residue of my saliva, runny, sat at the back of my throat. My body was reacting. It was ready to shudder, to break down, to cry, to torment. I bit my pettiness away and went for a walk, tracking the weeds along the sidewalk right to McCarren Park, a few blocks away. The hair on the nape of my neck stood against the breeze as I

watched joggers on the ochre-red track. My gaze was searching for Ky. I inhaled, smelling the leaves of sassafras shake through me, fragrant with desire. I felt his kiss on my lips, repetitively, preferring my dreams on this cool, cool night.

At work the next day Kat cried in my arms about Roman. It was strange to see how this man's death affected the two closest people in my life in unrelated ways, punctured by the same pain. We stood by the grand baking ovens and took a reprieve from the business of the lunch rush. I pulsed her hand (in the space between her thumb and pointer finger, as she had taught me, for its unique acupressure) as tears scattered across her face like lost stars.

Death was a strange beast that I didn't know how to tackle. When Alyssa died, the mourning overtook my soul, but consoled me. Grief was a consolation back then, but now it felt insincere. I felt detached from the pain and therefore much better at being a stand-in, like a death doula. Maybe that was my fate? I thought of the intricacies and formality of funerals, what Ky must be going through balancing it all. I held Kat as she cried.

After work, I walked across the East River, moving past the gentrified Williamsburg pads. They stood upright like vapid tin intrusions, littering the corners of the place I called home. As I walked idly, I caught the eye of a biker careening down from Greenpoint and felt myself blush. I cursed myself, feeling pathetic. Any kind of human interaction always made me feel strange and giddy, like I was sharing a secret that nobody knew. There was something oddly sensual in that fantasy, nerves jittering in the aftermath.

I turned toward a narrow park on my left, making my way across the cobbled stone path down to the bank. The greenery was overwhelmingly placid. I faced the city's profile, rapacious buildings protruding out like jigsaw pieces that didn't fit, I stood, insignificant, against the tide of life, the tide that kept coming. "Bulletproof... I Wish I Was" blasted in my ears, the song accompanying the breeze, mirroring my disposition. Vaguely annoyed,

I took the headphones out of my ears and stuck them into my pocket. Right now, I wanted to hear the actual sounds of the city. Sitting down on a big blackened log to my right, I caught the eye of a guy sitting in front of me on a makeshift bench made from dried branches and scattered driftwood. I looked away quickly, thoroughly embarrassed. He was wearing fitted corduroys with a hooded khaki jacket and a maroon beanie. He looked back again, this time smiling. Fingering his pocket, he took out some tobacco, and gesturing toward it, he asked, "Do you want one?"

I was mute.

"They're not as nasty as the prepackaged ones."

"I don't smoke."

"Oh, but you should."

He came and sat next to me. We made eye contact again. The feeling enveloped me.

I concentrated on him and his actions. He was delicate with his craft, his fingers surprisingly nimble for a man so tall.

"You live around here?"

"Yup, North Ninth."

"Near Cafe Colette, right?"

An unease came over me.

"Don't worry. I've seen you before, you look familiar."

"You live around here, too?"

"Yup, at the north end of the park, just where it forks out."

"Oh, near Five Leaves?"

"That's it."

"Cool."

He exhaled and gray particles dissipated into the air. "You walk around a lot. You're always in your own world."

My hands went to my face as I muffled my laugh.

"What?" He asked as if he really wanted to know.

"No, nothing. It feels weird that I've been watched."

He exhaled again, a wolfish grin played on his face. "Well, it's not like I stalk you. I'm not your personal *stalker*."

I giggled, loud. "Aren't all stalkers personal?"

"Yeah... Okay. I don't know your life like that."

I laughed.

"Whatever, my point is, I am neither of those things. I've just seen you from time to time, that's all."

I gave him the thumbs-up, and a smile crept onto his face.

"Yup. It's pretty sweet."

He lifted the cigarette back to his lips and held it there as he wiped his right hand on his trousers and extended it toward me.

"Ralph."

I laughed unnaturally. I think I was trying to flirt.

"What?"

"The Simpsons..."

"Fuck, really? That's what you tell me? You can't be like, 'Oh, is that pronounced *Rafe*, like Ralph Fiennes'? Instead you compare me to a... cartoon?"

Baba hated *The Simpsons* because of Apu. He never explicitly told Alyssa and me that, but the theme song would come on the TV, sliding us into a dream, and a silent commotion would start as Baba would rush to bark, "Turn that off, *please*, both of you. I don't want to tell you twice." Alyssa would always smirk quietly, but I would feel sad. Sad for the traumas we can't face.

"Well, I wouldn't ask you that, because you just pronounced your name like Ralph anyway..."

"I could be tricking you, you know?"

I sighed. "Taylia." I delayed extending my hand.

"Tay-what?"

"L-i-a."

"That's actually nice."

I lifted my eyebrow. "Sure."

"No, really."

"Okay, *Ralph*."

I felt comfortable. Better yet, I felt confident.

After a few inhalations he put out his smoke on a rock and wiped his face with both hands. "It's a filthy habit, but God, do I love it."

Getting up abruptly, he fixed his jacket as he straightened out.

"Come to the bar at the Wythe one night, I bartend there on weeknights. They have a great rooftop bar, drinks on me. "

I smiled.

"I'll see you around, Taylia."

"Yeah."

He walked past me and I didn't turn around to see if he looked at me again. Prurient, and suddenly warm, I watched the waves wash past and looked out at the New York skyline. I'd done it! He was no Ky, but he was cute. Maybe I was getting better, maybe I was conquering my weaknesses. As I sat on the shore, I wondered if I would see Ralph again and how often in life we hope for things to be better, to be different.

Alyssa had taken up smoking. Buying overpriced Marlboros and leaning out of her bedroom window, coughing, spitting, but mainly reveling in her newfound habit. It gave her an edge, and I liked it. It reminded me of the girls in the movies, like Ally Sheedy in *The Breakfast Club*. Alyssa was cooler, though, but there was a severity she displayed that felt opulent. Like, it was a newfound zero-fucks attitude that was less mean and more defiant. In those moments, I still believed she couldn't hurt me.

She got a record player for her sixteenth birthday. It was one of those gifts that she felt truly described her: *I'm eclectic, I'm alternative, I listen to vinyl, I watch Ingmar Bergman films, I read Allen Ginsberg. I'm different. I'm different. I'm different.*

One of her earliest albums was *The Velvet Underground and Nico*. She bought it on First Avenue, in a dingy record store. The look on her face when she came home that night was irreverent. She sprawled onto my bed, eyes shining. She smelled like Tommy Girl.

"I know you're not old enough... but love is so great."

I wasn't listening, I was worried she was ruining my bed, which I had made earlier. I had creased every edge to smooth perfection.

She started singing "I'm Waiting for the Man," then walked out of the room singing even louder. The shift was palpable, her strutting around, indignant, entitled—something dark inside of her had begun to shimmer out. Was it the determination of love? The way it must embolden you *to be beloved*. To not have a question of doubt in your mind. I heard her chanting louder, fully aware that it was late, and Mama and Baba would do little to reprimand her, a mere hiss of disapproval. I could hear the lyrics echo against the panes of glass and mirror in the bathroom. *I'm waiting for my man.* I sensed her staring narrow and pointed toward her reflection, basking in her mirrored delight, her hair in smooth waves.

I was destined to be forever waiting. Why do we wait, and who is there to wait for? Doesn't the very idea of waiting imply that there is something or someone on the other end? Like gravity, was she who was waiting being pulled closer at lightning speed to whoever she was waiting for? Waiting felt useless. It felt cumbersome. I could feel the ache of the love that I was not having resonate, cold, in my bones.

But then I smelled him when I opened the front door. Ky was back so soon? I was surprised that Emi had not gone to the service— maybe it had been small? I wondered these things as I entered, suddenly wet, desirous.

I walked in cautiously. My nerves, like hot oil in a skillet, put me in a dance. Up the stairs—*no, what if he's there?* Down, okay. *Wait. Who's that in the kitchen? Fuck, fuck, fuck. That's him.* He coughed as if he could sense me waltzing. I balanced myself up the stairs, biting my nerves until I was in my room. All things would be easier handled once I was out of the apprehension zone.

I sat on the bed and waited. I picked up *The Namesake*, opened it, and placed it near me to ensure that if he were to come into the room I would have an alibi. *What are you doing?* I would look at him with no sign of affection, no sign of tenderness. *I'm reading, can't you tell?*

I waited on the bed for hours, my mind unable to process anything other than memories of him, past, present, and future. I listened to music, I flipped through several books, but nothing calmed me. My breathing had slowed to the point that even the slightest bit of exertion burned a hole through the rest of me. Perversely I lay there, drawing him in. Ky, my custodian, my companion. I waited. But he never came. Inquisitive, but tired, I fell asleep in dreams, mouth wide open, my saliva staining the pillow, arrested by him fully.

Later, I awoke with a start and said aloud, "It doesn't make any sense."

"What doesn't?"

"Did you see him kiss me?"

"I did."

"And?"

Alyssa shrugged.

"I need some input here."

She played with her hair. "I don't know what you want me to say."

I was annoyed.

"Come on, Taylia, this is what men are like."

"Ky's not like that."

She raised her eyebrows. "That's what we all think."

"No, it's not a fucking cliché, Lyse. It's the fucking truth."

Dejected, she lowered her voice like she was speaking with authority. "Okay, T."

I closed my eyes and focused on our whereabouts. We were in the Catskills at our summer house near the lake. We spent those days dusted in grime and dirt, our clothes stiff like cardboard from the buildup of the earth around us. We sat in the woods, lodged in between the trees, and hid as young brats do. Green pines, pungent, and the smell of fresh mildew, musty rot, damp leaves stuck together days after a rainstorm. I savored this memory. I was glad I remembered it.

She broke my meditation. "I never anticipated you'd feel like this."

"Like what?"

"Heartbroken."

"Is this what it feels like?"

She nodded. "I've been watching you."

"I just don't get it. He kissed me. He was so keen, and then nothing. Nothing! Did I do something? I wish I could go back and take it away, do whatever I did differently."

She sighed. "I know how you feel."

"Have you ever had your heart broken?"

She nodded.

"By Ryan?"

She was silent.

I didn't care, I was in my own head again. "It would have been easier if he hadn't said anything. If he hadn't shown he cared. Then he'd be like everyone else and right now I wouldn't feel so rejected."

She sucked on her bottom lip. "Life was never meant to be easy, my love."

And then she disappeared

I woke up to moans. It was as if she were being purposely loud. The rhythm of the bed headboard knocked me awake. The sounds of wood hitting the wall made it hard to concentrate on anything else.

"Ky."

"Harder."

"Yes, fuck me."

Jade sounded like a child who had just learned the word. I felt myself blushing and silently crawled out of bed and opened my door with a steady hand to ensure no creaks were made. The panting was instantly louder. It was as if I were in there with them, watching guilelessly as Ky moved in and out of Jade. Moments later I heard the panting lower; this time it was coming from him. He moved with urgency, his breath a pattern across

my ear's soul. There was something so distinctly animal about his call: he sounded wounded. I could picture his face, a score of painful expressions and an inextricable joy pulsing through his radiating body.

I headed out with the sun that morning. I didn't have work, but I also didn't have any thoughts that didn't concern him. I walked up Wythe, along the bike trail, and watched the skyline move past me. I took every step with an anxiousness that crept through me. I was cautious to look a certain way, because I wanted Ky to happen to see me and feel desire run through his vast and tenuous body.

Every tree, every sign, every car reminded me of him. I walked past a coffee shop and remembered how he had mentioned the coffee served there. Foolishly, I walked in, believing that I could forget about him for a few seconds as I tested the macchiato skills of the pink-haired barista. She said her name was Amber and we talked for a few minutes about the beans. I asked her what was good to eat around here and she mentioned a place on the right, just a few blocks down. "You won't miss it! It has one of those great New York awnings." I saw La Superior a few minutes later and walked in and ordered fish tacos from the waify white girl who served me. She winked at my choices, adding in that they were the best tacos she'd ever had. I smiled absent-mindedly. I wanted a distraction. *Anything.* I was desperate. But he was everywhere, on the grimy walls, on the ugly graffiti art, in every smudge that marked my reality.

I came down the same route back to Ky's. My steps were still cautious, still calculated. I'd force my mind somewhere but it would always move right back to *him.* When I walked into the house he was playing "Please, Please, Please, Let Me Get What I Want." I hated Morrissey and I wanted to groan at the universe's joke. He made no sign that he knew I was in the house, or that he even cared, and I walked up the stairs, sullen. I was frustrated by my loyalty. This man had shown me affection and now I was locked in, unable to muster any thought that didn't concern

him. I went to my room and paced around, hoping something would lift this weight off my chest. Almost maniacal, I opted for a bath. Crumbling what was left of my bubble bar, I prematurely climbed into the bathtub and sat in the lukewarm water with a frown. Waiting for the water to rise around me, I slapped my headphones onto my ears and lay back. The water finally got to the right height and I turned off the tap. Closing my eyes, I tried to transport myself into his thoughts. Was he thinking of me? If he was, why hadn't he come to see me? He could just say hi. That would be enough. Or a smile. He could knock, come in, and just smile. I would fantasize about that hello and smile for days to come and put meaning to the syntax and sound, to the rhythm of his voice. Would there be a hidden message in the pull of his smile? If the left side edged upward, was he trying to tell me that he loved me? *He kissed me. He kissed me. He kissed me.* He put his delicate, swollen pink lips to mine. I felt his eager tongue slide into my mouth, never once overbearing. That meant something. I was transported there again.

"*Taylia!*" A voice behind the music in my ears screamed my name. I didn't know this part of the song. *How odd—how had I never picked that up before?* A hand came out of nowhere, like a wave, and pulled my face up. I woke up and saw Ky kneeling before me. His hands were tightly clasped around my jaw and I was looking back at him. I pulled my headphones off and slowly realized what had happened.

"I—God. Fuck."

He had gotten up and had one hand on his hip and the other resting on the wall. He leaned into his hand and I watched him, groggy. The door was off the hinges.

"Taylia."

I was in the bath.

"What were you doing?"

Naked.

"I was so worried."

I was in the bath, naked.

"I thought you..." His voice trailed off.

Ky had seen my naked body.

He looked at my face again. I wanted him to see me, all of me.

"I thought you..."

I wanted him to touch my puckered skin and love me for all my inadequacies.

"I was just taking a bath," I whispered.

"I was outside and I was calling your name. And you didn't reply... and that got me nervous."

I smiled up at him, but he was looking away.

I wanted to come out of the water and stand there. I wanted him to look over at me and I wanted him to want me. I wanted him to watch me with desire me as I stood in the cold water, my whole body visibly crinkled, and tell me how much he wanted to fuck me.

He was still looking away.

"Ky, I'm fine."

He put his hand through his hair. Looking back past me, respectfully, he said, "Well that's good to know."

All serious, but there was a small hint of a smile at the edges of his mouth. I beamed up at him.

"How have you been?" he asked.

I haven't stopped thinking about you a moment since you've been gone.

"I've been good," I lied.

"Good."

"How was... the funeral?" I felt already stupid, but I knew it had to be on his mind.

"It was as expected."

"So, terrible?"

He made a sound like *hmm*. He had his back to me, and we were in silence for a few moments. I hesitantly moved my legs closer to my seated body, turning myself into a lopsided W

to ensure that I wasn't being completely indecent. He turned around and came closer, crouching with widened eyes.

"Listen, I wanted to ask you something."

"Okay." My heart slowed down just a little bit.

"It's about Jade."

"Oh."

He laughed. "She wants to stay here for a little bit, some nights, you know? Anyway, I said I'd ask you."

"That was nice of you."

"Taylia, I would like an honest reply."

I pulled my knees closer still, feeling chewed up. "It's your place."

"It's *our* place. Oh yes, and our other roommate, Emi, is fine with it."

"Why does she want to move in anyway?"

He sighed. "To look out for me in this 'dire time of need.'"

He sensed my lifted eyebrows.

"Her words, not mine."

"We, as in Emi and I, can look after you."

He rested against the bathroom wall. "I know." He gave me a smile.

"Maybe she just wants to use your body." I looked down; I knew my delivery was off and cringed. I couldn't bear to look at him.

"I wouldn't mind that." He didn't say it with a laugh as I expected him to. I looked up to see him staring at me. Now that we were looking at each other, I watched his mouth move: "I wouldn't mind it at all."

I looked down quickly, a rotation of the stars in my stomach. I felt him get up and walk toward the door. Gesturing to the debris, he croaked, "I guess I'll have to fix this somehow, maybe Emi can finally come in handy." Suddenly awkward, he walked away. The space howled between us.

I stayed in the bluish water, swelling from the moment. Awakened, pulsating like a life-sized artery, the idea of his tongue

moving through my crevices revived me. I felt sanctified like a Byzantine saint, and I was going to listen to my calling. Feeling this buzz, I got up and wrapped the towel around me with a dull fear. I half-heartedly slabbed on some Tahitian monoi body oil. I didn't know where he was, but I was going to find him. I walked toward his bedroom and entered without an invitation, without a knock. He was standing near the window, present. He was my sexual nexus. I moved toward him unabashedly.

"Ky."

He turned around and his eyes focused on mine. I pulled my towel off and stood there in front of him, a child of the sun, the limpid rays infusing me with power. I could feel my bones trembling. He held his breath.

"Ky."

"Yes, Taylia." I could hear it in his voice.

"I want you to..."

He came toward me fast and put his hand on my face. I knew he wanted to know, to make sure, that this—what we were about to do—was what I wanted before we did anything.

"You sure?"

I responded with absoluteness.

We looked at each other for eons before he sunk down and kissed me forcefully. He traced his tongue up my neck and jaw until he was back to my mouth. I felt his warmth envelop me as his tongue danced around mine for a millenia. He pushed me down onto the bed and brought his legs to mine, entwining them together. My hands went up his back that was suddenly bare, up his spine until it led me to his full head of hair, where I felt it move under my skin. He kissed me strongly on the mouth again, exploring every detail, then moved toward my pussy. There was a pause, and I was almost panting, suddenly hungry. I never wanted something as much as I wanted that. He felt perfect, just as I imagined, his tongue a dance, a slow, perfectly slimy beat. He sucked me like mango and got me so wet I could feel it drip down my thighs, sliding down to my crack. He stopped and

raised himself onto his knees, suddenly regal, hovering above me. He opened me up, and my body followed him, and as our torsos met I felt him rising against me. He fumbled and found his way inside. Suddenly we were together, breathless. *No hurt, no bruises.* The provocation of my skin ruptured through my very fibers, but it was dazzling. I was seduced by his rhythms, by his mercurial disposition, as his eyes caught mine, filling me with longing. The animal in me was moving and dancing on my chest, a puppet on a string. The rush I felt squealed against my nerves with pleasure. Just slightly under full consciousness, I lay, being fucked and feeling no edge, no hurt. And I embraced him fully as I felt him again. It was more than I could bear. He surged into me, again and again, watching every bit of tension move through my eyes. Our legs, tangled, and his body gently moving in and out, swaying to the tide of time.

Truth is what you've experienced. It's what you know. In the years of feeling unworthy of love I grew to believe that I was unlovable. My theories were proven and sustained by every bit of mistreatment I'd ever felt. Even Alyssa couldn't do much to dissuade me. *You're overreacting,* she would tell me. Code for: *You're exaggerating.* That's how people gaslight you. They do it in the subtlest of ways, making you doubt your intuition, your knowing. Alyssa had no desire to drive me insane, but sometimes, even I knew she wanted me to shut up and take it. I felt like sometimes even she was bored of me.

After everyone had gone to sleep, sometimes I'd stand in front of the bathroom mirror so long that my whole body would feel numb. Like when you're out in the cold for too long and the feeling overtakes you so much that you can't remember what it felt like to be warm. I'd trace my hands up my thighs and to my stomach. *Je me dégoûte.* I'd say it over and over again. I was afraid to say it in English, some part of me didn't want it to be true. I didn't want the ghosts to hear me say it, and know it, and see it.

I'd stand on the side and pull my stomach in as far as it would go. I reveled when I could see the lines of my rib cage, skin like cheesecloth being pulled over the edges of a rough surface. I was definitely bigger than the girls in the magazines. Dark hair shaded my lower back to my crack, and visible stretch marks bruised my hips like spiderwebs. I had big arms that stuck out and medium-sized, semiround tits that were set far apart from each other, giving them a disproportionate distance. How could anyone ever make love to this body? I felt that deeply, at that time, as my eyes lingered painfully on my tortured unappeal. I knew I would never be desired and loved simultaneously.

Ky was asleep when I woke, so I got up and walked to my room. Unsure of whether anyone could see me stark naked, I moved fast, trying to make no sound. I put on what was closest and plonked down onto the floor. It had happened, it had really happened. Life felt strangely intense, but positive. I looked down at my thighs and found them half unshaven and prickly. Out of laziness I often skipped shaving the backs of my legs or even large anonymous sections of the vast space of my thighs. I put my head to my hands. But shame couldn't fester in my current state. My heartbeat felt large in all the places where the energy was suddenly pumping. I felt embraced by the universe, the furtive voices of my self-disdain weak in the moment. The blood in my face moved with a throbbing madness; the tiny blue vein in my left temple pulsed as I thought of *that* night in waves. That night, with its terror, was like an eruption.

I replayed my sulky, brutalized self, a close-up observation of my agony, as I lay opposite Simon, hoping to be saved even in that moment. In my replay, he was a body with an all-consuming pride. A deathly pallor with an aquiline nose and that deranged gray glare. The overture of the night rung on repeat. But, now, where was I? In this moment, I stood suddenly at the edges of my dreams, soaring. I couldn't believe how the pendulum had swung. That I, a girl who could have felt *that* low, felt good, felt surreal, right now, *right now*. I got up and walked downstairs. I

felt famished. Agitated, I was met in the kitchen with a pile of dirty dishes. So I started washing them, existing for a time in my thoughts.

"Taylia."

I had not heard him come downstairs. He now stood behind me in the kitchen doorway. I had a soapy plate in my hands as he approached me.

He reached down and wiped a bit of foam off my dress, caressing me softly as he did so. I felt scared, anxious, momentarily unaware of myself again and of what to do next. I faced the other way so he couldn't see the questions on my face. I felt him come up from behind. With one hand he took my wrist and turned me to him. Tracing my skin softly, he pressed himself against me. I don't remember how we got upstairs.

Toward the end with Simon, I was bleeding under the loss of myself. And, for a split second there, I thought I saw *the* white light. Frankly, the notion of death, in that moment, seemed comforting. I had toyed with suicide for so much of my life, because anything had to be better than the life I had been dealt, even silence. Like that scene in Amélie where she thinks of all the people crying at her funeral, I felt sorry for myself, of course I did. So, dying felt like a solution, an absolution. As I looked toward the white light, my body bruised like a bashed-up fruit, my vagina blaring hot, hot heat, I felt myself transcend to a time so similar. *Alyssa, I'm coming for you,* I thought, as her breath was suddenly fixed in my pulse. I could feel her; in her moment of dying, she was all adrenaline. She was with me, even my blurred vision could tell. But then, all of a sudden, she was running toward her freedom. Without me.

White light, white light, white light.

I came back to myself. To Simon. But I was alive.

What surprised me about him the most was that he didn't talk about his mother with contempt; he didn't casually slip in

how he dreamed of slaying her while she was on her knees after he'd stabbed her thirty-seven times across the top half of her body. Surely the violence that he had administered to me would be detectable in his voice or the linger of his sneer. There had to be signs. Like a smoker's odor that always reeked through every perfume, the undernotes of tobacco lingering, there must be a way to sense terror in a man.

What was so shocking was that it was obvious, and I *had* always known he was a piece of shit. I had just pretended not to. Simon had an alchemical taste to his aura. The air tasted of steel when he was nearby, stale, like all the air around him trapped. I could see the violence in his eyes, like a glimmer. I just hadn't properly intuited the depth of his ferocity. How was he able to hide the pitless and unappeasable psychopath that lay dormant within him? And was there something wrong with me that it took me so long to recognize it, but really—to fear it?

20.

Kat and I sat in a restaurant near her house in Fort Greene. Beats of music passed through us, sinking us back into our wooden chairs. We had closed the café early that day, deciding on curried rice with saffron and raisins, chakalaka, and mojitos. Kat brought me here, the walls covered with variegated maps of Africa and pop-style portraits of the madiba himself, Nelson Mandela. The guitars hummed while we devoured our food like starved animals, drinking the fresh sweet-and-sour slush that tasted like the booze of a crushed flower. Then we ordered some more, and more.

"I brought some tarot for you *today*, my sweet Taylia."

I was drunkenly thrilled.

"Tarot—to be honest—should be the regular practice of *ev-ory-bo-day*." She sang it, and I joined in. We were drunk.

"I feel you."

"Are you ready for some spiritual praxis, hun?"

"Yes! I am!"

We were both definitely very drunk. She pulled the cards as we sang rhythmed oohs and aahs in response. "Page of Cups!" "Ace of Cups!" When the final card came, she placed it near my left arm and breathed in. "Two of Cups, all cups." My fortune teller gasped, "A suit of all cups, all upright." She paused. "This is quite something."

"Is it?"

"Oh, yah, Tay."

"Okay, okay, tell me!"

"Well, the cups represent emotionality, love... water signs..."

"I'm a Cancer!"

"Yeah, I know—wait, what's Ky?"

"Fuck... I don't know?"

"Okay, find that out, Taylia. Find that out!"

"Okay, okay." My mouth twitched as I repeated, *Ask Ky his birthday. Ask Ky his birthday*, in my mind, blasting it through the coils of my memory center. "Please, what else?"

"Okay, this is all positive. Seriously."

"For?"

"For *lurvve*, my baby."

I was in a trance.

The sky was suddenly luminous, and the screech of cicadas rushed in the late summer heat. A man on a bike went past our window and I watched him zigzag, his safety light blinking like lightning. The moon shone through the park ahead of us and framed the silhouettes of the cars on the street. We were both distracted in unison.

I smiled. "Kat."

"Yes, my love?"

"I feel happy."

She fluttered her eyes, as if she were Samuel Morse himself, mimicking the *tip tap tip tap tip tap* of the first Morse code message. She was now quiet, aureoled—my darling friend. "You're finally seeing what you have to offer this world, my love, and it's pulling you out of your manic, er, cataclysm, or what have you."

"I didn't know... Honestly, I didn't know that I could ever feel like this."

"When you're young everything feels impossible because they're things you haven't experienced before. Then, as you get older, you see that life is worth relishing, and sometimes there are patterns you can almost intuit. The noise dies down after a while, then maybe it picks up again... but sadness, these days, feels far, far away... Another drink?"

I nodded, slowly drifting.

"Just one more, right?"

We both grinned mischievously at each other.

It'd been more than a few months since Kat and Claudia had started dating, and there was an ease in Kat that I mirrored, well not entirely, but it was inspiring to see someone be so relaxed in love.

"Is the whole dating a woman thing hard?"

"Not entirely, like... there's more emotional honesty than before. The sex... is different, maybe more intense than with men. She only dates women, so sometimes I'm worried that I'm disappointing her."

"What? Impossible."

"Girl, it's been a transition. I don't know why being with a woman feels so different, but it does. It feels more weighted, you know? Because this shorthand exists: she understands me better than all the rest, maybe because we're similar. I don't know, but I love her deeper, I feel more aligned with myself than I ever have before. I just feel this intensity consumes me all the time. I don't know..." She slurred her last words. "Am I talking too much?" As confident as Kat could be, she had moments of self-consciousness, especially when she talked about

Claudia. She was giddy, in love. It was sweet, we were both reflections of each other.

"Are you serious? This is all I want to talk about," I assured her.

Kat smiled. "Being in love feels like such a feat."

"You *are* in love..." It was confirmed.

Her eyes lit up brighter as she touched her right incisor with her tongue, a little cheeky. "Maybe."

I watched the golden hour light move along her hands to mine, past my fingers. My body had always felt as if I were trying it on for size, never quite fitting, but now, beneath this honeyed glow that shone across us both, I felt full, thinking of love and its majesty. I grinned, seeing the light of the city change before us.

"How are you finding the job, by the way?" she asked. I liked how she controlled moods. It was her Capricorn nature, she steered things.

"It's good... I don't know if I'll ever have the rapport that you have with the customers. I feel like some of them are bummed out when they see it's me and not you at the counter."

"Well, they can suck it!"

I howled. "No, but seriously, I mean it's about them, but it's also about you, about us, this community you are cultivating. It's made me confront a lot of things about myself."

"Like what?"

"Like my fear of being unlikable."

"I think that's a burden put on all women, Tay."

"Really?"

She smirked.

"What?"

"Sometimes you feel so outta this world. Like, these things that are so simple..."

"You mean basic..."

"Yes." She giggled mercilessly, and I shook my head.

"I mean, I feel naive... most of the time."

"It's a Taylia charm. Because then you're not. Then all of a sudden it's clear you've seen some shit. But, truthfully, I've never met a kid from New York like you, so you're an anomaly."

"I'm not soft..."

"No, you are not. But you're you."

"As are you!"

"We're both unique... Also, is it just me, or does the air taste like champagne?"

We paused and took a moment. There was something about the sky. Just as I looked up toward it, a fleet of birds cuckawed above. There was a serenity to the moment that I didn't want to lose. Something about it reminded me of Dadi-ma.

"You know, you're really the first friend I've made since the death of my grandmother."

There was a beat. Kat, with her unique brand of patience, didn't say anything, almost stubbornly. I knew it annoyed her that she always had to cajole things out of me, and I was trying to be more accountable to my secrecy, to my fears, my anxious awkwardness. So I told her about Dadi-ma. About how this, our relationship, was one of sincere ease and something that I hadn't experienced in my adult life, ever.

Kat told me about the girls she had grown up with in Brooklyn, told me stories of grief as well as stories of generosity and community. That spirit was palpable in everything she did. So she told me about her youth and how much she loved Brooklyn, how there's a certain respect she had for Black people in Brooklyn.

"Honestly, if I could get something for Milk Thistle in BK, dude, are you effing kidding me? I'd get it in a heartbeat. Well, with the help of Ma, but you know, it'd be a worthy investment. The woman was born with a gift." She scratched her chin, in super planning mode. "But, okay, imagine more seating. Imagine a bigger menu—as in not just drinks and pastries. I'm thinking sort of like a nine-to-four eatery, you know, like how the Australians do. Those Australian lunch menus... kimchi fried rice with an egg and shiitakes roasted in bacon fat... I just made that up, but

just these elaborate, beautiful, luscious meals, pouring out with delicacy. I want this to just be good, like runny yolks on a chicken congee. I really want to play, I really want to maybe try and do the real cook thing."

I was incredibly moved, seeing her in her element, when she was linking ideas, inspiration, movements together to create something different. This was an exceptional quality of Kat's. There was a reason Milk Thistle had gotten prime real estate, for quite decent rent, in Manhattan—Kat was doing something invigorating. Yes, she served pastries as well as the highest-grade coffee—inspired by international baristas, using perfectly sourced, truly fair trade beans—but the space was also alive and Zen in a way. I could also see the vision clearly for her future Brooklyn outpost. She was dreaming, and I knew I had to ask her logistical questions to help harness the manifestation.

"Okay, what color walls?"

"A pale pink."

"A garden?"

"Absolutely."

"Ideal location?"

"Near the house. Are you kidding me?"

"Waffles?"

"Yeah, but, like, with buckwheat and a raspberry coulis... and crème fraîche."

"Grits?"

"Yes, but more authentically Cajun with a vinegary avocado side salad to cut the creaminess of the grits."

We continued the back and forth. Eventually tired by our visions, we sat silently, both looking out into the neighborhood. We both felt comfortable in our silences, a habit we had developed in the café, and I thought about how grateful I was for our connection, something that I believed was a true kinship. After a while she told me what was on her mind.

"What we have is so special." She paused. "I benefit from you being just as good a friend as a work companion. You're someone

who can help me through my rough patches, but also my creation period. You've been someone I can lean on privately... and I really appreciate it—"

"You're the same for me." We were psychic. We both smiled at each other, in love.

"I know."

A few days later it was hot, and Ky and I were in a deep, meditative semicoma when we decided to watch a movie, both craving satisfaction through entertainment. Jade had left after dinner last night, which meant she wouldn't be back for a few days. I don't know what had happened to her plans of staying with Ky, and I didn't ask. Besides, she was acting weird. My anxiety was coasting on a low setting, so I didn't care, even though I could tell something was off. I was numbing myself to the situation. I had told myself that it was okay, that I was okay in doing what I was doing, because Ky and I had a special kind of love.

She had looked at me funny the entire time we ate dinner together. Emi had cooked a paella and we were drinking Prosecco. There was so much parsley in the paella, tenderized with the mussels and shrimp, it was perfect. But, as we all ate, basically the entire time Jade's eyes scratched at me. Did she know something? It didn't matter; after dinner, she decided to leave, and I was relieved and excited to watch her go. I was going to fuck her boyfriend. It felt terrible to admit it to myself, so I danced around it. Ky and I had a connection, it was true. We still hadn't fully addressed what was happening, but we both knew *it was happening*. Our chemistry was rude. It was so greedy and lustful, but we hid it well. Both playing the part. Whether Jade knew it or not (which I momentarily felt bad for), she decided to leave us easily caught in each other's grasp. Now, after fucking three times in a row, Ky nominated watching *In the Mood for Love* by one of his favorite directors. I acquiesced, feeling paralyzed by the heat, and my plump pussy needed rest. By the end, I was marooned

in this tale of love, loss, and regret. The music held me for the whole damn movie, and those beautiful swaying hips of Maggie Cheung were intoxicating. But the end left me gutted, my skin tracked with tears. As the credits rolled, Ky spoke. "Thoughts?"

I felt hollow. "What does it mean to you?"

He was silent for a few seconds. "I guess, to me, it showcases life."

"How?"

"Well, the characters are complex, and in the end none of them get what they want."

I sat, numb from the words. "And that's life to you?"

"Well, yeah."

"That just sounds so sad."

He smirked. "Life is sad, Tay."

I knew this was true. Of course I knew it was true, my entire life had been a questionable mix of painful events. Even then, I hoped for something more, for something to be better.

"What did you think of it?"

"I fucking loved it."

He smirked.

"No, I did. I thought it was a beautiful love story, but..."

"But they're never together."

"Yeah, well, that part sucked. But they had love!"

"That's it? They had love? That's enough for you now?"

I looked over at him, disheartened. If he didn't believe in happiness, did that mean that he would never be happy with me? I mistook Ky for someone who believed that things could be better. Now, I felt consumed by a black surf. I felt fooled, suddenly sunken.

"What's going on in there?"

He was trying to be sweet, trying to lighten the mood. But I just shrugged. I felt scared to talk, afraid that my vulnerability would scream in the break of my voice.

"Life is sad, but still, sometimes there are extreme moments of serenity that make these shit lapses in time bearable. You

know?" he said, trying to salvage the moment, but suddenly, again, I felt brandished with the truth. I wasn't ready.

"One day I want to be happy." I said it with desperation again: "One day I want to be happy."

He looked hurt, like he was a parent telling his child the inevitable truths of the world. "Okay?"

It wasn't the answer I wanted to hear. Was it even an answer? I wanted to hear him say that I would one day be happy. That he would be the one to make me happy. That no matter what, he would try to do whatever he could in his power to make me happy.

"I can't."

It was as if he read my mind. "What?"

"I can't, Taylia."

"You can't what?"

"Do what you want me to do for you."

I felt halved in two.

"It doesn't mean that I don't care. But I can't do that for you."

I was hardly listening anymore. There was a ring in my ears.

We hadn't yet talked about it, but because he hadn't broken up with Jade, it became increasingly difficult to force the conversation about our relationship in any direction toward permanency or stability. At this point, his cavalier-ness had become a trigger point for me. I craved stability, like one craved fur coats. For me, stability was a declaration of something, a hymn of one's purpose. I didn't like the feeling of uncertainty anymore. I had spent too much of life living in that space. Now my heart felt creased, signaling weak arteries. I wanted permanence, goddamn it. I wanted to feel stable. At least, in one place in my life, I wanted to feel settled.

I assumed he felt nervous, and a little guilty, too. About the turn of events, and how this implicated the both of us. But I felt guilty, too. I knew Jade sensed something, and I knew that's why she had been so judgmental of me in the first place. Maybe she had been trusting her gut. It wasn't fair, but if she only knew

how much I dreaded facing myself each day. How, as time passed, that feeling had lessened, but that it was still a stubborn oak, with branches and roots right into the very depths of my heart, lodged in between my veins and flesh. If she only knew how much I had hated myself my whole life. How this was a response to that, too. She had just been in the cross fire, and I just wanted something to work out for me. For once. And, as much as doing this behind her back wasn't making me feel like a good person, it was making me feel desired. But I despised being a secret and blamed her for it. The cabin fever was setting in, costuming every emotion with a terrible feeling of simultaneous dread and sadness.

Dadi-ji had a thin, stark face and once told me, in between stagnant puffs of a cinnamon-colored cigar (like father, like son), that every man is on earth not just to exist, but to live. I remember him sitting in a "chair of ugly comfort" (as Mama would call them) against the washed-out wall. Kolkata walls looked tea stained, tapestries of brown-and-gray watercolors. In my memory, Dadi-ji sat and just continued to smoke. He died a few years after Dadi-ma, but we didn't go back to Kolkata as a family, just Baba. When he returned he had shaved all of his hair. He looked so weak, so lifeless—deflated, I assumed, from the sadness of losing both your parents.

There was a time in my life when I thought that living and existing were the same thing. Two plus two equals life. But as you grow older, or wiser, or maybe both, you start noticing the nuances between living and existing. I thought that once I met someone like Ky—a man to save me from myself—my life would have meaning. Pure, striking, pulsating meaning. I'd have purpose. Better yet, I'd be exempt from suffering, from my all-encompassing, boring pain. I was naive to think that being happy meant the absence of misery, because, well, it doesn't. Our next-door neighbors' youngest daughter, Maddie, died when

she was twenty-seven years old from a tumor the size of a Milk Dud lodged lumpy in her left lung. Diagnosed at twenty-five, she was dead two years later. The cancer ate her away, drifting her in and out of a semicoma in the last stages, distilling her body down to dusty sediment, like a sponge drying out in the sun. Her mother came by crying in variegated fits during the chemo, then through remission. By the time of her death, her mother's tears were more stunted; the misery had been subdued through its continuity, the heart striated by the agonizing dullness of repetition.

When I was younger, I envied Maddie. Even Alyssa was in awe of her. A summa cum laude graduate from Yale, she was an older girl with a tepid coolness that white girls with money from New York often had. She looked like Bijou Phillips and wore Missoni prints with a sense of fashionable ease. Maddie's parents were fiercely proud. But the coolest part of her life (or the thing I most envied) was that she had a college sweetheart, Matthew, whom she lived with.

He had bought them a two-bedroom apartment in the West Village with his inheritance three years into their relationship, filling it with midcentury furniture to Maddie's liking. It had a second bedroom that she used for writing, overlooking a diamond-shaped courtyard in the middle. It felt like a hacienda, misplaced for New York, but misplaced in a good way. I saw it all on Facebook.

I imagined she enjoyed the way the skinny, leafless trees shook in this courtyard during the fall's wind, how they muttered secrets to her as the seasons changed. On weekends Matthew and Maddie would sleep in together, *New Yorker*s stacked on their respective bedside tables. Matthew would make coffee in their stovetop Bialetti, pouring almond milk in his cup from a refrigerated mason jar, distilled out of a batch he made earlier that week with their trusty Vitamix. Sometimes they would promenade like real locals up to Chelsea Market and pick up bottles of cold milk from Ronnybrook (which Maddie preferred

in her coffee, using the glass bottles to hold tulips around the house afterward) and fresh loaves from Amy's Bread for the week ahead. They would walk past the traffic toward their home that they had built together, past the billboard of lifeless Calvin Klein models, and talk about their future children, about new restaurants they had to try; they were happy.

But none of the projected dreams came true. Maddie died against the backdrop of a pale dawn in the hands of Matthew, who no longer had anything to live for. I wondered if people would recall Alyssa's life like that.

21.

Alyssa's face was once alive, expressive.

It was almost spring, and she was smiling at the effervescent sun. Her eyes crinkled at the sides; I knew it was hurting her to look at the brightness with that much intensity, but she wanted to. She wanted to convince herself of her mind's perfected drama.

"Look at that cloud."

I followed her fingers to a large, slightly ominous off-white mass. "It's so big!"

She wasn't listening; she ran off, chasing. "You can almost fool yourself into thinking that you're spinning the speed of a thousand miles and circumventing the sun."

She had run so far ahead that I could only just make her out in the distance. The wind moved through her like a snake.

"What?" I yelled.

We were upstate again. This was one of the happy times, just before she changed. I remember the before and after so clearly. How there once used to be a charming ease to her. But when she

realized she was beautiful she did what a lot of pretty girls end up doing. She punished herself for the sin of beauty.

It was the summer solstice and the tilt of the planet's semiaxis caused the back of my shirt to dampen. The air was dulcet and warm, and I was peeling an orange, the light citrus blending and wafting through the space between Emi and me like a live spritzer.

I broke our cave of silence. "Does Ky ever talk about me to you?"

There was a spark in Emi's eyes that contained a deep, unnameable something I couldn't quite place, but it was very palpable. "Oh, this game?"

"I'm not playing games..."

"Hmm."

"No, seriously, I'm just asking."

"Oh, *okaaaaay*." He sipped on his grappa, a pure distillation of grape pips. My mind wandered to when I was a child and I asked Baba, "If I swallowed a seed and some soil, could I grow grapes in my tummy?"

"I sometimes wonder..."

"Wonder?"

"What he thinks about me."

"Well, I think it's pretty obvious."

"Obvious, how?"

He paused and bit his lip. I could sense him slowing down, the energy palpably shifted. I started to feel nervous, like I sometimes did as a child when I could intuit Mama's or Baba's anger like an electric shock in my body, pulsating on a low sedateness. For a few seconds, I was aghast, not knowing how I should broach him, but he finally answered.

"Have y'all told Jade anything yet?"

I felt slapped across the face, but I also knew I had no right to. "I... don't think he has..." I stumbled in half words. Though,

it was also *the truth*. I rarely wanted to bring it up with Ky, and I could sense and understand Emi's frustration, now that I could finally place it.

"I obviously don't want to overstep, Taylia. Kynan is his own person. He's a grown-ass man, so I'm not gonna give advice. But I think it's shitty to Jade, if I'm gonna be honest..."

He paused. "I don't think I ever told you what happened with my ex, but, basically"—he took a deep sigh—"she cheated on me. And Ky knows that, so it's weird to sort of witness it on this end. And, okay, Jade is a hard one to like immediately. But she's really fucking nice when you get to know her... Ky wouldn't be dating her otherwise. Or dated, or whatever the fuck you're doing... Like, is this a throuple, are y'all in an open relationship?" He paused again. "Okay, and I really, really mean it—no judgment—but I can't help but relate to Jade, and nobody deserves this. Okay, maybe All Lives Matter people deserve this shit, but, like, ordinary nonracist nonshitty people don't! It's dishonest and disrespectful to everyone involved."

I inhaled, knowing what he was saying was true, and it was hard to deny it. "I know. I agree, and I'm sorry."

He groaned. "Don't apologize to me! Figure it out with Ky, though. Before it hurts Jade more than it already will." Immediately after saying this, he threw down about two fingers of grappa, refilling the glass again. I could tell he was in pain. I could tell he resented having to tell me this.

"I'm sorta doing things I'd never imagined I'd ever do," I muttered, embarrassed. I wanted to tell him I felt ashamed, but also resisted being too vulnerable with him. There was a part of me, if I'm being honest, that felt adult to be in this situation. It felt gratifying to be in a position of some kind of power. I felt crazy, because inside of me existed a duality. I knew how unfair I was being—but maybe there was a part of me that felt justified. I deserved this. I deserved love after the life I had led. I knew that wasn't something to voice to Emi, he wouldn't understand. There was something so boyish to him, and it annoyed me. Ky had it,

too, at times. But Emi felt like a big, goofy idiot, guileless and gullible. I didn't respect him. I didn't know why. Maybe I was just witnessing him at a time in his life when he was removed from his best self, bloated in pain, and I found that quite weak and boring and was unsympathetic toward his turbulent emotions, and clearly his latent drug and alcohol abuse. In this moment, however, I paid attention, maybe because some part of me wished to be scolded. I wasn't sure.

"I mean, listen... I know Ky isn't a bad guy. He's my best friend..." He trailed off. "And I don't think you are, either, Taylia."

A voice came out of nowhere. "Yo, Emi. What's going on?"

We both swiveled toward the sound. It was Ky. The music froze dramatically, the Leonard Cohen record skipping on the last beat again and again and again. Emi threw back his head, this time sharply, gulping down the rest of the grappa. By the time I watched him take his second swallow I felt water standing in my eyes. I looked toward Ky but couldn't discern his full face, so I stared past him, toward the world I had dreamed up between us. He came toward me and paused.

"I'm sorry, man, I'm just being real." Emi took the bottle of grappa, with its bold blue Romanesque label, preparing for something.

"Dude, don't you think it's kinda whack that you're dragging Taylia into this?"

I felt like I was being wrapped in a heavy, itchy shroud. My breathing was quiet with a dull fear laced with excitement.

"Nah, man, it's the both of you... right? Two people in a relationship..."

"Yeah, okay, but I don't think Taylia deserves this, especially not from you. As much as I do, maybe..."

"Maybe? Okay, look, I'm not trying to be a dick. And I'm sorry, Taylia."

I shrugged.

"It just is alarming to me. That's all! And I think Jade oughta know."

Alanis Morissette played in my ear, I was distracted. I looked at Ky: he was in pain.

"I mean, I'm not disputing that. I'm just saying that you're coming for the wrong person."

"Okay, fair. My bad..."

I remained silent, detached.

Ky exhaled. "For what it's worth, this is not my proudest moment and I think of it all the time. It's just... it's hard." He paused for an eternity, then turned to me: "If I'm being honest, I don't know what to do." He paused again. "I don't know what to say, but I feel like I have to say the truth."

I was back in my body, but this time I felt so sad. He came to face me, searching for a light in my face, an entry point.

"I guess I'm having a hard time figuring out what I want..."

I guess I had also known this. Kat had said something to me about customers being predictable. It was a metaphor.

I heard him speak. "I'm not trying to say I don't want this. I do, but it's complicated. I was in a long-term relationship with someone. I absolutely thought Jade and I would be together for a long time... then you came into the picture, Taylia... and something shifted. I started wanting you in a way I no longer wanted Jade. Which is so unfair to her. But that's what happened. You and I fell in love, and who's to say that won't happen again and again?"

Emi pulled the air through his teeth. "Come on, bro, now you're just being selfish."

"I'm... I'm just trying to be honest. All I'm saying is this isn't easy for me!"

"Ky... truthfully"—Emi's words were comedically slurred— "you're being a dick, man."

It felt like that was my cue to exit. I had wanted to leave for a while but couldn't move, and now a sob kicked into my chest. I muttered an excuse and scuttled upstairs. Neither of them tried to stop me, which was a relief. This whole interaction was involuntarily thrust on to me, and I needed to process it. For myself.

That night we didn't make love. When Jade wasn't here, we'd sleep in my room, which should have been a sign. I respected Jade for knowing something felt off and avoiding it. She had class, she was giving it time. Maybe she was giving us time for reflection, to compose ourselves. We were all cowards, but I blamed Ky for his hallucinating inaction.

The moon shone through the curtains. I couldn't sleep. At a certain point in the night he curled up behind me but soon pulled away, my body frigid to his touch. Something felt off, suspended and frozen. I couldn't do this kind of instability again. Had I come so far only to be treated like dirt, *again*? To not be chosen, *again*? I felt like a turd on the side of the road, but unlike the other times I had felt this suffocating feeling, now I was alive. No longer a dead intention. I changed when I walked out of my parents' house. I had started betting on myself.

When I woke up, breakfast was beside me with a note that read, *I love you*. I kept running it through my head, hoping to settle my nerves, but instead I was distracted by the repetition of the word *jinn* in my mind, which in Arabic meant "hidden from sight." A word I had found researching the real meaning of *jihad*. What was opaque to me, hidden in sight? What had me arrested in motion? *I love you?* I called bullshit. Why now? I was traveling on my Möbius strip of thoughts. *I love you...* Ky had once said to me those were just words. It was everything else that counts.

With psycho-spiritual clockwork, Kat brought up Jade as well the next night. I was over for dinner. Claudia, whom I was meeting for the first time, was making ragout de truffles accompanied with pommes dauphinoise, delicacies she learned living in France. She poured a Crémant du Jura into a sleek, chandelier-like glass as an aperitif for both Kat and me. I watched the way Claudia looked at Kat, even while cooking, like Kat was her compass. Wearing a face of readied hunger and also constant

awe, she looked like she knew she was so lucky to have the woman of her dreams. And she was.

"I made something very simple, I hope you don't mind," she said. Her hands were delicate, lined with veins like my mother's. I could understand why Kat was attracted to her. Like a vortex, she was so embodied that she had a gravitational pull. It's a strange quality, but it was in the way she calmly arranged the plates onto the table, using silverware like a frame. She had a presence. I think I was forming a tiny crush.

As we all inhaled the food, sipping on a wonderful, cloudy, appley pét-nat from Portland, Kat asked me, gently, "Babe. I've been thinking about this for a while... What's going on with Jade?"

Maybe I had expected it, so I felt ready. "I don't know, I—"

Claudia interjected. "Wait, who's Jade?"

"Honey, let her speak..."

Claudia nodded, and they both looked at me, an audience.

"No pressure, LOL." I was trying to deflect hard, looking at Claudia, embarrassed by her inevitable judgment, any by handsome she was. "Ky's been cheating on his girlfriend, Jade, with me."

I felt like shit. I had intuited right, I could see Kat was trying to lessen the blow to Claudia, who seemed unnerved.

"Baby, it's complicated," she said, protecting me.

"How?" Claudia wasn't having it.

Kat looked at me, probing me to explain.

"I... I don't know, it's not like I ever thought I'd do this to someone. It's not like I get turned on by breaking up relationships. Ky and I... it's different." I guess I had never tried explaining it to anybody. "We're just really compatible. Our intensity matches the other's, which is a big one for me. I've never really met anyone that could face me with that feeling." I guess that was it, Ky could hold me. He had the capacity, the want to. Ever since the beginning of our relationship he had made such space, and I realized that's what bonded us. This awe-inspiring feeling we both felt around each other, or at least what I felt around him.

"But... Taylia, men who cheat are unreliable. It's simple."

I felt slapped.

"Okay, Claud, wait a second. Frankly, T—I like Ky. I really do. I don't think I would be so supportive of you if I didn't. I liked his brother, Roman, too. Clearly they were raised right. And to be completely honest, Ky is hot, and I think you guys are good together. And, so, I'm excited for what's to come. Because, and I really believe this, no matter what happens between you two, this is an important milestone for you to go through. It's an important transition to usher you into the next part of your life. That much is clear to me."

I looked at her, astounded, because I had been feeling that so much recently myself. It was as if she had the articulation in language that I understood abstractly. I agreed profusely, and she paused, gathering her thoughts,

"I know it's complicated, because nobody deserves this, so I'm sympathetic to Jade. But, over these last few months, you've really helped me understand Elijah, if I'm being honest."

Claudia held Kat's hand gently as she talked and tears began to stream. I moved closer to her in my chair, wanting all of a sudden to cocoon her, and so Claudia and I both held her at each side.

"I think it's easy to fall into narratives of people. And if someone's hurt you, then it's easy to replicate that." She paused, turning to Claudia. "My love, it took me such a long time to trust you. I trust easily in my life for most things—I mean, I'm not an idiot, I'm obviously psychic af —but I haven't always been lucky in love and the wound is deep."

She started to cry now, stuttering. Claudia and I shielded her more, wanting to make a haven for her to let it all out.

"But, my God, did I feel so fucking low when he left. I was in disbelief. Just pure effing disbelief. I couldn't believe this man I built this home with didn't want me anymore. And the hardest, hardest, *hardest* part was that I don't really blame him. It got too hard, we just were compatible to a certain point, but that's it, and

we had surpassed that marker. We just didn't want to admit it to each other, because it's not as if we hadn't both tried to salvage what we had, but it just wasn't working, and it's been easier to believe he was Voldemort than to see his perspective. He was a good man, but he was just a weak, indulgent man. He didn't know how to stand up for me, or us, and he grew lazy. But a lot of people grow lazy in love. And that's the problem. But for a long time he was good, and he loved me. It's taken me a long time to see it, and, Tay, truthfully I wouldn't have been able to have this kind of compassion if you weren't in this situation. Because seeing it from your side, and seeing your naïveté and maybe tenderness, made me see how complicated any given situation is. Honestly, so thank you. You've given me clarity. You've made me remember that people are complicated."

I was in shock. "Kat..." I started pulsing her hand, my full face on her chest, resting against her collarbone.

"Thank you for sharing that, my love," Claudia said, kissing her on the cheek, then on the mouth. Their love was so wholesome, so pure. "I guess I don't get it, but I get it... if that makes sense. Clearly, Taylia, I don't know the specifics and I'm sure it's much more complicated... as most interpersonal relationships are. I didn't mean to be judgmental."

I felt floaty and so held. "Thank you. But you were just being honest, and I get it." I smiled. "It's not been an easy road, because I know I'm in the wrong. I don't feel good about it most of the time, and I don't know if I ever will, until he tells her. And then I'll still feel like shit because I will have hurt her." That was the truth. But then some part of me lingered; that's when the anxiety started, and I felt restless. *Would he tell her? What if he never told her?* I felt suddenly panicked, but unwilling to share it with Kat and Claudia. I didn't want to ruin their night, this beautiful night.

"Anyway, it's a lot. Let's talk about something else..."

So I changed the subject and steered things in another direction.

The next morning, back at Ky's, I walked outside and watched the puffs of milky white move leisurely across the sky. I was thinking about the conversation from the night before and the anxiety I had felt, wondering if Ky would ever tell Jade. I hadn't been the same around him since Emi's outburst, and it was as if he was being cautious. Alert. I thought he had been writing, but I felt him come up behind me, curious but also mildly suffocating.

"What are you doing?"

"I'm watching the clouds."

"Just in case?" He mirrored my gaze. "I think there's one that looks like Bowie!"

I laughed despite my nervous mood, playing along momentarily. "Where?"

"There." He pointed at one that resembled no part of David Bowie.

"He's singing 'Velvet Goldmine.' Look, he's got the microphone to his face!"

Ky anticipated a laugh. I myself was expecting a laugh to come out. I waited for it to rise in my chest, but my mouth hurt at the crease and I didn't want to stretch the sides of my pitiful emotions and deflating self-worth.

"You okay there, kiddo?"

"Sure am."

"You're not overworking that pretty head, are you?"

"You mean with thoughts?"

It was supposed to be funny. We had fallen into a comedy routine in our daily banter. But today one member was slightly off; the show would not go on. My voice broke, and I ended up sounding sad rather than sassy. He picked up on it but stayed silent.

We stood together for a while, both in our worlds of imagination. I wanted to say what I wanted to say, but I couldn't. There were too many outcomes and answers that I was not ready to face. Not yet, anyway.

"What are you thinking about?"

I'm ten days late for my period. I'm ten days late for my period. I'm ten days late for my period. Fuck, fuck, fuck, fuck, fuck.

He suddenly seemed very far from me. My poker face was secure, but I felt like a mockery of myself. There was no suspicion in his face, but he knew I was blatantly lying. He could hear the echoes of my weariness play in the silence. Sorrow had become me, but the tension was unspeakable. Besides, I would deny everything. *Deny, deny, deny.*

Eventually, he smiled and kissed me on my forehead. "You mean the world to me."

As he walked away, I heard him hum "Sorrow."

In Arabic, etymologically, the word for fetus comes from *jinn.*

The next day there was a peculiar sense of metamorphosis. I had awoken that day tender, in tears. My mind was a labyrinthine explanation of terror. I had once heard that a lot of women don't generally know, but for me it was an intrinsic knowing. Like when you can taste the rain in the air and the clouds bloom and rise and the darkness embellishes the sky. The water pours only seconds after you realize it's going to gush and then it does, washing the bad away. Just like that, there was a shift. I felt a pull in my lower abdomen, like the hands of a ghost pulling at my womb. There was a distinguishable heaviness as a tangible weight began to crawl inside of me. The baby's soul was inhabiting my insides. I didn't react. I just numbed myself to the point that I was no longer exerting anything. No energy, no thoughts. I was just *overcome* with stillness.

We were so young. And Ky was still so dumb. I didn't know so much that I wanted to learn. Like ikebana and playing the guitar. I wanted to be able to say that I ran every day, to be fit and not have to hide my thighs, to be proud of my body. I wanted to be really good at chess and do crosswords and listen to Bach and not forget to take (or buy) my iron supplements. These were all things that I still wanted to do, to learn how to do. I wasn't ready for this.

The reality struck me and caused me to halt.

I wasn't ready for *this*.

The moment I knew for sure I was pregnant, just a few days later, the air was dense like liquid. I felt the tears I was crying evaporate into the air and hollow me out like a cave. My tears, my sweat, were rising to the surface and I was drying out like clay. I felt so low. I felt as if an energy had overtaken me and now controlled me. I was no longer Taylia. I was at the whim of the universe now. I was weak, I was nothing. *Me, have a baby? I couldn't even face myself.*

I walked past the cars with my headphones on. I was listening to *Figure 8* accidentally, and as I walked underneath the Williamsburg Bridge, "Everything Means Nothing to Me" came on. I smiled at the irony, at that little Spotify sign. I was in a lake of my own misery, but the song was pulling me through, sinuously, for two minutes and twenty-four seconds. When it stopped, I was in reality once more. My legs felt like stilts, pieces of bark, coarse in their fear of the unknown.

I walked onto Broadway, past the Marcy Avenue stop, and kept walking.

Finally, I reached my impending doom. I saw the stairs to the doctor's office and could already taste the metal against my tongue. I hadn't trusted the two take-home tests I had done a few days earlier. Those little plus signs meant nothing to me. Those stupid pink plastic pieces of shit meant nothing to me. I needed someone to shake me and scream at me and tell me, YOU ARE PREGNANT. Even though I knew I was, I still needed to hear it. I needed someone to know what I needed to do. I needed someone to ask all the right questions like, *What the fuck are you going to do?*

The office was busy with women with children, women with no children, and women who were very obviously about to have children. I swiped at my tears with the back of my hand.

"Taylia Chatterjee?"

I looked up as a pretty woman gestured me into a room. I felt slightly embarrassed that she was clearly South Asian, but some part of me wanted to be ruthless. I couldn't care right now.

"Hi, Taylia, I'm Dr. Kumar, nice to meet you. Please sit down."

"Okay." I looked at the floor and there were vacuum marks on the carpet.

"So, what can I do for you today?"

"I'm pregnant." I blurted it out in the hope that if I did the baby would miraculously leave me. *Then I would be free.*

"Okay."

"Am I pregnant?"

"I thought you just said..."

"I did the tests—you know, the take-home ones. I bought the packet with two of them in it, just in case, you know, and it was like, I don't know... like twenty bucks or something. It was from Duane Reade. I don't think that's really a reputable source for someone to tell you that you're pregnant, don't you think?"

"You mean *Duane Reade*?"

I nodded.

"Well, Taylia, they're formulated tests and they're pretty accurate. What did the test say?"

"Tests, I did both of them."

"Okay, well, what did these tests say?"

"They said that I was pregnant." I started to fully cry.

She passed me some tissues. I didn't want her to judge me, I was scared of that.

"Listen, it's okay, Taylia..."

I stopped listening. I looked toward the window. It was slightly ajar, and I could see the Williamsburg Bridge and that gigantic white savings bank. There seemed to be a thin screen blockading me from out there. I knew, by just looking at it, that there would be no issue to break it. I could catapult out the window like in the movies. I could play a song in my head to make it easier. *She's like the wind...* I'd fly out, pretending like I was in the arms of Patrick Swayze, limbs flailing unnecessarily, my heart in my chest, and a fetus I would never know in my body.

"Taylia. I know what you're going through is difficult, trust me, I know. Unplanned pregnancies are always hard, and I'm

guessing by your reaction that this was unplanned... You really need to figure out what exactly it is that you want to do from this point onward. You need to make a decision as to whether you'd like to keep this baby, or... not. Have you thought any of this through already?"

I was silent.

"Do you have a partner, or..."

He's going to leave you, Taylia.

He's going to leave you.

He's going to leave you and your sorry ass, and then you're going to have to look after your good-for-nothing baby by yourself.

"I..."

"...or family?"

They already left you.

"No."

Why do we ever do anything? Something always pushes us to the answers. But what are those answers, really? They're nothing of substance, right? In the larger detail of our lives, the decisions that we make are nothing more than that. Decisions that we made.

Made, past tense.

They're not the puzzle pieces forming together, or the corners that we cut in the maze to come to some realization. When we were younger, Alyssa loved watching *Labyrinth.* She was probably thirteen or so when she said that the labyrinth Sarah moved through symbolized human life. She sounded so smart to me then. But I realize now that she wasn't. And it doesn't. Life is random, with no meaning, no purpose, and definitely no point.

He was going to leave me. He was going to leave me and not Jade. He was going to leave me like my parents had. He was going to leave me. I was almost certain that he would.

So. I left him first.

22.

I walked from the doctor's office (equipped with my JanSport backpack, I had come prepared) to the café and sat there as Arnold and Elliott, and all our other regulars, came and went, sipping espresso, discussing books and articles by Ta-Nehisi Coates. A day earlier Kat and I had talked about the politics of being the neighborhood friendly Black woman and the psychological impact of being nice to white people all the time. It made me defensive of her as I watched Elliott and Arnold talk about *Between the World and Me* like these white men truly understood and actually wanted to unlearn the smearing unjustness of white privilege. That madness was a good way for me to temper the insanity I felt.

I struggled with the whiteness that lay dormant in me, and it was something that I didn't want to talk to Kat about. I guess I was embarrassed. Embarrassed by a lot of things, like how little I really knew, but also the overwhelming fear of facing racism in America in a way that was beyond theoretical. I wanted to be a person who could stand by my politics; I didn't want to be like my parents who had grown frail and ugly. I also didn't want to lean on her, even though I knew I would, and I preemptively felt shitty about having needs and not knowing who else to turn to. I focused on that thought—a loop, a complete distraction—and maybe it was a way for me to feel sad without acknowledging the real root of my sadness. I couldn't let the fear of leaving him overtake me. I had to be strong. For this baby, for me.

I could tell Kat sensed something was off; she kept looking at me with thin, concerned lips, but I avoided her stare. Taking orders, boxing pastries, I remained steadfastly particular, focusing on the details. But inside I felt like a madwoman. I felt fucking uncontained.

When the lull of the day came she asked me what was wrong.

"I'm pregnant," I said, looking away, focusing on the inviolability of motherhood, this deep moon inside of me that was growing like a bean. I tried to meditate on Kat's impressive poise.

She embraced me. "Oh, baby" was all she said, letting my face fall to her chest as I disappeared from the world momentarily like a quiet ghost.

Some part of Kat understood that there was a dark underbelly of my life that I was not ready to share. A puddle of black ink hovered over me, and even just a brush of a fingertip could be transformed into my hurt. So I avoided it. She understood the volatility and knew I couldn't afford that kind of interference, not now, not in this state. So she propped my spirits up with her love. She didn't ask questions. When I asked her if I could come and stay with her again, she nodded silently, maybe slightly afraid of me or for me. Or both.

From the very beginning there were endless hours when she would stay up late, massaging my back with her deftly soothing fingers. I'd wake up sometimes, my sheets and my body succored with Tiger Balm, tingling slightly. A trace of a faint smile would sometimes peek through the cracks, giving me an awareness that I was alive and that that, at the very least, was something.

I woke up, uncomfortable in the position I had been sleeping in. The clock showed the time: 6:56 A.M. As I looked around my darkened room, the same one I had stayed in before, my eyes adjusted to the shapes. Kat had taste, so the spare bedroom was nice, with heirlooms and linen, and even the ceiling, with its expansive crown molding, felt comforting. I was reminded of Kolkata, of sleeping next to Dadi-ma during her daytime nap. We wouldn't use the mosquito net then, so I'd stare at the ceiling, an archipelago of stains and leaks, of muddy water lines, as she snored. As I remembered her, a glimmer of light seeped through the shutters, outlining some objects on my nightstand. The hit of the early-morning rays in the room at Kat's made everything look ominous, creating shadowed illusions on the walls. I made

out the round curve of a big leather chair, an Alvar Aalto stool. I felt greedy, I felt lacking, in Kat's home. There was an incredible void that I needed to fill, and nothing fit, nothing was the right size. I wasn't quite showing yet, which only continued to breed a fickle uneasiness right through the very bones of my body. I was beginning to face myself.

I sat in bed for a while, my thoughts pushing me into an alternate reality. I had one daydream that I would replay in my head until I was satisfied. It involved Ky. It was a reality that I knew would never exist, and yet I continued to dream it, hoping that one day, soon, it—the dream—would be enough for me. I moved myself over to the armchair and lulled myself into my fantasy. The horizon peeked through the clouds, and I witnessed another beginning without his presence, without his comfort.

"Hey, you're up." Kat stood at the doorway.

"Yeah." I forced a smile.

I wanted to say, *Do you hate me? Do you hate how much space I'm taking up in your already busy life?* But I didn't say anything.

"How are you feeling?" she asked. "No headaches?"

"No headaches," I said.

"Hungry?"

"Sure am."

I got up and followed her to the kitchen and immediately looked at the microwave clock:

7:37.

Luc entered the kitchen. "Oh, you're up today," he said with surprise.

Next it was Isaac. He looked at me happily but kept his distance.

"What's wrong, Isaac? Come here." I gestured him toward me. He ran, halting at my feet, and looked cautiously over to see if his mother had seen him run. She hadn't. He relaxed his tiny bony shoulders, like a small bird, and grinned up at me. I brought my fingers to my lips and mimed *ssh*. He smiled and nodded.

"So what are you going to be doing today, dear Taylia?" Kat asked, passing me some eggs and day-old lavender polenta cake with homemade clotted cream.

"I'm gonna watch daytime television."

She smirked. "Sounds exciting."

"Television has a life of its own, Kat."

"Evidently... I mean, arguably, everything has a life of its own." She smiled, knowing something, taking a pause. "I've got a new crew member coming in today!"

In my absence, Kat had hired a new employee. I was glad that the pressure of performing was gone. It also meant that she was beginning to slowly, ever so slowly, start to rely on others. To ask for help, instead of putting too much on herself. I knew that, after me, Kat had realized she could afford to slow it down, to meet Claudia for lunch at Balthazar or catch a matinee at the Angelika. Before my very eyes I was seeing her resistance to life a little bit less and her floating in the feeling of abundance. It was extraordinary to watch her and Claudia bond, too. For their heads to sometimes lean on each other as they read their different newspapers together in the morning, after nights when Claudia had slept over. Or massage each other's feet as they watched TV with the boys and me, us all one big random-ass family. Claudia would bring by natural wines (her new favorite find) and lavish Kat with gifts: Palestinian za'atar, the book *In Praise of Shadows*, and a multicolored hexagonal pepper grinder. It was like they had memorized and rehearsed each other's love languages to a T. She reminded me of Roman, which made me think of Ky.

Kat never made me feel like I was in her way, but there were moments I felt it. I felt uncomfortable that I was there, just lingering. Like a disease, or a bacteria sitting, innocuous. My fat blooming body blazing from heat, deliriously eating food and demanding attention. I felt ashamed. To accept and embrace the love somebody gives you was half the battle. I knew both Kat and I were learning how to do that with each other, so that we could learn to do it with others, too.

In the mornings, depending on our interactions, Kat would sometimes pull one tarot card for herself, for us. Today she pulled the Magician, winking as she slid it in front of me. I googled the card and the explanations were littered with positive messages like "new beginnings" and "great expectations." I hummed a soft tune. The air had the intoxication of tuberose, an incense that Kat would light in the mornings. All of a sudden, I felt pink, I felt luminous, and in that moment I sat, calm. I turned on the TV and watched back-to-back episodes of *Love and Hip Hop: Atlanta*. The day felt inspiring.

23.

It happened on a gloomy day where the rain stuck on the windows like pristine, clear goop, crystal bindis in a row, teardrops, symmetrical. Kat was off at work, and the boys were at their grandmama's. I remember, because I was attempting to read Kat's copy of Bertrand Russell's *The Conquest of Happiness* when the voice on the radio, just as I hit the curve of a sentence, changed from the soft humming of Mozart's Fifth into the sweet, mellifluous sounds of Alyssa's soft vibrato. "Taylia?" she called as I sat still; she'd never come to me through the radio before. The line cracked and she repeated, in a higher, more rushed tone, "TAYLIA!" It was cacophonous. The voice repeated, in waves, an old adage that Alyssa would say when everything felt bleak. She'd impart this wisdom with her quintessential lightness. A naïveté that was always undercut by so much pain, so much torturous emotion. "Life will turn out!" She said it again and again, circling through the radio sounds like a calming saint. Then she was gone. *Life will turn out,* the faint whisper of life's inevitability.

I got up and walked out of the room. I went to the kitchen and opened the cupboard where the snacks were stored. Making a big mess, I helped myself to Triscuits and jelly, in memory of Emi, filling my mouth with the fancy fat raspberries from the jam Kat bought at the farmers' market. She liked making her own (and, frankly, hers *was* the best), but every now and again she'd treat herself, and by extension me. I ate the jam blissfully, laughing. Alyssa had just spoken to me through the radio, she'd never done that particular trick before. I gawked at everything like they were alive. Spout mouthed, I laughed and laughed, plummeting berries down my throat.

"Taylia!"

Out on the street, I turned around, bursting with hope. Instead I was faced with a familiar face that I had no memory of.

"Hey..."

The man sensed that I didn't know who he was.

"I don't know if I should be wounded that you very clearly don't know who I am."

"I'm sorry?"

"I'm being a jerk. Ralph. I'm Ralph. We shared a moment on the... er... shores of the East River that one time."

I suddenly remembered. "Oh, Rafe!"

There was a beat as he smiled. "What are you doing in this part of Brooklyn? Have you moved?" He was joking.

"Uh, yeah, I guess I have."

"Oh." He looked away and then back at me. "Well, what are you up to?"

I thought for a second. "I'm on my way to meet a friend for breakfast."

Kat and I had arranged a brunch date: the boys were at her sister's, and Claudia was out of town.

"I was just about to get some breakfast..."

"Yeah?"

"Yeah. Where are you going?"

"Buttermilk Channel..."

He smiled. "Oddly enough, me, too. I swear it always seems like I'm stalking you a little bit."

"How do you know you're not?"

"I don't."

I laughed appropriately. "Are you meeting anyone?"

"Mm-hmm." He pointed at his ragged old notebook.

"Well..." I paused. "Look, I'm sure my friend wouldn't mind if you joined us."

"Really?"

"Really."

"That'd be chill, Taylia."

I laughed loudly in public for the first time in a long time. Something about the way he said it, said *chill* so nonchalantly, tipping off his tongue, evoked a tender youthfulness. A youth that I realized, right then and there, that I'd never had. It struck me like whiplash. How fast I had grown up, how much I had been burdened with, because I never had "chill." Never been it, either. We were standing at the edge of the street, and it was awe-inspiring, like seeing the sky in front of you turn pink, like seeing a kaleidoscope for the first time. I couldn't believe it, couldn't believe how much time I had wasted on pain, on being in the purgatory of my family's decided disinterest in me. But I didn't want to be that version of me anymore. The one always in slight pain. I didn't want that for myself—or this baby. I wanted to learn how to be chill.

That day I managed to decrease the amount of times I thought about Ky. There was something endearing about Ralph that made me focus on him; he had an energy of being young and living in Brooklyn that was contagious. It was all in his demeanor, in his street wear, in his embrace of his twenties. We were wearing the same Stan Smith sneakers, and after years of feeling as if I were from another era, I felt my age in his presence. I was easing the burden of the last few months. I was someone I had never been.

While Ralph was in the bathroom, Kat announced she was going to leave and let me do my thing. I resented her for leaving me alone. She said she needed to go get her hair done at her salon, her ritual, but I also knew she was pushing me toward Ralph, and I was annoyed.

He was back at our table, about to sit down, looking a little too hopeful that Kat had left. "Oh, she's gone?"

I feigned an excuse.

He smiled, pausing. The tone shifted, more intimate. "I was hoping you'd come and see me, one day. At the Wythe."

I squinted, looked away, and chose to be earnest. "I don't do well in most social circumstances."

"You seem fine to me." He was serious.

I laughed to fill my turn to speak.

"You're cool, Taylia. Really," he reiterated.

I made a face.

"That's not a pickup line, but..." He was leaning in toward me. I wasn't sure what he was going to say, but I wasn't ready to hear it. "...I want to see you again. Not accidentally. Would that be all right?"

I wasn't sure what was all right anymore. "I don't know," I whispered, wanting to be heard and not at the same time.

"Taylia?" He hadn't heard me.

I breathed in everything around me and swallowed past the lump in my throat. "Yeah?"

He sensed my reservation. "It doesn't have to mean anything more than a getting-to-know-each-other kinda thing."

"I think that'd be better."

"Okay." He was hurt but still hoping.

I watched him from the corner of my eye to see if any part of him resembled Ky. There were some similarities, but there were also vast, vast differences. We were up, and Ralph slid on his heels, impatient, nodding to a tune as he shrugged at me cheekily. I'd never really been attracted to white men before, and maybe that had something to do with it. He wasn't my type, but his eagerness excited me.

"I want to kiss you."

I came out of it. "Not today."

I wasn't sure what that meant, though it seemed to be enough for Ralph.

"I can live with that." He dared to come closer, lingering near my face. I was ready to elbow him away, but he kissed me softly on the forehead and pushed my hanging hair behind my ears. His fingers were eager and slick like a pianist's. "You have very pretty eyes."

I kept my gaze down, modest, saying nothing. He rolled up, his sadness an answer to my silence.

"I guess I'll see you soon."

I nodded and smiled up toward his general direction. He stayed there momentarily, gazing back and puncturing me with his direct stare. I refused to lock eyes with him. Eventually, he turned and walked away.

"So?" Kat asked when I got home.

"So, what?"

"How'd it go?"

"Fine." I was still annoyed.

"And? Taylia?"

I shrugged. "He wants to see me again."

"And?"

"And I said that sounds nice."

"That sounds *nice*?"

The frustration was crawling up on me, like a rash. "I don't know if you realize this, but I'm pregnant. I can't start a relationship now, especially when all I do is think of him—" I stopped myself and put my hands to my face. "When I think about..."

"Tay?"

I pushed her voice away.

"When I think about..." I was hyperventilating. It felt all-consuming.

"Taylia, I know you're upset. But please remember that I'm your friend. You came to me, remember? But, just be conscious

of that this is hard for me, too, so please don't push me away, it's not fair to me otherwise."

I suddenly realized I was treating Kat like the mentor I never had, and I knew it was unfair. I wanted that relationship so badly, I replicated it without her consent.

I breathed in, hurt, but knowing. "Kat. I need to sleep, okay? I'm sorry, but I need to sleep."

I was already out before I heard her speak. I went to my room and stayed awake for ages, replaying old memories. For hours I stubbornly shook the sleep away and thought about him. I knew it was my own fault that I missed him, but I did, and that was that.

I had created a near-perfect image of Ky, and as I lay, the blue volts of my love's rage racing through me, I traced him on the ceiling, on the window where the fog had shaded the glass a mossy terra-cotta color, on my stomach so I could tell my baby who its father was, who its father *is*. I missed the half-intense gaze he'd give me every morning, when Jade wasn't home. I cringed over the detail but still missed him. He wanted to be present, batting his eyelashes so many times I could almost make believe he was singing me a love song in saturated blinks. The way he'd throw that smile at me, his lips a shade of peachy pink, and the way his jaw would feel under my hands, stubbled and comforting like a cat's tongue.

"Hi."

It was early and I had already been waiting a couple of hours to make sure it was an acceptable time to call. That morning I awoke from the baby's presence, my face patterned with creases from the sheets, my stomach burning from hunger. Later, I threw up, my internal skin puckered by the acid. Lying down on my arm, exhausted, I fenced myself off from the world. I wanted to be asleep, I wanted to make my bed there on the stale toilet and cold bathroom floor, but after a half an hour of stillness, I got up and faced my day.

"Taylia?"

"Yup, is this a bad time?"

"Not at all. I'm just half awake. What time is it?"

I looked at the clock on the microwave. It blazed a bright red 7:51 A.M. I probably overshot the acceptable time range to call someone in the morning.

"It's almost eight."

"Oh, whoa, I don't think I've been up this early in a while."

Strike one. "Okay..."

"I mean, it's good to hear from you."

"Listen, Ralph, I was wondering if you wanted to hang out later today." I expected a no, I had already given up on my invitation.

"Today?" He paused. "Yeah, that could work. Where are you staying now?"

"Around the general Fort Greene area."

He laughed, no doubt thinking of our stalking joke, as I had intended him to.

"There's this really great place by Dekalb..."

"Okay, how does twelve-ish work?"

"Can you do it earlier?"

"You're a morning person, aren't you?"

"Does eleven work?"

"Whoa! Okay. Well, I'm sure I can shoot for eleven for you."

"See you then... then."

I planned it out. Fifteen minutes to walk down, which meant that I had about two hours and a bit to figure out what I was doing in the other spaces of my day.

I texted him the address, and I got there before him and sat down outside. The chairs were warm from the sun, and I could see Fort Greene Park, the spirulina-green grass still milky with morning dew. The variation of the sky's patterns gave the city a different kind of warmth. When Ralph finally came he kissed me on the cheek and scanned my face for answers, resigning himself to his nearby seat when he got nothing.

"You are something else, Taylia."

I paused, taking my time. "I don't have many friends, Ralph. Actually Kat is my only friend. And I had another friend..." I regrouped. "I don't really have any family. They're all... gone. So I'm not good with this people stuff. I don't know what to say or when to say it. I know you don't believe me because you've only seen one side of me, but I am just learning... all of this... you know?" I paused. "Like, to let people in again, I mean."

When I had the courage, I looked at his furrowed brow, then focused on something behind him. I looked away shortly after.

"Are you trying to make me run away?"

"Are you going to?"

"No." He said it matter-of-factly.

"I guess I just want to get to know you and I want you to get to know me. I want to be friends and for me to learn more about myself. I feel like I don't know anything about myself, really."

"You think I'll teach you things about yourself?"

"Human interaction usually helps, right?"

He shrugged. "I don't think I know much better than you."

I felt apprehensive.

"Well, what do you want to talk about?"

I blinked. "What do you people talk about in these situations?"

He stopped and thought. "Tell me about yourself."

"Me?"

He gave me a confused nod.

Fuck.

And for the first time in my life I thought rationally: *What do I have to lose?*

I brought flowers home for Kat. Tulips the color of daffodils, because she loved tulips, and it was the season. I felt alive in a way I hadn't felt in a while, the way your body fills with adrenaline. I also felt grateful, in a strange way, as if the sun had nourished me with its radiance and courage had coalesced inside of me.

The pregnancy had been a tiny eternity; these last few months away from Ky were a way for my body to settle and shift the emotional construction toward something that felt grander than just me or him. I was becoming my own compass, and I could feel it. Weirdly, Ralph was helping me with this, as he was seeing me during this transformation. "You're smiling." It was Alyssa, who had returned to the hallway as I checked to see if Kat was home. I guess I was.

"No, I'm not," I said, swatting her away.

I had walked through to the back room, which was brightly lit, and there was Kat reading an anthology called *This Bridge Called My Back*, which was creased all over like it had been through the wash then hung out to dry. The red cover was bright like blood. Lemon oil laced through the front room and the kitchen.

"You're making lemon squares!"

She was beaming. "Hi, what did you do today?"

I looked around; Alyssa was gone. I was back in the moment, and with a snap I realized Kat had this remarkable way of getting me to apologize and confront my inner brat with her use of kindness as a tool for self-reckoning. I passed her the tulips, understanding this incredible journey she had started before the boys were born, to always be present with kindness, to emanate it—while not taking shit. I knew I had recently been moody. I wanted to tell her that the lack of unconditional love in my life had left me heavy, weary with the need to be seen. I wanted to tell her that because I had spent so much of my life walking on eggshells with my parents' moods, the presence of her compassion was jarring. Sometimes I shirked her kindness, like a fly, out of arrogance and fear of vulnerability. Maybe because I expected her to still hurt me. Like I was suspicious of what she gave me.

In the past, we had discussed this "power dynamic" between us and how miraculously we each played a role in the other's needs. Love—feeling it and having it—was a source of power. People just didn't realize it was the most honest source of it. So, with her love of transparency, we had concocted ways to help

aid each other. From me, but also in general, she needed reliability, care, and thoughtfulness. No mess in the house (or the café) and constant consideration (i.e., making sure I was on top of the shopping list and our everyday needs like paper towels or laundry detergent, or, most important, a ping to remind her we needed coffee beans to crunch at home).

Definitely an act of care first, gifts and quality time coming in second—she welcomed flowers and skin care products (she loved Goop or Josie Maran) and books. But dates? She *loved* dates. Dates from Egypt, from Yemen, from the Emirates. Dates paired with good biodynamic wine at local Brooklyn restaurants.

And me? I just needed to feel like I was worth loving. That was all. Or at least, that's what I was starting with. I was learning that needs could, and should, evolve. Sharing space with Kat made me realize that we both had to develop a shorthand. At the café, but also at home, with the boys. In many ways, I had become an aunt to Luc and Isaac, and they treated me as such, sometimes requesting my reading of the bedtime stories (we were going through the Harry Potter books in order; Kat had started on them young, to get their heads full of magic, and you can see how the Elijah-as-Voldemort metaphor was even more apt) and to accompany them to the park. We had become a family; in many ways, they were the first real family where I felt valued for being my own person.

"I just want to say, first, I love you." I didn't want Kat to feel like I was using her generosity and began to feel quite humbled by our relationship. She didn't owe me anything and yet here I was: I was well, there was no other way to describe it.

She kissed me on the cheek, laying the bouquet gently on the table, making a mental note, I knew, to find the perfect vase. I could tell, because her mind was so good at making checklists. There was a pause. I liked how though she wanted you to, she never really made it easy to apologize, there was a sternness to her, but a gentleness, too. She appreciated effort, she appreciated the earnestness that I had. As I thought this I knew that all she

wanted was for me to tell her more about my life. She had told me so many times, and I was trying to be more open with her as well. She got up and stood, facing me, snagging the ends of her navy-blue checkered sleeves. We both yearned for intimacy, and we hadn't had one-on-one time in a while. So, I acquiesced, and talked about the easiest conversation starter: Ralph.

"He's doing his master's at NYU, he's a TA."

Kat smiled. "You like 'em smart."

"Yeah, I do!" It came out effortlessly, with no hesitation from me. "It makes sense because Baba's really smart."

She pulled her eyebrows into a question mark.

"Baba is what I call my father..."

She nodded slowly.

"Both of my parents are smart, actually."

Her voice was quiet when she spoke. "I guess I just always thought they were dead."

Pinching fingers went up my spine. "Oh, no, no... they are both very much alive."

Clearing her throat of more questions, she said, "Well, it makes sense that you're smart then."

I exhaled. "I used to be smart. In school I was really smart. But in the last few years I've felt so displaced, I guess. I feel loose with energy but none of it is directed."

We were both still, together. She was the first to break the silence. "All you have to do is direct it somewhere. Take me, for example. I did it with ambition. I did it 'cause I had to. I want Isaac and Luc to see that life won't be handed to them but that *that* shouldn't stop them from going out there and getting what they want."

Sighing, I released something. "I know, but with myself? I don't know what to do. At school I wrote a lot, mainly poetry... but these last couple of years... everything feels stunted."

"I haven't seen you write in the time I've known you. Except that poem to Cillian."

I snorted. "That's because I don't... write..."

"Why? There's so much going on in that head."

My eyes were wide. Sometimes I still felt so scared of life.

"It's your prerogative, but sometimes you gotta let people in. You're carrying around this guilt and it's weighing you down. I know I'm not an artist, per se, but guilt is not inspiring." She sensed I was overwhelmed and changed direction. "Okay, let's change the subject... back to Ralph."

"What about him?"

"Girl, stop playin', are you, Taylia, going to sleep with Ralph?"

I shuddered at the thought of having sex. Chewing the inside of my cheek, I let it out like another exaggerated sigh: "I'm not ready. I mean, for him to see me"—I gestured at my body—"like this..."

"Oh, this crap again." Sigh. "I know this is your big lesson, Taylia. But! You really need to start letting that go."

"Maybe I'm just not a sexual person." But, thinking back to me and Ky, I knew that wasn't really true. "Besides, I'm pretty sure I just want to be friends with him... You know?" I looked up at her, my gaze direct. "You know?"

She sucked her teeth, her eyes almost blue. Sympathetic, her voice was suddenly tender: "Well, let the poor chump know then, won't you? Don't string him along, Taylia. Be gentle, and be quick. You got him wrapped around your li'l finger, let me tell you."

Suffocating, I coughed loudly.

A week later, Kat, Claudia, and I went shopping. We went to the Park Slope Beacon's Closet, and they both mourned the days of good vintage in New York.

"Though, I have to say Century 21 is lit," Claudia announced to me as Kat tried on clothes in the changing room. Upon hearing this declaration, Kat started to guffaw, which caused all of us to start cracking up loudly; we were a raucous bunch, feeling free. All Claudia could whisper, through laughs, was *"It's true, it's true!"* I ended up taking them out for dinner, for their passing

on of their joy. They had even helped me find a nice floral dress from the '90s. It was long, strappy, and elegant—and the first time I took effort to actively feel better about my physical self.

There was a trendy stationery store near Kat's that I went to the next day. It looked like Kate Spade had barfed on all the items, splotched in glittering colors, stringed confetti splendor. Yet, I resisted my negativity, sincerely needing an outlet to explore the breadth of my interior life, along with all the shapes and sizes of it, via some relatively cool, colorful shit. My lack of direction revolved around my lack of real purpose. So, I wanted to *try to* write. Or to document some of my feelings, somehow, somewhere. Even on a fluorescent green page.

Suffocated in the tight, bright place of the store, I stood forever at the pen station, testing a variety of pens with lavish colors like fuchsia rose and orange blossom. Though, through a composed stillness, I went for a monosyllabic pen color (vert) after a few brief tries. Accompanying my purchase of vert was a medium-sized camel-colored notebook with red letters bolded on the outside that read NOTEBOOK (no shit!). I headed home in a vague fog of acrid ink fume.

When I got home I sat at the kitchen table, and for the first half hour I stared at a sliced avocado that sat on an orange ceramic plate. I knew that if the pit was kept in the avocado it kept it's *green*-green lime green, but this poor guy was pitless, its flesh a barely dull brown, a sad sight; avocados went from God's gift to putrid real fast. Before my pregnancy, I used to love avocados, their silky interior goodness, their cratered baldness. Now they made me sick. Could I use it as a metaphor for something? I opened up the book and scrawled *Taylia Chatterjee* like I had something to say.

"Baby."

I opened one eye and saw that the microwave read 7:27. I put my hands to my sides and pulled myself up. Kat was beside me and I was still in the kitchen. She looked amused, but I felt heavy, my shoulders sore. "Fuck, I can't believe I fell asleep..."

"I tried calling you but you weren't picking up."

"I think I literally fell asleep, like, five hours ago."

With the gentleness of a saint, she put her hands on my shoulders, tenderly circulating her fingers up my strained neck. "You have to think of yourself and the baby now. You can't accidentally fall asleep on a table, boo. Even if it is really amusing to watch you."

I groaned. *Empty hours.* I had spent such good hours of the day asleep and unproductive. Whenever I awoke from a daytime nap my body would react with anxiety, as if I had been cocooned and prematurely disturbed. Always sweaty, the creases of my skin gummed together like melted candy, the baby heavy.

"The position felt nice when I rested my head, popping a squat kinda."

She giggled. "What were you doing?"

I paused, my head filling with water. "Writing."

"You're doing it, bitch!"

"I just wrote my name! That's all!" I placed my face in the comforting gap of my elbow.

Kat cackled. "It's the way of the universe, you gotta keep the momentum going. It's not gonna happen in a day, you know, Rome and blah blah."

The cold gleam of the streetlight shone as Kat walked to the stovetop and hummed a sweet tune, the sound vibrating behind her closed teeth.

"Do you ever feel like what if all this positivity doesn't work? That we're all just doomed."

Kat turned to me and rolled her eyes.

"What?" I said defiantly.

"Enough."

I wanted to whine, but I didn't. There was a long, long pause, then from a clear stutter, she emerged, suddenly serious, as if

this had been rehearsed: "I have something I want to tell you, Tay."

My heart stopped. Everything felt incredibly still.

"Some effed up shit happened to me when I was younger, and I've just been moving through it recently, so I thought I should tell you. You're basically my second wife, babe."

Suddenly jolted, I felt her pain. I knew it'd be hypocritical of me to probe, when I, in turn, had shared nothing of my trauma. But... my stomach churned. "Like... what? Of course, we don't need to talk about it—"

"I mean, it's okay..." She paused. "I guess I never really knew—I mean, I had always wondered... wondered why certain sexual things terrify me. Like, *terrify me.* How uncomfortable they make me, or even sad, damn... and it's always been this inexplicable, paralyzing thing... and Elijah always accepted it, and I made sure it never got in the way... but Claudia, she knew. My body just shut the fuck down one night... and she damn right knew, and she called it. This has all been unraveling the last few days."

"What'd she say?"

Kat sighed. "It was simple, she just had this look and said, 'Baby...' Our nonverbal communication, Taylia? Yowwwwie."

I sat, stunned.

"It happened a couple of times, with two different cousins. Tiffany and Stevie." She paused, looking at my face. "Sorry, that's heavy. I'm sorry. I didn't even ask if you're ready to hold this."

"I'm ready," I told her bluntly, looking her in the eye. I was starting to understand that many of us who had experienced this type of sexual trauma—abuse, molestation, rape—talked about it in code. She didn't have to say much more for me to understand completely. I took her hands and breathed in, tears in my eyes. She had started crying, too.

"It's nice to not always be strong, Taylia. I want to share that with you, because I think you need to hear it." She paused. "I like

that Claud makes me feel safe enough that I can be vulnerable. Because Black women can't afford to be vulnerable. Look at all this responsibility. The café, the kids. You." We both laughed. "But I want you to see this kind of love and believe it's possible for you, too."

I circled her hands with my fingers. I felt so selfish, like I was entitled to her love, all while she'd been housing this, healing this deep, dark wound. I couldn't believe how she'd handled all of this on her own. With two kids and a business. I felt like trash. "I'm sorry I'm such a piece of shit sometimes. You've given me so much..."

I trailed off, wanting not to embarrass myself and cry more.

"Claudia has been suggesting she wants to move in, maybe? She thinks it might be easier. She wants to be here with the boys more, she says she wants to show up for me more."

I inhaled. "Do you want her to move in?" I wasn't afraid of the answer.

She looked at me. "Kinda... yeah."

A little bruised, I smiled, feeling truly happy for her. I didn't know what that meant for me, but I was also beginning to trust that things would work out. Maybe because I inherently *had* started to trust Kat. I didn't push to know more about what had happened to her as a child, but I felt relieved that I wasn't alone, or something. It was hard to locate the full dimensions of what I was moving through emotionally, but it felt less lonely all of a sudden. Relief and sadness packed into one. Sitting within this rapid, sweaty, sedated feeling, we both sat in it.

It was here that I realized, for the first time fully, that maybe what I had lacked, for the entirety of my life, was the experience and understanding of another's. In all honesty, I had never really thought about it. Everything had always been about *me*. How *I was feeling*. Even when Alyssa died, I never fully contemplated the loss it was for Mama and Papa, let alone her boyfriend, Ryan. I had never reached out to him or looked back. Then after Simon, everything was *even more* about me. I had missed that part. I had missed the part that made me look bad.

Embarrassed, I massaged Kat's feet with shea butter and ran her a bath with Epsom salt and lavender oil. She asked me to bring in the Bose speaker and play some Etta James, and as she soaked her body, I sat next to her, forgetting why I was ever sad in the first place.

The next morning felt like a lurch, and all of a sudden a sinking feeling hit: I wanted to bring up her abuse again, but I knew I couldn't. I knew it wouldn't be fair for me to do that to her, but still I wanted to know. It was an itch. I wanted to hold her and kiss her cheeks. I felt protective of her; the idea that someone had done something to her made me sick, it sparked something inside of me that felt mythical, violent. Like a spirit was shooting through me, emblazoning my soul. I wanted to protect her; I wanted her to be happy.

Instead, she went to work early and left the boys under my care. Playgroup was twice a week, and because I wasn't working at the café, they were with me from three onward. Ideally, Kat would have them for the weekend—but I didn't mind if days, like today, she'd have to sneak into work. Truly, I enjoyed the distraction.

This morning, right after a breakfast of tofu scramble, I took the boys down to the park. As I watched them run around with their mini-lightsabers, baby boys playing—Luc in yellow overalls, Isaac in bright pink shorts and a lime-green T-shirt—I felt their youth, their spirit. Watching children play is magical, because it's so pure, so unfettered. Their energy bouncing like a light source, unadulterated. I was overwhelmed with joy, seeing them come alive fully. I knew in a few months there'd be another companion in the pack. My baby, kicking around, suddenly felt near, more palpable than I remembered.

Eventually the boys and I returned back home. I sat them down to watch an episode of *Adventure Time* as I cooked lunch. I liked the rhythm of doing so, my hand like a lever against my lower back. I fed them at Kat's table where we all laughed like a family. I entertained them, tricking them into eating their healthy

meal. The act of caring for them so intimately made me suddenly feel purposeful. It was as if the symmetry of all the mothers before me came to possess me, teaching me things I had not known before this very moment. Like the switch of motherhood came on, a light pulsating. I looked beyond the dining room and saw Dadi-ma smiling brightly and nodding: *See this is how it's done.* I blinked back, nursing a quiet admiration for myself and this achievement: I was beginning to accept that I was a mother. I had always been my own.

Suddenly, I was flushed with a memory of Dadi-ma stealing a ladoo for me from a vendor who was her friend. It was a prank, something ever so innocent, but she picked up this ladoo from its Pyrex container—one perfectly spherical orb, yellow like turmeric—and passed it to me. As I stuffed it into my mouth, the entire thing like a breakable gobstopper, she uttered her favorite American phrase, "*Hot diggity.*" It was always so funny that even she would laugh at the absurdity. She had a comedic quality to her; her access to fun was such a fluid emotion. I thought about how much she had taught me about laughter and play in the months I got to know her. How her innocence and sense of life were compounded by her excitement for it. Even at an older age she hadn't lost her playfulness. As I thought about children— Isaac and Luc and also my own soon-to-be child—I gathered parenting had a similar sense of wonder. Something I had never been given by my parents but now desperately wanted for my own child. As I dreamed of Dadi-ma, she sat before me, smiling, still at the dining table, and whispered, "Hot diggity."

I tried writing again the next day as I stared at Kat's vast plant collection and admired the thin pottery bowls they sat in, the leaves draping down like their own constellations, gravitational, placidly languid, dreaming their green-crushed dreams. I remembered Mama's love for plants. I'd watch her sometimes from my bedroom window that overlooked our garden, puttering along to and fro, a copper trowel in her left hand, red hair frizzy and winking. For her, it was a sanctuary; the dirt and the earthly

palette grounded her physically. It was a nourishment for her hands, for her soul, and it connected her to Alyssa in some way. Though, I understand now, it was also an escape from Alyssa, her treachery, her insurmountable, continued sadness. Inside the walls of Mama's garden, her moon-ladened Gibraltar, she created a retreat, a life no longer void of her prodigious daughter. She could have control over the lives of these plants, and, unlike her daughter's life, she could nurse these plants to prosperity and encourage spectacular growth, like jewels glinting, her resplendent riches. She was a bewitching light out there, thriving, grieving in her own way.

"Do you look like your mother?" Ky once asked cautiously. I smiled, and he grabbed at me, pressing his lips delicately onto my mouth. "I wasn't sure how you'd react."

"Right, because I am so moody." I was joking, but I guess I had always known it was true.

"So do you?" he asked, peeling himself off of me.

"I don't know..." I said. "She was—is—so beautiful..."

There were no other words to describe my mother. His right hand came to my cheek, brushing his warmth onto me.

"She's delicate and graceful in a way women no longer are. She used to exude so much confidence in a glare, or a smile, or her laugh. I feel like she embodied a kind of majestic aura, like women of a bygone era. Like Georgia O'Keeffe in all those portraits that Alfred Stieglitz took of her, there's this knowingness, a togetherness. Or like Meryl Streep walking out of an office in *Kramer vs. Kramer*, hair parted in the middle and a crisp white shirt unbuttoned a quarter way down. I didn't get that. It was passed directly on to Alyssa. I think—I mean, I know—that's why they both loved her so much... You always love anything that reminds you of yourself. Alyssa resembled the daughter they wanted. One who was astute, composed, smart but coy. They wanted a white-passing, beautiful daughter."

"I asked about you, not Alyssa." He whispered it, his breath lingering in my mouth.

I propped myself up on my elbows, pushing him to the side. "It's hard, Ky. I was always so unappealing. Next to Lyse, I was 'homely.' My hair was always frizzier, my skin always darker. Alyssa was this light-skinned, bright-eyed beauty. She was basically fucking white. It wasn't easy. I didn't feel Indian or white."

Even as I said it, I cringed. I had matured so much, and now I mourned all the time I had wasted hating myself for not being something it turns out I didn't even want to be. I sat silently for a while.

"I remember I had a journal. It was given to me by my aunt for my seventh birthday. Handmade by Bengali village women, I treasured their handiwork, so I would only ever write special things in it, mainly stories..."

"Like?" Ky asked.

"Stories of myself being perfect, or like Alyssa." I began to blush. "I thought if I wrote these stories down maybe they would come true. That maybe this fictional character would take over and turn me into something beautiful or different. But always, *always*, like, better..."

"But why still? You're older now. You know better now."

"I don't know who I am if I'm not trying to be Alyssa, making myself in her image."

"Just be yourself. That's all anyone can ask of you."

I lay in silence. "I don't know who I am."

He got up and stood in the shadows, examining me. "Don't let your wounds make you someone you're not, Tay."

24.

"What's another word for *soaked* that also starts with an *s*?"

Ralph and I were in the park doing crosswords.

"*Sodden?*"

"*Sodden*! Yes, you genius woman!"

His natural inclination was to kiss me, but I turned my lips to the side and he hit my cheek instead. Still, he smiled, unshaken.

"You're in another world today."

"Huh?" I asked.

"Point proven."

"What are you talking about?"

"Nothing, dear Taylia, nothing!"

I put down the crossword and rolled onto my back. My new notebook was nearby and I clutched at it, suddenly feeling the urge to write. Anything.

"Writing now, are we?"

"Mm-hmm."

"What are you writing?"

"Well, I can't write anything when you're hounding down my neck!" I tried to sound nice, but I wasn't sure if I succeeded. Ralph got up soon after, under the guise of thirsting for some ginger beer. I happily accommodated and doodled the nearby trees, shakily, across the lavender-colored hills, when a voice came at my side, assaulting my inner silence.

"Taylia?"

I wasn't looking up, but I knew that it wasn't Ralph. The voice asked me again, but this time it wasn't a question.

"Taylia. Holy shit."

I recognized who it was, though I didn't quite know what to say. I felt sick. I pushed myself up to a seated position slowly, easing my back into my posture. I looked up toward the sun. He stood there, all six feet two inches of him, and stared back at me with a candied smile.

"Hi."

"Hey!"

He came toward me, crouching down on his tiptoes. He was still handsome, still athletic, still Ryan. I took in his springy hair and the long muscles in his shoulders. He hadn't changed a bit.

Well, maybe he was more built. He gave me a steady, unblinking look, and I was transported back to my teenage self.

"How are you?"

The questions were whistling out of him. I extended my palm up to stop him, braced my stomach, and hurled the sticky puke out of me like an unwanted secret. I was a Catholic at confession, I wanted to be absolved. It came in dredges, and as I watched the stink pool up around his shoes, I expected him to walk away, disgusted. I expected him to frown at the string of yellow retch that moved out of me with calculated precision. I was familiar with the process. I welcomed the release. But he, instead, looked at me with a look so tender, so soft.

"Tay..."

Alyssa. Alyssa.

Can you hear me, Alyssa? Help me, Lyse. I can't do this anymore, Lyse.

I felt his hands on my face and then he pulled me toward him. No shyness involved, he opened himself up to me. A flower blooming, waiting. He was unafraid, and so I cried into him, swallowing past the harsh taste of life, breathing in the scent of him. Between the brown cloud of my hair and the landing rock of his shoulders, I felt comforted, I felt grounded. Then I collapsed.

The smell of bleach surrounded me when I woke up. Everything was milky, drenched in the diluted off-white color of limbo. I wasn't in my bed, at Kat's or Ky's, but my blinking eyes were able to make out that I was in a hospital. There were two figures with their heads bowed in the distance: one of them looked familiar, and the other, only just. My limbs felt weighty with an ache. I felt as if I had been smashed into a million little pieces and then stitched back together like a mismatched collage. I coughed loudly and instantly a head popped up.

"Are you doing okay?" It was Ryan. He came toward me.

"What happened?" I was unsure of the events. I remember puking and then drifting out of my body, but that was it.

"You collapsed. In my arms."

"How romantic."

He smiled. It was strange; we were so familiar even through the distance.

I heard a noise behind Ryan and soon saw Ralph's head come up from behind.

"Hey." He walked closer toward me, already marking his territory.

"Hey. Have you met Ryan?"

He didn't look over at him but instead answered with "Yeah. We spoke a little bit while you were, uh, asleep."

I nodded okay.

Ryan interrupted. "I'm sorry, but I'm just going to go and look for a nurse."

Ralph and I both watched him walk out.

"Who is he?" The jealousy was unsettling.

"He didn't tell you who he was?"

"No. He just said he's known you for years."

I shook my head in an upward direction to indicate that I agreed.

"Ex-boyfriend?"

"No. He's my sister's old boyfriend. I have known him for years, though. Family friends and all that stuff."

"Sure." He seemed more comfortable.

A nurse came back into the room. "Heya, you're awake."

"I am."

"You'll be pleased to know that the baby is fine."

I looked over at Ralph and saw Ryan at the doorway, looking away from the nurse, looking away from me. "Okay." I could hardly hear myself.

"You need to look after yourself."

I coughed loudly, not wanting to hear what she had to say anymore.

Ryan spoke up. "We'll be sure to look after her."

The nurse looked at me—"I'll come by a bit later"—and then smiled and walked out. I almost dreaded her exit as much as I also longed for it. I knew answers needed to be given.

"Ralph. Where do you live?" I heard Ryan ask.

"Not too far from here."

"Okay. Great. Well, I can take care of Taylia today."

I could see the tension rise up in Ralph's jaw. He peered over at me to see if I disagreed.

I didn't.

"Yeah, thanks, man." He walked to his chair and picked up his jacket and then came to me and kissed me on the cheek. "Get some rest. I'll call you later."

Ryan looked at the floor, I nodded, and Ralph walked out.

There was an unbearable silence until Ryan broke it. "Pregnant, huh?"

I cringed inside.

"Nobody knows what happened to you... But it looks like you're doing well?"

I didn't answer.

"You just sort of disappeared. Wasn't sure if I'd see you again."

Silence.

"What happened, Taylia?"

The inevitable question: *What happened, Taylia? What happened to you, Taylia?*

My throat was locked on mumbles, nothing audible was coming out. It surprised me that Ryan had evidently kept in touch with my parents, which was the only way he must've known any of this, of my leaving. What was even more fascinating was that they had kept the details of my departure very vague, obviously for easier conversational consumption. It was a pathetic way to control the narrative, to keep their victimization intact. I paused for an eternity, marking my words. "I grew up."

Ryan scoffed, though it wasn't mean. "You grew up? Is that why you're pregnant?"

My instinct was to shrug, to run. "I made a mistake."

As soon as I said it, I knew it wasn't true. I was pregnant because I had fallen in love with an idea. With being saved. With the bromides we tell ourselves about a good life. About a family unit. I was curious about what would happen if I had an ounce of control, holding Ky captive, licking his ear, whispering, "Come inside of me," like I was a regular Minnie Riperton. It felt powerful to rewrite the patterns of my skin, of my insides, with his gooey debris, his guttural oohs and aahs, his shaking body. It felt significant to be fucked and in love. But now he wasn't here. He was never really mine. This baby felt like a hollow gift, one that I had not yet unwrapped.

"That's not true," I corrected myself. "I am at a crossroads right now."

"A crossroads?"

"Yeah, a fucking crossroads, Ryan. There are many fucking turns and many fucking roads and I'm not sure which one to fucking take."

A smile crept along his lips. "Do you have any idea which one might be the best one?"

"I don't know. Probably the one that has been least traveled. Or whatever."

He nodded slowly. "Classic Taylia."

We sat in the hospital room for a little while longer. We waited for the nurse to give me instructions, and soon after I was discharged and taken home by my dead sister's ex. He didn't come up but left me at Kat's stoop. I watched him walk away, nostalgia hitting me hard, feeling warm with memories. The moon inside of me was still. I felt content.

"I can't believe they didn't call *me*! I'm your emergency contact!"

The next day, over a pineapple turnover, I was telling Kat the story of my hospital adventure.

"I was there with Ralph and Ryan, so I was just fine... Trust me."

"Who the hell is Ryan?"

How could I explain this to avoid further questioning?

"He's my sister's old boyfriend."

She was confused, I could see it in her eyes, the way they locked tightly on to something in the foreground, the irises pulsing in the particled morning light. She hugged her elbows and her eyes gleamed with emotion. "Didn't know you were meeting up with him..."

"I wasn't. I just saw him randomly in the park."

Her lips were puckered into a question mark, but she didn't string the words through.

"Actually"—I coughed—"he's a really nice guy. Would you, er, mind if I invited him over for dinner, maybe, one day?" I didn't even know if this was something I actually wanted, but I was trying to be chill.

She put her coffee mug down and gripped the sides with obscured fingertips. Her face looked funny with so much confusion. "You want him to come over?"

"Yeah."

"Wait, why?"

I wanted to shrug, but I didn't. I articulated: "I want to get to know him, I guess. As an adult."

She looked at me, wanting more. So, I breathed in.

"I don't think I've ever told you, maybe because talking about death never felt right. I never wanted to spoil the mood or whatever. But my sister killed herself a few years ago. And everything since then has been, I guess, fractured."

She looked at me, incredibly still, subdued. "I'm sorry," she said, mid-sigh. She grabbed my hand and stared into my eyes with a fierce and steady compassion. "I want you to be able to tell me these things. I want us to be able to lean on each other."

My tongue felt lifeless, tongue-tied. I managed to say, "I know." Then, after a few seconds, I said, "I want to be able to talk about this, too... but I never wanted to burden you."

"You can't be scared around me. Sometimes I feel like you're so nervous—where does that come from?"

I sucked my bottom lip. "That's just who I am, I guess. I'm always scared of fucking up, saying the wrong thing. But I'm changing, I'm getting braver."

She smiled, eyes glassy. "My love, the amazing thing about adulthood is that you get to be in control. You get to make your own family."

We were both silent.

"What was her name?"

I looked at Kat, tears suddenly in my eyes. "Alyssa," I said. I felt her, Alyssa, climbing inside of me, my sweet moon. In these past months, years, I realized how I had forgotten her former outlines and had now begun a new perspective of seeing her. A clearer image, where I wasn't pitted against her, even in my mind. I still missed her. Like a long-lost song.

"Alyssa," Kat echoed. "Alyssa Chatterjee."

I smiled, tears like the lines designating lanes in a swimming pool rushed down my cheek. "Yes." I nodded. "The one and only."

We sat, both in tears, through joy and sorrow. I remembered, again, how all life seemed beautiful at a distance, and how easy it was to fall into patterns of solipsism and sadness when you felt robbed of a good life. Kat talked to me about friends she'd lost to drugs or petty crimes, like weed possession, who were now serving lifetime jail sentences all because they were Black. She told me about her friend Nina who was murdered because she was a Black trans woman. Nina had been beautiful, sweet, gentle. Kat had known her through the queer and trans network and explained the cacophony of pain she'd felt when she'd first heard of her murder—the pain of being reminded, time and time again, how uncared for Black life was. Especially the lives of Black femmes. We talked of grief, this grief, that human life—in particular nonwhite human life—incurs and the resilience and weight of living. How, in turn, there was the pressure and guilt

of surviving. But also the gratitude for one more day. I told her about my need to give space for Alyssa to move through me. How soon after her death, I felt as if I owed her my life.

"I'm almost forty. My sister never killed herself, but I definitely have felt the brokenness of death. It sounds like Alyssa chose her fate. I know that's harsh, but there's a truth to it. You can't hold yourself back. All I can say, Tay: you just gotta bet on yourself, mourn, give yourself the time. Then be kind to yourself and those around you and keep it moving."

She made a joke about that being the most Capricorn thing she'd ever said, and we both laughed, but I knew she was right. I needed to unlodge Alyssa.

"Oh, BTW, I have something for you." She stood up and rummaged through her custom camel handbag, which sat crumpled next to her, finally handing me a piece of paper.

I looked down at it. There, in large, bold letters, it said SINGLE MOTHERS CLUB.

I didn't read on. "Kat, seriously?"

"Don't judge, Taylia. It'd do you good."

"Good for... How? People are still making flyers? Where did you find this?"

"It doesn't matter. And, obviously, to talk to other women who are going through similar emotions could help you. Besides, I wanna go, too, we can make it a date."

"What do they do?"

She sucked her teeth. "Read the damn pamphlet!"

"I don't want to."

"Namaste." A slim white woman walked into the wide room. There were all types of people in the class, though it was jarringly white. The room was filled with draping saris, and smelled like cheap, suffocating incense. No South Asian body besides my own could be seen, which made me sad. I thought about Dadi-ma, and how white girls say *namaste* with such relish, having

claimed the word, feeling entitled to it with such ferocity that we had forgotten the meaning of that which was once ours, all ours.

I looked at Kat with a raised eyebrow.

"Namaste," everyone replied.

"How's everyone doing today?"

"Good," some people replied.

"Her name is Jan," Kat whispered.

How had yoga, a practice of my ancestors for thousands of years, become known as a bougie white thing? My voice felt locked in my throat. *Why was I here?*

"It's quite a hot day, great for our class. We can get an extra workout!" Jan exclaimed.

Oh, how wonderful.

"I see we have a few new members today. Hello."

I looked around. All eyes were on me and Kat. Kat looked at me to lead, so I said hi uncomfortably.

"Welcome to our class."

Her stare was direct, yet strangely comforting. She had one of those soothing voices that you expected annoying (white) yoga teachers to have.

"Is this your first time?" she asked.

I wasn't sure what she was referring to, the baby or the class.

I tactically answered, "Ah, yeah."

"Wonderful." She put her palms together. "And your name is?" she asked.

"Taylia..."

"Taylia, namaste."

"Namaste," I replied, missing Dadi-ma in the softness of that word.

"Now this class is all about doing things that feel right for you, so please, if you feel at any point that you can't do something, just stop. Go at your own pace and don't forget to keep breathing."

I nodded and took a deep breath. Everyone then looked at Kat, who introduced herself with charming reluctance, and soon the class began.

"Judy, would you like to start us with a mantra?"

Jan sat down onto her unrolled mat. A voice nearby, which I figured belonged to Judy, started a Hindu chant. India, its broad temples, darling marigold mandalas, and salty turmeric with burning pungent onions, ignited my pulse. I watched Jan's skinny white body with contempt but then, somehow, extraordinarily, got pulled into the om. The om felt like mine, a rhythm for me. Its roots were embellished in my vinegary sweat, in the darkness of my body's plains, in my yellowed brownness; the om vibrated a frequency of a blessing. I felt the hatred diminish inside of me—*om, om, om*—I felt Dadi-ma's moon-shaped face guide me, her spirit rattling inside of me—*om, om, om, shanti om*. I came out of class, heaving in my own way, and saw that I had two messages on my phone. One was from Ralph, the other from Ryan. I read Ryan's first.

Hope you're doing okay, kid. If you're up for it, we should grab a coffee.

You choose the place and time. I'm flexible.

I felt giddy afterward, a swarm of bees rising in my stomach. I didn't even remember giving him my number, but he wanted to see me. I walked out of the studio with Kat, completely in my own world.

"It wasn't so bad, was it?" I heard her say.

I agreed.

Things weren't that bad.

"I wasn't sure if you'd get back to me."

We were sitting by the window in a restaurant in the West Village. I had let Ryan choose, as I had no idea for cool things outside of Kat's.

"Why not? Why wouldn't I?"

"Well, you've always been a bit aloof, haven't you, Taylia?"

He was wearing a gray fisherman's sweater. His hair was buzzed tighter than it used to be. He must've gotten a haircut

since I saw him. He looked like someone who cared about his life. I watched him, waiting.

"How are you doing? Are you feeling better?"

"Yes. Yes, I am." I wanted to tell him it was because of him. I was suddenly excited about things after such a long time of being so absent in my own narrative. But here was someone who knew me, knew me before it all happened. Knew the Taylia who wasn't afraid to dance to Louis Armstrong after Sunday dinners on warm summer nights. Those rare, rare nights I felt truly free. Mama, pink from wine and chatter, dancing to the rhythm; Baba, with a cigar in his mouth, crooning some old Bollywood tune as everyone cheered; Alyssa slow dancing with herself. It was the perfect familial alchemy. Ryan also knew the Taylia who was afraid of the Natural History Museum and the great vastness of Central Park—the Taylia with her unsullied teenage jealousy of Shirley Temple, with her curls all pretty and blond. He knew *my* weaknesses. But better yet, he knew Alyssa's.

"Are you hungry?"

I nodded.

"Good, they have a great falafel here." He ordered.

It was raining and the water pattered the outside of our shell like fingertips in the dark.

"Do you ever think about her?"

My heart braced itself. There she was, she had entered the room. She was truly omnipresent. "Yes. All the time. I think about her all the time..."

He nodded. For the first time in my life, I saw Ryan searching for something.

"Seeing you has brought it all back, Taylia." Pause. "Who she was, what she was. It's all coming back to me now."

I couldn't help singing the lyrics to "Céline." I inhaled slowly, biding my time.

"It's strange when things you think you've worked through resurface."

I nodded. "I know, it's weird." I wavered, looking for the right way to say it. "Actually, it's weirder because I never thought you liked me."

"Oh, Taylia..." He stumbled. "I never knew what to say around you. I could tell that you were protective of her. And she loved you more than anyone. I guess that was hard for me to get over. So, I avoided you."

The rain drummed.

"Do you hate her for it?"

I was about to reask the question, not sure if he had heard the first time, but he slowly answered me, knowing what I was asking. "Yes and no."

I nodded in understanding.

"I'd like to think that I'm way more mature than that..."

"I don't think it's about maturity..."

"No, no, let me finish." I gestured to him to do so. "I don't think it's about being mature in the traditional sense. But you and I both know that in the end... Alyssa wasn't thinking about me or you. Her pain had transcended *her* reality."

I sat there, numb. "Do you really think that?"

"She had a lot going on. Things that you probably never understood because you were so young. Plus, your parents drove her insane. And your mother had this ridiculous tendency to polarize people. According to her, Alyssa was all good..."

"And I was all bad."

"Yeah... I guess. Kind of."

"I do that, you know? I always told myself I'd never end up like them, but every now and then I'll catch myself saying something like my mother, like judging someone's awkward taste in patterns or color coordination with their clothes."

"You even have some of her mannerisms, like the way you scratch your chin with your forefinger."

I laughed. "Really?"

"Oh yeah. I mean, you can't really escape them, can you, Tay? They're your blood."

I looked past him, embracing the truth and inevitability of that statement. Our food came and we sat there, our conversation awkwardly paused.

"I miss her so much. Sometimes it's hard for me to believe she's not here. She just..." I whimpered, tears floating and rising like a tide, half-moons in my eyes. Ryan sat against the backdrop of the rain that beat against the sidewalk. He looked outside, and I desperately wanted to be given answers. "Don't you think she was perfect..."

I knew it was unfair of me to probe him like this. I felt as if I had suddenly turned into an addict. I wanted nothing more than to wallow in conversations of Alyssa with him. He lifted his left hand to his ear, as if blocking a twitch, and looked past me.

"Yes, I guess she was, in her own way." He paused, taking a sip of water. Neither of us had touched our food. We were participating in the awkward dance of consideration. He waited for me, and I, in turn, waited for him.

"Remember how she used to do that thing and lick her lips before she ate?" I said, mimicking her soft charms.

Ryan didn't look up; he knew what I was referring to. Half smiling, he answered me, sighing. "She always knew how to get her way."

From that I knew he was stepping away. His hands, in the air, begging for Alyssa's mercy. *Enough,* he was saying, *I've had enough.* He seemed suddenly powerless, his eyes closed in a hushed prayer. From whatever veil lifted, I understood that Ryan had undeniably been hurt and that I was, again, not the only victim of Alyssa's recklessness.

The next single mothers club meeting was an art class at a local artist's studio in Bushwick. I had often wondered what an artist's studio would resemble. Perhaps a lair of prints and charcoal sketches? A multicolored mosaic of colors, embellished with paint and European postcards? A messy bloom of potted and hanging plants, a green sanctuary within this harsh city?

Alyssa would frequently bring back books of famed artists from school, scattering the pages of her passions, dog-eared and belly open. She preferred artists with a bit more perversion, particularly admiring Egon Schiele, Amedeo Modigliani, and her favorite hedonist, Toulouse-Lautrec. His pictures of prostitutes and nymphlike naked women always exuded a freedom that I could tell she longed for. She would have fit well into the Belle Epoque era. Her face: pretty, yet daring. Her body: supple, eyes ensnaring men with extraordinary ease.

An hour before I was about to head out, Kat texted saying Ruth, her new employee, couldn't cover, so that she could no longer accompany me to the workshop. I felt as I had as a kid when I didn't get my way, huffing the blue expanse of fear and frustration of being alone. I put the phone down, welcoming the feeling like inviting in a ghost. This dread that I had of change was merely a pathetic fixation I had on familiarity, a strange compulsion with reliability. I was afraid of the emptiness of my mind and of the solitude that would inevitably follow. But I knew I needed to honor the fear, surpass it, and move on to my main trajectory, toward a place of halogen-like contentment, a fearless Taylia. I wanted to be strong like the women in the songs, to be redolent of the women proselytized in poetry, mounted in history. Unafraid of my failures or my shortcomings, I wanted to embrace it all: the murkiness, the tepid waters that stood before me. I took in a slow inhalation.

In my flash of anxiety, I imagined what it would be like to be strong. I was strong when Alyssa died and when I walked away from my parents' house, resolved in my resilience and the vindication that I was not to blame. That was the first time I took refuge in myself, realizing that within this broken corpse of a being lay a fire that was ready to emerge. I breathed in the agitation of wanting to be who I was already. In those moments, again, I could feel my sulky presence shifting, and I knew if you blinked you could see me, slowly, slowly. I was evolving.

As soon as I walked into the Bushwick artist's studio, a man came out of a back room, immediately introducing himself to

everyone as Mateo. As he talked to another student, I admired the beauty of the main room. With the large windows and high ceilings, it had mostly exceeded my expectations. I slowly began to blink approval of this Mateo character. He had olive skin with tattoos that lined his right forearm, and I could see that almost all his hair was gray. As he spoke, he spun and turned toward me. And then, as he looked directly at me, I saw that his eyes were sober, like a child's, unflinching and honest, resembling a pair of fish oil capsules Mama used to take every night before she went to bed.

"Hello?" he asked with an interesting inflection.

"Hi, I'm here for the art class."

"Well, you're in the right place, take a seat."

In that moment I noticed how needy I was, how much direct attention I craved. I sat down in a seat nearest to me, straight-away immersing myself in this new environment. This studio was a raw, unblemished canvas, with no arrogance attached. As I looked around, with shrill excited focus, I noticed a familiar face from the yoga class a few days earlier, one of the only other blaringly nonwhite faces besides Kat's and mine. Her long hair framed her broad, thick eyebrows and a strong nose. Today she wore a sleeved floral dress that matched her flushed cheeks and her pale pink lips. Just looking at her reminded me of Alyssa; she left me starry-eyed and famished.

Throughout the class I watched her. She kept mainly to herself but would often laugh fearlessly, her whole face transformed into a wide, open gummy release. She painted with verve, an unwill-ingness to compromise—asking Mateo for colors that weren't in her reach. "I really would love this cerulean blue when you have a chance!" She'd bask in his attention, smiling a cheeky grin. I wanted to be her friend.

In front of us, inside a circle, lay props, and the session was designed so that from every angle lay something seductively stimulating for our imaginations. I sat in front of some grapes and a solo khaki-green combat boot. Unsure of how to frame, I

breathed in and just painted what I saw, hoping the rest would come. Cringing at every stroke, I reminded myself that I couldn't be a perfect painter if I never tried. More important, I had already decided I wanted this woman to be my friend, so I walked toward her after class.

"I've seen you at the yoga classes..." I fumbled. "Or, really, just one class."

My words were like friction, which I felt, but she let her guard down slowly.

I stuck my hand out like a lever. "I'm Taylia."

She took it. "I'm Tahsin."

"I've heard that name before!"

She smiled as if she had a secret. "We must have met in a dream."

I wasn't sure if she was serious, she was still half smiling. "Yeah."

I stood there, temporarily feeling strange. I felt like I had known her, a flashing trance. That feeling made me reobserve her, a malachite-green hue resonating as we talked. *Who is she?*

"Are you enjoying the classes?" I asked.

"Yeah, it's a great concept, isn't it? Plus, it's nice to get away for a little bit. I don't really get much time off."

I sympathized. She talked fast, like she was nervous, too.

"But I have a beautiful healthy boy waiting at home for me, and that's enough motivation to remain in high spirits."

"What's his name?"

"Sufjan."

I smiled. "I wonder how many names *he's* inspired."

She picked up on my emphasis. "Oh yeah, the singer... No, not for me, I just liked the way it sounds in Arabic."

I laughed. "Oh! What does it mean?"

"Sufjan means 'comes with the sword.' I think it's a relic from the last bastion of the Muslim empire. I like it for its musicality. Anyway, how about you? Is this your first baby?" She gestured to my stomach.

"Yeah. Can you tell?" I said in my idiosyncratic, self-deprecating manner I had on lock.

She shook her head in an exaggerated no. I exhaled. "I never thought I'd be having children so young, but here I am."

"Right? Some days it's hard. Like really, undeniably hard, but then you come home and your little bub will smile at you with a toothless little grin and then, I kid you not, all of it—the shit on your hands, the three A.M. wake-up calls, the heavy udders that have replaced your boobs"—we both laughed—"will be..." She sighed. "...worth it. But I'm sure you've heard that."

"Well, I haven't heard exactly that." She smiled. "But, yeah, so they say."

"They say it for a reason."

My eyes lingered on her eyes for a few moments. She seemed confident, but always in thought, avoiding my direct gaze. I interrupted our silence. "Are you divorced?"

She raised her eyebrows, but half smiled again. "No." She paused and breathed in. "I'm widowed."

My brain thudded. "Oh, I'm so sorry."

Suddenly it hit me and I wondered if this interaction was even real. She had to be Roman's widow. Now I buzzed with a secret. I nodded with nerves, trying to hide what I knew in my sweaty, exhausted heart. She was Roman's wife! Roman's wife! It felt surreal to be standing near her, to smell her skin—like pure jasmine—and look into her eyes and see something akin to home. Instead of saying anything, I just zipped it up, tight inside my stomach, like vomit was urging to ooze out. This was my soon-to-be child's aunt. I felt mildly high.

"Thank you. How about you? You're not divorced, are you? You look too young to be divorced."

"Never married. It just got too hard."

"What do you mean?"

What did I mean?

"My relationship... it just got hard I guess..."

"It's okay. I'm sure it's complicated."

Was it?

"Yeah. It was. That's an easier answer anyway."

She laughed and I looked away, chewing the rubbery insides of my cheeks. There were words, frustrations, questions, coiled around my throat. I wanted her in my life, and I was desperate for her to approve of me, for her to say that I was her friend. I gave her my number and we told each other we'd meet up soon.

I walked back to Kat's that night with a gentle kind of eagerness. It was a nostalgic stirring, an awakening. I had found a possible friend, another like Kat. She was the type of woman that I always found I was drawn to. Self-assured and proud, and yet with an almost self-effacing sensibility, never detracting from the acquisition of true womanhood. Like a deep laugh in my stomach, a restless sense of wonderment brewed inside of me. She was also the closest link I had to Ky.

I looked forward to the single mothers club more than anything else in my week, and it became a tangible incentive that pushed me into shape. I found myself reading more, something I had not done resolutely for a while. My bad habit had been to offhandedly read the papers Kat left around the house in passing. Whether it was a week-old *New York Times* or a magazine, I would languidly take in a few pieces here and there, and that would habitually suffice my self-imposed reading quota. But now? Now, I was thirsty to read and to feel again. To be hungry and outraged. I wanted to feel life in a thrilling way.

When I got to Mateo's studio again, I worked on an abstract piece, focusing on the same boot that he had centered for us to paint, except from a different angle. I loved the catharsis involved in painting, in the drabness of the wet brushes after I cleaned them in baby mason jars. The swirls of colors oscillating through the water, the paint moving fast like cloaks of whirling dervishes. I wasn't a good painter, but the feeling I had as a little child, the desire of wanting to be good and perfect at everything, was quickly waning. I felt untwisted underneath

a golden sun, full with purpose. I was becoming something of my own design. Fucking finally.

Ryan called me the next day.

I was cooking a curry lentils recipe I had found in one of Kat's addictive Ottolenghi cookbooks. The garlic and onions were browning to a soft caramel when the phone buzzed and Ryan's name blinked like a flashing sign.

"Hello."

"Hey, kid, whatchya doing?"

"I am... cooking."

"You can cook?"

"Um, I used to cook all the time for you! Remember?"

"Oh yeah, I guess you're right. Well, what's the occasion?" he asked. I could see the smile on his face, his lips pursed to the side.

"Oh, nothing."

He laughed for real that time. "Wanna hang out?"

"Uh, yeah." And I did, I really, really did.

An hour and a half later he picked me up from Kat's and we walked around the block with a lilac-purple Tupperware container filled with curried lentils and a slightly burned, but still tasty, golden quinoa and sweet potato cake.

He opened the lid cumbersomely. "Don't be mad, but I wasn't expecting for it to actually look, you know, edible."

"Jeez, thanks, man."

"No, I mean, I can't remember if you were a good cook or not!"

I nodded my head, a little annoyed. After all those meals I cooked for him, I felt kinda disrespected. But it was in the wake of Lyse's death, so I forgave him quickly.

"Fork?"

I shook my head, instead passing him some chopsticks.

"Okay, that's strange."

I laughed and watched him contemplate the proportions. He eventually took a bite.

"That's actually not bad."

"Right."

"In theory, it could have been bad."

"Maybe."

"So, how you doing?"

"Well, I made a friend."

"That's nice, what are they like?"

"She's a she. She's nice. Friendly. Pretty."

"Pretty girls are always a great incentive."

I laughed. Ryan set down the Tupperware and stared at me.

"Where should we go?"

"Take me anywhere you'd like!"

We walked to a café nearby and we ordered some creamy tiramisu, a dulcet strawberry cheesecake, and a short, sharp espresso for Ryan. The air's circadian sense of rhythm was palpable. I wondered if he was seeing anyone. I wondered if I should ask.

"What are you thinking about?"

"This. This is strange, right?"

"Us? Yeah, this is strange. But a good strange." I smiled up at him.

"It's definitely weird seeing you. You're the same but then you're not."

"I'm not." And I wasn't.

"What were you then? And what are you now?"

I took a few moments before I answered. "I was weak..."

"And now you're not?"

I laughed. "No, I still am."

He joined my laughter.

"But, I mean, I feel older. It's not even a mental thing. It's like I can feel life in my body. My skin has changed, shifted, grown, stretched. Having a baby inside of you makes time a tangible thing." I paused just as the baby moved. She had begun to move. "I mean, I'm still unsure of what I'm going to do with my life, you know, but I'm not as nervous about it as I once was."

"Well, I remember when you didn't talk, not a peep!"

I smiled, remembering also. "I didn't need to talk, Alyssa did all the talking."

"Why did you always step down? Why didn't you ever challenge her?"

I shrugged as if it were obvious. "She was the *chosen one*."

I said it in a joking voice, but he scoffed. I felt defensive.

"She was... My parents loved her!"

"And they didn't love you?"

I paused. "No. They didn't."

"Tay, that's bullshit."

The tight rage, with a sudden jolt, was building. "Listen, you were an outsider looking in. You can't even begin to understand... I mean, why do you think I'm here?"

I didn't want to entirely open the Pandora's box of suffering; for now, I still wanted vagueness to subsume my past.

Without a beat, he asked, "Well, why are you here?"

I sat silently.

"Taylia? I've upset you."

I shrugged again.

"Hey, listen. I'm not saying that your issues of insecurity aren't valid. They definitely painted Alyssa as this—this... golden child and maybe it's unfair of me to question how much that had an effect on you. No doubt it was tough. I'm just saying that though I'm sure it was hard, maybe it would do you some good to look at it from another perspective. Glass half full, maybe?" He paused. "I mean, I don't know... I don't want to 'mansplain' your life to you or anything."

I winced at the usage.

"That's what all the kids are saying."

"You forget... You're a millennial, too. *Sorrrrrrry, dude!*"

He smiled. "Word."

I stopped deflecting, and for a second I indulged him. *Was it all as painful as I remembered?* Truth was, *I didn't know*. I wasn't sure. All I *knew* was this was what I felt, and that *that* was valid.

Ryan strategically moved the conversation away from my family. "How are you doing anyway?"

And I deliberately changed the subject, not wanting to unnecessarily linger. "I think I'm sick of Ralph."

"Ralph? The guy I met at the hospital? Not the baby daddy, right?"

I nodded.

"He seemed like a nice guy. Overprotective, but nice."

"He's a philistine."

"Big word, Taylia."

"Shut up. It's true." I felt myself acting dumb again. I had created my own drama. I was my own Alyssa, luring in a man whom I now no longer needed. I was being strong like her, feminine like her, wicked like her.

"Don't be an asshole to him." I didn't say anything, and he continued, going right back to the wound. "When you have that thousand-yard stare on your face, you look remarkably like your mother."

I jolted out of my daze. "My mother?"

"Yes."

"I didn't know you still had such a good relationship with my parents." I said it with disdain. I said it because, in some universe, maybe I was jealous that they liked their nonbiological son more than me.

I could see the words climbing up his throat: "I loved Alyssa, but I also hung around for your parents." He continued. "Two years into our relationship I began to understand the ins and outs of Lyse's character... She was predictable because, in a lot of ways, she just liked drama. Maybe I was drawn to that, at least as a teenager. Now, as an adult, it's different. But I guess I just really liked being around y'all. You were alive, in your own ways. I don't have siblings, so you became this—this... extended family for me... It felt nice to be welcomed into your home with all of you." As he talked to me his eyebrows pulled in like waves of compassion and immediacy, nudging me to listen, letting the

words sink in. "All four of you made up this indistinguishable serenity in my life."

Suddenly, my eyes were rigid against his face. "What the fuck was so great about my parents?"

This unfazed him, like he was almost too eager to go on this propaganda campaign. "Your parents were cool. I'd never met anyone like them before. Your dad was a weird Brown antisocial brainiac and your mom was obsessed with art in a way that was riveting and stimulating to me. They weren't like other parents I knew. You guys were just exciting to me. I don't know what to tell ya!"

I felt like I wanted to bark at him, but I just sat and absorbed this information, putting it into context. Ryan's parents were really rich Black entertainment lawyers who traveled a lot for work. They sent Ryan, their only child, to all the best schools, and I wasn't surprised to hear that even after Alyssa's suicide Ryan graduated (though years later) from Harvard Law. Unscathed.

"Ryan, don't."

"Don't what?" His voice was suddenly tinged with defiance.

My cheeks flushed over. "Respectfully... you don't know what you're talking about."

"Whatever they did, you don't need to keep punishing them for it. You know your father has, like, full-blown dementia now. Early onset. Like it's bad..." It sounded like an accusation, and momentarily my heart curled over. I knew Baba had been show- ing the signs for years, ever since Alyssa died, but I cared little to know much more about it now. My fury toward them had possibly saved my life, and I couldn't let go of it. And now, for the first time, Ryan, my dead sister's ex-boyfriend, was telling me how to think and to feel about *my* life—like he knew what it felt like to *ever* compete for love. Though Ryan's parents were busy throughout his life, and I'm sure the absence hurt, he was always the apple of their eye. They made sure to prioritize him, to love him. I could tell when I saw them engage with Mama and Baba, I could tell that Ryan was loved by the way he talked—

it was similar to Alyssa. Now a powerful executive at a fancy film production company, he had always been outstanding. A little boring, yes, but an overachiever. Like Alyssa. They had that much in common.

I knew it was unfair of me to project, but he couldn't know the traumas of my life. And I couldn't know his. But I also realized he had never even treated me like a person worth engaging with the many years he dated Alyssa. It was easy, in retrospect, to praise our fanciful, exotic life and all the things that *that* had offered him, but I wasn't a prop in a family play. I was a person. I had been mad at myself for never reaching out to him, but now I was figuring out that he had also never reached out to me. He never checked in, all the while still being chummy with my parents. It felt cruel. Why did people so rarely think of my needs? Why had I allowed myself to be glossed over so incessantly?

He was talking about my mother and how she was barely coping. I pictured her, the ghostly image moving through my stomach like a slippery mass. Her hair a dense cloud, and she, on her left knee, lifting the white powdery tights up Alyssa's legs. The memory was milky, delayed, lost in the puddle of a thousand recollections I had of being tossed to the side. Of being second. Of being fucking second. To Alyssa. What had she said to me moments before? *Taylia, come here?* Had she asked me to stand near her? Had she also asked to put the tights on? Had she asked me first? Before Alyssa? I can't remember. What did she say? Momentarily, I was caught in doubt. *Had it all been as hard as I thought it was?* I felt anger rise up again. Of course it was hard! I was a ball of clay that could be carved by the whims and desires of my parents. Too often mothers and fathers want their children to be pliable to their desires, the gatekeepers of their lost dreams. My nonlife—the existence on the other side of Alyssa's existence, the no-space of being where I had resided since I was a little girl—was my harrowing reality. I was the lesser child. Pointed out like an afterthought, a leftover, a messy fragment of

the equation... I knew I sounded dramatic, but it was my truth, and I hated Ryan for questioning me. He would never understand. But I was beginning to see my life fully.

Then there was the rape. I toyed with the idea of telling him, but I didn't want the questions. It would hurt too much to see them form. Besides, I felt myself unconsciously judging my own body, my own experience, still. I had to protect myself from being gaslit. I had to protect my mind and my heart from those who couldn't see it.

I knew Ryan hated Simon, but people always protect men. Even the ones they hate. I could see this in the statistics of the people (mainly women) who report rape and the even smaller numbers of people who find any redemption, any remote justice. Violence against women is too common and known, too ubiquitous, and yet the culture of shame creates the cycle of silence. The culture of shame.

I wish I could explain to Ryan what it feels like to have your body taken from you by violence that then lurks—for months, for years—like a ghost in the darkest corners of your mind, galvanizing like invisible smoke. How self-hatred creeps, and you are robbed of yourself. I wish I could explain to him that I still felt Simon as well. That I still had nightmares of their hands and the feeling of being ripped open. Rape is a kind of death. Of the self, mind and body. Survival looks like many things, but sometimes you do believe you deserved what happened to you, as a means of accepting your fate. Which is why there are such high suicide rates for survivors. At a certain point, you wonder what's left living for when your body no longer feels like yours. Where are you safe? To then watch the men, the people, who damaged you live, continue on, is another kind of death. It is to feel gutted out, constantly. It is to feel unsafe and unloved, constantly.

As I thought of Simon now I thought of claws. If it ever happened again, I know I could kill him. But when it came to Ryan and the truth, I saw Mama and Baba stare back at me, wreathed

in paranoia, the sham of care circling like a war wound in my stomach. I didn't want to feel judged by them, even if it was via somebody else, so I silenced myself and erased that specific smudge of my own experience. I didn't say any of this, presenting the version of myself who was irrational in her rage instead.

25.

When I was about thirteen, Alyssa found a journal my mother had kept in her early twenties. Inside the very first pages, dated September 29, 1982, my mother, before she was my mother, had inscribed:

> *Today Janice finally talked to me again. She didn't even say a hello when she walked up to me with all her fucking sass... But then she slowly opened her mouth and asked, in her annoying southern drawl, "How can you bear to kiss his lips?" I wanted to tell her how good it actually felt to be kissed by a man who respected you, who hadn't asked for "it" but who had instead told me that he'd wait for me "for as long as you need." But I just laughed her off, laughed off Janice with her stupid gap tooth. Now I sorta wished I hadn't laughed it off. Who does she think she is anyway? Maybe she's just jealous. I always thought she was. The thing is, I love him, Janice. I fucking love him.*

I was too young when I read it and the only thing that really resonated was the fact that my very own mother wrote *fucking*. My second thought was that this Janice was still very much a presence in my mother's life, which meant that Janice was a two-faced bitch. As I noticed the third and final thing, Alyssa simultaneously pointed it out to me. There were tear tracks down the page, blurring the words *lips* and *anyway*, smudging them into blue-inked clouds. For a moment, in that snapshot of time, my mother suddenly seemed very human to me: a tangible being with emotions and maybe even a heart. For the first time, I didn't feel sorry for myself but for her.

I fished around for Tahsin's number and called her, feeling grateful afterward that she happily accepted a meeting that in retrospect almost entirely felt like fate. We set a date, and on the day I waited frantically for her at our meeting place, outside the Whole Foods at Union Square. She worked in the city as an editor for a magazine, and we were meeting on her lunch break.

I tempered my apprehension with my inevitable excitement. I recalled what she looked like, the curves of her haunting face were etched into my brain. I had a day-old *New York Times* in my hand, but I couldn't read a full sentence without having to repeat each word every half a second, so I concentrated on the front page. There was a coffee stain from Kat's favorite ceramic mug creased into the first few pages and unintelligible scribbles written around the headline. I smiled, thinking of Kat reading the paper before work, only distracting myself for about three to four seconds.

Eventually Tahsin walked up to me. At that exact time I was watching the man in front of me sell his intricate crafted jewelry made of vintage spoons, but my glances were only a conduit for what I was actually doing: thinking nervously about Tahsin. She was smiling when she arrived, wearing a burgundy long-sleeved dress with a thin tan leather belt around her waist. Her shoes

were strappy, and her hair was down in waves and billowed around the corners of her face. A strand or two were caught in her red lips, like a fly to a Venus flytrap. I had worn a Canadian tuxedo that I thrifted from a Salvation Army. She hugged me first, and I hugged her back. It was a very embracing, full hug.

"I'm so happy to see you," I said, my mouth just above her shoulder.

"And I, you," she chanted back.

I knew it was only a courtesy, but it still felt so warm.

She pulled my arm to hers and asked, "Where should we go?"

I shrugged, so she took the initiative and we started walking.

"So, how have you been?"

"I don't know." I paused, trying to find the right words. "I had an interesting night last night."

"Oh yeah?"

I nodded.

"Like how?"

Where to start.

"Well, see, I don't have a very good relationship with my parents, in particular my mother."

She turned to me, concerned. "I'm sorry to hear that."

"It's okay," I said quickly, not wanting to cause her distress. "It's always been like that, I guess. Well, it's not really okay. But it's life, you know, so it's whatever."

She nodded. I wondered if she could understand.

"Anyway. I left home a while back. Things weren't working out... and my parents didn't want me in the house anymore... So I left, I guess... And, well, a few years before that my sister killed herself... So, anyway, my sister's ex and I recently reconnected, and last night he told me that I shouldn't let my parents suffer anymore, or, well, something to that effect, and I guess for the first time I started remembering my parents as humans who felt and had pain... which is just weird! Because things kind of shifted in my head after that... So now I'm in a weird place and I need to process it all."

I looked over at her. Her face was a blur of confusion. She put up her hands and mouthed, *What?!* "Taylia. Holy shit. That's a lot to deal with."

I shrugged, my safest default reaction, not knowing what else to do, knowing full well that my nonchalance was just a facade. I felt comfortable that she cared, as this was why I had turned to her. Sometimes we just need someone to tell us, *Wow, that's really hard.* It's as if having that someone acknowledge the pain creates a purpose for these things to have happened in the first place. Or that they would, somehow, be things that were lived and not merely conjured. We kept walking.

"So, what's the next step?"

"Nothing. I don't have one. I think, if anything, all I really want from my life is to accept the things that *have* been given to me." I emphasized the *have*, halving the air with my teeth, the two front ones cutting down lightly onto my bottom lip, resounding the whole word.

She stopped walking, the wind blowing her hair forward, and for a second her whole face was masked from me and others to her side. It looked like a curtain being stringed for a closing act, like her hair moved neatly and succinctly to a languid performance. As she turned to me, the music rose in my ears and I watched how beautifully she even turned her head. When our eyes finally met, hers were welled with tears, questions floating at the top.

"Taylia, honey..."

She grabbed my shoulders and pulled me into a full hug, and as we stood there, opposite the Walgreens, and she didn't let go for an eternity. Instead, she lingered in my hair, in my mind, and deep in my heart.

"Is it okay that I'm hugging you like this?"

I said yes. We kept hugging.

Minutes went by, passerbys continued on. Some stared, expecting a scene, an artwork, a remark, a protest. We just stood. Two people connected over pain, over heartache, over loss. She finally

let go of me and the timing seemed perfect, each of us fuller with something. We said nothing, but she held my hand and pulled me by her side so that our shoulders touched as we walked on.

"I'm sorry. I just think I really needed to hear that."

"How come?"

She exhaled. "After my husband died, I've been struggling with that idea, Taylia. I've been struggling with my faith, with God. How does a God that loves you take away something that meant the whole world to you? Can I worship a God that betrayed me in that way?"

I stayed silent. I had my own battles with God.

"Are you religious?"

I said I didn't know.

She laughed. "That's probably a good answer. Maybe people with true faith have to challenge God. Or at least that's what I've been telling myself."

We continued walking. Sometimes we were silent, other times she'd point out a store she liked and I'd mention how I'd never been there, or, sometimes, I'd make an observation, like the brightness of a woman's hair dyed a deep and effervescent violet. We were comfortable in our silence together.

We walked into a coffeehouse brimming with color. It was as if I had been transported into the '70s. The interior was wooden with flowers arranged on every table, like some eccentric dining hall at a *Freaks and Geeks*–themed summer camp. We walked through the small café to a quaint enclave in the back and made a place near some plants and a questionably placed fan. I ordered a white peach tea and Tahsin ordered a three-shot ristretto mocha.

She turned to me after ordering with a huge grin on her face. "Coffee is a weakness."

I nodded.

"Not a coffee fan, aye?"

"I just worked in a café, so coffee is very accessible to me all the time. I'd rather try something completely different... like a white peach tea!"

She laughed, quickly turning sober. "I can't imagine what you've been going through with the death of your sister and leaving, or rather being kicked out of your house, it sounds like?"

I agreed, also shifting into "serious" conversation mode.

"Where are you living now, by the way?"

"I live in Fort Greene. A very kind friend of mine has housed me for the last few months. Her name's Kat. She's also a single mother, we should all hang out."

Tahsin smiled a yes. Our drinks arrived and we started sipping. She oohed and aahed over hers. "You don't want to have a teensy-weensy try, do you?"

I ferociously declined.

"So, does your sister's ex... Okay, what's his name? We can't keep calling him that."

"Ryan."

"Okay, is Ryan suggesting that you go and pay your parents a visit, or... ?"

"I guess so."

"How does that make you feel?"

"Horrible. Going back to them would mean that I had forgiven them for everything."

"And you haven't?"

"No, not at all!"

She looked perplexed. "I don't know, love. I come from an Arab family where family is paramount. It's everything that you have. I understand that you never had that, but I'm just trying to look at it from an objective place."

"I appreciate that. Do you get along with your family?"

"Depends what you mean by that."

I laughed, thinking, technically, we *were* family. She and I— our children were cousins. Baby suddenly pushed, and I suddenly got quiet, seeing it as a sign, hoping she wouldn't notice.

"Look, every family has their own drama. It would be naive of me to say otherwise. I have had my ups and downs with my family, but they love me, and I love them. They've accepted a

lot of things in my life—I mean, I married a non-Muslim—but we've learned and grown together. We're not an ideal family, but we're happy. Which is something, I guess. Also, and this is the biggest thing recently, they've really been there for me since my husband died."

I deflected fast, not wanting to linger on Roman. "Do you have any siblings?"

"Yeah, a sister. She's pretty great."

I smiled sadly, remembering Roman talking about her around the dinner table.

She put her hand on my hand. "I know I keep saying this, but I'm sorry about your sister. That's just terrible."

"It happened a few years ago, which is weird to say. You'd think I'd be fully healed by now..."

She looked at me with a smile. "You'll heal when you're ready."

The words fluttered past my eardrums, down my spinal cord, and into my stomach. I felt lighter, calmer, and at peace. I felt tears rise up. *I'll heal when I'm ready.* Suddenly time no longer mattered, failure was no longer an option. I felt *with* life. "Ah, and I really needed to hear *that*."

We paused.

"Do you feel lonely without him? Your husband, I mean." I felt bad pretending as if I didn't know who her husband was. But I didn't feel ready to tell her.

She began with a sigh. "Every day, Taylia. It's always really hard when you're reminded of them because of a distinct memory you have of a thing that involves them, or your only memory of that thing is coiled around a memory of them. I'm sure you can understand. Sometimes I just touch things hoping I can feel the echo of his fingertips. When I don't, it's hard to accept that I'll never feel them again. He'll never push my hair back behind my ears or touch my hands... And that's"—she bit her lip—"that's when it's really, *really* hard." She looked down quickly; I knew it was because she was minimizing her chances of crying. I some-

times did that, too. She smiled even amid the tears, and I clasped my fingers around hers.

"I know it's not exactly the same thing, but I do understand. I felt like that after Alyssa died. It's hard to believe a person is dead when you can still feel their heartbeat everywhere. I was crazy. I wanted to relive everything in my memories of her, like go to her favorite cafés, believing that she would walk across the street and scream out, 'Tay, I've been looking around all over for you.' I have that dream still." I didn't tell her that it worked, that that's kinda what Alyssa did do, though not exactly as I had hoped. Apparitions of dead people weren't exactly the same as having them back in real life.

Tahsin closed her eyes so that a stream of tears spilled out of the corners. She was still smiling, but the smile was embedded with so much sadness. She got out a tissue and blew her nose, and then folded the tissue into a square and drew it to her eyes, where she brushed the edges of her soaked skin. She looked like a saint.

"Okay, enough of that." Her eyes were wide and open. "Today's about you."

"We can talk—"

She stopped me. "You." She paused. "So your sister's ex-boyfriend Ryan, huh?"

"I don't know what to do."

She took a sip of her coffee and then asked, "What are your options?"

"Well, to go see my parents, according to him."

"Is that a viable option?" she asked.

"No way. No fucking way."

"May I interject?"

I nodded. *Of course.*

"Sweetie, you're young. I know young people hate hearing this, but you don't really know what you want when you're young."

I breathed in defiance.

"I mean, to be fair, you never really know. But still. There are times when life *feels* right and an aha moment clicks in your head and things fall into place. I'm assuming seeing your parents doesn't give you that feeling, huh?"

I shook my head.

"Why?"

Tell her. Be open, Taylia.

I hesitated. I wanted to tell her about Simon, but I wasn't ready. Not yet. "They loved my sister more than me."

Without a beat, Tahsin asked, "So? I mean, don't get me wrong, love. That's horrible. I know, don't tell me that I don't understand sibling—or more specifically sister—rivalry. It's horrendous when you're growing up, especially when your parents play you against each other, but still. Look at yourself. You're amazing, you're smart, you're compassionate, *and* you're beautiful. What should it matter what your parents did or didn't do when you were growing up? I doubt they really loved you less, it just maybe feels that way."

I was shocked, both by the compliments and by how cavalier she was being of my pain.

"Taylia, sweetie? I haven't offended you, have I?"

I shook my head.

"I know it's easier said than done. I'm just putting my two cents in..."

"No, I want you to be honest."

"Okay, I will be then."

"I guess it's just a lot more complicated than you're making it out to be."

"Of course." As she said it, she put her hand on her heart.

"There was a lot of shaming and guilt-tripping involved. I guess that's why I feel so undeveloped as a person, you know? Like I shouldn't be having these problems in my twenties. So it just makes me feel like I'm slow... at life... or something."

"Honey, it's not a race." She smiled, and I cocked my head goofily. "Tell me about your sister."

26.

Mama is in the living room. She is angry, she is pulsing. She looks tough, the bruises of her anger apparent like swollen lumps on either side of her cheeks. Yet, despite her vexations, there is warmth—and it surges through her. She is a needy love, she is a confused love; the pain of unfulfillment travels fast through her blazing eyes. Every blink, every smile, every thousand-yard stare—is a call, to love.

"Alyssa, please don't wear that."

Alyssa laughs. At her. She is uncompromising to this woman, a stranger.

"Alyssa, don't be rude."

"Oh, Mom." *She's so condescending.* Oh, Mom. You're an idiot. Oh, Mom, what is wrong with you? Oh, Mom, I'm the best thing that ever happened to you. Oh, Mom. You're nothing without me.

So much said in so little words.

"Alyssa..."

"What? You're acting like a fucking cunt."

I am not there and there at the same time. I don't register. My facial expression remains intact, removed. I'm on Alyssa's side no matter what.

It felt like a dream lived, a past life. We were downstairs by the kitchen. The kettle was humming. I couldn't remember how old I was, but I knew I was old enough to do something. Or at least to know that what Alyssa was doing was wrong.

As I lay there not doing much of anything, I replayed it all in my mind. I tried to isolate the images of my mother that had formed in my brain. My mind focused on Alyssa, but I refocused it on Mama. She didn't do anything when Alyssa threw those words at her, assaulting the air, cutting through the energy like the slice of a guillotine. She just stood. The liquid around her eyes rose, creating a film that sat there on the edge of the cliff,

floating in the space between the lashes and her eyeballs. I rewatched her every move in my mind, haunted by her composition, disturbed by her preciseness, and for the first time I realized that she was used to this. Her face didn't transform into a mask of pain, but there was heartache etched all over. She bit her lips in a bid to pace the tears, and when Alyssa swiftly exited the room, laughing perniciously to herself, my mother let the tears reign over her.

I was there that day. I just sat as if I weren't. It wasn't my fight, it wasn't my war, but I let my mother weep and mourn, already at a loss for a child who had given up.

I got an abrupt message from Ryan on a Tuesday afternoon. I had ignored his last few attempts to meet again, so was surprised when the message just said, *We need to talk.*

There had never before been a sense of urgency with him, so I wondered what this message could possibly mean.

Why, is something wrong? I texted back.

His next message was as abrupt as the last. *Can you meet up later this evening?*

I felt nervous just awaiting his reply. We decided on 8:00, and at 8:02 he buzzed the door. I ran down, one hand on my belly.

"Hey." Inviting him up, I gestured a *come on,* but he paused. We both paused on the steps of Kat's brownstone.

"I have to tell you something, Tay. I should have told you this a while ago. Or maybe not, I don't actually know. But I'm gonna tell you this now because I think that it's right, or something."

He got out his iPad that had a dated message that read:

From: Alyssa Chatterjee
We all bleed for our wrongdoings. If not in this life, maybe in the next. I'm not ready to bring life into this world. It's not yours. I'm sorry. For everything.

I reread it at least five times before he said anything.

"She sent that to me the night before she killed herself."

I was dumbfounded. "Why?"

His head was cocked to the side. He was tired and angry. "Why? Why? Why... ?" His words were like a grater slowly tearing at the outer layer of my heart, shredding it to a pulp.

"Ryan?" *Was she pregnant? Was that what she was saying?*

"I hate her for leaving me to do the dirty work."

"Tell me."

His fingers were at his eyes. "A couple of months before she died, Alyssa was sleeping with Simon..."

I shook my head violently, *no, no, no.*

"She was seeing him because she needed him. Simon had something Alyssa needed." I knew he was trying to spell it out for me without saying the specific words, but I needed help.

"What? What did he have?"

His head was hung over the edge.

"Ryan?" I was shouting it at him. I needed to know. The answer was staring at me in the face with a smirk. Simon's smirk.

"She had an addictive personality, Tay..." He stopped talking midsentence, and I let him, my heart grinding to a stupefied halt. "She did it to herself, Taylia."

It was so cold. He had given up. Slowly he explained her pregnancy with Simon's baby. Her addiction. I wanted to projectile vomit. *Alyssa, my darling.* I wanted to weep, *Alyssa, Lyse. I'm sorry I wasn't there.*

"That sounds harsh, but it's true. She lacked self-control. She chose not to take advantage of the good life she was given. She decided to fuck up."

I could hear how hurt he was, but I didn't care. There were small tires of anger lodged underneath both sides of my throat. His response was so mean. Like a plug to my tears, I felt immeasurably sad for her. I knew this wasn't the whole truth, and in that moment, I mourned never getting the chance to know her side. The pain of holding back the deluge, even for a few moments,

sent a tight pull up my jaw, like a harness against my emotions. Couldn't he just forgive her and move on? He was still here, he was still living.

"Taylia..."

"Get the fuck out." I wanted to scream it, but before I inhaled another scratching breath, he had already left.

As I began to breathe normally again, I remembered that before she died, Alyssa wrote out, in her notebook left neatly on her bedside table, a quote from Mama's favorite book, *Family Lexicon*, by Italian writer Natalia Ginzburg. It was a line about Cesare Pavese, an Italian poet and writer who tragically killed himself. Though, I guess, suicide was always tragic.

"He looked beyond death and imagined death to the point where it was no longer death he imagined but life." She wrote it at the top of her Moleskine, leaving it open for all to see. It was scrawled with her favorite Kaweco fountain pen. The ink bled a little onto the pages, just the way Alyssa liked it. I remember, I remember reading it. I should have known.

She came as soon as I texted. In one hand she bore a stack of Ritter Sports, the ones with cornflakes in the chocolate, and in the other was Sufjan with an insistent gaze. Luc was behind me, holding on tightly to my stringy dress, hands shoved tightly against my fleshy calves.

"Who are you?" he asked Tahsin.

"I'm Tahsin. Who are you?"

"Luc." His questions didn't skip a beat. "Is that your baby?"

"Yes, it is. This is Sufjan."

"You know my mommy owns this place." Even under the circumstances, it was so cute that Tahsin and I both laughed. I tried to pick him up to kiss him, but he swatted my care. There was another short pause before he sprang off. "Okay, bye!"

Tahsin giggled. "Kat's not home?"

I shook my head. "I've been doing some babysitting to help her out. She's probably prepping the kitchen for tomorrow as we speak. She doesn't really ask for much help, but this is the least my giant amniotic sac of a body can do."

Tahsin cocked her eyebrows at me, judgmental. I watched her plop the chocolates onto the dining table while simultaneously pushing Sufjan upward in a graceful propelling motion.

"How are you really doing?"

"Well, I guess I don't know what to think..."

"Why? Don't you trust Ryan?"

I breathed in. "Yes. I do..." I guess I did, but I also didn't know him anymore and didn't know if I could trust his objectivity.

"Then? What's there to think?"

"I don't want to believe it, Tahsin. I just can't. It would mean too much."

"What? What would it mean? Other than she was complicated, and that she hid things. Even from you. I know that hurts... but you were coming to terms with that. If anything, this is a blessing. I think this is that for you. You just have to look at it like a blessing. Besides, you shouldn't hold her complexities against her."

I didn't. I just felt betrayed that she never told me. That she never confided in me.

"I'm just shocked."

"That is to be expected..."

"I just found out that my sister—" My voice broke.

Was pregnant? Drug addicted and pregnant? With Simon's child?

"Okay, sit down. I'll make us some tea."

I sat down, replaying every memory of her that could have pointed to the truth. How could she have done that to herself?

As if reading my mind, Tahsin remarked, "Taylia, people do stupid things, obviously to varying degrees, but she clearly felt like she was losing agency."

How could I tell her that this was also about Simon? How could I tell her about the disgusting overgrowth of despair that was Simon?

"Oh, and she only just left me all alone in this fucking world."

"Sweetie, please. Would you have wanted to be overshadowed by Alyssa your whole life? It's hard, but you have to find a positive in this..."

I felt a disorienting alignment pull up my spine. "A silver lining..." I said half-mindedly. "I guess. Yes. It's so great my sister killed herself so I can finally learn to be strong! Have you found the silver lining since Roman died, too?" I wanted to be cruel, but the question came out sedately, clear, with a certain piquancy.

"No," she said, "but I see him everywhere..."

My heart started hurting as I suddenly thought of Ky. I noted that she still talked about Roman in the present tense. I stared at Sufjan for a while, my mind suddenly absent. I could hear her speaking, but nothing was going in, she was just a voice outside of my paralyzing shell, her voice mildly operatic. I suddenly wanted to blame her for the fact that Ky never tried to get me back. He never even came looking for me. I guess he never really loved me, and I was also in the midst of accepting that.

"In time, I will heal. It's hard to start your life after death." I was back, listening to her. "Your natural inclination is to die with them, right? Like, you almost don't want it *to get easier*, because how dare it? And the thing is, did I even have a life outside of him? Do I just stop loving him? Do I just turn it off? I know that would make it easier, but how do you stop loving someone you love, and if life would have gone your way, they'd be loving you too... right here, right fucking now."

I could hear her voice stutter at the word *here*, and only then was I fully present again. I stared at her, knowing and not knowing her.

"It's strange, there's this word in Arabic, *Ya'aburnee*, which means 'I love you so much that I hope I die before you because I couldn't bear the pain of living without you.' I used to say it

to him all the time, and we'd laugh at its absurd moroseness. *Ya'aburnee.*" She started crying. "You look pale."

I looked up at her, unfazed by her tears. "Do I?"

She nodded.

I deflected by getting up at the zing of the kettle boiling and poured the hot water into two short ceramic mugs, wide with moon-shaped handles. Tahsin had scooped Sufjan into her left arm, drumming his diapered bottom as she cried melodically. I wondered at how much I didn't know about her. How I didn't quite understand the intricacies of her character yet. Was she just wearing a disguise of positivity? And if so, was she actually in chronic emotional pain underneath it all? I felt my eyes numb as I stared at her wiry silhouette, questioning what it was that made us who we are. She was so open, so authentic, but not vulnerable. There was no room for hurting anymore, only room for survival. She wanted to succeed. Even then, on some level I was a witness to her pain. It was deep like a well. I assumed some days the pain must rise more than others, floating to the top, usurping all.

I still hadn't mentioned Ky. I knew I wasn't ready, but I also was paralyzed by the idea of what to do next. Was I actually going to have this baby alone? Kat had done it, Tahsin was doing it, but was I going to actually join the single mothers club for eternity? Money was an obvious question. Kat owed me nothing, but I wondered if she'd let me work at the café again. If I could beg her to let me stay in this brownstone with her. How was I going to pay for everything? For this baby? With the small sum of money Dadi-ma left me? Forever? Life was beginning to come crawling in like an anthem.

27.

As my mother had married a man with toffee-colored skin and a Nehru nose, she knew she needed to prove that her husband was just the same, lacking in no way what a "normal" man had. He may have resembled a cabdriver, but he was a different breed of Indian. An Indian with a Western education, who despised incense and spoke with a well-adjusted transatlantic accent. His skin was sweet and odorless, unlike other dirty Indians (and never sticky on hot days). He despised religion, having never read the Bhagavad Gita or followed the silly customs of his family. He ate beef, drank wine, and never reeked of cheapness. Completely affable, he wore polo shirts that highlighted his handsome physique, resembling a more rugged and darker Imran Khan. He was the Commonwealth's dream who proved the Queen and her endeavors had done well to pillage and invest in Indian and foreign soil. He was cultured like *them*, like *her*. He was no longer barbaric, he was saved.

When we lived at Dadi-ma's, how easily Baba fell into wearing a lungi—a checkered blue sarong with hints of plum purple—in the daytime, reading newspapers with his feet, out of his Bata slippers, leaning like a bridge on Dadi-ma's glass coffee table, drinking garam garam chai. He would visit his mother after breakfast, as she'd lie on her high, hard bed, the mosquito nets twisted like braids to the side. He was lighter with her; speaking in Bengali gave him character that English never gave him. He had humor, he had dimensions. I lamented never knowing this Baba. I knew that he probably felt he had to wear a mask of stoicism to survive in America as a Brown man, and that tormented me.

Every morning I'd feed Dadi-ma red root, to strengthen her blood, and sat with her as the young girl, who usually swept the house, would wash Dadi-ma's floating feet and toes in a shallow

bucket. I'd tend to her hair, almost all white, like the beard of Gandalf, while she stroked her soft hands on the hems of her saree. We gobbled food, meals sectioning our days. In other hours, Baba lectured his visiting neighbors (I noticed he had a different vibrato in Bengali), while Mama would often read on the roof, in the rose garden, the peach and fuschia goblets already bloomed, and Alyssa would watch the Fashion network in the back room. In India, Baba's gender took hold again, and he was satisfied with the privilege of his birthright.

Are good memories just moments in time we choose to remember, or are they a sign of something greater? I looked back at the memories of my childhood and was surprised by what I had kept to bear with me through the days. A lot involved some kind of accomplishment. Like the time my fourth grade teacher said that I took *initiative,* and I knew that was a good thing, even if I didn't know what it meant entirely. These embellished moments were simply a result of my stunted self-esteem. I guess what I'm trying to say is if love had been fostered within me at a young age, would my life have been different? And would I look at it differently? I don't really know. But I'd like to think that I would. I'd come to realize that my self-effacing nature had become a roadblock to myself, and I never realized the way I viewed myself was deeply interconnected with Alyssa. So, to let go of that part of my life, the one that I had woven so tightly to my stunted heart, I needed to let go of Alysssa. Of what I deemed her to be. Especially in juxtaposition to me.

Tahsin and I had quickly become like *The Wives of the Dead,* bonded by loss. Both of us understood the disabilities that came with that kind of pain: the unwanted tears along the sidewalk, the accidental somnambulance that occurred in daylight, the confused feeling of one's heart continuing to drop, leaving an empty vessel—a heart-shaped lacuna. Our sudden bursts of emotion were as explainable and natural to each other as breathing and sleeping.

After art class Tahsin turned to me.

"Aye, Taylia?"

"Yes, Tahs."

She looked nervous.

"What?" I laughed.

"This guy, the guy you left. You never really talk about him..."

My positivity had its limits.

That's because it's none of your fucking business.

What I chose to say was the blanket answer to all uncomfortable inquiries: "I don't really feel like talking about it..." I stumbled. "Right now."

She wrinkled her nose.

"What was his name?"

I hadn't said his name in months. What would it sound like to say it again? How would my mouth feel to resonate that heart-twisting syllable, the sound of those letters again? How would my body react to his name being said aloud, and almost more important, how would Tahsin?

"I really... really would rather talk about how much you enjoyed Mateo's ass today!"

I hardly believed I had uttered it, but it had come out of *my* mouth. I didn't know if I should be proudly horrified. But my intuition knew one thing: Tahsin had a weakness for Mateo's spicy white (we still didn't know where he was from, but assumed Italian) butt. Tahsin laughed and nudged me playfully on the shoulder as we walked in the sunlight.

Later, I caught up with Ralph even though I didn't want to. When he called me to set something up, I said, "I don't like you, life," but what I had meant to say was his name. He laughed with familiarity, as if this were a candid joke of mine. I imagined his face as if it were right there. I imagined him smiling, eyelashes sprawled out like a fan as he thought of me.

When we eventually met up, he pulled me into a meaningful hug in a meaningful way. At first I didn't put my hands around him, but then something shifted and I involved myself both emotionally and physically. After a few moments he pushed me

forward, still holding on to me, and caressed the part of my cheek that was closest to my lips with his own. I wasn't repulsed; instead I looked up at him and saw him for what he was. And suddenly, it was that obvious. I looked at Ralph, finally clear-minded.

"I'm sorry. I can't do this anymore. It's not working for me."

I was learning new skills now, skills of straightforwardness, of honesty. With the heaviness of my voice, the directness of my glare, I knew Ralph understood me. I could tell he was skipping between words, but in the end he said nothing, so I walked away.

Letting go of Alyssa took a lot more willpower than I had initially anticipated. I had to rewrite the crusty neurological center of my brain, bright against blackness. It was the unknown, the uninhabited wilderness, that scared me. Living without Alyssa reinforced my innate fear of failure. My anxiety always swallowed me whole. My anxieties were their very own majestic organ. I was utterly afraid of ending up at square one again, so I had spent years steeping in my depression, a bitter tea leaf, sunken and rotting.

But, slowly, through the work of showing up for myself, in the smallest of ways, the pink membranes of my heart were starting to understand that I could fail without *being a failure*. That was it. When you accept that you're a real life human—a squishy, mortal, and malleable being of sorts—you begin to accept your mistakes. You accept that your life cannot ever be fixed, not like a fast-tongued solvable riddle. Instead, you must become intrigued by the messiness, the nuances and the in-between bits of yourself and your life, to survive. You have to accept change. At one point, you have to surrender.

I was beginning to understand that my mother wanted for me to excel only in her own image, maybe out of protection. It was a desperate requirement for a woman who, I came to realize, was stuck in her habitual racism, taught to her by her parents. Maybe she was drawn to Baba because of her self-actualizing hatred. So she dedicated herself to a cinnamon-eyed stranger out of a misplaced,

fleeting need for *change*. But white was the color she knew. And that permanence would haunt her. She loved Alyssa because she was closer to her, but also of a world she wanted to enter, a world that being Jewish also gave her—but her accidental whiteness, and generational emulation of whiteness, absolved her of. Now, I understood it: Mama was making sure we were all fitting in. She was doing it for all of us. Maybe she was trying to unlearn her racism, but in the end gave up on it. Both she and Baba were complicit. Through remembering that, I was finding compassion for her. I just wish she never stopped trying. I wish she and Baba had stood by their politics. Maybe that's why I felt okay leaving them—what did they have to teach me? I could love and respect them for all I had received, and let everything else go.

I had learned from both Kat and Tahsin the intricacies of being women—Black and Brown women—in a failing health-care system that cared little for your needs or pain threshold. How many women were dismissed, unseen and unheard. I thought of Dadima talking to me and Alyssa about her sister who died while giving birth. Complication from eclampsia. I remember being struck by the word. These days, with my baby, I knew that could easily be me. I had little money and even less support, but I would find a way. I wanted the birth to be a new beginning. To set a new standard into motion. I was optimistic, even when I wasn't.

"I'm going to put you in touch with Naima. She's a doula. She was mine with both the boys. She usually just works with Black women, but I asked for you, and she's down to take you on. You can do this, we will all help you," Kat assured me, with bluntness.

Tahsin was a similar help, conceiving a birth plan with me. I had decided to do a home birth, a forever masochist, and when I told Kat, she told me she'd get the kiddie pool ready. It felt powerful to be held by them both. The trauma of my rape was definitely present as the baby began to get bigger and bigger, and

I realized that there was no way that I could keep hiding. At least not from myself. The more I looked, the more I found myself in dark corners. I was resurrecting. The more I stared at those dark shadows of myself, the more I saw Dadi-ma, with her adoring eyes, mouthing, *Hot diggity.*

On the ground floor of the building right next to Kat's brownstone, there was an old Afro-Panamanian elder who would point at my belly every time he saw me and say, giving me the thumbs-up and harmonizing, "Baaaabycomesoon!"

Now things felt a little more stable, at the very least emotionally, and one lime-filled night, I made Kat a dinner consisting of rosemary lamb cutlets, with mint and peas on the side and buttery homemade gravy.

"Why does Claudia get to have all the fun with you?"

"*I meaaaaaannnnnn...*"

"Okay, okay, I get it. She offers you *things...*"

"And you don't know me like that, boo."

Kat had transformed over the past few months. She looked calmer, more resolved. I had been waiting to have a solo moment with her, so that she could talk to me about everything that had been coming up.

"I guess this stems from trauma, but I kept focusing on how it might end. Instead of embracing the now, the reality. Also, like, why does every 'successful' relationship have to be predicated on longevity? Sometimes it just doesn't work out, and it could still have been flourishing and vital... I just think that fear is our biggest captive, right? Like a dominating fear can stall you from the best kinda life."

I nodded voraciously, and the smell of tuberoses brushed past my nostrils like smelly clouds.

"I want to experience Claudia inside out. Not just date or fuck, but really experience her... and in order to truly do that you've gotta let go, you just *gotta* jump."

Her pupils were dilated, and she was glowing, lucid. Her teeth white against her radiating dark face, shining like pebbles under a haloed moon, she was wearing a fuschia lipstick and eyeliner, and a sixties pink and green smock. She looked beautiful. I smiled at her, knowing that I wanted to feel that sure in love, that resilient. I knew I didn't feel this kind of love for Ky, the one that Kat was describing, but that didn't scare me anymore. Seeing Kat in love made me see the possibilities of future love. Heteronormativity had defined so much of my desire... but was it even my own? Or a projection? I was suddenly open to possibilities. I pulled myself out of the situation and watched the space between Kat and I. What if I was queer? It wasn't something I had ever let myself explore, but the more I thought about it, the more it excited me. There was a tilting gold-and-violet orchid sitting between us, its flower a bloomed curl, stiff leaves buttressed up toward the light. The tiny yellow specks inside the funnel of its petals resembled a birthmark or freckles.

"Also, I want Isaac and Luc to grow up with two Black parents. I want my kids to grow up around Blackness, to be around Black love. To see Black women be strong and beautiful, and embracing. To be vulnerable and, you know, radically honest. To remind them that it's okay to be, and that they are loved. I've always wanted that, but when kids come into the picture it's more complicated, T. You want them to have the best— the best—the best—" Her voice broke. "Because this country won't give that to them, that's for damn sure."

I pulsed her hands with my fingers, wishing I had something to say. We were silent for a few minutes, both wanting to let that settle. She sighed a big, heady sigh, and we both stretched. I loved her, and I knew she loved me, too.

"I honestly don't know what the next few months are going to look like. But I want you to know, we will all figure it out together. Worse comes to worst, we'll help you find another place. You can come work at the café again if you want..."

Her words circled in my head like a prophecy. They hit me right in the bones. She had heard me. She was showing me all change didn't have to be bad, and that all no's weren't traumatic. I wanted to cry; I felt sedated, calm. Even though my belly felt like the ocean, I could feel that the baby was happy. And I was, too. I felt safe.

"I love you, Kat, and I'm here for the ride. Let's do this!"

She giggled, squeezing my hand. We were just about finished eating when she announced, "*Also*, this lamb, Taylia *Chatterjeeeeee*, was Italian-chef-kissing-fingers emoji!"

I grinned a deep grin, tears flaking near my eyes, and as she sipped her light gamay, she whispered quickly, as if to ease the mood, "Tarot?"

I nodded my head.

She shuffled languidly and pulled three cards: Ace of Cups, Ten of Swords, and the Empress. Putting on a British accent, she spoke with a slight lisp, her beautiful lips veiled: "Now what we have here is very simple, my dear Taylia. You have pulled yourself up from the deep rubble of yourself—the pain, the misery, the feeling of being attacked—cloistered in a corner by the deep workings of the universe. And you're untrusting, you've been failed by those forces that were deemed to protect you. You've been picked at, brutalized, hurt and hurt and hurt, but now you are rising, after the fleeing, *après le déluge*. The pain is releasing from the depths of you, and the subterfuge of the universe's design is finally showing you itself and its secrets. You are at the end and you are, my dearest, darling Taylia, ascending. There's just no two ways around it. You are ascending." She broke her trance.

I could see a luminous kind of light surface in front of her. The truth was there, in this suddenly bright room. And with *us*. As I looked directly into her eyes, the truth was resonating like floating dark red dots before her.

"Kat."

"Yes, Taylia."

I didn't break my gaze, but a mist was rising. Yet, for the first time, I felt unashamed.

"I was disowned by my parents. I was disowned by them because I was raped. I was raped by a family friend. Well, no, I was actually gang-raped by him and a few of his friends. And for this whole time, in the almost two years that has passed, I've tried to understand why. As if rape can be explained... But that's just it, we've—we've been socialized to wonder why when acts of violence are committed against us. *Why me? What did I do?* When in reality, I should be asking, *What happened to him for him to be so utterly fucked up?*"

I looked at her. Her eyes were lined with crimson, tears ready to trail down her cheeks.

"I'm not a victim, Kat. But I have felt like one, I have felt like one my whole life. It was a role I felt prescribed to me because I felt unworthy of being a survivor. Even way before the rape I felt like I didn't deserve to even live. That my body, my soul, was only a carrier of pain, and that I would never be good enough." I inhaled, my words broken in two by my heaving. "But I am good enough. I'm so fucking good enough."

Kat suddenly pushed her chest into my face, holding me as I thundered giant, heavy sobs into the groove of her neck and felt the yellow glowing catharsis of letting it all pass.

"Taylia, my love, my love."

I pulled away from her after a few moments, my head still down, curtained by hair. "I didn't tell you because I couldn't even say it to myself."

She pulled a string of hair behind my left ear. "You don't have to explain to me why you didn't tell me, Tay. You don't have to do that. This is bigger than that."

I looked at her and saw no judgment.

"All I can say is that you're not alone. You're not."

I sniffled, and a glistening trail of slime trickled up my nose.

"You knew the son of a bitch?"

I nodded.

"If I knew who he was"—she paused—"I'd fucking castrate him."

I smiled weakly, wanting the same end. I had felt a cold violence reach from the base of my tongue, remembering the copper taste of my split lips spilling blood. My rage felt purple.

"I watched that new documentary, *India's Daughter*."

The movie about Jyoti Singh Pandey, my sister. My sister who had been gang-raped by six male demons in India in 2012, then fucked by an iron rod that turned the inside of her body into red mush.

"I know it's too simplistic, but men are trash," I heard Kat say.

I wondered if the linoleum floor of the bus had marks from Jyoti's fingernails gouging at her freedom. I wondered if she—blinking eyes pooling with blood, as her organs, like bright red yams, failed from the rupturing of cocks and blue steel—prayed to Kali for revenge. Or if she prayed to Shiva for clemency from this unearthly brutality. I hoped those men saw her when they closed their eyes. I hoped her face lingered like a cold gray cough that starts off tight but then takes over, like a hurricane, beating faster and faster as the lungs lose air. I wanted them to suffer slowly. For little paper cuts to split their skin a million times, for them to be run over by the same blistering rickshaw wheel again and again and again.

I had no room for mercy, not for them, and definitely not for Simon. I wanted to slice him into neat little squares and let him rot in the sun so the maggots could slowly chew through his skin. If I saw Simon again, I would spit in his face, cursing him forever through the ages. I would haunt him, his dreams, his waking moments, and I would haunt him with my lips whispering, like sweet nothings, for his demise. I would make him suffer. I wanted him to die, like he killed me. But then, again, Jyoti was not here, and I was. I cried for her and all the lost women. Kat cried with me, too.

That night I dreamed of Baba, smoking a cigar, looking at me with his brown alchemist eyes, handsome and soft-spoken like

I'd never seen him before. "The greatest love is the love that's never shown, Taylia." He was saying it with an expression that was half stern, half earnest—but he felt mildly warm, he felt close. I spun his words around like cotton, fast and messy.

When we lived in India, he would take me to a grand old Imperial Chinese restaurant on a dusty street in Kolkata, carpeted in bloodred top to bottom. Waiting for my spicy wonton soup that was always too floury, I would play sudoku in an American newspaper. Baba would let me sketch the numbers in with his 0.5 mechanical pencil, his favorite width of lead, and I would hum, enumerating my advance.

Momentarily, I thought of Liza. Where was she now, after also being disowned? I thought of her brother, Vijay, and what he had done to me. I always fantasized telling her, the radical lesbian with a rapist for a brother. I wanted her to be angry with me, to feel the betrayal with me. I always hoped I'd see her for a split second in a crowd or serve her a dulcet coffee at the café. I wanted to tell her that her existence restored me. It made me believe I could choose myself, even if my family wouldn't. She made me see that I was—that my life was—worth choosing.

28.

Alyssa and I are watching *Kuch Kuch Hota Hai*. I desperately want to be Anjali, Alyssa is obsessed with Tina, and we both love Rahul. There's a moment during one of the songs when Rahul sees Anjali. There is love present in that gaze, and it's so palpable that my little heart flutters from the excitement that such a love could exist. An empyrean sort of love, reminiscent of an unconditionality that I so dearly craved.

Tum paas aaye, yun muskuraaye
Tumne na jaane kya sapne dikhaaye
...kuch kuch hota hai.

I dance to the TV, mirroring the moves of my Bollywood idols, hoping to adopt a semblance of their ineffable coolness. I glance over my shoulder, idly, and my mother watches, a little smile playing on the edges of her lips. I smile back at her. She whispers, "My little Bollywood queen," and I turn around shortly after. A few moments later I forget about this memory altogether, too absorbed by Shah Rukh Khan's good looks.

Alyssa is also glued to the TV, mimicking the way Rani uses her hand like a wave in that blue lace salwar, and me, the forever Kajol, the schlubbier of the two versions of what a girl could be, decked in a Nike headband and oversized tee. I'm about eleven; Alyssa is almost sixteen, a little more formative, her hips no longer straight but now ripe. I want to be like her, as well.

I remembered Mama watching the both of us, laughing and clapping to a rhythm that seemed cadenced to songs I know felt so foreign to her. In Kolkata, both Alyssa and I wanted kurtas, lehengas, and salwars to match our dreams of Bollywood, the most accessible (and cool) part of Indian culture. It was something that spoke to us, as outsiders who had a narrow definition of what it meant to be South Asian, but nonetheless felt it in our bones. It felt like relief to see some kind of representation, and though I know I liked being in India more than Alyssa, both of us desired the embrace in different ways. I guess what I'm trying to say is I think Mama craved it, too.

Tahsin came over with Sufjan cradled in her arms. She looked at me intensely.

"I don't know how to say this..." was how she started the conversation.

"Ah... say what?"

"I kind of maybe figured this out a while ago. But I wasn't sure..."

"Are you being intentionally evasive?"

"Taylia."

"Yes, Tahsin?"

The snake was right there, at the base of my throat.

"Ky misses you."

I had suspected right. Somebody just uttering his name sent waves of nostalgia/nausea/desire/sadness/happiness down-downdown and upupup my body. I could feel his presence and I missed him.

I looked at her, feeling fragile.

"When did you... *how* did you know?" Finally ready to open Pandora's box.

"He accidentally said your name a couple of times. At first I couldn't be sure. Taylia's an uncommon name, but this connection was too absurd. How could I meet my brother-in-law's... by accident? It seemed *too* strange, too unexpected. Then, after a while, it was obvious. I couldn't avoid the fact that perhaps, in some way, life was handing you to me and I had to figure out what to do with that. I didn't, and still don't, want to compromise our friendship, so Ky doesn't know that I know where you are... but"—she paused—"I think he should... Especially considering he doesn't know you're pregnant with what I'm assuming is his child?"

I nodded my head cumbersomely. Where to even begin.

"I figured it out, too, a while ago..." I muttered.

"You what?!"

I held on to the table in front of me, the big ball of my stomach a moon. Luc was watching *Yo Gabba Gabba!* and Isaac was playing with dominoes, making all sorts of symbols. Tahsin walked over and plonked Sufjan down next to the boys and came back to me. I watched Isaac walk over, sink down, and hand Sufjan a domino, which made me laugh. Children were so innocent, so open.

"Please, Taylia. Explain."

I didn't hesitate, knowing I'd had my time. "Well, when you mentioned Roman, I knew straightaway..."

"But... that was the first time I met you! You've known since *then*?"

I nodded my head. "I needed time, please don't be mad."

"I'm not mad!" Tahsin said with a raised voice, and both Luc and Isaac looked back. They were both *so* intuitive, so sensitive; they understood the good and bad sounds in their environment with very specific precision, enough to turn a head. "I'm not mad, but I'm confused. I'm a little annoyed, I guess, but I'm more confused. Why didn't you tell me?"

"Tahsin, there's so much... you don't know about me. It's not because I don't want to tell you, but it's because I don't know how... I don't even know how to utter everything to you."

"Just tell me..." she said, agitated.

"It's not that easy. I'm not good with questions or interrogation— not that I think you'd interrogate me... but my life has been fucked, kinda, and I don't always want to talk about it."

"But about Ky? Did he do something to you?"

There the snake was again, the ache in my throat.

"No..." I felt like I would cry. "He's great. But he's complicated. *It's complicated.*"

"I think he loves you, Tay. In his own way. I feel like I bullied that out of him."

I hadn't expected to hear that, and I suddenly felt overwhelmed with sadness. Even though it wasn't entirely appropriate to ask her more about Ky, I wanted to. What did she know? What had he said for her to think that he *loves me*?

"He chose Jade over me." I paused, choosing to articulate. I didn't even know if it was the truth, because I was beginning to question if he ever even wanted to choose me. "I don't trust people, Tahsin." I exhaled loudly, my eyes a sudden blur. "I don't trust people, and I'm so fucking tired of it. It's so exhausting to live like this." I had slumped down onto my seat like a rag doll with no spine.

"Where's Kat?" Tahsin asked, changing the subject. Perhaps too annoyed to continue the conversation, which I wouldn't blame her. At the sound of her name Luc and Isaac had congregated near my legs, holding on and leaning in.

"Mommy will be home soon, my loves..." I kissed their ears.

"I have to take a picture, they're so cute! They love you so much, Taylia. Look."

She passed me the phone and I saw the boys and me, a pietà-like figure, all plump, with these angels nursing their tiny heads on my thighs. I loved them both. I looked happy, beautiful. I did look like my mother. That made me feel warm.

I could tell Tahsin was plotting playdate ideas for Sufjan. Now he'd have more friends, older friends who might show him the way one day. She was sentimental like that; she preferred connectivity over stagnancy.

We all played dominoes and the boys showed off their toys. A little later, when they should have already been in bed, keys rustled at the front door, and the beep that indicated that it'd been opened went off. The boys looked at me, cheeky but slightly nervous, miming *shh* to Tahsin, who was now holding a sleeping Sufjan. Kat must've sensed it, because she walked right to the living room where we all sat, huddled near the games.

"Lord Almighty! What's going on here?" She smiled at the room.

"Hi, Mama," Luc, the charmer, started.

"Hi, baby, why aren't you in bed?" She was wearing her white clogs with a polka-dot jumpsuit.

"Auntie Taylia said we could play a little longer."

"I'm sorry, Kat, we were having so much fun. I—"

"I'm Tahsin." She was already up, ready to embrace Kat with a sleeping Sufjan in her arms. "I've heard so much about you, it's so nice to finally put a face to a name."

"Tahsin! Hello, how wonderful. Same here." She sat down by the boys and me, the dim light pouring onto all our faces so that we looked like paintings in the dark.

"How's Claudia?" I smiled.

"Who's Claudia?" Tahsin asked as Kat turned shy.

"She's my girlfriend..."

"Oh, wow! New?"

"I mean, it's been a while now, but it just happened so unexpectedly."

"An unexpected love? Oh, how delicious!" Tahsin hummed as I got up to make some tea for us all, grabbing a boysenberry cheesecake out of the fridge. I zoned out of the conversation, and when I came back in, this is what I heard:

"You know I actually know an Arabic word, and I actually use it a *fair* bit, Taylia will tell you." I slowed down what I was doing to watch Kat pause for effect and Tahsin's eyes alight with a tell omg. *"Khallas."*

She gasped. "Mashallah, your pronunciation is impeccable."

"Girl, I have so many Sudanese friends."

"Makes sense. Plus your name is Khadijah... Taylia once mentioned it to me."

I frowned, not understanding.

Kat explained. "Khadijah was Prophet Mohammad's first wife, technically the first Muslim as well. She was an entrepreneur, a divorcée fifteen years his senior... and she asked him, her employee, to marry her!"

Tahsin squealed. "Mashallah!"

By now, Luc and Isaac had joined Sufjan, fast asleep on Kat's legs. As I sat down, Kat slowly transitioned out of her seating, passing Luc to me and laying Isaac on the sofa behind us. All the speaking was muttered, but we were all enjoying this new modality; there was an excitement of being up when you normally weren't at a certain hour, with friends, cradled by their companionship.

"I hope this isn't too forward, but do you smoke, Tahsin?"

She smiled knowingly. "I think I smoke what you're smoking."

"That's what I like to hear!" Kat loud-whispered, grabbing her beautiful ornate weed box, which she opened only on special occasions. As Kat rolled, Tahsin filled me in.

"Kat and I were collectively agreeing about the fear of raising children in America."

I nodded, remembering what Kat had told me recently.

"The conversations that Black mothers need to have with their children... it's fucking devastating," she added. "I wonder, too, now without my son's father." Tahsin paused and looked at me, the truth all out. "Roman, who wasn't Muslim like me, would have maybe protected Sufjan from Islamophobia, but now I wonder what'll happen."

I cleared an itchy cough in my throat and took the floor, wanting all of a sudden to give Kat some sudden clarity. "Kat, Tahsin was married to Roman. As in Roman... Ky's brother."

"Wait, you knew Roman?" Tahsin gaped.

"I mean... I own a café next to his work and he was always there, almost every day."

"Wait, you made his last birthday cake!"

"Yes! That was me."

All of a sudden Tahsin launched over and embraced Kat, just the one side that was free, but she stuck her head in Kat's nook, cocooning herself.

"Thank you for that cake." She had started crying. "I always get so excited and emotional when I meet someone who also knew him. As if hearing you speak about him will bring him back."

There was a moment of silence as they sat like that, Kat gently pressing Tahsin above her right knee.

"Did Taylia tell you about my ex?"

"No, Taylia doesn't tell me anything!" She was still mad at me, and I welcomed it. Both of them deserved to be mad at me.

"Yo, you and me both." Kat laughed, having a better way of not letting it sting, knowing how sensitive I was, or maybe because we both were. "Well, Elijah left me. I don't know why—well, I do know, he just didn't want to do it anymore. He had enough of me, the kids... Or, really, once he tried to explain that *it*, meaning us, didn't feel right after the kids, and it's like, we got

the kids. You wanted them! Don't back out now, ya fool. But he did. So, much like what you're doing, I've raised these two babies on my own, and I keep thinking, all these years, did he think I wanted to do it? All of this? And alone? The effing nerve! But what I'm trying to say is that even folks that knew Elijah— because we were together a long time... it was Kat and Eli, man, we were a team—and even when those people who've known him come talk to me about memories about us... I still listen, because that's the perfect time to miss him. It's the time I allot to mourn him. And maybe that's a good way for you to do it, too. To give yourself the time to remember him."

"Habibti, thank you. That's very sweet, I like that."

I watched them both give each other what they had given me and what I hoped I had given them: solace, companionship, an ear—without a moment's hesitation. I wanted them to feel nurtured in this womb we had created in Kat's living room, a pumping heart.

"I think that's good advice for you, too, Taylia." Tahsin's eyes twinkled. "To give yourself a specific space to mourn."

I closed my eyes with a smile.

My heart beat fast at the memory of her. The tethered leaves on the trees outside my window ruffled and shook, causing my emotions to rupture. Alyssa once told me that love was re-dundant. She told me that love couldn't withstand *everything*, because in the end, someone always breaks. "And if you break enough times you reach the point of no return." That was said to me sometime around her last days. Then, I didn't know that she believed that hurt was the only consistent factor of her life. I wish I had known. *Fuck, Lyse. I wish you had trusted me.* I had trusted her word, because I thought she knew best. But what I'm realizing now is that she didn't have answers any more than I did. She had been hurt, and she was speaking from within that pain. Maybe by Simon, maybe by life, the unexpected pregnancy.

Had Mama and Baba known? They must've seen it in the autopsy. Their darling daughter. Obliterated by an unspeakable trauma that she couldn't face, so she hurt herself instead.

Eons ago, Alyssa, bangs parted to the side, gave me a wiry smile as her delicate kitten-shaped eyes watered over lightly, innocent, but in pain. "Oh, Tay. What do you think you'll be like when you grow up?"

I didn't know. "I don't know."

Tears stained her light honey-brown complexion, but she seemed unaware, or at least wanted me to be cavalier toward her emotions. She turned to me for a second, searching for me.

"I hope I get to see who you turn into."

When I looked at myself in the mirror, at this present moment, I stood aghast by how much had truly changed. My complexion was a little more freckled, the skin around my eyes a little more unruly. I was a dark golden-brown hue that emanated the endorphins charging through me. My big, fat belly stretched out like a gift I had not yet unwrapped. How did I come here, this place of acceptance? It seemed not so much a foreign entity, but a world unknown and exciting, brimming with hope but still familiar. As if I always knew that happiness resided in the spaces between and within me, even if I hadn't believed it.

Baba had never put much emphasis on happiness, but as kids we stayed on the lake up north on our summer holidays, daydreaming about Cary Grant in *The Philadelphia Story*, three-piece suits, his hair slightly frazzled and greasy. I don't know about Alyssa, but in those moments I would daydream about the feeling of being fully white, not just half white. If I was full white, maybe I could be a movie star? Like Kate Hepburn in a white one-piece. I always admired how sassy she was. She reminded me of Alyssa. We would often sing very loudly, our song of choice being "Ol' Man River," and without a moment's hesitation we would simultaneously both follow up with *"Oh my darling,*

oh my darling / Oh my darling, Clementine..." We must have heard the songs back-to-back on a cassette tape that Baba would play during bedtime, the melodies seared into our brains, rolling into one another like a natural symphony. Those days in summer were of happiness. Or as close to it as I had ever gotten.

One night I remember hearing sounds that my little body found exhilarating. At a young age, passion, even sexual passion, is coveted. It's seductive because it appeals to our human senses. It's not erotic, it's life.

I lurked by the ajar door, standing by the cavern of my interest. Inside, my parents were moving in motions unfamiliar to me, but they seemed content, sated. The movements were fast and concentrated, and the sighs rolling off the tops of their clavicles were filled with earnest, palpable desire. My mother ran her fingers across my father's back, tracing the loose hairs that grew sporadically. Navigating with her index, finally she placed her bare palm in the center of his sweaty middle region. They were happy, in love.

Years later, Simon and his parents joined us in the Catskills for a summer. He had started dealing cocaine and MDMA (then, later, heroin), claiming he had a "medical background" as a way to coax all his friends to take it. "I heard that you're trying to write songs. Oh, it's taking a while? Listen, I don't know if you're interested, but I have this thing that's really good for artistic creativity. Oh yeah, I heard Mallarmé used to take it all the time..." I could tell Alyssa and Simon were getting close, but it always seemed so transient, like neither of them had decided on the other.

As a kid I had learned that the samurai who had forsaken their duties were asked to perform a voluntary suicide known as seppuku. It was a ritual that involved slicing a tantō (a small knife) into your lower abdomen and disemboweling yourself from left to right. It was a part of the Bushido honor code, and the samurai volunteered to die like this to ensure that their deaths were noble. I was forever enchanted by this idea, by a people consumed by so much integrity that they were compelled

to voluntarily kill themselves. For the samurai, suicide absolved your sins.

Tahsin told me Muslims have a word, *nafs*, to identify the lower self, the unrefined self, the ego. They say that it is a little black spot in the heart that can be removed through the processes of spiritual development, refinement, and mastery of yourself. I didn't know what mastery of self referred to. But whatever I had done, I felt better. I was transforming, and since it began, Alyssa no longer visited me.

Something had shifted as well. In her absence—or maybe more accurately in the face of *my truth*—I realized I didn't need to be like Alyssa to be beautiful. I could be myself and everything I represented. I think this was partially why Dadi-ma protected me. She understood what her culture was like, what the world was like, how it upheld beauty like Alyssa's. The more white adjacent you were, the more you usually were revered. I'm not sure if my parents knew that; I don't know if either of them, frankly, had the sophistication. It took reflection to come to this place of understanding. A reflection I myself had only quite recently acquired. But I knew I was beautiful, with a face like Dadi-ma's, with skin dark and easily browned, with stretch marks, cellulite, and a juicy, fat belly. I was plump like ripe fruit; I was so intensely round like a delicious, cream-filled raspberry doughnut.

Going lingerie shopping with Tahsin, who had (maybe) been plotting a romance with Mateo (I didn't ask), I found myself facing the full-length mirror of a Journelle changing room. There was a cacophony of sounds outside the changing room: the buzzing of insects, that specific *cha-ching* sound from Venmo payments, Tame Impala's "The Less I Know the Better." I raised my dress. I was wearing a long-sleeved psychedelic printed smock that lay tight around my belly, and as I slid it off, slinkily, I looked at myself in the mirror. I had recently purchased underwear from Uniqlo, and the cotton stuck to my body like tiny claws, like the teeth of a Venus flytrap. My skin was tan, so caramel I wanted to lick it. I looked beautiful; better yet, I felt it. My

breasts with strong, bold areolas, I looked at my body and it felt like mine.

29.

Tahsin looked at me resolutely. I hadn't yet seen this face of hers, almost like a half-clownish scowl. I looked petulant, goading her. She bit her lip and began. "You know, the only time Roman and I used to fight was when we talked about money." She seemed hesitant, like she was sparing her words. "I think he didn't quite understand what it meant to be an immigrant and not come from a rich family... and how those two things really made my life extremely hard. Class is a deep issue for us. I still pay my parents' bills with my salary job. The sad reality is Roman's life insurance will help me, but I've spent so much of my life poor that I'm also terrified of everything being taken from me again. I mean, I had to lose my husband and best friend to feel monetarily stable. So I'm naturally scared for Sufjan, for his future. I live in that fear, always."

We were sitting on the grass at Fort Greene Park. My belly, at this point, was so big and robust that I had to scoop my waistband down just so I could sit comfortably on a picnic blanket. The boys were squirming out in front of us, the three of them on a mission for bugs, while Tahsin and I sat at home base, eating deli-style beef salami, fresh pesto on a focaccia, and Castelvetrano olives. As she was talking, she took big chunks out of the olives, her two front teeth against the pit, which she stored gracefully in her hand.

"So why did you fight?"

"Because"—she sounded lyrical—"he's rich. Ky and them, they're rich."

I felt my cheeks go red, maybe at the sound of his name, maybe at the rich part.

"And there's this... I don't know, maybe lack? Not sure if that's the right word, but I'll say lack, I guess, of fully understanding the scope of class."

I wondered why she was telling me this, but as soon as I thought this, I let my anxiety and insecurity go to the side.

"And when you're raised with money, it skews your perspective of what's possible and what kind of life you can have access to..."

"But I thought..."

She preempted me: "Yes, Ky and Roman grew up poor for a few years, but by their teens their parents had money, several property investments—you name it. So, for most of their lives, despite being two little Brown boys in New York, they still had nice things. And *that*, Taylia, is everything."

I looked at her, nibbling some of my beef salami. "My parents are rich."

"I can tell," she said, with no hint of sarcasm.

I blushed and looked toward the boys, who were poking at something in the grass, absolutely astounded in disgust and awe.

"How can you tell?" I asked finally.

"Your naïveté"—she paused—"and maybe even your secrecy."

I wanted to be less scared of saying things. I wanted to say what was on my mind and not be scared to fuck up or sound unintelligent. "I mean, for sure, class is real. I think that used to really eat Alyssa up, toward the end especially. Maybe it was some kind of ancestral pain where she felt like she couldn't live her life because of the poverty and pain of our lineage. So she was eaten up by it, by the old trauma that didn't want her to be happy." I hadn't yet articulated that to anyone.

"Uff, that's so deep." She licked some pesto off her finger. "Having a baby should make you think of all these things realistically. That's why I'm bringing any of this up, anyway."

"What'd you mean?"

"Are you going to get back with Ky?"

It hit me like a rock. "I don't know. Honestly."

"Okay, what I will say is: Ky is fine. I love him. He's my brother. Roman and I were together for seven years, so I'm sure you can understand I got to know Ky so well... This is all to say, he's no good as a partner. Y'allah." She smiled, exaggerating it with her eyes. "He's a dummy."

I burst out laughing, because I guess I had come to the same conclusion as well.

"This fake deep writerly shit. You know he's paid almost two hundred thousand a year to write the most basic, benign brand strategy?"

She shook her head and turned to look at the boys, who were now playing in a random pit of sand. I loved watching them roam free.

"Anyway, Taylia, the more I get to know you, the more I love this enchanting, brave person you are. You don't need him. Except maybe for his money."

We sat for a long time in the sun and heat.

"I'm thinking of all the women, Taylia. All the women that have been through what you've been through, habibti. This world is so unjust."

I had recently told her about my rape. I was moved that the story affected her.

We sat in that, as I thought of Dadi-ma and Alyssa, my two dead companions, again.

I broke the silence. "Tahs?"

"Hmm?" she asked, sniffling.

"So you think no more Ky?"

She looked at me hard, all our truths finally present. "He got you pregnant while still with Jade. Honestly? Fuck him."

I grinned. Maybe I had needed to hear this.

"Jade is definitely standoffish, but I think it's just anxiety."

"She's... so austere."

"Aha! *Austere* is the word..."

"She's always felt so rigid." Though, as I said, I knew I was being unfair. I knew I didn't like her because she didn't like me... and

I had fucked her boyfriend (many times) and now was pregnant with his child. So she had a point. Besides, he was still with Jade and had never tried to come and find me, but none of this really bothered me that much. I guess that's how I knew it was really over. He had given me this baby; maybe that's all our karmic responsibility was to each other. Like Kat had recently said, relationships didn't need to last for them to be important.

"Yeah, well, she's not. She's supercool, smart, talented. She's made Ky so much more interesting, and it's all her doing. Ky used to be a fuckboy..."

We looked at each other and laughed.

"Habibti, you don't need him. He doesn't deserve you! He doesn't deserve Jade, either, but that's her journey. But after all you've been through... nurture that heart of yours and fiercely love this baby. Kat, Claudia, and I, we got you." She reached over and squeezed my hand. "Ask him for child support, though." Her eyes glittered. "Take as much money from him as you possibly can."

We stared at each other for an eternity and then simply smiled.

After the park, Tahsin came over for dinner. Claudia was already there, I peeped, reading James Baldwin's *Blues for Mister Charlie*. She was wearing a blue checkered shirt, buttoned all the way up. When we came home she put the book down and started talking to Tahsin, who I could tell was also developing a quick crush. It was something about Claudia's aura. She was more reserved than Kat, with dark lips and a piercing onyx stare. She held gravity. Where Kat's energy was light, Claudia's was dark. Neither was stagnant, both were amorphous, mercurial. I had learned how to handle Kat in her bad moods, vice versa—and maybe our reliance on each other in that sense had led to a different kind of intimacy, a bond that felt like family. But Claudia was more mysterious, opaque to me. It was hot.

I took the boys upstairs to clean them off before Kat got there, and by the time I brought them down, both in their dinosaur one-

sies, Claudia told me she'd ordered jerk from the Islands, Kat's favorite take-out place. By the time Kat got home, a bottle of chilled Austrian Grüner Veltliner sat alongside copious amounts of jerk chicken, rice and peas, coconut shrimp, plantains and greens. That night we ate like kings.

On the way to bed, panting started above me, a few octaves higher, like an orchestra of groans. The soft moans wafted as I paused, haunted. My relationship to my body, to sex, was evolving. I got into bed, resolved. There, in that moment, I knew one day I would find what I was looking for romantically.

The thing is, I was grieving while I was preparing to have this baby alone. When I stepped out on Ky, I was clearly over his bullshit, but a small part of me had imagined maybe we would be together. But through time, it felt reminiscent of my parents' mediocre love. I had no time for that anymore, either—to be swayed with "maybes" and "I love you, buts..." I wanted devotion, dedication. I wanted a pulsing, empowered love.

I was rarely in the Lower East Side anymore, but the temperature was cool, and I missed my walks along the East River, over the bridge up to the Domino Sugar factory and past the big white arches of the Williamsburg Savings Bank. I felt weightless. The moon had passed over me, its orbit in Cancer, where it was home, soft and unalloyed. The sidewalks smelled of rain after it passed, and I walked alongside Kat and Claudia, out on an adventure for breakfast. They looked happy in the way companions do, Kat earlier resting her feet on Claudia's thick brown thighs as we drank on a bench outside the Juice Press. The latter's fingertips rhythmically rubbed at the cursed pain from Kat's bunions that were forming from the stress of being on her feet all the time. Weirdly, I was ready to get back to that life. I missed the flow of the café, of working alongside Kat.

We slowly began to walk, directionless, like three women who were free.

"Look at the light," Claudia exclaimed, her voice deep.

With smiles we all cooed, looking at the light shimmer across the city. It looked like magic.

"What if light is just God?" Claudia whispered.

One by one, we nodded our heads, a chorus witnessing majesty. I still wasn't sure what God was, but I was curious to know. Maybe my baby would bring me back to something.

I don't know how I sensed it, this disruption. She slid toward me, and as I smelled her, like a coriander glow, the back of my neck, where my hair met my skin, blazed. I hadn't seen her since Alyssa's funeral, but here she was, dressed in ivory linen, her shoes the color of blue porcelain.

"Taylia," she said in a whisper, and I heard my mother in the cadence.

"Zeina," I said confidently, because I was finally a woman who could meet another woman's gaze.

We stood there, four women, surrounded by secrets, and yet nothing felt cryptic, only open. I looked at her wide eyes and heard her croon an "OMG"; she came to me like I was an altar and embraced me, curling around my spine like a lover. She started crying, and I cried, too. Claudia and Kat held us. We all stood, a flood of grief.

"You're here," she kept saying, like a prayer.

As we circled each other, I felt the baby speak to me, and everything soon felt out of focus. It felt like eons, but I heard Kat say it first, then Zeina, as the water loosened inside of me, trickling to the cement beneath me.

Kat shouted at the two of them, "We need to get her back home now!"

I knew where the kiddie pool was, and Naima was on speed dial. I had been doing the pelvic floor exercises with Tahsin and going to doctor's examinations in tandem with biweekly fertility acupuncture visits in Park Slope. I felt prepared and even had the boys' hand-me-downs—crib, toys, bibs—everything I needed I had access to. I was safe, and so was this baby.

Nothing can shake us; we are strong. That mantra was my catharsis; my pain was being channeled toward the anger I felt in the past and the anger I felt now. I had moved past the cruelty of my rape. I heaved. Here I was in an inextricable amount of pain, but I felt relatively calm. I was present, I was focused. I was not hopeless, I was not lost. I pushed and kept pushing as Naima talked me through it. I looked at Kat and I remembered why I was there. I wanted this baby. More than anything, I wanted this baby.

I heard singing.

Bleeding steadily, the ribbon of red shot through me like puss oozing out of a sore. I clutched at the waves of bodies around me: Zeina, Kat, Claudia, and dear Tahsin, who had come to witness the birth. She must've gotten the signal. Finally, I could let go and there were loved ones who would catch me. I embraced the pain within this strange holiness of birth, with the mothers who stood beside me. The baby screamed to life, echoing across the ecosystem and my galaxy. I felt the towel wrap around me and I faltered, feeling fear at my lips, at my throat—what was I doing? Then, I felt the breath: a stillness perforated the space and I was frozen in suspension, full with love. Slowly, like a pull from a string, the connection was made. Forever tethered by our hands, our faces, our hearts that beat to the same drum, and our same veins of red, I saw my baby.

I didn't cry. I just got it. I could sense Dadi-ma there, her spirit looking at me. *Tumi bhalo aso, tumi bhalo aso. You are good, you are good.* She would often repeat it, as she sainted me with incense smoke from her morning pooja. I always thought she meant, with my broken translations from Baba, that I was a good kid, which I needed to hear then. But now I understood she was saying, *Your life is good.*

For a moment, I couldn't hear my baby.

"Where's my baby?" I screamed. I screamed for the ages, I screamed for my rights, I screamed for the women before me and after me who would bear this beauty of life. For the women and the torture faced by all of us, for our bodies that had been beat-

en but our hearts that were still strong. Naima slid her into my arms, and as I looked down I knew she was a fighter, with every breath she was a fighter. I bent my head and breathed in the fresh new musty scent of her; she smelled like me.

When I look up the name Taylia, I find no answers. The origin is unknown, potentially Hebrew, as Mama claims—but the name itself is a mystery. I embrace this, this random reality of my name, the rotation of stars sinking into me; I am undefinable. The name, like a loose broken T-shirt feels like it finally fits, it's a punchline that's landed. It is me, I am Taylia. I have felt unworthy of my name, of my being, for too long—but it's mine now, see. My pupils are dilated, everything is clear with a punchy aplomb, I see diamonds.

It's my name, and by God, I'm never giving it up.

You know, when I look at the moon, it's licked and jagged edges like a stone fruit orbiting the seas, I recognize Alyssa's faint curves, I see Dadi-ma in her shadha saree. They are the moon, its kinetic energy fuels me, reminding me of its quaint mercury. I am not alone, I have never been, I was always guided by the moon. Its dull circumference calms my anxiety. I am healing. For myself, for my child. I'm ending the cycle, I am becoming the moon, too.

In my mind, I walk up the stairs that I had hovered over for so many years, without realizing its life blood, its significance. In that moment, on the top-most stair, looking beyond the elegant trees, towards the full haloed moon, I sink into my thoughts, distracting my fear; will it rain today? My eyes scan the foliage, again, drawn in by the silence I breathe in twilight. I feel satiated, I feel poised, self possessed. Right now, there's no refuge in my fear, I breathe in. I knock on the door, a stranger amidst so much familiarity. She opens it briskly, with such ease. Her coloring is different, more sedated in age, but her crimson hair is flying with the wind, her skin is soft and milky, the same, *Mama*. My heart

rises. I want to scream, but there is an absence of saliva in my mouth so I smile a dry throated line and she smiles back at me, her eyes watering with a slivered sacredness.

She looks down onto the bundle in my arms, her small body cocooned, Dadi-ma's chain glinting on her tiny neck. Mama fingers the necklace quietly, enraptured by her fluttering red veined eyes. "What's her name?" her voice croaks. I don't say anything, I can't say anything. She's like the sun, she's like the moon, my faulty moon. I named my child something with teeth, and my mother understands this. She ushers me in, one hand on the small of my warm back, the other clutching my weary forearm where my young beauty sleeps, rests, my Alyssa, I've resurrected her. Beethoven's "Emperor" Concerto plays from Baba's study, unbelieving of this bliss my lips begin to tremble. Wrapped by my mother's embrace, frozen in the music, I hear her say: "Your father has been waiting for you..." I nod with a full lake of tears in my eyes, gushing, sublime. *I forgive myself, because I've forgiven you, too.*

"I've been waiting for you," she says. "I've been waiting for you to come home."

I opened my eyes, now in my room at Kat's, resting with my Alyssa. A few moments later, as I was still half lucid, Zeina walked in, sitting on the side of the bed. She brushed Alyssa's cheeks, cooing at her pinkness, and held my hand, pulsing the inner web, exactly where I would often pulse Kat's hand. She said the words quickly, spilling them out like gold stars.

"I'm proud of you mama."

I smiled back at first. Then I began to cry, to sputter, spit came out like a trail. It felt surreal, but important for this moment. I wanted to say thank you, but I just held her hand.

You see me, I thought. At last, you see me.

Acknowledgments

I owe this book to three people.

Firstly, Alexandra Ragheb.

I am absolutely in awe of you. You saw me, and carved me out. Thank you for investing in me, for telling me your truths, and trusting me. I love your Aquarian mind, dude. Here's to expansion, to the truth, to justice, to the takeover. Thank you for walking alongside me. Thank you for being a fire starter.

Oliva Taylor Smith

Thank you for respecting my mind, story and process from the very beginning. I cannot tell you what it meant to me for you to believe in this book that, I know, needed so much work. You've made me understand what I should expect from an editor. Your patience and resilience to help me with this story has moved me, I have so much gratitude for you, Olivia.

Tanaïs

Firstly, you should know I'm crying writing this. To my queer Bangla soul-sister… I'm so lucky to witness your brilliance, your consistency, and your power. You are a genius. Thank you for making this book better. Thank you for asking me to try harder, gently. You are infused in this story, and I am honored that we get to reflect each other. Thank you for helping me create a reference, and for being one, too. You are everything.

*

I wrote this book over eighteen years. I was twelve when I started it, and I've turned thirty the year it comes out. I can't tell you how much this feels like I'm ending a cycle, an old self. It is a spiritual death.

I am so grateful for all the countless people that read this over the years… from my eighth grade English teacher who read the first two chapters to my old friend in Sydney, Daniel Reynolds. What up! Thank you to my most recent readers in the last couple of years: Zeba Blay, David Ehrlich, Prinita Thevarajah, Lubna Hindi and Megan Williams. Y'all are some of my best friends, but also—I'm immensely grateful for your perspectives.

Thank you to Hanif, Tanaïs and Aria—and all my brilliant peers. To Monika and Eloisa, for your faith and consideration. To Unnamed Press and Mark Gottlieb.

Thank you to my father and my sister for being keepers of our familial pain. For being a sounding board, even when it wasn't easy. Thank you for being a witness to this story, thank you for trying so hard to accept me as I am. I see you trying, and I am filled with immense love. This story, in so many ways, is about all of us.

Thank you to all my closest friends and comrades who carried me through this dark as fuck life I've had. You know who you are. A special shout out to Mo Dafa and Hawa Arsala.

*

I wanted to write something about resilience. Not a lot of people believed in this book, so I owe my resilience to myself. To anybody writing a story they are being told is not sellable, keep going. Write for a purpose. Write for justice. Write to understand yourself. Write to heal. Write, and I can't exaggerate this enough, for the future. Write for the world you want.

Lastly, this book is for survivors. I believe in a world where we forgive ourselves. I believe in a world where we thrive. Thank you for surviving. You can heal. Let the pain guide you.

Onwards to global revolution, the end of patriarchy, capitalism and white inferiority. Onwards to true abolition and Black liberation. Ameen.